READER'S DIGEST
CONDENSED BOOKS

READER'S DIGEST
CONDENSED BOOKS

*Selected and edited
by Reader's Digest*

CONDENSED BOOKS DIVISION

THE READER'S DIGEST ASSOCIATION LIMITED, LONDON

www.readersdigest.co.uk

The Reader's Digest Association Limited
11 Westferry Circus
Canary Wharf London E14 4HE

For information as to ownership of
copyright in the material of this book,
and acknowledgments, see last page.

Printed in France
ISBN 0 267 42531 6

CONTENTS

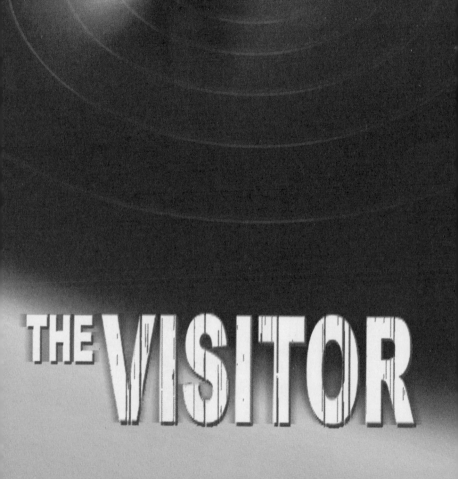

THE VISITOR

LEE CHILD

In one of the most difficult murder inquiries they've faced in a long time, the FBI are desperate for leads. All they have to go on is a description of the killer constructed for them by psychological profiler Julia Lamarr. He is, she believes, highly intelligent, probably from the military, a loner who knows investigative procedures inside out.

It's a profile that exactly fits Jack Reacher—the very man the Bureau have hauled in to help them crack the case.

Chapter 4

People say that knowledge is power. The more knowledge, the more power. Suppose you knew the winning numbers for the lottery? What would you do? You would run to the store, is what. You would mark those numbers on the playslip. And you would win.

Same for the stock market. Suppose you knew what was going to go way up? You're not talking about a hunch. You're talking about real, hard knowledge. Suppose you had it? What would you do? You'd call your broker, is what. You'd buy. Then later you'd sell, and you'd be rich.

Same for killing people.

Suppose you wanted to kill people. You would need to know ahead of time how to do it. Some ways are better than others. Most of them have drawbacks. So you use what knowledge you've got, and you come up with the perfect method.

You pay a lot of attention to the set-up. Preparation is very important. But that stuff is meat and drink to you, after all your training. The big problems will come afterwards. How do you make sure you get away with it? You use your knowledge, is how. You know how the cops work. You know what they look for. So you go through it all in your head, very precisely, and you don't leave anything for them to find.

JACK REACHER was sitting alone at a restaurant table in Tribeca, New York, gazing at the backs of two guys twenty feet away and wondering if it would be enough just to warn them off or if he would have to go the extra mile and break their arms.

It was a question of dynamics. The dynamics of the city meant that a brand-new Italian place like this was going to stay pretty empty until the food guy from the *New York Times* wrote it up or some celebrity was spotted in there two nights in a row. But neither thing had happened yet and the place was still uncrowded, which made it the perfect choice for a guy looking to eat dinner near his girlfriend's apartment while she worked late. The dynamics of the city also meant any bright new commercial venture would sooner or later get a visit from guys like the two he was watching, on behalf of somebody wanting a steady 300 bucks a week in exchange for not sending his boys in to smash it up with baseball bats.

The two guys were standing close in to the bar, talking quietly to the owner, a small nervous guy who had backed away until his backside was jammed against the cash drawer. His arms were folded tight across his chest, defensively. His eyes showed disbelief and panic.

It was a large, high-ceilinged room, easily sixty feet by sixty, which had probably started out as a factory. Now it was the type of Italian restaurant that has $300,000 invested up-front in bleached avant-garde decor, and that gives you seven or eight handmade ravioli parcels on a large plate and calls them a meal. The place was named Mostro's, which as far as he understood Italian translated as *Monster's*. He wasn't sure what the name referred to. Certainly not the size of the portions. But the food was good and the place was attractive. In Reacher's inexpert opinion he was watching the start of a big reputation.

But the big reputation was obviously slow to spread. Tonight there was just one other couple eating, five tables away. The guy was medium-sized, short sandy hair, fair moustache, light brown suit, brown shoes. The woman was thin and dark, in a skirt and a jacket. They weren't talking much.

The two guys at the bar were talking, that was for sure. They were leaning over, talking fast and persuading hard. They were dressed in identical dark wool coats. Reacher could see their faces in the mirrors behind the liquor bottles. Olive skin, dark eyes. Syrian or Lebanese, maybe. The guy on the right was making a sweeping gesture with his hand. It was easy to see it represented a bat ploughing through the bottles. The owner was going pale.

Then the guy on the left tapped his watch and turned to leave. His partner straightened up and followed him. He trailed his hand over the nearest table and knocked a plate to the floor. It shattered on the tiles. The sandy guy and the dark woman looked away. The two guys walked to the door, heads up, confident. Reacher watched them go out. Then the owner came out from behind the bar, knelt down and raked through the fragments of broken plate with his fingertips.

Reacher walked over to him. 'You OK?'

The guy shrugged and started pushing the shards into a pile.

'When are they coming back?' Reacher asked.

'An hour,' the guy said.

'How much do they want?'

The guy smiled a bitter smile. 'I get a start-up discount,' he said. 'Two hundred a week, goes to four when the place picks up.'

'Who were they?' Reacher asked quietly.

'Just some punks.'

'Can I use your phone?'

The guy nodded.

'You know an office-supply store open late?' Reacher asked.

'Broadway, two blocks over,' the guy said.

Reacher stood up and slid round behind the bar. He picked up the phone and dialled a number and waited until it was answered a mile away and forty floors up.

'Hello?' she said.

'Hey, Jodie.'

'Hey, Reacher, what's new?'

'You going to be finished any time soon?'

He heard her sigh. 'No, this is an all-nighter,' she said. 'Complex law, and they need an opinion like yesterday. I'm real sorry.'

'Don't worry about it,' he said. 'I've got something to do. Then I guess I'll head back on up to Garrison.'

'OK, take care of yourself,' she said. 'I love you.'

He hung up, came out from behind the bar and stepped back to his table. He left forty dollars under his espresso saucer, shrugged into his coat and headed for the door. 'Good luck,' he called.

The owner nodded vaguely and the couple at the distant table watched him go. He turned his collar up and stepped out to the side-walk. It was dark and small halos of fog were forming around the lights. He walked east to Broadway and scanned through the neon until he found the office store. He bought a small labelling machine and a tube of superglue. Then he headed north to Jodie's apartment.

His four-wheel drive was parked in the garage under her building. He drove it up the ramp and turned south on Broadway and west back to the restaurant. He slowed on the street and glanced in through the big windows. No patrons. Every table was empty and the owner was sitting on a stool behind the bar. Reacher came round the block and parked illegally at the mouth of the alley that led to the kitchen doors. He killed the motor and settled down to wait.

The dynamics of the city. The strong terrorise the weak. They keep on at it until they come up against somebody stronger with some humane reason for stopping them. Somebody like Reacher. He had no real reason to help a guy he hardly knew. It wasn't any kind of campaign. But equally he couldn't just walk away. He never had.

He fumbled the label machine out of his pocket. Scaring the two guys away was only half the job. What mattered was *who* they thought was doing the scaring. Nobody is afraid of a lone individual, because a lone individual can always be overwhelmed by sheer numbers. What makes a big impression is an *organisation*. He smiled and started to print letters in white on a blue plastic ribbon. When he had finished he laid the finished ribbons on the seat next to him. Then he unscrewed the cap off the tube of superglue and pierced the metal foil with the plastic spike, ready for action. He put the cap back on and dropped the tube and the labels into his pocket. Then he got out of the car and stood in the shadows, waiting.

The dynamics of the city. His mother had been scared of cities. She had told him *Cities are dangerous places. They're full of scary guys.* As a teenager he had seen that she was right. People on city streets were fearful and defensive. They kept their distance. He became convinced the scary guys were always right behind him. Then he realised *No, I'm the scary guy. They're scared of me.* It was a revelation. He saw himself reflected in store windows and understood. He had stopped growing at fifteen when he was already six foot five and 220 pounds. A giant. *They're scared of me.* From that point on he knew that for every city person he needed to be scared of, there were 999 others a lot more scared of him. He used the knowledge like a tactic, and the confidence it put in his walk redoubled the effect he had on people. The dynamics of the city.

Fifty-five minutes into the hour he moved out of the shadows and stood on the corner, leaning against the wall of the restaurant, watching the traffic coming towards him.

The two guys came back right on time in a black Mercedes sedan. It parked a block away and they stepped out of the car with their long coats flowing, opened the rear doors and pulled baseball bats off the seat. They slipped the bats under their coats, slammed the doors and glanced around, then strode confidently along the sidewalk. Reacher met them as they stepped up onto his kerb.

'In the alley, guys,' he said.

Up close, they were young, some way short of thirty. Wide necks, silk ties, suits that didn't come out of a catalogue. Gripping the bats with their left hands through their pocket linings.

'Who the hell are you?' the right-hand guy said.

Reacher glanced at him. The first guy to speak is the dominant half of any partnership, the one you put down first.

He stepped to his left and turned a fraction, blocking the sidewalk, channelling them towards the alley. 'Business manager,' he said. 'You want to get paid, I'm the guy who can do it for you.'

The guy paused. 'OK, but screw the alley. We'll do it inside.'

Reacher shook his head. 'Not logical, my friend. We're paying you to stay out of the restaurant, starting from now, right?'

They looked at him and looked at each other and stepped forward into the alley. They were happy enough. Big confident guys, bats under their coats, two against one. Reacher stepped back like he wanted them to precede him. Like a courtesy. They shuffled forward.

He hit the right-hand guy in the side of the head with his elbow. It was a short hard blow, well delivered. The guy went down like a trap door had opened up under his feet.

The second guy was almost on the ball. He got the bat clear of his coat and swung it ready, but he swung it way too far back and way too low. He aimed at the middle of Reacher's body. Two things wrong with that. A big backswing takes time to get into. And a blow aimed at the middle of the body is too easy to defend against.

Reacher caught the bat in both hands, before it had got up speed. He jacked the handle up and hurled the guy off balance. Kicked out at his ankles, tore the bat free and jabbed him with it. The guy went down on his knees and butted his head into the wall. Reacher kicked him over on his back. Squatted down and jammed the bat across his throat. He used his left hand to go into each pocket in turn. He came out with an automatic handgun, a thick wallet and a mobile phone.

'Who are you from?' he asked.

'Mr Petrosian,' the guy gasped.

The name meant nothing to Reacher. But he smiled incredulously. 'Petrosian? You have *got* to be kidding.'

He put a lot of sneer in his voice, like out of all the whole spectrum of worrisome rivals his bosses could possibly think of, Petrosian was so far down the list he was just about totally invisible.

'We've got a message for Petrosian,' Reacher said softly.

'What's the message?'

Reacher smiled again. 'You are,' he said. 'Now lie real still.'

He went into his pocket for the labels and the glue. Then he eased a thick worm of glue onto one of the labels and pressed it onto the guy's forehead. The label read *Mostro's has got protection already*.

'Lie still,' he said again.

He took the bat with him and turned the other guy face upwards. Used plenty of glue and smoothed the other label into place on his brow. This one read *Don't start a turf war with us*. He checked the pockets and came out with an automatic handgun, a wallet and a telephone. Plus a key for the Benz. He emptied the tube of glue into the first guy's palms and crushed them together. Chemical handcuffs. He hauled the guy upright and held him while he relearned how to stand. Then he tossed the car key to the second guy.

'I guess you're the designated driver,' he said. 'Now go give our best regards to Mr Petrosian. Beat it.'

The guy with the glued hands had a problem moving. The other guy had a problem helping him. He puzzled over it for a second and then ducked down and came back up between his friend's glued hands, piggybacking him. He staggered out of the alley.

The handguns were Beretta 9mm M9s, military issue. Reacher had carried an identical gun for thirteen years. The serial numbers on both guns had been filed off. Reacher stripped them in the dark and pitched the barrels, slides and bullets into the dumpster outside the kitchen doors. He laid the aluminium frames on the ground, scooped a handful of grit into the firing mechanisms and worked the triggers in and out until the grit jammed them. He pitched them into the dumpster. Then he smashed the phones with the bats and left the pieces where they lay.

The wallets held cards and licences and cash. Maybe 300 bucks in total. He rolled the cash into his pocket and kicked the wallets away into a corner. Then he straightened and walked back to the sidewalk. Glanced up the street. The black Mercedes was gone.

He walked back into the deserted restaurant. The owner was behind the bar, lost in thought. He looked up as Reacher peeled a ten from the stolen wad and dropped it on the bar.

'For the plate they broke,' he said. 'They had a change of heart.'

The guy just looked at the ten and said nothing. Reacher turned and walked back out. Across the street, he saw the couple from the restaurant standing on the opposite sidewalk, watching him. He climbed into his four-wheel drive and fired it up. Glanced over his shoulder. They were still watching him. He pulled out into the traffic. A block away, he used the mirror and saw the dark woman stepping out to the kerb edge, watching him go. Then she was lost from sight.

GARRISON IS ON THE EAST bank of the Hudson River, about fifty-eight miles north from Tribeca. Late on a fall evening, traffic is not a problem. With empty parkways, average speed can be as high as you dare to make it. But Reacher was anxious to stay out of trouble. So he drove slow enough not to be noticed and let the late commuters in their fast sedans scurry past him.

One hour and seventeen minutes later he turned into his driveway and the headlight beams swung towards the garage door and washed over two cars waiting nose-out in front of it. He jammed to a stop and their lights came on and blinded him just as his mirror filled with bright light from behind. He ducked away from the glare and saw people running towards him with guns.

A figure stepped close to his car. A hand came up and rapped on the glass next to his head. It was a woman's hand. A flashlight beam turned directly on it and showed it was cupping a bright gold badge in the shape of a shield with an eagle perched on the top. Reacher stared at it. It said *Federal Bureau of Investigation. US Department of Justice.* The woman pressed the shield against the window and shouted, 'Turn off the engine and place both hands on the wheel.'

He did so. The door opened and the light clicked on and spilled out over the dark woman from the restaurant. The sandy guy with the fair moustache was at her shoulder. She had the FBI badge in one hand and a gun in the other. The gun was pointed at his head.

'Out of the vehicle,' she said. 'Nice and slow.'

She stepped back, the gun tracking his head. He swung his legs out of the foot well and slid his feet to the ground.

'Turn around,' she said. 'Place your hands on the vehicle.'

He did as he was told. The sheet metal was cold to the touch and slimy with night dew. He felt hands on every inch of his body. They took his wallet and the stolen cash from his trouser pocket. Somebody leaned into the car and took his keys from the ignition.

'Now walk to the car,' the woman called.

She pointed to one of the sedans near the garage. He half turned and walked towards it. A guy in a dark blue bulletproof vest opened the rear door and stepped back. As Reacher folded himself inside, the opposite door opened up and the woman slid in alongside him, the gun, a SIG-Sauer, still pointing at his head. The front door opened and the sandy guy knelt in on the seat and stretched back for the woman's briefcase which was upright on the rear seat. The guy flipped the case open and pulled out a sheaf of papers.

'Search warrant,' the woman said to him. 'For your house.'

The sandy guy ducked back out and slammed the door. The car went silent. Reacher heard footsteps growing fainter through the fog.

'You're not asking what this is about,' she said.

It's not about what happened an hour and seventeen minutes ago, he said to himself. *No way was this all organised in an hour and seventeen minutes.* He kept quiet and absolutely still. He was worried about the whiteness in the woman's knuckle where it wrapped round the SIG-Sauer's trigger. Accidents can happen.

The woman shrugged at him. *Have it your own way,* she was saying. Her face settled into a frown. Not a pretty face, but interesting. Some character there. She was about thirty-five and there were lines in her skin. Her hair was jet black but thin. He could see her white scalp. It gave her a sickly look. But her eyes were bright. She glanced through the car window into the darkness, out to where her men were searching his house. She smiled. Her front teeth were crossed. The right one was canted sideways and it overlaid the left one by a fraction. An interesting mouth. It made her face distinctive. She was slim under her bulky coat and wore a black skirt and jacket and cream blouse. The skirt was short, and her legs were thin and hard under black nylon.

'Would you stop doing that, please?' she said. Her voice had gone cold, and the gun moved.

'Doing what?' Reacher asked.

'Looking at my legs.'

He switched his gaze up to her face. 'Somebody points a gun at me, I'm entitled to check them out head to toe, wouldn't you say?'

The gun moved closer. 'I don't like the way you're looking at me.'

He stared at her. 'What way am I looking at you?' he asked.

'Like you're making advances,' she said. 'You're disgusting.'

He stared at her thin hair, her frown, her crooked tooth.

'You think I'm making advances to you?'

'Aren't you? Wouldn't you like to?'

He shook his head.

AFTER TWENTY MINUTES the sandy guy with the moustache came back to the car and slid into the front passenger seat. The driver's door opened and a second man got in. He fired up the motor and in hostile silence they headed back to Manhattan.

They parked underground someplace south of midtown and forced him out of the car into a brightly lit garage. The woman turned a full circle on the concrete floor, examining the whole space. Then she pointed towards a black elevator door located in a distant corner. There were two more guys waiting there. Dark suits, white shirts, quiet ties. They watched the woman and the sandy guy as they approached. There was deference in their faces. But they were also comfortable, and a little proud. Like they were *hosts.* Reacher suddenly understood the woman and the sandy guy were not New York agents. They were from somewhere else.

They put Reacher in the centre of the elevator car and crowded in around him. One of the local boys touched a button, the door rolled shut and the elevator travelled upwards. It stopped hard with *21* showing on the floor indicator. The door thumped back and the local boys led the way out into a blank grey corridor.

The guy who had driven the sedan down from Garrison paused in front of the third door and opened it up. Reacher was manoeuvred into a bare space, maybe twelve by sixteen, concrete floor, cinderblock walls, all covered in thick grey paint like the side of a battleship. There was a single plastic garden chair in the corner.

'Sit down,' the woman said.

Reacher walked to the opposite corner from the chair and sat on the concrete floor, wedged into the angle of the cinderblock walls. Then everybody backed out into the corridor and closed the door on him. There was no sound of a lock turning, but there didn't need to be, because there was no handle on the inside.

He sat like that for the best part of an hour. Just waiting. Then the door opened and a grey-haired guy with thick spectacles stepped into the room.

'Time to talk,' he said.

Two junior agents took up station behind him.

Reacher jacked himself upright and stepped away from his corner. 'I want to make a call,' he said. The grey-haired guy shook his head.

'Calling comes later,' he said. 'Talking first, OK?'

Reacher shrugged. The problem with getting your rights abused was that somebody had to witness it for it to mean anything. And the two young agents were seeing nothing.

'So let's go,' the grey-haired guy said.

Reacher was ushered out into the grey corridor and into a big knot of people. The woman was there, and the sandy guy with the moustache, and there was an older guy with a big red face puffy with strain and blood pressure, and a younger guy with a lean face and shirt and tie. No jacket. They were buzzing. It was late in the evening, but they were all pumped up with excitement. And they were divided. There were two clear teams and there was tension between them. The woman stuck close to his left shoulder, and the sandy guy and the blood-pressure guy stuck close to her. That was one team. At his right shoulder was the guy with the lean face. He was the second team, alone and outnumbered and unhappy about it.

They walked down a narrow grey corridor and into a grey room with a long mahogany table filling most of the floor space. On one side, backs to the door, were seven plastic chairs. A single identical chair was placed in the exact centre of the opposite side.

Reacher paused in the doorway. Not too difficult to work out which chair was his. He sat down on it.

The two junior agents took up position against the walls at opposite ends of the table, like sentries. Their jackets were open and their shoulder holsters were visible. Opposite Reacher, the two teams were forming up. The grey-haired guy took the centre chair. Next to him on his right-hand side was the guy with the blood pressure, next to him was the woman, and next to her was the sandy guy. The guy with the lean face and the shirtsleeves was alone in the middle chair of the left-hand three.

The grey-haired guy leaned forward, his forearms on the shiny wood, claiming authority. 'We've been squabbling over you,' he said.

'Am I in custody?' Reacher asked.

'No, not yet.'

'So I'm free to go?'

The guy looked over the top of his spectacles. 'Well, we'd rather you stayed here, so we can keep this whole thing civilised for a spell.'

'So make it civilised,' Reacher said. 'Let's have some introductions. That's what civilised people do, right? They introduce themselves. Then they chat politely. I'm Jack Reacher. Who the hell are you?'

The guy nodded. 'I'm Alan Deerfield,' he said. 'Assistant Director, FBI. I run the New York Field Office.'

Then he turned his head to his right and stared at the sandy guy.

'Special Agent Tony Poulton,' the sandy guy said, and glanced to his left.

'Special Agent Julia Lamarr,' the woman said.

'Agent-in-Charge Nelson Blake,' the guy with the blood pressure said. 'The three of us are from Quantico. I run the Serial Crimes Unit and Special Agents Lamarr and Poulton work for me there.'

There was a pause and the guy called Deerfield turned the other way and looked towards the man on his left.

'Agent-in-Charge James Cozo,' the guy said. 'Organised Crime, here in New York City, working on the protection rackets.'

'OK now?' Deerfield asked.

Reacher nodded. 'OK,' he said. 'Pleased to meet you all. But you can't talk to me until you read me my rights. Whereupon you can't talk to me anyway because my lawyer could take some time to get here and even then she won't let me talk to you.'

'Your lawyer is Jodie Jacob, right?' Deerfield asked. 'Your girlfriend?'

'What do you know about my girlfriend?'

'We know everything about your girlfriend,' Deerfield said. 'She's at Spencer Gutman, right? Big reputation as an associate. They're talking about a partnership for her. But Spencer Gutman is a financial firm, right? Not much expertise in the field of criminal law. You sure you want her for your attorney? Situation like this?'

'What situation am I in?'

'Reacher, I already wasted an hour stopping these guys fighting over you. So now you owe me. Answer their questions, and I'll tell you when and if you need a damn lawyer.'

'What are the questions about?'

Deerfield smiled. 'Stuff we need to know, is what. To find out if we're interested in you.'

'Why would you be interested in me?'

'Answer the questions and we'll find out.'

'OK,' Reacher said. 'What are the questions?'

Lamarr leaned forward. 'You knew Amy Callan pretty well, didn't you?' she asked.

'Who?' Reacher said.

'You heard, you son of a bitch.'

Reacher stared at her. Then a memory of Amy Callan came back at him from the past and slowed him just enough to allow a contented smile to settle on Lamarr's bony face.

'You didn't like her much, did you?' she said.

There was silence. It built around him.

'OK, my turn,' Cozo said. 'Who are you working for?'

Reacher swung his gaze slowly to his right and rested it on Cozo. 'I'm not working for anybody.'

'*Don't start a turf war with us,*' Cozo quoted. '*Us* is a plural word. More than one person. Who is *us*, Reacher?'

'There is no us.'

'Bullshit, Reacher. Who sent you to that restaurant?'

Reacher said nothing.

'What about Caroline Cooke?' Lamarr said. 'You didn't like her either, did you?'

'Give us the whole story, Reacher, from the beginning,' Blake said.

Reacher looked at him. 'What story?'

'Who sent you to the restaurant?' Cozo asked again.

Reacher turned to him. 'Nobody sent me anywhere.'

Cozo shook his head. 'Bullshit, Reacher. You live in a half-million-dollar house on the river in Garrison and, as far as the Internal Revenue Service knows, you haven't earned a cent in nearly three years. And when somebody wanted Petrosian's best boys in the hospital, they sent you to do it. I want to know who the hell it is.'

'I'm not working for anybody,' Reacher said again.

'You're a loner, right?' Blake asked. 'Is that what you're saying?'

Reacher nodded. 'I guess.'

'I thought so. When did you come out of the army?'

Reacher shrugged. 'About three years ago.'

'Military policeman, right?'

'Right. I was a major.'

'So why did you muster out?'

'You wouldn't understand.'

'So, three years. What have you been doing?'

'Nothing much. Having fun, I guess.'

'Working?'

'Not often.'

'Doing what for money?'

'Savings.'

'They ran out three months ago. We checked. So now you're living off Ms Jacob, right? How do you feel about that?'

Reacher glanced at the wedding band on Blake's fat finger. 'No worse than your wife does, living off you, I expect,' he said.

Blake grunted. 'So you came out of the army, and since then you've been mostly on your own.'

'Mostly.'

'Bullshit, he's working for somebody,' Cozo said.

'The man says he's a loner, damn it,' Blake snarled.

Deerfield's head was turning left and right between them, like a spectator at a tennis game. He fixed Reacher with a quiet gaze. 'Tell me about Amy Callan and Caroline Cooke,' he said.

'What's to tell? Callan was small and dark, Cooke was tall and blonde. Callan was a sergeant, Cooke was a lieutenant. Callan was a clerk in Ordnance at Fort Withe near Chicago; Cooke was in War Plans at NATO HQ in Belgium.'

'Did you have sex with either of them?' Lamarr asked.

Reacher turned to stare at her. 'What kind of a question is that?'

'A straightforward one.'

'Well, no, I didn't.'

'They were both pretty, right?'

Reacher nodded. 'Prettier than you, that's for sure.'

Lamarr looked away. 'Did they know each other?' Blake asked.

'I doubt it. There's a million people in the army, and they were serving four thousand miles apart at different times.'

'Would you like to have had sex with them?'

Reacher smiled briefly. 'I can think of worse things.'

'Would they have said yes to you?'

'Maybe, maybe not.'

'You don't think they'd have rebuffed you?'

Reacher kept his gaze on Blake's eyes. 'No.'

There was a long pause.

'Do you approve of women in the military?' Deerfield asked.

Reacher's eyes moved across to him. 'What?'

'Do you approve of women in the military? Do you think they make good fighters?'

Reacher shrugged. 'Women can do it the same as anybody else. You ever been to Israel? Women fight in the front line there.'

'How did you meet Amy Callan?' Deerfield asked.

'She came to me with a problem she was having in her unit.'

'What problem?'

'Sexual harassment.'

'And what did you do?'

'I arrested the officer she was accusing.'

'And what did you do then?'

'Nothing. It was in the hands of the prosecutor. The officer won the case. Amy Callan left the service.'

'But the officer's career was ruined anyway.'

Reacher nodded. 'Yes, it was.'

'How did you feel about that?'

Reacher shrugged. 'Confused, I guess. My opinion was he was guilty. So I guess I was happy he was gone. But it shouldn't work that way, ideally. A not-guilty verdict shouldn't ruin a career.'

'So you felt sorry for him?'

'No, I felt sorry for Callan. But the whole thing was a mess. Two careers were ruined, where only one should have been.'

'What about Caroline Cooke?'

'Cooke was different. It was overseas. Belgium. She was having sex with some colonel. Had been for a year. It looked consensual to me. She only called it harassment when she didn't get promoted.'

'So you did nothing?'

'No, I arrested the colonel, because by then there were rules. Sex between people of different rank was effectively outlawed.'

'And?'

'And he was dishonourably discharged and his wife dumped him and he killed himself. And Cooke quit anyway.'

'And what happened to you?'

'I transferred out of NATO HQ.'

'Why? Upset?'

'No, because I was a good investigator. I was wasted in Belgium. Nothing much happens in Belgium.'

'You see much sexual harassment after that?'

'Sure. It became a very big thing.'

'Lots of good men getting their careers ruined?' Lamarr asked.

Reacher turned to face her. 'Some. It became a witch-hunt. Most of the cases were genuine, in my opinion, but some innocent people were caught up in it. The rules had suddenly changed.'

'Did you see Callan and Cooke after you had handed their cases over to the prosecutor?' Blake asked.

'Once or twice, I guess, in passing.'

'Did they trust you?'

Reacher shrugged. 'I guess so. It was my job to make them trust me. I had to get all kinds of intimate details from them.'

'You had to do that kind of thing with many women?'

'There were hundreds of cases. I handled a couple dozen, I guess, before they set up special units to deal with them all.'

'Suppose you saw one of those women again someplace? Would she remember you as a nice guy?'

Reacher nodded. 'It's a hell of an ordeal. Not just the event itself, but the process afterwards, too. So the investigator has to build up a bond. The investigator has to be a friend and a supporter.'

Blake nodded and the three agents from Quantico sat back, as if to say *OK, we're interested.* Cozo stared at Deerfield in alarm. Deerfield leaned forward, staring through his glasses at Reacher.

'Exactly what happened at the restaurant?' he asked.

'Nothing happened,' Reacher said.

Deerfield shook his head. 'You were under surveillance. My people have been following you for a week. Special Agents Poulton and Lamarr joined them tonight. They saw the whole thing.'

'You've been following me for a week? Why?'

'We'll get to that later.'

Lamarr reached down to her briefcase. She pulled out a file, opened it and took out a sheaf of papers covered in dense type. She smiled icily at Reacher and slid the sheets across the table to him.

In them Reacher was referred to as 'the subject'. They were a list of everything he had done in the previous week. They were accurate to the last detail. Reacher glanced at Lamarr's smiling face.

'Well, FBI tails are pretty good,' he said. 'I never noticed.'

'So what happened in the restaurant?' Deerfield asked again.

Reacher paused. *Honesty is the best policy*, he thought. 'I guess I committed a small crime to stop a bigger one happening.'

'You were acting alone?' Cozo asked.

Reacher nodded. 'Yes, I was.'

'So what was "*Don't start a turf war with us*" all about?'

'I wanted Petrosian to take it seriously, whoever he is. Like he was dealing with another organisation.'

Deerfield leaned over the table and retrieved Lamarr's surveillance log. He riffled through it. 'This shows no contact with anybody except Ms Jodie Jacob, and she's not running protection rackets.' He looked up at Reacher. 'Phone log is clear. You spoke to nobody except Ms Jacob. A quiet life. No contact with gangsters, no instructions by phone.' He turned to Cozo. 'You comfortable with that?'

Cozo shrugged. 'I'll have to be, I guess.'

'A concerned citizen, right, Reacher?' Deerfield said. 'You saw an injustice, you wanted to set it straight.'

Reacher nodded. 'I could have taken their guns. If I was connected, I would have. But I didn't. I disabled them and threw them in the dumpster.'

'You don't like injustice, right?'

'I guess not.'

'So why did you steal their money?'

'Spoils of battle, I guess. Like a trophy.'

'You wouldn't mug an old lady, but it was OK to take money off a couple of hard men.'

'I guess.'

There was silence.

'Know anything about criminal profiling?' Deerfield asked suddenly.

Reacher paused. 'Only what I read in the newspaper.'

'It's a science,' Blake explained. 'Special Agent Lamarr here is currently our leading exponent. Special Agent Poulton is her assistant.'

'We look at crime scenes,' Lamarr said. 'We look at the underlying psychological indicators, and we work out the type of personality that could have committed the crime.'

'What crimes?' Reacher asked. 'What scenes?'

'Amy Callan and Caroline Cooke,' Blake said. 'Homicide victims.'

Reacher stared at him.

'Callan was first,' Blake said. 'Very distinctive *modus operandi*, but one homicide is just one homicide, right? Then Cooke was hit. With the exact same MO. That made it a serial situation.'

'We looked for a link,' Poulton said. 'Between the victims. Not hard to find. Army harassment complainants who subsequently quit.'

'Extreme organisation at the crime scene,' Lamarr said. 'Indicative of military precision, maybe. A bizarre, coded MO. Nothing left behind. No clues of any kind. The perpetrator was clearly familiar with investigative procedures. Possibly an investigator himself.'

'No forced entry at either abode,' Poulton said. 'The killer was admitted to the house in both cases, by the victim.'

'So the killer was somebody they both knew,' Blake said.

'Somebody they both trusted,' Poulton said. 'A friendly visitor.'

There was silence again.

'We explored the psychology of the crime,' Lamarr said. 'We looked for an army guy with a score to settle. Maybe somebody outraged by the idea of pesky women ruining good soldiers' careers, and then quitting anyway.'

'Somebody with a clear sense of right and wrong,' Poulton added. 'Somebody confident enough in his own code to set these injustices right by his own hand. Somebody happy to act without the proper authorities getting in the way, you know?'

'Somebody both women knew,' Blake went on. 'Somebody they knew well enough to let right in the house, no questions asked.'

More silence.

'They never knew each other,' Lamarr said. 'They had very few mutual acquaintances. Very few. But you were one of them.'

'Profiling,' Blake said, 'is an exact science. It's good enough evidence to get an arrest warrant in most states of the Union.'

'It never fails,' Lamarr said, with a satisfied smile.

'So?' Reacher said.

'So somebody killed two women,' Deerfield said. He nodded to his right, towards Blake, Lamarr and Poulton. 'And these agents think it was somebody exactly like you. Maybe it *was* you.'

'No, it wasn't me,' Reacher said.

Blake smiled. 'That's what they all say.'

Reacher stared at him. 'You've got two women, is all. The army thing is probably a coincidence. There are hundreds of women out there, harassed out of the army. Why jump on that connection?'

Blake said nothing.

'And why a guy like me?' Reacher asked. 'That's just a guess. That's what this profiling crap comes down to, right? You've no evidence.'

'The guy didn't leave any behind,' Lamarr said. 'The perpetrator was obviously a smart guy, a loner, a brutal vigilante personality. That narrowed it down from millions to thousands to hundreds to tens, maybe all the way down to you.'

'Me?' Reacher said to her. 'You're crazy.'

Deerfield shrugged. 'Well, if you didn't do it, the Bureau's experts think it was somebody exactly like you.'

'Dates,' Reacher said. 'Give me dates, and places.'

'Callan was seven weeks ago,' Blake said. 'Cooke was four.'

Reacher scanned back in time. Four weeks was the start of fall, seven took him into late summer. Late summer, he had been battling the yard in Garrison. Three months of unchecked growth had seen him outdoors every day with scythes and hoes and other tools in his hands. He had gone days at a time without seeing Jodie. She had been tied up in the city with legal cases.

The start of fall, he'd transferred his energies to doing things inside the house. But he'd done them alone. Jodie had stayed in the city, working her way up the greasy pole. There were random nights together. But no trips anywhere, no ticket stubs, no hotel registers. No alibis. He looked at the seven agents ranged against him.

'I want my lawyer now,' he said.

THE TWO SENTRIES took him back to the small room. His status had changed. This time they stayed inside with him, one standing on each side of the closed door. Reacher sat on the plastic chair and ignored them for more than two hours.

Then, suddenly, the door opened and the sentries stepped out and Jodie walked in. She was wearing a peach dress with a wool coat over it, a couple of shades darker. She was a blaze of colour against the grey walls. Her hair was still lightened from the summer sun, her eyes were bright blue, and her skin was the colour of honey. It was the middle of the night, and she looked as fresh as morning. Every time he saw her, she looked more beautiful.

'Hey, Reacher,' she said. She bent down and kissed him.

He could see worry in her face. 'You talk to them?' he asked her.

'I'm not the right person to deal with this,' she said. 'Financial law, yes, but criminal law, I've got no idea.'

She waited in front of his chair, head cocked to one side.

He stood up and stretched, wearily. 'There's nothing to deal with,' he said. 'I didn't kill any women.'

'Of course you didn't. I know that. And they know that, or they'd have taken you straight down to Quantico. This must be about the other thing. They *saw* you do that. You put two guys in hospital.'

'It's not about that. They reacted too fast. This was set up before I even *did* the other thing. And they don't care about the other thing. I'm not working the rackets.'

She nodded. 'Cozo's happy. He's got two punks off the street, no cost to himself. But it's turned into a Catch-22, don't you see that? To convince Cozo, you had to make yourself out as a vigilante loner, and the more you made yourself out as a vigilante loner, the more you fitted this profile from Quantico.'

'The profile is bullshit.'

'They don't think so. You're in big trouble, Reacher. Whatever else, they saw you beat on those guys. I'm not the right person for this,' she said again. 'I don't do criminal law.'

'I don't need any lawyer,' he said.

'Yes, Reacher, you need a lawyer. This is for real.' She stepped into his arms, stretched up and kissed him, hard. 'I love you, Reacher, I really do, you know that, right? But you need a better lawyer.'

There was a long silence.

'They gave me a copy of the surveillance report,' she said.

He nodded. 'I thought they would.'

'Why?'

'Because it eliminates me from the investigation. Whoever's killing these women is working to a timetable. He's on a three-week cycle. Seven weeks ago, four weeks ago . . . The next one's probably already happened, this past week while they've had me under surveillance.'

'So why did they haul you in? If you're eliminated?'

'I don't know,' he said.

There were footsteps in the corridor outside. The door opened and Deerfield stepped into the room and spoke to Jodie. 'Your client conference is over, Ms Jacob,' he said. 'Please follow me.'

Deerfield led them back to the room with the long table. The two local agents followed him. A second chair had been placed on the far side. Deerfield pointed at, and Jodie moved round the end of the table and sat down with Reacher. He squeezed her hand under the shiny mahogany.

The same line-up was ranged against Reacher: Poulton, Lamarr, Blake, Deerfield, and then Cozo. Now there was a squat black audio recorder on the table. Deerfield pressed a red button. He announced the date and identified the nine occupants of the room.

'This is Alan Deerfield speaking to the suspect Jack Reacher,' he said. 'You are now under arrest on the following two counts. One, for aggravated assault and robbery against two persons yet to be identified. Two, for aiding and abetting a criminal organisation engaged in the practice of extortion.'

Deerfield smiled. 'You are not obliged to say anything. If you do say anything, it will be recorded and may be used in evidence against you in a court of law. You are entitled to be represented by an attorney. If you cannot afford an attorney, one will be provided for you by the state of New York. Do you understand your rights?'

'Yes,' Reacher said.

'Do you have anything to say at this point?'

'No.'

Deerfield reached forward and clicked the machine to *off*.

'I want a bail hearing,' Jodie said.

'No need,' Deerfield said. 'We'll release him on his own recognisance. Your client is free to go.'

REACHER WAS OUT OF THERE at just after three in the morning. Jodie had to get back to the office to finish her all-nighter, so one of the local guys drove her down to Wall Street. The other drove Reacher back to Garrison, doing fifty-eight miles in forty-seven minutes.

He jammed to a stop at the end of Reacher's driveway and took off again as soon as the passenger door slammed shut. Reacher watched the car disappear into the mist and walked towards his house.

He had inherited the house from Leon Garber, Jodie's father and his old commanding officer, back at the start of that summer. It had been a week of big surprises, both good and bad. Running into Jodie again, finding out she'd been married and divorced, finding out old Leon was dead, finding out the house was his. He had been in love with Jodie for fifteen years, since he had first met her on a base in the Philippines. She had been fifteen herself then, right on the cusp of womanhood, and she was his CO's daughter. He had crushed his feelings like a guilty secret. He felt they would have been a betrayal of her, and of Leon, and betraying Leon was the last thing he would have ever done, because he loved him like a father.

After Leon's funeral, he and Jodie had sparred uneasily for a couple of days before she admitted she felt the exact same things. It was a glorious sunburst of happiness.

So meeting Jodie again was the good surprise and Leon dying was the bad one, but inheriting the house was both good *and* bad. It was a half-million-dollar slice of prime real estate standing on the Hudson opposite West Point, but it represented a big problem. It *anchored* him in a way that made him profoundly uncomfortable. He had moved around so often it confused him to spend time in any one place. And the idea of property worried him. His whole life, he had never owned more than would fit into his pockets. He had once gone seven years without owning anything at all except a pair of shoes he preferred to the Defense Department issue. After mustering out he added a few clothes, a wristwatch, a toothbrush that came in half and clipped into his pocket like a pen. And that was it. Now he had a house. And a house is a complicated thing. There was insurance to consider. Taxes.

The only thing he had bought for the house was a gold-coloured filter cone for Leon's old coffee machine. He figured it was easier than always running to the store to buy the paper kind. At ten past four that morning, he filled it with coffee, added water and set the machine going. Before it had finished, he heard the crunch of tyres on his asphalt drive. Then a flashing red beam swept over his kitchen window. Doors opened and feet touched the ground. Two people. Doors slammed shut. The doorbell rang.

There were two light switches in the hallway. He pressed the one that operated the porch light and opened the door. Nelson Blake and Julia Lamarr were caught in the yellow spotlight. Blake's face was showing nothing except strain. Lamarr's was still full of hostility.

'Come on in,' Reacher said. 'I just made coffee.'

He walked away, back to the kitchen. 'Black is all I got,' he called. 'No milk or sugar in the house, I'm afraid.'

'Black is fine,' Blake said. He was standing in the kitchen doorway, staying close to the hallway, unwilling to trespass.

Lamarr was alongside him. 'Nothing for me,' she said.

'Drink some coffee, Julia,' Blake said. 'It's been a long night.'

The way he said it was halfway between an order and paternalistic concern. Reacher glanced at him, surprised, and filled three mugs. He took his own and leaned back on the counter, waiting.

'We need to talk,' Blake said.

'Who was the third woman?' Reacher asked.

'Lorraine Stanley. A quartermaster sergeant, serving in Utah someplace. They found her dead in California, this morning.'

'Same MO?'

'Identical in every respect.'

'Same history?'

Blake nodded. 'Harassment complainant, won her case, but quit anyway, a year ago. So that's three out of three. The army thing is not a coincidence, believe me.'

Reacher sipped his coffee. 'I never heard of her,' he said. 'I never served in Utah.'

Blake nodded. 'Somewhere we can talk?'

Reacher led the way into the living room. There were three sofas in a rectangle around a cold fireplace. Blake sat facing the window. Reacher sat opposite and watched Lamarr sit down facing the hearth.

'We stand by our profile,' she said.

'Well, good for you.'

'You were a plausible suspect,' Blake said. 'For the first two. Hence the surveillance.'

'Is that an apology?' Reacher asked.

'I guess so.'

'You got anybody who knew all three?' Reacher asked.

'Not yet,' Lamarr said.

'We're thinking maybe previous personal contact isn't too significant,' Blake said.

'You thought it was, couple of hours ago. You were telling me how I was this big friend of theirs, I knock on the door, they let me in.'

'Not you,' Blake said. 'Somebody like you. Maybe we were wrong. This guy is killing by category, right? Female harassment complainants who quit afterwards? So maybe he's not personally known to them, maybe he's just in a *category* known to them. Like the military police.'

Reacher smiled. 'So now you think it was me again?'

Blake shook his head. 'No, you weren't in California.'

'Wrong answer, Blake. It wasn't me because I'm not a killer.'

'You never killed anybody?' Lamarr said.

'Only those who needed it.'

She smiled in turn. 'Like I said, we stand by our profile. Some self-righteous son of a bitch just like you.'

Reacher saw Blake glance at her, half disapprovingly. He sat forward, forcing Reacher's attention his way. 'What we're saying is, it's possible this guy is or was a military policeman.'

'Anything's possible,' Reacher said.

'There's an *agenda* here,' Blake went on. 'And the way we read it there's army involvement. The victim category is too narrow for this to be random.'

'So?'

'As a rule, the Bureau and the military don't get along too well.'

'Well, there's a surprise. Who the hell *do* you guys get along with?'

Blake looked uncomfortable. 'Nobody gets on with anybody,' he said. 'You know how it is. Military hates the Bureau, the Bureau hates CIA. We need a go-between.'

'Me?'

'Yes, you. We think you could do it. We got your record. You were a hell of an investigator, in the service.'

'That's history.'

'Maybe you still got friends there, people who remember you. Maybe people who still owe you favours.'

'Maybe, maybe not.' He leaned back into the sofa, spread his arms wide across the tops of the cushions and straightened his legs.

'Don't you feel anything?' Blake asked. 'For these women getting killed? You knew Callan and Cooke. You liked them.'

'I liked Callan.'

'So help us catch her killer.'

'No.'

'You son of a bitch,' Lamarr said.

Reacher looked at Blake. 'You seriously think I would want to work with her? Can't she think of anything else to call me except "son of a bitch"?'

'What about an advisory role?' Blake asked. 'Purely consultative?'

Reacher shook his head again. 'No, not interested.'

'Would you agree to be hypnotised?' Blake asked.

'Hypnotised? Why?'

'Maybe you could recall something buried. You know, some guy making some threats, some adverse comments. Something you didn't pay too much attention to at the time. Might come back to you.'

'You still do hypnotism?'

'Sometimes,' Blake said. 'It can help. Julia's an expert. She'd do it.'

'In that case, no thanks. She might make me walk down 5th Avenue, naked.'

Blake looked away, then he turned back. 'Last time, Reacher,' he said. 'The Bureau is asking for your help as an adviser. You'd get paid and everything. Yes or no?'

'This is what hauling me in was all about, right?'

Blake nodded. 'Sometimes it works. You know, make them feel they're the prime suspect, then tell them they're not. Make them feel a sort of gratitude towards us. Makes them want to help us out.'

'Kind of cruel, don't you think?'

'The Bureau does what it has to do.'

'Evidently.'

'So, yes or no?'

'Take Ms Lamarr off the case and I might consider it.'

Lamarr glowered and Blake shook his head.

'I won't do that,' he said.

'Then my answer is no.'

Blake turned the corners of his mouth down. 'We talked with Deerfield before we came up here,' he said. 'You can understand we'd do that, right? As a courtesy? He authorised us to tell you Cozo will drop the racketeering charge if you play ball.'

'I'm not worried about the racketeering charge. I'll look like Robin Hood to a jury of Tribeca merchants.'

Blake wiped his lips with his fingers. 'Problem is it could be more than a racketeering charge. One of those guys is critical. Broken skull. If he dies, it's a homicide charge.'

Reacher laughed. 'Good try, Blake. But nobody got a broken skull tonight. Believe me, I want to break somebody's skull, I know how to do it. So let's hear the rest of the big threats.'

Blake looked at the floor. 'Cozo's got guys on the street, under-cover. Petrosian's going to be asking who did his boys last night. Cozo's guys could let your name slip. He's a hard guy, is what I hear.'

'I'll take my chances.'

Blake nodded. 'We thought you'd say that. We're good judges of character. So we asked ourselves how you'd react to something else. Suppose it's not *your* name and address Cozo leaks to Petrosian? What if it's your girlfriend's name and address?'

'I CAN'T BELIEVE they're acting like this,' Jodie said.

They were in her kitchen, four floors above lower Broadway. Blake and Lamarr had left Reacher in Garrison and twenty restless min-utes later he had driven south to Manhattan. Jodie came home at six in the morning looking for breakfast and a shower and found him waiting in her living room.

'They're desperate,' he said. 'And they're arrogant. And they like to win. They'll do what it takes. I have to call them by eight.'

Her coat was over the back of a kitchen chair. She was pacing ner-vously, back and forth in her peach dress. She had been awake and alert for twenty-three straight hours, but there was nothing to prove it except a faint blue tinge at the inside corners of her eyes.

'Maybe they're not serious,' she said.

'Safest strategy is assume they might be.'

'But why are they so desperate? Why the threats? And why you?'

'Lots of reasons. I was involved with a couple of the cases, I was locatable, I was senior enough that the current generation probably still owes me a few favours.'

She nodded. 'So what are we going to do?'

'I could go take Petrosian out.'

She stared at him, shook her head. Then said, 'We have a thing at the firm. We call it the so-what-else rule. Suppose we've got some bankrupt guy we're looking after. Sometimes we dig around and find he's got some funds stashed away that he's not telling us about. He's cheating. First thing we do, we say *so what else?* What else is he doing? What else has he got?'

'So?'

'So what are they really doing here? Maybe this is not about the women at all. Maybe this is about Petrosian. He's presumably a smart, slippery guy. Maybe there's nothing to pin on him. No evidence, no witnesses. So maybe Cozo is using Blake and Lamarr to get you to get Petrosian. They profiled you, right? Psychologically? They know how you'll react. They know if they use Petrosian to threaten me, your very first thought will be to go get Petrosian. Then he's off the street without a trial, which they probably couldn't win anyway. And nothing is traceable back to the Bureau. Maybe they're using you as an assassin. They wind you up, and off you go.'

'Then why didn't they just ask me straight?'

'They can't just ask you. It would be a hundred per cent illegal. And you mustn't do it, anyway, Reacher. A vigilante homicide, with their *knowledge*? Right under their noses? The Bureau would *own* you, the whole rest of your life.'

He leaned on the window frame and stared at the street below where the sounds of early morning were starting up.

'You're in a hell of a spot,' she said. 'We both are.'

He said nothing.

'So what are you going to do?' she asked.

'I'm going to think,' he said. 'I've got until eight o'clock. All I know is I can't go base myself at Quantico, Virginia, and leave you here alone in the same city as Petrosian. I just can't do that.'

JODIE WENT BACK to work. Before she left the apartment they kissed, long and hard, as if the feeling was going to have to last them long into the foreseeable future. Then Reacher sat alone and thought for thirty minutes. Then he was on the phone for twenty. At five minutes to eight he called Lamarr's number. She answered, first ring.

'I'm in,' he said. 'I'm not happy about it, but I'll do it.'

There was a brief pause. 'Go home and pack a bag,' she said. 'We're going to Virginia. I'll pick you up in two hours exactly.'

'No need. I'll meet you at the airport.'

'We're not going by plane.'

'We're not?'

'No, I never fly. We're driving.'

LAMARR ARRIVED exactly on time in a shiny new Buick.

'Where's your bag?' she asked as Reacher opened the passenger door and slid in beside her.

'I don't have a bag,' he said. His folding toothbrush was clipped into his inside pocket.

She looked away from him like she was dealing with a social difficulty and eased out into the traffic. She drove in silence. I-84 took them across the Hudson River and through Newburgh. Then she turned south on the Thruway and squirmed back in her seat, like she was settling in for the trip.

'You never fly?' he asked.

'I used to, years ago,' she said. 'But I can't now.'

'Why not?'

'Phobia,' she said simply. 'I'm terrified, is all.'

'Driving a car is a million times more likely to kill you.'

She nodded. 'I guess I understand that, statistically.'

'So your fear is irrational.'

'I guess,' she said.

There was silence. Just the hum of the motor.

'The Bureau got many irrational agents?' he asked.

She made no reply. Just reddened slightly under the pallor.

'We need to talk,' Lamarr said.

'So talk. Tell me about college.'

'We're not going to talk about college. We need to discuss the cases.'

He smiled. 'You did go to college, right?'

She nodded. 'Indiana State.'

'Psychology major?'

She shook her head. 'Landscape gardening, if you must know. My professional training is from the FBI Academy at Quantico.'

'Landscape gardening? No wonder the Bureau snapped you up.'

'It was relevant. It teaches you to see the big picture, to be patient.'

'So are there many irrational phobic landscape gardeners at Quantico? Any bonsai enthusiasts scared of spiders?'

'I hope you're real proud of yourself, Reacher, making jokes while women are dying. The Defense Department says there are ninety-one women who fit the same category as the murder victims. My stepsister is one of the eighty-eight who are left.'

He looked out of the window. 'I'm sorry. You must be worried about her.'

Soon they entered New Jersey. The road was wet and there were grey clouds ahead. They were chasing a rainstorm south.

She gripped the wheel and used the leverage to adjust her position in the seat. 'So let's discuss the cases,' she said again. He nodded. 'Locations are obviously random, but the victim group is very specific, right? He goes where he has to. Crime scenes have all been the victim's residence, so far. Single-family housing in all cases, but with varying degrees of isolation.'

'What about husbands and families?' Reacher asked.

'Callan was separated, no kids. Cooke had boyfriends, no kids. Stanley was a loner, no attachments.'

'You look at Callan's husband?'

'Obviously. Any married woman, we look at the husband. But he was alibied, nothing suspicious. And then with Cooke, the pattern became clear. So we knew it wasn't a husband or a boyfriend.'

'No, I guess it wasn't.'

'First problem is how he gets in. No forced entry. He just walks in the door.'

'You think there was surveillance first? Any evidence of a stake-out? Cigarette butts and soda cans piled up under a nearby tree?'

She shook her head. 'This guy is leaving no evidence of anything.'

'Neighbours see anything?'

'Not so far.'

'And all three were done during the day?'

'Different times, but all during daylight hours.'

'None of the women worked?'

'Like you don't. Very few of you ex-army people seem to work. Why is that?' she asked.

'Us *people*?' he repeated. 'In my case because I can't find anything I want to do. I thought about landscape gardening, but I wanted a challenge, not something that would take me two seconds to master.'

She fell silent again and the car hissed into a wall of rain. She set the wipers going and switched on the headlights and backed off the speed a little. 'Are you going to insult me all the time?' she asked.

'Making a little fun of you is a pretty small insult compared to how you're threatening my girlfriend. And how you're so ready to believe I'm the type of guy could kill these women.'

'So was that a yes or a no?'

'It was a maybe. I guess an apology would help turn it into a no.'

'An apology? Forget about it, Reacher. I stand by my profile. If it wasn't you, it was some scumbag just like you.'

The sky was turning black and the rain was intense. Up ahead, brake lights were shining red on the windshield. The traffic was slow-ing to a crawl. Lamarr braked sharply. 'Shit,' she said.

'Fun, right? And right now your risk of death is ten thousand times higher than if you were flying, conditions like these.'

She made no reply. She was concentrating, crawling forward into the deluge. 'Where were we?' she said after a while.

'He's staked them out sufficiently to know they're alone. It's day-light; somehow he walks right in. Then what?'

'Then he kills them.'

'In the house?'

'We think so.'

'You *think* so? Can't you tell?'

'He leaves no evidence,' she said. 'Absolutely nothing. No fibres, no blood, no saliva, no hair, no prints, no DNA, no nothing.'

'So maybe he's not killing them in the house.'

'He leaves the bodies in there. In the tub.'

'In the tub?' he repeated. 'All three of them?'

'Right,' she said. 'Naked. And their clothes are missing.'

'He takes their clothes with him?' he asked. 'Why?'

'Probably as a trophy. Taking trophies is a very common phenomenon in serial crimes like these.'

'He take anything else?'

She shook her head. 'Not as far as we can tell.'

'So he takes their clothes and leaves nothing behind.'

She was quiet for a second. 'He does leave something behind,' she said finally. 'He leaves paint.'

'Paint?'

'Army camouflage green. In the tub. He puts the body in there, naked, and then he fills the tub with paint.'

Reacher stared out at the rain. 'He drowns them? In paint?'

'He doesn't drown them. They're already dead.'

'Tell me about the paint,' he said quietly.

She looked at him, oddly. 'It's army camouflage basecoat. Flat green. Manufactured in Illinois by the hundred thousand gallons.'

He nodded, vaguely. He had never used it, but he had seen a million square yards of stuff daubed with it. 'Messy,' he said.

'But the crime scenes are immaculate. He doesn't spill a drop.'

'The women were already dead. Nobody was fighting. No reason to spill any. But it means he must carry twenty to thirty gallons into the house. That's a lot of paint. It must mean a hell of a lot to him. You figured out any significance to it?'

'Not really, not beyond the obvious military significance. Maybe covering the body with army paint is some kind of reclamation, you know, putting them back where he thinks they belong, in the military, where they should have stayed. It traps them. Couple of hours, the surface is skinning over. It goes hard, and the stuff underneath jellifies. Leave it long enough, I guess the whole tub might dry solid.'

Reacher stared ahead through the windshield. The horizon was bright. They were leaving the weather behind.

'Twenty or thirty gallons of paint is a major load to haul around. It implies a big vehicle. Very visible. Nobody saw anything?'

'We canvassed, door to door. Nobody reported anything.'

He nodded, slowly. 'The paint is the key. Where's it come from?'

'We have no idea. The army is not being especially helpful.'

'I'm not surprised. It's embarrassing. Makes it likely it's a serving soldier. Who else could get that much camouflage paint?'

She made no reply. She just drove south. The rain was gone and she switched the wipers off. He fell to thinking about a soldier somewhere, loading cans of paint. Ninety-one women on his list, some skewed mental process reserving twenty or thirty gallons for each one of them. Truckloads of it. Maybe he was a quartermaster.

'How is he killing them?' he asked.

She slid her hands to a firmer grip on the wheel. Swallowed hard and kept her eyes on the road. 'We don't know.'

'You don't *know*?' he repeated.

'We can't figure out how.'

Chapter 2

There are ninety-one altogether, and you need to do six of them in total, which is three more, so what do you do now? You keep on thinking and planning, is what. Because you need to outwit them all. The victims, and the investigators. More investigators all the time. New angles, new approaches. They're looking for you. They'll find you if they can.

The investigators are tough, but the women are easy. You planned long and hard, and the planning was perfect. They answer the door, they let you in, they fall for it. They're so stupid, they deserve it. And it's not difficult. It's like everything else. If you plan it properly, it's easy. Three more then you're home and dry.

'WHY DON'T YOU know how they died?' Reacher asked.

'There are no wounds, injuries. The crime-scene guys take the bodies out of the tubs; the pathologists clean them up and they don't find anything. No water or paint in the lungs, so they didn't drown.'

'No hypodermic marks? Bruising?'

Lamarr shook her head. 'Nothing. But remember, they've been coated in paint. That military stuff is full of chemicals, and fairly corrosive. It's conceivable the paint damage might be obscuring some marks on the skin. But whatever killed them was very subtle.'

'What about internal damage?'

She shook her head again. 'Nothing. No subcutaneous bruising, no organ damage. Toxicology was clear. No sexual interference.'

'Weird,' Reacher said. 'It's a very unsoldierly way to kill somebody. Soldiers shoot or stab or hit or strangle. They don't do subtle things.'

'We don't know exactly what he did.'

'But there's no *anger* there, right? If this guy is into retribution, where's the anger? It sounds too clinical.'

Lamarr yawned. 'That troubles me, too. But look at the victim category. What else can the motive be? And if we agree on the motive, what else can the perp be except an angry soldier?'

They lapsed into silence. The miles rolled by. Lamarr yawned again, and he glanced sharply at her.

'You OK?'

'I'm a little weary, I guess. It was a long night.'

'Well, take care.'

'You worrying about me now?'

He shook his head. 'No, I'm worrying about myself. You could fall asleep, run us off the road.'

She yawned again. 'Never happened before.'

He looked at her, long and hard. 'I'm going to sleep for an hour,' he said. 'Try not to kill me.'

WHEN HE WOKE UP, he could see that Lamarr was rigid with exhaustion, staring down the road with red unblinking eyes.

'We should stop for lunch,' he said.

She hesitated, ready to argue. Then her body suddenly went slack and she yawned again. 'OK,' she said. 'So let's stop.'

She drove on for a mile and coasted into a rest area in a clearing in some trees. The place was the same as a hundred others Reacher had seen, low-profile fifties architecture colonised by fast-food operations.

They got out and Reacher stretched his cramped frame in the cold damp air before strolling inside to line up for a sandwich.

The line shuffled forward and he changed his selection from cheese to crabmeat, because he figured it was more expensive and assumed she was paying. He added a large cup of black coffee and a doughnut, then found a table while she fiddled with her bag.

She joined him and he raised his coffee in an ironic toast. 'Here's to a few fun days together,' he said.

'It'll be more than a few days,' she said. 'It'll be as long as it takes.'

He sipped his coffee and thought about time. 'What's the significance of the three-week cycle?'

'We're not sure. Maybe he's on a three-week work pattern, two weeks on, one week off. He spends the week off staking them out, organising it, and then doing it.'

Reacher saw his chance. 'Possible,' he said.

'So what kind of soldier works that kind of pattern?'

'That regular?' He swallowed. 'Special Forces maybe.' He waited to see if she'd take the bait.

'Special Forces would know subtle ways to kill, right?'

He started on his sandwich. 'Silent ways, unarmed ways, improvised ways, I guess. But I don't know about *subtle* ways.'

'So what are you saying?'

'I'm saying I don't have a clue who's doing what, or why. You're the big expert here. You're the one who studied landscape gardening.'

She paused. 'We need more from you than this, Reacher. And you know what we'll do if we don't get it.'

'She gets hurt, you know what I'll do to you, right?'

She smiled. 'Threatening me, Reacher? Threatening a Federal agent? Now you're *really* stacking up the charges against yourself.'

He drained his cup and made no reply.

'Stay on the ball, and everything will be OK,' she said.

'I'll be a go-between. That's what I agreed to. But you need to tell me what you want.'

She nodded. 'Special Forces sound promising to me. First thing you'll do is check them out.'

He clenched his teeth to stop himself smiling. So far, so good.

THEY SPENT AN HOUR at the rest stop, then Lamarr gathered her bag and stood up from the table. They walked back to the Buick in silence. She fired it up and eased it out onto the highway.

The hum of the motor, the faint noise from the road came back and within a minute it was like they had never stopped at all.

'Tell me about your sister,' he said.

'My stepsister.'

'Whatever, tell me about her.'

'She's a rich girl who wanted adventure.'

'So she joined the army?'

'She believed the advertisements. You seen those, in magazines? They make it look tough and glamorous. She thought it was going to be all rappelling down cliffs with a knife between your teeth.'

'And it wasn't?'

'They put her in a transport battalion, made her drive a truck.'

'Why didn't she quit, if she's rich?'

'Because she's not a quitter. She pushed for something better. She saw some jerk of a colonel five times, trying to make progress. He suggested if she was naked for the sixth interview, that might help.'

'And?'

'She busted him. Whereupon they gave her the transfer she wanted. Infantry close-support unit. But you know how it works, right? No smoke without fire? The assumption was she *had* screwed the guy, even though she had busted him. In the end, she couldn't stand the whispers, and she quit.'

'So what's she doing now?'

'Nothing. She's feeling a little sorry for herself.'

'You close to her?'

'Not very,' she said. 'Not as close as I'd maybe want to be.'

'You like her?'

Lamarr made a face. 'What's not to like? She's very likable. She's a great person, actually. But I handled it all wrong. I was young, my dad was dead, we were real poor, this rich guy fell in love with my mother and finished up adopting me. I was full of resentment that I was being *rescued*, I guess. I figured it didn't mean I had to love *her*. She's only my *stepsister*, I said to myself. Then when my mother died, I was left feeling isolated and awkward. I didn't handle it well. So now my stepsister is just a nice woman I know. Like a close acquaintance. I guess we both feel that way. But we get along OK.'

'If they're rich, are you rich, too?'

She glanced sideways. 'I'm richer than you'd think. My stepfather is very fair with us, even though I'm not really his daughter and she is.'

'Lucky you.'

She paused. 'And we're going to be a lot richer soon. Unfortunately he's real sick. He's been fighting cancer for two years, but now he's going to die. So there's a big inheritance coming our way.'

'I'm sorry he's sick,' Reacher said.

She nodded. 'Yes, so am I. It's sad.'

There was silence. Just the hum of the miles passing under the wheels. 'Did you warn your sister?' Reacher asked.

'My stepsister.'

'Why do you emphasise she's your stepsister?' he asked.

She shrugged. 'Because Blake will pull me off if he thinks I'm too involved. And I don't want that to happen. I want to take care of this myself.' She was quiet for a moment. 'The family thing is awkward for me,' she went on. 'When my mother died, they could have cut me off, but they *didn't*. They have always been generous, very fair, and now I feel guilty for calling myself a Cinderella at the beginning.'

Reacher said nothing.

'You think I'm being irrational again,' she said.

He made no reply to that. Just watched the road.

'Did you warn her?' he asked again.

She glanced sideways at him. 'Yes, of course I warned her. I've called her again and again and told her not to let anybody through the door. Nobody at all, no matter who they are.'

'She pay attention?'

'I made sure she did.'

'OK. Only eighty-seven others to worry about.'

AFTER NEW JERSEY came eighty miles of Maryland, which took an hour and twenty minutes to cover. It was raining again, prematurely dark. Then they skirted the District of Columbia and entered Virginia and settled in for the final forty miles of I-95, through gentle forest all the way down to Quantico.

When Lamarr turned off the highway onto an unmarked road that wound through forest, Reacher sat forward and paid attention. He had never been to Quantico before. He was curious. The car rounded a tight bend, came clear of the trees and stopped at a checkpoint, a red-and-white striped pole across the roadway and a sentry's hutch made from bulletproof glass. An armed guard stepped forward. Over his shoulder, in the distance, was a long low huddle of honey-coloured stone buildings, a couple of high-rises standing among them surrounded by immaculate lawns. Except for the razor-wire perimeter and the armed guard, it looked like a college campus.

Lamarr had the window down and was rooting in her bag for ID. The guy clearly knew who she was, but rules are rules and he needed to see her plastic. He nodded as soon as her hand came clear of the bag. Then he switched his gaze to Reacher.

'You should have paperwork on him,' Lamarr said.

The guy nodded again. 'Yeah, Mr Blake took care of it.'

He ducked back into his hutch and came out with a laminated plastic tag on a chain. He handed it through the window and Lamarr passed it on. It had Reacher's name and his old service photograph on it. The whole thing was overprinted with a pale red V.

'V for visitor,' Lamarr said. 'You wear it at all times.'

'Or?' Reacher asked.

'Or you get shot. And I'm not kidding.'

The guard was raising the barrier. Lamarr buzzed her window up and accelerated through to a parking lot in front of the largest building. She eased into a slot and shut down. Checked her watch.

'Six hours,' she said. 'That's slow. The weather, I guess.'

'So now what?' Reacher asked.

'Now we get to work.'

He slipped the ID chain round his neck, opened his door and slid out. The plate-glass door at the front of the building opened up and Poulton, the sandy-haired guy, walked out. He was wearing a fresh suit, dark blue, with a white button-down shirt and a grey tie.

'I'll show you to your room,' he said. 'You can stow your stuff.'

'I don't have any stuff,' Reacher said to him.

Poulton hesitated. There was clearly an itinerary. A timetable to be followed. 'I'll show you anyway,' he said.

Lamarr walked away with her bag and Poulton led Reacher to an elevator. They rode together to the third floor and came out on a quiet corridor with thin carpet on the floor and worn fabric on the walls. Poulton walked to a plain door and unlocked it. Inside was a standard-issue motel-style room. Narrow entryway, bathroom on the right, closet on the left, bed, table and two chairs, bland decor.

Poulton stayed out in the corridor. 'Be ready in ten.'

The door sucked shut. There was no handle on the inside. There was a view of the woods from the window, but the window frame was welded shut. There was a telephone on the nightstand. He picked it up, hit nine and heard the dial tone. He dialled Jodie's private office line. Let it ring eighteen times before trying her apartment. Her machine cut in. He tried her mobile. It was switched off.

He put his coat in the closet, unclipped his toothbrush from his pocket and propped it in a glass on the bathroom vanity shelf. Rinsed his face at the sink. Then waited.

EIGHT MINUTES LATER he heard a key in the lock and looked up expecting to see Poulton at the door. But it was a woman. She looked about sixteen. She had long fair hair in a loose ponytail, white teeth in an open, tanned face. Bright blue eyes. She was wearing a man's suit, extensively tailored to fit. A white shirt and a tie. She was over six feet tall, long-limbed, and completely spectacular.

'Hi,' she said, smiling.

Reacher made no reply. Her face clouded and her smile turned a little embarrassed. 'So you want to do the FAQs right away?'

'The what?'

'The FAQs. Frequently asked questions.'

'I'm not sure I have any questions.'

'Oh, OK.' She smiled again, relieved.

'What are the frequently asked questions?' he said.

'Oh, you know, the stuff most new guys around here ask me. It's really, really tedious.' She made a face, resigned. 'I'm Lisa Harper. I'm twenty-nine, yes really; I'm from Aspen, Colorado; I'm six feet one, yes really; I've been at Quantico two years; yes, I date guys; no, I dress like this just because I like it; no, I don't currently have a boyfriend; and no, I don't want to have dinner with you tonight.' She finished with another smile and he smiled back.

'Well, how about tomorrow night?' he said.

She sighed. 'All you need to know is I'm an FBI agent, on duty.'

'Doing what?'

'Watching you,' she said. 'You're classified SU, status unknown, maybe friendly, maybe hostile. Usually that means an organised-crime plea bargain, you know, some guy ratting on his bosses.'

'I'm not organised crime.'

'Our file says you might be.'

'Then the file is bullshit.'

She nodded. 'I looked Petrosian up. He's Syrian. Therefore his rivals are Chinese. And *they* never employ anybody except other Chinese. Implausible they'd use you.'

'You point that out to anybody?'

'I'm sure they already know. They're just trying to get you to take the threat seriously.'

'Should I take it seriously?'

'Yes, you should. You should think very carefully about Jodie.'

'Jodie's in the file?'

'Everything's in the file.'

'You a profiler too?'

She shook her head. The ponytail moved with it. 'No, I'm operational. Assigned for the duration. So let's go.'

She held the door. It closed softly behind him as they walked to a different elevator. Inside, this one had buttons for five basement floors. Lisa Harper pressed the bottom button. Reacher stood beside her and tried not to breathe in her scent.

The elevator settled with a bump and the door slid back to reveal a grey corridor.

'We call this the Bunker,' Harper said. 'It used to be our nuclear shelter. Now it's BS. That stands for behavioural science.'

She led him along a line of doors in the left-hand wall, stopped him in front of one of them and knocked.

'I'll be right outside,' she said, opening up the door for him.

He went in and saw Nelson Blake behind a crowded desk in a small untidy office. There were piles of paper everywhere. No visitor chair. Blake was glowering at a muted television set, tuned to a political cable channel. A guy in shirtsleeves was reading something to a committee. The caption read *Director of the FBI*.

'Budget hearings,' Blake muttered. 'Singing for our damn supper.'

Reacher said nothing. Blake kept his eyes on the television.

'Case conference in two minutes,' he said. 'So listen up for the rules. Harper stays with you, all the time. Everything you do, everywhere you go, you're supervised by her. But don't get the wrong idea. You're still Lamarr's boy, only she stays here because she won't fly. And you'll need to get around some. And don't get ideas about Harper. Thing with her is, she looks nice, but you start messing with her, she's the bitch from hell, OK?'

'OK.'

Blake scrabbled in the pile of paper on his desk and came up with a large brown envelope. Held it out.

'With Cozo's compliments,' he said.

Reacher took the envelope. It contained photographs. Eight of them. Crime-scene photographs. Mutilated corpses. Pieces missing.

'Petrosian's handiwork,' Blake said. 'Wives and sisters and daughters of people who pissed him off.'

Reacher nodded. 'So where's Jodie?'

'How should I know?' Blake said. 'We're not tailing her. Petrosian can find her himself, if it comes to that. We're not going to deliver her to him. That would be illegal, right?'

'So would breaking your neck.'

Blake shook his head. 'I'm not worried about you, Reacher. Deep down, you're a good person. You'll help me, and then you'll forget all about me.'

Reacher smiled. 'I thought you profilers were supposed to be real insightful.'

THE CASE CONFERENCE was held in a long low room a floor above Blake's office. There was a long table made of expensive wood, surrounded by cheap chairs set at forty-five-degree angles so they faced the head of the table, where a large empty blackboard was set against the end wall.

Harper led Reacher to a seat at the furthest end from the blackboard. She sat one place nearer the action, and Blake took the chair nearest the board. Poulton and Lamarr came in together, carrying files, absorbed in conversation. Blake waited until the door closed behind them, then stood up and flipped the blackboard over.

The top right quarter was occupied by a map of the United States, dotted with a forest of flags. Ninety-one of them, Reacher guessed. Most of them were red, but three of them were black. Opposite the map, on the left, was an eight-by-ten colour photograph of a woman, squinting against the sun and smiling. She was in her twenties, pretty, a plump happy face framed by brown curly hair.

'Lorraine Stanley, ladies and gentlemen,' Blake said. 'Recently deceased in San Diego, California.'

Underneath the smiling face were more eight-by-tens pinned up in a careful sequence. The crime scene. There was a long shot of a small Spanish-style bungalow. Wide shots of a hallway, a living room, the master bedroom. The master bathroom. There was a shower stall on the right, and a tub on the left. Full of green paint.

'She was alive three days ago,' Blake said. 'Neighbour saw her wheeling her garbage to the kerb in the morning. Nobody saw anything after that. She was discovered yesterday, by her cleaner.'

'We got a time of death?' Lamarr asked.

'Approximate,' Blake said. 'Sometime during the second day. MO identical to the first two.'

'Evidence?'

'Not a damn thing, so far.'

Reacher was focusing on the picture of the hallway. It was a long narrow space leading past the mouth of the living room, back to the bedrooms. On the left was a narrow shelf at waist height, crowded with tiny cactus plants. On the right were more narrow shelves, fixed to the wall at random heights, packed with small china ornaments.

'She answers the door, this guy somehow wrestles her back through the hallway, into the bathroom, and then carries thirty gallons of paint through after her, and doesn't knock anything off those shelves. Where's the violence? Where's the anger?'

Blake shook his head. 'He doesn't do any wrestling. Medical reports show the women aren't touched at all. There is no violence.'

'You happy with that? Profile-wise? An angry soldier looking for retribution, but there's no uproar?'

'He *kills* them, Reacher. The way I see it, that's anger enough.'

'And what about the paint? How does he bring it to the house?' Reacher continued. 'We should go to the store and check out what thirty gallons looks like. He must have a car or a truck parked outside for twenty, thirty minutes at least. How does nobody see it?'

'We don't know,' Blake said.

'How does he kill them without leaving any marks?'

'We don't know.'

'That's a lot you don't know, right?'

Blake grimaced. 'Yes, it is, smart guy. But we're working on it. We've got eighteen days till the next killing's due, and with a genius like you helping us, I'm sure that's all we're going to need.'

'You've got eighteen days if he sticks to his interval,' Reacher said. 'Suppose he doesn't?'

Blake looked at Lamarr. 'Julia?'

'I stand by my profile,' she said. 'Right now I'm interested in Special Forces. They're stood down one week in three. I'm sending Reacher to poke around.'

Blake nodded, reassured. 'OK, where?'

Lamarr glanced at Reacher, waiting.

He looked at the three black flags on the map.

'Geography is all over the place,' he said. 'This guy could be stationed anywhere in the United States. So Fort Dix would be the best place to start. I know a guy there. A guy called John Trent. He's a colonel. If anybody's going to help me, he might.'

'OK,' Blake said. 'We'll call this Colonel Trent, get it set up.'

'Make sure you mention my name loud and often. He won't be very interested unless you do,' Reacher said.

'That's exactly why we brought you on board. You'll leave with Harper, first thing in the morning.'

MAYBE IT'S TIME to throw them a curve. Maybe tighten the interval a bit. Maybe cancel it altogether. That would really unsettle them.

Or maybe let a little of the anger show, too. Because anger is what this is about, right? Anger, and justice. Maybe it's time to make that a little more obvious. Maybe it's time to take the gloves off. A little violence could make the next one more interesting, too.

So what's it to be? A shorter interval? Or more drama at the scene? Or both? How about both? Think, think, think.

LISA HARPER took Reacher up to ground level and outside into the chill air just after six in the evening. She led him down a concrete walkway towards the next building. 'Cafeteria's in here,' she said.

She was ahead of him at another set of glass doors. She pulled one open and waited until he went inside. 'To the left,' she said.

There was a long corridor with the clattering sound and the vegetable smell of a communal dining room at the end of it.

'OK, help yourself,' she said. 'Bureau's paying.'

The cafeteria was a big double-height room, brightly lit, with a service counter along one side. Reacher joined a line of personnel, waiting with trays in their hands, Harper at his side.

The line shuffled up and he was served a filet mignon by a cheerful Spanish guy. He got vegetables from the next server in line, filled a cup with coffee from an urn, then looked around for a table.

'By the window,' Harper said.

She led him to an empty table for four, put her tray on the table and took her jacket off. Draped it on the back of her chair. Her shirt was fine cotton, and she wore nothing underneath it. That was pretty clear. She undid her cuffs and rolled her sleeves to the elbow, one by one. Her forearms were smooth and brown.

'Nice tan,' Reacher said.

She sighed. 'FAQs again? Yes, it's all over, and no, I don't especially want to prove it.'

He smiled. 'Just making conversation,' he said.

'I'll talk about the case. If you want conversation.'

'I don't know much about the case. Do you?'

'I know I want this guy caught. Those women were pretty brave, making a stand like that.'

'Sounds like the voice of experience,' he said, cutting into his steak.

'It's the voice of cowardice. I haven't made a stand. Not yet.'

'You getting harassed?'

She smiled. 'Are you kidding?' Then she blushed. 'I mean, can I say that without sounding bigheaded or anything?'

He looked at her over the rim of his cup. White cotton button-down shirt, a blue tie knotted neatly in place and rising gently over her small mobile breasts. Tanned face, white teeth, great cheekbones, the long blonde hair.

He grinned back. 'Yes, in your case I think you can.'

'It's just talk, you know, loaded questions, and innuendo. Nobody's said I should sleep with them to get promotion or anything. But it still gets to me. That's why I dress like this now. I'm trying to make the point, you know, I'm just the same as them, really.'

He made no reply. Just smiled again.

'Is there a camera in my room?' he asked. 'Video surveillance?'

'Why?'

'I'm just wondering if this is a back-up plan. In case Petrosian doesn't pan out. Blake assigned *you* to look after me, so you could get real close to me. So he's got something else to twist my arm with, like a nice intimate little scene, you and me in my room, on a nice little video cassette he can send to Jodie.'

She blushed. 'I wouldn't do a thing like that.'

'But he asked you to, right?'

She was quiet for a long time. Reacher drained his coffee. 'He practically challenged me to try,' he said. 'Told me you're the bitch from hell if anybody puts the moves on. But I wouldn't fall for it,' he said. 'I'm not stupid. I'm not about to give them more ammunition.'

She looked at him and smiled. 'So can we relax? Get past it?'

He nodded. 'Sure, let's relax. What do people do here in the evenings anyway?'

'Mostly they go home,' Harper said. 'But not you. You go back to your room. Blake's orders.'

'We're following Blake's orders now?'

She laughed. 'Some of them.'

HE SLEPT BADLY and woke before six. Dialled Jodie's apartment. Got the machine. Her office. No reply. Her mobile. Switched off.

He spent fifteen minutes in the shower with the water as hot as he could stand it, and once he was dressed he sat down to wait.

He waited forty-five minutes. There was a polite knock at the door, then it opened and Lisa Harper was standing there, smiling. 'Good morning,' she said.

He raised his hand in reply. She was in a different suit. This one was charcoal grey, with a white shirt and a dark red tie. An exact parody of the unofficial Bureau uniform, but a whole lot of cloth had been cut out of it to make it fit. Her hair was loose, hanging front and back of her shoulders, very long.

'We've got to go,' she said. 'Breakfast meeting.'

He took his coat from the closet as he passed. They rode down to the lobby together and paused at the doors. It was raining hard outside. She sprinted down the walkway, and he pulled his collar up and followed behind, watching her run. She looked pretty good.

Lamarr, Blake and Poulton were waiting for them in the cafeteria, in three of five chairs crowded round a table by the window. There was a coffee jug in the centre, surrounded by mugs, and a pile of newspapers. Harper took a chair and he squeezed in next to her.

'We called Fort Dix last night,' Blake said. 'Spoke with Colonel Trent. He seems to like you. Said he'll give you all day today.'

'That should do it.'

Lamarr nodded. 'Good. You know what you're looking for, right? Concentrate on the dates. Find somebody whose stand-down weeks match. My guess is he's doing it late in the week, because he's got to get back to base and calm down afterwards.'

Reacher shrugged. 'We do it by dates alone, we're going to come up with maybe a thousand names.'

'So narrow it down some. Get Trent to cross-reference against the women. Find somebody who served with one of them.'

Reacher smiled. 'Awesome brain power round this table. It could make a guy feel real intimidated.'

'You got better ideas, smart guy?' Blake asked.

'I know what I'm going to do.'

'Well, just remember what's riding on it, OK? Lots of women in danger, one of them yours.'

A MOTOR-POOL GUY brought a car to the doors and left it there with the motor running. Harper watched Reacher get in and then slid into the driver's seat. They drove out through the rain, past the checkpoint, out onto I-95. She blasted north through the spray and fifty minutes later made a right into the north gate of Andrews Air Force Base.

'They assigned us the company plane,' she said.

Two security checks later they were at the foot of an unmarked Learjet's cabin steps. They left the car on the tarmac and climbed inside. It was taxiing before they had their seat belts fastened.

'Should be a half-hour to Dix,' Harper said.

'McGuire,' Reacher corrected. 'Dix is a Marine Corps base. We'll land at McGuire Air Force Base.'

Harper looked worried. 'They told me we're going straight there.'

'We are. It's the same place. Different names, is all.'

She made a face. 'Weird. I guess I don't understand the military.'

'Well, don't feel bad about it. We don't understand you, either.'

Thirty minutes later they were on approach. There was cloud almost all the way down, then the ground was suddenly in sight. It was raining in Jersey. Dim and miserable. The Learjet touched down and taxied to a distant corner of tarmac. A green Chevy was racing through the rain to meet it. By the time the cabin steps were down, the driver, a Marine lieutenant, was waiting at the bottom.

'Major Reacher?' he asked.

Reacher nodded. 'And this is Agent Harper, from the FBI.'

The lieutenant ignored her, as Reacher knew he would.

'The colonel is waiting, sir,' he said.

'So let's go. Can't keep the colonel waiting, right?'

They drove out of McGuire into Dix, following narrow roadways through blocks of warehouses and barracks, and stopped at a huddle of brick offices a mile from the runway.

'Door on the left, sir,' the lieutenant said.

Reacher got out and Harper followed him into a spacious anteroom full of metal desks and filing cabinets. It was antiseptically clean and obsessively tidy. Three sergeants worked at separate desks. One of them glanced up and hit a button on his telephone.

'Major Reacher is here, sir,' he said into it.

There was a moment's pause and then the inner office door opened and a tall man stepped out, short black hair silvering at the temples. 'Hello, Reacher,' John Trent said.

Reacher nodded. Trent owed the second half of his career to a paragraph Reacher had omitted from an official report ten years before. Trent had assumed the paragraph was written and ready to go. He had come to see Reacher, not to plead for its deletion, not to bribe, but to explain, officer to officer, how he'd made the mistake, and that it was not malice or dishonesty. He had left without asking for a thing, and then sat and waited for the axe. It never came. The report was published and the paragraph wasn't in it. What Trent didn't know was that Reacher had never even written it. Ten years had passed and the two men hadn't spoken since. Not until Reacher had called him from Jodie's apartment the previous morning.

'Hello, Colonel,' Reacher said. 'This is Agent Harper, FBI.'

Trent shook hands with the agent.

'Pleased to meet you, Colonel,' Harper said. 'And thanks in advance for your cooperation.'

Trent smiled. 'I'll do what I can, but the cooperation will be limited. We're going to be examining personnel records and deployment listings that I'm just not prepared to share with you. Reacher and I will do it on our own. There are issues of national and military security at stake. You're going to have to wait out here.'

'All day?' she said.

Trent nodded. 'As long as it takes. You comfortable with that?'

It was clear she wasn't. 'I'm supposed to watch over him.'

'I understand that. Your Mr Blake explained your role to me. But you'll be right here, outside my office. There's only one door. The sergeant will give you a desk.'

A sergeant showed her to an empty desk with a clear view of the inner office door. She sat down slowly, unsure.

'You'll be OK there,' Trent said. 'This could take us some time. It's a complicated business. I'm sure you know how paperwork can be.'

Then he led Reacher into the large, inner office and closed the door. It had windows on two walls, a big wooden desk, leather chairs. Reacher sat down in front of the desk and leaned back.

'Give it two minutes, OK?' he said.

Trent nodded. 'Read this. Look busy.'

He handed over a faded green folder, one of a tall stack of files. Reacher opened it up and bent to examine it while Trent walked back to the door. Opened it wide.

'Ms Harper?' he called. 'Can I get you a cup of coffee?'

Reacher glanced over his shoulder and saw her staring in at him, taking in the leather chairs, the desk, the stack of files.

'I'm all set, right now,' she called back.

'OK,' Trent said. 'You want anything, just tell the sergeant.'

He closed the door again. Walked to the window. Reacher stood up. Trent unlatched the window and opened it as wide as it would go.

'You didn't give us much time,' he whispered. 'But we're in business.'

'They fell for it right away,' Reacher whispered back.

Trent nodded. Stuck his head out of the window and checked both directions. 'OK, go for it,' he said. 'And good luck, my friend.'

'I need a gun,' Reacher whispered.

Trent shook his head firmly. 'No,' he said. 'That, I can't do.'

'You have to. I need one.'

Trent paused. He was getting nervous. 'OK, a gun,' he said. 'But no ammunition. My ass is already way out on a limb on this thing.'

He opened a drawer and took out a Beretta M9. Same weapon as Petrosian's boys had carried, except Reacher could see this one still had its serial number intact. Trent took the clip out and thumbed the bullets back into the drawer, one by one. Then he clicked the empty clip back into the gun and handed it to Reacher, butt first.

'Take care,' he whispered as Reacher sat on the window ledge, swivelled his legs outside, and dropped to the ground.

He was in a narrow alley. The lieutenant was still waiting in the Chevy, ten yards away, motor running. Reacher sprinted for the car and it was rolling before his door was closed. The mile back to McGuire took little over a minute. The car raced out onto the tarmac and headed straight for a Marine Corps helicopter. Its belly door was standing open and the rotor blade was turning.

'Thanks, kid,' Reacher said.

He stepped out of the car and across to the chopper's ramp and ran up into the darkness. The door whirred shut behind him and the engine noise built to a roar. He felt the machine come off the ground and two pairs of hands grabbed him and pushed him into his seat. He buckled his harness and a headset was thrust at him. He heard the intercom crackle as the interior lights came on.

'We're going to the Coast Guard heliport in Brooklyn,' the pilot called. 'Close as we can get without filing a flight plan, and filing a flight plan ain't exactly on the agenda today, OK?'

Reacher thumbed his mike. 'Suits me, guys. And thanks.'

'Colonel must owe you big,' the pilot said.

'No, he just likes me.'

The guy laughed and the helicopter swung in the air then settled to a cruising speed.

The Coast Guard heliport in Brooklyn is sixty air miles northeast of McGuire. The Marine pilot made the trip in thirty-seven minutes. 'You've got four hours,' he said when they had touched down. 'Any longer than that, we're out of here and you're on your own, OK?'

'OK,' Reacher said. He unstrapped himself, slipped the headset off and followed the ramp down as it opened. There was a dark blue sedan with Navy markings waiting on the tarmac.

'You Reacher?' the driver yelled through the open passenger door. Reacher nodded and slid in alongside him.

The guy stamped on the gas. 'I'm Navy Reserve,' he said. 'We're helping the colonel out. A little inter-service cooperation.'

'I appreciate it,' said Reacher.

'So where we headed?' the guy asked.

'Manhattan. Aim for Chinatown.'

Traffic was light, but it was another thirty minutes before Reacher was where he wanted to be. The guy stopped short on a hydrant.

'I'll be waiting right here,' he said. 'Facing the other direction, exactly three hours from now. So don't be late, OK?'

'I won't,' Reacher said.

He slid out of the car and slapped twice on the roof. Crossed the street and headed south. He glanced at his watch. It was late morning and he started worrying he was too early.

After five minutes, he stopped walking. If any street was going to do it for him, this was the one. It was lined both sides with Chinese restaurants, bright gaudy façades in reds and yellows, a forest of signs in Oriental script. The sidewalks were crowded. Delivery trucks double-parked tight against cars. He walked the length of the street twice, inspecting the terrain, looking for his targets.

He glanced at his watch and saw his time ticking away. He looked into doorways. Nothing. He watched the alleys. Nothing. He walked a block south and tried another street. Nothing. He waited on a corner. Still nothing. He walked back to his starting point and checked his watch again. He had been waiting two hours. He had an hour left.

The lunch crowd died away to nothing and the street went quiet. A light drizzle started, and then it stopped. Low clouds moved across the sky. He walked east and south. Came back again and walked up one side of the street and down the other. Checked his watch. He had forty minutes left. Then thirty. Then twenty.

Then he saw them. Two guys. Chinese, of course. Young, shiny black hair worn long on their collars. They wore dark trousers and light windcheaters, with scarves at their necks, like a uniform.

They were very blatant. One carried a satchel and the other carried a notebook. They strolled into each restaurant in turn, slow and casual. Then they strolled out again, with one guy zipping the satchel and the other guy noting something in his book. Reacher crossed the street and moved ahead of them. Watched them go into a restaurant and approach an old guy at the register. The old guy reached into the cash drawer and took out a wad of folded bills. The guy with the book took it and handed it to his partner. Wrote something in the book as the money disappeared into the satchel.

Reacher stepped ahead, up to where a narrow alley separated two buildings. He ducked in and waited with his back to the wall. He timed the two guys in his head. Waited. Then he stepped out of the alley and met them head-on. They bumped right into him. He seized a bunch of windcheater in each hand and swung them through an explosive half-circle back-first into the alley wall. The guy with the satchel followed a wider arc, and therefore hit harder. Reacher caught him solidly with his elbow as he bounced off the wall and he went down on the floor. Didn't come back up again.

The other guy dropped the book and went for his pocket, but Reacher had Trent's Beretta out first. He stood close and held it angled low, down towards the guy's kneecap. 'Be smart, OK?' he said.

He reached down and racked the slide. The sound was muffled by the cloth of his coat, but to his practised ear it sounded horribly empty. The Chinese guy didn't notice. Too shocked. He just pressed himself to the wall like he was trying to back right through it.

'You're making a mistake, pal,' he whispered.

Reacher shook his head. 'No, we're making a *move*.'

'Who's we?'

'Petrosian,' Reacher said.

'Petrosian? You're kidding me.'

'No way,' Reacher said. 'I'm serious. Real serious. This street is Petrosian's now. As of today.' And he slammed him left-handed in the stomach. The guy folded forward and Reacher tapped him above the ear with the butt of the gun and dropped him neatly on top of his partner. He put the gun back in his pocket, picked up the satchel and tucked it under his arm. Walked out of the alley and turned north.

He was late, but he didn't run. Running in the city was too conspicuous. He walked away as fast as he could, threading his way along the sidewalks. He turned a corner and saw the blue car, *USNR* painted discreetly on its flank, moving away from the kerb. Now he ran.

He got to where it had been parked four seconds after it had left. Now it was three cars ahead. The light changed to red. The car braked to a neat stop and pedestrians swarmed out in front of it. Reacher ran to the intersection and pulled open the passenger door. Dumped himself into the seat, panting. The driver nodded to him. Didn't offer any kind of an apology for not waiting. Reacher didn't expect one. When the Navy says three hours, it means three hours. Not a second more, not a second less. *Time and tide wait for no man*. The Navy was built on all kinds of bullshit like that.

REACHER SPENT the flight back to Trent's office at Dix counting the money in the satchel. There was a total of $1,200 in there, six folded wads of $200. He gave the money to the pilot for the next unit party then tore the satchel along its seams and dropped the pieces through the flare hatch, 2,000 feet above Lakewood, New Jersey.

It had stopped raining at Dix. The lieutenant drove him back to the alley, and Reacher walked to Trent's window and rapped softly on the glass. Trent opened it up and he climbed back inside the office.

'We OK?' he asked.

Trent nodded. 'She's just been sitting out there, quiet as a mouse, all day. Must be real impressed. We worked right through lunch.'

Reacher handed back the empty gun. Took off his coat. Sat down. Picked up a file.

'Success?' Trent asked.

'I think so. Time will tell.'

'Don't forget your notes,' Trent said.

He handed over a sheet of paper with a list of maybe thirty names printed on it. Probably Trent's high-school football team. Reacher put it in his pocket, pulled his coat on and shook Trent's hand. Walked back into the anteroom where Harper was waiting.

'SO, YOU FOUND our guy yet?' Blake asked.

He, Poulton and Lamarr were sitting at the same table in the Quantico cafeteria.

'I've got thirty names,' Reacher said. 'He could be one of them.'

'So let's see them.'

'Not yet. I need more.'

Blake stared at him. 'Bullshit. We need to get tails on these guys.'

Reacher shook his head. 'Can't be done. These guys are in places where you can't go. You even want a warrant on these guys, you're going to have to go to the Secretary of Defense, right after you've been to the judge. And Defense is going to go straight to the Commander in Chief, who was the President last time I looked, so you're going to need a damn sight more than I can give you right now.'

'So what are you saying?'

'I'm saying let me boil it down. I want to see Lamarr's stepsister.'

'Why?' Blake asked.

Reacher wanted to say *Because I'm just killing time, and I'd rather do it on the road than stuck in here*, but he composed his face into a serious look. 'Because we need to think laterally,' he said. 'If this guy is killing by category, we need to know *why*. One of these women must have sparked him off, first time around. Then he must have transferred his rage from the personal to the general, right? So who was it? Lamarr's sister could be a good place to start. She got a transfer between two very different units. That doubles her potential contacts.'

It sounded professional enough.

'OK,' Blake said. 'We'll set it up. You'll go tomorrow.'

'Where does she live?'

'Washington State,' Lamarr said. 'Outside of Spokane.'

Reacher turned to Blake. 'You should be guarding these women.'

Blake sighed heavily. 'Do the arithmetic, for God's sake. Eighty-eight women, and we don't know which one is next. Seventeen days to go, *if* he sticks to his cycle. That's more than a hundred thousand man hours. We just can't do it. We don't have the agents.'

'Have you warned the women?'

Blake looked embarrassed. 'We can't. If we can't guard them, we can't warn them. Because what would we be saying? You're in danger, but sorry, girls, you're on your own? Can't be done.'

'We need to catch this guy,' Poulton said. 'That's the only sure way to help these women.'

Lamarr nodded. 'He's out there somewhere.'

'So eat and get to bed,' Blake said. 'It's a long way to Spokane. Early start tomorrow. Harper will go with you, of course.'

'To bed?'

Blake was embarrassed again. 'To Spokane, asshole.'

THE DECISION WAS MADE. *About the interval. The interval was history. Time to speed things up a little. Three weeks was way too long to wait now. You let the idea creep up on you. You look at it, consider it, see its value. You see its appeal and the decision is really made for you. You can't get the genie back in the bottle, not once it's out. And this genie is out. All the way out. Up and running. So you run with it.*

THE VISITOR

THERE WAS NO BREAKFAST meeting the next morning. The day started too early. Harper opened the door before Reacher was even dressed. He had his trousers on and was smoothing the wrinkles out of his shirt with his palm against the mattress.

'Love those scars,' she said.

She took a step closer, looking at his stomach with undisguised curiosity. 'What's that one from?' She pointed to his right side.

He glanced down at a violent tracery of stitches in the shape of a twisted star.

'My mother did it,' he said.

'Your *mother*?'

'I was raised by grizzly bears. In Alaska.'

She rolled her eyes, then moved her gaze to the left side of his chest. There was a bullet hole there, punched into the pectoral muscle.

'Exploratory surgery,' he said. 'Checking if I had a heart.'

'You're happy this morning.'

'I'm always happy.'

'Did you get Jodie yet?'

He shook his head. 'I haven't tried since yesterday.'

'Why not?'

'Waste of time. She's not there.'

'Are you worried?'

He shrugged. 'She's a big girl.'

'I'll tell you if I hear anything.'

'You better.'

'Where are they really from?' she asked. 'The scars?'

He buttoned his shirt. 'The gut is from bomb shrapnel,' he said. 'The chest, somebody shot me.'

'Dramatic life.'

He took his coat from the closet. 'No, not really. A soldier figuring on avoiding physical violence is like an accountant figuring on avoiding numbers.'

'Is that why you don't care about these women?'

He looked at her. 'Who says I don't care?'

'I thought you'd be more agitated about it.'

'Getting agitated won't achieve anything.'

She paused. 'So what will?'

'Working the clues, same as always.'

'There aren't any clues. He doesn't leave any.'

He smiled. 'That's a clue in itself, wouldn't you say?'

'That's just talking in riddles.'

'Better than talking in bullshit, like they do downstairs.'

THE SAME MOTOR-POOL GUY brought the same car to the doors. This time he stayed in the driver's seat, and drove them north on I-95 to the National Airport. It was still before dawn when they arrived at the airport terminal. Harper collected two economy-class tickets from the United desk and carried them over to the check-in counter.

'We could use some legroom,' she said to the guy behind the counter, and snapped her FBI pass down. The guy hit a few keys and came up with an upgrade. Harper smiled.

Business class was half empty. Harper took an aisle seat, trapping Reacher against the window like a prisoner. She stretched out. She was in a third different suit, this one a fine check in a muted grey.

When they had taken off, Reacher pulled the in-flight magazine out and started leafing through.

Harper had her tray unfolded, ready for breakfast. 'What did you mean?' she asked. 'When you said it's a clue in itself?'

He forced his mind back an hour and tried to remember.

'Just thinking aloud, I guess,' he said. 'Lamarr said you've got forensic tests I wouldn't believe. They can find a rug fibre, tell you where and when somebody bought it, what kind of flea sat on it, what kind of dog the flea came off. Probably tell you what the dog's name is and what brand of dog food it ate for breakfast.'

'So?'

'This guy killed Amy Callan and beat *all* of those tests, right?'

'Right.'

'So what do you call that type of a guy?'

'What?'

'A very clever guy, is what.'

She made a face. 'Among other things.'

'Sure, a lot of other things, but whatever else, a very clever guy. Because then he did it again, with Cooke. And *again*, with Stanley.'

'So?'

'So that's the clue. We're looking for a very, very, very clever guy.'

'I think we *know* that already.'

Reacher shook his head. 'I don't think you do. You're not factoring it in.'

'In what sense?'

'You think about it. I'm only the errand boy. You Bureau people can do all the hard work.'

The stewardess came out of the galley with the breakfast trolley. It was business class so the food was reasonable. Reacher smelt bacon and egg and sausage. Strong coffee. He flipped his tray open.

'How aren't we factoring it in?' Harper asked.

'Figure it out for yourself,' Reacher said.

'Is it that he's not a soldier?'

He turned to stare at her. 'That's great. We agree he's a really smart guy, and so you say *well, then he's obviously not a soldier*. Thanks a bunch, Harper.'

She looked away, embarrassed. 'I'm sorry. I didn't mean it like that. I just can't see how we're not factoring it in.'

He didn't reply. Just drained his coffee and climbed over her legs to get to the bathroom. When he got back, she was still contrite.

'Tell me,' she said.

'No.'

They didn't speak again, all the way to Seattle. Five hours, without a word. Reacher was comfortable enough with that. He was not a compulsively sociable guy. He just sat there, like he was making the journey on his own.

Harper was having more trouble with it. She was like most people. Put her alongside somebody she was acquainted with, she felt she had to be conversing. But he didn't relent.

Those five hours were reduced to two by the West Coast clocks. It was still about breakfast time when they landed. The arrivals hall had the usual array of drivers holding placards. There was one guy in a dark suit, striped tie, short hair. He might as well have had *FBI* tattooed across his forehead.

'Lisa Harper?' the guy said. 'I'm from the Seattle Field Office.'

They shook hands.

'This is Reacher,' she said.

The Seattle agent ignored him completely. Reacher smiled inside. *Touché*, he thought.

'We're flying to Spokane,' the agent said. 'Air-taxi company owes us a few favours.'

He had a Bureau car parked on the hard shoulder. He used it to drive a mile round the perimeter road to a cluster of huts and five acres of fenced tarmac filled with parked planes, all of them tiny, which called itself General Aviation. A guy met them outside one of the huts. He led them towards a white six-seat Cessna.

The interior of the plane was about the same size Lamarr's Buick had been, and a whole lot more spartan. It taxied out to the runway and lined up behind a 747 bound for Tokyo the way a mouse lines up behind an elephant. Then it wound itself up and was off the ground in seconds, wheeling due east.

The seat was cramped and uncomfortable, and Reacher started wishing he'd thought of a better way to waste his time.

At Spokane airfield a Bureau car was waiting on the tarmac, a clean dark sedan with a man in a suit leaning on the fender.

'From the Spokane satellite office,' the Seattle guy said.

The car rolled over to where the plane parked and they were on the road within twenty seconds of the pilot shutting down. The local guy seemed to know where their destination was. He drove east towards the Idaho panhandle, then turned north on a narrow road into the hills. There were giant mountains in the middle distance, snow gleaming on the peaks. The road had a building every mile or so, separated by thick forest and broad meadow.

The address itself might have been the main house of an old cattle ranch. It was boxed into a small lot by new ranch fencing. Beyond the fencing was grazing land; inside it the grass had been mown into a fine lawn. There was a small barn with garage doors punched into the side and a path veering off from the driveway to the front door. The whole structure stood close to the road and to its own fencing, which gave it a suburban feel. But the nearest man-made object was at least a mile away.

The local guy stayed in the car, and Harper and Reacher got out and walked together along the shale driveway towards the front door. The silence of the empty country fell on them like a weight. There was no bell push. Just a big iron knocker in the shape of a lion's head with a heavy ring held in its teeth. There was a fish-eye spyhole above it. Harper grasped the iron ring and knocked twice. The ring thumped on the wood.

There was no response. Harper knocked again. They waited. There was a creak of floorboards inside the house. Footsteps.

'Who is it?' a voice called. A woman's voice, apprehensive.

Harper held up her badge in front of the spyhole. 'FBI, ma'am,' she announced. 'We called you yesterday, made an appointment.'

The door opened to reveal a woman smiling with relief. 'Julia's got me so damn nervous,' she said.

Harper smiled back and introduced herself and Reacher. The woman shook hands with both of them.

'Alison Lamarr,' she said. 'Really pleased to meet you.'

She led the way inside. The hall was square and floored in old pine which had been stripped and waxed to a fresh colour a shade darker than the gold on Harper's badge.

'Can I get you coffee?' Alison Lamarr asked.

'I'm OK right now,' Harper said.

'Yes, please,' said Reacher.

She led them through to the kitchen, which occupied the whole rear quarter of the ground floor. It was an attractive space, waxed pine floor polished to a shine, new cabinets in unostentatious timber, a line of gleaming machines for washing clothes and dishes, electric gadgets on the countertops, yellow gingham at the windows.

Alison Lamarr was medium height, dark, and she moved with the bounce of a fit, muscular woman. Her face was open and friendly, tanned like she lived outdoors. She smelt of lemon scent and was dressed in carefully pressed denim and cowboy boots.

She poured coffee from a machine into a mug. Handed it to Reacher and smiled in a way that proved there was no blood relationship with her stepsister. It was a pleasant smile, interested, friendly—the kind that Julia Lamarr had no idea existed.

'Can I look around?' Reacher asked. 'Security check.'

'Be my guest.'

He took his coffee with him. The two women stayed in the kitchen. The whole house was solidly built out of good timber. The renovations were of excellent quality. All the windows were new storm units in stout wood frames, and each had a key. The front door was original, old pine two inches thick. A city-style lock. There was a back hallway with a back door, similar vintage and thickness. Same lock.

Outside there was a steel cellar door with a big padlock latched through the handles. The garage was a well-maintained barn, with a new Jeep Cherokee inside, and a stack of cartons proving the renovations had been recent. There was a new washing machine, still boxed up and sealed; a workbench with power saws and drills stored neatly on the surface.

He went back into the house and up the stairs. Same windows as elsewhere. Four bedrooms. Alison's was clearly the back room on the left, facing west over empty country as far as the eye could see. There was a new master bathroom, stealing space from the next-door bedroom. It held a toilet, a sink and a shower. And a tub.

He went back down to the kitchen. Harper was standing by the window, looking out at the view. Alison Lamarr was sitting at the table. 'OK?' she said.

'Looks good to me. This guy isn't into breaking doors down. So if you don't open up to anybody, nothing can go wrong.'

She nodded. 'That's how I figure it. You need to ask me some questions now?'

'That's why they sent me, I guess.'

He sat down opposite her. Tried to think of something intelligent to say. 'How's your father doing?' he asked.

'That's what you want to know?'

He shrugged. 'Julia mentioned he was sick.'

'He's been sick two years. Cancer. Now he's dying. He's in the hospital in Spokane. I go there every afternoon.'

'I'm very sorry.'

'Julia should come out. But she's all hung up on this stepfamily thing, as if it really matters. Far as I'm concerned, she's my sister, pure and simple. And sisters take care of each other, right? She's going to be the only relative I've got, my next of kin, for God's sake. Anyway, right now, that's not too important. What can I help you with?'

'You got any feeling for who this guy could be?'

'It's some guy who thinks it's OK to harass women. Or maybe not *OK*, exactly. But that the fallout should be kept behind closed doors.'

'Is that an option?' Harper asked. She sat down, next to Reacher.

Alison glanced at her. 'I don't really know. I'm not sure there is any middle ground. Either you swallow it, or it goes public in a big way. I just went ballistic.'

'Who was your guy?' Reacher asked.

'A colonel called Gascoigne. He was always full of shit about coming to him if anything was bothering me. So I went to him about getting reassigned. I wanted something more interesting to do.'

'So what happened?'

Alison sighed. 'At first I thought he was just kidding around.' She paused. Looked away. 'He said I should try next time without my uniform on,' she said. 'I thought he was asking for a date, you know, meet him in town, some bar, off duty, plain clothes. But then he made it clear, he meant right there in his office, stripped off.'

'Not a very nice suggestion.'

Alison made a face. 'He was pretty jokey about it, at first. It was like he was flirting. But clearly he figured I wasn't getting the message, so all of a sudden he got *obscene*. He described what I'd have to do, you know? Like a porno movie. Then it hit me, the rage, all in a split second, and I just went nuclear.'

'And you busted him?' Reacher asked.

'Sure I did.'

'How did he react?'

She smiled. 'He was puzzled, more than anything. I'm sure he'd done it lots of times before, and got away with it.'

'Could he be the guy?'

She shook her head. 'No. This guy is deadly, right? Gascoigne is a sad old man. I don't see him having that kind of *initiative*.'

Reacher nodded. 'If your sister's profile is correct, this is probably a guy from the background, a distant observer turned avenger.'

'Right,' Alison agreed. 'But at the end of the day, the target group is so specific, it *has* to be a soldier. Who else could even *identify* us? But it's a weird soldier, that's for damn sure. Not like any I ever met.'

'Nobody at all?' Harper said. 'No threats, while it was happening?'

'Nothing that I recall. I even flew out to Quantico and let Julia hypnotise me, in case there was something buried there, but she said I came up with nothing.'

Silence again. Harper nodded. 'OK. Wasted trip, right?'

'Sorry, guys,' Alison said.

'Nothing's ever wasted,' Reacher said. 'Negatives can be useful, too. And the coffee was great.'

Alison followed them out of her kitchen. Crossed the hall and opened her front door.

'Don't let anybody in,' Reacher said.

Alison smiled. 'I don't plan to.'

'I mean it,' Reacher said. 'It looks like there's no force involved. This guy is just walking in. So you might know him. Or he's some kind of a con artist, with a plausible excuse. Don't fall for it.'

He followed Harper out onto the shale path. They heard the door close behind them, and then the sound of the lock turning.

THE LOCAL BUREAU guy saved them two hours' flying time by pointing out they could hop from Spokane to Chicago and then change there for DC. Harper did the business with the tickets and they boarded a Boeing for Chicago. This time there was no upgrade. The economy seats put them close together, thighs touching all the way.

'So what do you think?' Harper asked.

'I'm not paid to think,' Reacher said. 'In fact, I'm not getting paid at all. I'm a consultant. So you ask questions and I'll answer them.'

'I did ask you a question. I asked you what you think.'

He shrugged. 'I think it's a big target group, but if the other eighty-eight do what Alison Lamarr is doing, they should be OK.'

'That's it?' Harper said. 'You think we should just tell the women to lock their doors?'

He nodded. 'I think you should be warning them, yes.'

'That doesn't catch the guy.'

'You can't catch him.'

'Why not?'

'Because of this profiling bullshit. You're not factoring in how smart he is.'

'Yes, we are. I've seen the profile. It says he's real smart. And profiling works. Those people have had some spectacular successes.'

'Among how many failures? It's not an exact science.'

'So you think the profile is worthless?'

'I know it is. It's flawed. It makes two incompatible statements.'

'What statements?'

He shook his head. 'No deal, Harper. Not until Blake apologises for threatening Jodie and pulls Julia Lamarr off the case.'

'Why would he do that? She's his best profiler.'

'Exactly.'

THE MOTOR-POOL GUY was at the National Airport in DC to pick them up. It was late when they arrived back at Quantico. Julia Lamarr met them, alone. Blake was in a budget meeting, and Poulton had signed out and gone home.

'How was she?' Lamarr asked.

'She was OK,' Reacher said.

'What's her house like? Is it very isolated?'

'Very isolated,' he said. 'But secure. Locked up tight as Fort Knox.'

She nodded. He waited.

'She wants you to visit,' he said eventually.

She shook her head. 'I can't. It would take me a week to get there.'

'Your father is dying.'

'My stepfather.'

'Whatever. She thinks you should go out there.'

'I can't,' she said again. 'She still the same? Dressed like a cowboy, tanned and pretty and sporty?'

'You got it.'

She nodded again, vaguely. 'Different from me.'

He looked her over. Her cheap black city suit was dusty and creased, and she was pale and thin and hard. Her eyes were blank.

'Yes, different from you,' he said.

'I'm the ugly sister.'

She walked away.

Chapter 4

Next morning Reacher was awake and waiting thirty minutes before Harper showed up. She unlocked his door and breezed in, looking elegant and refreshed, wearing the same suit as the first day. Clearly she had three suits and wore them in strict rotation.

They walked to the cafeteria. The whole campus was quiet, and Reacher realised it was Sunday. The weather was better. No warmer, but the sun was out. He hoped for a moment, as they walked between the buildings, that it was a sign that this was his day. But it wasn't. He knew that as soon as he saw Blake at the table by the window, alone. There was a jug of coffee, three mugs, a basket of doughnuts. The bad news was the pile of Sunday newspapers, opened and read and scattered, with the *New York Times* sitting on top in plain view. Which meant there was no news from New York. Which meant it hadn't worked yet, which meant he was going to have to keep on waiting.

Harper and Reacher sat down opposite Blake. He looked old and tired and very strained, but Reacher felt no sympathy for him. Blake had broken the rules.

'Today you work the files,' he said.

'Whatever,' Reacher replied.

'They're updated with the Lorraine Stanley material. So you need to spend today reviewing them and you can give us your conclusions at the breakfast meeting tomorrow. Clear?'

'Crystal.'

'Any preliminary conclusions I should know about? Any thoughts?'

'Let me read the files. Too early to say anything right now.'

Blake nodded. 'But we need to start making progress soon.'

'I get the message,' Reacher murmured.

AFTER BREAKFAST Harper took him to a quiet room filled with light oak tables and comfortable leather chairs. There was a stack of files about a foot high on one of the tables. They were in dark blue folders, with *FBI* printed on them in yellow letters.

The stack was split into three bundles, each one secured with a thick rubber band. He laid them out on the table, side by side. Amy Callan, Caroline Cooke, Lorraine Stanley. Three victims, three bundles. He checked his watch. Ten twenty-five. A late start.

'You didn't try Jodie,' Harper said.

'No point. She's obviously not there.'

'Worried?'

'I can't worry about something I can't change.'

There was silence. He pulled the Callan file towards him, took the rubber band off and opened up the folder. Harper took her jacket off and sat down opposite. The sun was directly behind her and it made her shirt transparent. He could see the curve of her breast swelling gently past the strap of her shoulder holster.

'Get to work, Reacher,' she said.

THIS IS THE TENSE TIME. You park at the kerb, leaving the car facing the right direction. You switch the engine off. You take the keys out and put them in your pocket. You put your gloves on.

You get out of the car. You stand still for a second, listening hard, and then you turn a complete circle, slowly, looking again. This is the tense time, when you must decide to abort or proceed. Think. Keep it dispassionate. It's just an operational judgment, after all.

You decide to proceed. You close the car door, quietly. You walk into the driveway. You walk to the door. You knock. The door opens. She lets you in. She's glad to see you. Surprised, a little confused at first, then delighted. She hasn't seen you in ages, since another life. You talk for a moment. You keep on talking, until the time is right. You'll know the moment, when it comes. You keep on talking.

The moment comes. You stand still for a second, testing it. You make your move. You explain she has to do exactly what you tell her. She agrees, of course, because she has no choice.

You make her show you the master bathroom. She stands there like a real-estate agent, showing it off. The tub is fine. You tell her to bring the paint inside. You supervise her all the way. It takes her five trips, in and out of the house, up and down the stairs. She's huffing and puffing, starting to sweat. You tell her to smile.

You tell her to find something to lever the lids off with. She nods happily and gets a screwdriver from the kitchen drawer. You tell her to take the lids off, one by one. She kneels next to the first can. She works the tip of the screwdriver under the metal flange of the lid and eases it upwards. She works around it in a circle. The lid sucks off. She moves on to the next can. Then the next. She's working hard.

You pull the folded refuse sack from your pocket. You tell her to place her clothes in it. She nods and smiles. Tugs off all her clothes. Drops them in the bag. She's naked. You tell her to smile.

You make her carry the bag down to the front door. She props it against the door. Then you take her back to the bathroom and make her empty the cans into the bathtub, slowly, carefully, one by one. She concentrates hard. The cans are heavy and awkward. The paint is thick. It runs slowly into the tub. The level creeps up, green and oily.

You tell her she's done well. She smiles, delighted at the praise. Then you tell her she has to take the empty cans back where she got them. But now she's naked. So she has to make sure nobody can see. She nods again. She threads them onto her fingers, five empty cans in each hand. She carries them outside. Runs all the way back.

You take her back up to the bathroom. The screwdriver is still on the floor. You ask her to pick it up. You tell her to make marks on her face with it. She's confused. You explain. Deep scratches will do, you tell her. Three or four of them. She smiles and nods. Scrapes the screwdriver down the left side of her face. A livid red line appears, five inches long. Make the next one harder, you say. She nods. The next line bleeds. Good, you say. Do three more. She nods and smiles. Good girl, you say.

She's still holding the screwdriver. You tell her to get into the bath, slowly and carefully. She puts her right foot in. Then her left. She sits. The paint is touching the underside of her breasts. You tell her to lie back, slowly and carefully. She slides down into the paint. Just right.

You tell her what to do. She doesn't understand at first, so you explain again. She nods. Her hair is thick with paint. She slides down. Now only her face is showing. She tilts her head back. She uses her fingers to help her. She does exactly what she's been told. She gets it right first time. Her eyes jam open with panic, and then she dies.

You wait five minutes. Then you do the only thing she can't do for herself. It gets paint on your right glove. Then you press down on her forehead with a fingertip and she slips under the surface. You peel your right glove off inside out and carrying it in your left hand you walk downstairs in the silence. Slip the glove into the refuse sack with her clothes. Open the door. Listen and watch. Carry the sack outside. Turn around and close the door behind you. Walk down the driveway to the road. Pop the trunk lid and place the sack inside. Open the door and slide in behind the wheel. Drive away.

THE CALLAN FILE started with a summary of her four-year military career. She had passed out of basic training and gone straight to the ordnance storerooms. She was a sergeant within twenty months, working at Fort Withe near Chicago in a warehouse full of the stink of gun oil and the noise of clattering forklifts. She had been content at first. Then the rough banter got too much and her captain and her major had started stepping over the line and getting physical. The dirty talk and pawing and the leering eventually brought her to Reacher's office.

After she quit she went to Florida. Lived there a year, got married and separated—then died there. The crime-scene photographs showed no damage to any doors or windows of her house and no disruption inside; just a white tiled bathroom with a tub full of green paint and a slick indeterminate shape floating in it.

The paint had a molecular structure that penetrated anything it was slapped onto. Removing it removed the skin. There was no evidence of bruising or trauma. The toxicology was clear. No air embolisms. There are many clever ways to kill a person, but the

Florida pathologists couldn't find any evidence of any of them.

'Well?' Harper said.

'She had freckles. I remember that,' Reacher said. 'A year in the Florida sun, she must have looked pretty good.'

'You liked her.'

He nodded. 'She was OK.'

The final third of the file was some of the most exhaustive crime-scene forensics he had ever heard of. Every particle of dust or fibre in Callan's house had been vacuumed up and analysed. But there was no evidence of any intruder.

'A very clever guy,' Reacher said. He pushed Callan's folder to one side and opened Cooke's. It followed the same format.

Cooke had joined as an officer, starting out a second lieutenant. She had gone straight to War Plans, where she had been promoted to first lieutenant and posted to NATO in Brussels where she started a relationship with her colonel. When she didn't get promoted to captain early enough, she complained about him.

Reacher remembered it well. There was no harassment involved, certainly not in the sense that Callan had endured. But the rules had changed: sleeping with somebody you commanded was no longer allowed, so Cooke's colonel went down, and then ate his pistol. She quit and flew home from Belgium to a cottage in New Hampshire, where she was eventually found dead in a tub full of setting paint.

The New Hampshire pathologists and forensic scientists told the same story their Florida counterparts had. A grey cedar house crowded by trees, an undamaged door; an undisturbed interior; a bathroom decor dominated by the dense green contents of the tub. Reacher skimmed through and closed the folder.

'What do you think?' Harper asked.

'I think the paint is weird,' Reacher said. 'It's so *circular*, isn't it? It eliminates evidence on the bodies, which reduces risk, but getting it and transporting it creates risk.'

'And it's like a deliberate clue,' Harper said. 'It underlines the motive. It's definite confirmation it's an army guy. It's like a taunt.'

'Lamarr says it has psychological significance. She says he's reclaiming them for the military. But if he hates them enough to kill them, why would he want to reclaim them?'

'I don't know. A guy like this, who knows how he thinks?'

'Lamarr thinks she knows how he thinks,' Reacher said.

Lorraine Stanley's file was the last of the three. Her history was similar to Callan's, but more recent. She was younger. She had been a sergeant in a giant quartermaster facility in Utah, the only woman in the place. She had been pestered from day one and her competence had been questioned. One night her barracks was broken into and all her uniform trousers were stolen. She reported for duty the next morning wearing her regulation skirt. The next night, all her underwear was stolen. The next morning she was wearing the skirt and nothing underneath when her lieutenant called her into his office. Made her stand easy in the middle of the room, one foot either side of a large mirror laid on the floor. The lieutenant ended up in the glasshouse and Stanley ended up serving out another year and then living alone and dying alone in San Diego, in the little bungalow shown in the crime-scene photographs, in which the California forensics people had found absolutely no evidence.

Reacher closed the file. 'Caroline Cooke was killed in New Hampshire and Lorraine Stanley was killed three weeks later in San Diego. That's about as far apart as you can get, right? Maybe 3,500 miles. And he's hauling hundreds of gallons of paint around.'

'Maybe he's got a stockpile stashed away someplace.'

'That makes it worse. Unless his stash just happened to be on a direct line between where he's based and New Hampshire and southern California, he'd have to detour to get it. It would add distance.'

'So?'

'So he's got a three-, four-thousand-mile road trip . . .'

Harper frowned. 'Say seventy hours at fifty-five miles an hour.'

'Which he couldn't average. He'd pass through towns and road construction. And he wouldn't risk breaking the speed limit.'

'So call it a hundred hours on the road.'

'At least. Plus a day or two surveillance when he gets there. That's more than a week, in practical terms. It's ten or eleven days.'

'So?'

'You tell me,' Reacher said.

'This is not some guy working two weeks on, one week off.'

'No, it's not.'

AT LUNCHTIME they walked over to the cafeteria again. The weather had settled to what fall should be. The air was warm but crisp. The lawns were green and the sky was a shattering blue.

They met Blake, who was on the way to the library. He looked aimless and agitated all at the same time. There was worry in his face. 'Lamarr's father died,' he said.

'Stepfather,' Reacher said.

'Whatever. He died, early this morning. The hospital in Spokane called for her. Now I've got to call Julia at home.'

'Give her our condolences,' Harper said.

Blake nodded vaguely and walked away.

'He should take her off the case,' Reacher said.

Harper nodded. 'Maybe he should, but he won't. And she wouldn't agree, anyway. Her job is all she's got.'

AFTER LUNCH they went back to the folders. Reacher arranged them on the table and stared at them, musing about the geography again. He leaned back and closed his eyes, thinking hard.

'Making any progress?' Harper asked after a while.

'I need a list of the ninety-one women,' he said.

'OK,' she said.

He waited with his eyes closed and heard her leave the room. Enjoyed the warmth and the silence for a long moment and then she was back with another thick blue file.

'Pencil,' he said.

She backed away to a drawer and found a pencil. Rolled it across the table to him. He opened the new file and started reading. First item was a Defense Department print-out, four pages stapled together, ninety-one names in alphabetical order. Then there was a matching list with addresses, and a thick sheaf of background information. Reacher flipped back and forth between pages; went to work with the pencil and twenty minutes later did a count.

'It was eleven women,' he said. 'Not ninety-one.'

'It was?' Harper said.

He nodded. 'Eleven,' he said again. 'Eight left, not eighty-eight.'

'Why?'

'Lots of reasons. Ninety-one was always absurd. A guy this smart would limit himself to what's feasible. A subcategory. What else did Callan and Cooke and Stanley have in common?'

'What?'

'Unmarried or separated, single-family houses in the suburbs or the countryside. Think about the MO. He needs somewhere isolated. No interruptions. No witnesses. He wants women who live alone.'

Harper shook her head. 'There are more than eleven of those. We did the research. I think it's more than thirty. About a third.'

'But you had to check. I'm talking about women who are *obviously* living alone and isolated. At first glance. We have to assume the guy hasn't got anybody doing research for him. All he's got is this list.'

'But that's *our* list.'

'All this information came straight from the military, right? He had this list before you did.'

FORTY-THREE MILES AWAY, the exact same list was lying open on a polished desk in a small windowless office in the darkness of the Pentagon's interior. It was two Xerox generations newer than Reacher's version, but otherwise identical. And it had eleven marks on it, against eleven names. Not hasty check marks in pencil, like Reacher had made, but neat underlinings with a fountain pen and a ruler.

Three of the eleven names had second lines struck through them.

The list was framed on the desk by the uniformed forearms of the office's occupant, and the wrists were cocked upwards to keep the hands clear of the surface. The right hand held a pen, which slowly scored a thick line straight through a fourth name. Then the pen lifted off the page.

'SO WHAT DO WE do about it?' Harper asked.

Reacher leaned back and closed his eyes again. 'I think you should gamble. I think you should stake out the surviving eight around the clock because the guy will walk into your arms within sixteen days.'

'Suppose you're wrong?' she said uncertainly.

'As opposed to what? The progress you're making?'

She still sounded uncertain. 'OK, talk to Lamarr tomorrow.'

He opened his eyes. 'You think she'll be here?'

Harper nodded. 'She'll be here.'

'Won't there be a funeral for her father?'

'She won't go. She'd miss her *own* funeral for a case like this.'

'OK, but you do the talking, and talk to Blake instead. Keep it away from Lamarr.'

'Why?'

'Because her sister lives alone, remember? So her odds just went all the way down to eight to one. Blake will have to pull her off now.'

'He won't pull her off.'

Reacher shrugged. 'Then don't bother telling him anything. I'm just wasting my time here. The guy's an idiot.'

'Don't say that. You need to cooperate. Think about Jodie.'

He closed his eyes again and thought about Jodie. She seemed a long way away. He thought about her for a long time.

FORTY-THREE MILES AWAY, the uniformed man stared at the paper, motionless, focusing on nothing, thinking hard, trying to recover. The best way to recover would be to talk to somebody. He knew that. *A problem shared is a problem halved.* But he wouldn't talk to anybody about this, of course. He smiled a bitter smile. *Faith in yourself*, that's what would do it.

There was a knock at his door.

'Wait,' he called.

He capped his pen and clipped it into his pocket. Folded the list and slipped it inside a drawer in his desk, weighted it down with a book. It was a Bible, King James Version. Slid the drawer closed and locked it. 'Come,' he called, putting the keys in his pocket.

The door opened and a corporal stepped inside and saluted. 'Your car is here, Colonel.'

BEFORE DAYBREAK the next day, Reacher stood at the window wrapped in a towel, staring out into the darkness. It was cold again. He shaved and showered, dressed, took his coat from the closet and put it on. Ducked back into the bathroom and clipped his toothbrush into the inside pocket. Just in case today was the day.

He sat on the bed and waited for Harper. But when the key went into the lock and the door opened, it wasn't Harper standing there. It was Poulton. Reacher felt the first stirrings of triumph.

'Where's Harper?' he asked.

'Off the case,' Poulton said.

'Did she talk to Blake?'

'Last night.'

'And?'

Poulton shrugged. 'And nothing.'

'You're ignoring my input?'

'You're not here for *input*.'

Reacher nodded. 'OK. Ready for breakfast?'

'Sure.'

The sun was coming up in the east and sending colour into the sky. It was a pleasant walk through the early gloom.

Blake was at the usual table in the cafeteria. Lamarr was with him, wearing a black blouse in place of her customary cream. There was coffee on the table, and doughnuts. But no newspapers.

'I was sorry to hear the news from Spokane,' Reacher said.

Lamarr nodded, silently.

'You're not going to the funeral?'

Lamarr took a teaspoon and balanced it across her forefinger. Stared down at it. 'Alison hasn't called me,' she said. 'I don't know what the arrangements are going to be.'

'You didn't call her?'

She shrugged. 'I'd feel like I was intruding.'

There was silence. Reacher poured coffee into a mug.

'You didn't like my theory?' he asked Blake.

'It's a guess, not a theory,' Blake said. 'We can't turn our backs on eighty women just because we enjoy guessing.'

'Well, the next woman to die will be one of the eleven I marked, and it'll be on your head.'

Blake said nothing and Reacher pushed his chair back. 'I want pancakes,' he said. 'I don't like the look of those doughnuts.'

He stood up before they could object and stepped away towards the centre of the room. Stopped at the first table with a *New York Times* on it. It belonged to a guy on his own who was reading the sports pages. The main section was discarded to his left. The story Reacher was waiting for was right there, front page, below the fold.

'Can I borrow this?' he asked, picking up the paper.

The guy nodded without looking.

Reacher tucked the paper under his arm and walked to the serving counter. He helped himself to a stack of pancakes and added syrup. Then he came back to the table and propped the paper in front of his plate and started to eat. He pretended to be surprised by the headline. 'Well, look at that,' he said, with his mouth full.

The headline read GANG WARFARE EXPLODES IN LOWER MANHATTAN, LEAVES SIX DEAD. The story recounted a brief and deadly turf war between two rival protection rackets, one of them allegedly Chinese, the other Syrian. The body count ran four to two in favour of the Chinese. Among the four dead on the Syrian side was the alleged gang leader, a suspected felon named Almar Petrosian.

'Well, look at that,' Reacher said again.

They had already looked at it. That was clear.

'Cozo call you to confirm it?' Reacher asked.

Nobody said a thing, which was the same as a yes.

Reacher smiled. 'Life's a bitch, right? You get a hook into me, and suddenly the hook isn't there any more. Harper wouldn't play ball with the *femme fatale* thing, and now old Petrosian's dead, so you got no more cards to play. And since you're not listening to a word I say anyway, is there a reason why I shouldn't walk right out of here?'

'Lots of reasons,' Blake said.

'None of them good enough,' Reacher said and stood up and stepped away from the table again. Nobody tried to stop him. He went out through the glass doors into the chill of dawn. Started walking.

AT THE GUARDHOUSE on the perimeter he ducked under the barrier and dropped his visitor's pass on the road. Walked on.

He heard the car behind him five minutes later, stopped and turned, waited for it. It was Harper, which was what he had expected. She drew level with him and buzzed her window down. 'Want a ride?' she asked.

'I-95 will do it. Going north.'

'Hitchhiking?'

He nodded. 'I've got no money for a plane.'

He slid in next to her and she accelerated away.

'They tell you to bring me back?' he asked.

She shook her head. 'They decided you're useless. Nothing to contribute, is what they said.'

He smiled. 'So now I'm supposed to get all boiled up with indignation and storm back in there and prove them wrong?'

She smiled back. 'Something like that. Lamarr decided they should appeal to your ego.'

'That's what happens when you're a psychologist who studied landscape gardening in school.'

'I guess so.'

'But she's right,' he said. 'I've got nothing to contribute. This guy's too smart for me, that's for damn sure.'

She smiled again. 'A little psychology of your own? Trying to leave with a clear conscience?'

'My conscience is always clear.'

'Even about Petrosian? Hell of a coincidence, don't you think? They threaten you with Petrosian, and he's dead within three days.'

'Just dumb luck.'

'Yeah? You know, I didn't tell them I was *outside* Trent's office all day?'

'And what's Trent's office got to do with anything?'

'I don't know. But I don't like coincidences. They could, you know, dig around. Might make it hard for you, later.'

He grinned. 'This is phase two of the approach, right?'

Her smile exploded into a laugh. 'Yeah, phase two. There are about a dozen still to go. You want to hear them all?'

'Not really. I'm not going back. They're not listening.'

She drove on. 'Jodie's home,' she said after a while. 'I called Cozo's office. Apparently they had a little surveillance going. She's been away. Got back this morning, in a taxi. Looked like she'd come from the airport. She's working from home today.'

'OK, so now I'm definitely out of here.'

'We need your input, you know.'

'They're not listening. And they're wasting their time with this profiling shit. They need to work the clues.'

'There aren't any clues.'

'Yes, there are. How smart the guy is. And the paint, and the geography. They're all clues. They should work them. Starting with the motive is starting at the wrong end.'

'I'll pass that on.'

She pulled over at the junction with the interstate.

'You going to get into trouble?' he asked.

'For failing to bring you back?' she said. 'Probably.'

He was silent. She smiled.

'That was phase ten,' she said. 'I'll be perfectly OK.'

'I hope so,' he said, and got out of the car. He walked north to the ramp and stood there, watching her car turn back towards Quantico.

A MALE HITCHHIKER standing six foot five and weighing 230 pounds is on the cusp of acceptability. But Reacher was showered and shaved and dressed quietly. That shortened the odds, and there were enough trucks on the road with big confident owner-drivers so that he was back in New York City within seven hours of starting out.

He was quiet for most of the seven hours, partly because the trucks were too noisy for conversation, and partly because he wasn't in the mood for talking. The old hobo demon was whispering to him again. *Where are you going?* Back to Jodie, of course. *OK, smart guy, but what else? What the hell else? Yardwork behind your house? Painting the damn walls?* He sat next to a succession of drivers and felt his brief unsatisfactory excursion into freedom ebbing away. His final ride was on a vegetable truck delivering to Greenwich Village. He got out and walked the last mile to Jodie's apartment, concentrating on his desire to see her.

He had his own key to her lobby, and went up in the elevator and knocked on her door. The peephole went dark and light again and the door opened and she was standing there, in jeans and a shirt, slim and beautiful. But she wasn't smiling at him.

'Hey, Jodie,' he said.

'There's an FBI agent in my kitchen,' she replied.

He followed her into the apartment, through to the kitchen.

The Bureau guy was a young man in a blue suit, white shirt, striped tie. He was holding a cellphone up to his face, reporting Reacher's arrival to somebody else.

'Wait here, please, sir,' he said after he'd made the call. 'About ten minutes.'

'What's this about?'

'You'll find out, sir. Ten minutes is all.'

Jodie sat down. There was something in her face. Something

halfway between concern and annoyance. The *New York Times* was open on the countertop. Reacher glanced at it. 'OK,' he said.

He sat down too. They waited in silence. Then the buzzer sounded from the street and the Bureau guy went into the hallway. They heard the apartment door open. Footsteps on the maple floor.

Alan Deerfield walked into the kitchen. He had sidewalk grit on the soles of his shoes and it made him loud and invasive.

'I got six people dead in my city,' he said. 'So I came to ask Ms Jacob here a couple questions.'

Jodie didn't look up. 'What questions?' she said.

'Where have you been, the last few days?'

'Out of town,' she said. 'On business.'

'Where out of town?'

'London. Client conference.'

'Reacher knew you were there, right?' Deerfield said.

She shook her head. 'No, I didn't tell him. It was a last-minute trip.'

'So he was a worried man. Right after he got to Quantico, he was trying to get you on the phone. Office, home, mobile. That night, same thing again. Couldn't get you. A worried man.'

Jodie glanced at Reacher. Concern in her face, maybe a little apology. 'I should have told him, I guess.'

'Hey, that's up to you. But the interesting thing is, then he stops calling you. Suddenly he's not calling you any more. Now why is that? Did he find out you were safe over there in London?'

She started to reply, and then she stopped.

'I'll take that for a no,' Deerfield said. 'So as far as Reacher knew, you were still right here in town. But he's suddenly not worried any more. Maybe because he knows Petrosian isn't going to be around for much longer.'

Jodie's eyes were focused on the floor.

'He's a smart guy,' Deerfield said. 'My guess is he whistled up some pal of his to set the cat among the pigeons up here in Chinatown, and then he sat back and waited for the tongs to do what they always do when somebody starts messing with them. And he figures he's safe. Because while Petrosian is getting the good news with the machete, he's locked into a room down in Quantico. A smart guy.'

Deerfield turned to Reacher. 'So am I on the money?' he asked.

Reacher shrugged. 'Why should anybody have been worrying about Petrosian?'

Deerfield smiled. 'Oh, sure, we can't talk about that. We'll never admit Blake said a word to you on that subject. I just want to be sure what I'm dealing with here. If you stirred it up, just tell me and maybe I'll pat you on the back for a job well done. But if by some chance it was a genuine dispute, we need to know about it.'

'I don't know what you're talking about,' Reacher said.

'So why did you stop calling Ms Jacob?'

'That's my business.'

'No, it's everybody's business,' Deerfield said. 'Certainly it's Ms Jacob's business, right? And it's mine, too. So tell me about it, Reacher. Petrosian was a piece of shit for sure, but he's still a homicide, and we can crank up a pretty good motive for you. We could call it a conspiracy with persons unknown. Careful preparation of the case, you could be inside waiting for the trial.'

Jodie stood up. 'You should leave now, Mr Deerfield. I'm still his lawyer, and this is an inappropriate forum for this discussion.'

Deerfield nodded slowly, and looked around the kitchen, like he was seeing it for the first time. 'Yes, it sure is, Ms Jacob,' he said. 'So maybe we'll have to continue this discussion someplace more appropriate. Maybe tomorrow, maybe next week, maybe next year.'

He turned on the spot, walked out of the apartment.

'So you took Petrosian out,' Jodie said, after they heard the door slam shut.

'I never went near him,' Reacher replied.

She shook her head. 'Save that stuff for the FBI, OK? You engineered it. You took him out, as surely as if you were standing right next to him with a gun. And Deerfield *knows*.'

'He can't prove it.'

'That doesn't matter,' she said. 'Don't you see that? He can *try* to prove it. And he's not kidding about jail. A suspicion of gang warfare? The courts will back him up all the way. It's not an empty threat. He owns you now. Like I told you he would.'

Reacher said nothing.

'Why did you do it?'

He shrugged. 'Lots of reasons. It needed doing.'

There was a long silence.

'So why did you stop calling me?' she asked eventually.

He looked down at his rough hands. 'I figured you were safe,' he said. 'I figured you were hiding out someplace.'

'You figured,' she repeated. 'But you didn't know.'

'I assumed,' he said. 'I was taking care of Petrosian, I assumed you were taking care of yourself. We know each other well enough to trust assumptions like that.'

'Like we were comrades,' she said softly. 'In the same unit, a major and a captain maybe, in the middle of some dangerous mission, relying on each other to do our separate jobs properly.'

He nodded. 'Exactly.'

'But I'm not a captain. I'm not in some unit. I grew up in the army, just like you did, and I could have joined up if I'd wanted to, just like you did. But I didn't want to. I wanted to go to college and law school. I wanted to live in a world with rules. And now I'm afraid, caught up in something I don't want to be caught up in.'

'I'm sorry.'

'And you're not a major any more. You're a civilian.'

He nodded. Said nothing.

'And that's the big problem, right?' she said. 'You're getting me caught up in something I don't want to be caught up in, and I'm getting you caught up in something you don't want to be caught up in. The civilised world. The house, the car, living somewhere, doing ordinary things. My fault, probably,' she went on. 'I *want* those things. Makes it hard for me to accept that maybe you don't want them.'

'I want you,' he said.

She nodded. 'I know that. And I want *you*. You know that, too. But do we want each other's lives?'

The hobo demon erupted in his head, cheering and screaming. *She said it! She said it! Now it's right there, out in the open! So go for it! Jump on it! Just gobble it right up!*

'I don't know,' he said.

'We need to talk about it,' she said.

But there was no more talking to be done, not then, because the buzzer from the lobby started up an insistent squawk. Jodie stood up and hit the door release and moved into the living room to wait. Reacher stayed where he was. He felt the elevator arrive and heard the apartment door open. He heard urgent conversation and fast light footsteps through the living room and then Jodie was back in the kitchen with Lisa Harper at her side.

Chapter 5

'It's all gone crazy,' Harper said. 'Alison Lamarr.'

'Shit,' he whispered. 'When?'

'Yesterday. He's speeding up. He didn't stick to the interval.'

'How?'

'Same as all the others. The hospital was calling her because her father died, and there was no reply, so they called the cops, and the cops found her. Dead in the tub, in the paint, like all the others.'

'But how the hell did he get in?'

Harper shook her head. 'Just walked right in the door.'

'Shit, I don't believe it.'

Harper glanced around Jodie's kitchen, nervously. 'Blake wants you back on board,' she said. 'He's signed up for your theory in a big way. Eleven women, not ninety-one.'

'So what am I supposed to say to that? Better late than never?'

'He wants you back,' Harper said again. 'This is getting way out of control. We need to start cutting some corners with the army. And he figures you've demonstrated a talent for cutting corners.'

It was the wrong thing to say. It fell across the kitchen like a weight.

'You should go, Reacher,' Jodie said. 'Go cut some corners. Do what you're good at.'

HE WENT. Harper had a car waiting at the kerb on Broadway. It was a Bureau car, borrowed from the New York office and it took them straight to Newark airport, for a flight to Seattle. Blake wanted them to go direct to the crime scene.

They ran to the gate and were the last passengers to board.

'How's Lamarr taking it?' Reacher asked, when they were in their seats.

Harper shrugged. 'She's not falling apart. But she's real tense. She wants to take complete control of everything. But she won't join us out there. Still won't fly.'

'A country this size, it's kind of limiting, isn't it? Especially for a Federal agent. I'm surprised they let her get away with it.'

She shrugged again. 'It's a known quantity. They work around it.'

The engine noise built louder and the plane rolled forward, accelerating all the way. It came up off the ground and the earth tilted sharply below them.

'Did you think about the geography?' Reacher asked. 'Spokane is the fourth corner, right?'

She nodded. 'Eleven potential locations now, all random, and he takes the four farthest away for his first four hits.'

'But why?'

She made a face. 'Demonstrating his reach?'

'And his speed, I guess. Maybe that's why he abandoned the interval. To demonstrate his efficiency. He's a cool, cool customer, I wonder who the hell he is?'

Harper smiled grimly. 'The trick is to find out.'

YOU'RE A GENIUS, is who you are. An absolute genius. Four down! And the fourth was the best of all. Alison Lamarr! The look on her face as she opened the door! The dawning recognition, the surprise, the welcome!

There were no mistakes. Not a single one. You replay your actions in your head. You touched nothing, left nothing behind. You brought nothing to her house except your still presence and your quiet voice. The terrain helped, of course; nobody for miles around. It made it a real safe operation. Maybe you should have had more fun with her. You could have made her sing. Or dance!

But you didn't, because patterns are important. Patterns protect you. Stick to the pattern, that's the key. And keep on thinking. Plan ahead. You've done number four, and sure, you're entitled to savour it for a spell, but then you have to just put it away and prepare for number five.

THE FOOD ON THE PLANE was appropriate for a flight that left halfway between lunch and dinner and was crossing all the time zones the continent had to offer. Reacher fuelled up on coffee and fell back to thinking. Mostly he thought about Jodie.

He recalled the day in June he had walked back into her life; the exact second he had laid eyes on her and understood who she was. He had felt a flood of feeling as powerful as an electric shock. It was something he had rarely felt before. Rarely, but not never. He had felt the same thing on random days since he left the army. He remembered stepping off buses in towns he had never heard of in states he had never visited. He remembered the feel of the sun on his back and long roads stretching out straight and endless in front of him. The drifter's life. Its charm was a big part of him, and he missed it when he was stuck in Garrison or holed up in the city with Jodie. He missed it bad. Real bad. About as bad as he was missing her now.

THE ROAD outside the Lamarr place was blocked by a gaggle of cars. There was a local police black-and-white with its roof lights flashing, a pair of plain dark sedans, a black Suburban and a coroner's wagon. The vehicles were all beaded with raindrops.

Harper and Reacher stepped out of the Bureau car and walked over to the Suburban. Nelson Blake slid out of the passenger seat to meet them. His face was nearer grey than red, like shock had knocked his blood pressure down. He was all business. No apologies, no pleasantries.

'Not much more than an hour of daylight left, up here,' he said. 'I want you to walk me through what you did the day before yesterday, tell me what's different.'

Reacher nodded. He suddenly wanted to find something. Something important. Not for Blake. For Alison.

'Who's been in there already?' he asked.

'Just the local uniformed guy,' Blake said. 'The one that found her. Nobody else has been in. I wanted your input first.'

'So she's still in there?'

'Yes, I'm afraid she is.'

'OK,' Reacher said. 'Front door was unlocked?'

'Closed, but unlocked.'

'OK.' He walked past the parked vehicles and on past the mouth of the driveway. He walked twenty yards up the narrow road.

'Where does this go?' he called.

Blake was ten yards behind him. 'Back of beyond, probably.'

Reacher strolled back to join him. 'You should check the mud on the verges, maybe up around the next bend. Our guy came in from the Spokane road, most likely. Cruised the house, kept on going, turned round, came back. He'd want his car facing the right direction for the getaway.'

Blake nodded. 'OK. I'll put somebody on it. Meantime, take me through the house.'

He called instructions to his team, then joined Reacher and Harper at the front door. 'Put these on your feet,' he said. He pulled a roll of large-size food bags from his coat pocket. They put a bag over each shoe and tucked the plastic edges down inside the leather.

'I knocked on the door. She opened up, second knock,' Harper said. 'I showed her my badge in the spyhole.'

'She was pretty uptight,' Reacher said. 'Told us Julia had been warning her.'

Blake nodded sourly and nudged the door with his bagged foot.

'We all went through to the kitchen,' Harper said.

They filed into the kitchen. The floor was still waxed to a shine. The range was cold and empty, but there were dishes in the sink and one of the drawers was open an inch.

'Anything different in here?' Blake asked.

'Dishes in the sink,' Reacher said. 'And that drawer was closed.'

They crowded the sink. There was a plate, a water glass, a mug, a knife and a fork. Smears of egg and toast crumbs on the plate.

'Breakfast?' Blake said.

'Or dinner,' Harper answered. 'An egg on toast, that could be dinner for a single woman.'

Blake pulled the drawer with the tip of his finger. There was an assortment of household tools in there.

'OK, then what?' he asked.

'I stayed here with her,' Harper said. 'Reacher looked around.'

'Show me,' Blake said.

He followed Reacher back to the hallway, leaving Harper alone.

'I checked the parlour and the living room,' Reacher said. 'Looked at the windows. I figured they were secure so I went outside, checked the grounds and the barn.'

'We'll do the upstairs first,' Blake said.

'OK.'

Reacher led the way, conscious that maybe thirty hours ago the guy had followed the same path.

'I checked the bedrooms. Went into the master suite last.'

They walked the length of the master bedroom. Paused at the bathroom door. 'Let's do it,' Blake said.

They looked inside. The place was immaculate. No sign that anything had ever happened there, except for the tub. It was seven-eighths full of green paint, with the shape of a small muscular woman floating just below the surface, which had skinned over into a slick plastic layer, delineating her body. The head was tilted backwards. The mouth slightly open, the lips drawn back in a grimace.

'Shit,' Reacher said. He stood there and tried to read the signs. But the bathroom was exactly the same as it had been before.

'Anything?' Blake asked.

He shook his head. 'No.'

'OK, we'll do the outside.'

They trooped down the stairs, silent. Harper was waiting in the hallway. Blake just shook his head, like he was saying *Don't go up there*. Reacher led him out into the yard.

'I checked the windows from outside,' he said.

'Guy didn't come in the damn window,' Blake said. 'He came in the door.'

'But how the hell?' Reacher said. 'When we were here, you'd called her ahead on the phone, Harper was flashing her badge, and Lamarr *still* practically hid out in there.'

'Like I told you right at the beginning, these women *know* this character. They trust him. He knocks on the door, they check him out in the spyhole and they open right up.'

The cellar door was undisturbed. The garage door in the side of the barn was closed but not locked. Reacher led Blake inside. The new Jeep was there, and the cartons. The big washing-machine carton was there, flaps slightly open, sealing tape trailing. The workbench was there, with the power tools neatly laid out on it.

'Something's different,' Reacher said. 'Let me think.'

He stood there, opening and closing his eyes, comparing the scene in front of him with the memory in his head.

'The car has moved,' he said.

'It would have. She drove to the hospital after you left.'

Reacher nodded. 'Something else. Let me think.'

Then he saw it. 'Shit.'

'What?'

'That washing-machine carton. She already had a washing machine. Looked brand-new. It's in the kitchen, under the counter.'

'So? It must have come out of that carton when it was installed.'

Reacher shook his head. 'No. Two days ago that carton was new and sealed up. Now it's been opened. OK. Now we know how he transports the paint. He delivers it ahead of time disguised in washing-machine cartons.'

THE PROBLEM with rerunning it like a video over and over again is that little doubts start to creep in. You go over it and you can't remember if you really did all the things you should have done. The more you question it, the less sure you get.

You sit there cold and sweating for an hour and at the end of it you know you made a mistake. You forgot to reseal the carton. That's a fact now, and it needs dealing with. Because resealing the cartons guaranteed a certain amount of delay. You know how investigators work. A just-delivered appliance carton in the garage or the basement was going to attract no interest at all. Your best guess was that the primary investigators would never open it at all. You were proved right three times in a row. Maybe much later when the heirs came to clear out the houses they'd open them up and find all the empty cans, whereupon the shit would really hit the fan, but by then it would be way too late.

But this time, it would be different. They'd do a walk-through in the garage, and the flaps on the box would be up. They'd glance in, and they wouldn't see Styrofoam packaging and gleaming white enamel.

THEY BROUGHT in portable arc lights from the Suburban and arrayed them around the sturdy brown carton like it was a meteor from Mars. The manufacturer's name was screen-printed with black ink on all sides, along with the model number. Inside the box were ten empty three-gallon paint cans. No manufacturer's name. No trademark. Just a small printed label stencilled with *Camo/Green*. Standard-issue field supply.

'OK, so how did it get here?' Blake said.

Reacher frowned. 'Like I said, it was delivered, ahead of time. By a shipping company. FedEx or UPS or somebody.'

Blake sighed, like the world had gone mad. Stared at the box. Walked all round it. One side showed damage where the surface of the cardboard had been torn away. 'Shipping label,' he said.

'Maybe one of those little plastic envelopes,' Reacher suggested. 'You know, *Documents Enclosed*. The guy must have torn it off. Afterwards. So it can't be traced.'

'But how can the delivery happen?' Blake asked. 'Say you're Alison Lamarr, just sitting there at home, and UPS or FedEx show up with a washing machine you never ordered? You wouldn't accept the delivery, right?'

'Maybe it came when she was out,' Reacher said.

'Wouldn't the driver need a signature?'

'The guy probably specified no signature required.'

'Why didn't she unpack it?'

Reacher made a face. 'She figures it's not really hers, why would she unpack it? She just calls UPS or FedEx. Tells them to come pick it up. Maybe she tore off the envelope herself. Carried it into the house, to the phone, to give them the details.'

'Well, if the details are in the house, we'll find them. Crime-scene people are going in, soon as the coroner is through.'

'Coroner won't find anything,' Reacher said.

Blake looked grim. 'This time, he'll have to.'

'So you're going to have to do it differently. You should take the whole tub out. Maybe fly it back to Quantico.'

'How the hell can we take the whole tub out?'

'Tear the wall out. Tear the roof off. Use a crane.'

Blake thought about it. 'I guess we could. We'd need permission. But all this must be Julia's now. She's next of kin, I guess.'

Reacher nodded. 'So call her. Get her permission. And get her to check the field reports from the other three places. This delivery thing might be a one-off, but if it isn't it changes everything. It means the guy isn't driving truckloads of paint all over the place. He could be using the airlines, in and out quick as you like.'

BLAKE WENT BACK to the Suburban to make his calls, and Harper found Reacher and walked him fifty yards up the road to where agents from the Spokane office had spotted tyre marks in the mud on the verge where a car had turned. It had gone dark and they were using flashlights.

'Probably a midsize sedan,' one of the Spokane guys said, looking at the tyre marks. 'Fairly new radial tyres, maybe a fourteen-inch wheel. We'll get the exact tyre from the tread pattern. And we'll measure the width between the marks, maybe get the model of car.'

They left the Spokane guys setting up miniature waterproof tents over the marks and walked back towards the house. Blake was waiting. 'We've got appliance cartons listed at all three scenes,' he said. 'No information about contents. Nobody thought to look. We're sending local agents back to check. Could be an hour. And Julia says we should go ahead and rip the tub out.'

Reacher paused, immobilised by a new line of thought, then said, 'You should check on something else. You should get the list of the eleven women, call the seven he hasn't got to yet. Ask them if they've had any deliveries they weren't expecting. Because if this guy is speeding up, maybe the next one is all ready and set to go.'

EVENTUALLY YOU RELAX. You've got a lot of talent. Everything was backed up, double-safe, triple-safe. You know the investigators won't find where the paint came from. Or who obtained it. Or who delivered it. You're too smart for them. Way too smart. So you relax.

But you're disappointed. You made a mistake. And now you probably can't use the paint any more. But maybe you can think of something even better. Because one thing is for sure. You can't stop now.

THEY WAITED an hour and a half, crowded inside the Suburban. The evening crept towards night, and it grew very cold. Dense night dew misted the outside of the windshield. Breathing fogged the inside. Suddenly a loud electronic blast broke the silence. Blake fumbled the phone out of the cradle. Reacher heard the indistinct sound of a man's voice, talking fast. Blake listened hard with his eyes focused nowhere. Then he hung up and stared at the windshield.

'What?' Harper asked.

'Local guys went and checked the appliance cartons,' Blake said. 'They were all sealed up tight. But they opened them anyway. Ten paint cans in each of them. Used cans, exactly like we found.'

'But the boxes were sealed?' Reacher said.

'Resealed,' Blake said. 'They could tell, when they looked closely. The guy resealed the boxes, afterwards.'

'Smart guy,' Harper said. 'He knew a sealed carton wouldn't attract much attention.'

'But not totally smart any more,' Reacher said. 'Or he wouldn't have forgotten to reseal this one, right? His first mistake.'

'No shipping labels anywhere?' Harper asked.

Blake shook his head. 'All torn off. And you haven't heard the really good news yet.'

'Which is what?'

'The other little matter you came up with.'

'One of the other women got a delivery, right?' Reacher said.

Blake shook his head. 'Wrong. All *seven* of them got a delivery.'

'YOU'RE GOING to Portland, Oregon,' Blake said. 'You and Harper. So you can visit with an old friend of yours, Rita Scimeca. I believe you handled her case some years back. A lady lieutenant who got raped down in Georgia. She lives near Portland now. She's one of the eleven on your list. The closest to where we are now. You can get down there and check out her basement. She says there's a brand-new washing machine in there. In a box.'

'Did she open it?' Reacher asked.

Blake shook his head. 'No. A couple of Portland agents are on the way over there right now. They told her not to touch it.'

'If the guy's still in the area, Portland could be his next call.'

'Correct,' Blake said. 'That's why there's somebody on the way over.'

Reacher nodded. 'So now you're guarding them? What's that thing about barn doors and horses bolting?'

Blake shrugged. 'Hey, only seven left alive, makes the manpower much more feasible.'

It was a cop's sick humour in a car full of cops, but it still fell flat. Blake coloured slightly and looked away. 'Losing Alison gets to me, much as anybody,' he said. 'Like family, right?'

'Especially to her sister, I guess,' Reacher said.

'Tell me about it,' Blake said. 'She was burned as hell when the news came in. Never seen her so agitated.'

'You should take her off the case.'

Blake shook his head. 'I need her.'

SPOKANE TO THE VILLAGE east of Portland measured about 360 miles on the map Blake showed them. They took the Buick the local agent had used to bring them in from the airport.

'Call it six hours,' Harper said. 'You drive three and I'll drive three.'

The road ran southwest through hilly terrain. Reacher put the headlights on full beam and eased the speed upwards. Harper reclined her seat, her head tilted towards him. Her hair glowed red and gold in the lights from the dash. They passed a town called Sprague and the road straightened. Reacher accelerated towards eighty miles an hour, but minutes later a long low sedan blasted past them.

'Maybe that's the guy,' Harper said sleepily. 'Maybe he's heading down to Portland, too. Maybe we'll get him tonight.'

'I've changed my mind,' Reacher said. 'I think the guy flies.'

'And then what?' Harper said. 'He rents a car at the local airport?'

Reacher nodded in the dark. 'That's my guess.'

'Risky,' Harper said. 'Renting cars leaves a paper trail.'

'So does buying airplane tickets. But this guy is real organised. I'm sure he's got cast-iron false ID. Following the paper trail won't get anybody anywhere.'

Harper stretched. Reacher caught a breath of her perfume as she moved. 'So he gets off the plane, picks up the car, drives a half-hour to Alison's place, spends a half-hour there, drives a half-hour back, and gets the hell out. He wouldn't hang around, right?'

'Not near the scene, I guess,' Reacher said.

'So the rental car could be returned within about two hours. We should check real short rentals from the airports local to the scenes.'

Reacher nodded, and they fell silent for a spell.

'Tell me about Rita Scimeca,' Harper said.

'She was a little like Alison Lamarr, I guess. She had the same feel about her. Tough, sporty, capable, unfazed by anything. She was a second lieutenant. Great record. She blitzed the officer training.'

He fell silent at the wheel picturing Rita Scimeca in his mind, as fine a woman as the army would ever get.

'So here's another puzzle,' he said. 'How is the guy controlling them? Think about it. He gets into their houses, and thirty minutes later they're dead in the tub, naked, not a mark on them. No disturbance, no mess. How is he doing that?'

'Points a gun, I guess.'

Reacher shook his head. 'Two things wrong with that. If he's coming in by plane, he doesn't have a gun. You can't bring a gun on a plane.'

'*If* he's coming in by plane. That's only a guess right now.'

'OK, but I was just thinking about Alison Lamarr. She had infantry training. Either she'd have got mad and started a fight, or she'd have bided her time and tried to nail the guy somewhere along the way. But she didn't, apparently. Why not?'

'I don't know,' Harper said.

'And you're never going to find out because you're all so blinded by this profiling shit that you're wrong about the motive.'

Harper stared out of the window at the blackness speeding past. 'You want to amplify that?'

'Not until I get Blake and Lamarr sitting still and paying attention. I'm only going to say it once.'

THEY STOPPED FOR GAS just after they crossed the Columbia River. Reacher filled the tank and Harper went inside to the bathroom. Then she came out and got into the car on the driver's side, ready for her three hours at the wheel. Twisted the key and fired it up. Took off again south and eased her way up to a cruise. Reacher dozed.

It was nearly three in the morning when they got to Scimeca's village. There was a gas station and a general store on the through road, both closed up tight. There was a cross street running north into the lower slope of the mountain. Harper nosed up it.

Scimeca's house was easy to spot. It was the only one with lights on. And the only one with a Bureau sedan parked outside. Harper stopped and turned off her lights, and the motor died with a little shudder. Silence enveloped them. The sedan door opened and a young man in a dark suit stepped out. Reacher and Harper slid out into the chill air.

'She's in there, safe and sound,' the local guy said to them. 'She's waiting for you.'

Harper nodded. The house in front of them was a big square clapboard structure, built side-on to the street so it faced the view to the west. There was a generous front porch with railings, and the slope of the street made room for a garage under the house at the front. The garage door faced sideways, under the end of the porch.

Harper skipped up the steps in the centre of the porch but Reacher's weight made them creak in the night's silence, and before the echo of the sound came back from the hills the front door was open and Rita Scimeca was standing there watching them.

'Hello, Reacher,' she said.

'Scimeca,' he said back. 'How are you?'

She used her free hand to push her hair off her brow.

'Reasonable, considering it's three o'clock in the morning and the FBI has only just got around to telling me I'm on some kind of hit list with ten of my sisters, four of whom are already dead.'

'Your tax dollars at work,' Reacher said.

'So why the hell are you hanging out with them?'

'Circumstances didn't leave me a whole lot of choice.'

'Circumstances?' she repeated. 'Well, whatever, it's kind of good to see you.'

'Good to see you, too.'

She was a tall woman, muscular, not in the compact way Alison Lamarr had been, but in the lean, marathon-runner kind of way. She was dressed in jeans and a shapeless sweater, and had medium-length brown hair, worn in a long fringe above bright brown eyes. She had heavy lines all around her mouth. It was nearly four years since he had last seen her, and she looked the whole four years older.

'This is Special Agent Lisa Harper,' he said.

Scimeca nodded. 'Well, come on in, I guess,' she said.

Harper stepped inside and Reacher filed after her. The door closed behind them. They were in the hallway of a newly painted, nicely furnished little house. Warm and cosy. There were wool rugs on the floor. Polished mahogany furniture. Vases of flowers everywhere.

'Chrysanthemums,' Scimeca said. 'I grow them myself. Gardening's my new hobby.'

Then she pointed towards a front parlour. 'And music,' she said. 'Come see.'

The room had a grand piano in the back corner. Shiny black lacquer. A German name inlaid in brass.

'Nice instrument,' Reacher said. 'So, you're doing OK?'

She looked him in the eye. 'You mean have I recovered from being gang-raped by three guys I was supposed to trust with my life?'

'Something like that, I guess.'

'I thought I'd recovered. As well as I ever expected to. But now I hear some maniac is fixing to kill me for complaining about it. That's taken the edge off of it a little bit, you know?'

'We'll get him,' Harper said, in the silence.

Scimeca just looked at her.

'Can we see the new washing machine?' Reacher asked.

'It's not a washing machine, though, is it?' Scimeca asked.

'It's probably paint,' Reacher said. 'Camouflage green, army issue. The guy kills you, dumps you in the tub and pours it over you.'

'Why?'

Reacher shrugged. 'Good question. There's a whole bunch of pointy heads working on that right now.'

Scimeca nodded and turned to Harper. 'You a pointy head?'

'No, ma'am, I'm just an agent,' Harper said.

The older woman led the way to the garage. A new car filled the space, a Chrysler sedan. They walked single file along its flank and Scimeca opened a door in the garage wall. The musty smell of a basement bloomed out at them. 'There you are,' she said.

There was a carton standing in the middle of the floor. Same size, same brown board, same black printing, same manufacturer's name. It was taped shut with shiny brown tape.

'Got a knife?' Reacher asked.

Scimeca nodded towards a work area. There was pegboard screwed to the wall, and it was filled with tools hanging in neat rows.

Reacher took a linoleum knife off a peg, slit the tape and eased the flaps upwards. He saw five paint-can lids, reflecting the overhead light. He lifted one of the cans up to eye level. Rotated it. The label was printed with the words *Camo/Green*.

'When did this come?' he asked Scimeca.

'I don't remember,' she said. 'Maybe a couple of months ago.'

'A couple of *months*?' Harper said.

Scimeca nodded. 'I guess. I don't really remember.'

'You didn't order it, right?' Reacher said.

Scimeca shook her head. 'I already got one. I assumed it's for my room-mate,' she said. 'She moved out, couple of weeks ago.'

'But you didn't ask her?'

'Why should I? Who else could it be for?'

They stood in silence, three jagged shadows in the yellow light.

'I'm tired,' Scimeca said. 'Are we through?'

'One last thing,' Reacher said. 'Tell Agent Harper what you did in the service.'

'Why? What's that got to do with anything?'

'I just want her to know.'

'I was in armaments proving. We tested new weapons incoming from the manufacturer.'

Harper glanced at Reacher, equally puzzled.

'OK,' he said. 'Now we're out of here.'

Scimeca led the way through the garage and up into the foyer.

'Goodbye, Reacher,' she said, opening the front door. 'It was nice to see you again.' She turned to Harper. 'You should trust him. I still do, you know. Which is one hell of a recommendation, believe me.'

The front door closed behind them as they walked down the path.

'She had a room-mate,' Harper said. 'So your theory is wrong. Looked like she lived alone, but she didn't. We're back to square one.'

'Square two, maybe. It's still a subcategory. Nobody targets ninety-one women.' They got into the car. 'So now what?' he said.

'Back to Quantico.'

IT TOOK NEARLY nine hours of plane-hopping. When they reached DC, a Bureau driver met them and drove them south into Virginia. Reacher slept most of the way, the rest was just a blur of fatigue.

Harper led the way into the building and they took the elevator four floors underground to the seminar room where Blake, Poulton and Lamarr were at a table with drifts of paper in front of them. Blake and Poulton looked busy and harassed. Lamarr was as white as the paper in front of her, her eyes jumping with strain.

'Let me guess,' Blake said. 'Scimeca's box came a couple of months ago and she was vague about why. No paperwork on it.'

'She figured it was for her room-mate,' Harper said. 'She didn't live alone. So the list of eleven doesn't mean anything.'

But Blake shook his head. 'No, it means what it always meant. Eleven women who *look* like they live alone to somebody studying the paperwork. We checked with all the others. Eighty calls. None of them knew anything about unexpected cartons. So Reacher's theory that there are eleven women in the loop still holds.'

Reacher glanced at him, gratified. And a little surprised.

'Hey, credit where it's due,' Blake said.

'I'm sorry for your loss,' Reacher said to Lamarr.

'Maybe it could have been avoided,' she said. 'You know, if you'd cooperated like this from the start.'

There was silence.

'So we've got seven out of seven,' Blake said. 'No paperwork on any of the cartons.'

'You chasing the delivery companies?' Reacher asked.

'We don't know who they were,' Poulton said.

'There aren't too many possibilities,' Reacher said. 'Try them all.'

Poulton shrugged. 'And ask them what? Out of all the ten zillion packages you delivered in the last two months, can you remember the one we're interested in?'

'You have to try,' Reacher said. 'Start with Spokane. Remote address like that, middle of nowhere, the driver might recall it.'

Blake nodded. 'OK, we'll try it up there. But only there.'

'We need to catch this guy,' Lamarr said.

'Not going to be easy, now.' Blake said. 'Obviously we'll keep round-the-clock security on the seven who got the packages, but he'll spot that from a mile away, so we won't catch him at a scene.'

Lamarr nodded. 'He'll disappear until we take the security off.'

'How long are we keeping the security on?' Harper asked.

'Three weeks,' Blake said. 'Any longer than that, it gets crazy.'

Silence again. Poulton butted his papers into a pile. 'So we've got three weeks to find the guy,' he said.

Blake laid his hands on the table. 'Plan is we spell each other twenty-four hours a day. One of us sleeps while the others work. Julia, you get the first rest period, twelve hours, starting now.'

'I don't want it. I need to be involved right now.'

Blake looked awkward. 'Well, want it or not, you got it. They just flew your sister's body in for the autopsy. And you can't be involved in that. I can't let you.'

Chapter 6

The pathology lab at Quantico was no different from others Reacher had seen. It was a large low space, brightly lit, its walls and the floor lined with white tiles. In the middle of the room was a large examination table sculpted from gleaming steel and surrounded by a cluster of wheeled carts loaded with tools.

'Gowns, gloves and overshoes,' said Stavely, Quantico's senior pathologist.

He pointed to a steel cupboard filled with folded nylon gowns and boxes of disposable gloves and footwear. Harper handed them out to Reacher, Blake and Poulton.

They smelt the paint as soon as the technician pushed the gurney in through the door. The body bag lay on it, bloated and slick and smeared with green.

'Take her to X-ray first,' Stavely said.

The technician steered the gurney towards a closed room off the side of the lab. He was gone for a moment and then he stepped back into the lab and eased the lead-lined door closed behind him. There was a distant powerful hum which lasted a second and then stopped. He went back in and came out pushing the gurney again.

'Roll her off,' Stavely said. 'I want her face down.'

The technician stepped beside him, grasped the nearer edge of the bag with both hands and lifted it half off the gurney, half onto the table. Then he walked round to the other side, took the other edge and flipped the bag up and over. It flopped zipper-side-down.

'Get the film,' Stavely said.

The technician ducked back to the X-ray room and came out with large grey squares of film which mapped Alison Lamarr's body. He handed them to Stavely. Stavely shuffled them like a dealer and held one up. Ducked away to a light box against which he held the film.

'Look at that,' he said.

It was a photograph of the midsection. Reacher saw the outlines of ghostly grey bones: ribs, spine, pelvis, with a forearm and a hand lying across them at an angle. And another shape, so bright it shone pure white. Metal. Slim and pointed, about as long as the hand.

'A tool of some sort,' Stavely said.

'The others didn't have anything like that,' Poulton said.

Stavely clipped the grey photographs in sequence on the light box and studied them. 'Her skeleton is relatively undamaged. There are no fresh injuries. So she wasn't killed by blunt trauma.'

He hit the switch and the light behind the X-rays went out. He turned back to the examination table. 'OK, let's go to work.'

He pulled a hose from a reel mounted on the ceiling and turned a small faucet built into its nozzle. A stream of clear liquid started running. A heavy, slow liquid with a sharp, strong smell.

'Acetone,' Stavely said. 'Got to clear this damn paint.'

He used the acetone sluice on the body bag and on the steel table. The chemical stink was overpowering as green liquid eddied sluggishly to the drain below.

'Ventilator,' Stavely said.

The technician twisted a switch behind him and the fans in the ceiling changed up from a hum to a louder roar.

Stavely handed the hose to the technician and used a scalpel to slit the bag lengthwise from end to end. He made sideways cuts top and bottom and peeled the rubber back in two long flaps. Alison Lamarr's body was revealed, face down, slimy with paint. The skin turned greenish-white as the paint was washed off. Stavely used his gloved fingertips to peel the crust away from her body, and the acetone ran continuously, rinsing the green stream into the drain.

'Roll her over,' Stavely said.

She moved easily. The acetone mixed with the slick paint was like a lubricant against the steel of the table. She slid face up and lay there, her skin greenish-white and puckered. Her eyes were open, the lids rimmed with green. She wore the last remaining piece of the body bag stuck to her skin from her breasts to her thighs, like an old-fashioned bathing suit protecting her modesty.

Stavely probed with his hand and found the metal implement under the rubber. 'A screwdriver,' he said, pulling the object out.

The technician washed it in an acetone bath and held it up. It was a quality tool with a heavy plastic handle.

'Matches the others,' Reacher said. 'In her kitchen drawer.'

'She's got scratches on her face,' Stavely said suddenly, using the hose to wash her face. Her left cheek had four parallel incisions running down from the eye to the jaw. 'And I think they're self-inflicted.'

'Are you sure?'

Stavely was circling the head of the table, looking for the best light, examining the hand that held the screwdriver.

'I can't be sure. You know that. But probability suggests it. What are the chances the guy would have put them in the only place she could have put them herself?'

'He made her do it,' Reacher said.

'How?' Blake asked.

'I don't know how. But the scratches were probably an after-thought. I think he makes them put the paint in the tub themselves, and the screwdriver is to get the lids off with. If he'd been thinking about the scratches, he'd have made her get a knife from the kitchen as well as the screwdriver.'

'But why?' Blake said. 'Why make her scratch herself like that?'

'Anger?' Reacher said. 'Punishment? Humiliation? I always won-dered why he wasn't more violent.'

'But how did he kill her?' Blake asked.

Stavely had the final section of the body bag peeled back and was washing paint away from her midsection with the acetone jet.

'Is it possible you can kill somebody and a pathologist can't tell how?' Reacher asked.

Stavely shook his head. 'Not this pathologist,' he said. He shut off the acetone stream and let the hose retract into its reel on the ceiling. 'Fundamentally, there are two ways to kill a person. Either you stop the heart, or you stop the flow of oxygen to the brain. But to do either thing without leaving a mark is a hell of a trick.'

'How would you stop the heart?' Blake asked.

'Short of firing a bullet through it?' Stavely said. 'Embolism would be the best way. A big bubble of air, injected into the bloodstream, hits the inside of the heart like a stone. It's usually fatal.'

'You'd see the hypodermic hole, right?'

'Not on a corpse like this. The skin is ruined by the paint. But you'd see the damage to the heart. I'll check when I open her up, but I'm not optimistic. They didn't find anything like that on the others.'

'What about oxygen to the brain?' Blake asked.

'Suffocation, in layman's terms,' Stavely said. 'It can be done with-out leaving much evidence. Classic thing would be a pillow held over the face. Pretty much impossible to prove. But this is a young and strong person. She would have fought like crazy.'

Reacher looked away. The room was silent and cold.

'I think she was alive,' he said. 'When she went in the tub.'

'Reasoning?' Stavely asked.

'There was no mess. None at all. What was she, one twenty? One twenty-five pounds? Hell of a dead weight to heave into the tub without making some kind of a mess.'

'Maybe he put the paint in afterwards,' Blake said. 'On top of her.'

Reacher shook his head. 'It would have floated her up, surely.'

'We'd need to experiment,' Stavely said. 'But I agree she died in the tub. The first three, there was no evidence they were touched at all. No bruising, no abrasions, no nothing. My guess is they did whatever they did strictly under their own power.'

'Except kill themselves,' Harper said.

Stavely nodded. 'Obviously, this isn't suicide.'

'And they weren't drowned,' Blake said.

Stavely nodded again. 'The first three weren't. No fluid in the lungs. We'll know about this one soon, but I would bet against it.'

'So how the hell did he do it?' Blake muttered.

Stavely stared down at the body. 'Right now, I have no idea,' he said. 'Give me a couple of hours, I might find something.'

THEY LEFT THEIR GOWNS, gloves and overshoes in a tangle by the door and exited the pathology building. They took the long way back to the main building, as if the chill air would rid them of the stink of paint and death. In the seminar room Julia Lamarr was sitting alone at the table.

'You're supposed to be out of here,' Blake said to her.

'Any conclusions?' she asked quietly. 'From Stavely?'

Blake shook his head. 'Later. You should have gone home.'

'I told you. I can't go home. I need to be on top of this.'

'It was an order, you realise that?'

'And I ignored it,' Lamarr said. 'So what are you going to do? We need to work. We've only got three weeks to catch this guy.'

'That's plenty of time,' Reacher put in. 'If we talk about his motive, right now.'

Lamarr stiffened in her seat. Turned to Blake, appealing. 'We can't start arguing this all over again.'

'We have to,' Reacher said.

'Relax, people,' Blake called. 'Just relax. We've got three weeks, and we're not going to waste any of it arguing.'

'You're going to waste all of it, if you keep on like this,' Reacher said. 'You're wrong about his motive and it's keeping you from looking in the right places.'

'His motive is clear,' Lamarr said icily. 'Do we need this?'

Blake was silent. Then he nodded. 'You've got three minutes, Reacher. Give us what you've got.'

Reacher took a breath. 'This is a very smart guy, right? He's committed four homicides, bizarre, elaborate scenarios, and he hasn't left the slightest shred of evidence behind. He's only made one mistake, and that was a fairly trivial one, because it's not getting us anywhere.'

'So?' Blake said. 'What's your point?'

'His intelligence is of a specific type. It's practical, efficient, intensely rational. He deals with *reality*.'

'So?' Blake said again.

'So think about it. Any guy who gets in a big tantrum about this harassment issue is a guy who's *irrational*. And any guy who goes around looking for revenge against victims has got a screw loose. He's not rational. He's not dealing with reality. He's an idiot.'

'So?'

'So our guy is not motivated by anger at these women. It's not possible. You can't be rational and irrational, all at the same time.'

'We *know* what his motive is,' Lamarr said. 'What else could it be? The target group is too exact for it to be anything else.'

Reacher shook his head. 'A deranged guy couldn't commit these crimes.'

Lamarr clamped her teeth together. 'So what's his real motive, smart guy?' she asked, her voice low and quiet.

'I don't know,' Reacher said.

'You don't know? You question my expertise and you don't *know*?'

'It'll be something simple. It always is, right? Something simple and obvious. And lucrative enough to be worth protecting.'

'He's protecting something?' Poulton asked.

Reacher nodded. 'I think maybe he's eliminating witnesses.'

'Witnesses to what?'

'Some kind of a racket, I suppose. Something big.'

'Inside the army?' Lamarr asked.

'Obviously,' Reacher said.

Blake nodded. 'OK. So what is it?'

There was silence. Then Lamarr buried her face in her hands and started rocking backwards and forwards in her chair. Reacher stared at her. She was sobbing, like her heart was breaking.

'Julia?' Blake called. 'You OK?'

She took her hands away from her face. It was contorted and anguished. 'I'm sorry,' she gasped. 'I've made a terrible mistake. Because I think Reacher's right. I screwed up. I missed it. I should have seen it before.'

'Don't be sorry,' Blake said. 'It's the stress.'

She lifted her head and stared at him. 'Don't you see? My sister died because I wasted all this time. It's my fault. *I killed her*. Because I was wrong.'

Blake stared at her, helplessly. 'You need to take time out,' he said.

She wiped her eyes. 'No, no, I need to work. I already wasted too much time. So now I need to think.'

'You should go home. Take a couple of days.'

Reacher watched her. She was collapsed in her chair like she had taken a savage beating and her face was blotched red and white. She hauled herself upright in her chair and fought to breathe. 'Maybe later I'll rest,' she said. 'But first I *work*. First, we *all* work. We've got to think. What racket is he protecting?'

'Give us what you've got, Reacher,' Blake said. 'You didn't go this far without something on your mind.'

'OK, what was Amy Callan's job?'

'Ordnance clerk,' Poulton said.

'Lorraine Stanley's?' Reacher asked.

'Quartermaster sergeant.'

Reacher paused. 'Alison's?' he asked.

'Infantry close-support,' Lamarr said, neutrally.

'And before that.'

'Transport battalion.'

Reacher nodded. 'Rita Scimeca's job?'

'Weapons proving,' Harper put in. 'Now I see why you made her tell me.'

'Why?' Blake asked.

'What's the potential link between them?' Reacher asked.

'You tell me.'

'What did I take from those guys at the restaurant?'

Blake shrugged. 'I don't know. That's Cozo's business.'

'They had handguns,' Reacher said. 'Beretta M9s, with the serial numbers filed off. What does that mean?'

'They were illegally obtained.'

Reacher nodded. 'From the army. Beretta M9s are military issue. Now if this is some army guy protecting a racket, the racket most likely involves weapons theft, because that's where the money is. And these women were all in a position where they could have witnessed weapons theft. They were transporting and testing and warehousing weapons, all day long.'

Blake shook his head. 'It's too coincidental,' he said. 'What are the chances all these witnesses would also be harassment victims?'

'It's only an idea,' Reacher said. 'But the chances are actually pretty good, the way I see it.'

Lamarr leaned forward, fingers drumming on the table, life back in her eyes. 'No,' she said. 'Think about it *laterally*. They weren't harassment victims *and* witnesses. They were harassment victims *because* they were witnesses. If you're some army racketeer and you've got a woman in your unit who's not turning a blind eye to what you need her to be turning a blind eye to, what do you do about it? You get rid of her, is what. And what's the quickest way to do that? You make her uncomfortable, sexually.'

There was silence. Then Blake shook his head again. 'No, Julia,' he said. 'It's way too coincidental. On the other hand, what are the chances Reacher just happened to stumble across the back end of the same racket that's killing our women? A million to one.'

Lamarr stared at him. '*Think*, for God's sake,' she said. 'He's not saying he saw the *same* racket that's killing our women. There must be hundreds of rackets in the army. Right, Reacher?'

Reacher nodded. 'Right,' he said. 'The restaurant thing set me thinking along those lines, is all, in general terms.'

There was silence again. Blake coloured red. 'There are hundreds of rackets?' he said. 'So how does that help us? How are we going to find the right one? Needle in a damn haystack.'

'And what about the paint?' Poulton asked. 'If he's eliminating witnesses, he'd walk up and shoot them in the head with a silenced .22. He wouldn't mess with all this other stuff.'

Reacher looked at him. 'Exactly,' he said. 'Your perception of the motive is defined by the *manner* of the killings. Think about it. If they *had* all got a silenced .22 in the head, you'd have been more open-minded about the motive. Sure, you'd have considered the harassment angle, but you'd have considered other things, too. More ordinary things. You'd be all over the army looking for scams. But the guy deflected you by dressing it up with all this bizarre bullshit. He hid his true motive. He manipulated you, because he's smart.'

'Julia?' Blake said.

Lamarr said, slowly, 'It's possible he could be right. I think we should check it out, maximum effort.'

'But he's wrong,' Poulton said, riffling through paper, his voice was loud and joyful. 'Caroline Cooke makes him wrong. She was in War Plans at NATO. Never anywhere near weapons or warehouses.'

Reacher smiled. 'Cooke was an officer candidate. Fast-track type. People like that, they send them all over the place first, getting an overview.'

The room went quiet again. Then the silence was broken by Stavely hurrying into the room, big and busy and intrusive. He was dressed in a white lab coat, and his wrists were smeared green where the paint had lapped up above his gloves. Lamarr stared at the marks then closed her eyes and swayed like she was about to faint.

'I want to go home now,' she said, quietly.

She pushed back her chair and stood up. Walked unsteadily to the door, her eyes fixed on the remnants of her sister's last moments of life daubed across Stavely's stained wrists. Then she wrenched her gaze away and walked out.

'I know how he kills them,' the pathologist announced. 'Except there's a problem.'

'What problem?' Blake asked.

'It's impossible.'

'LIKE I TOLD YOU,' Stavely said, when he was seated, 'you stop the heart, or you deny oxygen to the brain. So first, I looked at her heart. It was perfect. Completely undamaged. Same as the other three. So the only remaining possibility is that he denied them oxygen.'

'But you said there are no signs of strangulation,' Blake put in.

Stavely nodded. 'There aren't. That's what got me interested.' He turned to Reacher. 'Did she have a cold, when you met her?'

'No,' Reacher said. 'She seemed pretty healthy to me.'

Stavely looked pleased. 'There was some very, very slight swelling inside the throat. It's what you'd get, recovering from a head cold. Normally I'd ignore it completely. But the other three had it too. That's a little coincidental.'

'So what does it mean?' Blake asked.

'It means he pushed something down their throats,' Stavely said. 'Something soft, something which would slip down and then expand a little. Maybe a sponge. Were there sponges in the bathrooms?'

'I didn't see one in Spokane,' Reacher said. 'Before or after.'

'You sure?' Blake asked.

Reacher nodded. 'Totally.'

Blake looked back to Stavely. 'So that's how he's doing it? Sponges down their throats?'

Stavely stared at his big red hands, resting on the tabletop. 'Sponges, or something similar. Something soft enough not to cause trauma internally, but dense enough to block the airway.'

Blake nodded, slowly. 'OK, so now we know.'

Stavely shook his head miserably. 'Well, no, we don't. Because it's impossible. There's no way you can force something into somebody's mouth against their will, without leaving bruises on their cheeks, their jaws. Their lips would be bruised and cut. And they'd be biting and scratching and kicking. Traces under their nails. It would be a fight to the death, right? And there's no evidence of fighting. None at all.'

'Maybe he drugged them,' Blake said. 'Made them passive.'

Stavely shook his head again. 'Nobody was drugged,' he said. 'Toxicology is absolutely clear, all four cases.'

The room went silent again.

'I told you, this is a smart guy,' Reacher said to Blake. 'Way too smart. Four homicides, and you *still* don't know how he's doing it.'

'So what's the answer?'

'I don't know,' Reacher said. 'But I intend to find out.'

'Yeah, like how?'

'Easy. I'll go find the guy, and I'll ask him.'

'You think you can find the guy?' Blake said.

'I'll have to, won't I? You guys aren't getting anywhere.'

'You're an arrogant bastard, you know that? I'm gambling big time here. With a lot at stake.'

'Seven women and your career.'

'So what do you need to find the guy?'

'Remuneration,' Reacher said.

'You find the guy, I'll speak to Deerfield up in New York, get the Petrosian thing forgotten about.'

'Plus a fee.'

Blake nodded. 'I'll think about it. And Harper goes with you, because right now the Petrosian thing ain't forgotten about.'

'OK. I can live with that,' he said. 'I'll need you to set me up with Cozo. I'll start in New York and I'll need information from him.'

'I'll call him. You can see him tonight.'

Reacher shook his head. 'Tomorrow morning. Tonight, I'm going to see Jodie.'

FORTY-ONE MILES AWAY, the colonel was two miles from his office. He had taken the shuttle bus from the Pentagon's parking lot and had got off near the Capitol. Then he had hailed a cab and headed back over the river to the National Airport's main terminal. His uniform was in a leather one-suiter slung on his shoulder, and he was cruising the ticket counters at the busiest time of day, completely anonymous in a teeming crush of people.

'I want Portland, Oregon,' he said. 'Open round-trip, economy.'

A clerk entered the code for Portland and his computer told him he had plenty of availability on the next nonstop.

'Leaves in two hours,' he said.

REACHER AND HARPER got a ride in a plain Bureau Chevrolet and were at the airport in DC before dark. They lined up for the shuttle with the lawyers and the lobbyists. Harper chose seats at the back.

'No rush to get off,' she said. 'You're not seeing Cozo until tomorrow. And we can talk back here. I don't like people listening.'

'Talk about what?'

'The scratches on her face,' she said. 'I need to understand what that's about.'

The engines wound up to a scream and the plane lumbered towards the runway.

'I think it proves my point,' Reacher said. 'I think it's the single most valuable piece of evidence we've got so far.'

'Why?'

He shrugged. 'I think it proves the guy is hiding behind appearances. It proves he's pretending. Somewhere, he is reviewing his progress, and he's thinking *Oh my God, I'm not showing any anger*, and so on the next one he tries to show some, but he's not really feeling any, so it comes across as really nothing much at all.'

'Why Alison, though? Why did he wait until number four?'

'A guy like this, he's thinking and refining all the time, I suppose.'

'Does it make her special in some way? Significant?'

'That's pointy-head stuff. Don't stray into their territory, Harper.'

Harper nodded. 'The motive is probably money.'

'Has to be,' Reacher said. 'Always love or money. And it can't be love, because love makes you crazy, and this guy isn't crazy.'

The plane stopped at the head of the runway. Paused for a second and accelerated. Lifted heavily into the air.

'Why did he change the interval?' Harper asked.

Reacher shrugged. 'Maybe he just did it for fun. Nothing more disruptive for you guys than a pattern that changes.'

'Will it change again?'

'It's over,' Reacher said. 'The women are guarded, and you'll be making the arrest pretty soon.'

'You really want this guy, right?'

'Yes, now I do.'

'For Amy Callan? You liked her, didn't you?'

'She was OK. I liked Alison Lamarr better, what I saw of her. But I want this guy for Rita Scimeca.'

'She likes you, too,' she said. 'I could tell. Did you have an affair?'

He shook his head. 'I only met her after she was raped. *Because* she was raped. She wasn't in any kind of a state to be having affairs. Still isn't, by the look of it. We got very friendly, but it was like a big brother and little sister, always completely platonic.'

'And now this guy is setting her back, and it's making you mad.'

'I feel responsible for Rita, he's messing with her, so he's messing with me.'

'And people shouldn't mess with you.'

'No, they shouldn't.'

'Or?'

'Or they're in deep shit.'

'You *are* kind of arrogant, you know?' she said. 'Prosecutor, judge, jury, executioner, all in one? What about the rules?'

He smiled. 'Those *are* the rules,' he said. 'People mess with me, they find that out pretty damn quick.'

Harper frowned. 'We're going to do this according to *my* rules, OK? We find the guy and arrest him.'

'I already agreed to that.' He yawned and closed his eyes. 'Wake me when we get there.'

THIS TIME *there will be guards. So this time will be difficult. Very difficult. But not impossible. Putting guards into the equation will elevate the whole thing up a little nearer to interesting. A challenge to relish.*

So what do the guards mean to you? Who are the guards? Out here in the sticks, first impression is you're dealing with dumb-ass local cops. But out here in the sticks there aren't enough cops to keep up a twenty-four-hour watch. So they'll be looking for help, and you know for sure that help will come from the FBI. The way you predict it, the locals will take the day, and the Bureau will take the night.

Given the choice, you aren't going to tangle with the Bureau. So you'll take the day, when all that stands between you and her is some local fat boy in a car full of cheeseburger wrappers and cold coffee. The day is a more elegant solution. Broad daylight. You love the phrase. 'The crime was committed in broad daylight,' you whisper to yourself.

Getting past the locals in broad daylight won't be too hard. But you're going to have to invest some time in careful, patient observation. Fortunately, you've got a little time. And it won't be hard to do. The place is mountainous. So you just get yourself concealed high up on some peak or knoll. Then you settle in, and watch. And you wait.

A BUREAU CAR met Reacher and Harper at La Guardia, and after the driver had dropped Harper at her uptown hotel, he drove Reacher to Jodie's place.

Reacher let himself into the apartment. Nobody home yet. He lay down on the living-room sofa and closed his eyes. Figured he'd catch ten minutes.

When he woke up he found her bending over him, kissing his cheek.

'Hey, Reacher,' she said softly.

He pulled her to him and held her in a silent embrace. She hugged back, hard.

'How was your day?' he asked.

'Later,' she whispered.

He pulled her down on top of him. She struggled out of her coat and let it fall. The silk lining whispered and sighed. She was in a wool dress with a zipper all the way down her spine. He unzipped it slowly and felt the warmth of her body underneath. Her hands scrabbled at his shirt. He pushed the dress off her shoulders.

She stood up and her dress fell to the floor. She held out her hand and he took it and she led him to the bedroom. They stumbled out of their clothes as they walked.

She pushed him down on the bed, with her hands on his shoulders. She was strong, like a gymnast. Urgent and energetic and lithe on top of him. He was lost. They finished filmed in sweat in a ruck of tangled sheets. She was pressed against him, her heart hammering on his chest. Her face was tucked into his shoulder and he could feel the smile against his skin. The shape of her mouth. She was beautiful in a way he couldn't describe. Somehow shot through with energy and passion. Crackling with restless intelligence, like electricity.

'Now you can ask me about my day,' she said.

'How was your day?'

She put her hand flat on his chest and pushed herself up onto her elbow. 'It was great. They're going to make a partnership offer.'

He smiled. 'Who to?'

She smiled back. 'Guess.'

He pretended to think about it. 'They'd go for somebody special, right? The smartest, hardest-working associate they got?'

'That's usually what they do.'

He nodded. 'Congratulations, babe. You deserve it. You really do.'

She smiled happily and threaded her arms round his neck. 'Partner,' she said. 'What I always wanted.'

'You deserve it,' he said again.

'There'll be a party. Will you come?'

'If you want me to. If I won't ruin your image.'

'You could buy a suit. Wear your medals. You'd blow them away.'

He was quiet for a spell, thinking about buying a suit. If he did, it would be the first suit he'd ever worn.

'Have *you* got what you want?' she asked.

He wrapped his arms round her. 'Right now?'

'Overall?'

'I want to sell the house,' he said.

She lay still for a moment. 'OK. Not that you need my permission.'

'It burdens me,' he said. 'I can't handle it.'

'You should think carefully. It's the only asset you've got.'

'Not to me. The house is a burden. And I could live the rest of my life on the money I get for it.'

She was silent.

'I'm going to sell my car, too,' he said.

'I thought you liked it,' she said.

'It's OK. For a car. I just don't like owning things.'

'Owning a car isn't exactly the end of the world.'

'It is to me. Too much hassle. Insurance, all that kind of stuff.'

'How will you get around?'

'Same as I always did, hitch rides, take the bus.'

'OK, sell the car,' she said. 'But maybe keep the house. It's useful.'

He shook his head, next to hers. 'It drives me crazy.'

He felt her smile. 'You're the only person I know who *wants* to be homeless,' she said. 'Most people try real hard to avoid it.'

'There's nothing I want more,' he said. 'Like you want to make partner, I want to be free.'

'Free of me, too?' she asked, quietly.

'Free of the house,' he said. 'It's a burden. You're not.'

She unwrapped her arms from his neck and propped herself on an elbow. 'I don't believe you.'

'The house makes me feel bad,' he said. 'You make me feel good.'

'So you'd sell the house but you'd stick around New York?'

He was quiet for a moment. 'I'd maybe move around a little. You're busy a lot of the time. We could make it work.'

'We'd drift apart.'

He shook his head. 'I don't think so.'

She was silent.

'It won't change anything,' he said.

'So why do it?'

'Because I have to.'

THEY FELL ASLEEP like that, in each other's arms, with a strand of melancholy laced through the afterglow. Morning came and there was no time for more talk. Jodie showered and left without asking him what he was doing or when he'd be back. He showered and dressed and locked up the apartment and rode down to the street where he found Lisa Harper waiting for him, leaning on the fender of the Bureau car.

'You OK?' she asked.

'I guess.'

'So let's go.'

The driver fought traffic twenty blocks uptown and went underground into the same crowded garage Lamarr had brought him to. They used the same elevator in the corner. Rode up to the twenty-first floor. Stepped into the same grey corridor. The driver preceded them like a host and pointed to a door on his left.

'The return of the vigilante,' James Cozo said when they entered the room. He closed a file and pushed back from his desk. 'So what do you want?'

'Addresses,' Reacher said. 'For Petrosian's boys.'

'The two you put in the hospital? You going to hurt them again?'

'Probably.'

Cozo nodded. 'Suits me, pal.'

He pulled a file from a stack and rooted through it. Reversed the open file on the desk and tossed a pencil on top of it. 'They live together. They're brothers. Copy it down yourself. Don't want my handwriting anywhere near this, literally or metaphorically.'

The address was near 5th, on 66th Street.

'Nice neighbourhood,' Reacher said. 'Expensive.'

'Lucrative operation.' Cozo smiled. 'Or it was until you got busy down in Chinatown. Take a taxi,' he said to Harper. 'And you stay out of the way. No overt Bureau involvement here, OK?'

THEY CAUGHT A CAB uptown and got out at 60th Street.

'We'll walk the rest of the way,' Reacher said.

'We?' Harper said. 'Good. I want to stay involved.'

'You have to stay involved. I won't get in without you.'

The address led them six blocks north to a plain, medium-height apartment building. Air conditioners built through the walls under the windows. No doorman, but clean and well kept.

The street door was open. The lobby was narrow, with a single elevator at the back. Reacher touched the elevator button and the door rolled back. They stepped in. Pressed eight.

'You knock on their door,' Reacher said. 'Get them to open up. They won't if they see me in the spyhole.'

She nodded and the elevator stopped on eight. They stepped out on a dull landing and found the apartment they were looking for.

Reacher stood flat against the wall and Harper stood in front of the door. She took a breath and knocked on it. There was a rattle of chain from the inside and the door opened a crack.

'Building management,' Harper said. 'I need to check the air conditioners.'

Wrong season, Reacher thought. But Harper was more than six feet tall, had blonde hair more than a yard long and her hands in her pockets so the front of her shirt was pulled tight. The chain rattled again and the door swung back. Harper stepped inside.

Reacher peeled off the wall and followed her in before the door closed again. It was a small, dark apartment. The living room held a sofa and two armchairs, and Harper. And both of the guys Reacher had last seen leaving the alley behind Mostro's.

'Hey, guys,' he said.

They both had broad strips of hospital gauze taped to their foreheads, a little longer and broader than the labels Reacher had stuck there. One of them had bandages on his hands. They were dressed identically in sweaters and golf trousers. Without their bulky overcoats they looked smaller. They watched him, with fearful eyes.

Reacher felt his aggression drain away. 'Sit down,' he said.

They sat on the sofa. 'Petrosian's dead,' the first guy said.

'We know that already,' Reacher said back.

The brother with the bandaged hands was older. The spokesman. 'What do you want?' he asked.

'Information. In exchange for not sending you back to hospital.'

'OK,' the guy said.

Harper smiled. 'That was easy.'

'Things change,' the guy said. 'Petrosian's dead.'

'Those guns you had,' Reacher said. 'Where did you get them?'

'Petrosian gave them to us,' the guy said.

'Where did he get them from?'

'We don't know.'

Reacher smiled. 'Well, they came from the army.'

'He bought them and gave them to us,' the younger brother said.

Reacher shook his head. 'No, he didn't. He sent you to pick them up someplace. Probably in that Mercedes you were using.'

The brothers stared at the wall, thinking, like there was a decision to be made. 'Who are you?' the older one asked eventually.

'I'm nobody,' Reacher said. 'Not a cop, not FBI, not anybody. So there's an upside and a downside here. You tell me stuff, it stays with me. Doesn't have to go any further. I'm interested in the army, not you. The downside is, if you *don't* tell me, I'm not concerned with sending you off to court with all kinds of civil rights. I'm concerned with breaking arms and legs.'

There was silence.

'New Jersey,' the older brother said. 'Through the Lincoln Tunnel, there's a roadhouse set back where Route 3 meets the turnpike. Somebody's Bar. Mac something. Like Irish.'

'Who did you see in there?'

'Guy called Bob.'

'How does it go down?'

'You go in the bar, you find him, you give him the cash, he takes you in the parking lot and gives you the stuff out of his car.'

'A Cadillac,' the other guy said. 'An old DeVille, some dark colour.'

'What stuff?'

'Berettas.'

'What time of day?'

'He's always there by evening time, eight o'clock,' the younger brother said. 'That's what Petrosian told us.'

Reacher nodded. 'So what does Bob look like?'

'Like you,' the older brother said. 'Big and mean.'

Chapter 7

'OK, what now?' Harper said, as she headed south on 5th.

In order to preserve some respectable distance between the FBI and Reacher's activities, James Cozo had withdrawn the Bureau's sedan and the services of its driver and given Harper the keys to an anonymous black Nissan Maxima.

'Bob's not around until eight,' Reacher said. 'We've got the whole afternoon to kill.'

'So what do we do?'

'First we eat,' Reacher said. 'I missed breakfast.'

She drove the Nissan into a commercial parking garage on West 9th Street, and they found a bistro with a view of Washington Square Park. The air was cold, but the sun was out.

'I told Jodie I'm selling the house,' Reacher said.

She looked across at him. 'She OK with that?'

He shrugged. 'She's worried. I don't see why. It makes me a happier person, how can that worry her?'

'Because it makes you a footloose person.'

'It won't change anything.'

'So why do it?'

'That's what she said.'

Harper nodded. 'She would. People do things for a reason, right? So she's asking herself, OK, *why* doesn't he want to own a house?'

'Because I don't want the hassle. She knows that. I told her.'

'But you need to convince her. You know, make her believe you're going to stick around, even though you're selling the house.'

'I told her I might travel a little, too,' he said.

She stared at him. 'That's not very reassuring, Reacher.'

'She travels. She's been to London twice this year. I didn't make a big fuss about it.'

'You know what?' Harper said. 'Before you convince *her* you're going to stick around, maybe you should convince yourself.'

'I am convinced.'

'Are you? Or do you figure you'll be in and out, as and when?'

'In and out a little, I guess.'

'You'll drift apart.'

'That's what she said.'

'Well, I'm not surprised.'

He said nothing. Just drank his coffee and ate his Danish.

'It's make-your-mind-up time,' Harper said, as she picked up the bill. 'On the road or off the road, you can't do both together.'

THE WAY YOU predict it, it's going to be a straight half-each split between the local police department and the Bureau, with changeovers at eight in the evening and eight in the morning. You saw it happen at eight in the evening yesterday, so now you're back bright and early to see it happen again at eight this morning.

You're not dumb enough to rent a room anywhere close by, so you wind your way through the mountains and leave your car on a gravel lay-by half a mile from your spot.

You climb up a small hill maybe 100 feet high. There are scrawny trees all over the place, a little more than shoulder-high. They have no leaves, but the terrain keeps you concealed. You drop to your knees and shuffle forward to where two giant rocks rest on each other, giving a wonderful view of Lieutenant Rita Scimeca's house through the triangular gap between them. The Bureau car is right there, parked outside. A clean Buick, dark blue. One agent in it. You use your field glasses. The guy is still awake. He's not looking around much. Just staring forward, bored out of his skull.

The house has a wire fence all the way round the perimeter of the yard. There's an opening onto a short driveway. A single garage door stands at the end of it, under the end of the front porch. There's a path off the driveway that loops round through some neat rockery planting to the front door. The Bureau car is parked at the sidewalk right across the driveway opening, facing down the rise. That puts the driver's line of vision directly in line with the mouth of the path. Intelligent positioning.

If you walk up the hill to the house, he sees you coming all the way. You come on him from behind, he maybe spots you in his mirror, and he sees you for certain as soon as you walk up the looping path.

You see movement. A black-and-white Crown Victoria enters the road. Stops flank to flank with the Buick. You don't see it but you know the windows are buzzing down. Greetings are being exchanged. Information is being passed on.

The black-and-white moves up the hill and turns in the road. The Buick moves away down the hill. The black-and-white rolls forward and stops. Exactly where the Buick was, inch for inch. The cop turns his head to the right and gets exactly the same view of the path the Bureau guy had. Maybe not such a dumb-ass, after all.

HARPER WANTED to see the city. Reacher walked her south through Washington Square Park and all the way down West Broadway to the World Trade Center. It was about a mile and three-quarters. They sauntered slowly. The sky was bright and the city was teeming.

'We could go up to the restaurant,' Reacher said. 'Bureau could buy me lunch.'

'I just bought you lunch,' Harper said.

'No, that was a late breakfast.'

'You're always eating,' she said.

'I'm a big guy. I need nutrition.'

They checked their coats in the lobby and rode up to the top of the building. Harper showed her badge and they got a table for two, right at a window facing directly back up West Broadway.

'Awesome,' she said.

The view *was* awesome. Far below them the city was khaki in the fall light. Packed, intricate, infinitely busy.

'Bob's out there someplace,' she said. 'He's not our guy, right?'

'He's small-time,' Reacher said. 'Selling out of the trunk of his car? Not enough at stake to make it worth killing people. He's a storeman. A nine-to-five guy.'

'So how can he help us?'

'He can name names. He's got suppliers, and he knows who the other players are. He'll point us in a new direction. That's about all we can count on from Bob.'

YOU WAIT and you watch her house. You keep the field glasses tight to your eyes and you watch. You have to be sure. And by now you're sure the cop in the black-and-white is a permanent fixture. He eats in his car, he uses her bathroom from time to time, and that's it.

Either he has to be moved, or you have to go in right past him. At first you toy with the idea of a diversion. What would it take to get him out of there? A major automobile accident at the crossroads, maybe. But that would be hard to stage.

Maybe a bomb threat. But where? At the station house? That would be no good. The cop would be told to stay where he was until it was checked out. And a bomb threat would mean a phone call. Where from? Calls can be traced. And there are no payphones near where you're crouched. You can't use your mobile because eventually the call would appear on your bill.

But the more you think about it, the more your strategy centres around the phone. There's one person you can safely let hear your voice. But it's a geometric problem. Four-dimensional. Time and space. You have to call from right here, in the open, within sight of the house, but you can't use your mobile. Impasse.

REACHER DROVE out of the city that evening. Harper preferred not to in the dark and the rush hour. And rush hour was bad. Traffic was slow up the spine of Manhattan and jammed at the entrance to the tunnel. They inched forward deep under the Hudson River.

Eventually they were on Route 3, which angled slightly north towards the New Jersey Turnpike. It was a shiny night, damp asphalt everywhere, sodium lights with evening-fog halos strung like necklaces. There were lit billboards and neon signs left and right.

The roadhouse they were looking for was in the back of a lot where three roads met. It was labelled with a beer company's neon sign which said *MacStiophan's*. Reacher parked the Nissan near the door. Slid out and looked around.

'No Cadillac DeVille,' he said. 'He's not here yet.'

'We're a little early,' Harper said. 'I guess we'll wait.'

'You can wait out here,' he said. 'If you prefer.'

She shook her head. 'I've been in worse places.'

It was hard for Reacher to imagine where and when. The outer door led to a lobby with a sisal mat worn smooth with use. The inner door led to a dark space full of the stink of beer and smoke. The walls were dulled and sticky with fifty years of cigarettes.

There were eight customers in the body of the room, with glasses of beer in front of them. All of them were men, staring hostilely at the newcomers. None of them was a soldier.

Reacher stepped up to the bar and rolled a stool out for Harper.

'What's on draught?' he asked the bartender.

The guy was maybe fifty, grey-faced, paunchy.

'Haven't seen you in here before,' he said.

Harper smiled. 'No, we're new customers.'

'What do you want?' the guy said.

'Two beers,' Reacher said.

'Apart from that? People like you don't come in a place like mine without you're wanting something.'

'We're waiting for Bob,' Harper said.

'Bob who?'

'Bob with the old Cadillac DeVille,' Reacher explained. 'Comes in here eight o'clock every night.'

The guy smiled. Yellow teeth, some of them missing. 'Well, you've got a long wait, then.'

He took two glasses from an overhead rack and filled them. Placed the beers on the bar. Harper pulled a wallet from her pocket and dropped a ten-dollar bill between the glasses.

'Keep the change,' she said. 'So why the long wait for Bob?'

The guy slid the ten into his pocket. 'Because Bob's in jail.'

'What for?'

'Some army thing. I don't know the details, and I don't *want* to know the details. The Military Police just came in and grabbed him right here, in this room. Couple of months ago, I guess.'

THEY LEFT THE BEER untouched on the bar and headed back to the parking lot. Unlocked the Nissan and slid inside.

'Couple of months is no good,' Harper said. 'Puts him right outside the picture.'

'He was never in the picture, but we'll go talk to him anyway.'

'How can we do that? He's in the army system somewhere.'

He looked at her. 'Harper, I was a military policeman for thirteen years. If I can't find him, who can? Regional MP HQ for this region is Fort Armstrong, outside of Trenton, less than two hours away.'

'We don't want to waste time,' she said. 'Check it first.' She smiled and opened her bag. Came out with a folded cellular phone the size of a cigarette packet. 'Use my mobile,' she said.

THE TARGET you're watching is a woman of about twenty-three or four. She's dressed comfortably like she's got a long flight ahead and she's leaning back in her chair with her head tilted left and her phone trapped between her shoulder and chin. She's smiling as she talks, and playing with her nails. Turning her hands in the light to look at them. This is a lazy chat with a girlfriend.

On the floor near her feet is a small designer backpack, all covered in little loops and catches and zippers. It's clearly so complicated to close that she's left it gaping open. She checks her watch and wraps up the chat. Flips her phone closed and drops it in her backpack. Picks up her wallet and goes off to get coffee.

You're on your feet instantly. Car keys in your hand. You hustle straight across the court, ten feet, twenty, thirty. You're swinging the keys, looking busy. She's in line. About to be served. You drop your keys and they skid across the tiles. You bend to retrieve them. Your hand skims her bag. You come back up with the keys and the phone together. The keys go back in your pocket. The phone stays in your hand. Nothing more ordinary than somebody walking through an airport lounge holding a mobile. You smile to yourself. Now the crucial call is going to end up on someone else's bill. Safe as houses.

THE PHONE CALL to the Fort Armstrong duty officer revealed nothing, but the guy's evasions were voiced in such a way that Reacher took them to be confirmation.

'He's there,' he said. 'I guarantee it.'

They pulled off into the next service area to get gas and a map.

'We're on the wrong road,' Reacher said, craning over the yard-square sheet. 'Route 1 would be better.'

'OK, next exit,' Harper said. 'Use 95 to jump across.'

She used her finger to trace south down Route 1. Found Fort Armstrong on the edge of the yellow shape that represented Trenton.

'Close to Fort Dix,' she said. 'Where we were before.'

Less than two hours later they drew up at a vehicle barrier outside a two-storey guardhouse. A sentry peered through the window and came out to the car. Reacher buzzed his window down.

'You the guy who called the captain?' the heavy black guy asked. Low voice, slow accent from the deep South.

Reacher nodded.

The sentry grinned. 'He figured you might show up. Go ahead in.'

He stepped back into the guardhouse and the barrier came up. Reacher drove towards a low symmetrical building with white-washed steps leading up to double doors in the centre.

'Duty office,' Reacher said.

Two carriage lamps mounted on the door pillars lit up, the doors opened inwards and a man in uniform stepped through the gap.

'That was me, about a million years ago,' Reacher muttered.

The captain waited at the top of the steps, sheltered from the drizzle. He was a head shorter than Reacher, but he was broad and looked fit. His uniform jacket was buttoned, but his face looked open enough. Reacher slid out of the Nissan and walked round the hood. Harper joined him at the foot of the steps.

'Come in out of the rain,' the captain called.

His accent was East Coast urban. Bright and alert. A decent guy. Reacher went up the steps first. Harper followed.

'This is Lisa Harper,' Reacher said. 'She's with the FBI.'

'Pleased to meet you,' the captain said. 'I'm John Leighton.'

The three of them shook hands and Leighton led them along a corridor to his office. Old desk, new computer, old filing cabinet, new phone. Every surface overloaded with paper.

'We'll try not to take up too much of your time,' Reacher began.

'Don't worry. I called around, after you called me, naturally. Friend of a friend said I should push the boat out. Word is you were a solid guy, for a major.'

Reacher smiled. 'Well, I tried to be.'

'So how can I help?' Leighton said, gesturing for them to sit down.

Harper ran through it all from the beginning. Leighton listened attentively, interrupting here and there.

'I know about the women,' he said. 'We heard.'

She finished with Reacher's smoke-screen theory, the possible army thefts, and the trail which led from Petrosian's boys in New York to Bob in New Jersey.

'His name is Bob McGuire,' Leighton said. 'Quartermaster sergeant. But he's not your guy. We've had him two months, and he's too dumb.'

'We figured that,' Harper said. 'Feeling was he could name names, maybe lead us to a bigger fish. Somebody doing enough business to make it worth killing witnesses.'

Leighton nodded. 'Theoretically, there might be such a person,' he said cautiously.

'You got a name?'

Leighton shook his head. 'Now we're computerised we can keep track of everything better than we used to. For instance, we know how many Beretta M9s have been delivered, we know how many have been legitimately issued, and we know how many we got in store. And if those numbers didn't add up, we'd be worrying, believe me.'

'So do the numbers add up?'

'They do now. That's for damn sure. Nobody's stolen an army Beretta M9 in the last year and a half.'

'What was Bob McGuire doing two months ago?' Reacher asked.

'Selling out the last of his stockpile. He'd been thieving ten years, at least. A little computer analysis made it obvious. Him, and a couple dozen others in different locations. We put procedures in place to dry up the stealing and we arrested a couple dozen guys. The leakage stopped.'

'You got them *all*?' Harper asked.

Leighton nodded. 'All of them. Big push, worldwide. There weren't that many. Computers did the trick.'

'Well, there goes that theory,' Harper said. She stared at the floor.

'Maybe not,' Leighton replied quickly. 'We've got a theory of our own. Like I told you, we've got a couple dozen guys waiting for trial, all the leaks accounted for. But the way we picked them up was we sent undercover guys in, to buy the stuff. Entrapment. Bob McGuire, for instance, he sold a couple of Berettas to a couple of lieutenants in a New Jersey bar.'

'We were just there,' Harper said. 'MacStiophan's.'

'Right,' Leighton said. 'Our guys bought two M9s out of the trunk of his car, two hundred bucks apiece. So then we haul McGuire in and we start looking for the money. And we find about a half of it, either in bank accounts or in the form of stuff he's bought.'

'So?' Reacher said.

'So nothing, not right then. But we're pooling information and the story is pretty much the same everywhere. They've all got about a half of their money missing.'

'Enter the theoretical big fish,' Reacher muttered.

Leighton nodded. 'Exactly. How else to explain it? We started to figure some big guy in the shadows, maybe organising everything, offering protection in exchange for half the profit.'

'Or half the guns,' Reacher said.

'Right,' Leighton said. 'A scam inside a scam.'

There was a long pause.

'Looks good from our point of view,' Harper said. 'Guy like that, he's smart and capable. He has to run around taking care of problems in various locations. Could explain why he's interested in so many different women. Not because all the women knew *him*, but because maybe each one of them knew one of his clients. So who is he?'

Leighton rubbed his eyes. 'We have no idea. We've got two dozen guys, all of them with their mouths shut tight. We figure the big guy's really put the frighteners on.'

There was silence in Leighton's office. Just the brittle patter of rain on the windows.

'Well, we need his name, I guess,' Reacher said. 'I should go talk to McGuire for you.'

Leighton smiled. 'I figured you'd say that. And I was all set to say no, it's improper. But you know what? I just changed my mind.'

THE CELL BLOCK was underground, like it always is in a regional HQ. Leighton used an old-fashioned bell pull outside the iron door and it opened after a second to reveal a bright hallway with a huge master sergeant standing in it. Leighton led them in out of the rain.

Inside, the walls were faced with white porcelain glaze. There was a cubbyhole office on the right, with a wooden rack of keys on four-inch metal hoops; a big desk, piled high with video recorders taping flickering images from twelve monitor screens. The scenes showed twelve cells, eleven of which were empty. In the twelfth there was a humped shape under a blanket on the bed.

'Quiet night at the Hilton,' Reacher said.

Leighton nodded. 'Right now McGuire's our only guest.'

'The video recording is a problem,' Reacher said.

'Always breaking down, though,' Leighton said. He bent over the desk. Touched a switch. The recorders stopped humming. 'See? Very unreliable system.'

'It'll take a couple hours to fix,' the sergeant said. 'At least.'

The sergeant took a hoop of keys off the wooden board and moved to the inside door. Unlocked it and swung it back. Reacher stepped through and the sergeant locked the door again behind him. Pointed to a staircase. 'After you.'

The staircase led to another locked door at the bottom. Then a lobby, with three locked doors to three blocks of cells. The sergeant unlocked the middle door. Flipped a switch and fluorescent light flooded a bright white area forty feet by twenty. There was an access zone the length of the block and about a third of its depth. The rest of the space was divided into four cells delineated by heavy iron bars. Three of the cells were empty, with their gates folded back. The fourth was locked closed. McGuire sat up, surprised by the light.

'Visitor for you,' the sergeant called. There were two tall wooden stools in the corner of the access zone. The sergeant carried the nearer one over and placed it in front of McGuire's cell. Walked back and sat on the other. Reacher ignored the stool and stood gazing silently through the bars. McGuire was pushing his blanket aside and swinging his feet to the floor. He was wearing an olive undershirt and olive shorts. He was a big guy. More than six feet tall, more than 200 pounds. Heavily muscled, a thick neck, big arms, big legs. Thinning hair cropped close, small eyes, a couple of tattoos.

'Hell are you?' McGuire said. His deep voice matched his bulk. Reacher made no reply. He walked over to where the master sergeant was sitting and whispered in his ear. The guy nodded and stood up and handed Reacher the hoop of keys. Went out through the door and closed it behind him. Reacher walked back to McGuire's cell.

'What do you want?' McGuire said.

'I want proof.'

'Of what?'

'Of exactly how dumb a piece of shit like you really is.'

McGuire paused. His eyes narrowed, pushed into deep furrows by his brow. 'Easy for you to talk like that,' he said. 'Standing on the other side of these bars.'

Reacher took a pace forward. 'Want me to open the cell gate? Even things up a little? Keys are right here.'

McGuire's eyes narrowed more. He nodded. 'Yeah, open the gate.'

Reacher unlocked the gate. Swung it open. McGuire stood still. Reacher walked away, hung the hoop of keys on the doorknob.

'Sit down,' he gestured. 'I left the stool there for you.'

McGuire came out of the cell. 'What do you want?' he said again.

'It's complicated,' Reacher replied. 'You're going to have to juggle a number of factors.'

'What factors?' McGuire asked, blankly.

'First factor is I'm unofficial, OK?' Reacher said. 'It means I'm not an army cop, I'm not a civilian cop, in fact I'm not anything at all. So if I leave you walking on crutches, there's nothing anybody can do to me. And we got no witnesses in here. Second factor is whatever the big guy says he'll do to you, I can do worse.'

'What big guy?'

Reacher smiled. 'Now it gets sophisticated. Third factor is, if you give me the guy's name, he goes away somewhere else, for ever. You give me his name, he can't get to you. Not ever, you understand?'

'What name? What guy?'

'The guy you were paying off with half your take.'

'No such guy.'

Reacher shook his head. 'We're past that stage now, OK? We know there's such a guy. So don't make me smack you around before we even get to the important part.'

McGuire tensed. Breathed hard.

'So concentrate,' Reacher said. 'What you need to understand is, if you rat him out it actually makes you safe, the rest of your life, because people are looking at him for a bunch of things a whole lot worse than ripping off the army.'

'What's he done?' McGuire asked.

Reacher smiled. *So the guy exists.*

'He killed four women. You give me his name, they'll put him away for ever. Nobody will ask him about anything else.'

McGuire was silent. Thinking about it. It wasn't the speediest process Reacher had ever seen.

'Last factor,' Reacher said gently. 'You need to understand, sooner or later you'll tell me anyway. It's just a question of timing. You can tell me right now, or you can tell me in a half-hour, right after I've broken your arms and legs.'

'You ain't going to do nothing,' McGuire said.

Reacher turned and picked up the wooden stool. Flipped it upside-down and held it chest-high with his hands round two of the legs. Took a firm backhand grip and snapped his elbows back. The legs tore away from the rungs. The rungs clattered to the floor. He reversed the stool, held the seat in his left hand and splintered a leg free with his right. It was about the size and weight of a baseball bat.

'Now you do the same,' he said.

McGuire tried hard. He turned over his stool and grasped the legs. His muscles bunched and the tattoos swelled, but he got nowhere.

'Too bad,' Reacher said. 'I tried to make it fair.'

'He was Special Forces,' McGuire said. 'He's real tough.'

'Doesn't matter,' Reacher said. 'He resists, the FBI will shoot him down. End of problem.'

McGuire said nothing. Reacher swung the leg of the stool.

'Left or right?' he asked. 'Which arm you want me to break first?'

'LaSalle Kruger,' McGuire said. 'Supply battalion CO. He's a colonel.'

STEALING THE PHONE was candy from a baby, but the reconnaissance is a bitch. Timing it right is the first priority. You need to wait for full dark, the daytime cop's final hour. Because somebody's last hour is always better than somebody else's first hour. Attention will have waned. Boredom will have set in. He'll be thinking ahead to a beer with his buddies or a night with his wife.

So your window extends to about forty minutes, say seven to seven forty. You drive back from the airport and you approach on the through road. You drive straight through the junction three streets from her house. You stop at a hiker's car park 200 yards further north. You get out of your car and you work your way west and north through lightly wooded terrain. You're about level with your first position, but on the other side of her house, behind it, not in front.

You ease through the brush and come out at her fence. Stand motionless in the dark and observe. Drapes are drawn. It's quiet. You can hear a piano playing, very faintly. The house is built into the hillside, at right angles to the street. Facing you is the side wall, dotted with windows.

*No doors. You ease along the fence and check the back of the house.
No doors there, either. So the only ways in are the front door on the
porch, and the garage door facing the street. Not ideal, but you've
planned for it. You've planned for every contingency.*

'OK, COLONEL KRUGER,' Leighton said. 'We're on your ass now.'

They were back in the duty office, damp from the jog through the
night-time rain, flushed with elation. Now Leighton was scrolling
through a menu on his computer screen, and Reacher and Harper
were sitting side by side in front of his desk.

'OK, he's in the personnel listings,' Leighton said.

'Has he been in trouble?' Reacher asked.

'Can't tell, yet. You think he'll have an MP record?'

'Something happened,' Reacher said. 'Ex-Special Forces, and now
he's working supply? What's that about?'

'It needs explaining. Could be disciplinary, I guess. But I'm afraid
I can't let you look at our computer stuff. You know how it is, don't
you? Anyway, this could take all night.'

'Could you trace some missing camouflage paint, too?' Harper
said suddenly.

'Maybe,' Leighton said. 'Theoretically, I guess.'

'Eleven women on his list, so look for about three hundred gallons,' she said. 'Put Kruger together with the paint, that would do it
for me.'

Leighton exited the personnel listings and clicked on another
menu. Then he paused. 'The army is going to just love me, right?
Kruger's our guy, and I'm busting my ass all night so we can give
him away to the Bureau.'

'I'm sorry,' she said. 'But the jurisdiction issue is clear, isn't it?
Homicide beats theft.'

Leighton nodded, suddenly sombre. 'Like scissors beats paper.'

*ONCE YOU'VE SEEN enough of the house you step away from the fence
and duck into the brush. You work your way back to the car in the dark,
dust yourself off, slide in and head back down through the crossroads.
You've got about twenty minutes to complete part two of your task.
There's a small shopping centre two miles west of the junction, left-
hand side of the road. An old-fashioned one-storey mall, shaped like a
squared-off letter C. A supermarket in the middle like a keystone,
small single-unit stores spreading either side of it. You pull into the
parking lot at the far end and you nose along, looking. You find what
you want, three stores past the supermarket. You smile to yourself.*

Then you turn the car around and idle back through the lot, checking it out, and your smile dies. You don't like it. You don't like it at all. It's completely overlooked. So you drive round behind the arm of the C, and your smile comes back again. There's a single row of overspill parking back there, facing plain painted delivery doors in the back walls of the stores. It's perfect.

You drive back into the main lot and you park up alongside a small group of other vehicles. You wait and watch for ten minutes, and then you see the Bureau Buick heading by, reporting for duty.

'Have a nice night,' you whisper.

LEIGHTON RECOMMENDED a motel a mile down Route 1 towards Trenton. It was cheap, clean, and the only place for miles around. Harper drove, and they found it easily enough.

'Number twelve is a nice double,' the desk clerk said. 'Down the row a piece.'

Harper nodded. 'OK, we'll take it,' she said.

'We will?' Reacher said. 'A double?'

'Talk about it later,' she said.

She paid cash and the desk guy handed over a key.

Reacher walked to it through the rain, and Harper brought the car over and parked it in front of the cabin. She found Reacher waiting at the door.

'What?' she said. 'It's not like we're going to sleep, is it? We're just waiting for Leighton to call. May as well do that in here as in the car. I'm too excited to sleep, anyway.'

He just shrugged and waited for her to unlock the door. She opened up and went inside. He followed.

It was a standard motel room. There were two chairs and a table at the far end by a window. Reacher sat in the right-hand chair. Put his elbows on the table and his head in his hands. Kept very still.

'What is it?' Harper asked. 'Something's on your mind.'

'It is?'

She nodded. 'Sure it is. I can tell. I'm a woman. I'm intuitive.'

He looked straight at her. 'Truth is I don't especially want to be alone in a room with you and a bed.'

She smiled, happily, mischievously. 'Tempted?'

'I'm only human.'

'So am I,' she said. 'If I can control myself, I'm sure you can.'

He said nothing.

'I'm going to take a shower.'

'Christ,' he muttered.

IT'S A STANDARD motel room, like a thousand you've seen coast to coast. Doorway, bathroom on the right, closet on the left, bed, dresser, table and two chairs. You hang your coat in the closet, but you keep your gloves on. No need to leave fingerprints all over the place.

You walk through the room and you sit in the left-hand chair. You lean back, close your eyes, and start to think. It has to be tomorrow. You plan the timing by working backwards. You need dark before you can get out. But you want the daytime cop to find her. You accept that's just a whim, but hey, if you can't brighten things up with a little whimsy, what kind of life is that? So you need to be out after dark, but before the cop's last bathroom break. Somewhere around five thirty.

OK, five thirty. You're going to allow a full half-hour for this one. So you need to be inside and started by five. Then you think it through from her point of view, and it's pretty clear you need to be making the phone call at about two o'clock.

HARPER CAME OUT of the bathroom wearing nothing but a towel. Her face was scrubbed and her hair was wet. Cornflower-blue eyes, white teeth. Without make-up she looked about fourteen, except she was more than six feet tall. And that kind of height made a standard-issue motel towel seriously deficient in terms of length.

'I think I'd better call Blake,' she said. 'I should really check in.'

'Keep it vague, OK? Quantico gets involved at this point, they'll pull Leighton off. He's only a captain. They'll haul in some two-star asshole, and then we'll never get near the facts for the bullshit. Just say we're seeing some guy tomorrow who might have something.'

'I'll be careful,' she said. She sat down and opened her phone.

'Be real vague, OK?' he said again.

She nodded. 'Don't worry.'

'I guess I'll shower, too.'

She smiled. 'Enjoy. I won't come in, I promise.'

He went into the bathroom and closed the door. Harper's clothes were hanging from the hook on the back. All of them. The underwear was white and lacy. He thought about setting the shower icy cold, but decided to rely on will power alone. So he set it hot and stripped off his clothes. He stood under the shower for a long time, trying to relax. Then he gave up and turned the handle to cold. He held it there, gasping. One minute. Two. He shut it off and groped for a towel.

She knocked on the door. 'Are you done? I need my clothes.'

He lifted them off the hook. Opened the door a crack and passed them through. She took them and walked away. He towelled himself dry and dressed. Then rattled the door handle and came out. She was standing by the bed, wearing some of her clothes. The rest of them were folded over the back of the dresser chair. Her hair was combed back. Her phone was closed, lying next to the ice bucket.

'What did you tell him?'

'That we're meeting some guy in the morning, nothing specific.'

She was wearing the shirt, but the tie was draped over the chair. So were the suit trousers. Her legs were lean and long.

'He have anything to say?'

'Poulton's in Spokane,' she said. 'The car rental thing came to nothing, just some woman on business. But the UPS guy is coming through with stuff. He's pulling the records.'

'Won't say LaSalle Kruger on the paperwork, that's for sure.'

She sat down on the edge of the bed, her back to him. 'Probably not, but that doesn't matter any more, does it? We found him. We should celebrate,' she said, and turned to face him.

Reacher propped the pillows on the far side of the bed, sat down and leaned back against them. Looked up at the ceiling and concentrated on the sound of the rain battering on the roof.

She turned to face him. The first two buttons on her shirt were undone. 'It's Jodie, isn't it?' she said.

He nodded. 'Of course it is.'

'Wasn't for her, you'd want to, right?'

'I do want to.' He paused. 'But I won't,' he said. 'Because of her.'

She looked at him, and then smiled. 'I like that in a guy, I guess. Steadfastness.'

He said nothing. She sighed, just a tiny sound. She moved away, just an inch. But enough to ease the crisis.

'So you're going to stick around New York,' she said.

He nodded again. 'That's the plan.'

'She'll be sorry about the house. Her father willed it to you.'

'She might be,' he said. 'But she'll have to deal with it. The way I see it, he left me a choice. The house, or the money I'd get for it. He knew what I was like. He wouldn't be upset.'

The room went quiet again. The rain was easing.

She sat down on the bed, opposite him. 'I still feel like celebrating. Celebration kiss,' she whispered, leaning into the space between them. 'Nothing more, I promise.'

He looked at her and reached round with his left arm and pulled her close. Kissed her on the lips. She tilted her head and opened her mouth. He felt her tongue deep in his mouth, urgent. It felt good. He opened his eyes and saw hers, too close to focus on. They were shut tight. He let her go and pulled away, full of guilt.

'Something I need to tell you,' he said.

She was breathless, and her hair was a mess.

'I'm not being straight with you,' he said.

'How not?'

'I don't think Kruger's our guy.'

'*What?*'

'He's Leighton's guy,' Reacher said. 'But I don't think he's ours.'

'*What?* This was *your* theory, Reacher.'

He shrugged. 'I just made it up. I didn't mean any of it. I just wanted some kind of a plausible excuse to get me out of Quantico for a spell. To give myself time to think. And it was an experiment. I wanted to see who would support it and who would oppose it. I wanted to see who really wants this thing solved.'

'I don't believe this,' she said. 'We *all* want it solved. What is this to you? A *game?*'

There was pounding at the door. Loud, insistent. He stood up, ran his hand through his hair and walked towards the door. A new barrage started up.

'OK,' he called. 'I'm coming.'

The pounding stopped. He opened the door. Leighton was standing on the stoop, raindrops on the shoulders.

'Kruger's our guy,' he said.

He pushed past, inside the room. Saw Harper buttoning her shirt.

'Excuse me,' he said, surprised.

'It's hot in here,' she said, looking away.

'He's our guy, for sure,' he went on. 'Everything fits like a glove.'

Harper's mobile started ringing. Leighton paused. Gestured *I can wait.* Harper flipped the phone open and listened. Reacher watched the colour drain out of her face.

'We're recalled to Quantico,' she said. 'They got Caroline Cooke's full record. You were right, she was all over the place. But she was never anywhere near weapons. Not ever, not for a minute.'

'That's what I'm here to tell you,' Leighton said. 'Kruger's our guy, but he isn't yours.'

Leighton walked the length of the room and sat down at the table. 'First thing, there was no list,' he said, looking at Harper. 'You asked me to check thefts of paint, where the women worked, so I needed a list of the women to do that, obviously, so I tried to find one, but I couldn't, OK? So I made some calls, and what happened was when your people came to us a month ago, we had to generate a list from scratch. It was a pain in the ass, trawling through all the records. So some guy had a bright idea, took a short cut, called one of the women herself on some fake pretext. We think it was actually Alison Lamarr, and she supplied the list. Seems they'd set up a big support group among themselves.'

'Scimeca called them her sisters,' Reacher said. 'Remember that? She said four of my sisters are dead.'

'Then Kruger's records started coming in, and the dates and places didn't match. Not even close.' Leighton paused for breath. 'So I checked out why he went from Special Forces to supply battalion. He was a top boy in the Gulf. Big star, a major. They were out in the desert, behind the lines, looking for mobile Scud launchers; small unit, bad radio. And when they start the artillery barrage Kruger's unit gets all chewed up under friendly fire. Bad casualties. Kruger himself was seriously hurt. So they gave him the promotion all the way up to colonel and stuck him somewhere his injuries wouldn't disqualify him, hence the desk job in supply. My guess is we'll find he started running the rackets as a kind of revenge or something. You know, against the army. The guy lost both his legs. He's in a wheelchair. No way he's running up and down any stairs to any bathrooms.'

Harper stared at the wall. 'Shit,' she said. 'Bad idea.'

'I'm afraid so, ma'am. And you need to hear about the paint, too.'

'More bad news?'

'Weird news,' Leighton said. 'I started a search for reports about missing camo green, and the only definitive thing was hidden in a closed-access file. A theft of a hundred and ten three-gallon cans. They fingered a supply sergeant in Utah.'

'Who was he?'

'She,' Leighton said. 'She was Sergeant Lorraine Stanley.'

Total silence.

'But that's impossible,' Harper said. 'She was one of the victims.'

Leighton shook his head. 'I called Utah. Spoke to the investigating officer. He says it was Stanley, no doubt about it. They didn't proceed against her because she'd just come off the harassment thing, not long before. They just watched her, until she quit.'

'One victim stole the paint?' Reacher said. 'And another provided the list of names?'

'That's how it was, I promise you.'

REACHER DROVE FAST and it took a fraction under three hours from the outskirts of Trenton all the way back to Quantico.

'OK,' Harper said. 'Let's go get our asses chewed.'

Reacher killed the motor and the lights and they looked at each other for a second then slid out of the car. Inside the building it was quiet. Nobody around. They went down in the elevator to Blake's underground office. Found him sitting at his desk, staring at a curled sheet of paper, his face totally blank.

'Fax in from UPS,' he said gently. He looked beaten, confused. 'Guess who sent the paint to Alison Lamarr and all the others?'

'Lorraine Stanley,' Reacher said.

Blake nodded. 'Correct. From an address in Utah that turned out to be a self-storage facility. And guess what? She sent one of the cartons to herself, but she didn't even *have* her own place when she put the paint in the storage facility. She waited until she was settled, then went back up to Utah and dispatched it all. What do you make of that?'

'I don't know,' Reacher said.

'And Poulton just called from Spokane. He just got through interviewing the UPS driver. The guy remembers the delivery pretty well. Alison was there when he called. She was listening to the ball game, radio on in the kitchen. She asked him inside, gave him coffee, they heard the grand slam together. A little hollering, a little dancing around, another coffee, he tells her he's got a big heavy box for her.'

'And?'

'And she says *Oh, good*, and clears a space for it in the garage. He brings it in, dumps it, and she's all smiles about it.'

'Like she was expecting it?'

Blake nodded. 'That was the guy's impression. Then she tears off the Documents Enclosed thing and carries it back to the kitchen. He follows, to finish up his coffee. She pulls the delivery note out of the plastic, shreds it up into small pieces and dumps them in the trash.'

'So what's your take?'

Blake shook his head. 'I have no idea.'

'I apologise,' Reacher said. 'My theory led us nowhere.'

Blake made a face. 'It was worth a try.'

'Is Lamarr around? I should apologise to her, too.'

Blake shook his head. 'She's at home. Hasn't been back. Says she's a wreck, and she's right. Can't blame her.'

'A lot of stress. She should get away.'

'Where to?' Blake sighed. 'She won't get on a damn plane. And I don't want her driving anyplace, the state she's in.' Then his eyes hardened. 'I'm going to look for another consultant. When I find one, you're out of here. You're getting nowhere. You'll have to take your chances with the New York people.'

'OK,' Reacher said.

Blake looked away and Harper took her cue and led Reacher out of the office. Into the elevator, up to the third floor. They walked together through the corridor to the familiar door.

'Why was she expecting it?' Harper said. 'Why was Alison expecting the box of paint, when all the others weren't?'

He shrugged. 'I don't know.'

Harper opened his door. 'OK, good night,' she said.

'You mad at me?'

'You wasted thirty-six hours.'

'No, I invested thirty-six hours.'

'In what?'

'I don't know, yet.'

'You're a weird guy.'

'So people say.' He kissed her chastely on the cheek, and she walked back to the elevator.

He stepped into his room. Walked to the bed and lay down, still in his coat. It was three in the morning, too late to call Jodie. He stared up at the ceiling. Tried to see Jodie up there, but all he saw instead were Lisa Harper and Rita Scimeca. He thought about Scimeca's face, the hurt in her eyes. Her rebuilt life out there in Oregon, the flowers, the piano, the buttoned-up defensive domesticity. He closed his eyes and then opened them and stared hard at the white paint above him. He thought about Harper's body, the way she moved, the guileless smile, her frank engaging stare. Rolled onto his elbow and picked up the phone. Dialled Harper's cellphone number.

HARPER DIDN'T KNOCK, just used her key and walked right in. She was in shirtsleeves, rolled up to the elbows.

'What's this all about?'

'I want to ask you a question,' he said. 'What would have happened if we'd already known about the paint delivery and we'd asked Alison Lamarr about it? What would she have said?'

'The same as the UPS guy presumably.'

'No,' Reacher said. 'She would have lied to us.'

'She would? Why?'

'Because they're all lying to us, Harper. We've spoken to seven women, and they all lied to us. Vague stories about room-mates and mistakes? All bullshit. If we'd got to Alison before, she'd have given us the same kind of a story.'

'How do you know?'

'Because Rita Scimeca was lying to us. That's for damn sure. I just figured that out. She didn't have any room-mate. It just doesn't fit. You saw how she lives. Everything was so neat and clean and polished. Obsessive. Living like that, she couldn't stand anybody else in her house. And she didn't need a room-mate for money. You saw her car, some big new sedan. And that piano. You know how much a grand piano costs? More than the car, probably.'

'So what are you saying?'

'I'm saying she was expecting the delivery, just like Alison was. Just like they *all* were. The cartons came, they all said *Oh good*, just like Alison did.'

'It's not possible. Why would they?'

'Because the guy has got some kind of a hold over them,' Reacher said. 'He forced Alison to give him their own list of names, he forced Lorraine Stanley to steal the paint, he forced her to send it out at the right time, he forced each one of them to accept the delivery, he forced each one of them to destroy the delivery notes immediately.'

Harper stared at him. 'But how? How would he *do* all that?'

'I don't know,' Reacher said.

'Blackmail?' she said. 'Threats? Fear?'

'I don't know. They weren't an especially fearful bunch, were they?'

'So what do you want me to do?' Harper asked.

'Just keep on thinking, I guess. Blake won't listen to me any more. I've exhausted my credibility with him.'

She sat down on the bed next to him. He was looking at her, something in his eyes.

'What?' she said.

'Is the camera on?'

She shook her head. 'They gave up on that. Why?'

'Because I want to kiss you again.'

'Why should I want to kiss *you* again?'

'Because you liked it before, too.'

She blushed. 'Just a kiss?'

He nodded.

'Well, OK, I guess,' she said.

She turned to him and he took her in his arms and kissed her. She moved her head like she had before. Pressed harder and put her tongue into his mouth. He moved his hand down to her waist. She kissed harder. Her tongue was urgent. Then she put her hand on his chest and pushed herself away. 'We should stop now,' she said.

'I guess.'

She stood up, tossed her hair behind her shoulders.

'I'm out of here,' she said. 'I'll see you tomorrow.'

When she had gone he lay back on the bed. Didn't sleep. Just thought about obedience and acquiescence, means, motives and opportunities. And truth and lies.

SHE CAME BACK at eight in the morning, showered and glowing and wearing a different suit and tie. She looked full of energy. He was tired and crumpled, but he was standing inside the door with his coat buttoned, waiting for her, his heart hammering with urgency.

'Let's go,' he said. 'Right now.'

Blake was in his office, at his desk, same as he had been before.

'Today you work the files again, Reacher,' Blake said.

'No, I need to get to Portland. Will you lend me the plane?'

'The plane?' Blake repeated. 'Are you crazy? Not in a million years.'

'OK,' Reacher said. He moved to the door. Took a last look at the office and stepped into the corridor. Harper crowded past him. 'Why Portland?' she asked.

He looked at her. 'Truth, and lies.'

'What does that mean?'

'Come with me and find out.'

Reveille had been 0600 the whole of Rita Scimeca's service career, and she stuck to the habit in her new civilian life. She slept six hours out of twenty-four, midnight until six in the morning, a quarter of her life. Then she got up to face the other three-quarters.

Today, she was scheduled to work on Bach. She was trying to perfect the *Three-part Inventions*. She loved the way they moved forward, on and on, inescapably logical, until they ended up back where they started. But they were very difficult pieces to play.

The fifth was one of the hardest in the canon, but it was Rita Scimeca's favourite. The tone had to be whimsical, but it had to sound utterly serious, too, for the effect to develop properly. It had to sound polished, but insane. Secretly, she was sure Bach was crazy.

She played the piece all the way through twice, and was reasonably pleased with what she heard. She decided to play for three hours, then stop and have some lunch.

YOU TAKE UP your position early. Early enough to be settled before the eight o'clock changeover. You watch it happen. It's the same deal as yesterday. The Bureau guy, still awake, but no longer very attentive. The arrival of the local cop. The flank-to-flank pleasantries. The Buick starts up, rolls away down the hill; the local cop car crawls forward and settles into its space. The engine dies, and the guy's head turns. He sinks low in his seat, and his last shift as a cop begins. After today, they won't trust him to direct traffic around the Arctic Circle.

'SO HOW DO WE get there?' Harper asked as she climbed into her own little yellow two-seater. Reacher realised he had never seen it before. He folded himself into the passenger seat, and she dumped her bag in his lap. Shoulder room was tight.

'We'll have to go commercial,' he said. 'Head for National, I guess. You got credit cards?'

She was shaking her head. 'They're all maxed out,' she said. 'They'll get refused. What about you?'

'I'm always broke,' he said, thinking fast.

He opened her bag and took out her phone. Closed his eyes and tried to recall sitting in Jodie's kitchen, dialling the number. Tried to remember the precious sequence of digits. He entered them slowly. Heard the ring tone for a long moment. Then the call was answered.

'Colonel John Trent,' a deep voice said.

'Trent, this is Reacher. You still love me?'

'What?'

'I need a ride, two people, Andrews to Portland, Oregon.'

'Like when?'

'Like right now, immediately.'

'You're kidding, right?'

'No, we're on our way there. We're a half-hour out.'

Silence for a second.

'Andrews to Portland? OK,' Trent said. Then the line went dead.

'So is he doing it?' Harper asked.

Reacher nodded. 'He owes me,' he said. 'So let's go.'

She let in the clutch, drove out of the Bureau lot, and blasted along the approach road. Rush-hour traffic was heavy on the I-95. Harper flicked the tiny car right and put it on the shoulder. Hauled past the stalled traffic on the inside.

'So what is the key?' she asked, eventually.

'Means, motive, opportunity. The holy trinity of law enforcement. We know everything we need to know. Some of it we've known for days. But we screwed up everywhere, Harper. Big mistakes and wrong assumptions.'

'What mistakes?' she said. 'What assumptions?'

'Very, very ironic ones, in the circumstances,' he said. 'But it's not entirely our fault. I think we swallowed a few big lies, too. So big and so obvious, nobody saw them for what they were.'

WHEN THEY REACHED Andrews, a captain showed them to a waiting room on the second floor. It was a utilitarian space, lit by fluorescent tubes, linoleum on the floor, plastic chairs round low tables.

'Talk to me,' Harper said when the guy had gone. 'What is it?'

'Start with the motive,' he said. 'Who's got a motive?'

'I don't know.'

'Go back to Amy Callan. Suppose she'd been the only victim? Who would you be looking at for a motive?'

'Her husband. Dead wife, you always look at the husband,' she said. 'Because motives are often personal.'

Reacher nodded. 'OK, so suppose it *is* Amy Callan's husband. How does he avoid suspicion?'

'He can't avoid it.'

'Yes, he can. He can avoid it by finding a bunch of women with some kind of a similarity with his wife and killing them, too. Doing it in some bizarre fashion that he knows is going to get everybody rushing off on some flight of fancy. In other words he can take the spotlight off himself by burying the personal connection in a crowd. Like where's the best place to hide a grain of sand?'

'On the beach.'

'Right,' he said.

'So you're saying all but one are decoys. Sand on the beach.'

'Camouflage,' he said. 'Background noise.'

'So which one? Which one is the real target?'

Reacher said nothing.

The captain came back and led them out to a waiting staff car.

'Have a pleasant flight,' he said.

The car drove them a mile round the perimeter track and then cut across towards a brand-new Boeing standing alone on the apron. The captain had explained that it was a transport plane, undergoing a flight test that was being rerouted to Portland. There was a wheeled ladder at the forward cabin door. Flight crew in uniform clustered at the top, with clipboards thick with paper. 'Welcome aboard,' the co-pilot said. 'You should be able to find an empty seat.'

There were 260 of them. It was a regular passenger plane with the fripperies stripped out. No televisions, no in-flight magazines, no stewardess call buttons.

'So which one is the real target?' Harper asked again.

'You can figure it out,' Reacher said.

The plane turned. Headed for the runway. A minute later it was in the air, smooth, quiet and powerful. Then it climbed hard over the sprawl of DC, settling to a westward cruise.

IT'S TWO O'CLOCK and the local cop is still right there in front of her house. Time for the call. You open the stolen mobile. Dial her number. You hear the connection go through. You hear the ring tone. You crouch low in the lee of your rock, ready to speak.

She picks up. 'Hello?' she says.

'Hello, Rita,' you say.

She hears your voice. You feel her relax. 'Yes?' she says.

You tell her what you want her to do.

'NOT THE FIRST ONE,' Harper said. 'That would be random. Leading us away from the scent. And the second establishes the pattern.'

'I agree,' Reacher said. 'Callan and Cooke were background noise.'

'But he wouldn't leave it too late,' Harper said. 'He's got a target, he'd want to hit it before anything unravelled, right?'

'I agree,' Reacher said again.

'So it's the third or the fourth.'

Reacher nodded. Said nothing.

'But which one?' Harper asked. 'What's the key?'

'Everything,' Reacher said. 'Same as it always was. The clues. The geography, the paint, the lack of violence.'

'Lorraine Stanley stole the paint,' Harper said. 'The lack of violence proves the guy is faking it. But what does the geography prove?'

'We talked about that,' Reacher said.

'It demonstrates scope.'

'And speed. And mobility,' he added. 'Don't forget mobility.'

'Why is a demonstration of mobility important?' Harper asked.

'That's one of the lies,' Reacher said. 'We just swallowed it whole.'

LUNCH WAS A COLD wrinkled apple and a square of Swiss cheese, which was about all Rita Scimeca's refrigerator had to offer.

Afterwards, as she washed the plate there was a ring on the bell. It was the cop wanting to use the bathroom again. She waited in the hallway until he came back out of the bathroom. Watched him all the way back to the car. Locked the door again and stepped into the parlour. Sat at the piano.

She played for another hour and a half. Her touch improved until it was better than it had ever been. Her mind locked onto the notes and she brought the speed to a point just a little slower than the tempo was marked. But it sounded magnificent. She was pleased.

She pushed back on the stool, knitted her fingers and flexed them above her head. Then she went to the coat closet and took out her jacket. She unlocked the door to the basement stairs and went down to the garage. Used the keychain remote to open her car and switched on the garage door opener. Slid into the car and started the engine while the door rumbled upwards.

She backed onto the driveway and hit the button to close the door again. Twisted in her seat and saw the police cruiser parked in her way. She got out and walked towards it.

'I'm going to the store,' she said through the open window. 'I'll be about an hour.'

'OK, but I wait here,' he said. 'We're watching the house, not you personally. Domicile-based crimes, that's what we do.'

'Fine. Nobody's going to grab me at the store.'

YOU SEE THE GARAGE DOOR open, you see the car come out, you see the door close again. You see her stop on her driveway, and you see her get out. You watch the conversation with the local cop. You see her reverse out onto the roadway and take off down the hill. You smile to yourself and stand up. You go to work.

SHE MADE THE LEFT at the bottom of her hill, and then the right onto the road towards the city of Portland. After two miles she slowed for the left into the shopping centre. Waited for an oncoming truck to labour past and swooped into the lot. Parked up alone behind the stores. Got out and walked towards the supermarket.

Inside she took a cart and walked every aisle, selecting things she figured she was out of. She ended up with little enough in the cart to get her into the express line at the check-out.

The girl put it all into one paper sack and she paid cash for it and walked out with the sack cradled in her arms. Turned right on the narrow sidewalk and headed for the hardware store.

She juggled the grocery sack into one arm and pulled the door. A bell rang. It was an old-fashioned place and there was an old guy in a brown coat at the register. He nodded a greeting. She walked past the tools and the nails and found the paint section. She put her groceries on the floor and took a colour chart from a rack.

'Help you, miss?' the old guy said.

'I want a dark green colour,' she said. 'Does this stuff mix with water?'

He nodded. 'They call it latex but that just means water-based.'

'I think I'll take the olive. I want it to look kind of military.'

'OK,' the old guy said. 'How much?'

'One can,' she said. 'A gallon.'

He carried it back to the register for her and rang up the sale. She paid cash and he put it in a bag with a free wooden stirring stick.

'Thank you.' She carried the grocery sack in one hand and the hardware bag in the other. Walked along the row of stores then looped round behind the last one to the overspill parking lot out back. Hurried to her car. Dumped her bags on the back seat and climbed in.

THE COP SAW the approaching figure when it was still about a 100 yards away down the hill. The guy was tall and he had thick grey hair neatly trimmed and brushed. He was dressed in army uniform. Eagles on the shoulderboards, eagles through the lapels: a colonel. A clerical collar where the shirt and tie should be. A military chaplain, approaching fast up the sidewalk.

The guy stopped a yard from the cop's right headlight. Just stood on the sidewalk, looking up at Scimeca's house. The cop buzzed the passenger window down. He called, 'Excuse me? Can I help you?'

The colonel looked around and put one hand on the car roof and the other on the door. Ducked his head in through the open window. 'I'm here to visit with the lady of the house,' he said.

'She's not home,' the cop said. 'And we've got a situation here.'

'A situation?'

'She's under guard. Can't tell you why. But I'm going to have to ask you to step inside the car and show me some ID.'

The colonel hesitated for a second, like he was confused. Then he opened the passenger door, and folded himself into the seat. He put his hand inside his jacket and came out with a wallet. Flipped it open and pulled out a worn military ID. The cop checked it over, nodded. 'OK, Colonel,' he said. 'You can wait in here with me, if you like.'

RITA SCIMECA MADE the left off the main road and the right into her street. The cop was parked across her drive again. Somebody was in the front seat next to him. She stopped on the crown of the road, ready to turn in, hoping he'd take the hint and move, but he just opened his door and got out, like he needed to talk to her. She opened her window and he walked across to her.

'There's a guy here to see you. An army padre. His ID is OK.'

'Get rid of him,' she said.

The cop was startled. 'He's all the way from DC.'

'I don't care. I don't want to see him.'

The cop said nothing. Just glanced back over his shoulder. The colonel was getting out of the car. Easing up to his full height on the sidewalk. Walking over. Scimeca slid out of her car and stood up.

'Rita Scimeca?' the padre asked, when he was close enough.

'What do you want?'

'I'm here to see if you're OK,' he said. 'After your problems.'

'*My problems?*'

'After the assault.'

'And if I'm not OK?'

'Then maybe I can help you.'

His voice was warm and low and rich. A church voice.

'The army send you?' she asked. 'Is this official?'

'I'm afraid not,' he said. 'I've argued it with them many times.'

'If they offer counselling, they're admitting liability.'

'That's their view,' the colonel said. 'Regrettably. So this is a private mission, against orders. But it's a matter of conscience, isn't it?'

Scimeca glanced away, pulled her jacket tight round her.

'Why me in particular?' she asked. 'There were a lot of us.'

'You're my fifth,' he said. 'I started with the ones who are obviously living alone, who might need my help most. I've been all over the place. Some fruitful trips, some wasted trips. I try not to force myself on people. But I feel I have to try.'

'Well, you've wasted another trip, I'm afraid,' she said. 'I don't want your help.'

'Are you sure? Please think about it. I came a long way.'

She didn't answer. Just glanced at the cop, impatiently. He shuffled his feet, calling the colonel's attention his way. 'I'm going to have to ask you to leave now, sir,' he said. 'We've got a situation here.'

The colonel was still for a moment. 'The offer is always open,' he said eventually. 'I could come back, any time.'

He turned abruptly and walked back down the hill, moving fast. Scimeca watched him for a while and slid back into her car.

The cop walked back to his cruiser. Reversed it up the hill with his door hanging open. She turned into her driveway. Pushed the button on the remote and the garage door rumbled upwards. She drove inside and pushed the button again. Saw the cop moving back into position before the door came down and left her in darkness.

She opened her door and the dome light clicked on. She pulled the little lever and popped the trunk. Got out of the car, took her bags from the back seat and carried them upstairs. Placed them side by side on the kitchen countertop and sat down on a stool to wait.

IT'S A LOW-SLUNG CAR, so although the trunk is long enough and wide enough, it's not very tall. So you're lying on your side, cramped. Getting in was no problem. She left the car unlocked, just like you told her to. You watched her walk away to the store, and then you just stepped over and opened the driver's door and found the lever and popped the trunk. Closed the door again and walked round and lifted the lid. Nobody was watching. You rolled inside and pulled the lid closed on top of you. It was easy.

It's a long wait in there. But you feel her get back in and you follow the turns in your mind so you know when she arrives back at her place. You hear the cop talking. There's a problem. Then you hear some idiot padre, pleading. What the hell is going on? What if she asks him in? But she gets rid of him. You hear the ice in her voice. You smile in the dark when you feel the car move off again. Then the engine shuts down and it goes very quiet. She remembers to pop the trunk. You knew she would, because you told her not to forget. Then you hear her footsteps moving away and you hear the basement door open and close. You ease the trunk lid upwards and you climb out. You pull your gloves on tight.

'HELLO, RITA,' the visitor said.

Rita looked up and saw the visitor she was expecting. 'Hello.'

The visitor gazed at her from the doorway, eyes enquiring. 'Did you buy the paint?'

'Yes, I did,' she said.

'So, are you ready?'

'I don't know,' she said.

The visitor smiled. 'I think you're ready. What do you think?'

She nodded, slowly. 'I'm ready,' she said.

The visitor was silent for a long moment, just watching carefully. 'You did good with the padre.'

'He wanted to help me.'

'Nobody can help you.'

'I guess not,' Scimeca said.

The visitor stepped into her kitchen. 'Show me the paint.'

Scimeca took the can out of the bag and held it up by the wire handle. 'It's olive green,' she said. 'Closest they had.'

The visitor nodded. 'Good. You did very well. Now you need to concentrate, because I'm going to tell you what I want you to do.'

'OK,' she said.

'First thing, you have to smile for me. That's very important. It means a lot to me.'

Scimeca came up with a shy, weak smile. She held it, desperately.

'That's nice,' the visitor said. 'Got to be happy in our work, right? We need something to open the can. Have you got a screwdriver?'

'Of course,' Scimeca said. 'I've got eight or nine.'

'Go get a big one for me, would you? And don't forget the smile.'

THE VISITOR

AFTER LANDING at Portland International, Reacher and Harper stood waiting for a taxi. Head of the line was a battered Caprice with a chequerboard stripe down the side. The driver wasn't local. He needed to check his map before he headed east towards the slopes of Mount Hood. As the gradient steepened, the old car dug deep and rumbled upwards.

'Who is it?' Harper asked.

'The key is in Poulton's report from Spokane.'

'It is?'

Reacher nodded. 'Big and obvious. But it took me some time to spot it.'

'The UPS thing? We went through all of that.'

He shook his head. 'No, before that. The Hertz rental car.'

SCIMECA CAME BACK with a large screwdriver in her hand. 'I think this is the best one,' she said. 'For the purpose.'

The visitor looked at it. 'I'm sure it's fine. So where's your bathroom?'

'Upstairs.'

'Bring the paint,' the visitor said. 'And the screwdriver.'

Scimeca picked up the can.

'Do we need the stirring stick, too?' she called.

The visitor hesitated. *New procedure, needs a new technique.*

'Yes, bring the stirring stick.'

Scimeca picked up the items and led the way up the stairs. Across her bedroom and into the bathroom. 'This is it,' she said.

The visitor pulled out a black plastic garbage sack from her coat pocket. 'OK. Put the stuff down on the floor. I need you to put your clothes in here.'

Scimeca looked confused. 'What clothes?'

'The clothes you're wearing,' the visitor said.

Scimeca nodded, vaguely. 'OK.'

'I'm not happy with the smile, Rita,' the visitor said. 'Make it a real big one. You want to make me happy, right? So put your clothes in the bag. And smile.'

Scimeca took off her sweater. It was a heavy knit item with a tight neck. She hauled the hem up and stretched it over her head. Leaned over and dropped it in the bag. She unbuttoned the jeans and pushed them down her legs. Kicked off her shoes and stepped out of the jeans. Rolled the shoes and the jeans together and put them in the bag. Pulled off her socks and underwear and tossed them in the bag. She stood there, naked, waiting.

'Run the bath,' the visitor said.

Scimeca bent down and put the stopper in the drain. Then she opened the faucets, three-quarters hot and one-quarter cold.

'Open the paint,' the visitor said, 'then pour it in the tub. Be careful. I don't want any mess.'

Scimeca levered off the lid then picked up the can, clamped it between her palms and carried it to the tub. Twisted from the waist and tipped it over. The paint was thick. It smelt of ammonia. The swirl from the faucets caught it. It eddied into a spiral pattern and sank like a weight. She held the can upside-down until the thick stream thinned, and then stopped.

'Now get the stirring stick. Mix it up.'

Scimeca picked up the stick and knelt at the edge of the tub. Worked the stick into the thick sunken mass and stirred. The colour changed as the paint dissolved. It went from dark olive to the colour of grass growing in a damp grove.

'OK, that'll do. Put the stick and the screwdriver in the can.'

Scimeca pulled the stick out of the water and shook it carefully. Stood it upright in the empty can. Stood the screwdriver next to it.

'Put the lid back on.'

She picked the lid up by its edge and laid it across the top of the can. It canted up at a shallow angle, because the stirring stick was too tall to let it go all the way down.

'You can turn the faucets off now.'

She turned back to the tub and shut off the water, which was up to within six inches of the rim.

'Now I want you to put the can down in the basement,' the visitor said. 'Right where the carton was. Can you do that?'

Scimeca nodded. 'Yes, I can do that,' she said.

She raised the metal hoop. Eased it up alongside the unsteady lid. Carried the can out in front of her, down the stairs and through the hallway, down to the garage and through to the basement.

When she returned to the bathroom, slightly out of breath, the visitor said, 'Now you have to get into the tub.'

Scimeca stepped to the side of the tub and raised her foot. Pointed her toe and put it in the water, then brought the other in after it. Stood there in the tub with the paint up to her calves.

'Now sit down. Carefully.'

She put her hands on the rim and lowered herself down.

'Arms in.'

She let go of the rim and put her hands down beside her thighs.

'Good,' the visitor said. 'Now slide down, slowly and carefully.'

She shuffled forward in the water and lay back, felt the warmth moving up her body. She felt it lap over her shoulders.

'Head back.'

She tilted her head towards the ceiling. She felt her hair floating.

'Have you ever eaten oysters?' the visitor asked.

She nodded. 'Once or twice,' she said.

'You remember how it feels? They're in your mouth, and you just suddenly swallow them whole? Just gulp them down?'

She nodded again. 'I liked them,' she said.

'Pretend your tongue is an oyster,' the visitor said.

She glanced sideways, puzzled. 'I don't understand.'

'I want you to swallow your tongue. I want you to just gulp it down, real sudden, like it was an oyster.'

'I don't know if I can do that.'

'Push it back with your finger. It worked for the others.'

'OK.' She raised her hand. Opened her mouth.

'Put your finger right under your tongue,' the visitor said. 'And push back hard.'

She opened her mouth wider and pushed back hard.

'Now swallow.'

She swallowed. Then her eyes jammed open in panic.

Chapter 9

The cab pulled up nose to nose with the police cruiser. Reacher was the first one out, partly because he was tense, and partly because he needed Harper to pay the driver.

'Everything OK?' he asked the cop.

'Who are you?' the cop said.

'FBI,' Reacher said. 'Is everything OK here?'

'Can I see a badge?'

'Harper, show this guy your badge,' Reacher called.

The taxi backed off and pulled a wide kerb-to-kerb turn in the road. Harper reached into her bag and came out with her badge, gold on gold, the eagle on top with its head cocked to the left. The cop glanced across at it and relaxed.

'It's all quiet here,' the cop said, through his window.

'She in there?' Reacher asked him.

The cop pointed at the garage door.

'Just got back from the store,' he said.

'She went out?'

'I can't stop her from going out,' the cop said.

'You check her car?'

'Just her and two shopping bags. There was a padre came calling for her. From the army, some counselling thing. She sent him away.'

Reacher nodded. 'She would. She's not religious.' He turned to Harper. 'OK,' he said. 'We're going inside.'

They walked up the path, up the steps to the door. Harper pressed the bell. Waited ten seconds and pressed again. Noise, echoes, silence.

'Where is she?' she said.

He looked at the big heavy lock on the door. Probably new. The door frame was probably Oregon pine. The best construction timber in history. 'Shit,' he said. He stepped back to the edge of the porch. Sprang forward and smashed the sole of his foot against the lock. Felt the timbers yield.

'What the hell are you doing?' Harper said.

He hit the door again, once, twice, three times. The frame splintered and part of it followed the door into the hallway.

'Upstairs,' he gasped.

He raced up, with Harper at his back. He ducked into a bedroom. A made bed, dimpled pillows, a telephone and a water glass on the nightstand. A connecting door, ajar. He stepped across the room and shoved it open. He saw a bathroom.

A tub full of hideous green water.

Scimeca in the water.

And Julia Lamarr.

Julia Lamarr, turning and rising and twisting off her perch on the rim of the tub, whirling round to face him. She was wearing a sweater and trousers and black leather gloves. Her face was white with hate and fear. He seized her by the front of the sweater and spun her round and hit her once in the head, a savage blow. It caught her solidly on the side of the jaw and her head snapped back. She went down like she was hit by a truck. He turned back to the tub. Scimeca was arched up out of the slime, naked, rigid, eyes bulging, head back, mouth open in agony.

Not moving. *Not breathing.*

He put a hand under her neck and held her head up, then straightened the fingers on his other hand and stabbed them into her mouth. He scrabbled in her throat and hooked a finger round her tongue and eased it back up out of her throat. He bent down to blow air into her lungs but as his face got near hers he felt a convulsive exhalation from her and a desperate cough and then her chest started heaving. Giant ragged breaths sucked in and out. He cradled her head. She was wheezing. Tortured sounds in her throat.

'Set the shower running,' Reacher shouted.

Harper ran to the stall and turned on the water. He lifted Scimeca under the shoulders and knees. Stood up and stepped back and held her in the middle of the bathroom, dripping green slime everywhere.

'Got to get this stuff off her,' he said, helplessly.

'I'll take her,' Harper said, gently.

She caught her under the arms and backed into the shower. Jammed herself into a corner of the stall and held the limp body upright like a drunk. The shower turned the paint light green, and then reddened skin showed through as it rinsed away. Two minutes, three, four.

Harper was soaked to the skin and her clothes were smeared with green. She was tiring. 'Get towels,' she gasped. 'Find a bathrobe.'

They were on a row of hooks, directly above where Lamarr was lying inert. Reacher took two towels and as Harper staggered forward out of the stall, he held one in front of him and caught Scimeca through the thickness of the towel. He wrapped her in it, carried her out of the bathroom, into the bedroom. Laid her down gently on the bed. Leaned over her and wiped the wet hair off her face. She was still wheezing hard. Her eyes were open, but they were blank.

He caught her wrist and felt for the pulse. It was there, strong and fast. 'She's OK,' he said. 'Pulse is good.'

'We should get her to the hospital,' Harper called. 'She'll need sedation. This will have blown her mind.'

'She'll be better here,' Reacher said. 'She'll wake up, and she won't remember a thing.'

Harper stared at him. 'Are you kidding?'

He looked up at her. 'She was hypnotised.'

He nodded towards the bathroom. 'That's how she did it all,' he said. 'Everything, every damn step of the way. She was the Bureau's biggest expert.'

'When did you know?' Harper asked.

'For sure?' he said. 'Last night.'

'But how?' she said.

Reacher took the bathrobe from her and laid it over Scimeca's passive form. Bent his head and listened to her breathing. It was still strong, and it was slowing. She looked like a person in a deep sleep.

'I just went round and round it all,' he said. 'Right from the beginning, for days and days. Thinking, thinking, thinking, driving myself crazy. I knew they were wrong about the motive, I knew it all along.

But I couldn't understand it. They're smart people, right? But they were *so wrong*. I was asking myself why? *Why?*'

'And you knew Lamarr was driving the motive,' Harper said. 'Because it was her case, really. So you suspected her.'

He nodded. 'Exactly. Soon as Alison died, I had to think about Lamarr doing it, because there was a close connection, and like you said, close family connections are always significant. So then I asked myself what if she did them all? What if she's camouflaging a personal motive behind the randomness of the first three? But I couldn't see how. Or why. There were no family issues. No unfairness about the inheritance, for instance. No jealousy there. And she couldn't fly, so how could it be her?'

'But?'

'But then the dam broke. Something Alison said. I remembered it much later. She said her father was dying but *sisters take care of each other, right?* I thought she was talking about emotional support or something. But then I thought what if she meant it another way? Like she'd take care of Julia financially? Like she knew the inheritance was all coming her way and Julia was getting nothing and was all uptight about it? But Julia had told me everything was equal, and she was already rich, anyway, because the old man was generous and fair. So I suddenly asked myself: what if she's lying about that? What if the old guy *wasn't* generous and fair? What if she's *not* rich? She certainly doesn't look rich.'

'And then I thought, what if *everything* is a lie? What if she's lying about not flying? What if that's a big lie too, so big and obvious nobody thinks twice about it? I even asked you how she gets away with it. You said everybody just works around it, like a law of nature. Well, we all did. We just worked around it. Like she intended.'

'Well, she fooled me,' Harper said. 'That's for sure.'

Reacher stroked Scimeca's hair. 'She fooled everybody. That's why she did the far corners first. To make everybody think about the geography, the range, the reach, the distance. To move herself right outside the picture.'

Harper was quiet for a second. 'But she was so upset. She *cried*, remember? In front of us all?'

Reacher shook his head. 'She wasn't upset. She was frightened. It was her time of maximum danger. Remember how she refused to take her rest period. Because she knew she needed to be around, to control any fallout from the post-mortem. And then I started questioning the motive, and she got tense as hell because I might be heading in the right direction. But then I said it was weapons theft, and she cried, but not because she was upset. She cried with *relief*.'

Harper nodded. 'She backed you up on the weapons theft thing.'

'Exactly,' Reacher said. 'She jumped on the bandwagon, because she saw the bandwagon was heading in the wrong direction. She was thinking hard, improvising like crazy, but she wasn't thinking hard *enough*, because that bandwagon was always bullshit. There was a flaw in it, a mile wide.'

'What flaw?'

'It was an impossible coincidence that the eleven witnesses should all be living alone. I told you it was partly an experiment. I wanted to see who *wouldn't* support it. Only Poulton wouldn't. Blake was out of it, upset because Lamarr was upset. But Lamarr backed it all the way. And then she went home, with everybody's sympathy. But she didn't go home. She came straight here and went to work.'

Harper went pale. 'She actually confessed. Right then and there, before she left. Remember that? She said *I killed my sister*. Because of wasting time, she said. But it was true. It was a sick joke.'

'She's sick as hell. She killed four women for her stepfather's money. And she enjoyed it. Sick as hell but very smart, too. Can you imagine the planning? She must have started two years ago. Her stepfather fell ill about the same time her sister came out of the army. She started putting it all together then, meticulously. She got the support-group list direct from her sister, picked out the ones who obviously lived alone, then she visited all eleven of them. Walked in everywhere she needed to because she was a woman with an FBI shield, just like you walked past that cop just now. Then she maybe gave them some story about how the Bureau was trying to finally nail the military. Said she was starting a big investigation. Sat them down in their own living rooms and asked if she could hypnotise them for background information on the issue. She even got Alison to come to Quantico for it. Remember that? Alison said she'd flown out to Quantico so Julia could hypnotise her for deep background. But there were no questions about deep background. Just instructions for the future. What to do, just like she told all of them what to do. She told them all to expect another visit from her, and in the meantime to deny everything if they were ever asked about anything.'

Harper closed her eyes. 'She was off duty the day Alison died. It was Sunday. Quantico was quiet. I never even thought about it. She knew nobody would think about it, on a Sunday. She knows nobody's there.'

'She's very smart,' Reacher said.

Harper opened her eyes. 'And I guess it explains the lack of evidence everywhere. She knows what we look for at the scene.'

'And she's a woman,' Reacher said. 'The investigators were looking for a man, because she told them to. Same with the rental cars. She knew if anybody checked they would come back with a woman's name, which would be ignored. Which is exactly what happened.'

'But what name?' Harper asked. 'She'd need ID for the rental.'

'For the airlines, too,' Reacher said. 'But I'm sure she's got a drawerful of ID. From women the Bureau has sent to prison. Innocent feminine names, meaning nothing.'

Harper looked rueful. 'I passed that message on, remember? From Hertz? *It was nothing*, I said, *just some woman on business.*'

Reacher nodded. 'She's very smart. I think she even dressed the same as the victims, while she was in their houses. Like she's in here now wearing an old sweater like Scimeca's. So any fibres she leaves behind will be discounted. She asked us what Alison was wearing, remember? Is she still all sporty and tanned and dressed like a cowboy? she asked. We said yes, she is, so no doubt she went in there wearing denim jeans and boots.'

'And she scratched her face because she hated her.'

Reacher shook his head. 'No, I'm afraid that was my fault,' he said. 'I kept on questioning the lack of violence, so she supplied some, the next time around. I should have kept my big mouth shut.'

Harper glanced at the bathroom door. Shuddered. Glanced away. 'How did you figure the hypnotism thing?'

'Like everything else,' Reacher said. 'I thought I knew who and why, but the *how* part looked impossible, so I just thought around it. It took me a long time. But eventually, it was the only possibility. It explained everything. The passivity, the obedience, the acquiescence. She just re-established the spell and told them what to do, step by step. They did everything themselves. Right down to swallowing their own tongues. The only thing she did herself was what I did, pull their tongues back up afterwards, so the pathologists wouldn't catch on.'

'But how did you know about the tongues?'

He was quiet for a beat. 'From kissing you,' he said.

'Kissing me?'

He smiled. 'You've got a great tongue, Harper. It set me thinking. Tongues were the only things that fitted Stavely's autopsy findings. But I figured there was no way to *make* somebody swallow their own tongue, until I remembered Lamarr was a hypnotist, and then the whole thing fell together.'

Harper shivered. 'Where would she have stopped?'

'Maybe one more. Six would have done it. Sand on the beach.'

Reacher turned towards Lamarr. 'Go wake her up,' he said. 'Make the arrest, start the questioning. You've got a big case ahead of you.'

Harper stepped out to the bathroom. The bedroom went quiet. No sound anywhere, just Scimeca's breathing. Then Harper came back in, white in the face. 'She won't talk to me,' she said.

'How do you know? You didn't ask her anything.'

'Because she's dead.'

Silence.

'You broke her neck.'

Then there were loud footsteps in the hallway below them, coming up the stairs, in the corridor outside.

The cop stepped into the room. 'What the hell's going on?' he said.

SEVEN HOURS LATER, Reacher was locked up in a holding pen inside the FBI's Portland Field Office. It was hot in the cell. His clothes dried within an hour, stiff as boards and stained olive with paint. Apart from that, nothing happened. He guessed it was taking time for people to assemble.

After midnight things started happening. He heard sounds in the building. Arrivals, urgent conversations. First person he saw was Nelson Blake. He must have flown in on the Learjet.

Blake walked past the bars and glanced into the cell, something in his face. *You really screwed up now*, he was saying.

Past one o'clock in the morning, Alan Deerfield arrived, from New York. He walked in, silent and morose, the same contemplative look he'd used all those nights ago. Then a local agent came in and unlocked the door. 'Time to talk,' he said.

He led Reacher out of the cell block and into a conference room. Deerfield and Blake were sitting on one side of a big table. There was a chair opposite. He walked round and sat down in it. Blake sat forward. 'I've got a dead agent,' he said. 'And I don't like that.'

Reacher looked at him. 'You've got four dead women,' he said. 'Could have been five.'

'We had the situation under control. Julia Lamarr was right there rescuing the fifth when you killed her.'

The room went silent again. Reacher nodded, slowly. 'That's your position?' he asked.

Deerfield looked up. 'It's a viable proposition. She makes some kind of breakthrough in her own time, she overcomes her fear of flying, she gets herself out here in the nick of time, she's about to start emergency medical procedures when you burst in and hit her. She's a hero, and you go to trial for the murder of a Federal agent.'

'The cop see her get in the house?'

Deerfield shrugged. 'We figure he fell asleep. You know what these country boys are like.'

'He saw a padre come calling. He was awake then.'

Deerfield shook his head. 'Army will say they never sent a padre.'

'How did she get in?'

'Knocked on the door, interrupted the guy. He bolted out past her, she didn't chase him because she wanted to check on Scimeca.'

'The cop see the guy running out?'

'Still asleep.'

'And she took the time to lock the door behind her, even though she was rushing upstairs.'

'Evidently.'

The room went quiet.

'Scimeca come round yet?' Reacher asked.

Deerfield nodded. 'We called the hospital. She's fine.'

Blake smiled. 'But we won't pursue her for a description of her attacker. That would be grossly insensitive, given her circumstances.'

'Where's Harper?' Reacher said.

'On suspension,' Blake said.

'For not following the party line?'

'She's unduly affected by a romantic illusion,' Blake said. 'She told us some fantastic bullshit story.'

'You see your problem, right?' Deerfield said. 'You hated Lamarr from the start. So you killed her for personal reasons and invented a story to cover yourself. But it's not a very good story, is it? You can't put Lamarr anywhere near any of the scenes.'

'Where's her car?' Reacher asked. 'She drove up to Scimeca's place from the airport, where's her car?'

'The perp stole it,' Blake said. 'She surprised him, he took off in her car.'

'You going to find a rental in her real name?'

Blake nodded. 'Probably. We can usually find what we need to.'

'You see your problem, right?' Deerfield said again.

Reacher nodded. 'Well, I guess this means I'm not going to get paid,' he muttered.

Deerfield made a face, like there was a bad smell in the room. 'This is not a joke, Reacher,' he said. 'Let's be real clear about that. You're in big trouble. You can say you had suspicions. But nobody will listen. And it won't matter anyway, because our counsel will say that even *if* you had mistaken but sincere suspicions, you should have gone straight for Scimeca in the tub and let Harper deal with

Lamarr behind you. It was two against one. It would have *saved* you time, right? If you were so concerned about your old buddy?'

'It might have saved me half a second.'

'Half a second could have been critical,' Deerfield said. 'Our counsel will make a big point out of it. He'll say spending precious time hitting somebody proves something, like personal animosity.'

Reacher looked down at the table.

'And you can't claim it was accidental,' Blake put in. 'You once told me you know all about how to break someone's skull; no way would it happen by accident. That guy in the alley, remember? Petrosian's boy? And what goes for skulls goes for necks, right? So it wasn't an accident. It was deliberate homicide.'

'OK,' Reacher said. 'What's the deal?'

'You're going to jail,' Deerfield said. 'There's no deal.'

'Bullshit, there's no deal,' Reacher said. 'There's always a deal.'

'Well, we could compromise,' Blake said. 'We could call Lamarr a suicide, tormented that she couldn't save her sister.'

'And you could keep your big mouth shut,' Deerfield said.

'Why should I?' Reacher said.

'Because you're a smart guy. Don't forget, there's absolutely nothing on Lamarr. You could come up with a little meaningless circumstantial stuff, but what's a jury going to do with that? A big man hates a small woman? He's a bum, she's a Federal agent? He breaks her neck, and then he blames her for it? Some fantastic story about hypnosis? Forget about it.'

'So face it, OK?' Blake said. 'You're *ours*, now.'

Reacher shook his head. 'No, thanks.'

'Then you go to jail.'

'One question, first,' Reacher said. 'Did I kill Lorraine Stanley?'

Blake shook his head. 'No, you didn't.'

'How do you know?'

'You know how we know. We had you tailed, all that week.'

'And you gave a copy of the surveillance report to my lawyer, right?'

'Right.'

Reacher smiled. 'So maybe you can lock me up for Lamarr, but you can't ever claim I'm also the guy who killed the women, because my lawyer has got your own report proving that I'm not.'

'So what?' Blake said. 'You're locked up anyway.'

'Think about the future,' Reacher said. 'You've told the world it's not me, and you're swearing blind it's not Lamarr, so you've got to be seen to keep on looking, right? Think about the negative headlines. ELITE FBI UNIT GETS NOWHERE, TENTH YEAR OF SEARCH. You'd just have to swallow them. And you'd have to keep the guards in place, you'd have to spend more and more budget, year after year, searching for the guy. Are you going to do that?'

Silence in the room.

'No, you're not going to do that. And not doing that is the same thing as admitting you know the truth. Lamarr is dead, the search has stopped, it wasn't me, therefore Lamarr was the killer.'

More silence. Reacher smiled. 'So now what?'

They recovered. 'We're the Bureau,' Deerfield said. 'We can make your life very difficult.'

'My life's already very difficult,' he said. 'Nothing you guys can do to make it any harder. But you can forget the threats, anyway. Because I'll keep your secret.'

'You will?'

Reacher nodded. 'I'll have to, won't I? Because if I don't, it'll all just come back on Rita Scimeca. She's the only living witness. She'll get pestered to death, prosecutors, police, newspapers, television. I don't want that to happen. So, your secret is safe with me.'

Blake stared at the tabletop. 'OK,' he said. 'I'll buy that.'

'But we'll be watching you,' Deerfield said. 'Always.'

'Well, don't let me catch you at it. Because you guys should never forget what happened to Petrosian. OK?'

IT FINISHED LIKE THAT, as a tie, as a wary stalemate. Reacher stood up and left the room. He found an elevator and made it to street level. Nobody came after him. He pushed open the main oak doors and stepped out into the chill of the night.

'Hey, Reacher,' Harper called.

She was behind him in the shadow of a pillar flanking the entrance. He turned and saw the gleam of her hair and a stripe of white where her shirt showed at the front of her jacket.

'Hey, yourself,' he said. 'You OK?'

She stepped across to him. 'I will be,' she said. 'I'm going to ask for a transfer. Maybe over here to Oregon. I like it.'

'Will they let you?'

She nodded. 'Sure they will. This is going to be the quietest thing that ever happened.'

'It never happened at all,' he said. 'That's how we left it, upstairs.'

'So you're OK with them?'

'As OK as I ever was.'

'I'd have stood up for you,' she said. 'Whatever it took.'

'I know you would. There should be more like you.'

'Take this,' she said.

She held out a slip of flimsy paper. It was a travel voucher, issued by the desk back at Quantico. 'It'll get you to New York.'

'What about you?' he asked.

'I'll say I lost it. They'll wire me another one.'

She kissed his cheek. 'Good luck,' she said and started walking.

'To you, too,' he called back.

HE SLEPT THROUGH four hours in the air and touched down at La Guardia at one o'clock in the afternoon.

He used the last of his cash on a bus to the subway and a subway ticket into Manhattan. Got out at Canal Street and walked south to Wall Street. He was in the lobby of Jodie's office building a few minutes after two o'clock. Her firm's reception area was deserted. He stepped through an open door and wandered down a corridor lined with law books. Left and right of him were empty offices.

He came to a set of double doors and heard the heavy buzz of conversation on the other side. He pulled the right-hand door and the noise burst out at him and he saw a conference room jammed full of people in dark suits, snowy white shirts and quiet ties. There was a long table under a heavy white cloth loaded with ranks of sparkling glasses and bottles of champagne. Two bartenders were pouring the foamy golden wine as fast as they could. People were drinking it and toasting with it and looking at Jodie.

She was rippling through the crowd like a magnet. She turned left and right, smiling, clinking glasses, and then moved on randomly into new acclaim. She saw Reacher at the door at the same moment he saw himself reflected in the glass over a Renoir drawing on the wall. He was unshaven and dressed in a crumpled, stiff khaki shirt covered in green stains. She was in a thousand-dollar dress. A hundred faces turned with hers and the room fell silent. She hesitated for a second, like she was making a decision. Then she fought her way through the crowd and flung her arms round his neck.

'The partnership party,' he said. 'Congratulations, babe. And I'm sorry I'm late.'

She drew him into the crowd and people closed around them. He shook hands with 100 lawyers the way he used to with generals from foreign armies. *Don't mess with me and I won't mess with you.* The top boy was an old red-and-grey-faced man of about sixty-five. His suit must have cost more than all the clothes Reacher had ever worn in his life. But the mood of the party meant there was no edge in the old guy's attitude.

'She's a big, big star,' he said. 'I'm gratified she accepted our offer.'

'Smartest lawyer I ever met,' Reacher said over the noise.

'Will you go with her?'

'Go with her where?'

'To London,' the old guy said. 'Didn't she explain? First tour of duty for a new partner is running the European operation for two years.'

Then she was back at his side, smiling, drawing him away. The crowd was settling into small groups, and conversation was turning to work matters. She led him to a space by the window.

'I called the FBI uptown,' she said. 'I was worried about you, and technically I'm still your lawyer. I spoke with Alan Deerfield's office, but they wouldn't tell me anything.'

'Nothing to tell. They're straight with me, I'm straight with them.'

'So you delivered, finally.' She paused. 'Is there going to be a trial?'

He shook his head. 'No trial.'

'Just a funeral, right?'

He shrugged. 'There are no relatives left. That was the point.'

She paused again, like there was something important coming up. 'I have to go to work in London,' she said. 'Two years.'

'I know,' he said. 'The old guy told me. When do you go?'

'End of the month.'

'You don't want me to come with you.'

'It'll be very busy. It's a small staff with a big workload.'

'And it's a civilised city.'

She nodded. 'Yes, it is. Would you *want* to come?'

'Two straight years?' he said. 'No. But maybe I could visit.'

She smiled, vaguely. 'That would be good.'

He said nothing.

'This is awful,' she said. 'Fifteen years I couldn't live without you, and now I find I can't live *with* you.'

'I know,' he said. 'Totally my fault.'

'We've got until the end of the month.'

He nodded. 'More than most people get. Can you take the afternoon off?'

'Sure I can. I'm a partner now. I can do what I want.'

'So let's go.'

They left their empty glasses on the window ledge and threaded their way through the knots of people. Everybody watched them, and then turned back to their quiet speculations.

LEE CHILD

From his earliest days at primary school, Lee Child has been drawn like a magnet to the world of entertainment. The head-mistress of the school, a woman with 'a huge show-business streak', staged a musical twice a year, he remembers, and he was desperate to star in one. 'Then I had the trauma of discovering that I couldn't sing or act, so I became a spear carrier—but a very enthusiastic one!'

At King Edward's Grammar School, Edgbaston, Child joined the drama group and in his spare time helped out behind the scenes at the Birmingham Rep. Later, as an undergraduate at Sheffield, he says he 'spent almost the whole time in the university theatre'.

Then it was time to earn a living and he struck lucky with his very first application to Granada TV in Manchester where he was taken on as a tech-nical assistant. The next eighteen years, as he moved steadily up the ranks to the job of transmission controller, were 'a lot of fun', and included work on major productions like *Brideshead Revisted*, *Prime Suspect* and *Cracker*.

In June 1995, as part of a major cost-cutting drive, Child was made redun-dant. He re-evaluated his skills and decided that what television had given him was an instinctive grasp of pacing, dialogue, suspense—all the things that make a good novel. So while many of his colleagues invested large sums in cinematic equipment in order to set themselves up as independent producers, Child spent just £4 on some stationery items and sat down at the kitchen table to write. Four months later, *Killing Floor* was not only complete but had been sold to a publisher. 'I took the call during a pub quiz night in Kirby Lonsdale,' he recalls. 'We had a big celebration!'

Tripwire and *The Visitor* followed and have established Lee Child firmly in the best-seller charts. With more Jack Reacher stories already in the pipeline he looks set to stay there.

Nicholas Sparks
THE RESCUE

Volunteer firefighter Taylor McAden is renowned for his bravery, his willingness to be first into the flames. But when it comes to love, he won't risk his heart for anyone.

Until the night a fierce storm hits North Carolina and Taylor takes part in a desperate rescue mission to save a vulnerable little boy...

Chapter 1

It would later be called one of the most violent storms in North Carolina's history. It had begun in an instant. One minute it was cloudy and dark, but not unusually so; in the next, lightning, gale-force winds and blinding rain exploded from the early-summer sky.

The system had blown in from the northwest and was crossing the state at nearly forty miles an hour. All at once, radio stations crackled with emergency warnings. People who could, took cover inside, but people on the highway, like Denise Holton, had no place to go. Rain fell so hard in places that traffic slowed to five miles an hour and Denise held the wheel with white knuckles, her face a mask of concentration. At times, it was impossible to see the road through the windshield. Her headlights seemed useless and she wanted to stop, but where would it be safe? People were swerving all over the road, as blind as she was.

And then, just as suddenly as it had started, the storm weakened and it was possible to see again. Cars began to speed up. Denise speeded up as well, staying with them. She glanced at the gas gauge and felt a knot form in her stomach. She knew she had to stop soon. She didn't have enough to make it home. Ten minutes passed before she heaved a sigh of relief. Gas, less than a mile away, according to the sign.

She stopped at the first open pump, filled the tank and then helped Kyle out of his car seat. He held her hand as they went inside to pay. Denise grabbed a can of Diet Coke, then searched the refrigerators along the back wall and found strawberry-flavoured milk for Kyle. It was getting late and he loved milk before bedtime. Hopefully, he'd sleep most of the way back.

By the time she went to pay she was fifth in line. In the aisles behind her, she heard a mother arguing with her young son. Denise glanced over her shoulder. The boy appeared to be about the same age as Kyle, four and a half or so. His mother seemed as stressed as Denise felt. The child stomped his foot. 'But I want the cupcakes!'

His mother stood her ground. 'You've had enough junk today.'

'But *you're* getting something.'

And so it went. Denise put her hand on Kyle's shoulder. He was sipping his milk through a straw, standing quietly. She finally reached the register and paid with cash. The argument between mother and son continued unabated as she received her change. She turned and smiled at the mother behind her, as if to say, *Kids are tough, sometimes, aren't they?*

In response, the woman rolled her eyes. 'You're lucky,' she said. 'This one here never shuts up.'

Denise nodded then left the store. Walking towards the car, she suddenly felt the urge to cry.

'No,' she whispered to herself, 'you're the lucky one.'

WHY HAD THIS HAPPENED? Why, of all the children, was Kyle the one?

Back in the car Denise hit the highway again, staying ahead of the storm. For the next twenty minutes, as the rain fell steadily, she made her way back to Edenton, North Carolina. To see the road better, she pulled the shoulder strap of the seat belt over her head so that she could lean forward over the steering wheel.

Despite the stress of the storm and the long day's driving, all she could think of was Kyle. After his birth she had taken one look at him and couldn't believe there was anything more beautiful in the world. That feeling hadn't changed, although she wasn't in any way a perfect mother. These days, she simply did the best she could, looking for joys in the little things. With Kyle, they were sometimes hard to find.

Kyle had been born three years to the day after her mother had died of a brain aneurysm. He was, she felt sure, a gift from God, sent to replace her family. Other than him, she was alone in the world. Her father had died when she was four, she had no siblings and her grandparents on both sides had passed away. Kyle immediately became the sole recipient of the love she had to offer. But fate is unpredictable. Though she showered Kyle with attention, it somehow hadn't been enough. Now, she led a life she hadn't anticipated, a life completely dedicated to her son.

She glanced in the rearview mirror. 'What are you thinking about, sweetie?'

Kyle was watching the rain as it blew against the windows, his head turned sideways. His blanket was in his lap. He hadn't said anything since he'd been in the car and he turned at the sound of her voice. She waited for his response. But there was nothing.

FOR THE PAST three months Denise Holton had lived in a house that had once been owned by her maternal grandparents. After their deaths, it had become her mother's, then eventually it had been passed down to her. It wasn't much—a small ramshackle building set in three acres, surrounded by oak and cypress trees. The two bedrooms and the living room weren't too bad, but the kitchen was in dire need of modern appliances and the porches were sagging. But because she could live there rent-free, it was exactly what she needed.

Staying in Atlanta, the place where she'd grown up, would have been impossible. Once Kyle was born, she'd used the money her mother had left her to stay at home with him. At the time, she had considered it a temporary leave of absence. Once he was a little older, she had planned to go back to teaching. The money would run out eventually and she'd have to earn a living. Now, four years later, she was still at home with Kyle and teaching was a vague and distant memory. Instead she worked the evening shift at a busy diner called Eights, on the outskirts of Edenton. The owner, Ray Toler, was a sixty-something black man who'd run the place for thirty years. He and his wife had raised six kids, all of whom went to college. Copies of their diplomas hung along the back wall and everyone who ate there knew about them. Ray made sure of that.

He was a man who understood how hard it was for single mothers. 'In the back of the building, there's a small room,' he'd said when he hired her. 'You can bring your son with you, as long as he doesn't get in the way.' Kyle went to bed in a cot in that small room as soon as she started on her shift; hours later, she loaded him in the car and took him home.

She worked four nights a week, five hours a shift, earning barely enough to get by. She'd sold her Honda for an old but reliable Datsun two years ago, pocketing the difference. That money, along with everything else from her mother, had long since been spent. She hadn't bought new clothes for herself since the Christmas before last; she had $238 in the bank.

None of those things mattered though. Only Kyle was important. But never once had he told her that he loved her.

NOW IN THE CAR, Denise remembered sitting with the doctor in his office earlier that day while he read the results from the report on Kyle.

'"The child is male, four years, four months old at the time of testing . . . Though IQ falls within the normal range, he is severely delayed in both receptive and expressive language . . . Probable Central Auditory Processing Disorder (CAPD), though cause can't be determined . . . Overall linguistic ability estimated to be that of a twenty-four-month-old."'

Barely that of a toddler, she couldn't help but think.

'There's a note here that says you've had him evaluated elsewhere.'

Denise nodded. 'I have.'

He shuffled through the papers. 'The reports aren't in his file.'

'I didn't give them to you.'

His eyebrows rose slightly. 'Why?'

'Kyle has been misdiagnosed again and again over the past two years—with everything from deafness and autism to Pervasive Development Disorder to Attention Deficit Disorder. Do you know how hard it is for a parent to hear those things, to believe, learn everything about them and finally accept them, before being told they were diagnosed in error?'

The doctor didn't answer. Denise met his eyes and held them before going on. 'I wanted Kyle's language skills tested independently so that I could know specifically where he needed help.'

He paused. 'Does he see a speech or behavioural specialist?'

'No. I work with him at home. He went to therapy three times a week for over a year, but it didn't seem to help. He continued to fall further behind, so I pulled him out last October. Now it's just me.'

'I see.' It was obvious he didn't agree with her decision.

Her eyes narrowed. 'You have to understand, even though this evaluation shows Kyle at the level of a two-year-old, that's an improvement from where he once was. Before he worked with me, he'd never shown any improvement at all.'

DRIVING ALONG the highway three hours later, Denise thought about Brett Cosgrove, Kyle's father. Tall and thin with dark eyes and ebony hair, she'd first seen him at a party. She was twenty-three at the time, single, in her second year of teaching. She asked her friend Susan who he was: she was told that Brett was in town for a few weeks, working for an investment bank. She glanced his way, he glanced back, and their eyes kept meeting for the next forty minutes before he finally came over and said hello.

They left the party a little after eleven, had drinks in the hotel bar, and ended up in bed. It was the last time she saw him. He went back to New York, back to his own life. And she went back to hers.

At the time, it didn't seem to mean much; a month later, while sitting on the bathroom floor one Tuesday morning, her arm round the commode, it meant a whole lot more. She went to the doctor who confirmed what she already knew. She was pregnant.

She called Brett on the phone. He listened, then sighed with what sounded like exasperation. He offered to pay for the abortion. As a Catholic, she said it wasn't going to happen. What did she want him to do? he asked her angrily. She said she didn't want anything, she just needed to know if he wanted to be involved in the child's life. No, he said. He was engaged to someone else.

She'd never spoken to him again.

IN TRUTH, IT WAS EASIER to defend Kyle to a doctor than it was to herself. Even though he'd improved, the linguistic ability of a two-year-old wasn't much to cheer about. Kyle would be five in October.

Still, she refused to give up on him, even though working with him was the hardest thing she'd ever done. She drilled him on the mechanics of speech for four hours a day, six days a week. Some days, he said everything she asked him to, some days he didn't. Some days he could comprehend new things easily, other days he seemed further behind than ever. Conversation was still far beyond his ability.

Yesterday, they'd spent the afternoon on the banks of the Chowan River. He enjoyed watching the boats and it provided a change from his normal routine. Usually, when they worked, he was strapped in a chair in the living room. That helped him focus.

They had been sitting in a clover patch, just the two of them. Kyle had been staring at the water.

Denise asked: 'Do you see any boats, sweetie?'

Kyle didn't answer. Instead, he lifted a tiny jet in the air, pretending to make it fly.

She touched his hand, making sure she had his attention.

'Kyle? Say, "I don't see any boats."'

'Airplane.' *Owpwane.*

'I know it's an airplane. Say, "I don't see any boats."'

He raised the toy a little higher, one eye focused on it. After a moment, he said, 'Jet airplane.' *Jet owpwane.*

Denise tried again. 'Say, "I don't see any boats."'

Nothing. She pulled a tiny piece of candy from her coat pocket.

Kyle saw it and reached for it. She kept it out of his grasp.

'Kyle? Say, "I don't see any boats."'

Like pulling teeth, the words finally came out.

He whispered: 'I don't see any boats.' *Duh see a-ee boat.*

Denise leaned in and kissed him, then gave him the candy.

'That's right, honey. Good talking! You're such a good talker!'

Kyle ate the candy, then focused on the toy again.

Denise jotted his words in her notebook. She glanced upwards, thinking of something he hadn't said that day.

'Kyle, say: "The sky is blue."'

After a beat: 'Owpwane.'

THEY WERE IN the car again, now twenty minutes from home. In the back of the car, she heard Kyle fidget in his seat and she glanced in the rearview mirror. The sounds soon quietened and she was careful not to make any noise until she was sure he was sleeping again.

Kyle. Yesterday was typical of her life with him. A step forward, two steps backwards, always a struggle. Would he ever catch up?

Once someone had asked her if she would have had Kyle if she had known what was in store. 'Of course,' she'd answered quickly, just as she was supposed to. And deep down, she knew she meant it. Despite his problems, Kyle was a sweet child, the sweetest she'd ever known, and when he smiled he was just so beautiful. She would smile back and for a split second, she'd think that everything was OK. She'd tell him she loved him and the smile would grow wider. Sometimes she felt as if she was the only one who noticed how wonderful he actually was.

Another mile and she'd be home. She was driving through the Nameless Swamp, a mysterious place as old as time. There were no other cars on the highway. Then, suddenly, rounding a curve at nearly sixty miles an hour, she saw it standing in the road, less than forty yards away: a doe, fully grown, frozen in the oncoming headlights.

Denise slammed on the brakes, heard the tyres screeching as they lost their grip on the rain-slicked surface, felt the momentum forcing the car forward. Still, the doe did not move. She was going to hit it. Denise screamed as she turned the wheel hard, missing the deer by a foot. It finally broke from its trance and darted away safely.

But the turn had been too much for the car. She felt the wheels leave the surface of the asphalt, felt the *whump* as the car slammed to earth again. It seemed as if everything was moving in slow motion, then at full speed, then slow motion again. She heard the twisting of metal and shattering of glass as she blasted into the tree and the front of the car exploded towards her. Her head shot forward, slamming into the steering wheel. Then there was nothing.

Chapter 2

'Hey, lady, are you all right?'

With the sound of the stranger's voice, the world came back slowly, as if she were swimming towards the surface in a cloudy pool of water. Denise couldn't feel any pain, but on her tongue was the salty-bitter taste of blood.

'Don't move . . . I'm gonna call an ambulance.'

The words barely registered. Everything was moving in and out of focus, including sound. Slowly, she turned her head towards the shaded figure in the corner of her vision. A man . . . dark hair . . . yellow raincoat.

The side window had shattered and she felt the rain blowing into the car. Shards of glass were in her lap, on her trousers . . . blood on the steering wheel in front of her . . . *so much blood*. Nothing made sense . . . She closed her eyes and felt pain for the first time. Forced herself to concentrate. She was in the car . . . dark outside . . .

'Oh God!' With a rush, it all came back. The deer . . . swerving out of control. She turned in her seat. Squinting through the blood in her eyes, she focused on the back seat—Kyle wasn't in the car. His safety seat was empty; the back door on his side of the car was open.

'Listen, don't try to talk. You're pretty banged up. My name is Taylor McAden and I'm with the fire department. I've got a radio in my car. I'm gonna get you help.'

She did her best to make her words as clear as possible. 'You have my son, don't you?'

He shook his head. 'No, I just got here. Your son?'

It was then that the first jolt of fear shot through her. 'My son was in the back! Have you seen him?'

Denise struggled to get out of the car, but the seatbelt across her lap held her fast. She unbuckled it, ignoring the pain in her wrist and elbow, and forced the door open. Her knees were swollen from smashing into the console and she almost lost her balance as she stood.

'I don't think you should be moving—'

Holding on to the car for support, she ignored the man as she moved round to where Kyle's door stood open. In disbelief, she bent inside to look for him. Her eyes scanned the floor, then back to the seat again, as if he might magically reappear.

'You haven't seen him? A little boy . . . brown hair?'

'No, I—'

'You've got to help me find him! He's only four!'

She whirled round, the rapid movement almost making her lose her balance. She grabbed hold of the car again. The corners of her vision faded to black as she struggled to keep the dizziness at bay.

The scream came out despite the spinning in her mind. 'KYLE!'

Pure terror now. Concentrating, closing one eye to help her focus. Oh God. She could feel her feet slipping in the mud-soaked grass as she staggered towards the road.

Finally understanding, the man ran after her. His eyes scanned the area around him. 'I don't see him . . .'

'KYLE!' She screamed as loud as she could.

The sound prompted Taylor into action. They took off in opposite directions, both shouting Kyle's name, both stopping to listen for sound. The rain, however, was deafening. After a couple of minutes, Taylor ran back to his car and made a call to the fire station. Then he took off at a lope, shouting Kyle's name over and over.

He found Kyle's blanket, in the swamp about fifty yards from the spot where Denise had crashed, snagged on the undergrowth that covered the area.

'Is this his?' Taylor asked.

Denise started to cry as soon as it was handed to her. After thirty minutes of searching, Kyle was still nowhere to be seen.

SITTING IN THE BACK of the ambulance with a blanket wrapped round her, Denise's mind was racing. She was cold and still dizzy, unable to focus for more than a few seconds at a time. The ambulance attendant suspected concussion and wanted to bring her in immediately. She steadfastly refused. She wouldn't leave until Kyle was found. He could wait ten minutes, he said, then he would have no choice.

More people arrived. A state trooper, more men from the fire department, a trucker who saw the trouble and stopped. They stood in a circle, in the middle of the cars and trucks which had their headlights on. The man who'd found her—Taylor?—had his back to her. She suspected he was filling them in on what he knew.

Taylor and the trooper stepped up into the ambulance and exchanged glances before Taylor gently put his hand on Denise's shoulder. 'I know this is hard, but we have to ask you a few questions before we get started. It won't take long.'

The trooper squatted before her. 'I'm Carl Huddle with the State Trooper's office. I know you're worried, and we are too. Most of us out here are parents, with little ones of our own. We all want to find

Kyle, but we need to know some general information.'

They went over the basics for the report: names and address, the reason she was driving, the accident itself. When it was all on paper, Sergeant Huddle looked up at her expectantly.

'Are you kin to J. B. Anderson?'

John Brian Anderson had been her maternal grandfather and she nodded.

Sergeant Huddle cleared his throat—like everyone in Edenton, he'd known the Andersons. He glanced at his flip pad again.

'Taylor said that Kyle is four years old?'

Denise nodded. 'He'll be five in October.'

'Could you give me a general description—something I could put out on the radio? In case someone finds him, and calls the police.'

Denise turned away, trying to order her thoughts. 'Um . . . three and a half feet tall, forty pounds or so. Brown hair, green eyes, just a normal little boy of his age.'

'Any distinguishing features? A birthmark, things like that?'

She focused as best she could. 'He's got two moles on his left cheek, one larger than the other,' she offered. 'No other birthmarks.'

'Do you remember what he was wearing?'

She closed her eyes, thinking. 'A red shirt with a big Mickey Mouse on the front. And jeans. White shoes.'

'How about a jacket?'

'No. I didn't bring one. It was warm when we started to drive.'

As the questioning went on, lightning, three flashes close together, exploded in the night sky.

'Do you still have family in the area? Parents? Siblings?'

'No. No siblings. My parents are deceased.'

'How about your husband?'

Denise shook her head. 'I've never been married.'

'Has Kyle ever wandered off before?'

Denise rubbed her temple, trying to keep the dizziness at bay.

'A couple of times. At the mall once and near my house once. But he's afraid of lightning. I think that might be the reason he left the car.'

'Would he be afraid to go into the swamp in the dark?'

Fear cleared her mind just a little. 'Kyle isn't afraid of being outside, even at night. I don't know that he knows enough to be afraid.'

'Do you know what time it was that you saw the deer?'

'I don't know . . . maybe nine, nine fifteen.'

Instinctively, both men glanced at their watches. Taylor had found the car at 9.31pm. It was now 10.22pm. More than an hour had passed since the accident. Both Sergeant Huddle and Taylor knew they had to get started right away. A few hours in this rain without proper clothing could lead to hypothermia.

'Anything else we should know? Miss Holton? A nickname maybe? Something he'll answer to?'

'No, just Kyle. But . . .' It was then that the obvious hit her.

Shock, fright, anger, denial seemed to wash over her at once. *He can't answer them!* She lowered her face into her hands.

'Miss Holton?'

Drawing a ragged breath, Denise said, 'Kyle doesn't talk very well. He . . . he can't understand language for some reason.' She turned from one man to the other, making sure they understood. 'You'll have to find him. Simply shouting for him won't do any good. He won't answer—he can't. You'll have to find him.' Unable to say anything else, she started to sob.

'We'll find him, Miss Holton,' Taylor said. 'We'll find him.'

FIVE MINUTES LATER, as Taylor and the others were mapping out the search pattern, four more men from Edenton arrived to help. The first step was to park the cars and trucks as close to the edge of the swamp as possible. They were left with headlights set on full beam, about fifteen yards apart, to provide extra light for the search.

Eleven men would be involved and the search would start from where Taylor found the blanket. From there, they would fan out in three directions—south, east and west. East and west paralleled the highway, south was the direction in which Kyle's blanket had lain. One man would stay behind, near the trucks, on the off chance that Kyle returned. He would send a flare up every hour on the hour, so that the men would know exactly where they were.

After Sergeant Huddle had given them a description of Kyle and what he was wearing, Taylor spoke. He, along with a couple of other men who had hunted in the swamp before, laid out what they were up against. Here, on the outer fringes, the ground was damp, but it wasn't until a half-mile further into the swamp that water formed shallow lakes above the ground. Mud was a real danger, though; it closed in around the foot and leg, making it difficult for an adult to escape, let alone a child. Mud pockets combined with rising water would make a deadly combination. On the plus side, trees and vines made the going rough, hopefully limiting the distance Kyle might have travelled.

'But,' Taylor went on, 'according to the mother, it turns out that the boy probably won't answer if we call. Look for any physical sign of him—you don't want to walk right by.'

THE SEARCH TEAM reached the spot where the blanket was found and began to fan out. Taylor, along with two other men, headed south, deeper into the swamp, where visibility—even with a flashlight—was a few yards at most. Within minutes, Taylor couldn't see or hear anyone.

He pressed forward. Though he didn't have any children himself, he was godfather to the children of his best friend, Mitch Johnson, and he searched as though looking for one of them. Mitch was also a volunteer fireman and Taylor wished fervently that he was out here. Mitch knew the swamp almost as well as Taylor did and they could use his experience. But he was out of town for a few days.

As the distance from the highway grew, the swamp became denser and darker with every step. The water had risen past his ankles, making movement even more difficult. Taylor checked his watch: 10.56. Kyle had been gone for an hour and a half, maybe more. *How long before he got too cold? Or . . .*

He did not want to think beyond that.

He knew the swamp better than anyone. It was here that he'd shot his first deer at the age of twelve; every autumn he still ventured forth to hunt ducks as well. He had an instinctive ability to track nearly anything, seldom returning from a hunt empty-handed. When asked to explain his skill, he simply replied that he tried to think like a deer. People laughed at that, but Taylor said it with a straight face and they quickly realised he wasn't being funny. *Think like a deer? What the hell did that mean?*

They shook their heads. Perhaps only Taylor knew.

He closed his eyes. Where would a four-year-old go? Which way would he head?

His eyes snapped open at the burst of the signal flare in the evening sky, indicating the turn of the hour. Eleven o'clock. *Think.*

DENISE, STILL SHIVERING and dazed, had begged to stay, but was told that it was better for Kyle if she went with the ambulance. She would only hinder things, they said. Now she was at the hospital in Elizabeth City, thirty miles to the northeast.

The emergency room was crowded, but because of her head wound, she was taken in immediately. She was only partially conscious, speaking gibberish, repeating the same word over and over: 'Kyle'.

ANOTHER THIRTY MINUTES passed, and Taylor McAden had moved into the deeper recesses of the swamp. It was incredibly dark now. Trees and vines grew even closer together, and moving in a straight line was impossible. The water was halfway up his shins and he hadn't seen anything. He'd checked in on his walkie-talkie a few minutes earlier—everyone else said the same thing. Nothing. Not a sign of the boy anywhere.

Kyle had been gone for two and a half hours. *Think*.

The wind gusted and rain stung his cheeks as lightning flashed in the eastern sky. *Kyle was small and afraid of lightning . . . stinging rain . . . gusting wind.*

Taylor stared up at the sky, concentrating, and felt something beginning to emerge in the recesses of his mind.

He grabbed his walkie-talkie and spoke quickly, directing everyone back to the highway. He would meet them there.

'It has to be . . .' he said to himself.

TAYLOR'S MOTHER, Judy McAden, couldn't resist calling the fire station. She worried about her son every time he went out, hadn't wanted him to be a fireman and told him so, though she finally stopped pleading with him once she realised he'd never change his mind. He, like his father, was stubborn.

All evening long, she'd felt instinctively that something bad had happened. Finally, she'd made the call, expecting the worst, but instead learned about the little boy—'J. B. Anderson's grandkid'—who was lost in the swamp. Taylor was involved in the search. The mother was on the way to the hospital in Elizabeth City.

After hanging up, Judy sat back in her chair, relieved that Taylor was OK, but worried about the child. Like everyone else in Edenton, she'd known the Andersons. But more than that, Judy had also known Denise's mother when they were both young girls. That had been a long time ago—forty years at least—and she hadn't thought about her in years. But now the memories of their youth came rushing back. She'd had no idea that her friend's daughter had moved back to Edenton.

And now, her son was lost . . .

Judy didn't debate long—she had always been the take-charge type and, at sixty-three, hadn't slowed down at all. Years earlier, after her husband had died, she had taken a job at the library and had raised Taylor by herself. Not only had she met the financial obligations of her family, but she had done what it usually takes two parents to do. She took Taylor to ball games, went camping with the scouts and volunteered at his school. Although those days were behind her, she still worked at the library thirty hours a week and was busier than ever.

Though she didn't know Denise, Judy was a mother herself and understood fear where children were concerned. She pulled on her raincoat, knowing that the mother needed support. Even if Denise Holton didn't want to see her—or couldn't because of her injuries— Judy knew she wouldn't be able to sleep if she didn't let her know that people in the town cared about what was going on.

Chapter 3

At midnight, the flare once again ignited in the evening sky. Kyle had been gone for three hours.

Taylor was nearing the highway, and saw that more than a dozen extra vehicles had arrived. And more people. Even at a distance, he recognised most of them. People who'd defied the storm, people who had to work the following day. People who Denise had probably never met. Good people, he thought.

The mood, however, was gloomy. Those who'd been searching were soaking wet, exhausted and dejected. As Taylor approached, Sergeant Huddle turned, his face illuminated by the flashlights. 'So what's the news? Did you find something?'

'No, but I think I have an idea of which way he headed. It's just a guess, but I think he was moving to the southeast.'

Like everyone else, Sergeant Huddle knew of Taylor's reputation for tracking. 'Why?' he asked.

'Well, that's where we found the blanket and if he kept heading that way, the wind would be at his back. I don't think a little boy would try to fight the wind—I just think he'd go with it. The rain would hurt too much. And I think he'd want to keep the lightning at his back too. His mother said he was afraid of lightning.'

Sergeant Huddle looked at him sceptically. 'That's not much.'

'No,' Taylor admitted, 'it isn't. But I think it's our best hope.'

'You don't think we should continue covering every direction?'

Taylor shook his head. 'We'd be spread too thin.' He wiped his cheek with his hand, collecting his thoughts. 'Look,' he went on, 'we've got, what? More than twenty people now? We could fan out wide and cover everything in that direction.'

Huddle squinted at him doubtfully. 'But what if you're wrong? It's dark out there . . . he could be moving in circles for all we know.'

Taylor had learned to trust his instincts. 'Trust me, Carl,' he said.

'It's not that easy. A little boy's life is at stake.'

'I know.'

With that, Sergeant Huddle sighed and turned away. Ultimately, it was his call. He was the one officially coordinating the search.

'All right,' he finally said. 'We'll do it your way. I just hope to God you're right.'

TWELVE THIRTY now. Arriving at the hospital, Judy McAden approached the front desk and asked to see Denise Holton, her niece. The clerk checked the records. Denise Holton, she explained, had been moved to a room upstairs, but visiting hours were over. If she could come back tomorrow . . .

'I see,' Judy said, sounding defeated. 'Do I have to stop here before I go up to see her? Tomorrow I mean?'

'No. Just head up to room 217 and inform the nurses at the station when you get there. They'll direct you to her room.'

'Thank you.'

Judy stepped away from the desk and a middle-aged man with his arm in a makeshift sling moved forward.

Judy made sure that the lady's attention was focused on the man, then she walked through a set of double swinging doors that led directly to the main area of the hospital. In a matter of minutes, she was sailing past a vacated nurses' station, heading for room 217.

Denise was still awake because sleep was simply an impossibility. There was a clock on the wall alongside her bed and she was staring at it, watching the minutes pass with frightening regularity. Kyle had been missing for nearly four hours.

She wanted to be out looking for him and the fact that she wasn't was more painful than her injuries. In the past hour, the dizziness had abated only slightly. Bright lights hurt her eyes and when the doctor had asked her a few simple questions, she'd seen three images of his face. She hated herself for her weakness. What kind of mother was she? She couldn't even look for her own child!

Denise had begged one of the nurses to call the police to find out what was happening, but the nurse had gently refused. Instead, she'd said that as soon as they heard anything, they would let her know. Until then, the best thing she could do was to calm down, to relax.

Relax. Were they crazy?

JUDY McADEN opened the door slightly and made her way inside. Even in the semidarkness, she immediately recognised Denise as the young woman who often used the computers at the library. The one with the cute little boy who liked the books about airplanes. Oh, no. The cute little boy.

Denise, however, didn't make the connection as she squinted groggily at the lady standing before her. 'Do I know you?' she croaked.

Judy started towards the bed. She spoke softly. 'Sort of. I've seen you in the library before. I work there.'

'What are you doing here?' Denise's words came out slurred.

What, indeed? Judy couldn't help but think. 'I heard about your son getting lost. My son is one of those looking for him.'

Denise's eyes flickered with a mixture of hope and fear. 'Have you heard anything?'

Judy shook her head. 'No, nothing. I'm sorry.'

Denise pressed her lips together, staying silent. She seemed to be evaluating Judy's answer. Finally, she turned away. 'I'd like to be alone.'

Still uncertain of what to do, Judy said the only thing she herself would have wanted to hear. 'They'll find him, Denise.'

At first, she didn't think Denise had heard her, but then she saw the younger woman's jaw quiver, followed by a welling in her eyes.

'But what if they don't?'

Judy moved closer, reached for her hand and gave it a squeeze. 'They will.'

Denise faced Judy with red and swollen eyes. 'I don't even know if they're still looking for him . . .'

Unsure if she had heard correctly, Judy furrowed her brow. 'Do you mean to say no one's kept you informed of what's happening out there?'

'I haven't heard a thing since I was put in the ambulance.'

At once, Judy glanced around for the phone, her confidence rising with the knowledge that there was something she *could* do.

She sat in the chair beside the small table in the corner of the room and picked up the phone. Dialling quickly, she reached the fire station in Edenton.

'This is Judy McAden and I'm here with Denise Holton—the one whose boy's in the swamp. I'm at the hospital, and it seems that no one's told her what's happening out there. She needs to know what's going on . . . I see . . . Uh-huh . . . Oh, OK, thanks, Joe. Call here if you find out anything, anything at all. And we'll check back in a little while.'

Judy hung up the phone and went to the bed again. 'They haven't found him yet, but they're still out there. The weather's cleared up some and they think Kyle was moving to the southeast. They went that way about an hour ago . . .'

Denise felt a lump rise in her throat as her nausea returned. *Kyle was still out there.*

IT WAS COMING up to 1.30am. The temperature—originally in the sixties—was nearing forty degrees now, and the searchers began to realise that if they hoped to find the little boy alive, they needed to get to him in the next couple of hours.

They'd now reached an area of the swamp that was a little less dense, where the trees and bushes grew further apart. Here they were able to search more quickly, and Taylor could see three men—or rather their flashlights—in each direction. There were twenty-four searchers in total, covering an area nearly a quarter of a mile wide.

Taylor had hunted in this part of the swamp before. Because the ground was elevated slightly, it was usually dry, and deer flocked to the area. A half-mile ahead, the elevation dropped again to below the water table, and they would come to an area known as Duck Shot, that was filled with dozens of duck blinds during the hunting season. It was the farthest point Kyle could have reached.

If, of course, they were going in the right direction.

IT WAS NOW 2.26am. Kyle had been missing for five and a half hours.

Judy brought a wet flannel to Denise's bedside and gently wiped her face.

'What's your name?' Denise asked eventually.

'I'm Judy McAden. I guess I forgot to mention that when I first came in.'

'And you work in the library?'

Judy nodded. 'I've seen you and your son there on more than a few occasions.'

'Is that why . . .?' Denise asked, trailing off.

'No, actually, I came because your mother and I were friends a long time ago. When I heard you were in trouble . . . Well, I didn't want you to think that you were in this all alone.'

Denise squinted, trying to focus on Judy. 'My mother?'

Judy nodded. 'We grew up together.'

Denise tried to remember if her mother had mentioned Judy McAden, but concentrating on the past was like trying to decipher an image on a fuzzy television screen. As she was trying to remember, the telephone rang.

It startled them both, the sound shrill and ominous.

A FEW MINUTES EARLIER, Taylor had reached Duck Shot. Still he was trying to put himself in Kyle's shoes. The wind alone would have steered the boy in this direction and heading this way would have kept the lightning behind him . . . Then, where was he? *Think.*

Lightning flashed again, startling him. As the night sky was illuminated, he saw it in the distance, rectangular and wooden, overgrown with foliage. One of the dozens of duck blinds.

Duck blinds . . . They looked almost like a kid's playhouse, with enough shelter to keep much of the rain away . . . Had Kyle seen one? No, it couldn't be. But . . .

Taylor felt the adrenalin race through his system. He did his best to remain calm. Maybe—that's all it was. Just a great big maybe.

He rushed to the first duck blind he'd seen, his boots sinking in the mud, making a sucking sound as he fought the ground's spongy thickness. The blind hadn't been used since last fall and was overgrown with vines and brush. He poked his head inside. Sweeping his flashlight around the interior, all he saw was ageing plywood.

Another bolt of lightning lit the sky and Taylor caught a glimpse of another duck blind, not fifty yards away. One that wasn't as shrouded as the one he'd just searched. Taylor took off again, believing . . .

Shining his light inside the second blind, he almost stopped breathing.

A little boy, sitting in the corner, muddy and scratched, filthy, but otherwise seemingly OK. Taylor blinked, thinking it was a mirage, but when he opened his eyes again, the boy was still there, Mickey Mouse shirt and all. 'Well hello, little man. I take it you must be Kyle.'

Kyle looked up at him with an expression of surprise on his face. 'Hewwo,' he said exuberantly, and Taylor laughed aloud. Grins immediately spread across both their faces. Taylor dropped to one knee and the little boy scrambled to his feet and then into his arms. He was cold and wet, shivering, and when Taylor felt those small arms wrap around his neck, he felt tears well in his eyes.

'He's OK, everyone . . . I repeat, he's OK . . . I've got Kyle with me right now . . .'

With those words spoken into the walkie-talkie, a whoop of excitement arose from the searchers and the word was passed along to the station, where Joe called the hospital. It was 2.31am.

Judy retrieved the phone from the table, then sat it on the bed so that Denise could answer it. She was barely breathing as she picked up the receiver. Then, all at once she brought her hand to her mouth to stifle the scream. Her smile, so heartfelt and emotional, was contagious and Judy had to fight the urge to jump up and down.

When she'd hung up the phone, Denise sat up and spontaneously hugged Judy while filling her in. 'They're bringing him to the hospital. He's cold and wet and they want to bring him in as a precaution, just to make sure everything's OK. He should be here in an hour or so—I can't believe it.'

The excitement brought the dizziness back, but this time Denise couldn't have cared less. Kyle was safe. That was the only thing that mattered now.

THEY REACHED the hospital a little after 3.30am, Taylor riding in the ambulance with Kyle. The doctors were waiting for him. So were Denise and Judy.

Judy had surprised the nurse on duty by walking up to the station in the middle of the night to request a wheelchair for Denise. A little cajoling was necessary—though not much. 'They found her son and they're bringing him here. She wants to meet him when he arrives . . .' The nurse went ahead and granted the request.

The ambulance rolled up and the back door swung open. Kyle was wheeled out on a gurney as Denise struggled to her feet. Once inside the hospital doors, the doctor and the nurses stepped back so that Kyle could see his mother.

In the ambulance he'd been stripped down and then wrapped in warm blankets to get his body temperature back up. They had done the job. His face was pink, and in every respect he looked far better than his mother did.

Denise bent closer so that Kyle could see her and he sat up immediately. He climbed into her embrace and they held each other tightly. 'Hewwo, money,' he said.

Denise laughed. 'Hi, sweetie,' she said. 'Are you OK?'

As the gurney was rolled to the examination room, Judy hung back, watching Denise and Kyle go, not wanting to interrupt. As they disappeared from view, she sighed, suddenly realising how tired she was.

She walked out of the emergency room and began to search for her keys. Looking up, she spied Taylor talking to Carl Huddle near his patrol car and breathed a sigh of relief.

Taylor saw her at the same time, sure at first that his eyes were playing tricks. 'Mom, what are you doing here?' he asked incredulously.

'I just spent the evening with Denise Holton—you know, the child's mother? I thought she might need some support.'

'And you just decided to come down? Without even knowing her?' They hugged each other. 'Of course.'

Taylor felt a surge of pride. His mother was a hell of a lady.

Judy pulled back, giving him the once-over. 'You look terrible, son.'

Taylor laughed. 'Thanks. I actually feel pretty good, though.'

'I'll bet you do. You did something wonderful tonight.'

Judy looped her arm through Taylor's and they started towards the parking lot. After a few steps, she glanced at him.

'You're such a nice young man. How come you're not married yet?'

'I'm worried about the in-laws.'

'Huh?'

'Not my in-laws, Mom. My wife's.'

Judy playfully pulled her arm away. 'I take back everything I said.'

Taylor chuckled to himself as he reached for her arm again. 'Just kidding, Mom. You know I love you.'

'You better.'

When they reached the car, Taylor took the keys and opened her door. Once Judy was behind the wheel, he asked, 'Are you sure you're not too tired to drive?'

'No, I'll be fine. It's not that far. By the way, where's your car?'

'Still at the scene. I rode with Kyle in the ambulance. Carl's gonna take me back.'

'I'm so proud of you, Taylor.'

THE FOLLOWING DAY dawned cloudy with sporadic rain, though most of the storm had passed out to sea. Denise and Kyle were still in the hospital and had been allowed to sleep in the same room. Although Kyle could have been discharged, the doctors wanted to keep Denise in for an extra day of observation.

They spent the morning watching cartoons. Both were on her bed, pillows behind them, wearing ill-fitting hospital gowns. Kyle was watching Scooby-Doo, his favourite.

'He's running,' Kyle said, pointing at the screen. *Eez runny.*

'Yes, he's running from the ghost. Can you say that?'

'Running from the ghost,' he said softly. *Runny fraw ah goz.*

She looked at him tenderly. 'Were you scared last night?'

'Yes, he's scared.' *Yes, eez scairt.*

Denise didn't know whether he was talking about himself or Scooby-Doo. Kyle didn't understand the differences between pronouns, nor did he use tenses properly. Running, ran, run . . . It all meant the same thing.

Earlier, she'd tried to talk to him about his experience, but hadn't got very far. Kyle hadn't answered any of her questions.

With a slow push, the door squeaked open. 'Knock, knock.'

Denise turned as Judy McAden peeped inside.

'I hope I'm not coming at a bad time.'

'No, of course not. We're just watching TV. C'mon in.' Using the remote, Denise turned down the volume slightly.

'I just wanted to come by to meet your son. He's quite the topic of conversation around town now.'

Denise angled her head, glancing proudly at Kyle. 'Well, here he is, the little terror. Kyle, say hello to Miss Judy.'

'Hello, Miss Judy,' he whispered. *Hewwo, Miss Jeewey*.

Judy pulled up a chair and sat beside the bed. She patted him on the leg. 'Hello, Kyle. How are you? I heard you had a big adventure.'

After a moment of silence, Denise prodded her son. 'Kyle—say, "Yes I did."'

'Yes I did.' *Yes, I di*.

'Kyle doesn't talk too well yet,' Denise offered quietly.

Judy nodded. 'That's OK, isn't it, Kyle? I'm not as much fun as watching cartoons anyway.' She turned to Denise. 'So how are the two of you holding up?'

'Well, Kyle here is healthy as can be. From the looks of him, you'd think that nothing at all happened last night. Me, on the other hand . . . Well, let's just say I could be better.'

'Will you be getting out soon?'

'Tomorrow, I hope. Body willing. I'm sorry I didn't get a chance to thank you last night, but—well . . .'

'Oh, don't worry about that. I'm just glad everything worked out the way it did. Has Carl stopped by yet?'

'Carl?'

'He's the state trooper. The one from last night. Taylor told me this morning that Carl still had to wrap up a few things.'

'Taylor? That's your son?'

'My one and only.'

Denise struggled with memories from the night before. 'He was the one who found me, right?'

Judy nodded. 'He was trying to find some downed power lines when he came across your car.'

'I guess I should thank him, too.'

'I'll tell him for you. But he wasn't the only one, you know. They had more than twenty people by the end. People from all over town.'

Denise shook her head, amazed. 'But they didn't even know me.'

'People have a way of surprising you, don't they? There are a lot of good people here. Edenton's a small town, but it has a big heart.'

AN HOUR AFTER LUNCH, Carl Huddle met up with Denise and finished the remaining paperwork. Light-hearted and far more alert than the evening before, Denise answered everything in detail.

When they were finished, Sergeant Huddle folded everything into a manila file then rose to leave. 'Well, I should be going. You probably need some rest.'

Denise sat up higher in the bed. 'Well . . . um . . . before you go—can I ask you a couple of questions about last night? With all the commotion I really haven't learned what went on.'

'Sure. Ask away.'

'How were you able to find him? I mean, it was so dark and with the storm . . .' She paused, trying to find the right words.

'Well, I'd like to say it was all skill and training, but it wasn't. We got lucky. Damn lucky. Taylor figured that Kyle would follow the wind and keep the lightning behind him. Sure enough, he was right.' He nodded towards Kyle and went on. 'You've got one tough boy there, Miss Holton. His being OK had more to do with him than any of us. Most kids would have been terrified, but your little boy wasn't. It's pretty amazing.'

'Denise's brow furrowed as she thought about what he'd just told her. 'Wait—was that Taylor McAden?'

'Yeah, the guy who found you.' He scratched his jaw. 'Actually, he was the one who found both of you. He found Kyle in a duck blind and Kyle wouldn't let go of him until we got him to the hospital. Clamped onto him like a crab claw.'

'Thank you, anyway. Without you, Kyle probably wouldn't be here.'

'No problem. I love a happy ending, and I'm glad we had one.'

After saying goodbye, Sergeant Huddle slipped out of the door. As it closed behind him, Denise looked upwards, towards the ceiling, without really seeing it. Taylor McAden? Judy McAden?

She couldn't believe the coincidence, but then everything that happened last night had fluke written all over it. The storm, the deer, Kyle wandering away. Everything. Including the McAdens.

Later that afternoon, she wrote thankyou notes to Carl and Judy as well as a general note (addressed care of the fire department) to everyone involved in the search. Lastly, she wrote her note to Taylor McAden, and, as she did so, she couldn't help but wonder about him.

Chapter 4

Three days after the search for Kyle Holton, Taylor McAden made his way to Cypress Park Cemetery, the oldest cemetery in Edenton. He knew exactly where he was going and he cut across the lawn, stopping only when he reached the shade of a giant willow tree. Here, on the west side of the cemetery, was a granite block, twelve inches high and simply inscribed. Directly in front of it, in a small metal tube set into the ground, was a bouquet of eleven dried carnations, one for each year of his mother's marriage. She left them every May, on her anniversary, as she had for the past twenty-seven years.

Taylor knelt down and ran his finger over the polished granite. The words were simple:

Mason Thomas McAden
Loving father and husband
1936–1972

Taylor was now thirty-six, the age his father had been when he'd passed away. In his mind, his father would always be thirty-six, never younger, never older, looking the way he did in the photo that still sat on the mantelpiece in the living room.

It had been taken a week before the accident, on a warm June morning. In it, his father was stepping off the back porch, fishing pole in hand, on his way to the Chowan River. Taylor's mother had been hiding behind the truck, and when she had called Mason's name he had turned and she'd snapped the picture. The film had been sent away to be developed and because of that, it hadn't been destroyed with the other photos. Judy didn't pick it up until after the funeral, when she had looked at it, cried, then slipped it into her bag. To others, it wasn't anything special—a man in mid-stride, hair uncombed, a stain on the shirt he was wearing—but for Taylor it had captured the very essence of his father. It was there, that irrepressible spirit that defined the man in his expression, the gleam of his eye, and that was the reason it had affected his mother so.

A month after his father had died, nine-year-old Taylor had sneaked the photo out of her bag and had fallen asleep holding it. His mother had found it pressed between his hands, smudged with tears. The following day, she'd had a copy made and framed for Taylor.

His father looked so young in the picture, his eyes and forehead showing only the faintest suggestion of wrinkles that would never have the chance to deepen. Why, then, did he seem so much older than Taylor felt right now? His father had always seemed so wise, so sure of himself, so brave. In the eyes of his nine-year-old son, he was a man of mythic proportions, a man who understood life and could explain nearly everything.

In the weeks immediately after his father died, time had blurred into a series of fragmented memories: the funeral, staying with his grandparents, suffocating nightmares when he tried to sleep. It was summer—school was out—and he spent most of his time outside, trying to blot out what had happened. His mother wore black for two months, mourning the loss. Then, finally, the black was put away. They found a new place to live, something smaller, and nine-year-old Taylor knew exactly what his mother was trying to tell him. *It's just the two of us now. We've got to go on.*

After that fateful summer, Taylor had drifted through school, earning decent but unspectacular grades. With his mother's care, his adolescent years were like those of most others who lived in this part of the country. Yet, in many ways, he was considered a loner. Mitch was his only real friend, and in the summer they'd go hunting and fishing, just the two of them. Though Mitch was married now, they still did whenever they could.

Once he graduated, Taylor bypassed college in favour of work, plastering and learning the carpentry business. The owner was an alcoholic who cared more about the money he'd make than the quality of the work. After a confrontation that nearly came to blows, Taylor quit working for him and started taking classes to earn his contractor's licence.

He supported himself by working in the gypsum mine near Little Washington, and by the time he was twenty-four he'd saved enough to start his own business. No project was too small and he often underbid to build up his business and reputation. By the age of twenty-eight, he'd nearly gone bankrupt twice, but he stubbornly kept on going. Over the past eight years, he'd nurtured the business to the point where he made a decent living, enough for him to lead the simple life he desired. A life that included volunteering for the fire department, even though his mother had tried strenuously to talk him out of it. It was the only instance in which he'd deliberately gone against her wishes.

Of course, she wanted to be a grandmother. Every now and then she let that slip, but Taylor tried to change the subject. He hadn't come close to marriage and doubted whether he ever would, though in the past he'd dated two women fairly seriously. The first time was in his early twenties. Valerie was coming out of a disastrous relationship when they'd met, and Taylor was the one she turned to in her time of need. She had wanted something more serious, but Taylor told her honestly that he might never be ready. In time, they simply drifted apart.

Then there was Lori. She had moved to Edenton to work for the bank. She was a loan officer, working long hours, and hadn't had the chance to make any friends. Then Taylor walked into the bank to apply for a mortgage. He offered to introduce her around; she took him up on it. Soon they were dating, but eventually she, too, wanted more than Taylor was willing to commit to. They broke up.

Both Valerie and Lori claimed that there was something inside Taylor that they were unable to reach. And though he knew they meant well, their attempts to talk to him about this distance of his didn't—or couldn't—change anything.

Now, he stood up, his knees aching from the position he'd been kneeling in. Before he left the cemetery he said a short prayer in memory of his father, and then, bent over to touch the headstone one more time.

'I'm sorry, Dad,' he whispered. 'I'm so sorry.'

MITCH JOHNSON was leaning against Taylor's truck, watching his friend leaving the cemetery. In his hand he held two cans of beer, and he tossed one to Taylor as he drew near.

Taylor caught it in mid-stride, surprised, his thoughts still deep in the past. 'What are you doing here?'

'I sort of figured you'd need a beer about now,' Mitch answered simply.

'Am I that predictable?'

'Hell, Taylor, I know you better than I know my own wife.'

Taller and thinner than Taylor, Mitch was six foot two and weighed 160 pounds. Most of his hair was gone—he'd started losing it in his early twenties—and he wore wire-rimmed glasses. He worked at his father's hardware store and was regarded around town as a mechanical genius, able to repair everything from lawn mowers to bulldozers. Unlike Taylor, he'd gone to college, majored in business, and had met a psychology student named Melissa Kindle before moving back to Edenton. They'd been married twelve years and had four children, all boys. Taylor had been best man at the wedding.

The two of them had joined the volunteer unit at Edenton fire station at the same time. Though Mitch considered it more a duty than a calling, he was someone Taylor always wanted along when a call came in.

Taylor leaned against the truck. 'How's Melissa doing?'

'She's good. Her sister drove her crazy at the wedding, but she's back to normal now that she's home. So now it's just me and the kids who are driving her crazy.' Mitch's tone softened imperceptibly. 'So, how're you holding up?'

Taylor shrugged without meeting Mitch's eyes. 'I'm all right.'

Mitch didn't press it, knowing that Taylor wouldn't say anything more. His father was one of the few things they never talked about. He cracked open his beer and Taylor did the same.

'I hear you had yourself a big night in the swamp while I was gone.'

'Yeah, we did.'

'Wish I could've been there.'

'We could have used you, that's for sure.'

'Yeah, but if I'd been there, there wouldn't have been all that drama. I would have headed straight to those duck blinds. I couldn't believe it took you guys hours to figure that out.'

Taylor laughed before taking a drink of beer and glancing over at Mitch. 'Does Melissa still want you to give it up?'

Mitch nodded. 'You know how it is with the kids and all. She doesn't want anything to happen to me.'

'So you're considering it?' Taylor asked.

Mitch took a long pull from his beer before answering. 'Yeah, I guess I am.' He paused. 'You know, it's not just Melissa—it's me too. I've been at it for a long time and it just doesn't mean what it used to. I'd sort of like to be able to spend some time with the kids without having to go out at a moment's notice.'

'You sound like your mind's made up.'

Mitch could hear the disappointment in Taylor's tone and he took a second before nodding. 'Well, actually, it is. I'll finish the year, but that'll be it for me. I just wanted you to be the first to know.'

Taylor didn't respond. Mitch cocked his head. 'But that's not why I came out here today. I came out to lend you some support.'

Taylor seemed lost in thought. 'Like I said, I'm doing all right.'

'Do you wanna head somewhere and have a few beers?'

'No. I gotta get back to work.'

'Well, how 'bout dinner Wednesday? You want to stop over then?'

'That'd be great.'

'All right, then.' Mitch nodded and pushed away from the truck as he fished the keys from his pocket.

'Thanks,' Taylor said.

'You're welcome.'

'I mean about you coming by today.'

'I knew what you were talking about.'

DENISE HOLTON was seated at the Formica table in her small kitchen, poring over the insurance papers in front of her, doing her best to make sense of them. Her car was totalled, and she'd only had third-party liability insurance. Her boss, Ray, bless his heart, told her to take her time coming back, and eight days had gone by without her earning a penny. The regular bills—phone, electricity, water, gas—were due in less than a week. And to top it all, she had just had the bill from the towing service who'd removed her vehicle from the side of the road. With a couple of hundred bucks in the bank, this was a big problem.

Fortunately, though, they'd offered to give her seventy-five dollars for the remains of her car and call it even. She could cover the regular bills with what was left in the current account, and still have enough for food if she was careful. It was a good thing Ray let them eat for free at the diner. She'd called Rhonda—another waitress at Eights—and she'd agreed to help Denise get to and from work. She'd have to start riding her bicycle for errands around town.

Denise left the kitchen to check on Kyle. Sleeping soundly. She headed outside and sat on the back porch, wondering again if she'd made the right decision to move here. Even though she knew it was impossible, she found herself wishing she could have stayed in Atlanta. It would be nice sometimes to have someone to talk to. With the exception of Rhonda at the diner (who was twenty and single)—and Judy McAden—Denise didn't know anyone in town.

And then, of course, there was the whole man thing. Brett was the last man she'd dated and, in reality, it hadn't even been a date. A roll in the sack, perhaps, but not a date. What a roll though, huh? Twenty minutes and boom—her whole life changed. What would her life be like now, if it hadn't happened? True, Kyle wouldn't be here, but . . . But what? Maybe she'd be married with a couple of kids, maybe she'd even have a house with white picket fence round the yard. It sounded good, but would her life be any better?

Kyle. Sweet Kyle. Simply thinking about him made her smile. No, she decided, it wouldn't be better. If there was one bright spot in her life, he was it.

WITH EARLY-MORNING sunlight slanting through the windows, Kyle padded through the bedroom and crawled into bed with Denise, ready to start the day. He whispered, 'Wake up, Money, wake up,' and used his little fingers to try to lift her eyelids. He thought it was hilarious. 'Open your eyes, Money,' he kept saying, and despite the ungodly hour, she couldn't help but laugh as well.

A little after nine, to make the morning even better, Judy had phoned to see if she could visit the following afternoon. After gabbing with her a little while Denise hung up the phone, thinking about her mood the night before and the difference a good night's sleep made.

After breakfast, she got the bikes ready, and helped Kyle put his helmet on. They started towards town under a blue and cloudless sky, Kyle riding out in front. Last December, Denise had spent a day running along holding on to his bicycle seat until he'd got the hang of it. He had always had above-average motor skills, a fact that surprised the doctors. To him, riding his bike was an adventure and he rode with reckless abandon. Even though the traffic was light, Denise found herself shouting instructions every few seconds.

'Stop' was the only command he really understood, and whenever she said it he hit the brakes, put his feet on the ground, then turned round with a big toothy grin, as if to say, This is so much fun. Why're you so upset? Denise was a nervous wreck by the time they reached town. She knew then and there that riding a bicycle just wasn't going to cut it, and she decided to ask Ray for two extra shifts a week. Save every penny and maybe she'd be able to afford another car in a couple of months.

Edenton had a small downtown, but from a historic perspective the town was a gem. Houses dated back to the early 1800s and had nearly all been restored to their former glory over the past thirty years. Giant oak trees lined both sides of the street and shaded the road, providing pleasant cover from the heat of the sun.

Though Edenton had a supermarket, it was on the other side of town, and Denise decided instead to drop into Merchants, an old-fashioned store that sold everything from food to automotive supplies. She filled a small plastic basket with the few things she needed—milk, oatmeal, cheese, eggs, bread and candy (for working with Kyle)—then went to the cash register. The total came to less than she expected, which was good, and the owner packed everything into two brown paper bags. And that, of course, was a problem she'd overlooked. She would have preferred plastic bags so she could have slipped the loops over her handlebars. How was she going to get all this home?

She glanced at her son and noticed he was staring through the glass door, an unfamiliar expression on his face.

'What is it, honey?'

He answered, though she didn't understand what he was trying to say. It sounded like *fowman*. Leaving her groceries on the counter, she bent down so she could watch him as he said it again. Watching his lips sometimes made understanding him easier.

'What did you say?'

'Fowman.' This time, Kyle pointed through the door and Denise looked in that direction. All at once, she knew what he'd meant.

Taylor McAden was standing outside the store, holding the door partially open while talking to someone outside. As Taylor ended his conversation, Kyle ran up to him and Taylor stepped inside without really paying attention to where he was going. He almost bowled Kyle over before catching his balance.

'Whoa, sorry—didn't see you . . .' he said instinctively. 'Excuse me.' He took a step backwards, blinking in confusion. Then, recognition crossing his face, he broke into a wide smile, squatting so he could be at eye level. 'Oh, hey, little man. How are you?'

'Hello, Taylor,' Kyle said happily. *Hewwo, Tayer*. Without saying anything else, he wrapped his arms round Taylor as he had that night in the duck blind. Taylor—unsure at first—hugged him back, looking content and surprised at the same time.

Denise watched in stunned silence. After a long moment, Kyle finally loosened his grip, allowing Taylor to pull back. The boy's eyes were dancing, as if he'd recognised a long-lost friend. 'Fowman,' he said again, excitedly. 'He's found you.' *Eez foun you*.

Taylor cocked his head to one side. 'What's that?'

Denise moved towards the two of them. 'He's trying to say that you found him,' she said quietly. Taylor glanced up and saw Denise for the first time since the accident, and for a moment he couldn't look away. Despite the fact he'd seen her before, she looked . . . well, more attractive than he'd remembered. Her face was lovely, almost mysterious, accentuated by high cheekbones and exotic eyes, long dark hair pulled into a ponytail.

'He's found you,' Kyle said again, breaking into Taylor's thoughts.

'That's right, I did,' he said, 'but you, little man, were the brave one.'

Denise watched him as he spoke to Kyle. Despite the heat, he was wearing jeans and Red Wing work boots that were covered with dried mud and well worn. His white shirt was short-sleeved, revealing tight muscles in his sun-darkened arms—the arms of someone who worked with his hands all day.

'Sorry about almost knocking him over back there,' he said quietly. 'I didn't see him when I came in.' He stopped, as if not knowing what else to say, and Denise sensed a shyness she hadn't expected.

'It wasn't your fault. He kind of snuck up on you.' She smiled. 'I'm Denise Holton, by the way. I know we met before, but a lot of that night's fairly foggy.' She held out her hand and Taylor took it. She could feel the calluses on his palm.

'Taylor McAden,' he said. 'I got your note. Thanks.'

'Fowman,' Kyle said again, louder than before. 'Big fowman.'

Taylor furrowed his brow and reached out, grabbing Kyle by his helmet in a friendly, almost brotherly way. 'You think so, huh?'

Kyle nodded. 'Big.'

Denise laughed. 'I think it's a case of hero worship.'

'Well, the feeling's mutual, little man. It was more you than me.'

If Taylor noticed that Kyle didn't understand what he'd just said, he didn't show it. Instead, he winked at him. Nice.

Denise cleared her throat. 'I haven't had the chance to thank you in person for what you did.'

Taylor shrugged. 'Ah, that's all right,' he said. 'Your note was plenty.'

For a moment, neither of them spoke. Kyle, meanwhile, wandered towards the candy aisle. Both of them watched as he stopped halfway down, focusing intently on the brightly covered wrappers.

'He looks good,' Taylor finally said into the silence. 'Kyle, I mean. After all that happened, I was sort of wondering how he was doing.'

'He seems to be OK. Time will tell, I guess, but right now I'm not too worried about him. The doctor gave him a clean bill of health.'

'How 'bout you?' he asked.

'Still a little sore here and there, but otherwise I'm fine. It could have been worse.'

'Good, I'm glad. I was worried about you, too.'

There was something in the quiet way he spoke that made Denise take a closer look at him. Though he wasn't the most handsome man she'd ever seen, there was something about him that caught her attention—a gentleness, perhaps, despite his size. An unthreatening perceptiveness in his steady gaze. Glancing at his left hand, she noticed he wasn't wearing a ring.

She quickly turned away, wondering where the thought had come from and what had brought it on. Why would a ring matter?

'So I take it you're in town for a few errands?' Small talk, Taylor knew, but for some reason, he was reluctant to let her leave.

'Yeah, we needed to grab a few things. How about you?'

'I'm just here to pick up some soda for the guys.'

'At the fire department?'

'No—I only volunteer there. I'm a contractor—I remodel homes, things like that.'

For a moment, she was confused.

'You volunteer? I thought that went out twenty years ago.'

'Not here it hasn't. As a rule, it's not busy enough for a full-time crew, so they depend on people like me when emergencies come up.'

'I didn't know that.' The realisation made what he'd done for them seem even greater than before.

Kyle peered up at his mother. 'He's hungry,' he said. *Eez hungwy*.

'Well, we'll be home very soon. And then I'll make you a grilled cheese sandwich when we get there. Does that sound OK?'

He nodded. 'Yes, it's good.' *Yes, ess good.*

Denise, however, didn't move fast enough for Kyle. Instead, she looked at Taylor again. Kyle reached up and tugged his mother by the hem of her shorts and her hands automatically went down to stop him. 'Let's go,' Kyle added. *Wess go.*

'We're going, honey.'

Kyle and Denise's hands engaged in a little battle as she peeled his fingers away and he tried to grab the hem again. She took him by the hand to stop him.

Taylor stifled a chuckle by clearing his throat. 'Well, I'd better not keep you. A growing boy needs to eat.'

'Yeah, I suppose so.' She gave Taylor an expression of weariness common to mothers everywhere.

'It was good seeing you again,' she added, hoping he could tell that she actually meant it.

'You too,' he said.

Kyle waved with his free hand. 'Bye-bye, Tayer,' he said.

'Bye, little man.' Taylor grinned before heading towards the refrigerators along the wall to get the soda he'd come for.

Denise turned to the counter. The owner was immersed in *Field and Stream* magazine, his lips moving slightly as he perused the article. He saw her approaching and set his magazine aside.

She motioned towards the bags. 'Would you mind if we left these here for a few minutes? We have to get some other kinds of bags that loop over the handlebars . . .'

Despite the fact he was halfway across the store, Taylor strained to hear what was going on.

Denise continued. 'We're on our bikes and I don't think I can get this all home. It won't take long—we'll be right back.'

He heard the manager answer. 'Oh, sure, no problem. I'll just put them behind the counter here for now.'

Soda in hand, Taylor started towards the front of the store. Denise was shepherding Kyle out, her hand on his back.

'Hey, Denise, wait up . . .'

She turned and stopped as Taylor approached.

'Were those your bikes outside the store?'

She nodded. 'Uh-huh. Why?'

'I couldn't help but overhear what you told the manager.' He paused. 'Can I give you a hand getting your groceries home?'

Though she knew he was trying to be kind, she wasn't sure she should accept.

He held up his hands, as if sensing her indecision, an almost mischievous grin on his face. 'I won't steal anything, I promise.'

She swallowed, thinking of the trip across town and back again. 'If you're sure it's not out of your way . . .'

'No, it's not out of my way at all. Just let me pay for this and I'll help you carry your things to the truck.'

LATER THAT WEDNESDAY evening, Melissa, Mitch and Taylor were in the back yard, steaks and hot dogs sizzling over charcoal. The air was bruised with humidity and the yellow sun hovered low in the sky. While Mitch stood ready, tongs in hand, Taylor nursed a beer. After bringing them up to speed on what had been happening, he mentioned that he'd seen Denise again at the store and that he'd dropped off her groceries.

'They seem to be doing fine,' he observed.

Though it was said in all innocence, Melissa eyed him carefully, leaning forward in her chair. 'So you like her, huh?' she said, not hiding her curiosity.

'I didn't say that,' Taylor said quickly.

'You didn't have to. I could see it in your face.' Melissa turned to her husband. 'He likes her.'

'You're putting words in my mouth.'

Melissa smiled wryly. 'So . . . is she pretty?'

'What kind of question is that?'

Melissa turned to her husband again. 'He thinks she's pretty, too.'

Mitch nodded, convinced. 'I thought he was kind of quiet when he arrived. So what's next? You gonna ask her out?'

Taylor turned from one to the other, wondering how the conversation had spun in this direction. 'I hadn't planned on it.'

'You should. You need to get out of the house once in a while.'

'I'm out all day long . . .'

Melissa giggled. 'You know we're just teasing.'

Her eyebrows danced up and down and despite himself, Taylor laughed. Melissa was thirty-four but looked—and acted—ten years younger. Blonde and petite, she was quick with a kind word, loyal to her friends, and never seemed to hold a grudge about anything.

Taylor took another drink from his beer. 'Why are you so interested?'

'Because we love you,' Melissa answered sweetly.

And don't understand why I'm still alone, Taylor thought.

THE DAY after Denise had run into Taylor at Merchants, she'd spent the morning working with Kyle. Now that summer had arrived, he seemed to work best if they finished before noon. After that it was too warm in the house for either of them to concentrate.

After breakfast, she'd called Ray and fortunately he'd consented to her working a couple of extra shifts. Starting tomorrow night, she'd work every evening except Sunday.

She found herself thinking about Taylor McAden. Just as he'd promised, the groceries had been placed on the front porch, in the shade. He'd offered to put their bikes in the back and give them both a ride, too, but Denise had said no. It had less to do with Taylor than Kyle—he was already getting on his bike and she knew he was looking forward to another ride. She didn't want to ruin that for him.

Part of her had wanted to accept Taylor's offer. She'd been around long enough to know that he'd found her attractive—the way he looked at her made that plain—yet it didn't make her uncomfortable as the scrutiny of other men sometimes did. The way he'd looked at her was more appreciative somehow, less threatening, and she'd found herself flattered.

Denise was still thinking about Taylor as Judy pulled up outside in the shade of a blooming magnolia tree. She was just finishing the dishes, and waved before going to meet Judy at the front door.

They seated themselves on the front porch so they could keep an eye on Kyle who was playing with his trucks near the fence, rolling them along make-believe roads. On a small wooden table sat two glasses of sweet tea. Judy took a drink from hers.

'I used to live right down the road from here,' she said. 'Do you know the Boyle place? That white house with the green shutters, big red barn out back?'

Denise nodded. She passed it on the way into town.

'Well, that was where I lived when I was little. Your mom and I were the only two girls who lived out this way so we ended up doing practically everything together. She was probably the best friend I ever had.'

'Why didn't she keep in touch after she moved?' Denise began. 'I mean . . .' She paused and Judy cast her a sidelong glance.

'You mean why, if we were such good friends, didn't she tell you about it?'

Denise nodded and Judy collected her thoughts.

'I guess it had to do with her moving away. We kept in touch for a few years, but then I lost contact with her. It took me a long time to understand that distance can ruin even the best of intentions.'

Denise set her glass on the table. 'So you didn't know my father?'

'No. But I do remember your grandparents heading off to the

wedding and being a little hurt that your mother hadn't sent me an invitation. Not that I could have gone of course. I was married by then and my husband and I were struggling financially and with the new baby—well, it would have been impossible to make it.'

'I'm sorry about that.'

'Nothing to be sorry for. Your father came from a very respectable Atlanta family and by that point in her life, I think your mom was a little embarrassed about where she'd come from. She was quite a tomboy when she was young. Not that your father minded, obviously, since he married her. But I remember that your grandparents didn't say much after they'd returned from the wedding. I think they knew they didn't fit into their daughter's world any more. Practically overnight she turned into a Southern lady, complete with white gloves and table manners.'

'I knew Mom wasn't close to her parents, but she never told me any of this.'

'No, I don't expect she did. But please don't think poorly of your mother. I certainly don't. She was always so full of life, so passionate—she was exciting to be around. And she had the heart of an angel, she really did. She was as sweet a person as I ever knew.' Judy turned to face Denise. 'I see a lot of her in you.' And then, as if knowing she'd said too much, she added, 'But listen to me, droning on like some senile old woman. Let's talk about you for a while. Why did you move to Edenton?'

Denise sighed. 'It's tough to know where to start. I guess mainly it has to do with Kyle. I think I told you he has trouble speaking?'

Judy nodded.

'Well, right now, they say he has an auditory processing problem. Basically, it means that for some reason understanding language and learning to speak are hard for him. I guess the best analogy is that it's like dyslexia, only instead of processing visual signals, it has to do with processing sounds. It's like he's hearing Chinese one second, German the next. But in the beginning, they weren't sure how to diagnose him, and, well . . .' Denise ran her hand through her hair. 'Are you sure you want to hear all of this? It's kind of a long story.'

Judy patted Denise on the knee. 'Only if you feel like telling me.'

The older woman's earnest expression suddenly reminded Denise of her mother. Strangely, it felt good to tell her about Kyle, so she went on. 'Well, at first, the doctors thought he was deaf. Then, they thought he was autistic. After that came PDD, or Pervasive Development Disorder, which is sort of like autism, only less severe. Then, they said he was retarded with ADD—Attention Deficit

Disorder—thrown in for good measure. It wasn't until maybe nine months ago that they finally settled on this diagnosis.'

'Where was the father during all of this?'

Denise shrugged. 'The father wasn't around. I hadn't expected to get pregnant. Kyle was an "oops" if you know what I mean.'

She paused and the two of them watched Kyle in silence. Judy seemed neither surprised nor shocked by the revelation.

'After Kyle was born, I took a leave of absence from the school where I was teaching. My mom had died, and I wanted to spend the first year or so with the baby. But after all this started happening, I couldn't go back to work. I was shuttling him all day long to doctors and evaluation centres and therapists until I finally came up with a therapy programme that we could do at home. None of that left me with enough time for a full-time job. I'd inherited this house but I couldn't sell it, and eventually the money ran out. So I guess the short answer to your question is that I had to move here, so that I could live rent-free and keep working with Kyle.'

Judy stared at her before finally patting her on the knee again. 'Pardon the expression, but you're a helluva mother. Not many people would make those kinds of sacrifices.'

Denise watched her son play in the dirt. 'I just want him to get better.'

Judy leaned back in her chair. 'You know, I remember watching Kyle when you were in the library. Never once did the thought occur to me that he was having any problems at all. He seemed like every other little boy there.'

'But he still has trouble speaking . . .'

'So did Einstein and Teller, but they turned out to be the greatest physicists in history.'

'How did you know about their speech problems?'

'Oh, you'd be amazed at the amount of trivia I've picked up over the years. I'm like a vacuum cleaner with that stuff, don't ask me why.'

'You should go on *Jeopardy*.'

'I would, but the host is so cute, I'd probably forget everything I know as soon as he said hello.'

'What would your husband think if he knew you'd said that?'

Judy's voice sobered slightly. 'He passed away a long time ago.'

'I'm sorry,' Denise began. 'I didn't know.'

'It's OK.'

'So . . . you never remarried?'

'No. I just didn't seem to have time to meet someone. Taylor was a handful—it was all I could do to keep up with him.'

'Boy, does that sound familiar. It seems like all I do is work with Kyle and work at the diner.'

'You work at Eights? With Ray Toler?'

'Uh-huh. I got the job when I moved here.'

From there, the conversation drifted easily to Denise's job and the endless projects that seemed to occupy Judy's time. Half an hour later, Kyle tired of playing with his trucks and he put them under the porch before wandering up to his mother. 'Can I have some macaroni and cheese?' *Ca-ah haf son concor cheese?*

'Macaroni and cheese?'

'Yes.'

'Sure, sweetie. Let me go make some.'

They all went into the kitchen, Kyle leaving dusty footprints on the floor. He went to the table and sat while Denise opened up the cupboard.

'Would you like to stay for lunch?'

Judy checked her watch. 'I'd love to but I can't. I have a meeting about the festival this weekend.'

'Festival?'

'Yeah. It's an annual event and gets everyone in the mood for summer. I hope you're coming. Kyle would love it.'

Denise's mind immediately leapt to the cost involved.

'I don't know if we can,' she finally said, thinking of an excuse. 'I have to work Saturday night.'

'Oh, you don't have to stay long—just come by during the day if you'd like. It is a lot of fun.'

Judy picked up her bag from the counter and they walked to the front door and stepped out onto the porch again.

'Thanks for coming by,' said Denise. 'It was nice to have adult conversation for a change.'

'I enjoyed it,' said Judy, giving her an impulsive hug.

Denise suddenly realised what she'd forgotten to mention. 'Oh, I didn't tell you that I ran into Taylor yesterday at the store.'

'I know. I talked to him last night.'

After a beat of awkward silence, Judy adjusted her bag strap. 'Let's do this again some time, OK?'

'I'd like that.'

Judy made her way down the steps and onto the gravel walkway. When she reached her car she turned to face Denise again. 'You know, Taylor's gonna be at the festival this weekend with the rest of the fire department. Their softball team plays at three.'

'Oh?' was all Denise could think to say.

'Well, just in case you do come by, that's where I'll be.'

Denise waved as Judy slipped behind the steering wheel and cranked the engine to life, the faint outline of a smile playing softly on her lips.

Chapter 5

'Hey there! I wasn't sure you two were going to make it,' Judy called out happily.

It was Saturday afternoon, a little after three, when Denise and Kyle made their way up the stand towards Judy.

'Hey, Judy . . . I didn't know that Edenton had so many people. It took us a while to make it through the crowds.'

Denise and Kyle had taken their time walking their bikes through town, both of them enjoying the energy of the festival. The streets had been closed to traffic and were teeming with people. Banners stretched across the road and craft stalls lined both sidewalks. In the central square, the carnival was in full swing.

Kyle wedged himself between Judy and his mother. Settling down, he pulled out one of the toy airplanes he'd brought with him.

Judy nudged him in the ribs. 'Hi, Kyle. How are you?'

With a serious expression, he held up his toy for her to see. 'Owpwane,' he said enthusiastically.

Though Denise knew it was his way of trying to communicate on a level he understood she nonetheless prodded him to answer correctly. 'Kyle, say, "I'm fine, thanks,"'

'I'm fine, thanks.' *I'n fie, kenks*. He turned his attention back to his toy. Denise slipped her arm round him and nodded towards the action on the field.

'So who exactly are we rooting for?'

'Either team, really. Taylor's at third base for the red team—that's the Chowan Volunteers. They're with the fire department. The blue team—the Chowan Enforcers—that's the police, the sheriffs and local troopers. They play for charity every year. The losing team has to pony up five hundred dollars for the library.'

'So the library wins either way?'

'That's the whole point,' Judy said. 'Actually, though, the guys take it very seriously. There are a lot of egos on the line out there. You know how men are.'

'What's the score?'

'Four two. The fire department is leading.'

For the next hour, Denise and Judy watched the game, chatting about Edenton and cheering for both teams. Kyle, however, grew bored and took to climbing and jumping, running here and there. With so many people around it made Denise nervous to lose sight of him, and she stood up to look for him on more than a few occasions.

Whenever she did, Taylor found his eyes darting towards her. He'd seen her arrive with Kyle, oblivious to the heads turning as she strode past. But Taylor had seen the men admiring the way she looked, her white shirt tucked into black shorts, long legs stretching down to sandals, dark wind-blown hair flowing past her shoulders. Her presence was distracting, and he couldn't seem to stop glancing her way. Once, his stare lasted a little too long and she waved.

He waved back with an embarrassed grin and turned away, wondering why on earth he suddenly felt like a damned teenager again.

IN THE SEVENTH INNING, the Volunteers were trailing fourteen to twelve and Taylor was waiting for his turn to bat. Kyle had taken a break from his activities and was standing near the fence when he saw Taylor taking his practice swings.

'Hewwo, Tayer,' he said happily.

Taylor turned at the sound of his voice and approached the fence.

'Hey there, Kyle. Good to see you. How you doing?'

'Eez fowman,' Kyle said pointing.

'I sure am. Are you having fun watching the game?'

Kyle held his airplane up for Taylor to see. 'Owpwane.'

'You're right. That's a nice airplane.'

Kyle handed it through the fence and Taylor hesitated before taking it. He examined it as Kyle watched him, a look of pride on his little face. Taylor heard his name being called to the plate.

'Thanks for showing me your airplane. Do you want it back?'

'You can hold it,' Kyle said. *You kin hode it.*

'OK, this'll be my good-luck charm. I'll bring it right back.' He made sure that Kyle could see him put it in his pocket. 'Is that all right?'

Kyle didn't answer, but he seemed to be fine with it.

Taylor jogged to home base.

Both Denise and Judy had seen what had just transpired.

'I think Kyle likes Taylor,' Denise said.

'I think,' Judy answered, 'the feeling's mutual.'

ON THE SECOND PITCH, Taylor smashed the ball into right field and took off at a full clip towards first base, while two others in scoring position made their way round the bags. The ball hit the ground and bounced three times before the fielder could reach it. Taylor rounded second, charging hard, and the ball reached the infield just as he arrived safely at third. Two runs had been scored, the game was tied. Then Taylor scored again. On his way to the dugout, he handed Kyle the airplane, a big grin on his face.

'I told you it would make me lucky, little man.'

'Yes, the airplane is good.' *Yes, ee owpwane ess goo.*

It would have been the perfect way to end the game, but alas, it wasn't meant to be. The Enforcers scored the winning run when Carl Huddle knocked one out of the park.

Denise and Judy made their way down from the seats, ready to head over to the park where food and beer were waiting. Judy pointed out where they'd be sitting.

'I'm helping to set up,' Judy said. 'Can I meet you over there?'

'Go ahead—I'll be there in a couple of minutes. I have to get Kyle.'

Kyle was still standing near the fence, watching Taylor gather his gear in the dugout when Denise approached him. He didn't turn, even after Denise had called his name, so she had to tap him on the shoulder to get his attention. 'Kyle, c'mon, let's go.'

'No,' he answered with a shake of his head.

'The game's over.'

Kyle looked up at her. 'No—he's not.' *No—eez not.*

'Kyle, would you rather go play?'

'He's not,' he said again, frowning, his tone dropping an octave. Denise knew exactly what that meant—it was one of the ways he showed frustration at his inability to communicate. It was also often the first step towards a screamfest, and more than anything, she didn't want to have that happen here.

'Kyle, he's not what?'

'No!' he said. He was angry now, his cheeks turning red. He shook his head in frustration, groping for the words. 'Eez not . . . Kye,' he finally said.

Denise was completely lost now. 'You're not Kyle?'

Kyle shook his head. 'Eez not Kye. Eez linno man.'

She ran through it again, making sure she understood what he was saying. 'Little man?' she asked.

Kyle nodded triumphantly and smiled, his anger receding.

'Eez linno man,' he said again and all Denise could do was stare at him. Little man. Oh Lord, how long was *this* going to last?

At that moment, Taylor approached, his gear bag thrown over his shoulder. 'Hey, Denise, how are you?'

Denise turned her attention to him, still flummoxed. 'I'm not exactly sure,' she answered honestly.

The three of them began walking across the park together and Denise recounted her exchange with Kyle. When she was finished, Taylor patted Kyle on the back. 'Little man, huh?'

'Yes. Eez linno man,' Kyle said proudly in response.

'Don't encourage him,' Denise said with a shake of the head.

'But he is a little man,' Taylor said in Kyle's defence. 'Aren't you?'

Kyle nodded, pleased to have someone on his side. Taylor unzipped his gear bag and pulled out an old baseball. He handed it to Kyle. 'Do you like baseball?'

'It's a ball,' Kyle answered. *Ess a baw*.

'It's not just a ball. It's a baseball,' he said seriously.

'Yes,' Kyle whispered. 'It's a baseball.' *Yes. Ess a bessbaw*.

He held the ball tightly in his small hand and seemed to study it, as if looking for a secret that only he could understand. Then, glancing up, he spotted a children's slide in the distance. All of a sudden, that took priority over everything else.

'He wants to run,' Kyle said. 'Over there.' He pointed to where he wanted to go. *Ee wanta wun . . . O'er dare*.

'OK, go ahead,' she said. 'Just don't go too far.'

Kyle dashed towards the kid's play area. Luckily, it was right next to the tables where they would be sitting—Judy had chosen the spot for just that reason.

'That little man thing isn't really a problem, is it?' Taylor asked.

'It shouldn't be . . . he went through a phase where he pretended to be Godzilla a couple of months ago. He wouldn't answer to anything else.'

'Godzilla?'

'Yeah, it's pretty funny, when you think back on it. But at the time, oh my. I remember we were at the store once and Kyle slipped away. I was walking through the aisles calling for Godzilla and you wouldn't believe the looks that people were giving me.'

Taylor laughed. 'That's great.'

'Yeah, well . . .' She rolled her eyes, communicating a mixture of contentment and exasperation. Glancing at him, her eyes caught his and lingered just an instant too long, before each of them turned away. They walked on in silence.

Out of the corner of his eye, however, Taylor still watched her. She was radiant in the warm June sunlight. Her eyes, he noticed, were the colour of jade. She was shorter than he was—maybe five six—and she moved with the easy grace of a person who knew her place in the world. He sensed her intelligence in the patient way she dealt with her son, and most of all, how much she loved him. To Taylor, those were things that really mattered. Melissa, he knew, had been right after all.

THE TABLES were piled high with enough food to feed a small army, which about equalled the number of people milling about in the area. Off to the side, where burgers and frankfurters were being grilled, were four large coolers filled with ice and beer. As they neared the coolers, Taylor tossed his gear bag off to one side, piling it with the others. He grabbed a beer. 'Would you like one?'

'Sure.'

He handed a can to her and she opened it. The beer was refreshing on such a hot day.

Taylor took a long pull just as Judy spotted them. She put a stack of paper plates on one of the tables, then walked over and gave Taylor a quick squeeze. 'Sorry your team lost,' she said playfully. 'But you owe me five hundred bucks.'

'Thanks for the moral support.'

Judy laughed and squeezed him again before turning her attention to Denise.

'Well, now that you're here, can I introduce you around?'

'Sure, but let me check on Kyle first.'

'He's fine—I saw him when he came over. He's playing on the slide.'

As if by radar, Denise was able to locate him almost immediately. He was indeed playing but he looked hot.

'Um . . . would it be OK if I got him something to drink?'

'Absolutely. What does he like? We've got Coke, Sprite, root beer?'

'Sprite.'

Taylor saw Melissa and Kim—Carl Huddle's pregnant wife—coming over to say hello. Melissa was wearing the same triumphant expression that she'd had the night he'd been over for dinner.

'Let me take it to him,' he offered hurriedly. 'I think a few people are coming over to say hello to you.'

'Are you sure?' Denise asked.

'I'm positive,' he answered emphatically, and took another pull from his beer as he headed towards Kyle.

Judy introduced Denise to Melissa and Kim and, over the next half an hour or so, to a dozen other people. Nearly all of them had children. Names were coming quickly—their own and their kids'—making it impossible for Denise to remember them all, though she did her best.

Lunch for the kids came next. They rushed to the tables from all over as the hot dogs were pulled from the grills.

Kyle didn't come with the rest of the children, and, strangely, Denise didn't see Taylor either. Curious, she looked towards the play area, and it was then that she saw the two of them. When she realised what they were doing, her breath caught in her throat.

Frozen, she watched as Taylor gently lobbed the baseball in Kyle's direction. Kyle stood with both arms straight out and close together. He didn't move a muscle as the ball sailed through the air, but as if by some magic, the ball dropped directly into his little hands.

Taylor McAden was playing catch with her son.

KYLE'S NEXT throw was off the mark—as many of them had been— and Taylor scrambled as the ball went past him, finally coming to a stop in the short grass. As he stepped over to retrieve it, he saw Denise approaching.

'Have you been doing this the whole time?' she asked, unable to hide her amazement. Kyle had never wanted to play catch before. Her surprise, though, wasn't limited to Kyle; it had to do with Taylor. He was playing with Kyle. Nobody played with Kyle.

Taylor nodded. 'Pretty much. He seems to like it.'

Kyle saw her and waved. 'Hello, Mommy.' *Hewwo, money.*

'Are you having fun?' she asked.

'He throws it,' he said excitedly. *Ee frows it.*

Denise couldn't help but smile. 'I see that. It was a good throw.'

Taylor pushed up the peak of his hat. 'He's got quite an arm sometimes,' he said, as if to explain why he'd missed Kyle's throw.

'How did you get him to do it?'

'What? Play catch?' He shrugged. 'Actually, it was his idea. After he finished his Sprite, he sort of sailed one at me. So I tossed it back and gave him some pointers on how to catch it. He caught on fast.'

'Throw it,' Kyle called out impatiently. *Frow it.*

'Here it comes,' Taylor said, lobbing the ball. It hit Kyle on the wrist before falling to the ground. Kyle immediately picked it up, aimed, then threw the ball back. This time, the ball was on target and Taylor was able to catch it. 'Good one,' he said quickly.

The ball went back and forth a few more times before Denise called out to Kyle, 'OK, sweetie, last one.'

Kyle knew what that meant and he eyed the ball carefully before throwing it. It went off to the right and once again Taylor wasn't able to catch it. Coming to a stop near Denise, she retrieved it just as Kyle started towards her.

'That's it? No argument?' Taylor asked, obviously impressed by Kyle's good-naturedness.

'No, he's pretty good at things like that.'

When Kyle reached her, she gave him a hug. 'Would you like to play on the slide?'

Kyle nodded and immediately headed towards the play area.

Once they were alone, Denise faced Taylor. 'That was really nice of you, but you know you didn't have to stay out here the whole time.'

'I know I didn't. I wanted to. He's a lot of fun.'

She smiled gratefully, thinking how seldom she'd heard someone say that about her son.

'I'm ready for a burger now,' Taylor said. 'I take it you've eaten?'

'Actually, I haven't, but we can't stay. It's almost five and I've still got to feed Kyle and get ready for work.'

'He can eat here—there's plenty of food.'

'Kyle doesn't eat hot dogs or chips. He's kind of a picky eater.'

Taylor nodded. For a long moment, he seemed to be lost in thought. 'Can I give you a lift home?'

'We rode our bikes here.'

Taylor nodded. 'I know.'

As soon as he said it, she knew it to be a key moment for both of them. She didn't need the ride and he knew it; he'd asked despite the fact that his friends and food were waiting nearby. It was obvious that he wanted her to say yes; his expression made that clear.

It would have been easy to say no. Her life was complex enough— did she really need to add something more to the mix? And she barely knew him . . . The thoughts registered in quick succession but despite them, she surprised herself by saying, 'I'd like that.'

Mitch and Melissa watched as Taylor, Denise and Kyle departed.

Mitch leaned towards his wife's ear, so that others wouldn't overhear him. 'So, what did you think of her?'

'She's nice,' Melissa said honestly. 'But you know how Taylor is. Where this all goes from here will really depend on him. I just hope that this time, he doesn't hurt anyone.'

TAYLOR LOADED THE BIKES into the back of his Dodge four-by-four with its oversized wheels, then, because the truck was high, helped Kyle scramble inside. Denise was next and Taylor accidentally brushed against her as he showed her where to grab to hoist herself up.

He started the engine and they headed towards the outskirts of town with Kyle between them. As if knowing she wanted to be alone with her thoughts, Taylor didn't say anything. From the corner of her eye, Denise could see him concentrating on the road.

Up ahead was Charity Road and Taylor slowed the truck, making the turn, then accelerating again. They were almost home.

A minute later, Taylor reached the gravel driveway and turned in, gradually applying the brakes until the truck came to a complete stop. He left the engine idling and Denise turned towards him, curious.

'Hey, little man,' he said. 'You wanna drive my truck?'

Kyle hesitated.

'C'mon,' Taylor said, motioning. 'You can drive it.' He pulled Kyle onto his lap, placing his hands on the upper part of the steering wheel while keeping his own hands close enough to grab it if necessary. He slowly let the clutch out and the truck began to inch forward.

'All right, let's go.'

Kyle, a little unsure, held the wheel steady as the truck began to roll up the drive. His eyes widened as he realised he really had control, and all at once he turned the wheel hard to the left. The truck responded and moved onto the grass, heading towards the fence before Kyle turned the wheel the other way.

He broke into a wide grin and turned towards his mother, a *look-what-I'm-doing* expression on his face. He laughed in delight, before turning the wheel once more.

'He's driving!' Kyle exclaimed. *Eez dryfeen!*.

The truck rolled towards the house, missing every tree (thanks to Taylor's adjustments in course) before finally stopping. Opening the driver's side door, Taylor lifted Kyle down.

As they watched him scramble to keep his balance before starting towards the house, neither of them said anything and Taylor finally turned away, clearing his throat.

'Let me go get your bikes,' he said.

Jumping out of the cab, he moved to the back of the truck and opened the rear latch. Denise sat unmoving. Once again, Taylor had surprised her. Twice in a single afternoon, he had done something kind for Kyle, and it had touched her deeply. As his mother, she could love and protect Kyle, but she couldn't make other people accept him. It was obvious, though, that Taylor already did. He treated Kyle like a normal little boy. After four and a half years, Kyle had finally made a friend. She composed herself before opening her door and jumping down.

Taylor lowered the bikes to the ground, then hopped out of the truck in one easy, fluid movement.

'Thanks for driving us home,' she said.

'I was glad to do it,' he replied quietly.

Standing close to him, she couldn't escape the images of Taylor playing catch with her son or letting Kyle steer the truck, and she knew then that she wanted to know more about Taylor McAden. She wanted to spend more time with him.

'Would you like to come in for a glass of tea?' she asked.

'That's sounds good, if it's OK.'

They rolled the bikes round to the back of the house, leaving them on the porch, then walked inside followed by Kyle.

'Let me get your tea,' she said, trying to hide the sudden nervousness in her voice.

From the refrigerator, she pulled out the jug of tea, then added a few ice cubes to the glasses. She passed one to Taylor, conscious of how close she was to him. Turning to Kyle, she hoped that Taylor wouldn't guess what she was feeling. 'Do you want something to drink?'

Kyle nodded. 'He wants some water.' *Ee wonse sum wonner*.

Thankful for the interruption of her thoughts, she got that as well and handed it to him.

'You ready for a tub? You're all sweaty.'

'Yes,' he said, and took a drink from his small plastic cup.

'Can you give me a minute to get his tub ready?' she asked Taylor.

'Sure, take your time.'

Denise led Kyle from the kitchen and a few moments later, Taylor heard the water start up. By the back door, he saw a small wooden table with a series of textbooks arranged across the top. Curious, he walked over and scanned the titles. Every one of them had to do with child development. On the shelf below were thick blue binders, labelled with Kyle's name.

The water shut off and Denise returned to the kitchen, conscious of how long it had been since she'd been alone with a man.

'Interesting reading,' Taylor said and motioned towards the binders. 'What are those?'

'Those are his journals. Whenever I work with Kyle, I record what he's able to say and how he says it so I can follow his progress.'

'It sounds like a lot of work.'

'It is.' She paused. 'Would you like to sit down?'

Taylor and Denise sat at the kitchen table and she explained Kyle's problem.

'Why is language so hard for him?'

'That's the magic question,' she answered. 'Nobody really knows the answer.'

Taylor stared into his glass. 'You know, he doesn't talk all that badly,' he said sincerely. 'I understood what he was saying, and I think he understands me, too.'

Denise ran her fingernail through one of the cracks in the table, feeling it was a kind—if not completely true—thing to say. 'I think that has a lot to do with you, not just Kyle. You're very patient with him, which most people aren't. You remind me of some of the teachers I used to work with.'

'You were a teacher?'

'I taught for three years, right up until Kyle was born.'

'Did you like it?'

'I loved it. I worked with second graders and that's just such a great age. Kids like their teachers and are still eager to learn. It makes you feel like you can really make a difference in their lives.'

Taylor took a sip, watching her closely over the rim of his glass. 'Are you going to go back to it?'

'Some day,' she answered. 'Maybe in a few years. We'll have to see what happens in the future.' She sat a little straighter in her seat. 'But what about you? You said you were a contractor?'

Taylor nodded. 'Twelve years now.'

'And you build homes?'

'I have in the past, but generally I focus on remodelling. When I first started, those were the only jobs I could get because no one else wanted them. I like it, too—to me, it's more challenging than building something new. You have to work with what's already there and nothing is ever as easy as you suspected it would be.'

'So what do you like to do? In your spare time, I mean?'

'My job and the fire department keep me fairly busy, but if I can get away, I go hunting.'

'That wouldn't be popular with my friends in Atlanta.'

'What can I say? I'm just a good old boy from the South.'

Denise was struck by how different he was to the men she used to date. He seemed content. He wasn't yearning for fame or glory, he wasn't striving to earn zillions of dollars, full of plans to get ahead. In a way, he almost seemed to be a throwback to a time when the world wasn't as complicated as it was now, when simple things were the things that mattered most.

Kyle called out from the bathroom and Denise turned at the sound of his voice. Glancing at her watch, she saw that Rhonda would be there to pick her up in half an hour and she wasn't ready.

Taylor finished the last of his glass. 'I should probably be going.'

Kyle called out again and this time Denise answered. 'I'll be there in a second, sweetie.' Then to Taylor: 'Are you going back to the barbecue?'

Taylor nodded. 'They're probably wondering where I am.'

She gave him a mischievous smile. 'Do you think they're whispering about us?'

'Probably. But don't worry. I'll make sure they know that it didn't mean anything.'

Her eyes leapt to his, and under his gaze she felt something stir inside her, sudden and unexpected. Before she could stop the words, they were already out. 'It meant something to me.'

Taylor studied her in silence, considering what she'd said, as an embarrassed blush began to surge through her cheeks.

'Are you working tomorrow evening?' he finally asked.

'No,' she said a little breathlessly.

Taylor took a deep breath. 'Can I take you and Kyle to the carnival tomorrow?'

'I'd like that,' she said quietly.

Chapter 6

Sunday was mercifully cooler than the day before. Hazy clouds had blown in that morning keeping the sun from venting its full fury, and the evening breeze picked up as Taylor pulled up the driveway.

Denise stepped out onto the porch, dressed in faded jeans and a short-sleeved shirt. She hoped she didn't look as nervous as she felt. It was her first date in what seemed like for ever. She'd spent almost an hour trying to find something to wear. It wasn't until she saw that he was wearing jeans as well that she breathed a little easier.

'Hey there,' he said. 'I hope I'm not late.'

'No, not at all,' she said. 'You're right on time.'

It took only a minute before they were ready to go. As she locked the door on the way out, Kyle took off, running across the yard.

'Hewwo, Tayer,' he called out.

Taylor helped Kyle into the cab, just as he'd done the day before.

'Hey, Kyle. Are you looking forward to the carnival?'

'It's a monster truck,' he said happily. *Ess a monstew twuck.*

After scrambling onto the seat, the boy climbed behind the wheel again, trying unsuccessfully to turn it from side to side.

Denise heard Kyle making engine sounds as she drew near. 'He's been talking about your truck all day,' she explained.

Taylor nodded towards the cab. 'Should I let him drive again?'

'I don't think he's going to give you the chance to say no.'

As Taylor made room for her to climb up, she caught a trace of his cologne. Nothing fancy, but she was touched that he'd put it on. Kyle scooted over to make room for him, then immediately crawled into Taylor's lap once he was seated.

Taylor grinned as he turned the key. 'All right, little man, let's go.'

They made a big figure 'S', bumping haphazardly over the lawn before finally reaching the road. At that point, Kyle scooted off Taylor's lap, satisfied, and Taylor turned the wheel, heading into town.

The ride downtown took only a few minutes.

They turned right onto a side street, found a parking space close to the main road and walked towards the carnival.

'So, Kyle, what do you want to do?' Denise asked.

He immediately pointed to the mechanical swing—a ride in which dozens of metal swings rotated in circles, first forwards then backwards. Each child had his own seat and they were screaming in terror and delight. Kyle watched it going round and round, transfixed.

'Do you want to ride the swing?' Denise asked him.

'Swing,' he said, with a nod.

'Say, "I want to ride the swing."'

'I want to ride the swing,' he whispered. *Wonta wide ee sweeng*.

'OK.'

Denise spotted the ticket booth and began to reach into her bag. Taylor, however, raised his hands to stop her.

'My treat. I asked, remember?'

After Taylor had bought the tickets, they waited in line until the ride stopped and emptied. Nervously, Denise led Kyle to his seat. She lifted him in then lowered the safety bar for him as Taylor waited outside the gate.

She put his hands on the bar. 'Now, hold on and don't let go.'

Kyle's response was to laugh in delight.

'Hold on,' she said again, more seriously this time, and Kyle squeezed the bar.

She walked back to Taylor's side and prayed that Kyle would listen to her. A minute later the ride slowly began to pick up speed. By the second rotation, the swings were beginning to fan out, carried by their momentum. As Kyle swung by, it was impossible not to hear his high-pitched giggle. As he came back round, she noticed his hands were still right where they should be. She breathed a sigh of relief.

'It's the first time he's ever been on a ride like this,' she told Taylor.

'Haven't you ever taken him to a carnival?'

'I didn't think he was ready for one before.'

'Because he has trouble talking?'

'Partially.' She hesitated under Taylor's serious gaze. Suddenly she wanted more than anything for him to understand Kyle.

'People sometimes think that language is just about conversation, but for children, it's much more than that. It's how they learn about the world. It's how they learn that burners on the stove are hot, without having to touch them. It's how they know that crossing the street is dangerous, without having to be hit by a car. Without the ability to understand language, how can I teach him those things? If Kyle can't understand the concept of danger, how can I keep him safe? When he wandered away into the swamp that night . . . Well, you yourself said he didn't seem to be frightened when you found him.' She looked at Taylor earnestly. 'It makes perfect sense—to me at least. He didn't know enough to be afraid. I can't tell you how many close calls there have been. Climbing too high and wanting to jump, riding too close to the road, wandering away, walking up to growling dogs . . .'

She closed her eyes for a moment before going on.

'But those are only part of my worries. Most of the time, I worry about the obvious things: whether he'll ever be able to go to a regular school, whether he'll ever make friends.'

She paused. 'I don't want you to think that I regret having Kyle, because I don't. I love him with all my heart. But it's not exactly what I imagined raising children would be like.'

'I didn't realise,' Taylor said gently.

As if suspecting that she'd confided too much, she offered a rueful smile. 'I probably made it sound pretty hopeless, didn't I?'

'Not really,' he lied. In the waning sunlight, she was radiant.

She reached over and touched his arm. Her hand was soft and warm. 'I know I made it sound terrible, but I didn't tell you about the good things.'

Taylor raised his eyebrows slightly. 'There are good things too?' he asked, prompting an embarrassed laugh from Denise.

'Next time I need to pour my heart out, remind me to stop, OK?'

Though she tried to pass the comment off, her voice betrayed her anxiety. Taylor suspected that he was the first person she'd ever really confided in, this way and that it wasn't the time for jokes.

'So tell me about the good things,' he said quietly.

Denise glanced briefly at Taylor. 'Kyle's getting better. Last year, his vocabulary was only fifteen to twenty words. This year, it's in the hundreds, and at times, he puts three and four words together in a single sentence. And for the most part, he makes his wishes known now. He tells me when he's hungry, when he's tired. He's only been doing that for the last few months.'

She took a deep breath. 'You have to understand . . . Kyle works *so* hard *every* day. While other kids play outside, he has to sit in his chair, staring at picture books, trying to figure out the world itself. It takes him hours to learn things that other kids might learn in minutes. But you know, he just keeps on trying, day after day, word by word. And he doesn't complain, he just does it.'

She took a ragged breath, struggling to maintain her composure. 'You have no idea how far he's come, Taylor. If you knew where he started and how many obstacles he's overcome so far—you'd be *so* proud of him . . .' Despite her efforts, tears began to flood her eyes. 'And you'd know that Kyle has more *heart*, more *spirit*, than any other child I've ever known . . . He is the most wonderful little boy that any mother could wish to have. Despite everything, he is the greatest thing that's ever happened to me.'

All those years of wanting to say those words to someone. All those feelings—both the good and the bad—it was such a relief to finally let it all go. She was suddenly intensely thankful that she'd done so, and hoped in her heart that Taylor would understand.

Unable to respond, Taylor tried to swallow the lump that had formed in his throat. Without a word, he reached for her hand and took it gently in his. With her free hand, she wiped at a tear that had drifted down her cheek, and sniffled.

'That was the most beautiful thing I think I've ever heard,' he finally said.

The ride ended and Kyle called out from his seat, 'Swing!' He almost sang the word. *Sweeeng!*

'Do you want to ride the swing again?' Denise shouted.

'Yes,' he answered, nodding.

Taylor had to let go of Denise's hand so he could walk over and present the additional tickets. When he returned, the moment had passed; Denise was leaning on the barrier, resting on her elbows, and he decided simply to let it go. Yet standing beside her, he could still feel the lingering sensation of her touch on his skin.

They spent another hour at the carnival, riding the Ferris Wheel—the three of them crammed into the wobbly seat with Taylor pointing out the places that could be seen from the top—and the Octopus, a gut-twisting ride that Kyle wanted to ride over and over again.

Denise relished every minute of it. It was gratifying to watch Kyle trying—and *enjoying!*—new things. Everything was just right, as she had barely dared to hope it would be.

ONCE THEY GOT HOME, Denise got a cup of milk and led Kyle into his room. She helped him change into his pyjamas, and by the time she finished reading him a story, his eyes were already closing. Quietly slipping from the room, she left the door partially open.

Taylor was waiting for her in the kitchen, his long legs stretched out under the table.

'Would you like something to drink?' she asked.

'What do you have?'

'Iced tea.'

'And?'

She shrugged. 'Water?'

He couldn't help but smile. 'Tea's fine.'

She poured two glasses and handed one to him. They made their way out onto the porch and sat in the rockers, Denise closest to the door so she could listen for Kyle if he woke up.

'Now this is nice,' Taylor said, after making himself comfortable. 'Sitting outside. I feel like I'm on an episode of *The Waltons*.'

Denise laughed. 'Don't you like to sit on the porch?'

'Sure, but I hardly ever do it. I never seem to have time any more.'

'A good old boy from the South like yourself?' she said, repeating the words he'd used the day before. She grinned. 'I would have thought a guy like you would sit outside on your porch with a banjo, playing song after song, a dog lying at your feet.'

'If I didn't know you were from the South, I'd think you were insulting me.'

'But because I'm from Atlanta?'

'I'll let it slide this time.' He felt the corners of his mouth curling into a smile. 'So what do you miss about the big city?'

'Not a lot. I suppose if I were younger this place would drive me crazy. But I don't need big malls or fancy places to eat, or museums any more.'

'So what was your life like? Growing up in Atlanta, I mean?'

'Probably a little bit like yours.'

'What do you mean?' he asked curiously.

She met his eyes. 'We were both only children, raised by widowed mothers who grew up in Edenton.'

At her words, Taylor felt something flinch inside.

Denise went on. 'You know how it is. You feel a little different because other people have two parents, even if they're divorced. It's like you grow up knowing that you're missing something important that everyone else has, but you don't know exactly what it is. I remember hearing my friends talking about how their fathers wouldn't let them stay out late or didn't like their boyfriends. It used to make me so angry because they didn't even realise what they had. Do you know what I mean?'

Taylor nodded, realising with sudden clarity how much they had in common.

'But other than that, my life was pretty typical. I lived with my mom, I went to Catholic schools, shopped with my friends, went to the proms, and worried every time I got a pimple.'

'You call that typical?'

'It is if you're a girl.'

There was a brief lull in the conversation before Taylor finally spoke again. 'Do you mind if I ask you a question?'

'It depends on the question,' she answered, trying not to tense up.

Taylor glanced away. 'Where's Kyle's father?'

Denise had known it was coming. 'He's not around. I didn't really even know him. Kyle wasn't supposed to happen.'

'Does he know about Kyle?'

'I called him when I was pregnant. He told me straight up he didn't want anything to do with him.'

'Has he ever seen him?'

'No.'

'Do you ever wish he was around?'

'Oh, heavens no,' she said quickly. 'Not him. I mean, I would have liked Kyle to have had a father. But it wouldn't have been someone like him. And besides, for Kyle to have a father—the right kind, I mean, and not just someone who calls himself that—he'd also have to be my husband.'

Taylor nodded in understanding.

'But now, Mr McAden, it's your turn,' Denise said. 'I've told you everything about me, but you haven't reciprocated.' She was silent for a moment, then finally met his eyes. 'Tell me about your father,' she said softly.

The words startled him. It wasn't the question he'd expected and Taylor felt himself stiffen slightly.

The moon had risen and now hovered above the tree line. In the milky light, an occasional bat skittered by. Denise had to lean in close in order to hear him.

'My father passed away when I was nine,' he began.

Denise watched him carefully. He was speaking slowly, as if gathering his thoughts, and she could see his reluctance in every line of his face.

'But he was more than just my father. He was my best friend too.'

He hesitated. 'He and I were inseparable. As soon as five o'clock would roll round, I'd camp out on the steps and wait for his truck to come up the driveway. He worked in the lumber mill and I'd run for him as soon as he opened his door and jump into his arms. He was strong—even when I got bigger, he never told me to stop. I'd put my arms round him and take a deep breath. He worked hard and even in winter, I could smell the sweat and sawdust on his clothes. He called me little man.'

Denise nodded in recognition.

'My mom always waited inside while he asked me what I did that day. And I'd just talk so fast, trying to say as much as I could before he went inside. But even though he was tired he never rushed me. He'd let me say everything on my mind and only when I was all talked out, would he finally put me down. Then we'd head inside.'

Taylor swallowed hard, doing his best to think about the good things. 'Anyway, we used to go fishing every weekend. We'd go out in the boat and sit together for hours. Sometimes he'd tell me stories and he'd answer whatever questions I asked as best he could. My father never graduated from high school, but even so, he was pretty good at explaining things. And if I asked him something he didn't know, he'd say that too.

'I never saw him get angry, I never once heard him raise his voice. When I'd act up, all he had to do was say, "That's enough now, son." And I'd stop because I knew I was disappointing him. I guess I just didn't want to let him down.'

Taylor took a long, deep breath.

'He sounds like a wonderful man,' Denise said, knowing she'd stumbled upon something important about Taylor, but uncertain of its shape and meaning.

'He was.'

The finality of his voice made it clear that the discussion was closed, although Denise suspected there was far more to be said.

'How old were you when your father died?' he asked, breaking the silence.

'Four.'

'Do you remember him like I remember mine?'

'Not really. I just remember images, him reading me stories or the feeling of his whiskers when he kissed me. I was always happy when he was around. Even now, not a day goes by when I don't wish I could turn back the clock and change what happened.'

As soon as she said it, Taylor turned to her with a startled expression, knowing she'd hit it right on the head. How had she known? In just a few words, she'd explained the very thing he'd tried to explain to Valerie and Lori. But even though they'd listened with compassion, they'd never really understood. But now he'd finally heard someone else echo the things that he had known, and for the second time that evening, he reached for her hand.

They held hands in silence, fingers loosely intertwined, each afraid that speaking would break the spell. Lazy clouds, silver in the moonlight, lay scattered in the sky and the air had cooled slightly. A sea breeze had blown through earlier, leaving a stillness in its wake. Denise sipped her tea, listening as insects buzzed noisily around the porch light. The evening was coming to an end, she could feel that.

He finished his glass, then set it down.

'I should probably go. I have an early day tomorrow.'

'I'm sure,' she said.

He stood up. 'You're a good mother, Denise.' He was loath to release her hand. 'Even though it's hard, even though it's not what you expected, I can't help but believe that everything happens for a reason. Kyle needed someone like you.'

With reluctance, he turned away. The floor of the porch creaked as he moved to the steps, Denise beside him. She looked up at him.

He almost kissed her then, but couldn't tell if she really wanted that from him, and at the last second, he held back. The evening had already been more memorable than any evening he'd spent in a long time and he didn't want to spoil it. Instead, he took a small step backwards, as if to give her more space.

'I had a wonderful time tonight,' he said.

'So did I.'

He wanted to tell her that she had something inside her, something he'd looked for in the past but had never hoped to find. He wanted to say all these things but found that he couldn't.

He smiled faintly, then made his way down the steps in the moonlight, towards his truck.

Standing on the porch, she waved one last time as Taylor headed down the drive, his truck's headlights shining in the distance.

After he had left, Denise walked inside. The kitchen was quiet, and she could hear the crickets chirping outside. She looked out of the window. The sky was full of stars, stretching to eternity, and she stared at them, smiling, thinking of Taylor McAden.

TAYLOR WAS SITTING in his kitchen two evenings later, doing paperwork, when he got the call. An accident on the bridge between a gasoline tanker truck and a car.

Grabbing his keys, he was out of the door less than a minute later; within five minutes, he was one of the first on the scene. Stopping his truck, he scrambled out without shutting the door. Cars were backed up in either direction on both sides of the bridge, and people were gawping at the horrific sight.

The cab of the tanker had rolled up onto the back of the Honda, completely crushing the rear, before smashing through the wire barrier that lined the bridge. The driver of the tanker had locked the wheel as he'd slammed on the brakes and the vehicle had slewed across both lanes of the road. The car, pinned beneath the front of the cab, hung off the bridge, balanced precariously. Its roof had been torn open as it ripped through the wire along the side of the bridge, and the only thing that kept it from falling into the river eighty feet below was the weight of the tanker's cab, and that looked far from stable. Its engine was smoking badly and fluid was leaking onto the Honda beneath.

When Mitch saw Taylor, he came rushing forward to fill him in.

'The driver of the truck's all right, but there's still someone in the car. Man or woman, we can't tell yet—whoever it is is slumped over.'

'What about the tanks on that truck?'

'Three-quarters full.'

'If that cab explodes, will the tanks go with it?'

'The driver says that it shouldn't if the lining wasn't damaged in the accident. I didn't see a leak, but I can't be sure.'

Two fire trucks arrived and seven men jumped out already in their fire-retardant suits. They took one look at the situation, started barking orders and went for the hoses. Mitch and Taylor scrambled for the suits that had been brought for them and slipped them over their clothing.

Sergeant Huddle arrived; so did an additional two police officers from Edenton. After a quick consultation, they used a bullhorn to order people to vacate the area.

The truck was now smoking more heavily. Controlling the fire would be critical; rescuing the trapped passenger, however, was foremost in everyone's mind. But how to reach the passenger? Jostling the car or adding weight might be enough to cause it to tip.

'Let's use the ladder on the truck,' Taylor urged. 'We'll extend it out over the car and we'll used the cable to haul the person out.'

'It might not support the two of you,' Joe said quickly. As the chief and only full-time employee of the fire department, he was always the calming influence in a crisis like this.

'What other choice do we have? I'll be out and back before you know it,' Taylor said.

Joe had expected him to volunteer. Twelve years ago, during Taylor's second year with the crew, Joe had asked him why he was always the first to volunteer for the riskiest assignments. Taylor struck him as a man with something to prove. But Taylor offered a simple explanation: 'My dad died and I know what it's like for a kid to grow up alone. I don't want that to happen to anyone else.'

Taylor collected the rope he needed and attached it to his harness with a clip. When the fire truck was in place, Taylor climbed up and secured the other end of the rope to the ladder a few rungs from the end. A cable was also run from the rear of the truck, up to the ladder itself. On the hook at its far end a safety harness was attached.

Taylor lay on his belly as the ladder slowly began to extend towards the car. Keep balanced . . . Stay as far back as possible . . . When he still had ten or twelve feet to go he felt the ladder growing a little unsteady, creaking beneath him.

Eight feet. He was close enough now to reach out and touch the front of the truck. He could feel the heat from the flames, could see them lapping at the mangled roof of the car. As the ladder extended, it began to rock slightly.

Four feet. He was over the car now . . . getting close to the front windshield. And then the ladder came to a rattling halt. Taylor looked back over his shoulder, to see if some glitch had occurred. But by the expressions on the other firemen's faces, he knew that the ladder was extended as far as it would go.

The ladder wobbled precariously as he untied the rope attached to his own harness. Grabbing the other harness for the passenger, he began inching forward, towards the end of the ladder.

Eighty feet below, the water was the colour of coal. He could hear himself breathing as he moved forward; he could feel his heart thudding in his chest. Beneath him, the ladder bounced and shuddered with every movement and he could hear the flames licking beneath the truck. Then, without warning, the car beneath him started to rock. The nose dipped slightly and straightened, then dipped again before finally righting itself. He heard a low moan.

'Don't move!' Taylor shouted instinctively. He secured his rope on the final rung, tying the knot quickly. Pulling his legs forward, he squeezed through the rungs, doing his best to move as fluidly and slowly as possible. The ladder rocked as if it would break in two. He settled himself as if he were on a swing. Holding on to the rope with one hand, he reached downwards towards the passenger with the other, gradually testing the ladder's strength. Pushing through the windshield to the dashboard, he saw that he was too high, but he caught sight of the person he was trying to save. A male in his twenties or thirties, about the same size as Taylor. Seemingly incoherent, he was thrashing his arms and legs, causing the car to rock violently. The passenger's movement was a double-edged sword, Taylor quickly realised. It meant that he could probably be removed from the car without the risk of spinal injury; it also meant that his movement might finally tip the car.

His mind racing, Taylor reached up and grabbed the safety harness, pulling it towards him. The cable grew tight.

'More cable!' he shouted, and a moment later he felt it slacken and he began to lower it. Once it was in position, he shouted for them to stop. He unhooked one side of the safety harness so that he could hopefully work it round the man's body and reattach it.

He bent down again, but saw with frustration that he still couldn't reach. He needed another couple of feet.

'Can you hear me?' Taylor called into the car. 'If you can understand what I'm saying, answer me.'

He heard the moan again and, though the passenger shifted, it was obvious that he was at best semiconscious.

Taylor quickly evaluated the scene. The front of the car seemed to be undamaged and the man was lying half on the seat, half on the floor beneath the steering wheel, wedged in, but looking as if he could be pulled out through the sheared opening in the roof. The truck was radiating extreme heat now and sweat began to drip down Taylor's face.

Suddenly, he heard a loud whooshing sound and flames exploded from the engine of the truck, leaping towards him. He pulled up, instinctively covering his face as the flames receded again.

'You OK?' Joe shouted.

'I'm fine!'

No time for debate . . . Taylor reached for the cable, pulling it towards him. He quickly worked the hook that held the safety harness, until it was centred beneath him. Then he unhooked his own harness from the support rope. Crouching low enough to reach the passenger, he reached for the safety harness. and with one hand tried to work it round the passenger's chest, beneath his arms.

Flames began to sear the roof of the Honda, only inches from his head. Rivers of sweat poured into his eyes, blurring his vision. Adrenalin surged through his limbs.

'Wake up!' he shouted. 'You've got to help me here!'

The man, finally woken by some flicker of self-preservation, raised his head slightly.

'Put the harness under your arm!'

He didn't seem to understand but the new angle of his body presented an opportunity. Taylor immediately worked one end of the harness towards the man's arm then slipped it underneath.

'Help me! Wake up! We're almost out of time here!'

The man's other arm, wedged between his body and the steering wheel, looked stuck. Without worrying what might happen now, Taylor shoved the body. The ladder dipped precariously, as did the car. Somehow, however, the shove was enough. This time, the man opened his eyes and began to struggle out from between the steering wheel and the seat. The car was rocking heavily. Weakly, the passenger freed his other arm, then raised it slightly as he tried to crawl onto the seat. Taylor worked the safety harness round him, cinching it tight.

'We're gonna pull you out now. We're almost out of time.'

The man simply rolled his head, suddenly drifting into unconsciousness again.

'Bring him up!' Taylor screamed. 'Passenger is secure!'

The cable tightened and the ladder began to groan and shudder. But instead of the passenger coming up, the ladder seemed to be lowering . . .

Taylor could feel it on the verge of buckling, before, finally, he and the passenger began to rise. Up an inch. Then another.

Then the cable stopped recoiling. Instead, the ladder began to descend again. Taylor knew instantly that it couldn't support both of them.

'Stop!' Taylor shouted. 'The ladder's gonna go!'

He had to get off the cable and he had to get off the ladder. After making sure once more that the man wouldn't get snagged, he retreated hand over hand across the ladder, like a kid crossing the monkey bars. One rung . . . two . . . three . . . four. The car was no longer beneath him and yet he could still feel the ladder creeping lower.

It was while crossing the rungs that the flames ripped into a frenzy, straining with deadly intensity at the gas tanks. He'd seen engine fires numerous times—and this one was seconds away from blowing.

He looked towards the bridge. As if in slow motion, he saw the firemen, his friends, motioning frantically with their arms, screaming at him to hurry, to get off the ladder, to get to safety before the truck exploded. But he knew there was no way he could make it back to the fire truck in time and still get the passenger out.

'Pull him out!' Taylor shouted hoarsely. 'He's got to come up now!'

Then, dangling high above the water, he loosened his grip and let go. In an instant, he was swallowed by the evening air. The river was eighty feet below.

'THAT WAS THE DUMBEST, most moronic thing I've ever seen you do,' Mitch said matter-of-factly, fifteen minutes later when they were sitting on the banks of the Chowan River. 'I mean, I've seen some stupid stunts in my life, but that one takes the cake.'

'We got him out, didn't we?' Taylor said. He was drenched and had lost one boot while swimming for safety. In the aftermath, after the adrenalin drained away, he felt his body retreating into a kind of exhausted lull. He felt as if he hadn't slept for days, his muscles seemed rubbery, his hands were shaking uncontrollably.

After hitting the water, the pressure had sucked him under and held him for several seconds. He was spun and twisted like a rag in a washing machine, before fighting his way to the surface where he drew a gasping breath. By the time he'd swum to the bank, he was nauseated and dizzy, the events of the past hour finally hitting home. That was when his hands had begun to tremble.

Mitch had found him sitting in the mud, legs drawn up, head resting on his knees.

'You shouldn't have jumped,' he said, patting him on the back. 'But I'm just glad you're all right.'

Taylor was too tired to speak.

LATER THAT EVENING, once the situation on the bridge was under control, Taylor got in his car to head home. As he'd suspected would happen, Joe grilled him in earnest, walking him through every decision and the reasons for it. Taylor did his best to convince his boss that he hadn't acted recklessly. 'Look,' he finally said, 'I didn't want to jump. But if I hadn't, neither of us would have made it.'

To that, Joe had no reply.

Taylor was still shivering as he made his way home. He'd left the lights on in his haste to leave and the house was welcoming when he stepped inside. He set his keys on the counter and made his way to the bathroom where he took a quick hot shower.

Afterwards, he ran a brush through his hair, then walked through the house, turning everything off before slipping into bed.

He needed to sleep, but when he closed his eyes, images of the past hours replayed in his mind like a movie. And in each case, they were different from what had actually happened. In one sequence after another, he watched helplessly as everything went wrong. He saw himself reaching for the victim, heard the crack as the ladder snapped in two, sending both of them to their death . . . Or he watched in horror as the victim reached for his outstretched hand, just as the car tipped over the bridge . . . Or . . .

The nightmare he'd been living with since childhood—

His eyes snapped open. His hands were trembling again, his throat dry. Breathing rapidly, he could feel the adrenalin surge into his system. Turning his head, he checked the clock. The red glowing digital lights showed that it was nearly eleven thirty.

He turned on the lamp by his bedside and began dressing quickly. He didn't understand his decision, not really. All he knew was that he needed to talk. To Denise.

THE PARKING LOT at Eights was almost empty when he arrived. Taylor pulled his truck into the space nearest the door and checked his watch. The diner would be closing in ten minutes.

He pushed open the wooden door and heard a small bell jingle, signalling his entrance. Ray, who was cleaning up in the back, turned at the sound of the door and waved. 'Hey, Taylor. Long time no see. You comin' in to eat?'

'Oh, hey, Ray.' He looked from side to side. 'Not really.'

Ray shook his head, chuckling to himself. 'Somehow, I didn't think so,' he said, almost mischievously. 'Denise'll be out in a minute. You here to ask if you can drive her home?'

When Taylor didn't answer right away, Ray's eyes gleamed. 'Did you think you were the first to come in here, that lost puppy-dog look on your face? There's one or two a week hoping for the same thing.' He grinned. 'She's somethin', ain't she? Pretty as a flower. But don't worry, she ain't said yes to one of 'em yet.'

'I wasn't . . .' Taylor stammered, suddenly at a loss for words.

'Of course you were.' He winked. 'I'll tell her you're here.'

All Taylor could do was stare as Ray vanished from sight. Almost immediately, Denise came out from the kitchen area.

'Taylor?' she said, clearly surprised. 'What are you doing here?' She started towards him, smiling curiously.

'I wanted to see you,' he said quietly.

As she walked towards him he took in her white, work-stained apron over a marigold-yellow dress, white sneakers. Her hair was pulled back into a ponytail and her face was shiny from perspiration.

She was aware of his appraisal, but as she neared, she saw something else in his eyes, something she'd never seen before.

'Are you OK?' she asked. 'You look like you've seen a ghost.'

'I don't know,' he muttered, almost to himself.

She stared up at him, concerned, then looked over her shoulder. 'Hey, Ray? Can I take a quick break here for a second?'

'Take your time, sweetheart. I'm just about done here, anyway.'

She faced Taylor again. 'Do you want to sit down and talk?'

It was exactly the reason he'd come, but Ray's comments had thrown him off.

'Maybe I shouldn't have come,' he said.

Denise smiled sympathetically. 'I'm glad you did,' she said softly. 'What happened?'

Her eyes searched his, never turning away. Those wonderful eyes. God, she was lovely. Taylor swallowed, his mind whirling, confused by the faint smell of her shampoo, his desire to put his arms round her and tell her everything about the waking nightmares, how he longed for her to listen . . . 'There was an accident on the bridge tonight,' he said abruptly.

Denise nodded. 'I know. It was quiet here all night. Hardly anyone came in because the bridge was closed. Were you there?'

Taylor nodded.

She reached out, her fingers gently taking hold of his arm. 'Hold on, OK? I've got a few things to do and then I'll be ready to go. Why don't you wait for me? We can talk at my house.'

TAYLOR CARRIED Kyle to the truck, the boy's head on his shoulder. Once inside, Kyle curled round Denise, never waking in the process.

Once they were home, the procedure was reversed, and after sliding Kyle from Denise's lap, Taylor carried him into the house to his bedroom. He put Kyle in his bed and Denise pulled the sheet over him. She left the door half open as they both crept out.

In the living room, Denise turned on a lamp as Taylor sat on the couch. She sat on a separate chair.

Neither one of them had said anything on the way home, but once they were seated, Denise went straight to the point.

'What happened on the bridge tonight?'

Taylor told her everything; the rescue, what Mitch had said, the images he'd been tormented by afterwards.

When he had finished, Denise leaned forward. 'You saved him?'

'I didn't. We all did,' he said, automatically making the distinction.

'But how many of you went out on the ladder?'

Taylor didn't answer and Denise rose from her seat to sit next to him on the couch.

'You're a hero,' she said, a small grin on her face. 'Just like you were when Kyle was lost.'

'No, I'm not,' he said, images of the past surfacing, against his will.

'Yes, you are.' She reached for his hand. For the next twenty minutes, they talked about inconsequential things. The simple drift of the conversation was soothing; Denise did her best to keep Taylor's thoughts away from the accident and it seemed to be working. His answers came more slowly and his breath settled into a deeper rhythm as the demands of the day finally began to take their toll.

Denise held his hand, watching as his eyes closed and he nodded off. Rising from the couch, she retrieved a blanket from her bedroom. With a slight nudge, Taylor laid down and she draped the blanket over him.

Only partially awake, he mumbled that he should go; Denise whispered that he was fine where he was. 'Go to sleep,' she murmured as she turned off the lamp.

She went to her own room and slipped out of her work clothes, then into her pyjamas. Crawling into bed, she closed her eyes. The fact that Taylor McAden was sleeping in the other room was the last thing she remembered before she, too, nodded off.

'HEWWO, TAYER,' Kyle said happily.

Taylor opened his eyes, squinting against the early-morning sunlight pouring in the living-room window, and saw Kyle standing over him. It took a second to register where he was. Checking his watch, he saw that it was a little after six in the morning.

'Good morning, Kyle. How are you?'

'He's sleeping.' *Eez sweepeen*.

'Where's your mom?'

'He's on the couch.' *Eez on-ah coush*.

'I sure was.' Taylor stretched his arms out to the side and yawned.

'Good morning,' he heard behind him. Over his shoulder, he saw Denise coming out of her room, wearing pink pyjamas and socks

He stood up. 'Good morning. I reckon I must have dozed off last night.'

'You were tired.'

'Sorry about that.'

'It's OK,' she said.

Kyle had wandered to the corner of the living room to play with his toys. Denise walked over and kissed him on the top of his head. 'Good morning, sweetie. Are you hungry?'

'No.'

Denise returned her attention to Taylor. 'How about you? Are you hungry?'

'I don't want you to have to cook up something special.'

'I was going to offer you some Cheerios,' she said quickly, eliciting a smile from Taylor.

'And milk?' he asked.

'No, we use water in our cereal here,' she said seriously.

He looked at her, wondering whether or not to believe her, and Denise laughed, the sound melodic.

'Of course we have milk, you goob.'

'Goob?'

'It's a term of endearment. It means I like you,' she said with a wink.

'In that case, I'd be glad to stay.'

'So WHAT'S on your agenda today?' Taylor asked. They'd finished breakfast and Denise was walking him to the door.

'Same as always. I'll work with Kyle for a few hours and then, it sort of depends on what he wants to do—play in the yard, ride bikes, whatever. Then it's off to work tonight.'

'Back to serving those lecherous men?'

'A gal's gotta pay the bills,' she said archly, 'and besides, they're not all so bad. The one who came in last night was pretty nice. I let him stay over at my place.'

'A real charmer, huh?'

'Not really. But he was so pathetic, I didn't have the heart to turn him down.'

'Ouch.'

As they reached the door, she nudged him playfully. 'You know I'm kidding.'

'I hope so.' The sun was beginning to peek over the trees as they stepped out onto the porch. 'Hey, listen, about last night . . . thanks for everything.'

'You already thanked me earlier, remember.?'

'I know,' Taylor said earnestly. 'But I wanted to do it again.'

They stood without speaking until Denise took a small step forward. She could see the surprise in his eyes when she kissed him softly on the lips. It wasn't more than a peck, really, but all he could do was stare at her afterwards, thinking how wonderful it was.

'I'm glad I was the one you came to,' she said.

Still dressed in pyjamas, her long hair a tangled mess, she looked absolutely perfect.

Chapter 7

Later that day, at Taylor's request, Denise showed him Kyle's journal. Sitting in the kitchen they flipped through the pages. Each one was filled with Denise's goals, as well as specific words and phrases, pronunciations, and her final observations.

'See, it's just a record of what we do. That's all.'

Taylor flipped to the very first page. Across the top was written a single word: Apple. Beneath that was Denise's description of the very first day she'd worked with Kyle.

'Can I?' Taylor asked, motioning to the page. Denise nodded and he read slowly, taking in every word. When he finished, he looked up. 'Four hours? Just to say the word apple?'

'Actually, he didn't say it exactly right, even in the end. But it was close enough.'

'How did you finally get him to do it?'

'I use a type of behavioural modification programme, one that was originally designed out at UCLA. They've had a lot of success with autistic children over the years by rewarding good behaviour and punishing negative behaviour. I modified the programme for speech. Basically, when Kyle says what he's supposed to, he gets a piece of candy. When he doesn't say it, no candy. If he doesn't even try or he's being stubborn, I scold him. When I taught him how to say apple, he cried and fussed, he kept trying to get out of the chair, he screamed. If someone had heard us that day, they would have thought I was torturing him. I must have said the word five or six hundred times. It was terrible, truly awful for both of us, but you know when he finally said it, all the frustration and anger and fear went away. I remember how excited I was. That was the first time I knew for certain that Kyle had the ability to learn. I'd done it, on my own, and I can't describe how much that meant, after all the things the doctors had said about him.' She shook her head wistfully, remembering that day.

'After that, we just kept trying new words, one at a time. He got to the point where his vocabulary was huge, but he still didn't have the ability to understand that language was actually *used* for something. So then we started with two-word combinations, like "big truck" or "big tree", and I think that helped him grasp that words are the way people communicate. After a few months, he could mimic almost everything I said, and so I started trying to teach him what questions are.'

'Was that hard?'

'It's still hard. Harder than teaching him words, because now he has to try to interpret inflections in tone, then understand what the question is, then answer it. All three parts of that are difficult for him and that's what we've been working on for the last few months.'

'He's come a long way,' Taylor said, beginning to grasp just how hard all this must have been.

'Yes, he has. He's got a long way to go, though. He's good with some questions, like "what" and "who", but he doesn't understand "why" and "how" type questions. He doesn't really converse yet either—he just makes a single statement. Things like that are the reason I'm glad I've kept that journal. Whenever Kyle has a bad day I'll open this up and remind myself of all the challenges he's made it through so far. One day, once he's better, I'm going to give this to him. I want him to read it, so that he knows how much I love him.'

'He already knows that.'

'I know. But some day, I want to hear him say that he loves me.'

'Haven't you tried to teach him that?'

'No. Because I want to be surprised on the day that he finally does it on his own.'

DURING THE NEXT week and a half, Taylor spent more and more time at Denise's house, always dropping by in the afternoons, once he knew she'd finished working with Kyle. Twice, Taylor played catch with Kyle while Denise watched from the porch; then he taught him to hit the ball with a small bat and tee that Taylor had used when he was young. Swing after swing, Taylor retrieved the ball and set it back on the tee, only to encourage Kyle to try again. By the time Kyle was ready to stop, Taylor's shirt was soaked through. Denise kissed him for the second time after handing him a glass of water.

On the second Sunday after the carnival, Taylor drove them to Kitty Hawk, where they spent the day at the beach. Taylor pointed out the spot where Orville and Wilbur Wright made their historic flight, and they read the details on a monument that had been erected in the Wright brothers' honour. They shared a picnic lunch, then waded in and out of the surf as terns fluttered overhead.

On the way back, they stopped at a farmer's road-stand where they picked up some fresh corn on the cob. That evening Taylor had his first dinner at Denise's house. The sun and wind had worn Kyle out and he fell asleep immediately afterwards. Taylor and Denise talked in the kitchen until almost midnight. On the doorstep, they kissed again, Taylor's arms wrapped around her.

A few days later, he let Denise borrow his truck to head into town to run some errands. By the time she got back, he'd rehung the sagging cabinet doors in her kitchen. 'I hope you don't mind,' he said, wondering if he'd overstepped some invisible line.

'Not at all,' she cried, clapping her hands together, 'Can you do anything about the leaky sink?' Thirty minutes later, that was fixed as well.

On Wednesday of the following week, Taylor invited both Denise and Kyle to his home. Similar to Denise's in many ways, it was an older house on a large parcel of land. Kyle loved the toolshed out back and after pointing out the 'tractor' (in actuality, a lawn mower), Taylor took him for a ride on it round the yard. Kyle beamed.

Watching them together, Denise realised that her initial impression that Taylor was shy wasn't completely accurate. But he did hold things back about himself, she reflected. Though they'd talked about his job and his time with the fire department, he was strangely silent about his father, never volunteering more than he had that first night. Nor had he said anything about the women he'd known in the past. It didn't really matter, of course, but the omission perplexed her.

He'd stumbled into her life when she least expected it, in the most unlikely of ways. He was already more than a friend. But that night, lying in bed, she found herself hoping and praying that the whole thing was real.

'HOW MUCH LONGER?' Denise asked.

Taylor had surprised her by bringing over an old-fashioned ice-cream maker, complete with all the ingredients needed. He was cranking the handle, sweat running off his face, as the cream churned, thickening slowly.

'Five minutes, maybe ten. Would you like to take over?'

'No, that's OK. It's more fun watching you do it.'

Taylor played the martyr as he pretended to struggle with the handle. She giggled.

Taylor stopped and wiped his forehead with the back of his hand. 'Are you doing anything Sunday night?'

She knew he was going to ask. 'Not really.'

'Do you want to go out for dinner?'

'Sure. But you know Kyle won't eat anything at most places.'

'I meant, could I take just you? Without Kyle this time? My mom said she'd be happy to come over and watch him.'

Denise hesitated. 'He doesn't know her too well.'

'How about if I pick you up after he's already asleep? You can put him in bed, tuck him in and we won't leave until you're sure it's OK.'

She relented then, unable to disguise her pleasure. 'You've really thought this through, haven't you?'

'I didn't want you to have the opportunity to say no.'

'In that case, I'd love to go.'

AFTER GIVING Kyle a bath and putting on his pyjamas, Denise read three books to him while he drank his milk, his eyes half open. After pulling the curtains, she closed the door, Kyle already sound asleep.

She took a shower then stood with a towel wrapped round her, trying to decide what to wear. She decided on a simple black cocktail dress. It had been in the back of her closet for years, still draped in a plastic sheath from a dry-cleaner's in Atlanta. She couldn't remember the last time she'd worn it, but after slipping it on, she was pleased to see that it still fitted well.

After drying and styling her hair, she put on a little make-up, then sprayed perfume on her neck and wrists. In her top drawer, she kept a small jewellery box from which she withdrew a pair of hooped earrings. It was then that she heard Judy knocking. Taylor arrived two minutes later.

FONTANA'S RESTAURANT brought a touch of elegance to Edenton. Dimly lit and with first-rate service, it was popular with couples celebrating anniversaries and engagements.

Taylor and Denise were seated at a small table in the corner, Taylor nursing a Scotch and soda, Denise sipping chardonnay.

'Have I told you how nice you look tonight?' he asked.

'Only twice,' she said, 'but don't feel you have to stop. I don't mind. Not when it comes from a man dressed as spiffy as you.'

'Spiffy?'

She winked. 'It means the same thing as goob.'

The dinner that followed was wonderful, the food delicious and the setting undeniably intimate. Over dessert, Taylor reached for Denise's hand across the table. He didn't let go for the next hour.

As the evening wore on, they immersed themselves in each other's lives. It was the first time they'd ever had a conversation in which Kyle's name never came up.

As they stepped out onto the deserted street after dinner, Denise noted how different the old town seemed at night, like a place lost in time. As they neared Taylor's truck, they passed a door that had been propped open. Stencilled on the glass was *Trina's Bar*. When she peeked in, Denise saw three couples talking quietly over small circular tables. In the corner was a jukebox playing 'Unchained

Melody'. Denise stopped in her tracks when she recognised it.

'I love this song,' she said.

'Would you like to go inside?'

She debated as the melody swirled around her.

'We could dance if you'd like . . .' he added.

'No. I'd feel funny with all those people watching. And there's not really enough room, anyway.'

The street was devoid of traffic. A single light, set high on a pole, illuminated the deserted sidewalk. Denise took a step, away from the open door. The music was still playing softly behind them, when Taylor suddenly stopped. She looked up at him curiously.

Without a word, he slipped one arm round her back, pulling her closer to him. With a trusting smile, he raised her hand to his mouth and kissed it. Suddenly realising what was happening, Denise followed his lead, closing her eyes and leaning into him. Taylor's arm drifted up her back and they rotated in slow circles, swaying gently with the music. Suddenly it didn't matter whether anyone was watching. Except for his touch and the feel of his warm body against hers, Denise thought, nothing mattered at all as they held each other close, beneath the flickering streetlight.

JUDY WAS READING a novel in the living room when the two of them returned. Kyle, she said, hadn't even stirred while they'd been away.

'Did you two have a good time?' she asked, eyeing Denise's flushed cheeks.

'Yes, we did,' Denise answered. 'Thanks for watching Kyle.'

'My pleasure,' she said sincerely, getting ready to leave.

While Denise went to check on Kyle, Taylor walked Judy to the car. He didn't say much, and Judy hoped that it meant that Taylor was as taken with Denise as she seemed to be with him.

Taylor was back in the living room, squatting by a small cooler he'd removed from the back of the truck, when Denise emerged from Kyle's room. Lost in what he was doing he didn't hear her approach. Silently, Denise watched as he opened the cooler and removed two crystal flutes. He set them on the small table in front of the couch. Reaching in again, he pulled out a bottle of champagne. and a plate of strawberries, neatly wrapped in cellophane. Then, from the corner of his eye, he caught sight of Denise and froze, an embarrassed expression on his face. Smiling bashfully, he stood up.

'I didn't know whether you liked wine or champagne, so I just took a chance.'

'Wonderful,' she murmured, 'I haven't had champagne in years.'

Taylor popped the cork and poured two glasses. He handed one to her and all she could do was stare at him, wondering how long it had taken him to plan this.

'To you,' he said as they tapped their glasses together. She took a sip. The bubbles made her nose twitch, but it tasted wonderful.

He motioned to the couch and they sat close to one another, her knee pulled up and resting against his thigh.

'What are you thinking?' she asked.

'I was thinking about what would have happened had you never been in the accident that night.'

'I would have had my car,' she declared, and Taylor laughed.

'But do you think I'd be here now, if it hadn't happened?'

Denise considered it. 'I don't know,' she finally said. 'I'd like to think so, though. My mom used to believe that people were destined for one another. I guess part of me still believes it.'

Taylor nodded. 'My mom used to say that, too. I think that's one of the reasons she never remarried. She knew there could never be anyone to replace my father.' He drained the last of his champagne. 'What about you? Did you think you'd be married by now?'

'Of course,' she said wryly. 'I had it all worked out. Graduate at twenty-two, married by twenty-five, my first child at thirty. It was a great plan, except that absolutely none of it worked out the way I thought it would.'

'You sound disappointed.'

'I was,' she admitted, 'for a long time. My mom had this idea of what my life would be like and never missed the opportunity to remind me. She meant well, I know she did. She wanted me to learn from her mistakes. But when she died . . . I guess for a while I forgot everything she'd taught me.'

'Because you got pregnant?' he asked gently.

Denise shook her head. 'No, though that was part of it. It was more that after she died, I felt like she wouldn't be looking over my shoulder all the time, evaluating my life. And of course, she wasn't, and I took advantage of that. It wasn't until later that I realised the things she said weren't meant to hold me back, they were for my benefit so that all my own dreams could come true.'

'We all make mistakes, Denise—'

She held up a hand, cutting him off. 'Like I said, I'm not disappointed any more. These days, when I think about my mom, I know she'd be proud of the decisions I've made over the last five years.' Denise hesitated. 'I think she'd also like you.'

'Because I'm nice to Kyle?'

'No,' she answered. 'Because you've made me happier in the last two weeks than I have been in the last five years.'

It was at that moment that Taylor McAden fell in love with Denise Holton. He stared at her, humbled by the emotion behind her words. She was so honest, so vulnerable, so incredibly beautiful. All the years of loneliness had led to this, here and now. He reached out and took her hand, feeling the softness of her skin as a well of tenderness rose within him.

Denise closed her eyes, willing this moment to last for ever. She knew intuitively the meaning of Taylor's touch, the words he'd left unspoken. Not because she'd come to know him so well. She knew because she'd fallen in love with him at exactly the same time.

IN THE LATE EVENING, silver moonlight spilled through the bedroom. Taylor lay on the bed, Denise resting her head on his chest. She had turned on the radio and faint strains of jazz muted the sounds of their whispers.

She lifted her head from his chest, marvelling at the beauty of his naked form. With guilty pleasure, she recalled their bodies intertwined in passion, her own soft whimpers as they'd become one and she'd given herself to him without reserve.

When Taylor saw her staring, he reached over and gently traced her cheek with his finger, a melancholy smile playing on his lips, his eyes unreadable in the soft grey light. 'You're perfect,' he whispered.

'I'm not, but thank you. For everything.'

He pulled her close to him and the two of them finally fell asleep.

WHEN SHE WOKE the following morning, Denise was alone. The bed covers on Taylor's side had been pulled up and his clothes were nowhere to be seen. Checking the clock, she saw that it was a little before seven. Puzzled, she got out of bed, put on a short silk bathrobe, and checked the house quickly before finally glancing out of the window.

Taylor's truck was gone.

Frowning, she returned to the bedroom to check the bedside table; no note. None in the kitchen either.

Kyle staggered sleepily out of his bedroom as she was pondering the situation.

'Hewwo, Money,' he mumbled, his eyes half closed. Just as she answered, she heard Taylor's truck coming up the drive. A minute later, Taylor was opening the front door, a grocery bag in his arms.

'Oh, hey,' he said. 'I didn't think you two would be up yet.'

'Hewwo, Tayer,' Kyle cried, suddenly alert.

Denise pulled her robe a little tighter. 'Where did you go?'

'I ran to the store.'

'At this hour?'

'It opens at six.' Taylor closed the door behind him. 'Sorry about leaving this morning, but my stomach was growling. So I decided that I would make you two a real breakfast. Eggs, bacon, pancakes, the works.'

Denise finally smiled. 'You don't like my Cheerios?'

'I love your Cheerios. But today is special.'

'Why is today so special?'

He glanced towards Kyle who was now focused on the toys piled in the corner. Certain his attention was occupied, Taylor set the bag of groceries on the table and put his arms round Denise, his hands running down her back, then inching lower. She looked embarrassed, her eyes flashing towards Kyle.

'Stop,' she said, meaning it, but not really wanting him to.

Taylor pulled away with a wink. 'Well, today is special for the obvious reason,' he said conversationally. 'But even more so because after I make your gourmet breakfast, I'd like to take you and Kyle to the beach.'

'But I have to work with Kyle and then head into the diner.'

'I know. And I'm supposed to go over to Mitch's this morning to help fix his roof. But I'm willing to play hooky if you are.'

'But you can't back out on me now,' Mitch protested. 'I've already pulled everything out of the garage.'

'Well, put it all back in,' Taylor said good-naturedly into the phone's mouthpiece. 'Like I said, I'm not going to be able to make it.'

As he talked, he moved the bacon around with a fork in the sizzling pan and the aroma filled the house. Denise was still in her short robe, scooping coffee grounds into the filter, and the sight of her made Taylor wish that Kyle would disappear for the next hour or so. His mind was barely on the conversation.

'Four cups or six?' Denise asked.

'Make it eight. I love coffee.'

'Who's that?' Mitch asked, everything suddenly coming clear now. 'Hey . . . are you with Denise?'

'Not that it's any of your business, but yes.'

'So you were with her all night?'

'What kind of question is that?'

Denise smiled, knowing exactly what Mitch was saying.

'You sly dog . . .'

'So about your roof,' Taylor said loudly, trying to get the subject back on track.

'Oh, don't worry about it,' Mitch said, suddenly affable. 'You just have yourself a nice time. It's about time you finally found someone.'

'Goodbye, Mitch,' Taylor said, cutting him off. Shaking his head, he hung up the phone.

Denise pulled the eggs from the bag. 'Scrambled?' she asked.

'With you looking so good, how could I not feel scrambled?'

She rolled her eyes. 'You really are a goob.'

TWO HOURS later, they were on a blanket on the beach near Nags Head, Taylor applying sunscreen to Denise's back. Kyle was nearby, using a plastic shovel to scoop sand from one spot to another.

For Denise, memories of the previous evening were revived as she felt the lotion being caressed into her skin.

'Can I ask you a question?' she said.

'Sure.'

'Last night . . . after we'd . . . well . . .' She paused.

'After we'd done the horizontal tango?' Taylor offered.

'Don't make it sound so romantic,' she protested and Taylor laughed. She was unable to repress a grin.

'Anyway . . .' she went on, regaining her composure. 'Afterwards, you got sort of quiet, like you were . . . sad or something.'

Taylor nodded, looking out to the horizon.

Watching the waves as they rolled up the shore, Denise gathered her courage. 'Was it because you regretted what happened?'

Taylor's eyes followed hers, tracking the waves. 'No. It wasn't that at all. Last night was wonderful—you were wonderful. The whole thing was so perfect . . . I guess it makes me sad to think there's never going to be a first time with you again.'

At that, he grew quiet once more. Denise decided to let the subject go. Instead, she leaned back against him, comforted by the reassuring warmth of his encircling arms. They sat that way for a long time, lost in thought.

Later, as the sun began its midafternoon march across the sky, they packed up their things, ready to head home. Kyle was walking ahead of them, carrying his bucket and spade as he weaved through the sand dunes. All along the footpath, a sea of orange and yellow flowers bloomed, their colours spectacular. Denise bent down and plucked one, bringing it to her nose.

'Around here, we call it the Jobellflower,' Taylor said, watching her.

'It was named for Joe Bell, who lived on this island a long time ago. Supposedly, Joe had been in love with a woman, but she ended up marrying someone else. Heartbroken, he moved to the Outer Banks, where he intended to live the life of a recluse. On his first morning in his new home, however, he saw a beautiful woman walking along the beach in front of his house. Every day, at the same time, he would see her, and eventually, he went out to meet her. They talked all day, then the next and soon they were in love. At the same time, a small batch of flowers began to grow right behind his house, flowers never seen before in this area. As his love grew, the flowers continued to spread and by the end of the summer, they'd become a beautiful ocean of colour. It was there that Joe kneeled and asked her to marry him. When she agreed, Joe picked a dozen blossoms and handed them to her, but she recoiled, refusing to take them. Later, on their wedding day, she explained her reason. "This flower is the living symbol of our love," she said. "If the flowers die, then our love will die as well." This terrified Joe so he began to plant Jobellflowers all along the beach as a testimony to how much he loved his wife. And every year, as the flowers spread, they fell deeper and deeper in love.'

When he was finished, Taylor bent down, picked a few more of the blossoms, then handed the bunch to Denise.

'I like that story,' she said, kissing him on the cheek.

'SO WHAT'S HAPPENING with Denise?' Mitch asked. 'Melissa ordered me not to let you leave until you filled me in on the details.'

They were at Mitch's house on Monday, doing the roof repairs that Taylor had so successfully put off last week.

Taylor laughed. 'Well, you can tell Melissa that we're doing fine.'

'And?'

'And what?'

'Does she make you happy?'

It took a moment for Taylor to answer. 'Yeah,' he said finally, 'she really does.' He searched for the right words. 'I've never met anyone like her before. She's pretty, she's intelligent, she makes me laugh . . . And you should see the way she is with her son. He's got some problems with talking, and the way she works with him—she's so patient, so dedicated, so loving . . . It's really something.'

'She sounds great,' Mitch said, prising another nail loose.

'She is.'

'Can I give you some advice?'

'Could I stop you?'

'No, not really.'

Taylor adjusted his position on the roof, making his way towards another shingle. 'Then go ahead.'

'Well, if she's everything you say she is and she makes you happy, don't screw it up this time.'

Taylor stopped in mid-motion. 'What's that supposed to mean?'

'You know how you are in things like this. Remember Valerie? Remember Lori? If you don't, I do. You go out with 'em, you pour on the charm, you spend all your time with them, you get them to fall in love with you . . . and then wham—you end it.'

'You don't know what you're talking about.'

'No? Then go ahead and tell me where I'm mistaken.'

Reluctantly, Taylor considered what Mitch had said. 'They were different from Denise,' he said slowly. 'I was different.'

'It's not me you have to convince, Taylor. I'm only telling you because I don't want to see you kicking yourself later.'

For a few minutes they worked in silence. Finally Taylor shook his head. 'You're a pain in the ass, do you know that?'

'Yeah, I know. Melissa tells me that, too, so don't take it personally. It's just the way I am.'

'So DID YOU two finish the roof?'

Taylor, holding a beer in his lap, nodded. It was a couple of hours before Denise began her shift and they were sitting on the front steps as Kyle played in the yard. Despite his best efforts to the contrary, Taylor's thoughts kept returning to the things Mitch had said. There was some truth in Mitch's words, he knew, but he couldn't help wishing his friend hadn't brought the matter up.

'Yeah,' he said. 'It's done.'

'Was it harder than you thought it would be?' Denise asked.

'No, not really. Why?'

'You just seem distracted.'

'I'm sorry. Just a little tired, I guess.'

Denise scrutinised him. 'Are you sure that's all?'

Taylor brought the beer to his lips and took a drink. 'I guess so.'

'You guess?'

'Well, Mitch said some things to me today . . .'

'Like what?'

Taylor drew a deep breath. 'He told me that if I'm serious about you, that I shouldn't mess things up this time.'

Denise felt her breath catch in her throat at the bluntness of his comment. 'What did you say?'

'I told him he didn't know what he was talking about.'

'Then why is it bothering you?'

'Because it just pisses me off that he thinks I might mess up. He doesn't know anything about you, or us. And he doesn't know how I feel, that's for damn sure.'

'How do you feel?'

He reached for her hand. 'Don't you know?' he said. 'Haven't I made it obvious yet?'

OVER THE SUMMER the relationship between Taylor and Denise settled into a routine. They spent most afternoons together—to escape the heat, Taylor's crew started early in the morning and would finish by two o'clock—and Taylor continued to shuttle Denise to and from her job at the diner, whenever he could.

One warm night towards the end of July, he took her up to Elizabeth City and they went dancing. As they moved around the floor he looked at her as if she were the only person in the world. Later, in bed, as a thunderstorm raged outside, he pulled her close. 'This,' he confided, 'is as good as it gets.'

Kyle blossomed. Gaining confidence in his speech, he began to talk more frequently, though much of it still didn't make sense. By late summer, he'd learned to hit the ball off the tee consistently and his ability to throw had improved dramatically.

But, as idyllic as everything seemed, there were moments when Denise sensed an undercurrent of restlessness in Taylor that she couldn't pin down. He would sometimes get that unreadable, almost distant look after they made love. He would hold her and caress her as usual, but she could sense something in him that made her uncomfortable, something dark and unknowable. It scared her sometimes, although when daylight came, she often berated herself for letting her imagination run away with her.

Towards the end of August, Taylor left town to help fight a major fire in the Croatan forest for three days, a dangerous situation made deadly by the searing August heat. When he returned to Edenton, he drove straight to her house. With Ray's permission, she took the evening off, but Taylor was exhausted and fell asleep. Again, he had the shakes, but this time, they didn't stop for hours. He refused to talk about what had happened and Denise held him in her arms, concerned, until he was finally able to nod off again. Even in sleep, his demons gave him no relief. Twisting and turning, he called out, his words incomprehensible, except for the fear she heard in them.

The next morning, he apologised, but offered no explanation.

Somehow, she knew it wasn't simply memories of the fire that were eating him up; it was something else.

Her mother had once told her that there were men who kept secrets bottled up inside and that it spelt trouble for the women who loved them. Denise instinctively knew the truth of the statement, yet it was hard to reconcile with the love she felt for Taylor McAden. She loved the way he smelt; she loved the rough texture of his hands, and the wrinkles around his eyes whenever he laughed. She loved everything about him.

She also found herself dreaming of walking down the aisle with him. She could tell herself that they hadn't been together long and that if he asked her tomorrow, she would have the wisdom to say exactly that. Yet . . . in her most brutally candid moments, she admitted to herself, that she was far more likely simply to say, *Yes . . . yes . . . yes.*

'YOU SEEM NERVOUS,' Taylor commented, studying Denise's reflection in the mirror as she put the finishing touches to her make-up.

'I am nervous.'

'But it's only Mitch and Melissa. Nothing to be nervous about.'

'For you, maybe. You already know them. I only met them one time, three months ago. What if I make a bad impression?'

'You won't.' He slipped both arms round her, still staring at her in the mirror. 'Hey, have I told you how wonderful you look?'

After eyeing their reflection in the mirror, she turned to face him. 'Good enough for a barbecue with your friends?'

'You look fantastic,' he said sincerely, 'but even if you didn't, they'd still love you.'

Thirty minutes later, Taylor, Denise and Kyle were walking towards the front door as Mitch appeared from round the back of the house, beer in hand. 'Hey, y'all,' he said. 'Glad you could make it. The gang's out back.'

They followed him through the gate, past the azalea bushes, before reaching the deck.

Melissa was sitting at an outdoor table, watching her four boys jump in and out of the swimming pool.

'Hey there,' she called out, getting to her feet.

Taylor hugged Melissa and gave her a kiss on the cheek. 'You two have met, right?'

'At the festival,' Melissa said easily. 'But that was a long time ago. How are you doing, Denise?'

'Good, thanks,' Denise said, still feeling a little nervous.

Mitch motioned to the cooler. 'You two want a beer?'

'That sounds great,' Taylor answered. 'Denise?'

'Please.'

As Taylor went to fetch the beers, Mitch settled himself at the outdoor table, adjusting the umbrella to keep the sun off. Melissa made herself comfortable beside Denise. Kyle, wearing a bathing suit and T-shirt, stood shyly by his mother's side.

Melissa leaned towards him. 'Hi, Kyle, how are you?'

'I'm fine, thanks.' *I'n fie, kenks.*

Melissa smiled. 'Good. Would you like to get in the pool with the other boys? They've been waiting all day for you to show up.'

Kyle looked from Melissa to his mother.

'Do you want to swim?' Denise asked, rephrasing the question.

Kyle nodded excitedly. 'Yes.'

'OK, go ahead. Be careful.'

Kyle ambled towards the water and stepped in, the water up to his knees. He bent over and splashed, as if testing the temperature, before breaking into a wide grin. Denise and Melissa watched him as he finally waded in.

'How old is he now?'

'He'll be five in a few months.'

'Oh, so will Jud.' Melissa pointed towards the far end of the pool. 'That's him over there, holding on to the side, by the diving board.'

Denise saw him. Same size as Kyle, buzz haircut. Melissa's four boys were jumping, splashing, screaming—in short, having themselves a great time.

'All four kids are yours?' Denise asked, amazed.

'Today they are. You let me know if you want to take one home, though. I'll give you the pick of the litter.'

Denise felt herself relaxing a little. 'How old are they?'

'Ten, eight, six and four.'

'My wife had a plan,' Mitch cut in. 'Every other year, on our anniversary, she'd let me sleep with her, whether she wanted me to or not.'

Melissa rolled her eyes. 'Don't listen to him. His conversation isn't meant for civilised people.'

Taylor returned with the beers, opening Denise's bottle before setting it in front of her. 'What are y'all talking about?'

'Our sex life,' Mitch said and Melissa punched him in the arm. 'Watch it, buster. We've got a guest here. You don't want to make a bad impression, do you?'

Mitch leaned towards Denise. 'I'm not making a bad impression. Am I?'

Denise deciding that she liked these two, smiled. 'No.'

'See, I told you, honey,' Mitch said victoriously.

'She's just saying that. Now leave the poor lady alone. Why don't you and Taylor go clean the grill or something.'

Mitch turned towards his friend. 'I don't think we're wanted, Taylor.'

'I think you're right, Mitch.'

Melissa whispered conspiratorially to Denise, 'These two should have been rocket scientists. Nothing gets by them.'

'C'mon, Taylor,' Mitch said, pretending to be offended.

They rose from the table and headed towards the grill, leaving Denise and Melissa laughing.

'Now, how long have you two been married?'

'Twelve years. It only seems like twenty.' Melissa winked and Denise felt as if she'd known her for ever.

'So how was it down in the Croatan?'

When Joe had asked for volunteers to fight the forest fire a few weeks earlier, only Taylor had raised his hand. Mitch had shaken his head when Taylor had asked him to come along.

What Taylor didn't know was that Mitch had learned from Joe exactly what had happened, that Taylor had nearly been killed when the fire suddenly closed in around him. Had it not been for a shift in the wind that cleared enough smoke for Taylor to find his way out, he would have been dead. His latest brush with death hadn't surprised Mitch at all.

Taylor took a drink of his beer, his eyes clouding with the memory. 'Pretty hairy at times—you know how those fires are. But luckily no one got hurt. You should have come along. We could have used more men out there.'

Mitch shook his head as he worked the scraper back and forth on the grill. 'No, that's for you young guys. I'm getting too old for things like that.'

'You're still going to give it up?'

'Yep. A few more months and then that's it.' Mitch paused before going on. 'You know, you might want to consider giving it up, too,' he added conversationally.

'I'm not gonna quit, Mitch,' Taylor said immediately. 'I'm not like you. I'm not afraid of what might happen.'

'You should be. If you really care about Denise and Kyle, you gotta start putting them first, like I put my family first. What we do is dangerous, no matter how careful we are, and it's a risk that we don't have to take.' He was silent as he set the scraper aside. Then, his eyes met Taylor's. 'You know what it's like to grow up without a father. Would you want to do that to Kyle?'

Taylor stiffened. 'Christ, Mitch—'

Mitch raised his hands to stop Taylor from continuing. 'Before you start calling me names, it's something I had to say. Ever since that night on the bridge. A dead hero is still dead, Taylor.' He cleared his throat. 'I don't know. It's like over the years you've been testing fate more and more often. It scares me sometimes.' He put his hand on Taylor's shoulder. 'I always worry about you. Like you were my brother.'

'WHAT DO YOU THINK they're talking about?' Denise asked, watching Taylor. She saw the change in his demeanour, the sudden stiffness.

Melissa had seen it as well. 'Probably the fire department. Mitch is giving it up at the end of the year. I expect he told Taylor to do the same thing.'

'But doesn't Taylor enjoy being a fireman?'

'I don't know if he enjoys it. He does it because he has to.'

'Why?'

Melissa looked at Denise, a perplexed expression on her face. 'Well . . . because of his father.'

'His father?' Denise repeated.

'Didn't he tell you?' Melissa asked carefully.

'No.' Denise shook her head, afraid of what Melissa was getting at. 'He just told me that his father had died when he was a child.'

Melissa nodded, her lips together.

'What is it?' Denise asked, her anxiety plain.

Melissa glanced away. 'Taylor's father died in a fire,' she said.

A cold hand seemed to settle on Denise's spine.

MITCH AND TAYLOR were standing by the grill, cooking hot dogs for the five kids at the table. After swimming for a couple of hours, Kyle was famished.

Denise and Melissa had moved away to sit down closer to the pool. Ever since Denise had learned about Taylor's father, she had been trying to piece the rest of it together in her mind. Melissa seemed to divine the direction of her thoughts.

'Taylor?' she said.

Denise smiled sheepishly. 'Yeah.'

'How are you two getting along?'

'I thought it was going pretty well. But now, I'm not so sure.'

'Because he didn't tell you about his father? Well, I'll let you in on a secret: Taylor doesn't talk about it to anyone, ever. Not to me, not to anyone he works with, not to Mitch.'

'That makes me feel better.' Denise paused. 'I think.'

Melissa put her iced tea aside. 'How is he with Kyle?'

'Kyle adores him. Taylor's like a little boy when they're together.'

'Taylor's always been good with kids. My kids feel the same way about him. They'll call to see if he can come over to play.'

'Does he come?'

'Sometimes. Not lately. You've been taking up all of his time.'

'Sorry about that.'

Melissa waved off the apology. 'Don't be. I'm happy for him. You, too. I was beginning to wonder if he'd ever meet somebody. You're the first person in years he's actually brought over.'

'So there've been others?'

Melissa smiled wryly. 'He hasn't talked to you about them, either?'

'Nope.'

'Well, girl, it's a good thing you came over,' she said conspiratorially, and Denise laughed.

'What happened to them?'

'Now that I can't tell you. Taylor doesn't talk about that, either. All I know is that one day they seemed to be doing fine and the next thing you knew, it was over. I never did understand why.'

'That's a comforting thought.'

'Oh, I'm not saying it's going to happen with you. He likes you a lot more than he liked them. I can see it in the way he looks at you.'

Denise hoped Melissa was telling the truth. 'Sometimes . . .' she began, then trailed off, not knowing how to say it.

'Sometimes you're scared about what he's thinking?'

She looked at Melissa, startled by the acuity of her observation.

Melissa went on. 'Even though Mitch and I have been together for a long time, I still don't understand everything that makes him tick. But in the end, it's worked out because we both want it to. As long as you two have that, you'll be able to make it through anything.'

A beach ball came flying across from the table where the kids were sitting, bonking Melissa on the head. Loud giggles broke out.

Melissa rolled her eyes but otherwise paid no attention as the ball rolled away. 'You might even be able to put up with having four boys, like we do.'

'I don't know if I could do that.'

'Sure you could. It's easy. All you have to do is wake up early, get the paper, and read it leisurely while drinking tequila shooters.'

Denise giggled.

'Seriously, do you ever think about having more kids?' Melissa asked.

'Not too often. It's not something I can do alone, is it?'

'Do you think Taylor would be a good dad?'

'I know he would.'

'So do I,' Melissa agreed. 'Have you two ever talked about it?'

'Marriage? No. He hasn't brought it up at all.'

'Mmm,' Melissa said, 'I'll try to find out what he's thinking.'

'You don't have to do that,' Denise protested, flushing red.

'Oh, I want to. I'm as curious as you are. But don't worry, I'll be subtle. He won't even know what I'm getting at.'

'SO, TAYLOR, are you gonna marry this wonderful girl or what?'

Taylor was in the middle of taking a drink and he inhaled a bit of it, causing him to choke. He brought his napkin to his face, his eyes watering. 'Excuse me?'

The four of them were eating their meal—steaks, green salad, cheddar-cheese potatoes and garlic bread. They'd been laughing and joking, having a good time and were halfway done when Melissa dropped her bombshell. Denise felt the blood rush to her cheeks.

'I mean, she's a babe, Taylor,' Melissa went on matter-of-factly. 'Smart, too. Girls like her don't come along every day.'

'I haven't really thought about it,' Taylor said defensively.

Melissa leaned forward, patting his arm as she laughed out loud. 'I don't expect an answer, Taylor—I was kidding. I just wanted to see your expression. Your eyes got big as saucers.'

'That's because I was choking,' Taylor answered.

She leaned towards him. 'I'm sorry. But I just couldn't resist. You're easy to pick on. Just like bozo over here.'

'Are you talking about me, darling?' Mitch broke in, trying to offset Taylor's obvious discomfort.

'Who else calls you bozo?' Melissa leaned over and gave her husband a quick kiss on the cheek.

'Are they always like this?' Denise whispered to Taylor, praying he wouldn't think she'd put Melissa up to the question.

'Ever since I've known them,' Taylor said, but it was obvious that his mind was elsewhere.

'Hey, no talking behind our backs,' Melissa said. Turning towards Denise, she moved the conversation back onto safer ground. 'So tell me about Atlanta . . .'

Her wink was so inconspicuous that neither Mitch nor Taylor caught it.

'I'M GONNA get you!' Mitch shouted as he ran through the yard, chasing Jud, who was screaming with delight and fear.

It was an hour after dinner, the sun had finally set and Mitch and Taylor were playing tag with the boys in the yard. Mitch, his hands on his hips looked round at the five kids, his chest heaving.

'You can't get me, Daddy!' Cameron taunted.

'OK, now you asked for it!' Mitch said, trudging towards him, heading past Taylor and Kyle.

'Run, Daddy, run! . . .' Will teased, knowing Cameron was agile enough to stay well away from his father.

Mitch chased one son after the other. Kyle, who had taken a little while to pick up on the game, finally understood it well enough to run with the other kids, and soon his screams were joining with theirs. After one too many near misses, Mitch surged towards Taylor. 'I need a little break, here,' he gasped. 'They're faster than they look, and they change directions like jack rabbits.'

'It just seems that way when you're old like you,' Taylor replied.

'C'mon!' Cameron shouted to Taylor. 'You can't catch me!'

Taylor rubbed his hands together. 'All right, here I come!'

He took a giant step towards the kids and with a jubilant scream they scattered in different directions. But Kyle's voice, cutting loudly through the night air, suddenly made Taylor stop his charge.

'C'mon, Daddy! C'mon, Daddy!'

Daddy.

Taylor, frozen for a moment, simply stared in Kyle's direction. Mitch, who'd seen his friend's reaction, teased: 'Is there something you haven't told me, Taylor? He just called you Daddy.'

But Taylor barely heard what Mitch had said. Lost in thought, the word repeated in his mind. *Daddy.* Though he knew it was simply Kyle mimicking the other children—part of the game—it nonetheless brought Melissa's statement to mind again. *So are you going to marry this girl or what?*

'I'm not his daddy,' Taylor muttered to himself.

'Not yet, anyway.' Though Mitch whispered the words to himself, Taylor heard them as clearly as he'd heard Kyle a moment before.

WITH THE EVENING finally winding down, Denise volunteered to help Melissa in the kitchen. The kids were watching a movie in the living room, sprawled all over the floor, while Mitch and Taylor straightened things out on the deck.

'Hey, why so glum?' Mitch asked Taylor as he filled a plastic garbage bag with the remains from the table.

Taylor shrugged. 'Just preoccupied. That's all.'

'About what?'

'Just work stuff. I'm just trying to figure out everything I've got to do tomorrow. Since I've been spending so much time with Denise, I've let my business slide a little. I've got to get back into it.'

'Haven't you been heading in every day?'

'Yeah, but I don't always stay all day. You know how it is. You do that long enough and little problems start cropping up. One thing I've learned is that when things go wrong, they go wrong in a hurry.'

Mitch felt a strange sense of *déjà vu*. The last time Taylor had used that expression, he'd been dating Lori.

THIRTY MINUTES LATER, Taylor and Denise were driving home, Kyle between them. There was an air of tension in the truck that could not easily be explained by either of them. But it had kept them quiet enough that Kyle had already fallen asleep, lulled by the silence. What was supposed to have been a friendly night out with friends, Denise knew, had become something far more important.

She glanced at Taylor uncertainly. From the corner of his eye, he caught her glance and turned to face her.

'Did you have a good time tonight?'

'Yeah, I did,' Denise answered quietly. 'I like your friends.'

'One thing you've probably learned is that Melissa will say the first thing that pops into her head, no matter how ridiculous it is.'

His comment did nothing for her nerves. Denise wondered why the things Taylor hadn't said suddenly seemed more important than the things he had. *How well do I know you, Taylor McAden? And where are we going from here?*

Denise drew a deep breath, willing herself to keep her voice steady. 'Taylor—why didn't you tell me about your father?'

Taylor's eyes widened just a little. 'My father?'

'Melissa told me that he died in a fire.'

She saw his hands tighten on the wheel, but he didn't respond, just kept his eyes on the road ahead. Denise waited before realising he wasn't going to answer her question.

'Did you become a fireman because of your father?'

Taylor expelled a sharp breath. 'I'd rather not talk about it.'

'Maybe I can help . . .'

'You can't,' he said, 'and besides, it doesn't concern you.'

'It doesn't concern me?' she asked in disbelief. 'What are you talking about? I care about you, Taylor, and it hurts me to think that you don't trust me enough to tell me what's wrong.'

'Nothing's wrong. I just don't like to talk about my father.'

Once again silence descended in the truck. This time, however, it was tainted with fear.

AFTER TAYLOR HAD carried Kyle into his bedroom, he waited in the living room until Denise had changed her son into his pyjamas. When she came back out, she noticed that Taylor was standing near the door.

'You're not going to stay?' she asked, surprised.

'No, I can't. I've got to get to work early tomorrow.'

He said it without a trace of bitterness or anger.

Denise moved closer to him. 'You sure?'

'Yeah, I'm sure.'

She reached for his hand. 'Is something bothering you?'

Taylor shook his head. 'No, not at all.'

She waited to see if he would add anything else, but he didn't.

'All right. See you tomorrow?'

Taylor cleared his throat. 'I'll try, but I've got a full schedule tomorrow. I don't know if I'll be able to swing by.'

Denise studied him carefully, wondering. 'Even for lunch?'

'I'll do my best,' he said, 'but I can't make any promises.'

Their eyes met only briefly before Taylor glanced away.

'Will you be able to take me into work tomorrow night?'

For a brief, flickering instant, it almost seemed to Denise as if he hadn't wanted her to ask. *Her imagination?*

'Yeah, sure,' he finally said. 'I'll take you in.'

Chapter 8

Kyle kept asking about you this afternoon,' Denise said casually. Good as his word, Taylor was waiting in the kitchen as she collected the last of her things, though he hadn't come by with much time to spare before she had to head off to Ray's. They'd kissed only briefly and he seemed a little more distant than usual, though he'd apologised for it, attributing it to hassles at the worksite.

'Oh yeah? Where is the little guy?'

'Out back. I don't think he heard you come up. Let me go get him.'

After Denise opened the back door and called for him, Kyle came running for the house. A moment later, he burst inside.

'Hewwo, Tayer,' he said, a big grin on his face. Ignoring Denise, he surged towards Taylor and jumped. Taylor caught him easily.

'Hey, little man. How was your day?'

Denise couldn't help but notice the difference in Taylor's demeanour as he lifted Kyle up to eye level.

'He's here,' Kyle shouted gleefully.

'Sorry I was so busy today,' Taylor said, clearly meaning it. 'Did you miss me?'

'Yes,' he answered. 'I missed you.'

It was the first time Kyle had answered a new question properly, without being told how to do it, and it shocked both of them into silence. For just a second, Denise's worries from the night before were forgotten.

If Denise expected that Kyle's simple statement would alleviate her concerns about Taylor, however, she was mistaken.

Not that it went bad right away. In fact, for the next week or so, in many ways things didn't seem different at all. Though Taylor—still citing work as the reason—had stopped coming by in the afternoons, he continued to drive Denise to and from the diner. They'd also made love the night Kyle had spoken.

Yet, things were changing. Nothing dramatic, it was more like the unwinding of twine, a gradual unfurling of everything that had been established during the summer. Less time together meant less time to simply hold each other or talk, and, because of that, it was difficult for her to ignore the warning bells that had sounded the night they'd had dinner with Mitch and Melissa.

Of course, it might simply be that Taylor really was preoccupied with work. At night, after picking her up, he looked tired enough for Denise to know that he wasn't lying to her about working all day. They still hadn't had an argument and he was still great with Kyle. On the surface, everything seemed the same, and she wondered if she was making too much of the whole thing.

She kept as busy as she could, doing her best not to dwell on what might be happening between them. She threw herself into her work with Kyle with renewed energy. Now that he was speaking more, she began working on more complex phrases and ideas, while also teaching him skills associated with school, such as the concept of numbers which seemed to make no sense to him at all. She cleaned the house, worked her shifts, paid her bills—in short, she lived her life much the same as she had before she'd met Taylor McAden. But even though it was a life she was used to, she nonetheless spent most afternoons looking out of the kitchen window, hoping to see him coming up the drive. Usually he didn't.

Despite herself, she heard Melissa's words once more. *All I know is that one day they seemed to be doing fine and the next thing you knew, it was over . . .*

'IT'S JUST for a few days,' Taylor said.

They were sitting on the couch in the living room while Kyle watched a cartoon on television. It was Tuesday and Taylor had just come by to take her into work. Her pleasure at his earlier arrival had evaporated almost immediately when he'd informed her that he was leaving for a few days.

'When did you decide this?' Denise asked.

'Just this morning. A couple of the guys asked if I wanted to go along. South Carolina opens the hunting season two weeks earlier than we do around here, so I figured I'd head down with them. I feel like I need a break.'

Are you talking about me or work?

'So you're leaving tomorrow?'

Taylor shifted slightly. 'Actually, it's more like the middle of the night. We'll be leaving around three.'

'You probably shouldn't pick me up tonight,' Denise offered. 'You need a little sleep.'

'Don't worry about that. I'll be there.'

Denise shook her head. 'No, I'll ask Rhonda if she'll bring me home.'

Taylor slipped his arm round Denise, surprising her. He pulled her close. 'I'll miss you.'

'You will?' she said, hating the plaintive note in her voice.

'Of course. Especially around midnight. I'll probably wander out to my truck through force of habit.'

Denise smiled, thinking he'd kiss her. Instead, he turned away, motioning with his chin towards Kyle.

'And I'll miss you, too, little man.'

'Yes,' Kyle said, eyes glued to the television.

Taylor got off the couch, and crept on all fours towards Kyle. 'Are you ignoring me, Kyle?' he growled.

Once Taylor was close, Kyle realised his intent and squealed as he tried to get away. Taylor grabbed him easily and they began to wrestle on the floor.

'I'm gonna get you,' Taylor bellowed and for the next few minutes, there was pandemonium. Then Taylor let Kyle pull away.

'Hey, when I get back, I'm going to take you to a baseball game. If that's OK with your mom, of course.'

'Baseball game,' Kyle repeated wonderingly. *Basebaw game*.

'It's fine with me.'

Taylor winked at Kyle. 'Did you hear that? Your mom said we can go.'

'Baseball game!' Kyle cried, louder this time. *Basebaw game!*

At least with Kyle, he hasn't changed.

Denise glanced at the clock. 'It's about that time,' she said, sighing. She rose from the couch to collect her things. A couple of minutes later, they were on their way to the diner. When they arrived, Taylor walked with Denise to the front door.

'Call me?' she said.

'I'll try,' Taylor promised.

They stood gazing at each other for a moment before Taylor kissed her goodbye. Denise went in, hoping that the trip would help clear his mind of whatever had been bothering him. Perhaps it did, but she had no way of knowing. For the next four days, she didn't hear from him at all.

SHE HATED waiting for the phone to ring. The whole thing made her feel helpless, a sensation she detested. She wasn't, nor ever had been, the helpless type, and she refused to become that now. So he hadn't called . . . so what? She forged on. On Friday, she took Kyle to the park, on Saturday, they went for a long walk in the woods. On Sunday, she took Kyle to church, then spent the early part of the afternoon running errands.

With enough money now to begin looking for a car in the classified ads, she picked up two newspapers. Next stop was the grocery store. Denise was scanning the aisles, choosing carefully, not wanting to overload herself for the trip back home, when she heard her name being called. Turning, she saw Judy pushing her trolley towards her.

'I thought it was you,' Judy said cheerfully. 'How are you?'

'Hi, Judy. I'm fine.'

'Hey, Kyle,' Judy said.

'Hewwo, Jewey.'

'I didn't expect to see you here,' Judy said to Denise. 'I figured you'd be with Taylor. He told me he was going to spend the day with you.'

Denise ran her hand through her hair. 'He did?'

Judy nodded. 'Yesterday. He came by after he got home.'

'So . . . he's back?'

Judy eyed her curiously. 'Didn't he call you?'

'No.' Denise turned away, trying not to show her discomfiture.

'Well, maybe you were already at work,' Judy offered softly.

But even as she spoke the words, both of them knew it wasn't true.

TWO HOURS after she got home, Denise spotted Taylor's truck coming up the drive. Kyle was playing out front and immediately started running for the truck, racing across the lawn. As soon as Taylor opened the door, Kyle jumped up into his arms.

Denise stepped out onto the porch with conflicting emotions, wondering why her heart still leapt at the sight of him.

After Taylor put Kyle down, Kyle grabbed his hand and the two of them began making their way to the porch.

'Hey, Denise,' Taylor said warily, as if he knew what she was thinking.

'Hi, Taylor.'

When he tried to kiss her, she pulled back slightly.

'Are you mad at me?' he asked.

'I don't know, Taylor. Should I be?'

'Tayer!' Kyle said again. 'Tayer's here!'

'Could you go inside for a minute, sweetie?'

Turning round and reaching behind her, she opened the screen door and led Kyle inside. After making sure he was occupied with his toys, she returned to the porch.

'So what's up?' Taylor asked.

'Why didn't you call while you were gone?'

Taylor shrugged. 'I don't know . . . I guess I just didn't have the time. We were out all day and I was pretty worn out by the time I got back to the motel. Is that why you're mad?'

Without answering, Denise went on. 'Why did you tell your mother you were going to spend the day here if you didn't plan on doing so?'

'I did come by—what do you think I'm doing now?'

Denise exhaled sharply. 'Taylor, what's going on with you?'

'What do you mean?'

'You know what I mean.'

'No, I don't. Look—I got back into town yesterday, I was beat and I had a bunch of things to take care of this morning. Why are you making such a big deal out of this?'

'I'm not making a big deal out of this . . .'

'Yes, you are. If you don't want me around, tell me and I'll leave.'

'It's not that I don't want you around. I just don't know why you're acting the way you are.'

'And how am I acting?'

Denise sighed, trying to put it into words. 'I don't know, Taylor . . . it's hard to explain. You've changed. It's like you're not sure what you want any more. With us, I mean.'

'Just because I didn't call? I've already explained that.' He took a step closer to her, his expression softening. 'There just wasn't any time, that's all.'

Not knowing whether to believe him, she hesitated. Meanwhile, as if sensing something was wrong, Kyle pushed open the screen door.

For a moment, however, they simply stood without moving.

'C'mon.' Kyle reached for Denise's shirt.

Denise looked down, forcing a smile, her emotions warring within her. Again, his explanations seemed reasonable. Again, he was great with Kyle.

So why didn't she believe him?

AFTER KYLE was asleep that night, Denise and Taylor sat together on the couch in the living room. Denise felt better than she had for the past couple of weeks. The only light came from a small lamp in the corner and a radio was playing softly in the background.

'So when are you taking Kyle to his baseball game?'

'I was thinking about Saturday, if that's OK.'

'Oh, that's his birthday,' she said, disappointed. 'I was planning to throw a little party for him.'

'What time's the party?'

'Probably around noon or so. I still have to work that night.'

'The game starts at seven. How about if I take Kyle with me while you're at work?'

'All right. But don't keep him up too long if he gets tired.'

Taylor raised his hand. 'Scouts' honour.'

Denise rested her head against his shoulder. 'You're a good guy, Taylor. You've really made me feel special these last couple of months.' Reaching for his hand, she took it in hers, weaving their fingers together. 'Do you ever think about us? About where we're going with all this, I mean?'

Taylor didn't respond and Denise went on. 'I've just been thinking that we've been seeing each other for a few months now, but sometimes I don't know where you stand on all this. I mean, these last couple of weeks . . . I don't know . . . sometimes it feels like you're pulling away . . .'

She trailed off, leaving the rest unspoken, knowing she'd already said these things before. She felt his body stiffen just a little.

'I care about you, Denise, if that's what you're asking.'

'No, that's not it . . . or not all of it. I guess I just want to know if you're serious about us.'

He pulled her closer, running his hand through her hair. 'Of course I'm serious. But my vision of the future doesn't extend all that far. I'm not the brightest guy you've ever met.'

Hinting wasn't going to suffice. Denise took a deep breath.

'Well, when you think about the future, are Kyle and I in it?'

It was quiet in the living room as she waited for his answer.

Eventually, she heard him sigh. 'I can't predict the future, Denise. No one can. But like I said, I care about you and I care about Kyle. Isn't that enough for now?'

She lifted her head from his shoulder and met his eyes. 'Yeah,' she lied. 'That's enough for now.'

LATER THAT NIGHT, after making love and falling asleep together, Denise woke and saw Taylor standing by the window, looking towards the trees, but obviously thinking of something else. She watched him for a long time, before he finally crawled back into bed.

As he tugged at the sheet, Denise turned towards him. 'Are you OK?' she whispered.

Taylor seemed surprised at the sound of her voice. 'I'm sorry. Did I wake you?'

'No. I've been awake for a while now. What's wrong?'

'Nothing. I just couldn't sleep.'

'Is it something I did?'

He drew a long breath. 'No. There's nothing wrong with you at all.'

With that, he cuddled against her, pulling her close.

The following morning, Denise woke alone.

Taylor had slipped out unnoticed and calls to his house went unanswered.

She did her best to put it out of her mind, at least until she saw him again. He'd be by later to take her into work.

The morning and the afternoon passed slowly. Kyle was in one of his moods—not talking, grumpy, stubborn—and that didn't help her, but it did keep her from focusing on Taylor.

A little after five, she thought she heard his truck on the road out the front, but as soon as she stepped outside, she realised it wasn't him. Disappointed, she changed into her work clothes, made Kyle a grilled cheese sandwich, watched the news.

Six thirty and still no sign of him. Concern was giving way to a sinking sensation in her gut. He's coming, she told herself. Isn't he?

Against her better judgment, she dialled his number again, but there was no answer. She went into the kitchen, poured herself a glass of water, then returned to the living-room window. Looking out, she waited.

At five to seven she called Ray, apologising, and telling him she'd be a little late.

Denise tried Taylor again. Not in. She slammed the phone down angrily, then thought of who else to call. Not Rhonda—she was already at the diner. Judy? She dialled her number and let it ring a dozen times before hanging up. Who else did she know? Really, only one other person. She found the phone book. After punching in the right numbers, she breathed a sigh of relief as the call was answered.

'Melissa? Hi, it's Denise.'

'Oh, hey, how are you?'

'Actually I'm not too good right now. I hate to do this, but I'm really calling for a favour.'

'What can I do?'

'I know it's really inconvenient, but is it possible for you to drive me into work tonight?'

'Sure, when?'

'Now? I know it's last minute and I'm really sorry . . .'

'Don't worry about it,' Melissa interrupted. 'I'll be there in ten minutes. I just have to grab my bag and the keys.'

Denise hung up, then called Ray again, explaining with apologies again, that she'd be there by seven thirty.

This time, Ray laughed. 'Don't worry about it, honey. You'll get here when you do. No rush—it's kind of quiet right now, anyway.'

Gathering her things, she waited for Melissa, then led Kyle out of the door when the car appeared up the drive. Melissa rolled down the window as it slowed to a stop.

'Hey there. C'mon in, but excuse the mess.'

Denise buckled Kyle into the back seat and got in the front. The car made its way down the drive and turned onto the main road.

'So what happened?' Melissa asked.

'Taylor didn't show up.'

'And he said he would?'

'We didn't talk about it specifically,' Denise admitted, 'but he's been driving me all summer, so I just assumed he'd keep doing it.'

'Did he call?'

'No.'

Melissa's eyes darted in Denise's direction. 'I take it things have changed between you two.'

Denise nodded. 'You knew this was going to happen, didn't you?'

'I've known Taylor a long time,' Melissa answered carefully.

'So what's going on with him?'

Melissa sighed. 'To tell you the truth, I don't know. I never have.

But Taylor always seem to turn gun-shy whenever he starts getting serious with someone.'

'But . . . why? I mean, we get along so well, he's great with Kyle . . .'

'It's not you, trust me. Taylor really cares about you, more than I've seen him care about anyone—Mitch says the same thing. But sometimes I think that Taylor doesn't feel that he deserves to be happy, so he sabotages every opportunity. I think he can't help himself.'

Denise pondered that. Up ahead, she saw the diner.

'Again, the question is why?'

Melissa didn't respond right away. She began to slow the car.

'If you ask me, it's because he blames himself for his father's death.'

Denise felt her stomach roll. 'What happened back then?'

The car came to a stop. 'You should talk to him about that.'

'I've tried . . .'

Melissa shook her head. 'I know, Denise. We all have.'

DENISE WORKED her shift, barely concentrating, but because business was slow, it didn't really matter. Rhonda, who would normally have driven her home, left early, leaving Ray as the only option for getting her and Kyle home. Denise was tidying up just before it was time to lock up, when the front door opened.

Taylor. He stepped inside, waved to Ray, but didn't make a move towards Denise.

'Melissa called,' he said, 'and told me you might need a ride home.'

She was at a loss for words. Angry, hurt, confused . . . and yet undeniably still in love.

'Where were you earlier?'

Taylor shifted from one foot to the other. 'I was working,' he finally answered. 'I didn't know you needed a ride today.'

'You've been driving me for the last three months,' she said.

'But I was gone last week. You didn't ask me to drive you in last night so I just figured Rhonda would bring you. I didn't realise that I was supposed to be your personal chauffeur.'

Her eyes narrowed. 'That's not fair, Taylor, and you know it.'

Taylor crossed his arms. 'Hey, I didn't come here to get yelled at. I'm here in case you need a ride home. Do you want one or not?'

Denise pursed her lips together. 'No,' she said simply.

If Taylor was surprised, he didn't show it. 'All right, then,' he said. 'I'm sorry about earlier, if that means anything.'

It does and it doesn't, Denise thought. But she didn't say anything.

When Taylor realised she wasn't going to speak, he turned away, pulling the door open again.

'Do you need a ride tomorrow?' he asked over his shoulder.

Again she thought about it. 'Will you be there?'

He winced. 'Yes,' he answered softly. 'I will.'

'Then, OK,' she said finally.

He nodded, then made his way out of the door. Turning round, Denise saw Ray scrubbing the counter as if his life depended on it.

'Ray?'

'Yes, honey?' he answered.

'Can I take tomorrow evening off?'

He glanced up from the counter, looking at her as he probably would have looked at his own child.

'I think you'd better,' he answered honestly.

TAYLOR CAME by thirty minutes before her shift was supposed to start and was surprised when she opened the door, dressed in jeans and a short-sleeved blouse.

'C'mon in,' she said.

'Aren't you supposed to be dressed for work?'

'I'm not working tonight,' she said evenly.

Taylor followed her inside, curious. 'Where's Kyle?'

Denise sat. 'Melissa said she'd watch him for a while.'

Taylor looked around uncertainly and Denise patted the couch. 'Sit down.'

Taylor did as she suggested. 'So what's up?'

'We've got to talk,' she began. 'I took tonight off in the hope that you'd help me understand what the problem is.'

'Are you talking about what happened yesterday? I said I was sorry and I mean it.'

'It's not that, Taylor. I'm talking about you and me.'

'Didn't we just talk about this the other night?'

Denise sighed in exasperation. 'Yeah, we talked. Or rather, I talked. You didn't say much at all. But then, you never have. You just talk about surface things, never the things that are really bothering you.'

'That's not true—'

Denise stopped him by raising her hands. 'You don't come over much any more, you didn't call while you were away, you snuck out of here yesterday then didn't show up later.'

'I've already explained that . . .'

'Yes, you did—you explained each and every situation. But don't you see the pattern?'

He turned towards the clock on the wall, staring at it, stubbornly avoiding her question.

Denise ran her hand through her hair. 'But more than that, you don't talk to me any more. And I'm beginning to wonder whether you ever really did.'

Taylor glanced back at her and Denise caught his gaze. She decided to go to the heart of the matter, took a deep breath and let it out slowly. 'What happened to your father?'

'Why does that matter?' he asked, suddenly wary.

'Because I think that it might have something to do with the way you've been acting lately.'

Taylor shook his head, his mood changing to something just short of anger. 'He died, OK? I've already told you that.'

'And?'

'And what?' he burst out. 'What do you want me to say?'

She reached towards his hand and took it in hers.

'Melissa said that you blame yourself.'

Taylor closed his eyes, and when he opened them again, she saw a kind of fury there that she had never seen before.

'Christ!' he spat out. 'Can't you just drop it?'

His outburst surprised her and her eyes widened a little. 'No, I can't,' she persisted. 'Not if it's something that concerns us.'

He stood. 'It doesn't concern *us*! What the hell is this all about anyway?'

'I just want to know what's going on so we can work on it . . .'

'Work on what? We're not married, Denise,' he said flatly. 'What makes you think you have the right to pry?'

The words stung. 'I'm not prying,' she said defensively.

'Sure you are. You're trying to get into my head so you can try to fix what's wrong. But nothing's wrong, Denise, at least not with me. I am who I am and if you can't handle it, maybe you shouldn't try.'

He glared at her and took a step backwards. 'Look—you don't need a ride and I don't want to be here right now. So think about what I said, OK? I'm getting out of here.' With that, Taylor left the house as Denise sat on the couch, stunned.

Think about what I said.

'I would,' she whispered, 'if you'd made any sense at all.'

FLOWERS ARRIVED the day after their argument. The note was simple: *I'm sorry for the way I acted. I just need a couple of days to think things through. Can you give me that?*

Part of her wanted to throw the flowers away, to end the relationship right now. Another part wanted to plead for another chance. So what else is new? she thought to herself.

Outside her window, the sky was grey and cold, rain sheeting against the windows, strong winds bending the trees almost double.

She lifted the receiver and called Rhonda, then turned her attention to the classified ads. This weekend, she'd buy herself a car. Maybe then she wouldn't feel so trapped.

On Saturday, Kyle celebrated his birthday. Melissa, Mitch and their four boys and Judy were the only ones there. When asked about Taylor, Denise explained that he was coming by at around five to take Kyle to a baseball game. 'Kyle's been looking forward to it all week,' she said, downplaying any problem.

The hours ticked by, and at twenty past five, Denise was playing catch with Kyle in the yard, a nervous pit in her stomach.

Kyle looked adorable dressed in jeans and a baseball hat. With his new mitt—courtesy of Melissa—he caught Denise's latest toss.

'Taylor's coming,' he said. *Tayer's cummeen.*

Denise glanced at her watch for the hundredth time, then swallowed hard, feeling nauseated. She'd called three times; he wasn't home. Nor, it seemed, was he on his way.

'I don't think so, honey.'

'Taylor's coming,' he repeated.

That brought tears to her eyes. Denise approached him and squatted so she was at eye level. 'Taylor is busy. I don't think he's going to take you to the game. You can come with mommy to work, OK?' Saying the words hurt more than it seemed possible.

Kyle looked up at her, the words slowly sinking in. 'Taylor's gone,' he finally said. *Tayer's gone.*

Denise reached out for him. 'Yes, he is,' she said sadly.

Kyle dropped the ball and walked past her, towards the house, looking as dejected as she'd ever seen him. Denise lowered her face into her hands.

Taylor came by the following morning, a gift under his arm. Before Denise could get to the door, Kyle was outside, reaching for the package, the fact that Taylor hadn't shown up yesterday already forgotten. If children had one advantage over their elders, Denise reflected, it was their ability to forgive quickly.

But she wasn't a child. She stepped outside, her arms crossed, obviously upset. Kyle had taken the gift and was already unwrapping it, ripping the paper off in an excited frenzy. Deciding not to say anything until he was done, Denise watched as Kyle's eyes grew wider.

'Weggoes!' he cried joyfully. *Lego.*

'It sure is,' she said. Without looking at Taylor, she brushed a loose strand of hair from her eyes. 'Kyle—say thank you.'

'Kenk you,' he said, staring at the box.

'Here,' Taylor said, squatting, 'let me open that for you.'

Removing a small pocketknife from his trousers, he cut the tape on the box and removed the cover. Kyle reached in and pulled out a set of wheels for one of the model cars.

Denise cleared her throat. 'Kyle? Why don't you take that inside. Mommy's got to talk to Taylor.'

She held open the screen door and Kyle dutifully did as she'd asked. Setting the box on the coffee table, he was immediately engrossed in the pieces.

'I'm sorry,' Taylor said sincerely. 'There's really no excuse. I just forgot about the game. Was he upset?'

'You could say that.'

Taylor's expression was pained. 'Maybe I could make it up to him. There's another game this weekend.'

'I don't think so,' she said quietly. She motioned to the chairs on the porch. Taylor hesitated before moving to take a seat. Denise sat as well but didn't face him. Instead, she watched a pair of squirrels hopping across the yard.

'I screwed up, didn't I?' Taylor said honestly. 'You have every right to be angry with me.'

Denise finally turned to face him. 'I was. Last night, if you had come into the diner, I would have thrown a frying pan at you.'

The corners of Taylor's mouth upturned slightly then straightened again. He knew she wasn't finished.

'But I'm over that. Now I'm less angry than resigned. For the last four years, I had my life with Kyle,' she began. 'It's not always easy, but it's predictable, and there's something to be said for that. Then, you showed up.' She smiled, but it couldn't mask the sadness in her eyes. 'You were so good to him, and that meant the world to me. But even more than that, you were good to me.' Denise paused. 'When we first met, I didn't want to get involved with anyone. But little by little, I found myself falling in love with you.' She shook her head wistfully. 'You're everything I've ever wanted in a man. But as much as I care for you, I don't think you're ready for me or my son.'

Taylor rubbed his face wearily.

'I'm not blind to what's been happening to us these last few weeks,' she went on. 'You're pulling away from me—from both of us—no matter how much you try to deny it. It's obvious, Taylor. What I don't understand is why you're doing it.'

'I've been busy at work,' Taylor began halfheartedly.

'That may be true, but it's not the whole truth.' Denise took a deep breath, willing her voice not to break. 'I know you're holding something back, and if you can't, or don't, want to talk about it, there's not much I can do. But whatever it is, it's driving you away.' Her eyes welled with tears. 'Yesterday, you hurt me. Worse than that, you hurt Kyle. He waited for you, Taylor. For two hours. He jumped up every time a car went by, thinking it was you. But it wasn't and finally even he knew that everything had changed. He didn't say a single thing the rest of the night. Not one word.'

Taylor, pale and shaken, seemed incapable of speech. Denise looked towards the horizon, a single tear drifting down her cheek.

'I can put up with a lot of things. Lord knows, I already have. But I'm a grown-up and I'm old enough to choose whether I want to keep letting that happen. But Kyle . . .' She trailed off, wiping her cheek.

'You're a wonderful person, Taylor. You've got so much to offer someone, and I hope that one day you'll finally meet the person who can make sense of all that pain you're carrying around. You deserve that. In my heart, I know you didn't mean to hurt Kyle. But I can't take the chance of that happening again.'

'I'm sorry,' he said thickly.

'I am, too.'

He reached for her hand. 'I don't want to lose you.'

Seeing his haggard expression, she took his hand and squeezed it, then reluctantly let it go.

'But you don't want to keep me either, do you?'

He did not reply.

'So you ended it, huh?' Mitch said, clearly disgusted.

They were in a bar, a dingy place that opened its doors for breakfast, usually to a waiting crowd of three or four regulars. Now, however, it was late in the evening. Taylor hadn't called until after eight; Mitch had shown up an hour later. Taylor had started drinking without him.

'It wasn't me, Mitch,' he said. 'She's the one who called it off.'

'And I suppose it just came out of the blue, right? You had nothing to do with it.'

'It's over, Mitch. What do you want me to say?'

Mitch shook his head. 'You know, Taylor, you're a piece of work. You sit here thinking you've got it all figured out, but you don't understand anything.'

'Thanks for your support, Mitch.'

Mitch glared at him. 'Don't give me that crap. You don't need my support. What you need is someone to tell you to get your ass back over there and fix whatever it was you did wrong.'

'You don't understand—'

'Like hell I don't!' Mitch said, slamming his beer glass onto the table. 'You think I don't know? I probably know you better than you know yourself! You think you're the only one with a shitty past? I have news for you. Everyone has crap in their background. But most people don't go around doing their best to screw up their present lives because of it.'

'I didn't ask you to come here so you can give me advice, Mitch . . .'

'Well, you're getting the best advice I've ever given you. Do me a favour and listen to it, OK? Your father would have wanted you to.'

Taylor squinted at Mitch, suddenly tensing. 'Don't bring him into this. You don't want to go there.'

'Why, Taylor? Are you afraid of something? Don't forget, I knew your father, too. I knew what a great guy he was. He would have been disappointed by what you're doing now, I can guarantee it.'

The blood drained from Taylor's face. 'Screw you, Mitch. I don't need this.' He rose from the table. Turning away, he started for the door. 'You don't even know who I am.'

Mitch pushed the table away from his body, knocking over the beers and causing a few heads to turn. The bartender looked up from his conversation as Mitch stood and came up behind Taylor, grabbing him roughly by his shirt, spinning him round.

'I don't know you? Hell, I know you! You're a goddamn coward is what you are! You're afraid of living because you think it means giving up this cross you've been carrying around your whole life. But this time, you've gone too far. It isn't just Denise—you're hurting a little boy! God Almighty, doesn't that mean anything to you? What the hell would your father say to that, huh? "Good job, son. I'm proud of you, son"? Not a chance. Your father would be sickened, just like I am now.'

Taylor, his face white, grabbed Mitch and lifted him, driving him backwards, into the jukebox. Two men jumped off their stools, and moved away from the melee as the bartender rushed to the far end of the bar. Pulling out a baseball bat, he started back towards them.

Taylor raised his fist.

'What are you gonna do? Hit me?' Mitch taunted. 'Go ahead. I don't really give a damn.'

'Knock it off!' the bartender shouted. 'Move outside, now!'

Taylor pulled his arm back ready to strike, his hand shaking.

'I'll always forgive you, Taylor,' Mitch said calmly. 'But you gotta forgive yourself, too.'

Taylor, hesitating, struggling, finally released Mitch and turned away. Stifling the curses in his throat, he strode out of the door.

Chapter 9

Just before midnight, Taylor returned home to a message on his answering machine. Since leaving Mitch, he'd been alone, on the bridge where he'd plunged into the river only a few months earlier, doing his best to clear his mind.

Guessing that Mitch had left him a message, Taylor pressed the play button on the answering machine. To his surprise, it was Joe from the fire department.

'There's a warehouse fire, on the outskirts of town. Arvil Henderson's place. They're paint retailers . . . Lives are in danger. If you get the message in time, we'll need your help . . .'

The message had been left twenty-four minutes ago. Without listening to the rest of it, Taylor hung up and raced to the truck, cursing himself for having turned off his cellphone when he left the bar. Everyone else was probably already on the scene, and he'd be rolling in some thirty minutes late.

Gravel shot from his tyres as he turned the truck in the driveway; the engine roared as he pulled onto the road. He took every short cut he knew. In time, he could see the sky glowing orange in the distance and could hear the wailing of sirens.

The air was already thick with greasy black smoke, fuelled by the petroleum in the paint, and he could see the flames rising from the warehouse. Three pumper trucks were already there, hoses hooked to hydrants, blowing water towards one side of the building. He made a final turn, coming to a halt, the truck's tyres screeching. Pandemonium everywhere.

As he scanned the hellish scene, he noticed Mitch's car off to one side, although it was impossible to make him out in the chaos of bodies and vehicles.

Taylor leapt from the truck and scrambled towards Joe, who was barking out orders. Another fire truck arrived, this one from Elizabeth City; six men jumped out and started unwinding the hose while another ran towards a hydrant.

Joe turned as Taylor rushed towards him. His face was covered with black soot and he pointed towards the hook and ladder.

'Get your gear!' he shouted.

Taylor followed his orders, pulling out a suit, then tearing off his boots. Two minutes later, fully outfitted, he ran towards Joe again.

As he moved, the evening was suddenly shattered by a series of explosions. A black cloud mushroomed from the centre of the building, as if a bomb had gone off. Taylor covered his head.

Flames were everywhere now, the building being consumed from within. From the inferno, two men emerged, limbs on fire; hoses were trained on them and they fell to the ground, writhing.

Taylor ran towards the blaze, towards the men on the ground. More explosions as paint can after paint can exploded inside, the fire raging out of control. An external wall suddenly collapsed outwards, barely missing the men.

Taylor squinted, his eyes watering as he finally reached the two men. Both were unconscious, flames lapping within inches of them. He grabbed both of them by the wrists and began to pull them back, away from the fire. Paramedics rushed towards him.

Looking up from the injured men, Taylor saw Joe waving wildly again, three men crowded around him, three others closing in. It was then that Taylor turned towards the building and knew that something was terribly wrong.

He rose and began to rush towards Joe, a wave of nausea breaking over him. Drawing near, he heard the soul-numbing words.

'They're still inside! Two men! Over there!'

Taylor blinked, as a memory came to him.

A boy, nine years old, in the attic, calling from the window . . .

He looked towards the flaming ruins of the warehouse, and then, as if in a dream, he started towards the only portion of the building left intact. Gaining speed, he rushed past the men holding the hoses, ignoring their calls to stop. Straight ahead, black smoke was pouring out of a doorway.

Joe saw him and began screaming for him to stop. Unable to hear above the roar, Taylor rushed through the door, his gloved hand over his face, flames lapping at him. His eyes burned as he inhaled a lungful of acrid air and held his breath.

Everything blazed with unearthly fury. The walls, the ceiling . . . Above him, there was the splintering sound of a beam collapsing. Taylor leapt aside instinctively as it fell.

His lungs straining, he moved quickly towards the south end of the building, the only area left standing. To his left, he spied a window, and he lurched towards it. From his belt, he removed his axe and broke the glass in one swift motion, immediately leaning his head out, drawing breath.

Like a living being, the fire seemed to sense the new influx of oxygen and seconds later, the room exploded behind him with new fury. The scorching heat of the new flames propelled him away from the window, towards the south again.

After the sudden surge, the fire receded momentarily, a few seconds at most. But it was enough for Taylor to get his bearings and to see the figure of a man lying on the ground—a fireman.

Taylor staggered towards him, narrowly avoiding another falling beam. He reached the man, bending over, grabbed his wrist and hauled him up over his shoulder.

Moving on instinct alone, he struggled back to the window, closing his eyes to keep the smoke and heat from damaging them any further. He made it to the window and threw the man through the shattered pane. His damaged vision prevented him from seeing the other firemen rushing towards the body where it landed. All Taylor could do was hope. He took two harsh breaths and coughed violently. Then, taking another breath, he turned and made his way one more time into the roaring hell of acid-tongued flames and suffocating smoke. Taylor pushed through the wall of heat, moving as if guided by a hidden hand. One more man inside.

A boy, nine years old, in the attic, calling from the window that he was afraid to jump . . .

Taylor closed one of his eyes when it began to spasm in pain. As he pushed forward, a wall collapsed, toppling in on itself like a stack of cards. He felt like he was dying inside. His lungs screamed for him to take a breath of the burning, poisonous air around him. But he ignored the need, growing dizzier. He dropped to his knees, flames surrounding him in three directions, then pressed onwards, heading for the only area where someone might still be alive. Crawling now, the heat like a sizzling anvil . . .

Taylor knew he was going to die. He could feel the world beginning to slip away. *Take a breath*, his body screamed.

Crawling, inching forward, praying. Ahead of him, still more flames, an unending wall of rippling heat. It was then that he came across the body. With smoke completely surrounding it, he couldn't tell who it was. Feeling his insides weakening, his vision going black, Taylor groped the body like a blind man.

The man lay face downwards, arms out to the side, his helmet still on his head. Two foot of rubble covered his legs from the thighs down.

Taylor gripped both the man's arms and pulled. The body didn't budge. With the last vestiges of his strength, he painstakingly began to move the rubble. Flames closing in now, licking at the body. Piece by piece, he lifted the wreckage off, but the exertion had taken nearly everything out of him. He moved to the head of the body again and tugged.

This time it moved. Taylor put his weight into it and pulled again, but because he was out of air completely, his body instinctively reacted. Taylor expelled his breath and inhaled sharply. He suddenly went dizzy, coughing violently. He let go of the man and rose, staggering in pure panic now, every conscious thought evaporating in a rush of unadulterated survival instinct.

He stumbled back the way he had come, his legs moving of their own volition. After a few yards, however, he stopped, as if waking from a daze. At that second, the world suddenly exploded into fire and flames engulfed him as he lunged for the window. He threw himself blindly through the opening, his suit now on fire. The last thing he felt was his body hitting the earth with a thud, a scream of despair fading on his lips.

ONE PERSON DIED that early Monday morning. Six men were injured, Taylor among them, and all were taken to the hospital. Three were able to leave that night. Two of the men who stayed were those Taylor had dragged to safety—they were to be transferred to the burns unit at Duke University in Durham, as soon as the helicopter arrived.

Taylor lay in the darkness of his hospital room, one eye heavily bandaged, his thoughts filled with the man he had left behind who had died.

His mother sat with him for an hour, then left him alone with his thoughts. Taylor McAden never said a word.

DENISE SHOWED UP at Taylor's bedside on Tuesday morning, Kyle in tow. As soon as she arrived, Judy looked up from her chair, her eyes red and exhausted. She took Kyle's hand and silently led him downstairs.

Denise sat where Judy had been. 'I'm sorry about Mitch,' she said gently.

Taylor turned his head the other way.

THE FUNERAL was to be held three days later, on Friday.

Taylor was discharged from the hospital on Thursday and went straight to Melissa's. Her family had come in from Rocky Mount and the house was filled with people, including Mitch's family, who lived in Edenton.

Taylor stepped inside the front door, looking for Melissa. As soon as he saw her across the living room, his eyes began to burn and he started towards her. She was talking to her sister and brother-in-law but when she saw him she immediately made her way to him. He wrapped his arms round her, putting his head on her shoulder as he cried into her hair. 'I'm so sorry,' he said. 'I'm so, so, sorry.'

All he could do was to repeat himself. Melissa began to cry as well. The other family members left them alone in their grief.

'I tried, Melissa . . . I tried. I didn't know it was him.'

Melissa couldn't speak.

'I couldn't . . .' he finally choked out, before breaking down completely. They stood holding each other for a long, long time.

THE FUNERAL SERVICE, held at Cypress Park Cemetery, was overflowing with people. Every fireman from the surrounding three counties, as well as every law enforcement official, made an appearance.

Melissa and her four children sat weeping in the front row.

The minister spoke a little while before reciting the twenty-third psalm. When the time came for eulogies, the minister stepped aside, allowing close friends and family to come forward.

Joe, the fire chief, went first and spoke of Mitch's dedication and bravery. Mitch's older sister also said a few words, sharing remembrances from their childhood. When she had finished, Taylor stepped forward.

'Mitch was like a brother to me,' he began, his voice cracking. 'We grew up together and every good memory I have from that time includes him. He was the kind of man who added something to everything he touched. I was envious of his view of life. He saw it as a big game, where the only way to win was to be good to other people, to be able to look at yourself in the mirror and like what you see. Mitch . . .' He closed his eyes hard, pushing back the tears. 'Mitch was everything I've ever wanted to be . . .'

Taylor stepped back from the microphone, his head bowed, then made his way back into the crowd. The minister finished the service and people filed by the coffin, where a picture of Mitch had been placed. In the photo, he was smiling broadly. Like the picture of Taylor's father, it captured the very essence of the man.

ON WEDNESDAY, midmorning, Taylor sat in his kitchen, dressed only in a pair of jeans. He'd made scrambled eggs and bacon and had stared at the plate before finally throwing the untouched food down the disposal unit. He hadn't eaten anything in two days. He couldn't sleep, nor did he want to. Since the funeral, he hadn't left his house, refused to talk to anyone; instead, he let his answering machine pick up his calls. He didn't deserve those things. Those things could provide pleasure, they could provide escape—they were for people who deserved them, not for him. He was exhausted. He knew he could continue along this path for ever if he wanted. It would be easy, an escape. No, he couldn't go that far. He wasn't worthy of that, either.

He forced down a piece of toast. His stomach still growled, but he refused to eat any more than was necessary. Each hunger pang reminded him of his guilt, his own self-loathing. Because of him, his friend had died.

Just like his father.

Last night, while sitting on the porch, he had tried to bring Mitch to life again. Strangely, although he could remember Mitch's face, for the life of him, he couldn't remember what Mitch looked like when he laughed or joked or slapped him on the back. Already, his friend was leaving him. Soon, his image would be gone for ever.

Just like his father.

EARLY ON SATURDAY, woken by nightmares, Taylor forced himself out of bed. He hooked up the trailer to his truck, then loaded his mower onto it, along with a weed-wacker, edger and trimmer. Ten minutes later, he was parked in front of Melissa's house. She came out just as he finished unloading.

'I drove by and saw the lawn was getting a little high,' he said, without meeting her eyes. After a moment of awkward silence, he ventured, 'How're you holding up?'

'OK,' she said. Her eyes were rimmed with red. 'How about you?'

Taylor shrugged, swallowing the lump in his throat.

He spent the next eight hours working steadily, making her yard look as if a professional landscaper had come by. He didn't go inside to visit Melissa until he was finally ready to leave, and even then, he stayed only briefly.

'There are a few more things to do,' he said on his way out the door. 'I'll be by tomorrow to take care of them.'

MELISSA'S PARENTS left the following week and Taylor filled the void in their absence. As he'd done with Denise during the summer months, he began swinging by Melissa's home nearly every day. And though he still felt uncomfortable around her, he felt a sense of responsibility regarding the boys. They needed a father figure.

He knew what it was like to grow up without a father. He remembered longing for someone besides his mother to talk to. He remembered lying in his bed, listening to the quiet sounds of his mother's sobbing in the adjoining room, and how difficult it had been to talk to her in the year following his father's death. Thinking back, he saw clearly how his childhood had been stripped away. For Mitch's sake, he wouldn't let that happen to the boys. He would be there for them, doing the things that Mitch had done. Ball games and fishing trips. Odds and ends around the house. Whatever.

He was sure it was what Mitch would have wanted him to do. They were like brothers and brothers watched out for one another. Besides, he was the boys' godfather. It was his duty. The decision made, he began to eat again and all at once, the nightmares stopped. He knew what he had to do.

THE FOLLOWING WEEKEND, when Taylor arrived to take care of the lawn, he inhaled sharply when he pulled up in Mitch and Melissa's driveway. A real-estate sign. The house was for sale.

He sat in his truck as Melissa emerged from the house. Pushing open the door, he started towards her.

Melissa gave him a hug. 'How are you, Taylor?' she asked, searching his face.

Taylor took a small step back. 'All right, I guess,' he answered, distracted. He nodded in the direction of the road. 'You're selling the house?'

'Hopefully.'

'Why?'

Melissa's whole body seemed to sag. 'I just can't live here any more,' she answered. 'Too many memories.' She blinked back tears and stared wordlessly at the house. She suddenly looked so tired, so defeated. A ribbon of fear twisted inside him.

'Where're you going?'

'Rocky Mount.'

'But why?' he asked, his voice strained. 'You've lived here for a dozen years . . . you've got friends here. I'm here . . . Is it the house?' he asked quickly, searching. 'If the house is too much, I could build you a new one for cost, anywhere you want.'

Melissa turned to face him. 'It's not the house—that has nothing to do with it. My family's in Rocky Mount and I need them right now. So do the boys. All their cousins are there and the school year just started. It won't be so hard for them to adjust.'

'You're moving right away?' he asked.

'Next week,' she said. 'My parents have an older rental house they said I could use until I sell this place. It's right up the street from where they live. And if I do have to take a job, they can watch my boys for me.'

'I could do that,' Taylor said. 'I could give you a job doing all the billing and ordering and you could do it from the house.'

She smiled sadly. 'Why? Do you want to rescue me too, Taylor?'

The words made him flinch. Melissa looked at him carefully before going on. 'That's what you're trying to do, isn't it? Coming over last weekend to take care of the yard, spending time with the boys . . . I appreciate what you're trying to do, but it's not what I need right now. I need to handle this my own way.'

'I wasn't trying to rescue you,' he protested, trying to hide how pained he felt. 'I just know how hard it can be to lose someone and I didn't want you to have to handle everything alone.'

'Oh, Taylor,' she said in almost a motherly tone, 'it's the same thing.' She hesitated. 'It's what you've been doing your whole life. You sense that someone needs help and if you can, you give her exactly what she needs. And now, you're turning your sights on us.'

'I'm not turning my sights on you,' he denied quickly.

Melissa wasn't dissuaded. She reached for his hand. 'Yes, you are,' she said calmly. 'It's what you did with Valerie after her boyfriend left her, it's what you did with Lori when she felt so alone. It's what you did with Denise when you found out how hard her life was.' She paused, letting that sink in. 'You feel the need to make things better, Taylor. You always have. You may not believe it, but everything in your life proves that. Even your jobs. As a contractor, you fix things. As a fireman, you save people. It's who you are.'

Taylor turned away, his mind reeling from her words.

'That's not a bad thing, Taylor. But it's not what I need. And in the long run, it's not what you need, either. In time, once you think I'm saved, you'll move on, looking for the next person to rescue. And I'd probably be thankful for everything you did, except for the fact that I would know the truth about why you did it.'

'What truth is that?' he rasped out.

'That even though you rescued me, you were trying to rescue yourself, because of what happened to your father. And no matter how hard I try, I'll never be able to do that for you. That's a conflict you're going to have to resolve on your own.'

The words hit him with almost physical force. He felt breathless as he tried to make sense of his warring thoughts.

Melissa wrapped her arms around him, hugging him tightly.

'You've been like a brother to me, and I love the fact that you would be here for my boys. And if you love me too, you'll understand that I didn't say any of these things to hurt you. I know you want to save me, but I don't need it. What I need is for you to find a way to save yourself, just like you tried to save Mitch.'

He felt too numb to respond. In the early-morning sunlight, they stood together, simply holding each other.

'How?' he finally croaked out.

'You know,' she whispered. 'You already know.'

HE LEFT Melissa's home in a daze. It was all he could do to stay focused on the road. He felt as if his remaining strength had been stripped away. His life, as he knew it, was over, and he had no idea what to do. As much as he wanted to deny the things that Melissa had said, he couldn't. At the same time, he didn't believe them either. At least, not completely. Or did he? In his life, he'd tried to see things as concrete and clear, not steeped in hidden meanings. He didn't search for hidden motivations because he had never really believed that they mattered.

He couldn't understand why his father had died, and for a time, he'd talked to God about the things he was going through, wanting to make sense of it. In time, though, he gave up. Understanding it, would make no difference. It wouldn't bring his father back.

But now Melissa's words were making him question the meaning of everything he had once thought clear and simple. Had his father's death really influenced everything in his life? Were Melissa and Denise right in their assessment of him?

No, he decided. They weren't right. Neither one of them knew what had happened the night his father had died. No one, besides his mother, knew the truth.

Driving automatically, Taylor paid little attention to where he was going. Turning now and then, slowing at intersections, stopping when he had to, he obeyed the laws but didn't remember doing so. Melissa's final words haunted him. *You already know . . .*

Know what? he wanted to ask. *I don't know anything right now.*

He stopped the truck and began the short trek to his destination.

Judy was waiting for him at his father's grave, kneeling down, tending the weeds around the stone.

'What are you doing here, Mom?' he asked.

Judy didn't turn at the sound of his voice. 'Melissa called me and told me you'd come,' she said quietly. From her voice, he could tell she'd been crying. 'She said I should be here.'

Taylor squatted beside her. 'What's wrong, Mom?'

'I'm sorry,' she began. 'I wasn't a good mother . . .' Her voice seemed to die in her throat, leaving Taylor too surprised to respond. With a gentle finger, he removed a blade of grass from her cheek and she turned to face him.

'You were a great mother,' he said firmly.

'No,' she whispered, 'I wasn't. If I were, you wouldn't come here as much as you do.'

'What are you talking about, Mom?'

'You know,' she answered. 'When you hit bad patches in your life, you don't turn to me, you don't turn to your friends. You come here. No matter what the problem, you always come to the decision that you're better off alone, just like you are now.' She stared at him almost as if seeing a stranger. 'Can't you see why that hurts me? I can't help but think how sad it must be to live your life without people. And it's all because of me.'

'No . . .'

She didn't let him finish. Looking towards the horizon, she seemed lost in the past. 'When your father died, I was so caught up in my own sadness that I ignored how hard it was for you. I tried to be everything for you, but because of that I didn't have time for myself. I didn't teach you how wonderful it is to love someone and have them love you back.'

'Sure you did,' he said.

She fixed him with a look of inexpressible sorrow. 'Then why are you alone?'

'You don't have to worry about me, OK?' he muttered.

'Of course I do,' she said weakly. 'I'm your mother.'

Judy moved into a sitting position on the ground. Taylor did the same and reached out his hand. She took it willingly.

'Your father and I had a wonderful relationship,' she whispered. 'Your father made me happy, Taylor. He was the best person that I ever knew. Even if I'd known what would eventually happen to your father, I would have married him. Even if I'd known that we'd only be together for eleven years, I wouldn't have traded those eleven years for anything. Can you understand that? Loving someone and having them love you back is the most precious thing in the world. It's what made it possible for me to go on, but you don't seem to realise that. Even when love is right there in front of you, you choose to turn away from it. You're alone because you want to be.'

Taylor rubbed his fingers together, his mind growing numb again. 'I know,' Judy finally went on, 'that you feel responsible for your father's death. All my life, I've tried to help you understand that you shouldn't, that it was just a horrible accident. You were just a child. You didn't know what was going to happen, but no matter how many ways I tried to say it, you still believed you were at fault. And because of that, you've shut yourself off from the world. I don't know why . . . maybe you don't think you deserve to be happy.' Judy sighed. 'This summer, when I saw you with Kyle, do you know what I thought? I thought about how much you looked like your father. He was always good with kids, just like you. Just the way you used to look at your father always made me smile. It was an expression of awe and hero worship. Kyle looks at you in exactly the same way. I'll bet you miss him.'

Taylor nodded reluctantly.

'Is that because you were trying to give him what you thought you missed growing up, or is it because you like him?'

Taylor considered the question before finally answering. 'I like him. He's a great kid.'

Judy met his eyes. 'Do you miss Denise too?'

Yeah, I do . . . Taylor shifted uncomfortably. 'That's over now, Mom,' he said.

'That's a shame, Taylor,' she whispered. 'She was perfect for you.'

They sat without speaking for the next few minutes, until a light shower began to fall, forcing them back to the parking lot. Judy got in her car and smiled sadly at her son before pulling away, leaving Taylor standing in the rain.

HE'D LOST EVERYTHING. He knew that as he left the cemetery and began the short trip home.

She was perfect for you.

He finally admitted to himself that despite Mitch's death, everything, he hadn't been able to stop thinking about Denise. Her image had flashed through his mind over and over, but he'd forced it away with stubborn resolve.

His throat tightened as he remembered the first night they'd made love. As much as he wanted to deny it, he knew now that he'd been in love with her. So why then, hadn't he told her so? And more importantly, why had he ignored his own feelings in order to pull away?

In the truck, rain splashed against the windshield as if driving his thoughts home. Snatches of other conversations began to replay themselves in his mind.

Mitch warning him: *'Don't screw it up this time . . .'*

Denise, in all her luminous beauty: *'We all need companionship . . .'*

His response? *I don't need anyone . . .*

It was a lie. His entire life had been a lie and his lies had led to a reality that was suddenly impossible to fathom. Mitch was gone, Melissa was gone, Denise was gone, Kyle was gone . . . he'd lost it all. His lies had become reality. *Everyone is gone.*

The realisation made Taylor grip the steering wheel hard, fighting to keep control. He pulled the truck to the side of the road, his vision blurring. *I'm alone . . .*

He clung to the steering wheel as the rain poured down around him, wondering how on earth he'd let it happen.

Chapter 10

Denise pulled into the drive, tired from her shift. A few more minutes, a nice cup of cocoa and she'd be under the covers. The thought was intoxicating. As she neared the house, she slammed on the brakes at the sight of Taylor's truck.

Glancing towards the front door, she saw him sitting on the steps, waiting for her. Despite her exhaustion, her mind snapped to attention. A dozen possibilities raced through her head as she parked and shut the engine off.

Taylor approached the car as she got out. He looked terrible. His eyes were red-rimmed and raw-looking, his face pale and drawn. As he pushed his hands deep into his pockets, he seemed unable to meet her gaze. She searched for something to say.

'I see you got yourself a car,' Taylor offered.

The sound of his voice triggered a flood of emotions in her: love and joy, pain and anger, the loneliness and quiet desperation of the past few weeks. She couldn't go through all this again.

'What are you doing here, Taylor?' Her voice was edged with more bitterness than Taylor had expected.

Taylor took a deep breath. 'I came to tell you how sorry I was,' he began haltingly. 'I never meant to hurt you.'

She'd wanted to hear those words at one time but strangely, they meant nothing now. She glanced over her shoulder at the car, spying Kyle's sleeping figure in the back.

'It's too late for that,' she said.

He forced a smile, then lowered his gaze again before pulling his hands from his pockets. He took a hesitant step towards his truck, then stopped. 'Melissa's moving to Rocky Mount,' he said into the darkness, his back to Denise.

'I know. She told me a couple of days ago. Is that why you're here?'

Taylor shook his head. 'No. I'm here because I wanted to talk about Mitch.' Denise could barely hear him. 'I was hoping that you'd listen because I don't know who else to turn to.'

His vulnerability touched her and she almost went to his side. But she couldn't forget what he had done to Kyle—or to her.

'Taylor . . . it's really late. Maybe tomorrow?' she suggested softly. She thought he would leave then, yet strangely, he didn't move.

'I also wanted to tell you about my father,' he said slowly. 'It's time you knew the truth.'

From his strained expression, she knew how hard it had been for him to say the words. He seemed on the verge of tears as he stood before her; this time it was her turn to look away.

'All right,' she said.

HE DIDN'T LOOK at her from his position on the couch. With the room lit by only a single lamp, dark shadows hid his face.

'I was nine years old,' he began, 'and for two weeks, we were practically buried in heat. The temperature had hovered near a hundred, even though it was still early summer. Our house was old—it didn't have air conditioning or much insulation—and just lying in bed would make me sweat. It was impossible to sleep.'

He was staring at the coffee table as he spoke, his eyes unfocused, his voice subdued.

'Back then, there was this set of plastic army soldiers that I saw in the Sears catalogue. It came with tanks, jeeps, tents and barricades—everything a kid needs to have a little war, and I don't remember ever wanting anything more in my whole life. When I finally got the set for my birthday, I don't think I'd ever been more excited about a gift. But my bedroom was real small and there wasn't enough space to set it up the way I wanted, so I put the whole collection up in the attic. When I couldn't sleep that night, that's where I went.'

He finally looked up, a sigh escaping from him, something bitter and long repressed. He shook his head as if he still didn't believe it. 'It was late. It was past midnight when I snuck past my parents' door to the steps at the end of the hall. I was so quiet—I knew where every squeak in the floor was and I purposely avoided them so my parents wouldn't know I was up there. And they didn't.'

He brought his hands to his face and bent forward. His voice gained momentum. 'I don't know how long I was up there that night. I could play with those soldiers for hours and not even realise it. I just kept setting them up and fighting these imaginary battles. Even on that night, hot as it was, I couldn't think of anything else but those damn soldiers. I guess that's why I didn't smell the smoke.'

He paused, and Denise felt the hairs rise on her neck as he continued. 'I just didn't smell it. To this day, I don't now why. I didn't realise anything was happening at all until I heard my parents come scrambling out of their bedroom, making a huge ruckus. They were yelling and screaming for me and I remember thinking that they'd found out I wasn't where I was supposed to be. I kept hearing them call my name over and over, but I was too afraid to answer.' His eyes pleaded for understanding. 'I didn't want them to find me up there— they'd already told me a hundred times that once I was in bed, I was supposed to stay there all night. If they found me, I figured I'd get in big trouble. I had a baseball game that weekend and I knew they'd ground me for sure, so instead of coming out when they called, I came up with a plan to wait until they were downstairs. Then, I was going to sneak into the bathroom and pretend that I'd been in there the whole time. I turned out the light and hid behind some boxes to wait it out. I heard my father open the attic door, shouting for me, but I kept quiet until he finally left. Eventually, the sounds of them tearing through the house died down and I went for the door. I still had no idea of what was going on and when I opened it, I was stunned by a blast of heat and smoke. The walls and ceiling were on fire but it seemed so unreal; at first I didn't really understand how serious it was. Had I rushed through it then, I probably could have made it out, but I didn't. I just stared at the fire, thinking how strange it was. I wasn't even afraid.'

Taylor tensed, hunching over the table. 'But that changed almost immediately. Before I knew it, everything seemed to catch fire at once and the way out was blocked. That was when I first realised that something awful was happening. It had been so dry that the house was burning like kindling. I began to scream for my father. But he was already gone and I knew it. In a panic, I scrambled to the window. When I opened it, I saw my parents on the front lawn, running around in a panic, looking and calling for me. My mom seemed to sense where I was and she looked up at me. I can still see her eyes when she realised I was still in the house. They got real wide and she brought her hand to her mouth and then she just started screaming. My dad stopped what he was doing and he saw me, too. That was when I started to cry.'

A tear spilled out of the corner of his unblinking eye, though he didn't seem to realise it. Denise felt sick to her stomach.

'My dad . . . my big strong dad came rushing across the lawn in a flash. By then, most of the house was on fire and I could hear things exploding downstairs. The smoke started getting really thick. My mom was screaming for my dad to do something and he ran to the spot right beneath the window. I remember him screaming, *"Jump Taylor! I'll catch you! I'll catch you, I promise!"* But instead of jumping, I just started to cry all the harder. The window was at least twenty feet up, and it just seemed so high that I was sure I'd die if I tried. *"Jump, Taylor! I'll catch you!"* He just kept shouting it over and over: *"Jump! Come on!"* My mom was screaming even louder and I was crying until I finally shouted out that I was afraid.'

Taylor swallowed hard. 'The more my dad called for me to jump, the more paralysed I became. I could hear the terror in his voice and I just kept screaming back that I couldn't, that I was afraid. And I was, even though I'm sure now he would have caught me.'

A muscle in his jaw twitched rhythmically, and he slammed his fist into his leg. 'I can still see my father's face when he realised I wasn't going to jump—we both came to the realisation at exactly the same time. There was fear there, but not for himself. He just stopped shouting and he lowered his arms, and I remember that his eyes never left mine. It was like time stopped right then—it was just the two of us. I couldn't hear my mom any more, I couldn't feel the heat, I couldn't smell the smoke. All I could think about was my father. Then, he nodded ever so slightly and we both knew what he was going to do. He finally turned away and started running for the front door.

'He moved so fast that my mom didn't have time to stop him. By then, the house was completely in flames. The fire was closing in around me and I just stood in the window, too shocked to scream any more.' Taylor pressed the heels of his palms against his closed eyes, applying pressure. With great effort, he went on. 'It must have been less than a minute before he got to me, but it seemed for ever. Even with my head out of the window, I could barely breathe. Smoke was everywhere. The fire was deafening. Despite that, I could hear my father's voice in the house, calling that he was coming.'

Taylor's voice broke and he turned away to hide the hot tears that began to spill down his face. 'I remember turning round and seeing him rushing towards me. He was on fire. His skin, his arms, his face, his hair—everything. Just this human fireball rushing at me, bursting through the flames. But he wasn't screaming. He just barrelled into me, pushing me towards the window, saying, "Go on, son." He forced me out of the window, holding on to my wrist. When the entire weight of my body was dangling out the window, he finally let go. I landed hard enough to crack a bone in my ankle—I heard the snap as I fell onto my back, looking upwards. It was like God wanted me to see what I'd done. I watched my father pull his flaming arm back inside . . .'

Taylor stopped there, unable to go on. Denise sat frozen in her chair, tears in her eyes, a lump in her throat. When he spoke again, his voice was barely audible and he was shivering as if the effort of choking back sobs was tearing his body apart.

'He never came back out. I remember my mom pulling me away from the house, still screaming, and by then, I was screaming too.'

His eyes closed tightly, he lifted his chin to the ceiling. 'Daddy . . . no—' he called out hoarsely. The sound of his voice echoed like a shot in the room. 'Get out, Daddy!'

Denise moved instinctively to his side, wrapping her arms around him as he rocked back and forth, his broken cries almost incoherent.

'Please, God . . . let me do it over. Please . . . I'll jump . . . please, God . . . I'll do it this time . . . please let him come out.'

Denise hugged Taylor with all her strength, her own tears falling onto his neck as she pressed her face into him. After a while she heard nothing but the beating of his heart and the words he kept whispering over and over—'I didn't mean to kill him . . .'

DENISE HELD TAYLOR until he fell silent, spent and exhausted. Releasing him, she rose and went to the kitchen, returning a moment later with a can of beer.

She didn't know what else to do, or say. Taylor looked up from the couch as she handed him the beer; with a deadened expression, he opened it and took a drink.

She reached over, resting her hand on his leg and he silently took hold of it.

'Are you OK?' she finally asked.

'No,' he answered earnestly, 'but then maybe I never was.'

She squeezed his hand. 'Probably not,' she agreed. He smiled wanly. They sat in silence for a few moments before she spoke again.

'Why tonight, Taylor?' Though she could have tried to talk him out of the guilt he still felt, she knew that now wasn't the time.

'I've been thinking about Mitch ever since he died and . . . I don't know . . . I felt like it was starting to eat me alive.'

'Why me, then? Why not someone else?'

When he glanced up at her, his blue eyes registered nothing but regret. 'Because, I care about you more than I ever cared about anyone.'

Her breath caught in her throat. When she didn't speak, Taylor reluctantly withdrew his hand. 'You have every right not to believe me,' he admitted. 'I probably wouldn't, given the way I acted. I'm sorry for that—for everything. I was wrong.' He paused. 'I wish I could explain why I did the things I did, but I honestly don't know. I've been lying to myself for so long that I'm not even sure I'd know the truth if I saw it. All I know is that I screwed up the best thing I ever had in my life.'

'Yeah, you did,' she agreed, prompting a nervous laugh from Taylor. 'I guess a second chance is out of the question, huh?'

Denise was silent, suddenly aware that at some point this evening, her anger towards Taylor had dissipated. The pain was still there, though, and so was the fear of what might come . . .

'You used that one a month ago,' she said calmly.

He heard an unexpected glimmer of encouragement in her tone and looked up at her, his hope barely disguised. 'No hope, huh?'

Denise hesitated. She could feel her resolve crumbling as his eyes held her gaze, speaking more eloquently than any words he might say. All at once, she was flooded with memories of all the kind things he'd done for her and Kyle, reviving the feelings she had worked so hard to repress these past few weeks.

'I didn't exactly say that,' she finally answered. 'But we can't just pick up where we left off. There's a lot we have to figure out first and it isn't going to be easy.'

When he realised that the possibility was still there, Taylor felt a wave of relief wash over him.

'I'm sorry, Denise,' he repeated earnestly. 'I'm sorry for what I did to Kyle, too.'

She simply nodded and took his hand.

For the next few hours they talked with a new openness. It was nearly four in the morning when he rose to leave; Denise walked him to the door and watched him drive away. She reflected that she still didn't know where their relationship would go from here. As it had been from the beginning, it was up to Taylor.

THE FOLLOWING AFTERNOON he called to ask if it would be all right for him to stop by.

Still exhausted from the night before, she wanted time to mull things over. She needed that. So did he. But in the end, she reluctantly consented, more for Kyle's sake than her own. She knew that Kyle would be overjoyed to see him.

An hour later, Taylor arrived, and she could hear Kyle's excited screams from the front yard. 'Mommy! Taylor's here!' *Money! Tayer's here!*

She went to the front door, still feeling a little uneasy. Opening it, she saw Kyle charging towards Taylor's truck; as soon as Taylor stepped out, Kyle jumped into his arms as if Taylor had never stayed away, his face beaming. Taylor hugged him for a long time, finally putting him down just as Denise walked up.

'Hey there,' he said quietly.

She crossed her arms. 'Hi, Taylor.'

'Tayer's here!' Kyle said jubilantly, latching onto Taylor's leg.

Denise smiled thinly. 'He sure is, sweetie.'

Taylor cleared his throat, sensing her unease. 'I grabbed a few things from the store on my way over here. If it's OK to stay a while.'

Kyle laughed aloud. 'Tayer's here,' he said again.

'I don't think I have much of a choice,' Denise answered honestly.

Taylor grabbed a grocery bag from the cab of the truck and carried it inside. They spoke for a couple of minutes but he seemed to sense her ambivalence about his presence and finally went outside with Kyle. Denise started preparing the meal, thankful to be left alone. The monotony of the work was soothing.

As she stood over the sink, however, she occasionally glanced outside, watching Taylor and Kyle play in the dirt pile where they pushed Tonka trucks back and forth. Kyle climbed onto Taylor's squatting figure, covering him with dirt. She could hear Kyle laughing . . .

It's so good to hear that sound again . . . But . . . Denise shook her head. Even if Kyle has forgiven him, I won't forget. He hurt us once, he could hurt us again. She wouldn't allow herself to fall for him so deeply this time. She wouldn't let herself go.

But they look so cute together . . .

She sighed, refusing to allow the internal conversation to dominate her thoughts. She set the table, then decided to sit outside. She walked out into the crisp, fresh air and sat on the porch steps. She could see Taylor and Kyle, still immersed in their playing.

After a while, Taylor glanced towards the house and saw her, letting her know he had with a smile. Then he leaned close to Kyle and motioned with his chin, prompting Kyle to turn in her direction. The boy waved happily and both of them stood. Taylor brushed off his jeans as they started towards her.

'You two look like you were having fun,' she said.

Taylor grinned. 'I think I'll give up contracting and just build dirt cities. It's a lot more fun and the people are easier to deal with.'

She leaned towards Kyle. 'Did you have fun, sweetie?'

'Yes,' he said, nodding enthusiastically. 'It was fun.' *Ess fun*.

Denise looked up at Taylor again. 'The meal won't be ready for a while, so you've got plenty of time if you want to stay outside.'

'I figured as much, but I need a glass of water to wash down some of the dirt.'

Denise smiled. 'Do you want something to drink, too, Kyle?'

Instead of answering, however, Kyle moved closer and wrapped his arms round Denise's neck.

'What's wrong, honey?' Denise asked, suddenly concerned. With his eyes closed, Kyle squeezed more tightly and she instinctively put her arms round him.

'Thank you, Mommy. Thank you.' *Kenk you, money. Kenk you.*

'Honey, what's wrong?' she asked again.

'Kenk you,' Kyle said again, not listening. 'Kenk you, Money.'

'Honey . . .' Denise tried again, a little more desperately this time, suddenly feeling a flash of fear at what was happening.

Denise shot a *see-what-you've-done-now* look at Taylor when all of a sudden, Kyle spoke again, the same grateful tone in his voice. 'I wuff you, Money.' *I love you, Mommy.*

Denise closed her eyes in shock. As if knowing she still didn't believe it, Kyle tightened his grip around her, squeezing with ferocious intensity and said it a second time. 'I wuff you, Money.'

Oh my God . . . Tears suddenly began to spill from her eyes.

For five years, she'd waited to hear the words. For five long years, she'd been deprived of something other parents take for granted, a simple declaration of love.

'I love you too, sweetie . . . I love you so much.' Lost in the moment, she hugged Kyle as tightly as he was holding her.

I'll never forget this, she thought, memorising the feel of Kyle's body, his little-boy smell, his halting, miraculous words. *Never*.

Watching them together, Taylor stood off to the side, as mesmerised as she was. Kyle, too, seemed to know he'd done something right and as she finally released him, he turned to Taylor, a grin on his face.

Denise laughed at his expression, her cheeks flushed. She turned to gaze at Taylor, her expression full of wonder. 'Did you teach him to say that?'

Taylor shook his head. 'Not me. We were just playing.'

Kyle turned from Taylor back to his mother again, the same joyous expression on his face. 'Kenk you, Money,' he said simply. 'Tayer's home.'

Denise wiped the tears from her cheeks.

'I hope he's right,' Taylor said, his voice cracking slightly. 'Because I love you, too.'

It was the first time he'd ever said the words to her, or to anyone. Though he'd imagined they would be hard to say, they weren't. He'd never been so sure about anything.

Denise could almost feel Taylor's emotion as he reached for her hand. In a daze, she took it, allowing him to pull her to her feet, drawing her close. Before she knew it, she felt his lips against hers. The tenderness of the kiss seemed to last for ever until he finally buried her face in his neck.

'I love you, Denise,' he whispered. 'I love you so much. I'll do anything for another chance, and I promise I'll never leave you again.'

Denise closed her eyes, letting him hold her, before reluctantly pulling back. With a little space between them, she turned away, and for a moment Taylor didn't know what to think. He squeezed her hand, listening as she took a breath. Still, she didn't speak.

Above them, cumulus clouds, rolling white and grey, were drifting steadily, moving with the wind. On the horizon, dark clouds loomed. In an hour, the rain would come, full and heavy. But by then, they would be in the kitchen, listening as raindrops pelted the tin roof.

Denise sighed and faced Taylor again. He loved her. And she loved him. It was as simple as that. She moved into his arms.

Epilogue

From where she was sitting on the porch of their new house, Denise could see Taylor and Kyle perched on the sea wall, fishing poles in hand. She smiled wistfully, thinking how natural they looked together. Like father and son, which of course they were.

At the wedding, a small service held at the Episcopal Church, Kyle had served as ring-bearer, Melissa as maid of honour. Judy had dabbed at her tears from her seat in the front row as the rings were exchanged. After the ceremony, Taylor and Denise drove to a small bed and breakfast that overlooked the ocean. Next morning, they rose before the sun came up, and took a walk on the beach. With Taylor standing behind her, his arms round her waist, Denise simply leaned her head back, feeling warm and safe, as a new day unfolded.

When they returned from the honeymoon, Taylor had surprised her with a set of blueprints he'd had drawn up for a graceful home on the water, with wide porches, a modern kitchen and hardwood floors. They purchased a plot on the outskirts of town and began building within a month.

Denise had stopped working at Eights; she and Taylor went in for dinner now and then, simply to visit Ray. He was the same as always and joked that she could have her job back any time she wanted.

Though Taylor still suffered from the occasional nightmare, he'd surprised her with his devotion over the past year. Despite the responsibilities of building the house, he came home for lunch every day and refused to' work any later than six. They spent every weekend as a family.

Now, glancing through the window, she saw Taylor and Kyle walking towards the shed. She watched as Taylor hung his pole, then took Kyle's as well. A moment later, they were mounting the steps to the porch.

'Hey, Mom,' Kyle chirped.

'Did you catch anything?' she asked.

'No. No fish.'

Like everything else in her life, Kyle's speech had improved dramatically. It wasn't by any means perfect, but he was gradually closing the gap between himself and his peers at kindergarten. More importantly, she'd stopped worrying about it so much.

Taylor kissed Denise as he made his way inside. 'So, where is the little fella?' he asked.

She nodded towards the corner of the porch. 'Still asleep.'

'Shouldn't he be awake by now?'

'In a few minutes. He'll be getting hungry soon.'

Together they approached the basket in the corner and Taylor bent over, peering closely, as if he still couldn't believe he'd been responsible for helping to create a new life. He reached out and gently ran his hand over his son's hair. At seven weeks, there was barely any at all.

'He seems so peaceful,' he whispered.

Denise put her hand on Taylor's shoulder, hoping that one day the baby would look just like his father. 'He's beautiful,' she said.

Taylor leaned in close, kissing his son on his forehead. 'Did you hear that, Mitch? Your mom thinks you're beautiful.'

NICHOLAS SPARKS

In all Nicholas Sparks's novels, there is an element of autobiography. *The Notebook* was inspired by his wife's grandparents, who for sixty years were inseparable; *Message in a Bottle* owed much to his father's experiences after his wife died tragically young; and *A Walk to Remember* was written as a result of his younger sister's battle with cancer.

The Rescue also stemmed from Sparks's personal experience. His own son, like Kyle in his novel, has problems understanding language. 'The best description is probably dyslexia of sound. When you talk to him it's as if one second you are speaking Chinese, the next English and the next the sound is jumbled. He has to learn to talk through that jumble.' It's an unusual condition and, like Denise in his book, the author and his wife Cathy did a great deal of research into the subject. They found two books particularly useful: *Late Talking Children* by Thomas Sowell and *Let Me Hear Your Voice* by Catherine Maurice. 'Those books explained that we weren't alone in having a child like ours, although it often seemed that way, and they also showed we could do something about it,' says Sparks. 'The teaching techniques used by Denise in *The Rescue* are the ones my wife and I used.'

Nicholas Sparks is very much a family man and says that his two sons, Miles and Ryan, are 'the greatest thing that has ever happened to me. Although I do my writing at home, they never distract me—I'm not one of those writers who need absolute solitude to work. When I was working on *The Notebook,* for instance, I put the computer right next to the television so I could be with the boys. I'd lie on the floor typing on the keyboard, while they crawled all over me. It didn't bother me a bit.'

faith

Peter James

'I love you, Faith. I couldn't live without you.'

Hearing these words would once have made Faith Ransome happier than she ever dreamed possible. But her husband's protestations of love now chill her to the bone. Over the years, he has changed from the handsome young doctor who captured her heart, into a tyrant who tries to control her every move.

Leaving is the only answer. But she knows Ross will never, ever let her go . . .

One

Late on a wet May afternoon, Faith Ransome, walking around the downstairs rooms of her house, checking for errant bits of Lego, thought, Is this it? Is this my life? Is this all there is?

Alec, in the kitchen, called, 'Mummy! Come and watch!'

She stooped to recover a bright yellow piece from behind the sofa, and shivered, feeling a little queasy. It was cold in England after three weeks in Thailand. They'd been home four days and it felt longer.

'Muummmeeeee!'

Tuning out his voice, she walked upstairs, recovered another Lego brick from the landing, went into Alec's room, and put the two pieces in the box on the table. Spike, Alec's hamster, was trundling around inside the treadmill in his cage. She scooped up a few spilled grains from the tabletop and dropped them in the wastebin.

As she finished she heard the unmistakable mashing of tyres on gravel. Barking steadily, Rasputin, their black Labrador, lumbered from the kitchen, through the hall, into the drawing room where, Faith knew, he had leapt onto his chair in front of the bay window so that he could see his master.

He was home early.

'Alec! Daddy's home!' She sprinted for the bedroom, peered in, checked. Bed neat. Shoes, slippers, stray clothes, all put away. En suite bathroom. Basin spotless. Towels hung the way Ross liked them.

Hastily she took off the jeans, sweatshirt and trainers that were her habitual daytime clothes, pulled on black slacks, a white blouse, a

273

pale green cardigan. It wasn't that she felt like dressing up to greet her husband, she just wanted to avoid criticism.

In the bathroom she stared at her face in the mirror. She put on some eye shadow, mascara, dabbed a little powder on her perfect snub nose (her husband's craftsmanship, not her genes). She checked her hair. She was a natural blonde and favoured classic styles. Right now, it was parted to one side, cut just short of her jaw.

You don't look bad, girl, not for a thirty-two-year-old mum.

She hurried down the stairs, as the front door opened in a flurry of leaping dog, swirling Burberry raincoat, swinging black briefcase.

She took the case and the raincoat, thrust at her as if she was a hat-check girl. 'Hi,' she said. 'How was your day?'

'Total hell. I lost someone. Died on me.' Anger and pain in his voice as he slammed the door. Ross, six foot four, black hair gelled back, starched white shirt, red and gold silk tie, tailored navy suit, black brogues flossed to military perfection. He seemed close to tears.

At the sight of his son his face lit up. 'Hey, big guy!' Alex leapt into his arms and Ross held him tightly to his chest. 'What's been happening? How was your day?'

Faith smiled. No matter how low she felt, seeing the love between her husband and her son was the one thing that gave her strength and the resolve to make her marriage work.

She hung up his coat, set down the case, and went into the kitchen. She poured a three-finger measure of Macallan into a glass, then clinked four ice cubes into it. Ross followed her in and set Alec down. The boy's attention returned to the television.

'Who died?' Faith said, handing her husband the glass. 'A patient?'

He held up the rim to the window, checking for dirt before committing it to his lips.

One finger of whisky went down. She reached up, loosened his tie, halfheartedly put a comforting arm around him, then withdrew it.

'I scored two goals today, Daddy!'

'That's terrific!' Ross stood behind his son and wrapped his arms around him again. '*Two* goals?'

Alec nodded, torn between accepting praise and watching the screen.

Then the smile faded from Ross's face. He said again, 'Two goals!' But the sparkle had gone from his eyes. He patted Alec's head, then went down the hall to his study, sat down in his leather chair, levered it to its furthest back position, and closed his eyes.

Faith watched him. He was suffering, but she felt nothing for him. Part of her still wanted everything between them to be as it once was, although now it was more for Alec's sake, than her own.

'Died. I can't believe she did that to me.'

Quietly, 'What happened?'

'Allergic reaction to the anaesthetic. That's the second this year.'

Faith went to the humidor in the dining room, took out a Monte-cristo No. 3, clipped the end the way Ross liked it, and brought it back into the room. She held the flame of the lighter as he drew several deep puffs, rotating the end until it was burning evenly.

He blew a long jet of smoke at the ceiling, then, eyes closed, asked, 'How was your day?'

She wanted to say, Actually, it was a shitty day, the way most of my days are, but she didn't. She said, 'It was OK. Fine.'

He nodded, silently. Then, after some moments, said, 'I love you, Faith. I couldn't live without you. You know that, don't you?'

Yes, she thought. And that's a big problem.

FAITH LAY listening to the news from the clock radio, across the far side of the bed. Then a time check: 6.25am on Wednesday, May 12.

She reached for her contact lenses. Twenty minutes and she would have to get Alec up, fed, to school, and then . . . ?

The queasiness she'd been feeling for the past few days seemed worse this morning, and a thought struck her. Pregnant? *Oh God, please no*.

A year after Alec was born they'd begun trying for a second child but nothing had happened. After a year, Ross had arranged tests, but they'd shown everything was working fine. The problem, it seemed, was with him, but he refused flatly to go to any specialist. At first this had angered Faith, but increasingly she'd seen it as a blessing. She loved Alec but he was hard work. Depression had dogged her on and off since he was born, and her energy levels had been so low she didn't know how she could cope with another child. She knew that a big part of the reason she stayed in her marriage was that she couldn't imagine life without Alec. There was no way, in her depressed state, that Ross would have let her keep him if she had left.

From the bathroom, Ross called out, 'What are you wearing tonight, darling?'

Brain into gear, fast. 'I thought the black taffeta you bought me.'

'No—that's more suitable for a ball. This is just a dinner. You need to look right—it's really important tonight.'

She mouthed a silent curse. It was always *really important*.

All those dreams you had at school, all those glossy lives you looked at in magazines, of people who seemed to have it all. But she had never envied them. Her father, a gentle, uncomplaining man, had been bedridden throughout her childhood, and she'd worked since as far back as she could remember to help her mother keep the family.

Faith had never been ambitious for wealth. All she had ever sought to do with her life was to be a caring person and to make a difference to the world. She had always hoped that when she had children she could teach them respect, give them a happier childhood than she'd had and make them decent people.

But now, at thirty-two, her life was as remote from her modest origins as it was from her dreams. She was married to a plastic surgeon who was a seriously wealthy perfectionist, and they lived in a house that was absurdly grand. She knew she *ought* to count her blessings, as her mother told her. But she and her mother would always see things differently—she hoped.

Ten to seven and he was dressed, dabbing at a fleck of blood on his chin. On the bed she had laid out a dress, shoes, bag, necklace and earrings.

'OK, fine, good. Wear your hair up.' He cupped her face in his hands, kissed her lips lightly, and was gone.

FAITH DECIDED to drive into Burgess Hill, the nearest town, to do a major groceries shop. As she waited in the queue at the car-park barrier, staring out at the cloud-laden sky, she was aware that she was shaking slightly, her nerves jangling. That indefinable dark fear that was part of her depression never stayed away for long.

When did my life with Ross start to change?

Had there been a point in the past twelve years at which Ross, the kind, caring, fun-loving young houseman she had loved to death had turned into the vile-tempered monster whose arrival home she dreaded? Had that side of him always been there? Had her love for him blinded her to it? Or had he masked it?

Why was it only she who could see it? Why couldn't her mother, or her friends? But she knew the answer to that. Ross never gave them the chance—he could charm the birds out of the trees.

In those early days Faith had loved him so much she'd let him do anything. She had believed in him so completely that she'd endured the pain and discomfort of six operations and he had transformed her from being plain into someone, well, less plain. And in a way, it was flattering. As his reputation began its rapid ascent, she had enjoyed being taken to conventions where he had pointed out the reshaping he had done on her lips, eyes, mouth, cheeks, chin and breasts. That, at least, was one of the bonuses to have come out of twelve years of marriage: the huge boost to her self-confidence.

Life can be good again, she thought. Somehow I'm going to find a way to make it good—for Alec and for myself.

In a sudden fit of extravagance in the supermarket, she bought a couple of frozen lobsters—Ross's favourite—for their dinner tomorrow, some spicy chicken wings, for which Alec had acquired a taste in Thailand, as well as his favourite caramel-crunch ice cream. Then she remembered to buy a tin of Ambrosia rice pudding with sultanas for her mother, who was coming to baby-sit tonight.

Oh, Ross, why do I still keep trying to please you? Is it just to buy a few moments of peace? Or do I delude myself that if I'm sufficiently nice to you you'll release me from this marriage, and allow me to take my son with me?

She turned the Range Rover into the drive, past the grand stone balls topping the pillars and the smart brass sign, LITTLE SCAYNES MANOR. The approach to the Elizabethan house was stunning, down the tree-lined gravel drive, up to the gabled, ivy-clad façade.

It was in a beautiful location, close to the foot of the soft, rolling hills of the South Downs. Ten bedrooms, drawing room, library, a dining room, a huge kitchen with an oak floor. To visitors it was idyllic. Yet there was an atmosphere about the place that prevented Faith from feeling entirely comfortable. Sometimes, entering the house when it was empty, the large gloomy hallway, the sharp tick of the grandfather clock at the foot of the carved stairs, and the slits in the helmet visors of the armour Ross collected gave her the creeps.

Today it was OK. It was Wednesday and Mrs Fogg the cleaning lady was here: Faith could hear the whine of the vacuum cleaner up in one of the bedrooms. Speedily, she lugged the groceries into the kitchen. The nausea was back and her head felt warm as if she were running a slight temperature.

She removed from one of the bags the pregnancy testing kit she'd bought in Boots and squinted at the instructions. Then she carried the plastic pot, pipette and test disk into the downstairs cloakroom and locked the door. She urinated into the pot, drew some urine into the pipette and then released five drops of it onto the indent in the disk.

A red minus sign. She was praying for a red minus sign.

She looked everywhere except at her watch. She looked at the brass taps on the the brilliant white sink, the pile of *National Geographic* on the shelf by the seat. She noticed a spider's web up in a corner and made a mental note to tell Mrs Fogg. Then she looked down and raised the stick.

A red minus filled the window! With her relief, the nausea was gone.

two

Oliver Cabot was distracted by several things tonight, but principally by the woman at the next table, who had caught his eye twice and looked as bored with her companions as he was with his.

He had accepted the invitation to this dinner at the Royal Society of Medicine, not out of love for his profession or admiration for his hosts' organisation, which he mistrusted. Rather, he was interested in keeping up with medical advances. But right now this woman, on the far side of the table, with her streaky blonde hair framing her face— a cute face, pretty rather than classically beautiful—was reminding him of someone. At last he got it. Meg Ryan!

Meg Ryan was listening to a lean, bald man who was talking enthusiastically while she nodded. Her body language told Cabot that she had not taken to this man. He wondered what they were discussing. And as he did so she caught his eye again and immediately looked away.

'NORMALLY ASPIRATED, she'll give you two-eight-five BHP, but what I did, I took the cylinder heads to be polished.'

Faith had to look at his place card to remind herself of his name. Dighton Carver, Vice-President, Marketing had been talking about car engines for the past fifteen minutes. Before that he had talked about his divorce, his kids, his house and his power boat.

Her dessert lay untouched on her plate. The queasiness she'd felt this morning had returned and she'd barely eaten anything. This was one of those occasions that Ross enjoyed and Faith hated. Ross, the son of a Gas Board clerk, now a celebrated plastic surgeon, was being fêted by his profession. His name was there on the printed menu, featured in the same column as the Queen's gynaecologist. Ross Ransome MS, FRCS (Plast).

In spite of everything, she felt proud to see his name in print, knowing that, in her own small way, she had contributed towards his success. At Ross's insistence she'd had elocution lessons to change her suburban London accent. For years she'd dutifully read her way through the list of books Ross had prescribed for her: classics, the great poets, Shakespeare. He wanted her to be able to hold her own at any dinner table.

Many times she had wondered what it was about her that he had fallen in love with. He'd changed her face, her breasts, her voice, and re-educated her. Maybe he had been attracted to her because she was malleable, a *tabula rasa* he could shape into a perfect woman. Maybe that's what the control freak inside him needed.

He was watching her now, seated diagonally from her across the large round table, next to a man with a perfect tan and even more perfect teeth, who was talking to him intently.

Casting her eyes around the room, Faith saw that a man she'd noticed watching her was looking at her again. Their eyes met, and he smiled. Flattered, she looked away and suppressed a grin. It had been a long time since she had flirted with anyone and it felt good.

A little later she cast a furtive glance at his table. Her admirer was engrossed in conversation, and she had a chance to study him. He was in his mid- to late forties, she guessed, tall and lean, and wore wire-framed glasses. His face, beneath a tangle of grey curls, was serious and intellectual. He had a bigger, less perfect bow tie than the neat little black satin numbers that seemed to be standard here, and it gave him a rather reckless, louche air.

Who are you? she wondered. I really like the look of you.

The bang of the gavel snapped her out of her thoughts and a liveried toastmaster pronounced, 'My lords, ladies and gentlemen, please be upstanding for the loyal toast.'

SILENCE IN THE CAR. Ross driving fast. Darkness unspooling from the road ahead. Brahms playing, the violin mournful. The smells of Ross's cigar and leather filled the interior of the macho Aston Martin cocoon.

Faith's mind returned to the stranger in the crush at the bar after the speeches were over. He had been alone. All she needed to do was take four steps and she'd have been in front of him. Ross hadn't even been in the room. Just four steps. Instead, she'd bottled out.

'I saw you,' Ross said calmly.

'Saw me what?'

Silence. Just the violins and the night. She knew what. There was no point in going through the rigmarole of denial. Ross was calm but there was brooding anger inside him. Best to let it simmer and maybe by the time they were home he'd be too tired to make a big issue. Right now she didn't feel well enough for a fight.

It was twenty past twelve. She thought about Alec, tucked up and asleep by now. He'd be fine, he adored his grandmother, who spoiled him. Margaret enjoyed staying over—Ross had made a palatial space for her in the house, a whole suite of rooms. She'd be awake now, sitting in front of the sixty-inch television he'd bought for her, watching a movie. Faith thought again about the stranger at the dinner, wondered what life would be like with a different man . . . And then, suddenly, the nausea erupted inside her. 'Stop! Ross, pull over!'

The interior of the car seemed to close in around her. Hand rammed over her mouth, just one thought in mind as he pulled onto the hard shoulder, *Must not . . . Not in the car . . .*

They jolted to a stop. She threw the seat belt clear, found the door handle, stumbled out into the sharp, cold air. Then, on her knees on the tarmac, she threw up.

Moments later, as she threw up again, Ross's hand was on her forehead, holding her, then wiping her mouth with his handkerchief.

Back in the car with her seat reclined, the heater turned right up, he said, 'Probably that seafood cocktail. Duff prawn or something.'

She wanted to tell him he was wrong: he knew she'd been feeling like this for days. Instead, she lay back, her contact lenses feeling gritty and uncomfortable, dimly aware from the motion of the car, the stops and turns they made, that they were getting closer to home.

SHE WAS SITTING at the pine table in front of the Aga, listening to Rasputin barking, probably chasing a rabbit somewhere, and Ross calling him back in. The clock on the kitchen wall read ten past one.

She heard the patter of paws, then a key clattered as Ross locked up for the night. He came up behind her, rested his hands on her shoulders. 'Alec's sound asleep. How're you feeling now?'

'A little better, thanks.'

'The pills kicking in?'

'I think so. What were they?'

'They'll calm your system down.'

It irritated her that he always resisted telling her what pills he gave her, as if she were a child.

He smiled. 'There's something I want to show you before we go up—won't take a sec.'

She picked her evening bag up from the kitchen table and followed him down the corridor to his study. Whether it was the throwing up or the pills she did not know, but she was definitely feeling better.

Ross walked across to his computer, touched the keyboard and the screen came to life. Once Faith had liked the manly, solid feel of this room, but now she felt uncomfortable, like a child in a headmaster's study. It was spotlessly tidy with deep, leather-upholstered armchairs. Victorian seascapes on the walls, bookshelves lined with medical books. He worked at a handsome antique walnut desk, which she had bought for his birthday shortly after they'd moved here, and which had made a big dent in the savings she'd built up during her short career in catering.

She'd given up work at Ross's insistence shortly before their marriage. Although she loved her job, doing mostly directors' lunches for the small firm she'd joined, she had been happy to concentrate on making a home for herself and Ross.

Her face appeared on the computer screen.

'That's how you look now,' Ross said.

She yawned, trying to remember when the picture had been taken. On the beach outside their hotel in Phuket three weeks ago, she recalled, looking at the background.

Ross was pointing at her nose on the screen, making a curve with his finger along the bridge. 'A simple operation, just a few days of discomfort, and then . . .' He clicked the keyboard and her face disappeared, then reappeared again, with a new nose.

'Can we talk about this in the morning, Ross? I'm too tired.'

'I'll organise a room at the clinic. Your mother can take Alec—'

'No,' she said. 'I've told you, I don't want any more surgery.'

The anger that had been pent-up inside him since dinner was now coming out. 'Faith, do you know how many women would give their right arm for what you get free?'

Smiling acidly, she held out her right arm. 'Cut it off—you've cut bits off just about every other part of me.'

'Don't be ridiculous.'

'I'm not. If you don't like me the way I am, marry someone else.'

He looked so genuinely hurt that she felt a pang of guilt, which changed rapidly to anger. Ross was like a fine actor who had his audience in the palm of his hand. He had played with her mind and emotions for years, and she'd been sucked in. But not any more.

'Darling,' he said. 'Every plastic surgeon operates on his wife. When you come to conferences with me, you're the best credentials I have. People look at you and they see perfection.'

'Is that all I am to you? A *sample*?'

He moved closer to her, his voice raised. 'Listen, don't ever forget that you were nothing, you were just a plain little girl. I saw your potential. I made you a beautiful woman.'

'So why didn't you leave me as I was, if you can't bear to see other men looking at me? Why didn't you let me remain an ugly duckling?'

He stared at her, quivering, and although he had never struck her, she had a feeling that now he was going to. 'You weren't just looking at that man at dinner. He was undressing you with his eyes.'

She turned away. 'You're being ridiculous. I'm going to bed.'

Ross gripped her shoulders so hard she cried out in pain. Her handbag fell to the floor. 'I'm talking to you.'

She knelt and scooped up her bag. 'Well, I'm not talking to you any more tonight. I feel ill and I'm going to bed.'

As she reached the staircase the nausea got her again. She tried to hang on to the banister rail, but her grip slipped and she stumbled.

Ross caught her. Now his grip was gentle, his voice tender. 'I'm sorry, I didn't mean to hurt you. You just don't know how much you mean to me, you and Alec. I didn't have a life before you, not a real one. I didn't know what love was. Can you understand that?'

She stared at him dully. She'd heard this speech many times and, yes, she knew he meant it. But it had ceased to mean anything to her.

'You know how scared I get when you aren't well, don't you? I want you to see Jules tomorrow.'

Jules Ritterman was their family doctor. Faith did not care for him, but right now she felt too weak to argue. She just wanted to lie down, to sleep. Her head was swimming. 'I'll be OK,' she said.

'You've been feeling sick for a week. You may have picked up a bug in Thailand and if so it needs to be knocked on the head, OK?'

She tried to think it through. Seeing Jules meant going back up to London tomorrow. But it was Ross's birthday in a couple of weeks and it would give her a chance to do some shopping for him.

'OK,' she said, reluctantly.

'Besides,' he said, putting his arms around her and holding her tightly, 'we've got to get you right before we go into surgery.'

AT 6.05 in the morning, on May 13, Oliver Cabot, dressed in a track suit, gloves and trainers, removed the padlock and chain from his bicycle and wheeled it out of the communal hallway of his apartment building close to the Portobello Road. He shivered. There was a dampness in London that seemed to drive the cold deep into your bones, he thought. It had been a shock after life in southern California, and he still hadn't got used to it.

He pulled on his helmet, mounted the bike, zeroed the mileometer, then pressed down on the pedals. He built up speed as he swung left into Ladbroke Grove.

In spite of the cold, he liked London at this hour. There was something special about being out in a city ahead of the rest of the world. It all looked as it did every morning, but there was a change inside him today. The memory of that woman at the dinner last night. Her glances across the crowded room towards him. Faith Ransome. Eventually he'd asked someone who she was.

She's married, Oliver. Get her out of your head, man.

He pedalled along handsome terraced side streets up towards the Bayswater Road, crossed into Hyde Park and headed for the Serpentine. He cycled around it, watching the ducks, the reflections. *Something tells me you are not happy in your life, Faith. You were flirting with me last night. There was desperation in your face. So lovely, yet so* desperate.

What are you desperate about, Faith? Will I ever meet you again?

ON THE HARD COUCH behind the screen in the Wimpole Street consulting room, a strap tight around her arm, Faith held her breath. She'd never liked needles. She watched and did not watch at the same time. Out of the corner of her eye, she saw the hollow tube of the syringe steadily fill with crimson blood.

Two faces above her. A nurse and Dr Ritterman himself.

'OK, Faith,' he said, walking round to the far side of the screen. 'You may get dressed now.'

A few minutes later, Jules Ritterman was seated behind a desk studying her notes. A solemn, diminutive man of sixty, his face had the texture of parched leather. With his grey pinstriped suit, crinkly hair and unfashionably large glasses, he could have passed for a chartered accountant or a lawyer. According to Ross, Jules Ritterman was the top socialite general practitioner in London. He was GP to anyone who was anyone. It was typical of her husband, in his craving to distance himself from his humble roots, to have courted this man and made him a close friend.

Faith had never warmed to him. She wished she had a doctor she could talk to, but every time she had tried to discuss this with Ross, he became furious, refusing to see how she could want someone inferior.

Ritterman leaned forward. 'Well, Faith, I don't think there's anything to worry about. Probably a little hostile bacteria from your trip to Thailand. That's one of the hazards of travel, I'm afraid—encountering bugs our immune systems aren't familiar with. I'll have some analysis done on your blood and urine, just to make sure. And I'll have my secretary telephone a prescription through to Ross.'

'Why can't you give it to me?' It was always the same with Ritterman: she felt he treated her like a schoolgirl.

'Much easier. It will save you the bother of having to queue for it.'

'I don't mind that.'

His eyes slipped to his watch and the signal could not have been clearer. She left, feeling dissatisfied and belittled.

It was half past eleven. Outside, in the teeming rain, she took a cab to the General Trading Company in Sloane Street. Ross was a stickler for smart labels. Turnbull and Asser, Fortnum & Mason, Harrods. The General Trading Company was on his approved list.

Faith loved the rich atmosphere of the shop. It felt like being in a private club, its small interconnecting rooms packed with treasures. She tapped a glass display, pointing at a calfskin wallet, and asked an absurdly handsome male assistant if she could look at it.

'It's a wonderful wallet,' he told her, unlocking the cabinet.

She turned it over in her hands and savoured the rich aroma of the leather. Then she opened it and looked at the compartments inside. 'Would you know if it takes dollar bills? My husband always complains that English wallets are just that bit too narrow.'

'I'd better go and check up on that one,' the young man said.

But before he could move, a hand reached from behind Faith and laid a crisp, one-dollar bill on the counter. 'Here,' an American voice said, 'want to try this?'

Faith turned round, then stared in amazement at her admirer from last night. 'Er—thanks—er—hi,' she said, awkwardly.

He smiled. 'Hi! How did you enjoy the dinner?'

'The dinner was fine,' she said.

His smile told her he did not believe her.

She liked his face. It wasn't handsome in any conventional sense, but it was filled with warmth and sparkle, a wise, yet youthful face.

'Actually,' she confessed, 'it was incredibly dull.'

With an effort, she glanced away, aware she needed to stop the game. But it was good, just for a moment, to feel flattered by this tall man in his black polo neck, black jeans and black greatcoat.

Behind her, a triumphant voice said, 'Yes, look, a perfect fit!'

She turned and saw the assistant holding up the wallet with the dollar bill inside it.

'Fine, good,' she said. 'I'll take it.' She dug her purse from her handbag, handed her gold card to him, then turned back to her admirer. 'For my husband,' she said.

'Lucky man.' His eyes were flirting again. 'You have time for coffee?'

She looked back into his eyes. Danger flags were running up inside her head. She glanced at her watch: 11.45. She could spare half an hour. Her mother was collecting Alec from school today, so it would be OK if she was late back—and, anyhow, she would tell Ross she'd been shopping for his birthday. 'Sure,' she said. 'Why not?'

He put out his hand. 'I'm Oliver Cabot.'

'Faith Ransome.'

His eyes still fixed on hers, he said, 'Faith. A good name. The writer H. L. Mencken defined faith as 'illogical belief in the occurrence of the improbable'. Is that you?'

'Probably,' she said, with a grin, and signed her credit slip.

DOWNSTAIRS, in the basement café, Faith ordered green-leaf tea. As Oliver Cabot carried the tray to a vacant corner table, Faith followed at a distance, looking nervously around for any familiar faces.

Calm down, girl! she had to tell herself. *You're not having an affair with the man, for Christ's sake, just a cup of tea!*

But all the same, her nerves were jangling. Jangling because of her attraction to this stranger. She settled down at the tiny round table, and suddenly she no longer cared if anyone saw her. She was beginning to feel deliciously liberated, as if this was her own little revolution against the tyranny of Ross.

'So,' she said, 'what are you buying here?'

'I came to look at a wedding list—a colleague's getting married.'

'Great place to have a wedding list.'

'Actually, I told him to have it here. This is my favourite store in the whole world. It feels so quintessentially English.'

'It's always been my favourite shop too.'

They were silent for some moments.

Oliver was still in shock at seeing her here. If you *really* want something, he kept thinking, you can make it happen. *Power of the mind.* This morning, on his bicycle, he had been thinking about Faith and now she was here. A few years ago he would have dismissed it as coincidence. His medical training told him there was no such thing as telepathy. And yet, it had also taught him what many other doctors learned: that the most powerful drug in the world was the placebo: the power of the human mind.

She had on little make-up, and her eyes were warm, alert, but that desperation he had seen last night was there too. And there was something else, which he didn't like. Without saying anything, he reached across the table, took her left hand lightly by the wrist and began to study her palm. Her wrist was slender, sensuous, but he tried to block that from his mind. Tried to concentrate.

As Oliver Cabot gently traced her lifeline with his forefinger, a tiny erotic tickle coiled through Faith, startling her, as if a switch had been thrown deep inside her. The feeling she had had upstairs, that they were old friends, was deepening.

'That's your lifeline.' He pointed to it. 'It's broken just over a third of the way down which means you're going to have a change around your early thirties.' He paused. 'I guess that's where you are now, right?'

'Anything else you can tell from my palm?'

'Sure. How much else do you want to know?'

'Just the good stuff. You can edit out the rest.'

Smiling, he studied her. Then his expression darkened a fraction and he looked up at her with concern in his eyes. 'How's your health?'

She did not tell him that she was feeling queasy. 'It's fine, thanks.' With a nervous shimmy in her voice, she added, 'So what do you do exactly? Are you a doctor?'

'Did you hear of the Cabot Centre for Complementary Medicine?'

The name sounded familiar. She had a feeling there'd been some press coverage recently. Then she remembered. 'In *The Times* about a month ago? Was that you delivering a pretty blistering attack on the medical profession?'

He stirred his espresso thoughtfully. 'No disrespect to your husband, but the average conventional doctor in the Western world is a puppet on a string. A clerk, tied hand and foot to a medical system he helped build because he thought it would make the world a better place. Instead all it did was make a few organisations rich enough to afford absurd dinners like last night.'

'But you didn't have a problem accepting their hospitality?'

'I was there to snoop, although, actually, I am a paid-up, card-carrying doctor of medicine—I just don't practise as one.'

'Tell me about the Cabot Centre for Complementary Medicine.'

'We're doing interesting work. We have a homeopathy practice, osteopathy, acupuncture, hypnotherapy. Let me show you the stuff we're doing sometime—or is the wife of an eminent plastic surgeon forbidden to talk to quacks like me?'

She smiled. Ross always rejected alternative medicine. As far as he was concerned modern Western clinical medicine was the only kind anyone in their right mind should ever contemplate.

'Maybe your husband would like to come too?' Oliver asked. 'A lot of our treatments and therapies are for postoperative care.'

She felt disappointed. Was this just a sales pitch? And she could picture Ross's face. 'I don't think so—I mean, he's incredibly busy.'

She detected his relief and was glad. The invitation to include Ross had been a courtesy, nothing more. It *was* her he was interested in.

'How about tomorrow? I can check my diary—maybe you could come over and have some lunch afterwards?'

'I'd love to, but we live in Sussex.'

'Nice part of the world. OK, so next time you're in town?'

Their eyes met again. This was so dangerous. Getting entangled with another man was the last thing she needed. She had to sort out her life with Ross, and somehow find an exit for herself and Alec.

Oliver Cabot proffered a business card. 'Call me next time you're coming up.'

She slipped it into her handbag, intending to drop it into a waste-bin before she got home. 'Thanks,' she said. 'I will.'

'BRANDENBURG CONCERTO number two, in F, Jane,' Ross said to the scrub nurse, without looking up from his suturing. 'I think this is a number two in F morning, don't you?'

Under the bright octopus lamp, the young woman lay on the table, her eyes open, glazed, motionless as a cadaver. Ross was coming to the end of the thread. The scrub nurse, wordless, passed a fresh one up to him. This was how Ross liked his theatre to run. The old-style way. Like clockwork. Hierarchy. Discipline. A tight ship.

Strains of the Brandenburg Concerto filled the room. Ross pushed the needle through the thin flap of flesh, cropped only minutes earlier from the young woman's thigh, and then through the scar tissue on the terrible burns that covered her upper torso. Sally Porter, twenty-seven, a pretty girl before fire had ravaged her looks. He had operated on her ten times in the past two years, and he would probably have to operate at least another ten times, trying, one small step at a time, to give her back her life. He admired her stoicism in coping with the setbacks.

He finished the last of the sutures, stood back and nodded at the photographer, who stepped forward and took three pictures of his work. Then the registrar began to lay the strips of gauze in place, and the scrub nurse handed Ross the stapler . . .

Twenty minutes later Sally was hoisted up, lifted across onto a trolley, and wheeled out to the recovery room. The runner nurse turned off the CD.

Ross flipped his mask down, slackened the tapes of his gown, and began writing his notes, the registrar looking over his shoulder. He was interrupted by a young nurse holding a cordless phone. 'Mr Ransome, there's a call for you.'

'Who is it?' he asked, irritated. They were on a tight schedule.

The nurse covered the receiver with her hand. 'It's Dr Ritterman. The third time he's called.'

He slipped out of his gown, handed it to a nurse, then took the phone and went into the corridor.

'Ross,' Ritterman said, 'sorry to chase you like this.'

'No problem. What's up?'

'You recall you asked me to see Faith last week?'

'Yuh.' Ross entered the changing room. 'This nausea she's been having, Jules, it seems to have been going on a long time.'

'I had some tests done on her fluids,' the GP said, sounding hesitant, 'and I needed to have further analysis on what came back. I—is this a good time to talk, Ross?'

'Actually, no, I have to get back into the theatre.' But the GP's tone worried him. 'What is it, Jules? What do the tests show?'

'Look, Ross, I think we ought to have a chat about this. What time will you be finished today?'

Alarmed, Ross said, 'About six, but I have to dash to the flat and change. I have a livery dinner in the City at seven thirty.'

'I could pop in about six thirty for a few minutes—I'd have to be away before seven, we're going to the ballet.'

'What's wrong with her, Jules?'

'It's best if we discuss this face to face. It's not good, I'm afraid.'

ROSS, IN STOCKINGED FEET, braces of his dinner-suit trousers hanging loose, ushered Jules Ritterman into the living room of his small flat close to Regent's Park, and steered him to one of the two-seater chesterfields opposite each other in front of the fireplace. Gas flames leaped up among the imitation logs. Chopin played on the CD.

He felt strained and wanted desperately to hear what the doctor had to tell him, but he said, 'Can I get you a drink, Jules?'

'Well, just a very small whisky, thank you, if you have time. A livery dinner, you said?'

'Barber-Surgeons Hall. I'll have to leave just after seven.' He poured some Macallan into a crystal tumbler.

The doctor's eyes were roving approvingly over the antique furniture and the oil paintings on the walls. 'It really is a most charming place this, Ross. Are you using it a lot?'

'Three or four nights a week. It's a little small, but it suits me fine. Faith hardly ever comes to town these days.' He sat opposite the GP, glanced at his watch anxiously, and said, 'So?'

The doctor leaned forward. 'Um,' he said. 'I . . .' He raised his glass and stared at it. 'Look, there are a few more tests I could do, just to make certain, but I'm sure in my own mind, Ross. And I've had a couple of informed opinions as well. How familiar are you with a viral infection known as Lendt's disease?'

'*Lendt's* disease?'

'Named after Hans Lendt, the American immunologist who identified it. I've had a look at several case histories in the past week, and they share similar characteristics. All the known cases have contracted this disease after visiting areas in the Far East bordering the Indian Ocean and South China Sea which, of course, includes Thailand. The first symptom is prolonged nausea—the patient usually feels this for two to three months. Increasing disorientation with delusions follow. Night terrors. Terminal features include fluctuating levels of consciousness and hallucinations. Then a gradual loss of motor-control functions.' Ritterman fell silent.

Ross lifted his glass, turned it round and set it down again without drinking. His mouth was dry. 'What's the treatment?'

'There isn't one,' Ritterman said, baldly.

'Nothing?' It came from Ross's throat like a yelp of pain.

'There are clinical trials in progress but no specific treatment as yet. The disease was only identified eight years ago but it's growing rapidly. About three thousand people have been diagnosed with it and the numbers could double in the next twelve months.'

Ross fiddled with a stud in his dress shirt. 'What's causing it?'

'No one knows yet. Could be pollution. Could be that antibiotics are slowly destroying our immunity to some diseases.' Ritterman took a sip of his drink. 'I'm afraid Lendt's disease is terminal in a large number of cases.'

Ross stood up, walked over to the window and stared down at the rush-hour traffic. Faith, terminally ill. He felt as if his whole world was collapsing in on him.

'I want to understand this disease, Jules. I want you to let me have all your research sources. Faith is a great girl, she's strong, a fighter.'

Ritterman nodded, without conviction.

'What did you tell her when you saw her?'

'I told her the truth,' Ritterman said. 'That I thought it was probably some bacterial infection—just a tummy bug.'

'So she knows nothing about the Lendt's disease diagnosis?'

'Not yet.'

Ross was silent for some moments, thinking. Then he said, 'Who's doing the clinical trials?'

'Moliou-Orelan.'

Moliou-Orelan was a US pharmaceutical giant with an impressive record for fast-tracking drugs onto the market. 'They're a good outfit, Jules. How can we get Faith onto a trials programme?'

'I've been in touch with them already,' the GP said. 'They're being very secretive but I understand they've had positive results. I have a good contact who's working on someone in Research and Development there, and I think I can get her onto the trial. But I cannot guarantee what she'll be taking, you know that. No one can.'

Most drug trials involved two groups of people, one that took the drug itself, the other that took a placebo. In a double-blind trial—neither the doctors nor their patients knew which were which. Only a handful of employees at the pharmaceutical company running the trials held the keys to the codes.

'Jules, I don't want her taking a placebo, I want you to get the real thing. Do whatever you have to.'

'I'll do my best.'

Ross walked away from the window. 'Look—I'd rather you didn't say anything to her about how serious this is. Let me break it to her in my own time.' Shakily, he took a Havana from the humidor on a side table. 'You have to understand, Jules, Faith is a child. Emotionally, she has never grown up. She's vulnerable, needs protection.'

'I think she's mature and sensible, Ross. You're mistaken.'

'Maybe that's her act when she comes to you.'

Ritterman smiled. 'I don't think so.'

Ross began picking at the band on the cigar with his thumbnail. It was ten to seven, but he no longer cared about tonight's dinner. 'I know what's best for her, Jules. I don't think it would be good for her to know how serious this disease is, OK? Not now or at any time.'

'You're putting me in a difficult position. Faith is a very sick woman. What do you expect to achieve by keeping her in the dark?'

'What's the first rule of medicine?'

Ritterman shrugged. 'Do no harm.'

'Right. If you tell someone of Faith's mental fragility that they are going to die, they will die. They put themselves into a state of panic, it becomes a self-fulfilling prophecy. She will have a better chance of surviving if she doesn't know.'

Ritterman looked at his friend, thinking, Maybe it's you, Ross, who can't cope with the reality, not Faith. 'I don't agree,' he said. 'If patients know the truth, it gives them time to prepare for death.'

Ross lit the cigar and sent clouds of rich, heavy smoke swirling to the ceiling. 'I'm her husband. Surely I'm qualified enough to tell her?'

'Of course you are, but I can't lie to her if she asks me outright.'

'All you have to do is tell her she's picked up a virus and that you're giving her a course of treatment for it. End of story.'

'Well,' Ritterman said, reluctantly, 'I'll go along with it—for the moment—but I don't like it.'

Ross perched on an arm of the chesterfield opposite Ritterman, tears trickling down his face. 'She's not going to die. We are going to find a way. You've got to help me Jules. I couldn't live without Faith.'

'Of course. I'll do everything I can.'

three

The house was silent. Alec had been taken to Longleat by a school-friend's family. Faith missed him. She worried about him constantly when he was out of her sight, fretted about him travelling in a stranger's car, hoping he had his seat belt on properly. She wondered where he was now as she sat in the leather swivel chair in Ross's study, in front of his computer, logged on, entered her password, and checked her email.

Not much this morning—a brief message from an old friend who had moved to Los Angeles and some junk mail.

Today she was feeling particularly down, a combination of her curse being due and the bouts of nausea that were persisting, despite the tablets Ross had given her. It was almost a week since her consultation with Jules Ritterman yet she'd heard nothing. There was something else, too, that she was brooding about—her memory of that encounter at the General Trading Company. Several times she'd been tempted to lift the phone and take Oliver Cabot up on his offer to show her around the centre, but each time wisdom—or maybe nerves—got the better of her. Finally, though, she had rummaged in her handbag and pulled out Dr Cabot's business card from beneath a bunch of petrol receipts. Now she went onto the web, and carefully typed in the website address on the card.

Outside, Morris the gardener, pushed a laden wheelbarrow past the window. Rasputin padded over and barked.

'Quiet, boy! It's only Morris,' she said. 'We'll go walkies later.'

Suddenly, on the screen large letters proclaimed:

WELCOME TO THE CABOT CENTRE FOR COMPLEMENTARY
MEDICINE. YOU ARE VISITOR NUMBER 111926.

Then a picture of the Centre appeared—it looked like a tall, narrow church—with a photograph of Oliver Cabot dressed all in black, eyes twinkling behind those oval glasses.

She felt a tiny hump of excitement at the sight of him. Gripping the mouse she clicked in the top-right corner of the frame. Instantly his face filled the screen.

Crazy, she thought. I'm like an infatuated teenager.

She scrolled down and his image disappeared. A list of the services offered at the centre came up and below that it said: 'All our thera-pists at the Cabot Centre meet the highest international standards, and all, where policies permit, are practitioners accredited by major health-insurance companies. Come and visit our oasis of tranquillity in North London.'

There followed a phone number, fax number, email address and a link to other related sites. She read the phone number, then eyed the phone. A knot tightened in her throat.

He's just going to show me around the clinic, that's all, no big deal.

And maybe Dr Oliver Cabot could give her something to knock this bug on the head.

Picking up the receiver, she was about to dial when she saw a car nosing through the front gates. A white Mercedes estate. She watched it with a frown, displeased at the interruption. Then, as the door opened, she instantly recognised the driver.

Felice D'Eath, the world's most boring woman. Shit.

Faith had been co-opted with Felice onto a subcommittee of the NSPCC, organising this year's Halloween Ball. Although it was nearly six months away, the woman had been bombarding her with memoranda about every gift donated for the tombola.

Faith logged off the site and hurried to the door as a volley of raps from the knocker echoed around the hall. She'd call Oliver later.

In her reedy voice, Felice said, 'Oh, Faith, I'm so pleased to have caught you. I've got the car completely filled up with prizes.'

She peeled off her hat, shook free her brown hair and began unbuttoning her coat. 'You look pale, Faith—are you all right?'

'I'm fine.'

'You really don't look it. Anyway, let's sit down and discuss the tombola layout—I've had some thoughts about this—and we can go over the list. Last year they raised seven hundred pounds. I think we should try to double that at least, don't you?'

'Yes,' Faith said, resignedly, closing the door behind her. 'At least.'

WINCHMORE HILL was an area Faith barely knew. On the northern edge of London, it was a smart, leafy pocket, with a well-heeled air.

The building itself *was* an old church, Faith realised, as she stepped out of the cab. Shoehorned into a gap between two Victorian terraces, it was an imposing edifice of red brick and gargoyles.

She stepped up to the massive oak door and read the brass plaque beside it: THE CABOT CENTRE FOR COMPLEMENTARY MEDICINE.

Nervous, she dug her hands deep into her pockets, hugging her long raincoat tightly around her against the cold, gusting wind. Her hair whipped her face.

Come this far, no turning back now, girl.

She pushed the door open and stepped in. In contrast to the stern exterior, the interior was airy, modern and visually stunning: soft white walls hung with abstract paintings, plants and pieces of sculpture strategically arranged to break up empty spaces. New Age relaxation music played from speakers, and Faith could smell the pleasant aroma of a scented oil.

There was a reception desk directly in front of her. At it an attractive young woman wearing a navy polo shirt glowed with such an aura of health and vitality that Faith instantly felt a wreck. Displaying teeth to die for, she gave Faith a welcoming smile.

'I've come to see Dr Cabot,' Faith said, 'I have an appointment.'

The receptionist took her name, then pointed her to an encampment of seats beyond a screen of potted plants.

'Is there a lavatory?'

'Yes, just down to the right.'

Faith walked down a corridor and went into a spacious room, tiled in white, with massive white candles burning. She went into a cubicle, sat down and closed her eyes. The nausea, which had been coming and going all week, had returned.

She knelt at the lavatory and threw up. Her head was swimming, and it was several minutes before she felt better. She flushed the lavatory, then rinsed her mouth at a basin. She checked her face in the mirror, put on some lipstick and adjusted her hair. At least all the time I'm feeling grotty, Ross isn't saying anything about more plastic surgery, she thought.

Back in the waiting area, Faith perched on the edge of a sofa. She glanced at the magazines strewn on a side table and noticed a copy of the Hypnotherapy Research Society magazine, flagging an article by Dr Oliver Cabot on the front cover. She picked it up and began to read but had difficulty concentrating.

She had taken a lot of care deciding what to wear today. Casual smart but not too smart: a thin grey cashmere polo neck, black cotton jeans, black boots and her long camel coat. She looked good, she thought. Looking good but not feeling good.

'Mrs Ransome?' Faith turned. A woman in clothes identical to the receptionist's greeted her with a smile. Like the receptionist, she had a complexion so healthy it was unreal. 'Dr Cabot can see you now.'

Faith followed the woman along a corridor, past a sign that said RELAXATION THERAPY and another marked HYPNOTHERAPY.

'Faith!'

Oliver Cabot was standing in a doorway dressed in a black jacket, grey collarless shirt, black chinos and black suede brogues. He was even better-looking than when she had last seen him, but more serious. It felt as if she was visiting Oliver Cabot, doctor, rather than Oliver Cabot, friend. Yet as she reached him, his expression changed.

'Faith!' he said again, staring directly into her eyes, making her feel that she was the most important thing in his life. 'This is so great, I can't tell you! Great that you came! How *are* you?'

They were holding hands, Faith realised, but it seemed the most natural thing in the world to be standing in the doorway, soaking up the warmth from those crystal-clear grey eyes.

Happiness flooded through her and she felt something she had not felt for many years. She felt free.

ROSS FINISHED HIS ROUND in the day-surgery unit and went to grab a cup of coffee in the staff room. Tommy Pearman, his regular anaesthetist, followed him. A short, squat man with a figure like a bean-bag, his baggy blue surgical pyjamas made him look even more shapeless than he already was. A widower, he lived for his work and had accumulated over the years, through his medical-research connections, a terrifying array of bacteria and viruses, which he kept in a cold store at his home in Kent. He was brilliant at his job, and Ross trusted him implicitly.

'I've just seen Mrs Jardine,' Pearman said. 'She has a terrible cold, coughing up sputum. I'm not happy about her.'

Ross glanced at his list. Elizabeth Jardine was at the top for this afternoon. A full face-lift. She was fifty-seven, married to a film producer and off to Los Angeles in mid-July. A nice woman, he had liked her when she had first come to see him. She was desperate to have the operation before going to the States.

He mentally timed the list. After Elizabeth Jardine, a seven-year-old girl with a burn scar on her chest, then a nine-year-old boy with a patch of thickened skin on his scalp, preventing hair growth, and a woman with a skin tumour on the back of her calf. It was a lot to get through. Even so, he said, 'I'm reluctant to postpone. She's going to be very upset.'

Pearman shook his head. 'I really think you should take a look at her, see for yourself.'

Normally Ross would have trusted Pearman's judgment. The only thing holding him back was his concern for Elizabeth Jardine. 'Yes, OK, I'll go and see her in a minute.'

As he poured himself a cup of coffee, he said, 'Tommy, what do you know about Lendt's disease?'

The anaesthetist frowned. 'Rings a bell. I was reading something on it recently. Umm, viral, I think. Inflammatory symptoms. Attacks the brain's neurochemistry. Very rare. I can do a bit of homework on it, if you like?'

'I'd be grateful. There's a lot of stuff on the web about it—I took a trawl through it late last night.'

'What's your interest?'

'Relative of . . . of a friend of mine has it.'

'I'll see what I can come up with.'

'I'd appreciate it.'

OLIVER LOVED THE WAY Faith looked around his office, her eyes roaming the furniture, the walls, the pictures, the certificates. She seemed to notice *everything*.

He helped her off with her coat, and while he hung it in a cupboard she was looking at the framed black and white photograph of a little boy sitting up on the transom of a yacht, hair tousled by the breeze, grinning. *That's his kid*, Faith thought. *Oh, he's married. Why the hell did I imagine he was single?*

She caught Oliver's eye.

'Jake,' he said.

'Your son?'

He nodded, his face suddenly wretched. Then he ushered her to a deep sofa and said, 'Get you a drink? We have almost anything.'

Wondering why mention of his son made him look so unhappy, she said, 'Yes, I'd love a . . . ' She hesitated, not sure what she did want. Something to settle the queasiness. 'Tea.'

'Something herbal? Ordinary English?'

'Ordinary English with milk, please.'

She sat down and looked around to see what other clues about Oliver Cabot she could pick up. She liked the feel of the room: it was airy and bright, barely like an office at all—a couple of large, green plants, horizontal Venetian blinds half closed against the view, a framed reflexology chart, a dramatic photograph of Stonehenge, and a full-size Shell petrol pump, complete with nozzle.

No photograph of his wife. She wondered why not.

Smiling again, Oliver perched on the arm of a sofa opposite her.

Looking at the photograph of the kid, she probed, 'How old is Jake?'

A long pause, and then, 'He'd have been just coming up to sixteen right now.'

She felt a tightening in her throat. 'I'm sorry,' she said. 'I had no—'

He patted his thigh a couple of times. 'Don't worry about it, you didn't have any reason to know. You have kids?'

'A son, Alec. He's six.'

His secretary came in with tea for Faith and water for Oliver.

Faith was curious to know about this son who had died, but sensed he didn't want to talk about it. When the secretary left, she tried to keep him on the subject of his life. 'What does your wife do?'

'Marcy's a writer. She works in LA, writes television sitcoms, but we . . . ' He grimaced, good-naturedly. 'Let's say we inhabit the same planet but that's about the limit of what we have in common, these days.' Then he added, 'We're divorced.'

'I'm sorry,' she said.

He shifted off the arm of the sofa and sat down on it properly. 'You want to know something, Faith? People are lucky if they change together. Mostly they don't. They either stay together for the sake of their kids, living lives of quiet desperation, or they move apart.' He thought for a moment, then said. 'Tragedy can bring people closer together, but sometimes it throws them apart.' He crossed his legs, then reached forward and gripped the toes of his trainers, and stayed there, like a coiled spring. 'How about you?'

'I suppose . . . I sort of fit into the quiet-desperation category.'

'Too personal if I ask why you feel that?'

She would have loved to pour it all out to him, yet a part of her was thinking, Not here, not now, too soon. Way too soon.

His secretary put her head around the door. 'Sorry to interrupt, Dr Cabot, Mrs Martyns is on the line.'

He raised his eyes. 'Third time this morning. I'll call her back.'

'And a reporter called Sarah Conroy phoned from the *Daily Mail*. They're doing a piece on London's alternative clinics. I told her you'd call her back—she needs to speak to you before four o'clock.'

'Sure—remind me.'

She left and Oliver drank a little water, then dabbed his mouth with the back of his hand.

'I'm curious,' Faith said. 'Why the Shell pump?'

He turned to look at it, as if he had totally forgotten its existence. 'I saw it in a junk store. I guess its purpose here is that it has no purpose. We get too hung up on *meaning*. I like the irrational. Are you irrational, Faith?'

She used to love the irrational and the zany. She'd been a total addict of *Monty Python* . But there was no room in Ross's life for the irrational. 'I never wanted to be a grown-up,' she said.

He hunched his shoulders and gave her a big grin. 'There are times when I think life's too short to grow up. Part of me just wants to remain a kid. I—'

They were interrupted by a phone ringing. Oliver shot a glance at his desk. Then Faith realised it was coming from her handbag. She pulled out her Nokia, and glanced at the dial. It was Ross at the clinic. She pushed the END button with her thumb, killing the call, then she dropped the phone back in her bag. There'd be hell from Ross later, but right now she did not care one bit.

'THIS IS WHERE I come most days in my lunch hour,' Oliver said.

In the distance below them, the rooftops of London stretched far away into a grubby smudge beneath the threatening charcoal sky. The glacial wind tore at her hair but she scarcely noticed as she walked alongside him between the gravestones.

Oliver, in his long black coat, holding the bag containing their sandwiches, strode at an easy pace. She glanced at the names on the tombstones, then she looked up at him. 'Does death fascinate you?'

He stopped and pointed down at a headstone: *William Percival Leadbetter, 1893–1951.* 'You know what fascinates me? It's that little mark between the dates. I look down at someone's grave, and I think, That dash represents a human being's entire life. You and I are living out our dashes right now. It's not important when someone was born or when they died, what matters is what they did in between. And all we have here in this graveyard are just thousands of dashes. That makes me sad.'

'Do you think about your own death?'

'I think about life. I think what I can do with my little dash to make a difference. I—' He fell silent and they walked on for some moments. Then he said, 'You lose someone close and you realise how helpless we are. We can put people into space, but so many diseases still defeat us.' He tapped his head. 'We have the ability to beat any disease if we could just find the way to harness the power we have inside our heads.'

'I think that too,' she said. 'Is it true we use only a very small part of our brains, something like twenty per cent?'

'Around twenty per cent of what we know to be there. What we don't know is what else we are connected to that we could draw from.' They were approaching a bench. 'This is a good place to sit,' he said. 'You're not too cold?'

Faith was freezing, but the cold air, or maybe it was Oliver's company, had blown away her nausea. 'I'm fine.'

He dug into the bag and pulled out a tuna sandwich. As she began to unwrap it, her phone rang again. She checked the display, in case it was Alec's friends, but it was Ross again. Once more she pressed the END button and dropped the phone back into her bag.

'Where are you from in the States?' she asked.

'LA.'

'How long have you been in England?'

'Seven years, coming up to eight.' He was unwrapping his own sandwich, with long, slender fingers. Everything about this man was attractive to her, she realised, even the way he unwrapped a sandwich.

'I came to get away from the memories of my son. California haunted me. And, you know, this is a good place to be.'

'How did your son die?'

'Leukaemia. He had a form of the disease that nothing in conventional medicine could help, but my wife refused to go along with any alternative treatments.' He gave a wry smile. 'I gave up practising conventional medicine after his death—too many vested interests at stake. Modern medicine has itself in a box and I decided to dedicate my life to trying to get it out.'

'What kind of a box?'

The quiet was suddenly broken with the clatter of a fast-approaching helicopter, and at the same moment Faith's phone rang again. With an apologetic look at Oliver, she pulled it out of her bag. On the display no number was identified.

She pressed the green button to answer it.

'Where the hell are you?' Ross demanded.

The helicopter was passing right overhead.

'Can't hear you!' she yelled.

The voice became a few decibels louder. 'Faith, please tell me where you are and what you're doing.'

She hesitated. 'I'm in Knightsbridge.'

'Why didn't you tell me you were going to be in London, Faith? We could have arranged to do something this evening. *Les Sylphides* is on at Covent Garden.'

She wondered what Ross was on about: he had never before expressed the slightest interest in ballet. The noise of the helicopter was subsiding. 'Spur of the moment. I had to collect a birthday present for you.'

'You should have told me. I don't like it when you don't tell me things, Faith. And how's Alec getting home from school?'

'It's half term this week. He's with Nico Lawson.'

'He was with other people yesterday too. You should be there for him, Faith. He shouldn't keep spending time with different people.'

You hypocrite, she thought. In one breath you're telling me we could have had a night in town and in the next you're angry I'm not at home for Alec. I'm always at home for Alec. That's why I don't have a career. But she kept calm. 'It was his choice—it's Nico's birthday,' she said. 'I'm spending all of tomorrow with him.'

'It seems to be happening more and more, these days.'

She glanced at Oliver, embarrassed now. 'I don't think so. How's your day?'

'Fine, Faith. Who are you with?'

'I'm on my own.'

'I hope you're telling me the truth.'

'I'll see you tomorrow. Call me at home, later?'

'I don't like the sound of your voice, Faith.'

'I—I don't feel that brilliant.'

There was a long silence. Again she glanced at Oliver, who was turning his sandwich in his hand, as if inspecting it.

'Tell me how you're feeling, Faith? Is it the nausea?'

'Yes. I don't understand why I haven't heard anything from Dr Ritterman. You haven't heard anything?'

A little calmer suddenly. 'From Jules? No. I'll give him a call, chase him up. I love you, Faith. You do know that, don't you?'

'Yes.'

'I'll call you later,' Ross said. 'Love you.'

He was gone. She put the phone back in her bag.

Oliver looked at her. 'Hope I'm not causing you any hassle?'

'You're not.' She shrugged. 'My husband's very possessive.'

'Guess I can't blame him.'

She glanced away, blushing but smiling. 'Tell me about you,' she said. 'Tell me about *your* life since your divorce.'

'Well.' He looked coy. 'I've been celibate for eight years.'

'Why? Do you have a reason? Or you just haven't met anyone?'

'You know about the Jing Chi?'

Faith shook her head.

'It's the name the Chinese have for sexual energy. They believe that if you control it through celibacy it transforms into a higher energy you can use at a spiritual level for healing. I wanted to try that.' He bit into his sandwich again. 'I wanted to try to reach higher levels of consciousness and and so I made a decision. And I never met anyone who made me want to reverse that decision.' He looked at her again, focusing his clear grey eyes directly on her own. 'Until you.'

LEAH PHILLIPS was a mess. The seat-belt mountings in her mother's crappy little Russian car had sheared, and she'd taken out the windscreen face first, at forty miles an hour. The blades of a rotary mower, Ross thought, wouldn't have caused much more disfigurement. Blind in one eye, her face, gridded with scars, looked as if it had been soldered back together. The teenager was sitting in the chair in front of his desk, constantly glancing at her mother on the sofa a few feet away.

Even Ross, who had been hardened by countless harrowing sights, was moved by this one, but tried hard to let only reassurance show.

His office was designed to reassure. Rich, dark woods, leather upholstery, bookshelves lined with leather-bound medical tomes, a white marble bust of Hippocrates on a plinth.

'And your date of birth, Leah?' he asked.

She glanced again at her mother, who answered for her, in a timid, nervy voice, 'Nineteen eighty-three.'

He wrote down the details. Then shot a glance at the clock on his desk. Ten past three. This was the last of his afternoon patients and he was due back in theatre at four. It was an effort to concentrate when his mind was on Faith. Where the hell was she today? *In Knightsbridge.*

No, you're not in Knightsbridge. You're lying to me. Where are you really, Faith? You might as well tell me because I'm going to find out anyway.

He studied his notes. 'So, tell me, Leah, what can I do for you?'

'I want to look how I used to.'

'Leah was doing modelling work,' her mother said, 'with a top agency.' She passed him an envelope. 'These are of her.'

Ross shook out several professionally taken photographs of a strikingly beautiful young brunette. It was hard to believe this was the same girl, and he felt a swirl of anger at whoever in the A & E department after the crash had done this botch-up on her. It looked more like she had been treated by someone apprenticing in sheet metal work than by a doctor.

Putting the photographs down, he said as gently as he could, 'I think I can improve you, Leah, but it's going to take a long time. I can't promise what the results will be, and it's very important you both understand that.'

When they left, Ross closed the door, asked his secretary to hold any calls for a few minutes, then turned towards his computer, entered a command, followed by a password, and moments later was connected to his home computer. He soon had in front of him a log of every phone call made and received by Faith at home in the past seven days. At a single click of his mouse he could listen to a recording of any of them.

four

'I have to get going,' Faith said. She sipped the last of the cappuccino, feeling a flash of guilt that, for the past few hours with Oliver Cabot, she hadn't given Alec a thought.

There was a cheery fug in the café, which reminded her of her student days. Formica tabletops, the haze of cigarette smoke, the chatter of people at tables crammed close together. It was five past three. It would take her a good forty minutes to get to Victoria, half an hour on the Gatwick Express and a further twenty-five minutes' drive from there. Home just in time to have supper with Alec.

Across the table, Oliver, said, 'You know something, Faith, it's really been good seeing you.'

'Thank you. I've enjoyed myself too.'

'Can I see you again?'

Her attraction to him was scaring her yet boosting her. It felt so good being with him. She knew she ought to say no, but instead she heard herself say, 'I'd like to—yes.'

'Can you get away tomorrow?'

'It's half term and I'm taking my son and two friends of his out for the day.'

'Sometime next week?'

Hesitantly she said, 'Perhaps we'd better talk on the phone when I see how my diary is. It's Ross's birthday on Wednesday.'

Oliver raised his palms to her with a genial grin. 'Look, whenever. Cut yourself some slack when you have the chance. I'm not going anywhere.' He prodded around inside his empty coffee cup with his spoon, and scraped some remnants of froth from the sides. 'I just want you to know that I really do want to see you again. OK?'

As she stepped outside, the wind slashed her hair against her face, and then, suddenly, it seemed to have found its way inside her and was swirling in her belly. She was so cold she almost cried out, and then the nausea rose. The whole street seemed to come loose, and she saw the pavement tilt, coming straight at her face.

She was dimly aware of Oliver's arm catching her. He helped her back to her feet and she stood, unsteadily, supported by his arm around her waist. She breathed deeply, felt the air cooling her burning face, saw the lines of deep concern etched around his eyes.

'Want to go back inside?' he asked.

'No, I'm OK—just the—the air—'

'Let's go back in, sit down for a few minutes.'

'No, I have to get back. Can you call me a taxi? I'll be fine.'

'I'm not putting you in a taxi. I'll drive you.'

'Thanks, no, I'm OK, really.'

She felt a little better, until suddenly there was a blinding pain behind her eyes, as if she'd been stabbed through the head. Another bout of the nausea hit her, and she clutched him, everything around her a blur again. Her legs buckled.

THE SEAT in Oliver's dark blue Jeep was soft, like an armchair. She listened to the solid rattle of the diesel, the whir of the fan, felt the warm stream of air. She was concentrating hard on one thing.

Don't throw up. Don't throw up. Don't throw up.

He changed gear, pulling away from lights. 'Have you seen your doctor about this, Faith?'

Speaking was an effort. *What had the doctor said? Nothing.* 'Just . . . something I picked up . . . in Thailand . . . I'm—OK.'

'The hell you are.'

He was braking again, stopping at another light. He felt so strong, so good to be with. A deep, terrible fear seeped through her, a fear of what was wrong with her—a fear of Ross's anger.

'MR RANSOME, I simply fail to understand how you cannot see it,' Lady Geraldine Reynes-Rayleigh said during her consultation next day. 'Absolutely everyone else can. Absolutely *everyone*.'

Each syllable was articulated with slow, disdainful precision, as if speaking to him was something she considered utterly beneath her.

She had the kind of body a lot of women would kill for, especially at her age, which was fifty-two. The press gave her age as forty-seven, but her previous surgeon had nipped, tucked and liposuctioned away a good twelve of those years. Not many thirty-five-year-olds managed to look this good, Ross thought. Shame surgery couldn't do anything about her personality.

'I came to you, Mr Ransome, because everyone I spoke to said you were the number-one surgeon in this country,' she continued.

The true reason she had changed surgeons, Ross knew, was that her previous surgeon had found her so impossible that he had refused to operate on her again. Ross had usually been able to cope with troublesome patients, but he was bitterly regretting having taken this one on. She had wanted a face-lift but she was not happy with the results. It was inevitable, he realised now. She was not a woman it would ever be possible to please.

'The two sides of my face are simply not even—you absolutely *must* be able to see this.'

'Lady Reynes-Rayleigh, if you study the *Mona Lisa* you'll see that her face is asymmetrical, too.'

Plumed horses, parading through the folds of couture silk that encased her neck, rose up and down as she spoke. 'She's an old boot, if you want my opinion. I don't find the comparison flattering. You've also made a complete mess of my nose, so perhaps you would like to tell me what you intend to do about it?'

It took a supreme effort of self-will to restrain himself. He had done a superb job. But he knew that if he was rude to her, she could do him a lot of damage.

Putting on the charm he said, 'Are you prepared to face another operation?'

'I'm not a coward, you know. Do I look like a coward?'

'Of course not. But there are risks with every operation, Lady Reynes-Rayleigh—I do need to point that out.'

Acidly, she retorted, 'I've just said I'm not a coward, but I do have an extremely full diary. And I will expect you to compensate me for any extra expenses I incur, naturally.' With a smile that could corrode steel she added, 'My solicitors are preparing a list for you.'

KYLIE SPALDING was lying on the couch in Oliver Cabot's office, eyes shut, bony hands by her sides. She was nineteen, with long brown hair and a pre-Raphaelite face that, despite her painfully emaciated body, was gorgeous. When Oliver had first met her, three weeks ago, suffering cardiac arrhythmia and showing early stages of renal failure, she had been close to dying. Now she was close to living again.

'Tell me what it feels like when you eat.'

'Eat?' Her voice was slurred and slow.

Sitting beside her, he said, in the calm, steady voice he used in hypnotherapy, 'You like bananas, don't you, Kylie?'

A long pause and then, 'Uh.'

Kylie had bulimia, which had been preceded by anorexia nervosa. Her parents had brought her here in desperation, and already, after just two sessions, there was improvement—slight, but significant.

'I want you to imagine you're eating a banana, OK? Just hold this banana in your hands and take a real hard look at it. This is some banana, right?' No reaction, and that was fine: she was thinking about it. 'It's in great condition this banana, just how it should be for eating. I want you—just go very slowly—I want you to peel off the skin and take a look inside . . . It's firm, hard but sweet, you've never seen a banana this good before. Now I want you to take a bite.'

She mimed taking a bite.

'Terrific! Now tell me, how does it feel as you start to eat it?'

She sat bolt upright, her eyes wide, and began to retch into her cupped hands.

After some moments she pulled out her handkerchief and wiped her mouth. 'I—I'm sorry.'

He handed her a glass of water. She drank, gratefully, then he took the glass.

'I'm really sorry.'

'You don't have to be sorry, Kylie. I want you to close your eyes and try again now. You like bananas, right?'

She nodded, then closed her eyes.

'Now you have a new banana . . . ' and Oliver continued as before, soothing and relaxing, but his mind drifted away from his patient.

Faith Ransome, you are the most adorable woman I've ever met. But you are married. I know you are not happy, but I can't start messing with your marriage. I can try to help you with your health, but I have to stop these thoughts I'm having about you. Somehow I have to put a stop to them.

He looked up at the photograph of Jake, and thought about how he and Marcy had felt as they'd watched him slowly slip away from them, and he stared at Kylie and thought about her parents sitting downstairs in the waiting area right now, about the desperation in their faces when they'd first come to him. Kylie Spalding, there is no way I'm letting you do that to yourself or to your parents, he thought. There's no way anyone's going to lose you.

And then another thought bullied its way into his head. And there's no way, Faith Ransome, that I'm going to lose you, either.

ONCE, BUT IT SEEMED a long time ago now, the sound of those tyres on the gravel would have been like music to Faith. *Ross arriving home*. Once, she would have thrown herself at him as he came in at the front door, hugging and kissing him.

She could hear Rasputin barking wildly, racing down the hall to greet his master, and she could hear Alec, in his pyjamas, trailing after him. 'Daddy's home! Daddy's home!'

Looking through the gap in their bedroom curtains Faith could see the Aston Martin. She went out of the bedroom, leaving all the lights on, knowing that would irk him. There was a toy police car on its side on the landing floor and, further on, some Lego left over from a garage Alec had been trying to assemble. She left them where they were. Tonight he could go hang. Downstairs, above the commotion of the dog, she heard the front door opening, then Ross's voice, greeting first the dog, then Alec.

'Daddy, can I show you what I painted at school?'

Then Ross's voice again, bellowing. 'Rasputin! Quiet boy. *Quiet!*'

And for the first time in their married life, Faith decided she wasn't going downstairs. She walked on down the landing and into one of the spare bedrooms at the far end.

She switched on the light, closed the door behind her and sat down in a deep armchair. The room's décor was tasteful but impersonal, swagged curtains matching the floral bedspread, mahogany furniture, old copies of *Country Life* and *Vogue* on the bedside tables. Pictures they hadn't wanted in any of the other rooms hung here to fill wall space.

The silence of this room felt good, though. She closed her eyes and thought of Oliver Cabot. She tried hard to remember his face but it was elusive. Warmth was what she thought of most. Warmth and sadness, that deep, tender sadness when he talked about his son.

There was a pang inside her, a yearning of the kind she thought was left way behind in her past when she had crashed her bike and met the tall, charming, handsome young doctor. Ross. He'd put four stitches into her forehead, and she'd been terrified she would be scarred for life, yet within weeks of the stitches coming out there had been no mark at all. By then she was dating him. He had seemed so strong, so attentive, no hint of the control freak he would turn into.

'What the hell are you doing in here?'

She turned her head and saw him standing in the doorway, his face blazing with anger. She stayed put as he strode towards her.

'I said, what are you doing in here?' He stopped right in front of her, towering over her, shaking with rage.

'I live here,' she said, calmly. 'This is one of the rooms in my home, and I'm sitting in it. Do you have a problem with that?'

He stared back at her as if uncertain how to handle this. 'Where were you yesterday, Faith?'

'I told you, I was in London shopping for your birthday.'

'In Knightsbridge?'

'Yes. I went to the General Trading Company.'

'Helicopters don't fly over Knightsbridge. They're not allowed to.'

'Helicopters?'

'When I rang you on the mobile, and you answered, I heard a helicopter. You weren't in Knightsbridge. Don't ever think that because you have a mobile I don't know where you are. I checked with

Vodafone. They have cells all over the country, did you know that? I connected to you through their cell in Winchmore Hill in north London. Who were you with, Faith? Dr Oliver Cabot? Is that what you call being a *good mother*?'

She stared back at him floored. How the hell did he know that?

He strode out of the room and slammed the door behind him.

Faith listened to Ross's footsteps receding down the landing. Then it came to her. In the car after the dinner at the Royal Society of Medicine. The quiet but chilling way Ross had said, *I saw you*.

Had he put two and two together? The phone company telling him she was speaking from Winchmore Hill, and finding out—or knowing—that Oliver Cabot worked in Winchmore Hill? Was he having her followed? She had learned never to rule out anything with Ross. But asking her if she had been with Oliver Cabot had to have been a guess. All she had to do was deny it, and come up with some other good reason for being there. Or tell Ross to go to hell.

And that was what she decided now, anger emboldening her. *Go to hell, you bastard.* She stormed across the room and opened the door.

Just then Alec howled, as if he had had a terrible accident.

Faith sprinted down the landing, her stomach clenched. The child was screaming now, with pain and fear. She could see him lying on the flagstones curled up in a bundle, holding his head in his hands.

She reached the bottom of the stairs. Kneeling down, putting her arms around him, she said, 'Darling, what's happened?'

'D-D-D-D-Daddy hit me.'

And she could see now, the mark below his left eye, the bruising.

Her worst nightmare. Ross harming Alec. Ross had often told her how badly his own father had treated him. How he had beaten him. How he had blamed him for his mother leaving them. And Faith knew from what she had read that people who were abused by their parents often went on to abuse their own children.

Choking back her fury she checked Alec carefully to make sure nothing felt broken, then scooped him up in her arms and carried him through to the kitchen. She sat him down in a chair, then ran over to the freezer and pulled out a pack of frozen peas. She wrapped them in a kitchen towel, and pressed the bundle to his face.

He turned away, rejecting it, but she persisted, and slowly he calmed down.

'Why did Daddy hit you, darling?'

'I—I—I—' He began sobbing.

'It's bedtime, Mummy'll take you up.'

She carried him upstairs, screaming and protesting. Talking to him tenderly, trying to soothe him, she ran his bath, undressed him and got him into the water. He stopped crying.

He sat in the bath in silence as she soaped him, rinsed him and dried him. Then she carried him to bed and tucked him up. He lay there, uncommunicative, the left side of his face swollen and puffy.

She tried reading to him from his favourite book, *Charlie and the Chocolate Factory*, but he turned away with his thumb in his mouth. Finally she put the book down, kissed him good night and turned out the light. Instantly he started screaming.

She turned on the light again. 'What's the matter, darling?'

He stared at her in silence, with wide, fearful eyes, then suddenly he was whispering something to her. 'Please don't let Daddy come in here and hit me again.'

'He won't,' she said. 'I promise.'

She switched off the light, closed the door and stood outside. When she was sure he had settled, she went downstairs to look for Ross.

He was in his study, seated in front of his computer, suit jacket on the back of his chair, cigar burning in the ashtray.

She went in, closed the door behind her, then stood with her arms folded. 'You bastard,' she said. '*You hit my child, you bully.*'

There was no response.

'I'm giving you ten seconds to tell me why you hit him, or I'm going to call the police,' she said. 'And I'm going to divorce you.'

Without replying, and without turning his head from the screen, he tapped the keyboard. A second later, she heard her voice, crystal clear: 'Hi, Oliver? It's Faith Ransome.'

And then, equally clearly, she heard Oliver Cabot's voice. 'Faith! Hey, this is a surprise, great to hear you! How you doing?'

Ross turned towards her as she heard herself again.

'Fine, thanks. How are you?'

'Doing great. All the better for hearing from you!'

'I—I was wondering—is that offer to show me around your clinic still on?'

'And lunch? I said it was conditional on me buying you lunch.'

Trying to look anywhere but at Ross now, she heard herself laugh warmly, and say, 'Lunch would be great!'

IT WAS THE SILENCE that got to her. Those moments after Ross switched off the playback and leaned on his desk looking desperately hurt.

A previous version of herself, the Faith Ransome of a year back, would have reacted differently. She would probably, lamely, have given him a detailed explanation. But right at this moment she wasn't frightened of him. She was as close as she had ever come to attacking him with her bare hands.

'You're taping my calls?'

'With good reason.'

'What the hell gives you the right to think you can do that? Is that why you hit our child, you coward? You hit our child because it was easier than hitting me?'

He stood up violently, sending his chair rolling back across the room. 'I don't have any problem about hitting you, you bitch.'

'Why did you hit Alec? *How dare you hit him?*'

'You're not doing your job as a mother. You're letting him leave toys all over the place.' He took a menacing stride towards her. 'Someone's going to discipline that child, and if you haven't time to do it because you're too busy servicing your men friends, fine.' He stabbed his chest with his finger. 'I'll do it my way, in the language he understands. You're too soft with him, he needs discipline.'

'Discipline? After the things you've said to me about your father?'

Out of the corner of her eye she could see him clenching his fists and braced herself, certain that she was going to be struck.

'Is he a good lay, this Cabot?' His face was contorted in a sneer.

Keeping calm, she said, 'For God's sake, Ross, he's a *doctor*. I went to see him because he's a *doctor*. In case you've forgotten, I've been feeling like death for the past fortnight. I went to your friend, Jules Ritterman, OK? I went to see him over a week ago, and he's done absolutely nothing since then. I went to see Dr Cabot because I was *desperate*, Ross. I went to see him because he's a doctor.'

'He's not a doctor, he's a quack. A snake-oil salesman.'

'He's a doctor of medicine who happens to look beyond the horizons of the narrow little boxes most doctors keep themselves in, OK? I may be married to you but you don't own me, and if I want to see a doctor of my choice, I'm going to do that, and if you don't like it, divorce me.'

Backing off a fraction, he said, in a cracking voice that sounded more hurt than angry, 'Why didn't you discuss it with me?'

'Because you wouldn't have agreed.'

He stared at her through a mist of tears. *You made me mad. You made me hit the son I adore more than anything in the world, and now you are daring to answer me back. See what you are doing to me? Do you see? Do you see?*

He wanted to hit her, wanted to smash her so damned hard right in the middle of her face, punch those lips, stove in those teeth. This answering back was so out of character. Was this coming from *Dr* Oliver Cabot? Was this man poisoning her against him? Faith had never answered him back before. And she wouldn't be answering him back now if she knew the truth about what was wrong with her.

Taking a step towards her, he said, 'I love you, Faith. I love you more than anything in the world.' He put his arms on her shoulders and it hurt him to see her flinch. 'Don't you realise how much I love you? I want to make you better. Can't you see that?'

He tried to pull her closer to him, to hug her, but she resisted, kept a space like a block of wood wedged between them.

'Do you think I'd have sent you to Jules Ritterman if I didn't believe he's the best doctor in this country?'

'I don't like him and I don't intend seeing him again.'

The way she was staring at him, that look of defiance, as if she believed she was scoring some kind of triumph over him. Like the first spores of cancer in a biopsy, it had to be excised. He slapped her cheek so hard she staggered sideways, cracked her head on the corner of a bookcase, flailed with her hands, then went down, sprawling on the carpet, and lay still.

Motionless. Blood dribbling from her lip.

'Oh, Christ,' he said, kneeling down. 'Faith. Oh, sweet Jesus.' He was crying, touching her face with his hands. 'Darling? I love you. Darling? Are you OK?'

He pressed his face against Faith's, breathed in the smell of her hair. Then he reached down, held her slender wrist, feeling for a pulse. The solitary blink told him, yes, she was OK.

This thing she did, this not-moving business. Animals played possum to deceive predators, but Faith was doing it to panic him, to make him think he'd hurt her more than he really had. Her sad little way of trying to get back at him. He kissed her forehead and she moaned softly.

Droplets of blood stained the beige carpet. 'Hey!' he said. 'Hey, Faith, careful.' He lifted her face a little, dabbed at her lip with his handkerchief, stemming the blood, then saw the gash on the side of her head, where she had struck the bookshelf. It was one hell of a gash, he could see raw white bone exposed inside it. It needed stitches.

He lifted her onto her feet, then half carried her into the kitchen and propped her in a chair. She was limp, but conscious, not saying anything. That was her style: she often did this after she'd angered him, just stayed motionless, tracking him with her eyes.

He cleaned the wound, then froze it with a local anaesthetic and, with painstaking care, began to suture it. 'You're lucky it's me doing this, darling—this is the kind of gash that could leave you with a nasty scar if it's sewn by some Johnny-come-lately houseman.'

Carefully he pricked the skin, pressed the needle through. 'Three weeks and there won't be a mark.' He tried to look her in the eye, but each time her pupils swung away.

When he had finished, he covered the gash with a strip of flesh-coloured Elastoplast. 'There, all set.'

Still she refused to meet his eye.

Ross put his medical box away in his study, then came back into the kitchen to get water and a cloth to clean up the bloodstains from his carpet. His eye fell on a bone in front of the Aga. 'Rasputin been eating a bone in here?'

She ignored him.

He raised his voice. 'Faith, has the dog been eating a bone in here?'

She put her hands on the edges of her chair, gripping with her fingers, as if scared she was going to overbalance and fall off it.

Ross's voice softened. The anger was replaced with reproach. 'Faith, darling, I know you can hear me. *I'm deeply hurt.*'

He went out of the room, ran up the stairs and opened Alec's bedroom door. He could hear his son sobbing.

Even though the curtains were drawn it was still light in the room. Alec was facing away from him. Ross knelt by the bed, put his hand on Alec's shoulder and, to his horror, his son flinched.

'Hey, big guy!' he said softly. 'You didn't tell me if you scored any goals today. Did you?'

Alec continued to sob.

Ross leaned over and kissed his cheek. 'I love you. You've got to learn to be a little tidier, that's all, OK?' Ross bit his lip. This was him and his father all over again. He didn't want it to be that way, did not want Alec to go through the kind of hell he'd been through as a child. And yet . . . A child had to have discipline. A child had to realise there were rules that society lived by, and that if he did leave a toy car at the foot of the stairs, someone was going to stand on it and take a fall. Alec needed to learn that, and some lessons were painful.

You couldn't make an omelette without breaking eggs.

He kissed Alec once more. 'Good night, big guy, I love you.' He left the room with a heavy heart. Tonight he had done his duty, however painful it had been. *A child had to have discipline.*

FAITH STAYED PUT in the chair. When Ross was in these moods he was like a stranger, as if some other person were inside him. In the past she had kept quiet, thinking it would calm him, but that didn't work. Now she was standing up to him and that didn't work either.

'I don't smell anything cooking.'

She looked at Ross, who was standing in the kitchen doorway, shirtsleeves rolled up, sponge and bucket in his hands.

'Food?' he said. 'Dinner? I don't smell any dinner cooking. Why is that, Faith? Can you explain that to me?'

She closed her eyes, and in the giddying darkness behind her eyelids she searched for some place to crawl into. Her head was hurting so much, and it was all she could do to remain upright and conscious. She started sobbing uncontrollably.

Moments later she felt Ross's arms around her, cradling her like a baby, and her mind went back to all those nights, years ago when they had been so much in love, when they had been two spoons in bed together, her naked body held safe and firm by those same arms.

He was nuzzling her now, warm cigar breath on her cheeks. She turned her face sharply away.

'I love you, Faith. You don't know how much I love you.'

Suddenly, through her sobbing, she said, 'You hit Alec and you hit me. What are you? I don't know you any more. I used to be so proud of you, Ross. I used to look up to you and think I was the luckiest woman in the world to be married to you.'

She tried to pull free of him, but he held her tightly, gripped her face, forcing her to look at him.

'I'm the luckiest man in the world to be married to you, darling. I love you more than anything on this earth.'

'I hate you,' she said, struggling against him.

'You're the most beautiful thing that ever happened to me, Faith.'

'I hate you.' She broke free of him, stood up and walked across the kitchen. 'I hate you more than I ever knew it could be possible to hate someone.'

five

'Are you sure you want to know? I ask all my clients this question before I proceed. Are you *absolutely* sure you want to know?'

It was eleven on Monday morning. Ross, seated behind his desk in his Harley Street consulting room, replied, 'That's why you're here.'

Ross had never met a private investigator before, and Hugh Caven, seated in the chair normally occupied by his patients, did not fit his mental model at all. A thin, soulful-looking man in his late thirties, dressed in a grey suit, Bugs Bunny tie and clapped-out trainers, he had more the appearance of a has-been rock star than a detective. He was perfect for the job, Ross thought. And he had been highly recommended by one of the divorce-law partners at Ross's solicitors.

He spoke with an Irish accent, his voice soft but insistent. 'I always say this, Mr Ransome, because some people like the *idea* of finding out but then they have the problem of facing the *reality*. I think it's only fair to warn clients of the pain they might face if their suspicions prove true.'

Ross stiffened. 'Look, if I'd wanted a shrink I'd have phoned a shrink. I want my wife followed; I don't want a bloody sermon.'

Hugh Caven stood up. 'Then I'm afraid I'm not your man. Clients hire me, Mr Ransome, because they have a problem. You want some sleazy gumshoe with a long lens, look in the Yellow Pages. What you're asking me to do is to turn your life upside-down, your wife's life and, if she does have a lover, her lover's life as well.' His eyes opened wide. 'That's *three* lives, Mr Ransome.'

'Look, wait a second—I'm a little confused—'

'I don't think a man of your intelligence needs to be confused, Mr Ransome. We all have to rub along on this planet together, that's my philosophy. I like everybody to be civilised. If you don't want to be civilised, I don't need to work for you. It's a fine morning, I'll take the day off, go fishing down the Thames estuary on my boat. I'll be happier. You might be happier too.' He opened out his hands, palms outwards. 'You tell me.'

Do I want this cocky little shit working for me? Ross wondered. If not it would mean finding another agency, starting again. Losing valuable time. He took a deep breath and said, 'I'm listening.'

The private investigator nodded. 'Good. How about we sit down again?' He pulled his laptop computer out of its nylon bag, settled it on his thighs and opened the lid. 'I want you to think about the implications very carefully all the time I'm working for you, Mr Ransome. Any time you want out, you call the mobile number I'm going to give you.'

'You seem to have a problem with your conscience,' Ross said.

'I like to sleep at night.'

'I'd like to be able to sleep at night too,' Ross said. 'I'd like to sleep at night without wondering who my wife has been screwing.'

Caven busied himself with his computer. 'Address that you'd like me to use in communications with you, please.'

Ross gave him the address of his consulting room. 'What's your success rate in cases like this?'

Caven was still typing the address. 'If your wife is having an affair, Mr Ransome, I will find that out for you.'

'How long will it take you?'

Caven raised his hands in the air. 'Depends how careful she is. Could be a week if I'm lucky, could be a couple of months or more if she's being clever. And it depends how far you want me to go—and how much you're prepared to pay. Do you want just one person, or a full round-the-clock surveillance, nine men, three shifts of three? Are you happy to pay for phone taps? Audio bugging? Video surveillance? Satellite tracking? A transponder on the other man's car? There's a whole package of options I can offer you, depending on your budget and your urgency.'

'When can you start?'

'As soon as I have details of both parties, and your retainer, Mr Ransome, I can move as quickly as you want. I can start having the lady watched from this afternoon, if you like.'

'I want photographs,' Ross said. 'Clear photographs of her and her lover doing whatever it is they do to each other. You can do that?'

'You're the client, Mr Ransome. You can have as many photographs as you want.'

'It's not quantity, understand? *Quality.* I'm making myself clear?'

'Very clear. Quality. Not a problem. We're cool about quality.'

Ross reached down and pulled his chequebook out of a drawer. 'Money isn't an issue, Mr Caven. I want the best you've got.'

AT TEN TO TWELVE Faith pulled on her coat, stepped off the train at Victoria station and began to walk down the platform.

She'd spent an age deciding what to wear. Finally she had settled on a navy trouser suit, scarlet body, and ankle boots she'd paid an extravagant sum for. But she was glad she'd bought them: they made her feel good every time she wore them. Especially now.

Zipped into an inside pocket in her handbag, and safely switched off, was her old mobile phone. In her hand she carried the tiny brand new Nokia, with its new number, which she had bought earlier this morning with cash from her personal savings account.

When she reached the end of the platform she used her new phone to call Oliver Cabot's mobile number.

'Oliver? I'm here!'

A booming announcement almost drowned his reply. She could just hear, 'Make a left—I'm parked outside the Grosvenor Hotel.'

Excitement coursed through her and she had to make a conscious effort to stop herself breaking into a run. She hurried past the window of a foreign-exchange stall, a news vendor, ducked around a gaggle of Japanese students who were blocking the pavement. Then she saw the navy blue Jeep ahead, indicator winking.

Oliver!

He was standing there, anxiously scanning the crowds. He seemed even better-looking than the image she had carried in her mind during the past three long days.

'Hi! I'm sorry, the train was late!' She felt his outstretched arms close around her and they kissed, left cheek then right cheek. Gently, he pushed her back to arm's length, his smile changing to a frown.

'Your face—what happened?'

She'd been rehearsing this. 'Oh—I tripped on one of my son's toy cars, caught my head on the corner of a wardrobe. It's nothing.'

'Is it hurting?'

'No—it hurt like hell last night after the anaesthetic—' She stopped. She'd already said more than she intended.

'Anaesthetic? You had stitches?'

'Just a few.'

'Where? In hospital?'

'No, er, Ross happened to be around.' Her feigned innocence sounded just that. 'Couldn't really have a better person to do it!'

A traffic warden was approaching. Oliver ushered Faith into the car, started the engine, and as they pulled out into the traffic she felt snug, safe. Free.

He turned his head. 'Do you like Thai food?'

She hesitated. Thailand, where she'd recently been with Ross. And from where she had returned with the bug. The choice seemed a lousy omen, but she wasn't going to let it bother her. 'Love it.'

The wipers flicked away a few spots of rain. Oliver turned right, past the coach station, heading into Belgravia. There was an easy silence between them. She watched the traffic through the windscreen, detached from it by the cocoon of the car.

This felt so good. So dangerously good.

Then the dark shadow of Ross's attacks on Alec and her on Thursday evening was stalking her again. She'd had nightmares for the past four nights.

He'd been full of remorse the next day. On Saturday afternoon after playing golf he'd brought home a massive bunch of flowers for her, and an electric car for Alec, which he could actually sit in and drive. He'd taken her out to dinner on Saturday night. On Sunday he'd made her breakfast in bed, something he'd done maybe twice before in their entire married life.

But none of it had meant anything to her. She had done her best to get through the weekend without another confrontation—

'Your husband hit you, didn't he?'

Oliver startled her. Had he been reading her thoughts?

Slowly, she turned towards him and nodded.

THEIR WAITER CAME. Oliver selected the prawns in coconut sauce as a starter, lemon grass chicken, with a spicy nut salad to follow. To his secret delight, Faith ordered the same.

The happiness in her face seemed to him to fill the whole restaurant with light and warmth. He stared at her across the fresh linen, the gleaming glasses and the single-stem vase with purple orchid. It felt so good to see her pretty face all lit up with laugh lines, those gorgeous, alert blue eyes, the blonde sheen of her hair, her elegant clothes. He wanted to reach out and touch her, to hold her tight.

Protect her from her bastard husband.

Tapping his forehead above his left eye, he said, 'Tell me more about this.'

Raising her finger and touching the plaster, she looked embarrassed. 'I—' She was interrupted by the waiter presenting a bottle of Sancerre to Oliver for inspection.

He nodded, and the man poured some wine for him to taste. She continued, 'I—it—it wasn't deliberate. He didn't mean to—'

'Why are you defending him, Faith?'

'No, it's not that I'm defending him, it just needs to be in context.'

When the waiter left, Oliver picked up his glass. He held it towards her. 'Cheers.'

She raised her glass and chinked it against his. 'Cheers.'

He drank, set his glass down, and prompted her: 'You were saying about your husband?'

'He has a lot of good points.'

'You wouldn't have married him if he didn't.'

'Do you believe people can change?'

'Heraclitus said that you can't step into the same river twice.'

'Because we move on?'

'I think dumb people don't change because they're not affected by anything that happens to them. Intelligent people change constantly.'

She nodded. 'And can you change from being a kind, caring person into a monster? A psychopath?'

Oliver shook his head. 'We call them sociopaths. You are born one, you don't become one. But the smart ones know how to play the game. When you first meet them they are outwardly kind and caring, until they've gotten what they want. Then they don't need their masks any more and their true character emerges.'

He stared at her, and could see the fear in her eyes. She was too decent a person to have to live in fear. Fear was corrosive.

Your husband's a sociopath, Faith. And you're in danger because he's going to get worse. And one day he might just hit you so hard you won't get up again.

Faith was giving him a strange look and the colour was draining from her face. She placed both her hands on the table, steadying herself, as if fighting for control. Control of what? Was she having another bout of what she'd had last time?

Alarmed, he said, 'You OK?'

Even whiter now, she nodded but did not speak.

'Faith?'

She was shivering, staring wide-eyed at him. Then she got up and ran to the back of the restaurant, through to the lavatories.

When she returned, she was even paler than when she had left the table. 'I'm sorry,' she said.

'The bug?' he asked.

'Yes. It sometimes—comes on so suddenly.'

'You want to lie down?'

'I'll be OK, really.'

There was such an expression of defeat in her face that he felt a chill deep inside him. Was she more sick than she was letting on? *I've only just met you. Don't let me lose you before I've even got to know you.* He said, 'What's really wrong with you, Faith? I don't think you're telling me the whole story.'

In a frightened voice, that was barely even a whisper, she said, 'I don't know, no one will tell me.'

'You're married to a doctor and he won't tell you anything?'

'No.'

'You're going to come back to London tomorrow, Faith, to the clinic, and I'm going to take a good look at you, run some tests of my own, find out what's really going on. OK.' It wasn't a question.

Faith nodded, and the fear in her eyes was replaced with gratitude.

AT EIGHT THIRTY the following morning, Ross stood in a corner of the Harley Street operating theatre, face mask dangling below his chin, writing up his notes after the first operation of the day. He'd slept badly last night and the operation had not gone well.

It was the kind of work he enjoyed least. A repair. A skin graft he'd performed a month earlier on the neck of a man badly burned in a chemical plant accident had become infected. Now he'd had to crop a fresh flap of skin from the man's thigh and try again. The failure of the first graft had not been his fault, but he didn't see it that way. In his mind, all failures were his fault.

His failing marriage to Faith was his fault: he gave her too much freedom, too much time alone, too much money. And, in some way he didn't fully understand, he felt her illness was his fault and it was down to him to cure her. All these problems could be dealt with: they had to be taken in hand, the bad bits excised, like the necrotic flesh he'd just replaced. There were always solutions. And now, out of the corner of his eye, he saw his anaesthetist, Tommy Pearman.

Ross finished his notes and handed them to the scrub nurse to write up on the computer. Then he put an arm around the anaesthetist and propelled him towards the door. 'I need a quick word, Tommy.'

Out in the corridor, he said, 'Have you got any more for me on Lendt's disease, or the Moliou-Orelan drug.'

'Yes. In the phase two trial results they're getting just over thirty-five per cent survival rate beyond one year.'

Ross clutched him excitedly. 'Thirty-five per cent? That's excellent news, Tommy!'

'I wouldn't call it that. Sixty-five per cent of people with the disease die within twelve months—eighty per cent if they're not on the drug—and it's not a pleasant way to go. I don't think a thirty-five per cent cure rate is that impressive.'

'It's brilliant, Tommy! There wasn't anything and now there's thirty-five per cent. Thank you.' He left the anaesthetist and hurried into his office, closed the door, then rang Jules Ritterman.

'Ross! I was just going to call you!' Ritterman said.

'I just heard some information about the Moliou-Orelan trials.'

'That's what I was going to call you about. It's not brilliant, but there's some progress.'

'You have to get her on those trials, Jules, right now. You've just got to pull any strings you can.'

'I'm working on it. But it is only thirty-five per cent,' he cautioned, 'against twenty-five per cent for the placebo. That's only a ten per cent difference. And, as I told you, we'll have no way of knowing whether Faith will be given the drug itself or a placebo, which cuts the odds in half again.'

Ross barely heard the caveat. 'Faith is fit, she's a strong woman, and she has the right mental attitude. It's going to work, Jules, I know it.'

REPORT ONE. Tuesday 24 *May. Surveillance Operative HC.*

0915—Activity. The subject left Little Scaynes Manor unaccompanied, in dark green Range Rover registration S212 CWV. Subject proceeded to Gatwick Airport, car park 3, purchased ticket from Gatwick Express ticket office, boarded the 10.00 train to London Victoria, and sat on her own in the standard section.

At **10.03** subject made brief call from mobile phone to person (presumed from subsequent actions to be Dr Oliver Linden Cabot—home and office addresses at end of report). The following is the transcript of the recording made of the subject's end of the call by directional microphone (DM):

'*Hi, how are you? I'm on my way—should be in Victoria by ten thirty. Can't—sorry, can't—*' (15 seconds indecipherable due to passing train)—*same place as Friday? Me too . . . Bye.*'

10.07. Subject's rail ticket examined by inspector.

10.10. Subject acquired coffee from trolley. Passed rest of journey reading *Daily Mail* newspaper.

10.32—Activity. Arrival in Victoria. Subject left train, exited west from west concourse onto Buckingham Palace Road and met with male, mid-forties, American accent, six foot tall, thin build, wavy greying hair (later tentatively identified against his website photographs as Dr Oliver Cabot. Photograph 1.1 appendixed). Oliver Cabot was waiting in a navy Jeep Cherokee, registration P321 MDF (registered owner, the Cabot Centre for Complementary Medicine). Transcript from directional microphone (DM):

Dr OC: *Faith, hi, great, you made it. Great to see you.*

FR: *And you too. You didn't have to come and collect me again.*

Dr OC: *I wanted to. OK?*

FR: (reply inaudible from passing traffic)

Subject and Cabot enter Jeep Cherokee. Cabot in driving seat. Audio signal lost.

10.37—Activity. Jeep Cherokee departed from Buckingham Palace Road. No hook-up with GPS from transponder on Jeep Cherokee available, so surveillance maintained by taxi. Jeep Cherokee headed into North London. Journey time 43 minutes. Parked outside the Cabot Centre for Complementary Medicine.

11.25—Activity. Subject and Cabot exited Jeep and entered Cabot Centre. Observer unable to get close enough for audio.

11.28 Magnetic tracking transponder secured on underside of Dr OC's Jeep Cherokee.

11.31 Positive voice ID by window scanner microphone on subject and Cabot. Transcription from scanner on first-floor window:

Dr OC: *Glass of water you said? Sparkling?*
FR: *Still.*
Dr OC: *Coming up. OK, let me slip your coat off. Now, I want to start by taking a complete medical history from you. Let's begin with a few basics*—(Voice lost).

OLIVER PEERED out through the slats of the blinds. Suddenly he raised a finger to his lips, and walked towards the door.

Faith, puzzled by his behaviour, followed him through to his secretary's office and out into the corridor.

He closed the door quietly, then said, 'Is your husband having you followed, Faith?'

Oh, Christ. She felt a sudden heave of panic inside her as she flashed back to Ross confronting her on Thursday night with the recordings of her phone conversations. The possibility *had* occurred to her. 'Why do you ask?'

'A cab trailed us from Victoria—I'm pretty sure it was the same one all the way. I took a detour but the driver followed. Now there's a man in the street, lurking behind my car. He's talking on a mobile phone, keeps looking directly up at my office, angling the antennae towards my window, like he's trying to pick up our conversation.'

A few moments ago she had been feeling safe here with Oliver. Now she could sense the darkness of Ross closing around her. 'Anything's possible with him,' she said.

'I don't know much about surveillance except what I've read and seen in movies,' Oliver said, 'but I do know there are devices that can pick up sound waves bounced off glass. We'll go to another room where we aren't going to take that risk.'

Signalling Faith to be silent again, Oliver walked back into his office, then made his way stealthily to the window. There he stopped and pointed towards his Jeep.

Faith followed his finger, but all she could see at first were parked cars. Then she saw him. A slip of a man with shorn hair, wearing a leather jacket. He was holding a mobile phone with a wire trailing to his ear and his lips were moving.

She left the window, and joined Oliver in the corridor. After he had closed the door, he said, 'You haven't seen him before?'

'I don't think so.'

She followed him up a flight of stairs and along another corridor. He stopped outside a door, knocked, then went in. The windowless room was dark while he groped for a light switch, then twin fluorescents on the ceiling flickered into life.

It was a small consulting room with an array of high-tech equipment and an examination couch. There was a strong smell that Faith
always associated with modern offices and hire cars, the anodyne
smell of brand-new synthetic upholstery. It reminded her, suddenly,
of the Toyota they'd been driving in Thailand.

They'd been home barely a month but it seemed far longer than
that. Now her recollections of their holiday were more like a television travelogue she had watched than anything she had experienced.
The travelogue showed a tall man with a blonde wife and a small
son. The man played with his son and, when he wasn't doing this, he
was sitting at the bar, chatting to anyone who happened to be
around, the very model of charm itself.

They seemed like any other family on holiday, having a good time.
It was easy, Faith thought, to give the world the illusion you were
happy. Nobody knew what went on behind your locked doors.
Nobody knew that she prayed every night at dinner that Ross would
drink too much and fall asleep instead of wanting to make love.

Oliver tapped the keyboard in front of a computer and the screen
woke up. She saw her name appear at the top of a large, blank form.

'OK, I need your date of birth.'

She was feeling queasy again. The nausea she had woken up with
had gone when she had seen Oliver at Victoria. This queasiness was
of a different kind—not the sort born of illness, but the sort born of
fear. Fear of the man in the leather jacket down in the street.

She gave him her date of birth.

'Your GP—this Dr Ritterman—gave you a thorough checkup
when you went to see him?'

'Well, it seemed pretty thorough.'

'And you're generally in good shape, other than this thing?'

She shrugged. 'I try to keep in reasonable condition—I walk the
dog three or four miles every day, swim quite a lot in summer, go to a
local gym twice a week and do aerobics—well, before I went away.
But Jules Ritterman . . . ' she fell silent.

'What about him?' He gestured for her to sit.

She looked up at the thrumming light. 'He's never been commu-
nicative, and over this thing, he's said nothing at all. I don't know if
it's because there's nothing wrong or because there's something seriously wrong that he's keeping from me.'

'Why would he do that?'

'Because I'm just Ross's wife.' She bit her lip. 'Sorry, I don't mean
to sound bitter. It always hacks me off, being patronised.'

'It ought to. That shit is all part of the voodoo of conventional medicine. Like the way doctors always used to write things in Latin so you couldn't read their prescriptions.'

Oliver pulled up a chair close to her, and was silent for some moments, studying her. It was a comfortable feeling. She could smell the subtle, masculine scent of his cologne, could feel the energy coming off him; there was a quality about him that was pure animal, something muscular and powerful. And she could see something she had sensed before: the inner toughness of a man who has confidence in what he is doing, and is comfortable in his skin.

Something stirred deep within her: the need for this man that increased with every moment she spent with him.

She had to stop this, needed to remember why she was here: he might be able to make her better, that was all. She had to be able to say that to Ross, and to look him in the eye while she said it, because there was going to be a mighty confrontation when the private detective reported back.

'Oliver, I want you to promise you'll be honest with me. You will tell me straight if you find anything wrong with me, however bad it might be?'

'Let's work on the assumption that we're not going to find anything of the magnitude you're worrying about. OK?'

'Now *you're* patronising me!'

He laughed. 'You're right. I apologise. I want you to understand that if we *do* find something bad, whatever we find, we're going to deal with it. I promise you that.'

She believed him.

THEY WERE KISSING. Their faces pressed hard together. Cheek to cheek. Faith and Oliver Cabot. *Dr* Oliver Cabot. *In the street, for God's sake!*

Tight close-up, taken with a zoom lens, fast film, short depth of field, the small areas of background just a blur.

Ross rested the photograph against the wood-rimmed steering wheel of his Aston Martin and turned to the private detective in the passenger seat beside him. The man was exuding the stale, unpleasant odour of last night's tobacco.

'It's a joke,' Ross said. 'This man's a bloody quack. You tell me how this bastard has the gall to call himself a doctor.'

From the computer bag on his lap, Hugh Caven removed a sheet of paper and handed it to Ross. In a nonjudgmental tone, he said, 'This is Dr Cabot's curriculum vitae.'

Ross glanced down the sheet. A graduate of Princeton Medical

School, Cabot also had a doctorate in immunology from the Pasteur Institute and had been a consultant oncologist at St John's Hospital, Santa Monica. Then he had gained a doctorate in psychology and specialist training in hypnosis, before establishing the Cabot Centre.

Passing it back dismissively to the detective, Ross said, 'The man's a traitor to his profession.' He focused his attention on Caven's report. 'My wife and this charlatan were together for two hours inside this building, during which you have no idea what they were up to. Then he drove her back to Victoria Station. They could have been screwing for two hours.'

'With respect, Mr Ransome, I don't think so. I believe it was a bona fide medical examination. There was nothing improper in their body language when they emerged from the building, nor when they parted at Victoria Station. Nothing at all, in my experience, to suggest anything other than a professional relationship.'

Ross looked at him. '*Professional* relationship? You can go to all the alternative doctors in the world, Mr Caven. You can swallow all the useless homeopathic pills you want, you can have people stick acupuncture needles in you until you look like a hedgehog . . . I don't have time for that crap and I won't have truck with the con artists who peddle it.' He shook his head. 'Do you really want to put your faith in the kind of primitive stuff doctors were doling out two thousand years ago? I'll tell you something, Mr Caven. One hundred years ago, if you got acute appendicitis it was almost always terminal. Now it's little more than a minor inconvenience. People who turn their noses up at modern medicine make me sick. And I'm not having any Johnny-come-lately quack messing with my wife's health. Do you understand what I'm saying?'

'Very clearly, Mr Ransome.'

'My wife and Dr Oliver Cabot are either currently screwing each other or about to start screwing each other. I want the photographs. Another gift that our modern world has gained through science.'

Six

Rain was falling steadily outside. At the kitchen table, Faith sipped camomile tea to try to settle her stomach as she read the morning post. She was feeling lousy this morning. Upstairs, in their bedroom directly above, she could hear Mrs Fogg vacuuming. The machine clunked against the skirting board and Rasputin, lying in front of the Aga, lifted his head and growled at the ceiling. He was in a grumpy mood because she'd only taken him for a short walk.

'I know you don't mind the rain, but I do,' she said to him. 'Sometimes, just occasionally, we do what I want, not what you want.'

The dog looked at her hopefully, eyes bright, pink tongue out, panting. Ignoring him, she returned to her letters. Above her the vacuuming stopped and she could hear the rain thudding against the windows. Then the phone rang.

She answered it quickly, her heart lifting, in the hope that it might be Oliver, even though she'd told him only to use her new mobile number. But it was the Aga service engineer, calling to arrange a visit. She stood up and walked across the kitchen to her diary.

Then she sat down again, turned to the next letter and slit open the large, thick envelope. It was information she had requested on a course in nutrition at the Open University, together with an application form. She was glad it had arrived today and not tomorrow, Saturday, when Ross would have seen it. It would have been something else for him to get angry about—he didn't approve of her doing anything that smacked of independence.

She rubbed her eyes. The clock on the wall said twenty to ten. Ross would be home tonight, and Alec was going to stay the weekend on the Isle of Wight with a schoolfriend. She had mixed feelings about that. She was glad that he was going to be distanced from the bad atmosphere between herself and Ross, but it meant she was going to be stuck with Ross on his own. It was a long weekend. Bank Holiday. Three whole days.

She opened the local paper and turned to the property pages, looking at the classifieds for rental properties. The two-bedroom flats started at around eighty pounds a week. She was going to need around £10,000 a year just for rent and food for herself and Alec, and she needed to run a car on top of that, plus all the other costs of living. Hopefully she could get work in catering, but it would be a struggle. A struggle, yes, but better than this existence.

She could hear Mrs Fogg, in a spare room now. Her eyes felt raw, as if there was grit inside her contact lenses. It was probably from tiredness because she was barely sleeping, worrying about Ross and about what was wrong with her.

It was now three days since Oliver had examined her, and he'd told her it would take time to get the results from the blood tests. She thought about him constantly. Nothing had happened between them, yet she missed him, badly.

She picked up the cordless phone and dialled Dr Ritterman's number. His secretary answered, her usual cold, defensive voice.

'It's Faith Ransome, I'd like a word with Dr Ritterman, please.'

'You rang yesterday.' It sounded like an accusation.

'I did, and he still hasn't rung me back. I came to see him over a fortnight ago and now I want the results of my tests.'

'Dr Ritterman will be in touch when he has some news.'

'That's not good enough,' Faith said. 'I expect my doctor to return my calls. I'd like to speak to him now, please.'

'I'm afraid he's with a patient and cannot be disturbed. I'll tell him you phoned.'

'Look, I'd—'

But the woman had hung up.

Faith stared furiously at the receiver, on the verge of redialling, when Rasputin raced out into the hall, barking. Moments later the front doorbell rang.

Faith's heart sank. Felice D'Eath stood in the porch in a bright yellow sou'wester, clutching an ornate bottle of extra virgin olive oil in one hand and a basket of potpourri in the other. The tailgate of her Mercedes estate was open, piled high with another load of tombola prizes for the NSPCC ball.

'Beastly weather. You were expecting me, weren't you? Ten o'clock, you said?'

Faith had forgotten. As she helped unload the contents of the car, and lugged everything into the upstairs room where they were storing prizes, Felice reminded her twice, for good measure, that it was less than six months to the ball, and Faith silently wondered where she and Alec would be in six months' time.

She knelt amid a sea of prizes, most of them tat, being the dutiful committee woman, labelling each in turn under the command of Felice, who was reading out the list of gifts and their donors.

'I pity anyone who wins this,' Faith said, holding up a prancing china horse. 'Who on earth donated it?'

'I did.'

Faith felt her face burning with embarrassment.

'My first husband gave it to me—I've never been able to stand it.'

Relieved, Faith said, 'I didn't know you were married before.'

'I got rid of him ten years ago. Best thing I ever did.'

'Tell me more, Felice,' she said.

Suddenly the woman was interesting. With her wet weather clothes removed, in a jumper and black baggy trousers, she looked small and vulnerable. But her expression was proud.

'Jonathan was a bully, and one day I decided life was too short and I wasn't going to put up with him any more. I packed, collected the children from school and left home with them while he was at work.'

'And?'

'He came after me, made my life hell for a couple of years. But,' she shrugged. 'In the end it was worth it. Sometimes in life you have to stand up for yourself. You're lucky if you have a good marriage. You and Ross seem happy together.'

Faith smiled and held up the china horse. 'I suppose I should be grateful for small mercies. At least he never bought me one of these.'

ROSS CAME THROUGH the front door with a huge smile. He barely acknowledged Rasputin's greeting, just scooped Faith into his arms and held her tightly. 'Faith,' he said. 'My darling. My *darling*. God I missed you. I want to stop staying up in London, we shouldn't be apart so much. Do you miss me?'

A hesitation too faint for him to notice. 'Of course I do.'

Rasputin, upgrading his efforts at getting attention from his master, launched a volley of deafening barks.

She walked to the cloakroom and hung up his coat. When she came out, Ross was sifting through his post on the hall table.

Casually he said, 'You booked the tickets for *Life Is Beautiful*?'

'Yes. You said you wanted to see it.'

They had missed it on previous occasions when it had shown. Now it was on at an art-house cinema in Brighton.

'Where's Alec?' Ross said casually.

'Gone to the Isle of Wight for the weekend with the Caiborns.'

His face fell. 'I don't remember agreeing this.'

'We discussed it.'

'I'd never have agreed to it. I don't see enough of him as it is—I mean, I don't mind if he goes out for a day or something, but a whole *long* weekend? I miss him, don't you understand that?'

'I miss him too.'

He slipped his arms around her waist. 'At least I have you to myself for the whole weekend. You know something? I fancy you even more now than I did twelve years ago.'

She felt only revulsion for him, but she squeezed him back. She could feel his hardness, and could see the signal in his eyes. 'We have to leave in a minute,' she said. 'The film starts at eight.'

'I need a quick drink.'

'I'll get it for you,' she said, relieved to have an excuse to ease herself away from him.

He followed her into the kitchen, and leaned against a pine dresser, loosening his tie. 'We don't have to see the film, if you don't want to.'

'I do want to, very much.' Faith took a crystal tumbler from the display cabinet, held it against the spigot on the fridge and ejected several ice cubes into it.

Then she walked across to the cabinet where she kept the whisky. Ross was now peering at the framed photographs ranged along the pine shelves between the willow-pattern china. He picked up one of the two of them skiing in Zermatt, with the Matterhorn towering behind them. 'I can remember this being taken,' he said. 'It was our second wedding anniversary. It was freezing up there and you tried taking your bobble hat off but the wind hurt your ears. Do you remember?' There was a look of childlike joy on his face.

She poured three fingers of whisky. Handing him his glass, she said, 'I remember we climbed all the way up, and when we got to the top we saw there was a chairlift on the other side.'

He picked up a photograph of Alec sitting on a lawn, hugging Rasputin, and studied it. 'I love you, Faith,' he said, then took a sip of his drink. 'You don't have any idea how much I love you.'

The show of affection was puzzling her. It was unusual for him to be this loving without having been angry first, and she was not sure how to respond. She said nothing.

'How much do you think?' he insisted.

'I don't know. Tell me.'

He drained half the whisky in one gulp, replaced the photograph on the shelf. 'To the end of the universe and back—that much.'

He was scaring her. His mouth was smiling, but there was darkness in his eyes.

'Oh, by the way,' there was a forced casualness in his voice, 'I spoke to Jules Ritterman today. He apologised for not being in touch— some hiccup in the lab.'

'I rang him, too. His secretary hung up on me. I want a new doctor.'

He rotated his tumbler thoughtfully. 'No, he's a good man.'

'Ross, I'm not having my doctor's secretary hang up on me. I'm going to find myself a doctor I'm comfortable with.'

'So, anyway,' he continued, as if he hadn't heard her, 'there's nothing to worry about. You do have a bug, one of those tourist things, to which our Western immune systems are susceptible.'

'How do I get rid of it?'

He dug his right hand into his jacket pocket and pulled out a small cylindrical container, which he handed to her. On the exterior was printed in green letters on a white background, MOLIOU-ORELAN (UK) PLC, NOT FOR SALE, then several rows of numbers and letters.

Smiling, he said, 'Brand-new antibiotic—Jules managed to wangle some for me. Guaranteed to nuke any tummy bug.'

There was an eagerness in his voice that felt wrong to her.

'Isn't it better to take some established antibiotic? I'm not sure I like the idea of taking something new. What about side effects?'

'Moliou are a great company, good people, lot of integrity, I have total confidence in them. The problem with existing antibiotics is that we've all taken so many of them, the bugs are getting resistant to them. These are what you need, trust me.'

She unscrewed the lid, pulled out the cotton wadding, then tipped two tiny grey capsules into her palm.

'Take them with you,' Ross urged. 'Swallow them in the restaurant before we eat. We're going for a Chinese after the film, right? We'll go to the China Garden, have their crispy duck with pancakes. You love crispy duck, don't you?'

'I didn't think you cared for it.'

'No, I love it!'

He was acting very strangely, she thought. Was he worrying about his behaviour last Thursday when he'd struck her? Contrite about it? There was nothing he could have picked up from any phone bugging this week—she had been careful to say nothing at all over the phones at home, and her new mobile was now switched off and safely hidden in the cellar. At any moment she was expecting him to start quizzing her about her visit to Oliver Cabot's clinic.

But he said nothing about it, not a word. All weekend.

THREE DAYS was the longest Faith had ever been apart from Alec, and by Tuesday morning, she was missing him dreadfully. They'd spoken every day: Alec was having the time of his life.

From their bedroom window, she watched Ross's car disappear down the drive, her emotions in turmoil. Tightening the belt of her dressing gown, she went downstairs, her slippers slapping across the flagstones of the cold hall, and into the warmth of the kitchen.

Her breakfast place was laid on the table, the two capsules on the side plate so she wouldn't forget them, not that they'd made much of a difference so far. The bouts of nausea had continued to come and go over the weekend, and she was having a minor one now.

She went down the brick steps to the cellar, switched on the lights and walked past the racks of wines to the far end where the chest freezer sat. Reaching into the space between it and the wall, she retrieved her mobile phone and carried it upstairs.

She switched on the phone. There were three new messages.

Only one person knew the number.

'Faith, it's Oliver, seven thirty Friday evening, sorry I didn't get back to you sooner—I had to wait on some of the tests. Give me a call. I'll be on my home number or my cellphone all weekend.'

'Hi, Faith, Oliver again. Saturday morning. I'm going to be tied up with patients until noon. I'll be on my cellphone the rest of the day.'

There was anxiety in his voice, which seemed to increase with each message. In the final one there was distinct urgency.

'Faith, it's Oliver, Sunday, eleven. I really need to talk to you. Appreciate it may not be easy for you to call. If you get through to my voicemail, leave a message where I can call you back.'

Faith tried his home number. There was no answer. She tried him on his mobile and left a message.

At nine, Oliver rang her. At ten, she was on a train to London.

AT TEN, the Boeing 737 touched down at Malaga airport in Spain. Ross, carrying his leather briefcase, squinted against the brightness as he stepped out into the humid, kerosene-drenched sunlight.

He followed the other passengers down the gangway and into the bus. Ten minutes later, still carrying only his briefcase, he walked out through the customs area into the din of the arrivals hall, and scanned the sea of jostling placards. KUONI. THOMAS COOK. M.A. BANOUN. DR PETER DEAN. Then he saw the rather shabby rectangle of cardboard. SNR ROSS RANSOME.

The man looked like a pimp and spoke no English. He insisted on taking Ross's briefcase, then led him outside to a spotless white Mercedes with a chauffeur behind the wheel.

The pimp opened the rear door for Ross, handed him back his briefcase, then climbed into the front passenger seat. The interior temperature felt below zero.

In broken English the driver greeted him. 'You have good flight, Señor Ransome?'

Pulling on his seat belt Ross said, 'Thank you, it was fine.' He opened his briefcase, removed his mobile phone and the copy of the *British Journal of Plastic Surgery*, which he hadn't finished reading on the plane. Addressing both men he said, 'How is *il capitano*?'

The driver, easing the car away from the kerb, turned his head. 'Señor Milward? Señor Milward very well.'

'Good.' Ross dialled his secretary, Lucinda. She had no idea he was in Spain and he did not enlighten her. She knew only that he was taking this Tuesday off as part of the long weekend. He did not want anyone knowing he was here.

As they left the airport and wound up the fast road into the hills above, Lucinda went through his appointments for the following three days. On Thursday, she told him, he had the corrective operation on Lady Geraldine Reynes-Rayleigh. And a letter this morning from the woman's solicitor put him on notice that their client was dissatisfied with his work.

When he finished the call, he concentrated on his reading, trying to put aside his anger towards Lady Geraldine Reynes-Rayleigh.

An hour later, when he next glanced out, they were crawling past a parade of smart shops. A few minutes later, they pulled up on the quayside of the Puerto Banus yacht basin.

The chauffeur turned, gave him a glinty mile and said, 'Just a short walk, Señor Ransome. Two hundred metres.'

Ross stepped out of the air conditioning onto the quayside, into bleaching sunlight and a salty breeze tarred with the smell of rope and marine paint. He had been here once before about fifteen years back, on a golfing weekend, and hadn't cared for the place. It had a reputation for housing British villains taking advantage of Spain's lax extradition laws, as well as a few ageing dregs from the Third Reich eking out the last of their looted gains.

Putting on his sunglasses, he looked around. The port reeked of money. Flash boats lined the pontoons, young blondes on their sundecks. Paunchy middle-aged men dressed in shorts and yachting caps strutting on the bridge, holding beer cans.

Ross followed the pimp past a security guard, and along a pontoon where the largest yachts of all were berthed. It was quiet here, just the clattering of slack halyards, the flapping of ensigns and the faint beat of music coming from the interior of one floating villa.

The pimp stopped at the gangway of a boat that seemed more like a liner than a yacht. The name *Soozie-B-too* was emblazoned in gold on her rounded stern, and beneath was the name of the flag of convenience under which she was registered, *Panama*.

Two flunkeys in dark suits and designer sunglasses materialised from the aft saloon, and eyed Ross as he followed the pimp up the red carpeted gangway and onto the teak decking.

Ross pocketed his sunglasses as he entered the saloon, which was dim and vulgarly plush: white leather furniture, deep white carpet, gilded mirrors and a curved bar in one corner. There was a smell of cigar smoke, and Ross, his eyes adjusting to the gloom, could make out its source—the stocky figure of Ronnie Milward.

He was lounging on a sofa near the bar, wearing a dark polo shirt buttoned to the top, white trousers, crisp plimsolls, and sunglasses the size of patio doors. A smouldering cigar was clamped between his lips and a tall tumbler containing ice and the remnants of a pink drink sat next to the ashtray.

Ronnie Milward was in his late sixties but, with a sleek, tanned face and hair dyed black, he passed easily for a man in his mid-fifties.

He stood up and seized Ross's hand with a grip of steel. Then he swung his arms around Ross's midriff and gave him a huge bear hug. 'Hey, hey, hey! Good to see you, Ross, boy!'

Hugging him back, Ross said, 'Good to see you too, Captain.'

Milward gazed at him. 'Yeah, you look all right. Done some surgery on yourself, have you?'

'Just clean living.'

'Bollocks to that.'

They sat down. Even though they were berthed in harbour, Ross could feel a slight sensation of motion.

'So, how are you, Captain?'

'I'm drinking a Sea Breeze. Vodka and cranberry. Healthy, you know. Cranberries. Good for the cholesterol. You like one?'

Milward shouted, and a leggy red-headed woman in her mid-thirties appeared, wearing a chiffon shirt-waister and too many baubles.

'Mandy, this is Ross, most famous plastic surgeon in England.'

She gave him a vacuous smile. 'Nice to meet you.'

'When your tits start drooping, this is the man's going to do 'em.'

'Really?' she said.

'Get us two Sea Breezes, darlin', and some cashews.'

As she walked away, Ross studied with professional interest the parts of Ronnie Milward's face that weren't obscured by his ridiculous sunglasses. 'You're wearing well.'

'I'm clapped out on the inside,' he said. 'The joys of ageing.'

At least you're ageing in style, Ross thought. At least you're ageing on a £15 million yacht, free to spend your ill-gotten loot, instead of being locked up in a prison cell, which is probably the kind of old age you deserve.

Ronnie Milward was not his real name, nor was his face the one he had been born with. Ross had changed it for him in a discreet Swiss clinic, and £250,000 had changed hands, out of sight of the British tax man. Seeing this boat now, Ross regretted not having charged more.

Holding the flame of his gold lighter to the smouldering tip of the cigar and puffing hard, Milward said, 'You got to be away by three for your flight?'

'Yes.'

Mandy brought them their drinks and was about to sit down with them when Milward brushed her away. 'Push off and leave us in peace. Mr Ransome din't come all this way to talk about your tits.'

As she sauntered off, he turned to Ross. 'So, you want to see me, but you din't want to talk over the phone.' He stirred his drink with the plastic swizzle stick. 'What's on your mind?'

'You told me five years ago that you owed me a favour, Captain. I've come to call it in.'

Laying his cigar in the ashtray Milward said, 'I don't owe no favours, Ross. You did a job, I paid you. You want something, I'll see what I can do. That's how I work. Tell me what you want.'

'I want to know if you can arrange something.' From his briefcase, Ross removed a brown envelope. He shook two photographs out of the envelope and handed them to Ronnie.

Milward glanced at the first photograph, a face-on close-up of a man. The second was a longer shot, showing the same man in profile. He laid them down on the table. 'Am I meant to know him or what? Looks to me like that French singer geezer, wozzisname?'

'No, you don't know him. He's American, lives in London. His name is Oliver Cabot. *Dr* Oliver Cabot. He's screwing my wife.'

'You want someone to teach him a lesson?'

Picking up his glass, Ross drank some of the icy vodka. Then leaning forward and staring hard into those dark, impenetrable glasses, he lowered his voice and said, 'I want him dead.'

THE TAXI made a right turn off Notting Hill Gate. Faith looked out of the rear window to see if any other vehicle followed them. Nothing. She glanced at her Rolex: it was 11.25. To save her the trek across London to his clinic, Oliver had suggested they meet at his home.

Faith, I have the results back from your tests. I need to see you.

What the hell did they show?

The taxi slowed, then halted outside 37 Ladbroke Avenue. Faith climbed out, paid the driver then stood on the pavement looking warily around her. It was a fine morning, and the sky was cloudless.

Ladbroke Avenue was a grand residential street, wide and quiet and lined both sides with plane trees. Behind them rose imposing terraced houses, with columned porticoes and tall sash windows. The multiple entryphone panels showed that, like most London homes of this size, they had been carved up into flats. The quality of the cars parked along the street showed that they were still occupied by money: Mercedes, BMWs, Audis, Porsches and assorted off-roaders.

She checked both directions for any sign of the man in the leather jacket she had seen outside the clinic last week, or for anyone else who might be watching her. Then she walked up the steps to the columned porch, scanned the list of names and found Oliver's.

Moments later a voice crackled over the intercom. His American accent sounded more pronounced than usual. 'Hello?'

'It's Faith,' she said.

'Come right up—top floor, no elevator, I'm afraid.' There was a buzz then a sharp click, and she pushed the door. It yielded and she stumbled into a narrow hall with bare floorboards.

She walked past a row of mailboxes and a mountain bike propped against the wall, then began climbing the stairs. When she reached the third floor, she heard a door open above her.

A chirpy English voice said, 'I've checked all the sensors. The one in the bedroom was definitely on the blink and I've replaced it—no charge for that, it's still under warranty.'

Then Oliver's voice. 'Thanks. Appreciate it.'

She heard footsteps, then a man wearing a blue tunic with *Languard Alarms* sewn on the breast pocket, and carrying a toolbox, passed her on the stairs.

She was breathless, which surprised her. Before Thailand she'd considered herself reasonably fit.

'Faith?'

She stared back at him, puzzled. It was Oliver, and yet it wasn't. He was wearing a green sweatshirt over baggy blue jeans and trainers. The same build, the same hair colour, and almost the same voice. But this man looked older, and had subtly different features.

Stretching out a hand, he shook hers with a firm grip. 'I'm Harvey, Oliver's brother.'

Surprised, she said, 'Oh, hi. I didn't know Oliver had a brother.'

He grinned. 'I guess if I had a brother like me, I wouldn't go around bragging about it either.'

She laughed as he ushered her in and closed the door. 'He just called, the traffic was bad, he'll be right here. Can I fix you something to drink?'

She barely heard him. She was staring around in awe. 'Some tea, please. This place is incredible!'

'It's kind of a neat place,' he said.

It was like something out of a lifestyle television commercial: living room that finished in a fine metal staircase rising gracefully up to a crescent-shaped mezzanine sitting area. Picture windows looking out across miles of rooftops. A polished wooden floor covered with Persian rugs running the length of the apartment, and rich but spare furnishings with stunning Oriental pieces. Exotic fish swam slowly in a handsome tank.

Faith was entranced by the atmosphere. 'So much space and light! You both live here?'

'I'm just on a visit—I live in North Carolina. Ever been there?'

'Not to North Carolina. I've been to New York and Washington.'

'It's beautiful. I'm an hour's drive from the Blue Ridge mountains. Great place to live. Different pace from London.'

They went into a starkly modern kitchen. He filled the kettle. 'Guess you're pretty brave, letting an American make you tea.'

Smiling she asked, 'Are you over on holiday?'

'Work and holiday mixed.' He ducked down and produced a tin of biscuits. 'Cookies?'

'I'm fine, thanks. What work do you do?'

'Research. Quantum physics. I'm over to give a paper at a seminar in Switzerland next week, and I'm grabbing a few days' vacation in London either side, hanging out with my kid brother.'

It was strange watching him move, because there was so much of Oliver in him. Little gestures, expressions.

And then she heard Oliver. 'Hey, I'm sorry, the traffic!'

She turned, and he was standing in the kitchen doorway.

'Faith, good to see you.'

They kissed, each cheek in turn, Oliver holding her tenderly but firmly. But she sensed a distance and her fear deepened.

'My bro taking good care of you?'

'He's making me very welcome.'

Harvey raised a hand in the air. 'I'm outta here—going to check out your Royal Academy and the Tate. Oh, the alarm guy came, said he found the problem and fixed it. One of the sensors was toast.'

'Good,' Oliver replied. 'Thanks.'

'No problem. Nice meeting you, Faith. See you again.' He pumped her hand, then turned to Oliver. 'What time is the theatre tonight?'

'Seven forty-five,' Oliver said.

'Great!' And he was gone.

For a moment Faith and Oliver stood still, smiling at each other.

'Nice guy,' she said.

'He is,' Oliver replied, with feeling. 'Got a terrific wife and three great kids—they're in school right now which is why she isn't with him.' He looked at her for a moment. 'How have you been feeling?'

'Up and down. The attacks come and go.'

'Any change in their frequency?'

She nodded. 'They're getting more frequent—and stronger.'

The kettle rumbled, steam belched from its spout, then it clicked off. Oliver unscrewed the lid of a glass jar and pulled out two teabags.

'I wasn't followed,' Faith said.

He looked at her and she could see the worry in his eyes. Suddenly she felt uncomfortable, and walked back into the calming living area.

Oliver came out of the kitchen carrying two mugs, and they sat in deep sofas, looking out across the west London skyline.

Faith cradled her hot tea in trembling hands and, trying to ease the tension, said, 'So, tell me, how many hours have I left to live?'

'Plenty, Faith. But the news from your tests isn't good.'

'Wh-what did they show?'

'Did Dr Ritterman tell you *anything*?'

'No. After I rang again on Friday and gave his secretary a rocket, he phoned Ross, told him I have some bug, a tourist thing, and he's given me some antibiotics.'

'You have them with you?'

She opened her handbag and passed the Moliou-Orelan container to him. He read the label. 'Dr Ritterman provided these?'

'Yes—via Ross.'

He shook out one pill into his palm. 'What are your instructions?'

'I have to take two three times a day.'

'Faith, what did Ross tell you these were?'

Disturbed by his tone, she said, 'A new antibiotic. Do you know about them?'

'I know Moliou-Orelan, sure, but this is a new drug that's not on the market yet—it doesn't even have a brand name, only a code. Did he say anything to you about taking part in a clinical trial?'

'No.'

Oliver examined the pill for a few moments. 'Have you ever heard Ross mention something called Lendt's disease?'

'I don't think so, no. What is it?'

'You have it, Faith. I wish to God you didn't, but you do.'

She searched his face for comfort, and for the first time felt none. Outside, somewhere beyond the tranquillity of this room, a siren howled. And deep in her heart, she shuddered. 'What is Lendt's disease, Oliver? I want to know everything. Please tell me the truth. Tell me everything you know.'

Slowly, and in as positive a light as he could frame it, he told her.

It took time to sink in. And Faith didn't want it to, she wanted to keep talking, as if somehow if she talked for long enough they might arrive at some new way of looking at this *thing*, this Lendt's disease, this savage microorganism that invaded human bodies and killed eighty per cent of its victims within a year.

Oliver was showing her a picture of one now, a blow-up of a photograph taken through an electron microscope. It was hard to make out exactly what she was meant to be looking at. Then Oliver pointed to a white area, the shape of a kidney bean. ''Bout a hundred of those could sit on a pinhead.'

She stood up. Her eyes were moist but she wasn't about to cry: she was too shocked for that. *Four out of five dead within twelve months.*

She stared out of the window. A hundred or so yards away was a pretty roof garden, lush with leaves and hanging plants. May had ended; this might be the last spring she would see. Her last summer. The last Christmas. She was never going to see Alec grow up. Did Ross know? Was that why he'd been so sweet to her this weekend?

Oliver watched her standing silently, staring out of the window, and tried to understand what it must feel like to be given a death sentence. They'd never told Jake—he'd been too young for such news.

The thought occurred to him that he was meddling in someone else's life here, telling Faith something that her husband had deliberately not told her, maybe with the best intentions.

But then he thought about the sticking plaster above her eye. He did not know what Ransome's intentions had been; all he knew was that a man who hit a woman was not a man he would ever trust.

I'm going to make you better, Faith. Whatever it takes, you and I, we're going to beat this thing.

Oliver knew that twenty per cent of people would survive almost any disease for a longer period than the rest, simply because of their genetic make-up or immune system, or sheer will power. It wasn't about drugs. It was about luck and determination, and Faith was going to need both.

She was walking back towards him, looking utterly lost. He held out his arms and she sank into them, as if he were a piece of driftwood in a raging ocean. 'I'm scared,' she said. 'I'd like to be brave but I'm not. I'm sorry.'

'You *are* brave—and there's nothing you need to be sorry about.'

In a whisper she said, 'Why did Ross lie to me?'

'I can't tell you. I guess maybe he was trying to be kind, not wanting you to know the truth.'

He heard a tiny, halfhearted laugh.

She looked up at him and he stared into those bright blue eyes, so filled with fear and at the same time with trust.

Then she said, 'Make love to me.'

THE WHITE RENAULT van had REILLY & SONS BUILDERS. EST. 1951 in small letters on the side, and two ladders on the roof. It was parked fifty yards down the street from Oliver Cabot's flat, facing away from the front entrance, with a clear view through its rear windows of anyone entering or leaving the place.

Seated in the back of the van, in an old armchair bought from a junk shop, Hugh Caven listened to a Schubert concert on Classic FM. Mounted above his head was a bank of television monitors.

The van smelt as if a wet dog had slept in it. Barry Gatt, who'd done the night shift in here, had hygiene problems.

Caven's cellphone rang. 'Yup?' he answered.

'I've fixed the booster on the roof. You should have a picture now,' the voice the other end said. 'Five channels.'

'What about Sky?'

'Very witty, I like that.'

Caven reluctantly reduced the volume of the concert, stood up and pressed a button on the control panel. All five monitors flickered into life, showing the interior of a large flat. One showed the reception area beside the front door, another, part of what looked like the main living area, a third, the kitchen, the fourth an empty bedroom. But all Caven's attention was on the fifth. He saw two people he recognised instantly: Faith Ransome and Dr Oliver Cabot, standing next to a sofa, holding each other tight. He turned up the volume in time to hear Faith Ransome's voice. 'Make love to me.'

Caven had been afraid that this was going to happen. He'd selected the photographs that he had given to Ross Ransome carefully, and he had given him a less than accurate account of his observations of the behaviour of his wife and Dr Cabot.

He watched Dr Cabot ease himself away from her. 'Faith—I don't think that's a good idea. Not right now.'

Good man. Be strong! Caven urged, silently. Be really strong!

'I'm dangerously close to falling in love with you, Faith. I can't get you out of my mind when we're apart. There's something very special that you have . . . ' His voice tailed off.

'That's how I feel about you too,' she said.

He took her in his arms again. 'What I'm going to do is make you better, OK? I want to be your doctor. I can't be your doctor if I'm your lover—I need to keep an emotional distance. First I'm going to make you better and then—' He fell silent, just watching her.

'And then?'

'Then we'll see how you feel, about your life, about your marriage.'

Their faces were close now, nose to nose, lip to lip. Cabot cupped her cheeks in his hands and said, 'I wasn't telling you the truth just now, when I said I was dangerously close to falling in love with you, Faith. I am in love with you. I wish I wasn't, but I am.'

Caven's finger went to the STOP button on the video machinery. Normally, in his experience, people committing infidelities deserved all they had coming to them. But this woman was different: she was a decent person, and he was moved by her. He didn't want Ross Ransome, whom he disliked intensely, to see this.

He could stop the tape now, rewind it, erase it, tell Ross Ransome to take a hike—or tell him anything. Tell him, as he had before, that there really was nothing between the two of them.

Hugh Caven had a son and his wife was four months pregnant with their second child. Eight years ago he'd screwed up, big time, in his first business, importing cheap burglar-alarm equipment from Taiwan. A wholesaler who owed him a lot of money went bust, leaving Caven with an unsecured debt of £120,000, which threatened to take Caven's company down.

In an effort to prevent this happening, Caven attempted an insurance fraud, by setting fire to his warehouse. But he was tripped up by the forensic evidence, and spent two years in jail, during which he lost not only his business but also his home. He lost everything except his wife. For three years following his release he scraped a living first as a car-park attendant, then, falsifying his past, secured a job fitting bugging equipment for a private detective agency, which gave him the inspiration to set up on his own. Now he had his life back. And his business was going well.

Suddenly, the words of a Bob Dylan song began to play inside his head. It was the one about how many roads you had to walk down before you could be called a man.

Mouthing an apology to the two players on the screen, he remembered his priorities.

'SHOULD I STOP taking the Moliou-Orelan capsules?'

Oliver Cabot said, 'I want you to think back. When your husband first gave these to you on Friday evening, did you believe they were going to work?'

'Not really, no.'

'A lot of doctors are convinced that a drug will only work if the patient believes it's going to work.'

'And even if I believe this, there's only a thirty-five per cent chance?'

'Yes, and we don't even know the long-term prognosis for the thirty-five per cent. We're not gambling a few bucks on a roulette wheel;

this is gambling with your life. And I don't want to lose you, Faith.'

In a small, scared voice, she said, 'I don't want to lose you either.'

Ross, in his office, stared at the video on his television screen, his right hand clenched tight, his nails digging into his palm. *You bastard. You're talking about gambling with my wife's life—what odds are you offering her? Moliou-Orelan are worth a million of you. If you were a proper doctor, practising proper medicine, I'd have enough on this tape to get you struck off for professional misconduct.*

His phone rang. He ignored it. It rang again. He jabbed the PAUSE button on the video control, grabbed the phone and snapped, 'I told you I don't want to be disturbed, Lucinda.'

'You have three patients waiting—Mr Sirwan has been here over an hour—and you've got the BBC coming at five.'

'The BBC?'

'You agreed to do an interview for *Panorama* on breast implants.'

'Find me an hour in the morning.'

'I can't. You've got a completely full—'

He slammed the receiver down and pressed the PLAY button.

On the screen, Oliver Cabot said, 'Sit down, Faith, and we'll talk through what I'm going to do.'

Ross, his insides balled up tight like his fist, watched Faith sit down on a sofa. Oliver Cabot lit a low, fat candle on the coffee table, then sat opposite her. Faith had her back to the camera, and the weird fish-eye distortion of the lens gave Ross a view of Cabot's face.

'Conventional medicine tends to target the disease itself. What I try to do is understand an individual's immune system and find ways to boost that. I use hypnosis and other trance states, combined sometimes with pharmaceuticals as well, and natural remedies. There's a professor of immunology in the US who said very recently that the immune system is the mind. That's what I believe and that's what I want to work on with you. How do you feel about that?'

'That makes sense,' Faith said.

'I'd like to start by sending you to a lab I use, who will do a series of tests on your blood, which will help me understand clearly your immune system. Every human immune system is unique, and I need to establish which areas of yours we need to work on.'

'How quickly can they do them?'

'I'll phone them now—maybe you could go over there right away? They're five minutes by cab.'

'Please,' she said.

Ross's phone rang again, twice. He hit the PAUSE button. 'What is it, Lucinda?'

'Mr Seiler is on the phone from the Credit Shiel bank in Zürich—he says he needs to speak to you urgently.'

'Put Seiler on.'

A moment later, Ross heard the familiar accented English of the Swiss bank manager.

'Good afternoon, Mr Ransome. We received your fax and I just would like, please, your verbal confirmation. We are to transfer today the equivalent of twenty-five thousand pounds in euros to the account of the Benina Corporation SA in Puerto Banus. Correct?'

'Correct.'

'Thank you, Mr Ransome.'

Ross hung up and stared in grim satisfaction at the frozen, flickering image of Oliver Cabot on the screen. Ronnie Milward's down-payment was on its way. Half now, half on completion.

He switched off the VCR and told Lucinda to send in Mr Sirwan.

FAITH REMOVED one wooden chip too many from the precarious tower.

'Tim*berrrrrrrrr*!' Alec shouted.

She watched helplessly as, once again, all fifty-four pieces crashed down onto the kitchen table.

Alec, giggling, leaned back in his chair, pointing a finger at his mother. 'You did it! Silly Mummy!'

Fighting to stop herself crying, Faith knelt, ducking beneath the table to recover the pieces from the floor—and her composure. She knew why she kept losing: you needed a steady hand to play this game and she was shaking too much.

The only time she had stopped shaking was last night when she'd got back from London after the tests. Ross was staying in town till Friday and after Alec had gone to bed she'd demolished half a bottle of Chablis and for an hour, maybe even more, the buzz of the alcohol had sent her confidence soaring into orbit. Then, around eleven, the burned-out remnants of that confidence crashed back to earth.

At three in the morning she had lain in their massive four-poster bed, wide awake, in the claustrophobic grip of fear, fighting a terrible longing to phone her mother and tell her. The thought even crossed her mind that her mother already knew, that Ross had given her the news and said, 'Don't tell Faith, she won't be able to cope.' And, of course, her mother would go along with Ross. She always did.

Finally, Faith had gone down to Ross's study, and looked up Lendt's disease on the web. There were forty sites. Among them she found a help group for Lendt's disease sufferers. It contained information about the Moliou-Orelan trials, but she learned nothing new.

'Can we do it once more, Mummy?'

They'd played the game five times already, and she was tiring of it. It was seven o'clock. She didn't know what she wanted to do.

Oliver Cabot is going to make me better. I have to believe that. And if he doesn't?

She looked at Alec. *What would happen to you? You'd be Ross's.*

'Can we, Mummy? Once more?'

'Bed!' she said.

'Ohhhh. Please, Mummy?' That look on his face always got to her. Relenting, she said, 'Once more, and then bed—OK?'

Alec began to scoop the pieces back into the box, setting up the next game. While he was absorbed, Rasputin ran out into the hall, barking excitedly.'What is it, boy?' she called.

The sound of a key turning in the lock, the door opening, a man's voice. 'Hey, boy! Rasputin! Hey, hey, hey!'

Ross? She'd been trying to get hold of him all day, but what the hell was he doing at home? It was Thursday. He was meant to be staying in London until Friday.

He came through the kitchen door to a squeal of excitement from Alec, who launched himself at him. '*Daddy!* Daddeee!'

Ross scooped him up, held him in the air, and the sight angered Faith. Ten days ago Ross had struck him savagely, now he was hugging him, and Alec seemed to have forgotten all about it.

'Hey, big guy! I didn't see you all weekend! Missed you. You've grown!' He set the child back down on the ground. His face darkened. 'Shouldn't you be in bed? It's after seven.' He shot an accusatory glance at Faith, who remained seated at the table. 'I see. This is what happens during the week when I'm not here. You let all discipline go out of the window.'

'Why didn't you return any of my calls, Ross?'

'It's after seven. Why's he still up?'

Faith glanced at Alec. She hated him to see them arguing, but she was determined to hold her ground. Calmly she said, 'We're going to have one more game and then bedtime. You start, Alec.'

'He's going to bed, *now*!' Ross, a storm brewing in his face, looked around for something to be angry about. 'Why are there dirty dishes on the sideboard? Are they from lunch, Faith? Do you live like a slut when you're not expecting me home?'

Ignoring Ross, she said to Alec, 'You go first, darling.' Then continuing in the same calm voice she glanced at Ross and said, 'Why don't you relax in your study?'

She began to set up the pieces of the game, and could see Ross out of the corner of her eye, wavering. 'I left three messages for you with Lucinda,' she said. 'One yesterday and two today. I also left two messages for Jules Ritterman. I'd very much like to know why you haven't told me the truth about what is wrong with me.' She glanced at Alec, who seemed to be concentrating on the game.

Even so, he said, 'What *is* wrong with you, Mummy?'

She looked up at Ross. 'Would you like to tell him?'

'I have to send a couple of urgent emails.' Ross, the storm still gathering in his face, turned and walked out.

Forty minutes later, Faith switched off Alec's light and closed his door. Then she went downstairs, into Ross's study, and closed that door behind her also. Ross, sitting at his computer, continued to stare at the screen as he tapped a command.

'Why didn't you tell me I'm dying?' she said. 'Why did you tell me a load of rubbish about antibiotics?'

He picked up a container on his desk and held it up. There was no anger in his voice now, just hurt. 'You're not taking them, Faith. These were in your handbag and I have just counted them.'

'What gives you any right to go looking in my handbag?'

'What do you think gives you the right not to take these pills?'

'I have every right in the damned world not to take them.'

'You're wrong. You're my wife and Alec's mother and you have a duty to both of us—especially to him—to remain alive.'

'Why did you lie to me?'

He stood up abruptly, hands at his side, fists clenched and she stepped back, certain she was going to be struck.

But instead his face crumpled into tears. 'I love you, Faith. I can't bear the thought of losing you, I can't bear the thought that you might be going to die. Can you understand that?' He put his arms round her, pressing his wet face against her cheek. Then he checked himself. 'How do you know? Did Jules Ritterman tell you?'

She felt him clinging to her, and in spite of all her anger and hatred towards him, she felt pity for him. He was such a damaged man: so badly damaged from childhood that he could barely talk about it. His mother had died horribly when he was only eleven, burnt to death in a fire that was never properly explained, and his bullying father suffered a heart attack when Ross was in his early twenties.

'I went and got a second opinion,' she said, gently.

Nuzzling even closer to her, he said, 'Faith, oh, my darling, Faith. We may have had our ups and downs lately, but I do love you. We're going to beat this damned thing. I've got everyone I know who can help with something like this on the case. I'm getting you the best medical help in the world.'

'How come you're home?' she asked.

'I blew an interview with the BBC because I wanted to be with you. I'm here for you. I'll do anything in the world for you, my dear.'

Anything, she thought, *except the one thing I really want*.

AT TEN PAST ELEVEN the following morning, Ross passed a cluster of parked motorcycles and entered the front door of a modern, rather uninspired-looking office building in a mews just off Wigmore Street. The small sign on the door said WIGMORE LABORATORY.

Ross greeted the receptionist cheerily. The woman, in her late twenties, plain but chirpy, sat behind two small towers of Jiffy bags.

'Good morning, Mr Ransome. Who've you come to see?'

'Dr Gilliatt.'

A phone warbled. Before answering it, the receptionist leaned across and said, 'Please go up, Mr Ransome, third floor.'

Ross took the stairs and came out on a small landing. The door in front of him was labelled PATH/3. He went through and was warmly greeted by Susan Gilliatt, the lab's senior pathologist. He followed her into the windowless, L-shaped pathology laboratory. About ten people were at work in this room, all in white coats, a young team mostly, in their twenties and thirties. Some looked up as they passed, giving brief nods. They stopped behind a young man who was in deep concentration, releasing a single drop from a pipette into one of a whole row of Petri dishes, with a gloved hand.

'Niall is working on this problem now. He's been here around the clock for the past ten days.'

'Any progress?' Ross asked Susan Gilliatt.

'We've identified the strain—each one of those contains it.' She nodded at about two dozen plated Petri dishes sitting near the lab technician. Each dish contained a blood culture infected with a particularly virulent strain of septicaemia that had been found in a postoperative patient in the Harley-Devonshire Hospital, who had subsequently died.

'Any thoughts on how it might be transmitted?' he asked.

She shook her head. 'No, but the woman who died had recently been out in India. That's the most likely source of infection.'

Ross knew that the woman, who had come in for removal of fibroids, had been admitted in otherwise seemingly good health. Two days after the operation, performed by one of the country's foremost gynaecologists, she had developed the septicaemia, and four days later she was dead. Naturally the hospital was concerned that she might have contracted the infection there, and every effort was being made to understand the strain of the bacterium.

Niall sealed the dish he had been working on, got up from his chair and walked away up the laboratory. As he did so, Dr Gilliatt's pager began beeping.

She excused herself, then hurried to a wall phone a few yards away.

Ross glanced around for any hint of a closed-circuit camera, but could see nothing. Dr Gilliatt was on the phone.

He seized one of the Petri dishes, checked that the lid was secure and jammed it into his trouser pocket.

Trying to maintain his composure he looked around carefully. No one was in view, apart from Susan Gilliatt with her back to him. He reached out, and moved a few of the dishes closer to each other.

When the technician returned, he noted nothing amiss.

IT WAS TWENTY past two. The theatre was empty. Ross had maybe ten minutes if he was lucky. In his white clogs he crossed over to the scrub recess, where he was out of sight of anyone peering in through the small glass portholes in the theatre doors.

Although he'd rehearsed this carefully, now that he was doing it he felt vulnerable and exposed. He grabbed a pair of surgical gloves from the dispenser and pulled them on. Then he removed the Petri dish from the right-hand pocket of his surgical pyjamas. Holding it level, he unscrewed the lid and laid it carefully in the basin.

Holding his breath, he pushed the gloved fingers of his right hand into the culture in the dish, then knelt and wiped the fluid in the place he had already selected, to the right of a rivet underneath the sink. Standing up, he replaced the lid of the Petri dish securely and dropped it into the incinerator bin. He washed his gloved hands twice in sterilising gel, peeled off the gloves and dropped them, too, into the incinerator.

Then he left the theatre and sauntered casually along to the small rest lounge, where he fixed himself a cup of coffee.

AT TWO MINUTES past three, Lady Geraldine Reynes-Rayleigh, hooked up to drip lines, a breathing tube down her throat, was trolleyed into the theatre and lifted onto the steel operating table. While Tommy Pearman and his assistant monitored her carefully, the team began prepping her.

Ross stood at the sink, making a big deal of washing his hands and forearms. He wanted them to remember him doing it.

'I think we'll have Beethoven's Fifth, Jane,' he said.

Jane Odin, his scrub nurse, grinned. 'I'll check to see if we have it.'

'I brought it in myself,' Ross said. He nodded at his patient. 'Damned if I'm going to let that bitch listen to anything peaceful. If she wants to drag us through the mill, she can suffer with it.'

'Not a nice lady, by all accounts,' his scrub nurse said.

Everyone in the room was concentrating on the patient. Ross secured his mask, then slipped unobserved back into the scrub recess, knelt and rubbed his left hand beneath the sink, where, half an hour earlier, he had smeared the septicaemia culture.

Moments later he walked casually over to the operating table. All that was visible of Lady Reynes-Rayleigh, beneath the folds of green wrapping, was her nose.

The specialist registrar began discussing a car he was thinking of buying with Tommy Pearman. Jane Odin found the CD and put it on. As the rousing strains of Beethoven's Fifth burst out of the speakers, Ross stood still, keeping his left hand low, palm inwards, close against his gown but careful not to touch it.

Raising his right arm, he began to conduct an imaginary orchestra, and said, 'Everyone knows, of course, that Beethoven's Fifth stands for victory. The opening corresponds to V in Morse code.'

Looking around at the sea of blank eyes above the surgical masks he said, 'Don't tell me I'm operating with Philistines today! This is very apposite music because today we shall have victory over Lady Geraldine Reynes-Rayleigh's nose! Nasal speculum, Jane.'

He inserted the blade of the speculum into the left nostril and squeezed the handle, forcing the nostril wide open. Then leaving it *in situ*, he said, 'Osteatome.'

The scrub nurse proffered the chisel. He took it in his right hand and made a play of seeming dissatisfied with it, peering at the blade for a moment, then pinched it tightly between the fingers of his left hand, careful not to cut through the rubber.

'Do you want a different one?' the scrub nurse asked.

'No, it's fine.'

Feeling his way carefully with the dirty chisel, he pushed up until he could feel that the point was against the cribriform plate, which separated the cavity of the nose from the cranium. No one in the theatre could have any idea what he was doing. Discreetly he exerted more pressure, until he could feel the bone give and the tip of the chisel penetrate the cranium itself

Then he withdrew it, and could see, to his satisfaction, there was a tiny amount of blood on the tip. Enough to show he'd hit the target.

Beneath his mask, his lips moved, as he mouthed the great music to himself, feeling the adrenaline rush surging through his veins.

Then he began the reshaping of her nose. He did a great job, he was inspired, he was on a roll. His eyes beamed at his staff.

She was going to look *sensational*!

THE NEXT MORNING, after a meeting of the Little Scaynes Footpath Action Group, Faith pulled onto a garage forecourt, stopping short of the pumps, and switched on her mobile phone. It was nearly one o'clock. They were having a dinner party on Saturday night. Ten people were coming, four of them medics, including her least favourite, Jules Ritterman. She had all the shopping to do, and at three thirty she had to collect Alec and four of his friends.

Three sharp beeps told her she had a new message.

It was from Oliver. 'Faith, hi, wondering how you are. I should have the test results all back by tomorrow afternoon latest. I could see you Monday. Call me at the office.'

She played the message a second time, just to hear his voice again. *I'm behaving like a besotted teenager.*

Her desire for the American was intense, constant, dominating her every thought. Was she deluding herself about him? Was Ross right? Was he just a con man?

Never. She was certain that somehow Oliver Cabot was going to make her better, not the pills.

She should take two now. Oliver hadn't told her not to take them, but neither had he encouraged her to take them. She removed the Moliou-Orelan container from her handbag and tipped out two pills. Then, holding them in the palm of her hand, she climbed out of the car and dropped them into the litter bin.

That felt good.

THREE HOURS and eighteen minutes after her operation had begun, Lady Reynes-Rayleigh was heaved onto a trolley. Her cheeks, nose, jaw and forehead had been changed in accordance with her instructions, and were now covered with rows of neat stitches. Ross was highly admired for the quality of his sewing.

Less than five minutes after being taken into the recovery room, she began to regain consciousness. Another five minutes, and the breathing tube was removed from her throat. Tommy Pearman remained with her a short while, checking until he was confident that she was out of danger, then joined Ross in the changing room.

As Ross removed his coveralls, Pearman said, 'I must give you some stuff I printed out for you from the Net on Lendt's.'

'Have you found any more on the Moliou trials?'

'No, nothing.' Pearman slapped his belly, as if the mere act might reduce its girth. 'I really must do something about this.'

'You should take up running marathons.'

'My legs are too short.'

'Maybe they should have special marathons for fat midgets.' Ross put one foot on the bench and tied the laces of his black oxfords. 'Tell me something, you use ketamine a lot, don't you?'

'I've used it in certain circumstances for years—it's effective for burns patients, particularly when you have a lot of painful changes of dressings. Why?'

'It's related to LSD, isn't it?'

'Closely.'

'Do you use it in combination with other drugs?'

'No. It's a single-agent anaesthetic. I normally give it intravenously where it has a short half-life of about ten minutes.'

'How does a patient feel under it?'

Puzzled by his interest, Pearman said, 'They'll often hallucinate and feel delirious. One of the bad things is that although it has a short half-life its effect can go on repeating for up to forty-eight hours or even longer. Paramedics use it sometimes for people trapped in accidents—it numbs pain and constricts arteries, reducing blood loss. But it also causes horrific hallucinations and some patients get out-of-body experiences.'

'Can it be taken orally?'

'Well, yes, but I wouldn't administer it orally. It has a much longer half-life that way. At least an hour and a half, sometimes more.'

'Does it have any taste?'

Pearman gave him a strange look. 'I don't think so, no.'

'Any acidity?'

'It's neutral. You can look it up in the pharmaceutical books, or I can scan the details in and email them to you if you like?'

'I'd appreciate that,' Ross said. 'Thanks.'

Ross hung around in the changing room, checking his messages on his mobile phone while Pearman left. Then from a window in an empty office, he looked down at the street until he saw the anaesthetist's car emerge from the underground car park.

Immediately Ross walked along to the anaesthetics room which was unlocked, and went in. He found what he was looking for in the third cabinet he tried: a whole shelf stacked with vials of ketamine.

He slipped one into his jacket pocket.

Seven

Spider sat in his regular booth at the back of Trader Vic's in Park Lane, drinking his Hawaiian Sundowner and smoking Marlboro Lights. He liked this place, with its plush leather banquettes, its exotic flavour and smart clientele. It had sophistication. And it was always dark in here, whether day or night. He liked that the most. It was a discreet place to conduct his business.

Although he thought of this booth as his own, he was careful not to come here too often. He didn't want people starting to recognise him in places he went to. Doing that was like leaving tracks.

Spider had learned early in life that if he wanted respect, he had to work harder than most to earn it. If you had a badly repaired harelip and were only five feet four, with a weedy frame, you had to fight hard and mean. You had to develop other assets, taking on jobs that other people shied away from. There was a lot of money to be earned. And there were friends to be made. Lasting friends, who paid well. Friends like Ronnie Milward. *Uncle* Ronnie.

Ronnie was one of the few people who had been decent to Spider as a kid. He was never sure why—maybe it was because the old rogue had felt guilty for letting his dad take the fall in the armed robbery that jailed him for twenty years but Uncle Ronnie had always taken care of him and in return he took care of his uncle's business interests in England. Mostly he collected bad debts for him, and ensured that the cash from Ronnie's drug-dealings ended up in the right accounts abroad. But occasionally he handled other matters, also.

Spider was in a good mood. He opened the email from Ronnie once more and looked down at the tiny but crystal sharp picture on the handset of his telephone communicator. It showed a man with a lean, craggy face and a tangle of grey curls. He had an intellectual air, different from the sleazeball types Uncle Ronnie normally asked him to deal with.

There was some urgency, and that was good. Spider had his eye on a car. He was five grand light of the asking price, and Uncle Ronnie's fee of ten grand would solve that problem neatly.

'WHAT DID SHE THROW in the bin?'

Hugh Caven, seated on a sofa by the fireplace in Ross's London flat, said, 'Bin?'

'The rubbish bin on the garage forecourt. It says here in your

347

report that at one o'clock today she sat in her Range Rover on the garage forecourt listening to her mobile phone. Then she got out of the car and threw something in the rubbish bin.'

Caven hesitated. His loathing of this man deepened each time they met. But he did a quick calculation. He was employing three men on round-the-clock surveillance at Dr Oliver Cabot's flat, plus a further rota of three men on surveillance outside the Ransomes' country house, following Mrs Ransome wherever she went. Additionally he had rented time on a satellite, which picked up and relayed back to him all calls from Cabot's office and mobile phones. He was making more profit from this case than ever before. So he handed Ransome a sealed white envelope. 'My operative found several sheets of oily paper, and these.'

Ross tore open the envelope. Inside were two capsules he recognised instantly.

'The bitch is throwing her pills away—that bastard is persuading her to dump them. Can you believe it? My wife is dying, these pills are the only chance she has and he's talking her out of taking them.'

The detective sat in silence.

Ross looked down at the report again. 'I don't recognise that number. What number is he using?'

'It's a mobile phone.'

'It's not her phone,' Ross said. 'The bitch has got smart on me. She's using a phone I don't know about.'

'As I've said to you, Mr Ransome, I think you might find you're overreacting to this situation.'

'Overreacting? Is that how *you*'d feel if some charlatan was trying to kill your wife?'

IN BED, Faith closed her book. Her head was pounding. It was twenty past eleven.

She squeezed two paracetamols from their foil wrapping and swallowed them with a glass of water. Then she took out her contact lenses, put them in solution in their containers and replaced the lids.

She turned off her bedside light, leaned back against the pillow and closed her eyes.

'You OK?' Ross said.

'I have a bad headache.'

'How's the nausea? Are the pills helping it?'

'No, not so far.'

'You are taking them, aren't you, darling?'

'Of course I'm bloody taking them.'

She felt the bed sag slightly. Then his hand on her stomach, sliding down. She squirmed away. 'Ross, I really don't feel well.'

'You had a headache on Wednesday.'

'I'm ill, OK? I'm sorry.'

To her relief, Ross removed his hand. He leaned over and kissed her cheek. 'Good night, darling.'

Ross picked up the *British Journal of Plastic Surgery* from his bedside table, opened it and began to read. But he wasn't concentrating, he was listening to Faith's breathing.

Patience.

At ten past twelve he said, softly, 'Faith?'

She didn't respond.

He turned out the light and lay still, eyes wide open, waiting for them to adjust to the darkness. Then he slid out of bed and stood, motionless. In a whisper, he said, 'Faith?'

No response.

He walked round to her side of the bed, lifted the small case containing her contact lenses, and backed away from the bed to the bathroom. There he closed the door and locked it.

Pulling the toggle for the shaving light above his basin, he opened the hinged mirror of his cabinet, and took out a box of cologne.

Inside was the vial of ketamine he had put there earlier, with a small hypodermic syringe. He pierced the top of the vial with the needle, pushed it down into the fluid, and drew up a minuscule amount. He had no idea how much was needed. This was going to be trial and error. He would start with the smallest drop and see how that went.

He removed the lid from the contact lenses case, squirted in the ketamine, then screwed the lid back on. Working quickly now, he put the vial and the syringe back in the cologne and replaced it in the cupboard. Then he snapped off the light and, as quietly as he could, replaced the lenses on Faith's bedside table.

She slept on, undisturbed.

NICE NEIGHBOURHOOD. Plenty of flash wheels parked around here, no one about and the street lighting wasn't that good. Nice one. Cruising this quiet backwater of Notting Hill Gate in an unobtrusive rented Ford Mondeo, Spider made a mental note that this would be a good place to trawl on his next shopping spree for Uncle Ronnie, who had a lucrative business supplying luxury cars to export customers, mostly in the Middle East.

But tonight, it wasn't motors that were on Spider's mind. It was surveillance cameras. Every city had them now, perched high up in places where you didn't notice them, silently recording everyone beneath them. There might be cameras watching him now, but it was no problem. He had rented this Ford in a false name, with a false licence. That was the beauty of any system. Once you understood it, you could outwit it.

Spider lit a Marlboro, sucked the smoke in deep, blew it out. He made a right turn into Ladbroke Avenue.

Gotcha! Parked just four doors past number thirty-seven, the licence plate on the Jeep Cherokee told him all he needed to know. Dr Oliver Cabot was at home tonight.

Sweet dreams, Doctor, he thought, driving past. He lit another Marlboro and took a second cruise past Cabot's front door. Darkness. Seclusion. Fire escapes. Only four storeys high.

Chicken shit.

A NARROW STRIP of sunlight strobed on Faith's face through a tiny chink in the curtains. She woke smiling at some happy dream. Then, reality closed over her, like the cold waters of the deep.

A few days ago the future had stretched ahead of her, limitless. Now she lay wondering if she should make a list of all the things she wanted to do while she was still well enough to do them.

She shivered and a tear rolled down her cheek. I can't think like this. Can't admit it, have to be positive. Oliver is going to cure me. He's going to get rid of this thing. I feel fine today, I really do.

Outside the bedroom there was another sound. Grating voices, constant peaks and troughs of sound effects and music. A television cartoon. Which meant that Alec was awake.

It was Saturday. Downstairs there was a flurry of barking from Rasputin. Probably the papers arriving—it was too early for the postman. After a minute or so he quietened.

Now Ross was moving. She breathed in and out steadily, the way someone in deep sleep would breathe, eyes shut tight. *Please don't touch me. Don't start groping me.*

He grunted, then rolled over, and she knew, from years of sleeping beside him, that he was now looking at his watch, that in a few moments he would take a sip of water from the glass beside him.

'Faith?' Just a whisper, then louder. 'Faith? Are you awake?'

She lay still, facing away from him, tight and foetal.

Now silence. The bed moved, feet padded across the carpeted floor. She heard him in the bathroom, then the click of the door, and the soles of his slippers slapping along the landing and down the stairs. Excited barks from Rasputin in the kitchen, then louder barking as Ross opened the door for him and he rushed outside.

And she knew that, in a few minutes, Ross would be coming back upstairs, carrying a cup of tea and the newspaper.

She tried to go back to sleep but that was impossible. Instead, she started running through a list of everything to be sorted out for tonight. Twelve for dinner. Italian hors d'oeuvres starter, salmon en croûte, asparagus grilled with Parmesan, new potatoes, peas. Then she went through her checklist for the pudding ingredients. She worried that she didn't have enough cheese.

Ross was coming into the bedroom now. She heard the clink of a cup being placed on her table, inches from her face. The rustle of newspapers. She tensed waiting for the mattress to sag, the bedclothes to move. To her surprise, they didn't.

She heard running water in the bathroom. The radio came on and the shower door clicked shut.

She opened her eyes, and saw steam rising from her tea. The *Daily Mail*, with several bite marks from Rasputin and a small amount torn from the bottom of the front page, lay neatly folded beside it. The headlines, a little blurred, talked of the forthcoming wedding between Prince Edward and Sophie Rhys-Jones.

She reached across, picked up the case containing her contact lenses, took out each lens and inserted it.

Much better. Instantly the room and the newsprint were pin-sharp. She blinked a few times. The first few moments with the lenses were often uncomfortable, and today they felt worse than usual.

Big speculation in the paper about the vows Sophie was going to take. She would promise to obey her husband but said she was determined not to walk in his shadow. Faith admired her courage. She had learned that to be under a husband's shadow corroded your spirit.

Then, as she read the next line, all the words slipped off the page and she found herself looking at plain white newsprint.

It did not occur to her this was weird. She merely looked around her on the duvet, to try to find where the little black words had all gone. But she couldn't see them.

She picked up the newspaper and all the rest of the words slid off the pages like raindrops from a polished surface.

'Ross,' she said, 'there's something very strange—'

The walls of the room rippled like curtains in a breeze. She watched them, intrigued. 'Ross!' she called out. 'Ross, come and have a look at—'

Something crawled through her hair. With a shudder, she swung her legs out of the bed in panic, struck the bedside table. The cup fell to the floor in slow motion. Now, as she stepped on the carpet, the floor tilted away from her and she fell forward, plunging down into an empty lift shaft, screaming. 'Rossssss . . . Rosssssssss!'

Suddenly she was floating on the ceiling, looking down. She was looking down from the ceiling at her own body on the floor.

'Ross!' she screamed. 'Ross, help me, I'm dead, I'm dead.'

A change of sound. The shower switched off, then the click of the door, and then she watched Ross striding out of the bathroom, dripping wet, towel around his midriff. Watched him kneel beside her, cradling her head in his hands.

'Ross—please help me.'

The ceiling was pressing down on her. She was feeling shut in. Ross's lips were moving. Reading them, she could see he was calling her name, looking frantic. But she couldn't hear him.

Ross felt for her pulse. It was strong, steady, a little fast but that was fine. He looked at his watch: 7.48. Making a mental log of the time, he worked his arms underneath her, lifted her up and laid her on the bed. He moved the pillows away to ensure that her head was tilted well back, keeping her airways open, and checked inside her mouth for anything that might choke her.

Her eyes were open but unfocused, pupils dilated. He cursed. *Given her too damned much.*

Twenty minutes passed. He sat, holding her wrist, monitoring her pulse all the time, not daring to leave her.

'Cheese,' she said, her eyes springing open. 'We need cheese.'

'Are you hungry?'

In a deadpan voice she said, 'You're so funny, Ross. You're so funny, you make me laugh and you make me just keep on laughing.'

Then she turned her head and stared hard at him. Stared with eyes that were focused yet sightless. He looked away and as he did so she said, 'You're going to kill me, aren't you, Ross? Oscar Wilde said every man kills the thing he loves.'

'Why do you say that?'

'You'd prefer to kill me than lose me.'

'I'm not going to kill or lose you. I'm going to make you better, darling. We're going to beat this thing inside you.'

There was a long silence. Ross looked at his watch again. Another fifteen minutes elapsed. Then Faith said, 'You have to tell me what cheese to get for tonight's dinner.'

She kept having lucid flashes, he noticed, and this was good.

An hour and a half later there were signs that the drug was wearing off. But it was noon before Faith was stable enough to go down to the kitchen to start preparing dinner. She turned to him and said, shakily, 'Can you explain what happened to me this morning, Ross?'

'It's the disease advancing because you're not taking the pills,' he said. 'You must start taking them again.'

He made her take two capsules then left her in the kitchen and went upstairs. He opened the bathroom cabinet and took out the cologne box.

He would have a drink with Faith before the guests arrived, as they always did, to put themselves in a party mood. By his reckoning, just a quarter of the dose he gave her this morning should suffice.

IT WAS HALF PAST THREE, and Ross had gone to the golf course to play a quick nine holes, then he was collecting Alec from a birthday party. He wouldn't be back for at least another hour.

Faith snatched a break from her preparations in the kitchen, took her mobile phone from its hiding place in the bottom of her handbag, pulled on her Barbour and walked out through the French windows. She crossed the wide, flagstoned terrace then strolled down to the lake. It was meant to be summer but no one had told the weather that. Too cold to have drinks on the terrace tonight as Ross had planned.

She sat on a wooden bench and dialled the number. Moments later, Oliver answered. 'Faith! Hey! Where are you?'

'At home. Ross has gone out for a while so I thought I'd ring. I—I wanted to hear your voice.'

'It's good to hear yours. You sound down.'

'I had a bad experience this morning . . .'

Oliver listened in silence. When she had finished he said, 'We need to start your treatment as soon as possible. Would later on this afternoon work for you?'

'I—I can't. We're having a dinner party.'

'It's more important to get you right, Faith.'

'I'll be OK. I'll get through it somehow.'

'What about tomorrow?'

'No, I can't do tomorrow. But Monday's clear. Your message said Monday was good for you.'

'Monday's fine. Come to the apartment as early as you like.'

She did a quick calculation. One of the other mothers was doing the school run next week. She had to get Alec ready, that was all. 'I could be there by ten.'

'Call me tomorrow if you get a chance.'

'I'll try—it's going to be difficult. Ross wants us to go out for the day with Alec. He's suddenly got into the three of us doing family things together. Probably so that he won't feel guilty after I'm dead.'

'Faith, you're not going to die. Have you registered that?'

'OK,' she said, fighting back the tears.

AT FIVE TO EIGHT, Ross put a Brandenburg Concerto on the CD player. He always played Bach when guests were arriving: Baroque music stimulated the brain, put people in an upbeat mood.

He was dressed in his crimson brocaded smoking jacket, open-neck shirt, cravat, black trousers and Gucci loafers. Faith was wearing the simple short black dress from Nicole Farhi that he had put out for her. Plus her pearls and her black satin high heels.

'Here,' Ross said, holding out a glass, 'drink this. It'll perk you up.'

She took the ice-cold champagne flute, sat down on a side chair, so as not to dent the cushions of the freshly plumped sofas, and sipped. Ross came over and clinked glasses with her. 'Cheers, darling. You look beautiful.'

'You look very nice, too,' she replied.

'Christ, woman, lighten up. Hope you're not going to greet our guests looking this miserable.'

'I'm sorry, Ross, I don't feel well.'

'We've got some serious players coming. You're going to have to feel well.' He paced the room. 'Get that down your throat and you'll feel better.'

She took another tiny sip. The nausea was back, and she wished she could phone Oliver, just to hear his voice.

Ross peered out of the bow window. 'Bloody rabbits.'

She watched two grazing on the lawn. The sky had clouded over and a fierce wind was blowing. A Jaguar was coming in through the gates, two minutes early. Faith glared. Don't they know it's polite to arrive ten minutes late?

She drained half her glass, put it down on a side table and went to open the front door.

'Faith, how very nice to see you.'

Jules Ritterman was standing in the porch in a dark suit. His Nordic wife, Hilde, a foot taller, was standing grim-faced, holding the smallest box of chocolates Faith had ever seen.

It took Faith a moment to sort out their names. 'Hello—hi—good journey? Ross is here—he's expecting you—I mean—we—'

Oh, Christ, another car was coming down the drive now. She wasn't sure what she was supposed to do next. Invite them in. Yes. She took a step back, but now Ross was standing beside her. He shook Jules Ritterman's hand, kissed the Nordic iceberg.

'Can I take your coat?' Faith asked.

'Actually I don't wear one tonight,' Hilde said.

'No,' Faith said. 'Of course. Jules, can I take yours?'

'I'm not wearing one either, Faith.'

I'm not cracking up. Please, God, don't let me crack up.

Tyres crunched on the gravel. A modest-looking car. A modest-looking man and a modest-looking woman got out. They had matching grey hair, and almost matching haircuts. On the man it looked all right, on the woman it looked silly.

'This is His Honour Ralph Blakeham,' Ross said.

'And my wife, Molly,' the judge added.

Molly handed Faith a jar of homemade quince jelly. It slipped through her fingers and shattered on the porch tiles.

While Mrs Fogg cleared up the mess, the rest of the guests crowded in. In the kitchen, Faith sat on a chair, picking slivers of quince-coated glass off her shoes. She was up on the ceiling looking down; she could see herself, holding one shoe in her hand.

From the ceiling, she saw Ross storm in through the door. 'What the hell are you doing in here? Nobody's got any drinks.'

Faith stared down at him. Then, suddenly, she was staring up at him. He was seizing her arms, lifting her to her feet. He jammed her shoe back on, then gripped her hand and towed her along. She followed in small, tripping steps, trying to stay upright. The walls of the hall came in towards her, then stretched away into the distance.

'David deWitt,' Ross said. 'And his wife, Amanda. This is Faith.'

Looking down at them from the drawing-room ceiling, with Bach chiming around her, she heard the psychiatrist and his wife say they were delighted to meet her, and she knew she needed to reply.

She blurted the only words she could. 'Please help me, I'm dying.'

Now Ross was beside her, arm around her. 'Darling, it's all right. You're having another of your attacks. I'll take you upstairs—you can lie down for a while. I'll give you something to help you relax.'

'It's one of the symptoms,' she heard Jules Ritterman say.

'I'll fetch it from the car,' said another voice.

Her body was some way in front of her. She turned her head in panic. 'My body,' she said. 'Where's my body?'

A prick in her arm, like an insect sting.

In moments she was back in her body. She was lying on her bed. Anxious faces looking down at her. She smiled up at them in relief.

Then her eyes closed. She tumbled through the bed into a warm, blue ocean of sleep.

DRESSED in a lightweight track suit with a nylon rucksack strapped to his back, and thin cycling gloves, Spider pedalled along the quiet darkness of Ladbroke Avenue, a geeky guy in a smog mask and crash helmet who looked like he was returning home from a geeky Saturday night out.

The street was deserted. He was relieved that the navy blue Jeep Cherokee was still parked in the same place as it had been this afternoon. He looked up at Dr Cabot's windows. Dark. Good.

At the end of the street he made a left turn, then swung the bike into an opening between two buildings, past a row of lockup garages and into an empty, falling-down bike shed where he was invisible to anyone above.

He dismounted and heaved the rucksack off his shoulders. The Heckler and Koch P9 was a heavy brute, and the silencer made it heavier still. He also carried a photocopy of the floor layout of Dr Oliver Cabot's flat, obtained from the Planning Office, a photograph of Cabot downloaded from the Internet, a torch, a set of lock picks, a bolt-cutter, a glass-cutter and a strong suction cup for taking out window segments, an SP 300C Big Kahuna stun gun with a belt clip and a leather combat belt.

He began his preparations. First he strapped on the belt, then he secured the Big Kahuna and the clip to it. Double-checking that the safety catch was on, he jammed the loaded Heckler and Koch into his right-hand trouser pocket, which he had deepened and strengthened, and the silencer into his left-hand pocket. Next, he clipped onto the belt the torch and the bunch of lock picks. Finally, he closed the rucksack, slipped it back over his shoulders and checked his watch. Five past midnight. All set.

He pedalled back into Ladbroke Avenue. Not a soul in sight and only a few lights on here and there. He dismounted again, wheeled the bike up to the front door of number 37, and chained it carefully to the railings. As he climbed up to the front door, he freed the lock picks from his belt.

It wasn't much of a lock on the front door, a crappy household five-pin job, a decade old; one hard shove and it would probably have yielded, but he didn't want to draw attention to himself. He quickly sorted through the tungsten picks. He selected one, inserted the tip into the keyway, feeling for the first pin.

Found you, you little bastard.

Gently applying pressure, he levered the pin clear of the sheer line. Then he located the second pin, and lifted that one easily. Anyone watching him would think he was just a tenant having a problem with his key. The third, the fourth and fifth pins rose easily. Now he pushed the pick in the full length and gave it a twist.

The lock clicked. The door swung forward with a rustle of paper as it dragged a bunch of flyers from a pizza-delivery house along beneath it. A strip of light shone beneath a door to his left and he heard the faint sound of voices and music—someone watching a movie on television. The smell of curry filtered through his mask. He closed the door behind him. Switching on the torch, he crossed the floor and climbed the staircase.

The door to Dr Cabot's flat was secured by a sturdy mortise dead-lock. A pig to pick. It took him four minutes of deep concentration before he could push the door ajar, gently, an inch at a time, hoping there wasn't a safety chain as well.

Six inches. One foot. No chain. No pinpricks of red light, which would indicate an alarm system. Just big shadows moving on the wall. An illuminated fish tank.

He took a step forward and closed the door. There was enough light from the fish tank for him to see the room and work out the geography of the flat from the plans he had memorised.

He screwed the silencer to the Heckler and Koch and jammed the pistol down the front of his jacket. Then he unclipped the stun gun, put his finger on the trigger and went to the door that showed on the plans as a corridor to the bedrooms.

It was. The first door, on the right, which by his reckoning should be the master bedroom, was ajar. The curtains were open and there was enough light from outside to show that the bed was empty.

Suddenly, the light in the corridor brightened. Lights had been switched on in the living area. He heard footsteps across the oak floorboards, coming his way. He stood behind the bedroom door. Footsteps coming towards him. Someone whistling.

Spider gripped the stun gun, and with his right hand pulled out the Heckler and Koch and clicked off the safety catch. Holding his fingers on the triggers of both weapons, he peered down the corridor into the living area. He had a clear but narrow field of view.

A man ambled across it. He was a good six feet tall, with a mane of curly grey hair. Exactly as in the photograph.

Spider seized his opportunity. He came out quickly from the corridor, threw a quick glance around the room to make sure no one else had come in, walked up behind his victim and called, 'Dr Cabot?'

The man turned, startled, but before he had time to register anything, Spider jabbed the Big Kahuna against his arm and squeezed the trigger, dumping three hundred volts into the muscle.

Dr Cabot instantly went slack, as if all his bones had been removed from inside his skin. He took a step back, his eyes rolling, then went down backwards onto the floor with a grunt.

Spider knelt beside him and studied his face, comparing it against the photograph he had memorised. No question, this was his man.

The effect of a stun gun was short-lived. It wiped the stored blood sugar from all the body's muscles and short-circuited the neuromuscular system. Within a minute, if he gave him the chance, Dr Cabot would start to feel OK.

Spider dragged him across the floor, raised his shoulders and propped his head against a leather sofa—he didn't want to risk the bullet going through the floor into the flat below.

Lucidity was returning to his victim. Spider pressed the muzzle of the Heckler and Koch against the man's forehead, two inches above his nose, and gave the trigger a firm squeeze.

The silencer was good: the gun made just a dull phut, kicking sharply in his hands.

Breathing the acrid tang of cordite and the sweeter smell of singed flesh, Spider checked to see if he could find the bullet, but there was too much mess. It wasn't essential.

He left the flat, closing the door quietly behind him. Adrenaline was pumping and he was on a high. On silent footfalls he made his way back down the stairs. He had never felt so good about life.

As he started to make his way across the hall, he heard a loud crash. Then another. Blam . . . blam . . . blam . . .

In front of him, on the front door, wood splintered.

The door of the ground-floor flat opened and a man came out, naked, with a towel around his waist. 'What the hell?' he shouted.

At that moment the lock and the door jamb gave way, and the front door crashed open. A bald, tattooed hulk in a T-shirt and jeans barged into the hall.

The light came on.

'You!'

The bald hulk was pointing at Spider. 'You fucking murderer!'

Spider took a step back and tried to get the Heckler and Koch out of the front of his jacket, but it snagged on the fabric. The hulk was coming at him. A hand ripped away his mask, he smelt warm breath that reeked of fried onions, then something slammed into his stomach. He crashed against a wall and fell down hard.

Scrabbling back like a cornered rat, hand inside his jacket, tearing at the Heckler and Koch, he kicked out with his feet and heard a howl of pain from the hulk.

Spider had the gun out now, pointed at the hulk, and he jerked the trigger back. A neat round hole appeared on the hulk's cheek.

For an instant time stopped, as if he had pressed the PAUSE button on a video. He saw the hulk looking at him with an almost chiding expression, as if he were scolding a naughty child. He saw the man with the towel around him, hand over his mouth, staring in shock, halfway back into his doorway.

Then blood began to spurt, and the hulk rolled over to one side like a sack that had been released down a chute.

Spider scrambled to his feet. The naked man screamed, 'Please don't shoot me!' and retreated into his flat, slamming the door.

Spider realised his mask had gone.

The man had seen his face.

Spider stared out at the street. *Jesus, what a balls-up.* He heard the scraping of furniture. Threw himself against the door of the flat, then kicked the lock hard. From inside he heard a voice crying out, 'Please don't, I won't tell, I didn't see you!'

Then, outside, a siren. *Go.*

He took one more look at the door to the man's flat then, reluctantly, he went. Raced down the steps to his bike. The key to the padlock was at the bottom of his damned rucksack.

Siren getting closer.

He got the key out.

Siren even closer now.

He dropped the key. Tried to pick it up but the gloves made it too hard. Now he could see a glint of blue light skidding across the parked cars at the end of the street. *Abandon the bike.*

He ran, oblivious now of the route he had planned, the Big Kahuna swinging from his waist, the torch under his arm, the Heckler and Koch in his hand. His only thought right now was, *This is a balls-up. Oh, Jesus, what a balls-up.*

*e*ight

The ring of the phone came into her dream, teasing her from her snug warm shell of sleep. She opened her eyes. The phone rang again and now the bed was moving, Ross rolling, reaching for the receiver. Then his voice. 'Uh? Whozat? What d'you say? Oh, right, sorry, you woke me, bit of a late night . . . Yes.'

She lay still, grateful that the ringing had stopped. Her head was pulsing and she was feeling too nauseous to move. Something had been ripped away from inside her, some big piece of memory. Last night they'd been having a dinner party and now she was here in bed and it was morning. Sunday morning?

The clock on her bedside table said eight ten. Ross was sitting on the edge of the bed now, phone next to his stubbled cheek, hair sticking up like a scruffy kid. He sounded worried. 'Do you want me to come up? I can be there in an hour and a half if you need me.'

She felt giddy, closed her eyes, which made it even worse.

'Cross-contamination,' Ross said. 'That's what it sounds like. Is anyone else affected? . . . You'd better check on everyone. Could be in the air-conditioning, the water, the food, anything.'

Faith heard the click of the receiver going back on the cradle.

Ross said, 'It would have to be one of my patients, wouldn't it.'

Then the click of the television coming on and the sound of Ross padding through to the bathroom. The door shutting. Then a newscaster's voice. 'It seems from eyewitness reports that Dr Cabot's assailant may have shot the second man, Barry Gatt, because he tried to apprehend him.'

For an instant Faith thought she had imagined or misheard the name. The newscaster continued. 'The doctor, who was identified by his secretary this morning, came to England from America eight years ago following the death of his son from leukaemia. Dr Cabot founded the Cabot Centre for Complementary Medicine in North London in 1990.'

She sat bolt upright in bed. There, on the television screen, was the terraced Notting Hill Gate building where Oliver lived. The front steps were tented and police tapes cordoned off the pavement.

No. A sluice opened somewhere in her belly. Her blood was draining and ice-cold water was rising inside her. *Please no. Not Oliver.*

The newscaster was back on the screen. 'The assailant was dressed in cycling clothes, with a crash helmet and rucksack. The police are interested in talking to anyone who might have seen someone of this description in the vicinity of Ladbroke Avenue last night.'

A policeman appeared on the screen, but she found it hard to concentrate on his words. It was a particularly savage crime, he was saying, and it was too early to suggest a motive.

On the screen the scene changed. The newscaster said, 'Prime Minister Tony Blair arrives in Stormont this morning . . .'

Had she missed something? Whimpering, her nausea forgotten, Faith scrambled out of bed, grabbed the remote control and punched up Teletext, then selected the news headlines.

TWO DEAD IN NOTTING HILL SHOOTING. Page 105.

Ross came out of the bathroom naked. 'I may have to go to London,' he said. 'A patient has developed septicaemia . . .' He hesitated. 'What are you looking at?'

On screen, the story came up.

'Jesus,' said Ross.

Faith fell into his arms. 'No,' she said. 'It can't be him. Who would kill him, Ross? Why? He can't be dead.'

Ross sat her down on the bed and cradled her head in his arms. She was sobbing hysterically. 'Listen, my darling, I have to go to London. The clinic administrator's called a crisis meeting.'

'Don't go, please don't leave me.'

'I have to, angel.'

She flung her arms around his neck, holding on to him in terror. 'Please stay.'

'I'll get you something to calm you down.'

He released her, came back holding a glass of water. He put one pill in her mouth and she sipped and swallowed, then another.

'Please stay with me, Ross.'

'I'll ask Mrs Appleby to come over and look after Alec.' Mrs Appleby was a widow who lived in a cottage down the lane, and was always happy to baby-sit.

She felt him lifting her, then she was lying on her back. Downstairs she heard Rasputin barking.

After a while there was silence.

'MUMMY?'

Faith opened her eyes from deep sleep with a start, to see Alec standing over her. He was clutching a plastic Sumo wrestler with one of its hands missing. 'When are we going to Legoland, Mummy? You said we were going today. You promised.'

The curtains were open, and rain was lashing the window.

She glanced at the clock: 12.25. She'd slept the whole morning.

'You did promise, Mummy.'

Now it was all returning to her. *Oh God.*

Oliver. *Dead.*

She stared up at Alec, helpless, drifting. She needed time alone for a few minutes, time to think.

Alec was close to tears now. 'You *promised*, Mummy.'

She stared at him bleakly. 'Have you had breakfast yet, darling?'

'*Hours* ago. Daddy made it for me. He burnt the toast and my egg was all hard. And Rasputin's been sick in the hall.'

'Great.'

'Mrs Appleby cleared it up.'

'Did Daddy say when he would be back?'

'He said you're not very well. Are you going to get better?'

She took his free hand, squeezed his wrist. 'Of course I am. I'm going to get better because I love you.'

He sat down, pensively, on the bed. 'Are you going to get better in time to go to Legoland today?'

Despite herself, she smiled, and realised just how desperately she loved her son. She had to keep going for him. Whatever else, she wanted to make sure he had a normal upbringing. Maybe her mother could bring him up after she was gone.

'What time exactly do you think you will be better?' Alec enquired.

She smiled again. She loved the way he expressed himself.

'In *exactly* fifteen minutes.'

'I'm hungry, and Mrs Appleby says she has to go home now.'

'I'll make you something. A surprise. OK?'

'OK.' His face much brighter now, he jumped down from the bed and scampered out of the room.

Somehow she showered, dressed, paid Mrs Appleby and got Alec, clutching his Game Boy, belted into the back seat of the Range Rover. She started the engine, put on the wipers, opened the map on her lap and worked out a route to Legoland.

'You didn't make me any lunch, and I'm really, really, *really* hungry. You promised a surprise.'

She pulled out at the end of the lane into the main road. Swallowing a lump in her throat she said, 'I'm afraid the surprise is that you're going to have to wait for your lunch. I've had a bad surprise this morning so we're both having a lousy Sunday.'

After they had been driving for almost an hour, she saw the signs for a Happy Eater, pulled into the car park and they went inside. The place was packed and the smell of chips turned her stomach. A waitress came over with their menus. Alec chose a double burger with French fries, which Faith knew would be too much for him, but she ordered it anyway, and a coffee for herself.

Her mind was filled with the image of Oliver's face.

She got up, asked the waitress to keep an eye on Alec, made her way to the washroom, locked herself into a cubicle, sat down and wept into her hands.

It was several minutes before she felt composed enough to make her way back to the table. Alec's meal had arrived, so while he ate she went outside to make a phone call. She pulled her phone out of her handbag and switched it on. Before she had a chance to dial, the message indicator beeped. She jammed the phone to her ear and listened.

'Faith, hi, this is Oliver. Call me as soon as you can on my mobile.'

The message must be from yesterday. Fighting her emotions, she played it again. Just as it finished, the phone rang. Startled, she pressed the answer button. 'Hello?'

'Faith?'

It was Oliver. 'Faith, can you talk?'

Trembling, she said, 'Oliver?'

'Harvey's been murdered. My brother. Jesus, Faith, it's just so terrible, I—I can't believe what's happened.'

'You're alive?' It was all she could say.

'Harvey,' he said. He was crying. 'Oh, God, Faith, some bastard's killed my brother. I needed to speak to you. The police say it could have been mistaken identity. I just needed to hear your voice, Faith. I have to go—oh, Jesus. Can I call you later?'

'Yes.'

He said something she couldn't hear and hung up.

She stayed where she was, leaning against the misted-up glass, watching her son. The brother of the man she loved was dead. A nice man. She knew she should not be feeling elated.

But she couldn't help it.

SPIDER, in a crumpled white T-shirt and underpants, on his hard bed in his cramped flat, had not slept. Grey light filtered through the grimy, curtainless windows. Outside, a goods train was clanking past, making a noise louder than scaffolding collapsing. The television at the end of the bed was still on, as it had been all night.

It was Monday morning. He felt like shit. He'd seen the Identikit of himself on television half a dozen times already this morning. On ITV, on BBC 1, on Sky. An incredibly accurate likeness. It must have come from that screaming bloke who'd locked himself in his flat, and Spider was bitterly regretting letting him off the hook.

Now his phone was ringing. He picked up the receiver.

A man's voice said, 'You asshole.'

'This isn't smart, calling me at home, Uncle.'

'You don't have to worry about that. If you had more than half a brain inside you, you wouldn't be at home, not when there's a fifty-thousand-pound reward out for you. You'd be hiding in a cave on another sodding planet.'

On the edge of his bed now, Spider said, 'Reward? I ain't seen nothing about a reward.'

'You don't have my sources. The brother of one of your two balls-ups, Dr Oliver Cabot, agreed it with the police yesterday. They've already been circulating it in places where gun dealers hang out.'

Spider trembled. Fifty thousand pounds was big money. Big enough to tempt the weasel who'd sold him his piece?

'You didn't tell me he had a brother,' Spider said.

'I didn't tell you he had a mother either, or a father. Take my advice, lad, and get the hell out of there—vanish.'

The phone went dead.

IN THE MIDDLE of a consultation, Ross's intercom buzzed. He picked up the phone. 'Yes?'

'Mr Caven's in reception.'

'Tell him to make an appointment like everyone else.'

'He says it's urgent.'

'I'll see him for two minutes after I've finished with Mrs Levine.'

When his patient left, the private detective came in. He was looking pale, as if he hadn't slept. Ross closed the door and did not offer him a seat. 'This had better be good,' he said.

Caven handed him a brown envelope, looking at him with grave, accusatory eyes. There was a box-shaped object inside, which rattled. 'When you hired me, Mr Ransome, you told me you were wanting photographs. I think you should take a look at that.'

Ross removed the box from the envelope. There was a videotape inside it. He opened the cabinet containing the television and video recorder, and put in the tape. Still standing, both men watched the black and white footage in silence. The picture quality wasn't great, but it was good enough. It showed a wide-angle view of a large flat. The place was in darkness. Then suddenly light flared as the lens adjusted, and Ross could see more clearly. A man who looked like Dr Oliver Cabot was coming in at the front door.

As he walked across the wooden floor a figure appeared out of a doorway behind him, wearing a smog mask and biking helmet, a rucksack on his back, a pistol with a silencer in one hand and a black object in the other.

As if hearing his name called, the man who looked like Oliver Cabot turned. The other figure rammed the black object against Cabot's arm. Cabot staggered a few paces then fell over.

Ross and Caven watched in silence while the figure dragged the unconscious man across the floor, propped him up against a sofa, and shot him. The figure hurried to the front door and went out.

Ross turned to Caven, white-faced.

Caven said, 'You can turn it off. It's just a small section I've copied for your benefit.'

Shakily Ross walked over to his desk and buzzed his secretary. 'I'm going to be a few minutes, Lucinda. Hold the fort.'

It took Ross all his self-control not to blurt out, *I warned Ronnie Milward the place was under closed-circuit surveillance. I warned him!'*

Instead he looked everywhere in the room but at the detective, not wanting to catch his eye.

Hugh Caven sat down on the sofa. He cleared his throat. 'So. You suspect that Dr Cabot is committing adultery with your wife and you hire a private detective to establish this. Dr Cabot's brother, who could be his twin, is murdered in cold blood by what appears to be a professional assassin. Harvey Cabot is a good man, an eminent scientist, happily married, no obvious enemies. But Oliver Cabot has one very obvious enemy.'

Ross gave a smile that was devoid of any humour. 'Mr Caven, if I'm hearing what I think I'm hearing, that you're about to try to blackmail me, I just hope for your sake you've got a good solicitor. You've already committed two serious offences by installing those cameras—criminal damage and breaking and entering—and I'm sure you've contravened other laws with your bugging of Dr Cabot. I wouldn't advise you to compound them with an absurd attempt at blackmail. Get yourself out of my office and out of my life.'

Very quietly, Caven said, 'Mr Ransome, a second man was killed on Saturday night. He was one of my men, one of the best guys I ever worked with. He saw what was happening and tried to do something about it. You may be angry, but don't underestimate how angry I am. Barry Gatt was best man at my wedding.'

'Out,' Ross said, walking to the door. 'Send me your bill. I don't ever want to hear from you again or see you again.'

He tore open the door and shoved the detective through it, shouting, *'Get out of my life!'*

Then he slammed the door so hard plaster fell from the wall.

FAITH PAID THE TAXI and climbed out, pressing a pound coin into the hand of the doorman. Then she entered the lobby of the Marble Arch Hotel, and travelled up in a packed lift to the ninth floor, where she stepped out, checked the room numbers and found number 927. She knocked softly, and waited.

Oliver opened the door. He was barefoot, in a crumpled navy sweatshirt and jeans. His whole body seemed hunched and his unshaven face was gaunt, black rims around his eyes.

Faith was shocked. She threw her arms around him, wanting to comfort him. 'You poor darling,' she said. 'Oh, you poor darling.'

For a long while they stood there in silence, her face pressed against his chest, his hands massaging her back. 'Faith,' he murmured, 'How could anyone do this? Harvey was a wonderful guy. Everyone loved him. Who would want to kill him?'

Still holding each other, they moved into the room and Faith pushed the door shut behind her with her foot. She looked up into his sad grey eyes, and felt a sudden quickening sensation, as if an electrical current had been switched on inside her. They stood together and she could feel the same current inside him, could feel the dull thud of her heartbeat, then his.

Excitement ran deep inside her, their eyes locked and they were moving across the floor, lips caressing. His felt so soft, gentle, moist. She was pressing her body hard against him. Her hands were inside his sweatshirt on the firm flesh of his back, as he tugged at her blouse, pulling it free of her belt. She gasped, as his hands went round her stomach, his fingers pressing inside her waistband.

Then they were on the floor, clothes part on, part off and she was whispering his name, and he was cupping her face in his hands, kissing her forehead, her cheeks, her eyes.

She called his name as she felt herself being locked with him, gripped by him, filled totally and utterly by him. She closed her eyes, unable to believe this was real, that they were here, the two of them alone. Scarcely able to contain the bursts of pleasure exploding inside her, she prayed that this moment would never end.

ROSS, IN THE SPONGY vinyl armchair, was sitting too low for comfort. He felt as if he was peering up at the psychiatrist from the bottom of a cliff.

From his attire, Dr David DeWitt looked more like an architect, or an arts critic, perhaps, than a doctor. A gangling man in his early forties, he was wearing a crumpled brown corduroy suit, a dark shirt and a tie inspired by Jackson Pollock. With his inane perma-grin, he was listening to Ross with the expectancy of a man awaiting the punch line of a joke. But the shrink was high profile, constantly in the media and well connected. It was partly for these reasons Ross had cultivated him. The other reason was DeWitt's speciality in body dysmorphic disorder. His patients were normal-looking people who either imagined they were ugly or wanted some impossible ideal. He sometimes referred them to Ross, who would reassure them that nothing that he could do would help.

'Great seeing you on Saturday,' DeWitt said. 'A very good dinner.' He paused, then said, 'I'm sorry about Faith.'

'Yes.'

'Lendt's disease, you said?'

Ross nodded.

'But there is a glimmer of hope? This new drug?'

'The only hope. But it's not working.' Choking back well-rehearsed emotion, Ross dug out his handkerchief and dabbed his eyes.

'I'm sorry. She's such a lovely person. If there's anything I can do.'

'Thank you.' Ross pretended to pull himself together. 'Actually, there is, David, it's why I'm here.' Choosing his words carefully, he said, 'You've kicked up quite a controversy with your views on reforming the Mental Health Act. I heard you on the *Today* programme on Monday. Saw your piece in *The Times* yesterday.'

'Well, I believe the power to decide who is mentally ill and who should be detained in a secure institution should be in the hands of the medical profession and not determined by politicians.'

'So you believe that the medical profession should take a more proactive approach to the psychiatrically ill?'

'What exactly is your interest in all this, Ross?'

'I'm just coming to that.' Ross allowed his composure to deteriorate once again. 'David, you see, Faith—' He let his voice quaver. 'This disease is now affecting her mind. You've seen her yourself, for God's sake. And the Moliou-Orelan drug isn't working because she won't take the pills.'

'Why on earth not?'

'She thinks I'm trying to poison her. Instead she's going to some crazy alternative doctor who's into everything. Homeopathy, acupuncture, hypnotherapy, chicken entrails, you name it.'

DeWitt asked, 'How do you feel I can help you, Ross?'

'I need your cooperation. This is a big favour, David. You probably won't like it, but it's the only chance we have of saving her life. Sometimes you have to be cruel to be kind.'

ON THE BED, with Oliver's arm wrapped around her, the fingers of his other hand stroking her back, Faith lay serenely still, breathing in his scent, wondering what he was thinking.

Muted sounds of the London morning filtered through the double-glazed windows. She didn't know what the time was and she didn't care: Alec was being picked up from school by a friend's mother and would stay with her until Faith collected him.

It should feel strange, she thought, to be lying in bed with another man, but it seemed the most natural, beautiful thing in the world.

'I'm your doctor,' Oliver said quietly. 'I'm meant to be curing you, not sleeping with you.'

'I think you've just cured me,' she murmured. 'I'm better. I've never felt so good before.'

A thought flashed through her mind: *We didn't take any precautions.* But instead of being concerned she was glad.

'I love you,' she said.

His hand squeezed hers in silent acknowledgment.

She squeezed back, and said, 'Is it hard for you to go home?'

'Home?'

'Your flat? Ladbroke Avenue?'

'Crime scene. The whole building's sealed off. They let me in with a police officer to get a few things, said it would be about a week before I can go back. I don't even know if I'll want to go back, ever.'

'Do you—they—have any idea who killed Harvey?'

'If they do, they're not saying anything to me.'

'Who was the other man?'

'A private detective. Had a couple of convictions for assault some years back. He'd been a night-club bouncer, or something.' He released her hand and sat up a little. 'The police say it had the hallmarks of a professional killing. They asked if I had any enemies.'

His eyes searched hers and a shadow slid across her soul. It had occurred to her moments after she had heard the news.

'Ross is a bully,' she said, 'but I don't think he—'

'I didn't mean—' Oliver said, but she interrupted him.

'It was my first thought, too. But I know him. He lost a patient a couple of months ago and came home crying about it. He's a baby at heart, a baby who never had enough love.'

'Most psychopaths are people who never had enough love as children.'

'Not Ross,' she said. 'He's a lot of things but I don't think—'

They fell into a silence. Ross had always been fanatically jealous, and with Oliver he had been over the top. But she really didn't think he could kill anyone.

Ross STOOD in the phone booth in Marylebone High Street, surrounded by hookers' business cards. The phone was ringing, and after some moments a male voice answered in Spanish.

'I want to speak to Señor Milward,' Ross said. 'Tell him I'm calling from England, and I'm not happy. He'll know who it is.'

'A moment. You hold, please.'

The faint crackle of static. Ross shoved in a pound coin, then Ronnie Milward's distinctive voice came on the line. 'The boy blew it, he's being dealt with. What can I say?'

Ross was thinking about the £25,000 he had transferred to Milward's bank account in Zürich. 'What are you intending to do about it?' he asked.

'Might have helped if you'd mentioned the brother,' Milward said reproachfully. 'Caused a lot of grief, that.'

'You're saying it's my fault?'

'I think we should call it shared blame.'

'Meaning?'

'I'm happy to finish the job properly, but I wouldn't feel comfortable about a refund. I've had a lot of expenses.'

'Obviously not in your research department. And I'm not sure it's too smart to finish the job now.'

'Leave it a few weeks? See how the wind blows?'

'I think we'll do that. But if we call it off I'm looking for a refund.'

'I don't operate that way.'

Ross realised the line had gone dead. For a moment he thought Ronnie Milward had hung up on him. Then he saw, from the flashing display in front of him, that he'd forgotten to put in any more money.

SPIDER'S TOP-FLOOR bedsit was accessed by a narrow staircase, leading up from a front door sandwiched between a betting shop and a Chinese takeaway. The door led out onto a busy high street.

Spider, in his track suit, holding his rucksack in one hand, keys in the other, saw the blue baseball cap, the blue overalls just as he was pulling the front door shut behind him.

Like chameleons, the Firearms Squad could blend into any crowd, but those caps and those overalls always made them instantly recognisable to each other.

Baseball caps bobbing out of the crowd, towards him. For an instant he froze. *Jesus*. A swarm of them. They had been waiting.

A voice erupted from a megaphone. 'DROP THE RUCKSACK, PUT THE RUCKSACK DOWN ON THE GROUND. DROP THE RUCKSACK!'

He stepped back, slammed the door, vaulted up the stairs, made the first-floor landing before he heard the door splinter below him.

The voice seemed to be coming out of the walls at him. 'ARMED POLICE. WE HAVE THE BUILDING SURROUNDED. COME OUT WITH YOUR HANDS UP.'

He sprinted on up to his room, somehow got the key into the lock, twisted it, pushed open the door, slammed it shut, rammed the bed against it, hurled the small chest of drawers on top, then in desperation the television and the fridge.

Hammering on the door now. *'Police. Open up!'*

He pulled the Heckler and Koch from the rucksack, snapped off the safety catch. The door was splintering, the bed was moving. He backed away to the window, stared out down the fire escape.

Blue caps. *Shit.* Spider jammed the gun down inside his T-shirt, then lifted up the sash window. Two rifles with telescopic sights were trained on him, with two of the best marksmen in the world squinting through them.

But they wouldn't open fire unless he fired first, he knew that.

You have time, Spider, just think straight, man.

The legs of the bed scraped again. *'Armed police! Open up!'*

He swung himself out through the window, then stood to his full height on the rotten sill. The pointing was crap in the brickwork above him, plenty of fingerholds. Below, another megaphone bellowed, 'ARMED POLICE. YOU ARE SURROUNDED. CLIMB DOWN!'

He hauled himself up, finding a foothold on the top of the window. Had to get height, fast. Up again, hands on the guttering. Straining, taking all his weight on his hands, he pulled himself up. A voice shouted out of the window now, his bedsit window. *'Freeze!'*

He scrambled up the steeply pitched roof, sending tiles slithering down. It was wet from the rain, slippery as hell, his left foot momentarily lost purchase, and he lurched forward, crashing painfully down on his knee, then he was up again, almost at the top.

'YOU ARE COMPLETELY SURROUNDED BY ARMED POLICE. CLIMB SLOWLY DOWN. YOU WILL NOT BE HARMED IF YOU CLIMB DOWN. REPEAT, YOU WILL NOT BE HARMED IF YOU CLIMB DOWN.'

Below, sirens wailed. Spider glanced down and saw two Alsatians being released from the back of a police van. Ahead was the wall of a council low-rise. A vague plan was taking shape. He glanced up and, in that fraction of a second, didn't spot the cracked ridge tile, which split in half when he put his weight on it. It gave way beneath his right foot, and he was falling face first, surfing down the steep wet roof, tiles ripping past his face, tearing skin from his hands.

His jaw hit the guttering, which sheared from the wall, but somehow he seized it with one hand, and hung. Then the fixings came away from the brickwork and, with a shriek, he plunged down, head first into a greenhouse. He struck a roof pane, instantly severing his jugular vein, then crashed down on his back into a bed of tomatoes. Standing over him, snarling, was the last thing he would ever see: an Alsatian's face.

'SEA ROOM', sailors called it. Having plenty of deep-water ocean around you. Enough to drift in any direction without having to worry about rocks or sandbars or land. Hugh Caven called it 'thinking room'. It was where he went when he had a problem to solve.

The prow of the *Sandy Lady* rose with the swell, and behind him now, a long way west of his stern, was the Thames Barrier. The oil storage depots and refineries, the cranes, warehouses and power stations along the shoreline, faded into a charcoal smudge.

He needed to be out here this afternoon, in the Thames estuary in his sturdy little clinker-built boat, putting as much water as he could between himself and the world. 'I'm going to pay a visit to the thinking room,' he had told Sandy.

She understood.

And now, with the taste of salt on his lips, the comforting smells of petrol exhaust and seaweed in the air, the drone of the outboard behind him, his anger towards Ross Ransome was subsiding. He'd been thinking only last week that, with an extravagant client like Ross Ransome, he might be able to upgrade his boat. Now he was going to have a hard time getting a penny out of the bastard beyond the deposit. But that wasn't what he needed to think through now.

His employee Barry Gatt was dead. Barry had left a widow, Steph, with three sons. She was going to need money. And Barry needed justice. But . . . A big but. It had been a criminal offence to put those cameras in Dr Cabot's flat.

He should take the video to the police. Withholding evidence was an even bigger crime than either breaking and entering or illegal surveillance. Under the circumstances, the police might well let him off with a caution, if that. But he was a jailbird. A convicted criminal with a record. The police might just love this. .

What if they tried implicating him? He'd fallen foul of them during his work on a number of occasions, and, if they chose, they could make it very difficult for him.

But if he did nothing?

The crime-scene boys might find the cameras but he doubted that: they'd be looking at the ground, the walls, the furniture. Would they look up? And if they did, would they find those tiny cameras?

There had been a message on his voicemail this morning from a Detective Sergeant Anson, giving an incident-room number and two other numbers, and he hadn't yet returned the call. He couldn't until he'd decided what to say. Another good reason to be out here now.

It had been stupid going to Ross Ransome's office and showing him the tape. What the hell had he hoped to achieve by it? A confession?

Certainly the surgeon might be guilty. The guy was unstable: it wouldn't be beyond him to have someone killed.

Walk away from this one, Hugh, a voice said inside his head. *You can make amends to Steph without landing yourself in trouble. Ross Ransome's smart. You'll be the one who gets screwed, not him.*

He hesitated. The Dylan song came back to him, those words again about the roads. How many? How many roads would he have to walk? And he thought, *I don't know the answer.*

THE *DAILY MAIL* lay on the kitchen table. The front-page headline said: DOUBLE-KILLING SUSPECT DEAD IN FALL.

On the television screen, Bart Simpson was standing on a stage in the beam of a spotlight, singing. Alec, elbows on the kitchen table, spoon and fork in the air, spaghetti sliding onto his hand, chortled.

'Alec,' Faith chided, 'darling, elbows off, and put your fork and spoon down.' Her eyes returned to the *Mail.* She couldn't keep away from it. Paramedics had been unable to save the man.

Alec ignored her.

She glanced up again. 'Alec!'

He still ignored her.

She switched off the television.

'Mummy!'

'Bed!'

'But, Mummy, you always let me watch *The Simpsons.*'

She stood up, grabbed his arm, tugged him sharply from the table. 'You're going to grow up with good manners. People with good manners don't watch television at the dinner table.'

'But you were late tonight. Otherwise I could have had my supper and then watched them.'

She gripped him by the shoulders, struggling to contain the rage inside her. *Taking out my anger on my child*, she thought. *Taking out my resentment at having to leave Oliver yesterday afternoon to come home. And at not being able to see him all day today.*

Yesterday, after they had made love, Oliver had insisted on doing a little work on her, some hypnosis and visualisation. Afterwards she had felt rested and energised, but whether that was from their lovemaking, the hypnosis, simply being with him, or the herbal capsules he had given her, she didn't know. All she knew was that for twenty-four hours she had felt good for the first time in weeks. Normal.

I'm going to beat this, she thought.

'I want to see *The Simpsons,* Mummy.'

Rasputin ran into the hall, barking excitedly.

The front door was opening. Ross's voice. Her heart sank. What the hell was he doing at home? Ross was never at home on a Tuesday night. All this attention he had started paying her. Ironic. All the years when she had wanted him home he hadn't been around, and now, suddenly, he had become new Ross, caring Ross.

'Faith? Darling?'

Alec trotted out to him. 'Daddy, Mummy won't let me watch *The Simpsons*.'

Ross picked Alec up and kissed him. 'And why won't she let the big guy watch *The Simpsons*?' Turning his face towards her, he smiled.

'Alec,' Faith said, 'kiss Daddy good night and we'll run your bath.'

Ignoring her, the boy said, 'Bart was doing an audition and now I don't know if they're going to choose him.'

Ross lowered him to the floor. 'Go up and run your bath. Then I'll come up and read to you. Deal?'

Faith watched the lips pout, then the hesitation. Debating the toss. Sometimes his father had a strangely calming influence on him, and could get him to do things she couldn't. Alec nodded solemnly. Then, infuriatingly slowly, he began to climb the stairs.

Ross joined her in the kitchen. 'Pleased to see me home?'

'It's a surprise.'

'Nice surprise?' He came up behind her, slipped his arms around her waist. 'How about some champagne? To celebrate.'

'Celebrate what?'

'That we're going to beat this thing you have.'

She saw him glance at the headline of the newspaper. He would have seen in *The Times* that the suspect in the killing of Dr Harvey Cabot was dead. He would have heard it on the car radio. But he made no mention of it.

'What news of the patient who's so ill?'

'Not good. Meningoencephalitis. Her husband's threatening to sue.'

'They think she's picked this up in the Harley-Devonshire?'

'Seems probable. A case of septicaemia with the same strain of bacterium was diagnosed three days ago.'

'Is it going to affect the clinic?' She didn't know why she was asking the questions; she didn't care. It was something to distract him from nuzzling her neck.

'No.'

'Unless, of course, there are more cases?'

'I don't think that's likely,' he said emphatically.

'Why's that? If you've had two cases and don't know how they've caught it, how do you know there won't be more?'

'I'll get a bottle of Pol Roger up from the cellar.' He let go of her.

'What do you feel like eating?' she asked. 'I was only going to make myself a tuna salad. Are you OK with something from the freezer? Lamb chops? Pizza?'

He looked at his watch. 'Let's not worry about it for a while. We'll have a nice drink, a good talk. I'll go down to the cellar—still got one bottle of the eighty-three and it should be stunning.'

Faith glanced at her watch: 6.55. She'd promised Oliver she would call him at seven. They'd spoken briefly at lunchtime: he was distressed by the death of the suspect. He wanted answers, justice. The police had given him information that had not been released to the media. They were convinced that this was their man, but they had not yet found any connection between Harvey and the other dead man, Barry Gatt. They were lacking a motive, but still felt strongly that Harvey's death had been a professional hit.

She called down to the cellar. 'I'll just whiz out—won't take me ten minutes—see what they have at the fish counter at Tesco. They might have some scallops,' she said brightly.

Ross came barrelling up the steps. 'No, I don't need scallops. I'll have a tuna salad, that's fine. Let's go into the library, have a glass of champagne and relax. Yes?'

'I'll get the nice glasses out,' she said, trying to mask the reluctance in her voice. 'And I think there's a tin of those anchovy olives.'

'Why not? I'll go and take my tie off.'

In the bedroom, Ross checked his watch again. Seven. Opening the bathroom cabinet, he did a swift mental calculation. Timing was everything now. And quantity. That was crucial, too.

'CHEERS,' Ross said.

She raised her glass with a bleak smile.

'You'll never taste a finer champagne, I promise you,' he said.

She took her first sip. He was right, it was magnificent. What the hell? she thought, drinking another, larger sip. Maybe this would lift her mood. Oliver had told her of the importance of thinking positively.

It was after seven, she was thinking. She *must* speak to Oliver tonight. Tomorrow she would see him again. Tomorrow, she hoped, they would make love again. With luck, Ross would go into his study to work while she made supper. She would do it then.

Ross beamed at her. 'You look beautiful. I haven't seen you looking this good for weeks.'

He passed her the olives. She took one and drained the rest of her glass, needing suddenly to feel that alcohol inside her.

'That's it, down the hatch!'

'You look worried,' she said.

'Me?'

His voice sounded strange. Then, suddenly, he began to melt, turning to liquid, pooling into his chair. And there was a strange sensation inside her head, as if someone was rotating her brain.

Then she shivered as panic filled her. She was outside her body again. Not up on the ceiling this time, just disembodied. She heard a voice that might have been her own but she wasn't certain. The voice said, 'Ross, I'm feeling very strange.'

He was looking out of the window.

A car was coming down the drive. A taxi. She wasn't sure how she could move her mouth, but by thinking about it, it seemed to happen. 'Ross, please help me,' she said.

He walked out of the room as if he hadn't even heard her.

Voices. It sounded like the chatter of a cocktail party. The dog barked. She wanted to go and join them but she was scared. Another car was gliding down the drive, similar to the one her mother drove.

A voice she recognised said, 'Hello, Faith.'

A gangly man with glasses was standing in the doorway, looking at her. It was David DeWitt, the psychiatrist who had been invited here last Saturday night for dinner. Why was he back?

Then he came into the room, and standing in the doorway behind him was Michael Tennent, another psychiatrist, who had also been here for dinner on Saturday night.

'I think,' she heard herself say, 'that things in the kitchen are going astray. You'll have to remind me whether we've eaten or not—it's really hard to tell at the moment, with these long summer nights.'

'How are you, Faith?' David DeWitt said.

Suddenly, her mother was in the room, too.

'Mummy?'

Margaret was wearing something inappropriate for a dinner party: a lightweight nylon anorak. Maybe she was just going to baby-sit.

'Hello, darling.'

'You might not be able to hear me,' Faith said, 'because I'm dead. Could you explain this to Ross, Mummy? He keeps ignoring me.'

Jules Ritterman was in the room now. He said something to Ross but she couldn't hear the words. Then he came towards her, followed by Tennent, DeWitt and her mother.

Ritterman was speaking to her in a gentle, scolding way. 'Faith,' he said, 'Ross tells me that you won't take the medication that's been prescribed for you. Is that right?'

She heard her voice say, 'I'm dead, you see. It doesn't help taking things when you're dead.'

They were all asking her questions now. She heard Tennent say, 'Do you hear voices, Faith?'

DeWitt asked, 'Have you been experiencing visions?'

She answered the questions, but most of them drifted around inside her head. After a while everyone went out of the room but she could hear them talking in the hall, her mother among them.

She heard Ritterman say, 'It's normal practice to bring a social worker into a decision of this nature.'

Ross said, 'We can get round that, Jules. It can be a close relative instead of a social worker.'

Faith drifted in and out of consciousness. Suddenly they were all in the room again and her mother was standing in front of her. 'We love you, darling. We're doing this for you.'

Someone was rolling back her sleeve. Her arm was being held in a grip of iron. She felt a sharp prick. Some dense fluid forced its way into her muscle. She saw Ross's eyes. Jules Ritterman's eyes. Her mother's eyes. Her mother said, 'We all love you so much, darling.'

She heard a bird trilling outside. Then it stopped.

HUGH CAVEN sat at his desk, shoehorned between two filing cabinets in the headquarters of Caven Investigation Services, which occupied the rear spare room of his home. Home was a small, detached modern box, strewn with toys, in southwest London. He had a view from his desk down onto the strip of lawn. Sandy was pegging out washing. Sean, his three-year-old son, was playing with a boat in the tiny inflatable paddling pool.

Caven had one friend in the police and this man had just called him back with the information he needed. The police were satisfied that the dead man was the killer of Barry Gatt and Harvey Cabot, but they had yet to find a motive and were now looking into the dead man's background. They suspected it was a contract killing, but they'd been unable to find any connection so far between Gatt and Cabot.

Out in the garden Caven watched his wife peg out her laundry. She was a good mother, a good woman. He was lucky. Five years ago he had been in jail and had had nothing. Now he had a wife he loved, a kid he was proud of and a flourishing business.

And a close friend dead.

He could give the police the link they needed. He *must* do that. His instincts told him Ross Ransome was behind this. He couldn't recall ever disliking someone as much as that arrogant man. And yet . . .

He watched Sandy and Sean. She looked so beautiful and he was a lovely kid. *You two deserve the best I can give you—but what the hell is that? A father who sacrifices his principles for money? Or a father who risks going back to jail for his principles?*

SOMEWHERE BEYOND the walls of her room, the screaming had been going on all morning. For a while there was a series of low, terrible moans, then there were sharp, hysterical screams. It was bugging her.

But the Big Question was bugging her more.

It had been bugging her for a while, now—she couldn't tell exactly how long because her watch had gone. It had been replaced with a plastic tag, which had her name typed on it: Faith Ransome (Mrs).

She assumed someone had done this to help her. More useful at this moment to know her name than to tell the time. Everything they did here was helpful—wherever *here* was.

This wasn't the Big Question that bugged her. It was the thing on the back of her hand that had her baffled. She'd seen these dozens of times, in every hospital drama she'd ever watched on television, but she'd never had one herself before.

A tall metal rod with a metal arm, and a plastic bag suspended from a hook in the arm, out of which came the cord, which ran down into a connector that was attached by sticking plaster to the back of her hand. What the hell was the word?

She was having big retrieval problems with her memory. There was a lot all boxed up inside her head that she needed to deal with. Different boxes, an Alec box, a Lendt's disease box, an Oliver Cabot box. But there just wasn't time. The day seemed to be divided not into hours or minutes but into visits. The Pill Nurse visits. The Food Nurse visits. The Nurse Who Asked Her Questions visits. The Dr David DeWitt visits. The Ross visits. A lot of Ross visits.

They were all so friendly to her, probably because Ross was a medic, she assumed. The medical profession looking after its own.

Ross was coming into the room now. He kissed her forehead. 'How are you, my darling?' he asked.

'I'm really having nice time,' she said.

She saw his eyes glance up.

'This thing,' she said. 'Umbilical?'

Ross peered hard at her, then went to the door, which was open. He closed it, then walked back across the room, behind the bed, out of her line of sight. A shadow moved across her face and she looked up. The drip bag was moving. He was doing something to it. Disconnecting it.

A tiny swell of concern washed through her. 'What doing?'

'Checking,' he said. 'I want to make sure my darling has exactly the right amount—I don't want them being stingy with your supply.'

Now he was sitting in the chair beside the bed. There was a bulge in one jacket pocket. Had he taken the . . . ?

She looked up. The bag was there. He was just looking after her. Being a good husband.

Now he was standing at the sink. She heard running water. He was putting something in his pocket.

'I'm due in theatre in half an hour. I'll come by this evening,' he said, and kissed her. 'I love you, Faith.'

'I love you too,' she said.

The door clicked.

She looked up again at the drip bag. It was so good lying here, feeling so happy, so loved. She glanced away. *Umbilical*, she thought.

Her eyes closed then opened again. Christ, it was happening. The walls of the room seemed to inch in towards her, then move away. Panicking, she could feel perspiration running down her neck.

'Help me,' she said. 'Please help me, it's happening!'

She really was dying this time. Dying, leaving Alec behind, and Oliver Cabot. Where was Oliver? Why hadn't he—

Now the door was opening. A nurse was coming in with a man in a white coat, and she had seen the man before, a doctor. He leaned over, shone a torch into her eyes, checked her pulse.

She heard him say, 'She's had these before?'

'Twice,' the nurse said. 'It's a symptom of the disease.'

'Please get me back into my body,' Faith said. 'I must see my son before I die completely, before I go and don't come back.'

The man's voice replied, 'What you're having is just like a little panic attack, Faith. You're going to be fine.'

*N*ine

In his office at the Cabot Centre, Oliver punched up the 141 code to mask the identity of his phone, then dialled Faith's home number. Four rings then the sound of Ross Ransome's voice telling him no one was at home.

He dropped the phone back on the cradle.

What have you done with her? Have you killed her? You screwed up killing me and now you've killed her instead?

His next patient was downstairs in the waiting room, and he was already twenty minutes late for her appointment. It had been a mistake coming to work today. He'd thought it might distract him, take him away from the hotel room where he'd been incarcerated all day yesterday, waiting for the call from Faith that never came.

What explanation could there be? What were the options? Either she was deliberately not calling him, because she'd decided to bail out and go back to her marriage, or her husband was preventing her. He ruled out that she was deliberately not calling him. It wasn't in her nature. Which left her bully of a husband, who controlled her life, who was obsessed by her, who hit her.

He sipped water from the glass on his desk.

I need you, Faith, I really need you badly right now. And I don't like this silence from you. It's too loud. Way too loud.

THE DOORBELL RANG and Rasputin raced into the hall, barking. Alec followed him, shouting, 'Mummy's home! Mummy's home!'

'I don't think so, sweetie.' His grandmother had a quick look out of the library window to see who it was. She was always wary of opening the door to strangers.

There was a large blue off-roader on the drive, and a tall man in a suit, whom she had never seen before, standing in the porch.

She went across to the front door and, as a precaution, put on the safety chain. Alec peered up excitedly as she opened the door a few inches. The man looked well dressed and well groomed, she thought, but what did that count for in today's violent world?

'Can I help you?' she said, through the gap.

'I have an appointment at five o'clock to see Mrs Ransome.' His voice was pleasant, and he spoke with an American accent.

'Who are you, please?'

He proffered a business card through the gap, which she took and read: 'Don Rosslyn, Director. Research and Development. Moliou-Orelan Pharmaceuticals plc.'

There were two addresses, one in London and one in Berkshire. She returned the card to him. 'I'm afraid Mrs Ransome isn't here.'

'She's not?'

The man looked disappointed. She decided he didn't look like a rapist or a burglar, closed the door, released the chain, then opened it wider, keeping hold of Rasputin.

The man knelt down and began to make a fuss of the dog.

Alec said, 'My mummy's not well, she's in hospital but my daddy said she'll be able to come home soon.'

Still stroking the dog the man said, with surprise in his voice, 'She's in hospital?'

'I'm afraid my daughter is not well.'

The man stood up. 'I'm sorry. Actually, that's the reason I'm here. She's on a clinical drugs trial with my company. We have a new drug she's taking, which we're hoping will help her.'

Faith's mother said, 'I know all about it.'

'We're running a monitoring programme. I spoke to Mrs Ransome on Monday to make the appointment. We're learning about the efficacy of our drug as we go along, and by spending a little time with each of our patients we can get them to maximise the benefits. Can you give me the name of the hospital and the address?'

'I have it on a pad in the kitchen,' she said. 'I'll fetch it for you.'

FIVE MINUTES LATER, Oliver Cabot drove his blue Jeep Cherokee out of the front gates of Little Scaynes Manor.

A few hundred yards along the lane he pulled into a lay-by, called Directory Enquiries and asked for the number of the Grove Hospital, then dialled it.

'I'd like to speak to Faith Ransome,' he said.

'One moment.' There was a brief pause, then the woman came back, polite but cold. 'I'm sorry, she is not permitted telephone calls. I can put you through to the nursing station in her ward.'

'Sorry if this is a dumb question, but what kind of hospital are you?'

'We're a secure private hospital for psychiatric patients,' she said.

Oliver hung up.

Psychiatric hospital? Faith had been concerned about her bouts of dissociation. Had she had a really severe attack?

He put the car in gear. It would take him about an hour and a half, he estimated. He rang his secretary and asked her to make enquiries, any information she could find on the reasons Faith Ransome had been admitted there.

She rang him back forty minutes later. 'She's been sectioned under the Mental Health Act, Dr Cabot. She's on a twenty-eight-day order.'

IT WAS TEN PAST FIVE. In the rush-hour traffic it might take half an hour to get to the hospital. Then he needed to allow a further half-hour with Faith once he was there: he had to make sure he had enough time alone in the room to make one final switch. Tonight, he calculated, her existing supply of Moliou-Orelan capsules would be exhausted, and tomorrow they would start giving her these fresh ones. Ones he had doctored. Then life would be easier.

How the hell had he allowed himself to be bullied by Detective Sergeant Anson into meeting him at his flat at seven this evening?

Walking down the steps of the underground car park in Cavendish Square, Ross thought about the policeman's voice. It was precise and polite, no hint of emotion. Just duty. A voice in search of the truth. Ross wondered just how much the policeman knew or suspected.

Ross pushed open the door marked Level 2 and strode in the shadowy lighting past rows of parked cars. The Aston Martin was in his regular numbered bay. He pressed the button on the fob, and as the central locking clunked open, a figure stepped out of the shadows.

'Good afternoon, Mr Ransome. We need to talk.'

The soft Irish accent, the small frame, the pallid little face.

'You might need to. I don't.' Ross pushed past the private investigator, and opened the door of his car. 'And I've just heard from the police. They want to interview me. What did you tell them?'

'You have to believe me. I haven't said a word to the police.'

Struggling to contain himself, Ross put his hands on the investigator's shoulders and gripped them hard. 'You're pond life, Caven.'

'We need to be sensible, Mr Ransome. I can understand—'

Ross did something he had not done since his schooldays. He headbutted the man. Caven reeled backwards and sat down on the floor, blood running from his nose.

Ross climbed in the Aston Martin, slammed his door, rammed the key into the ignition, pulled out of the bay and accelerated, heading for the exit ramp. As he turned right, he saw the man emerge from the bay and lurch into a run after him. He followed the exit arrows, tyres squealing. As he started the turn to the final ramp up to the pay desk, he saw Caven come out of a door. He didn't want a further tangle with this man to delay him.

The barrier was down and the attendant in the booth was talking on the phone. Ross hooted twice. The attendant waved, and the barrier began to rise. Ross's car phone rang. Ignoring it, he accelerated hard up the ramp into daylight. The bastard was still running after him. He accelerated harder, eyes on the mirror.

Oh, Christ, no.

A great red wall in front of him.

He stamped on the brake pedal, heard the tremendous, deep metallic bang, then there was a burst of white light in front of his eyes and the car rocked to a halt.

An instant of numbed silence.

The bonnet had flown up and steam rose from the engine compartment. Airbags hung from the steering wheel and passenger dashboard. Beyond the bonnet he could see the crumpled side panels of a bus. A startled woman was peering down at him through one of its windows. The driver was climbing down from the cab.

Ross unclipped his seat belt and tried to open the door. It would not budge. Hot, sweaty and furious, he barged it with his shoulder. It still wouldn't move. His bloody car phone was still ringing.

He realised why his own door wouldn't open: the central locking was still engaged. He unlocked it, opened the door and climbed out.

'Not big enough?' An angry man's voice. 'Not bloody big enough? Not big enough for you to see? If you can't bloody drive it, you shouldn't bloody have it.'

Ross looked around anxiously. Someone was going to have to sort this mess out and he did not have time. He could get a taxi and phone the AA, tell them to come and collect the car, sort it out.

'Excuse me,' he said, and tried to push out through the crowd. An arm held him back. It was the bus driver.

'Where do you think you're going?'

'My wife's very ill,' Ross said.

'You're not going anywhere until the police have been.'

Ross pulled the man's arm away. 'I'm a surgeon and it's an emergency.'

The man grabbed him more tightly. 'You're staying here.'

Ross heard a siren. He balled his fist to hit the man, then restrained himself. 'You can let go, I'm staying.'

With threatening eyes, the driver released his grip. Ross stared back at his car. The bloody phone was ringing again, so he ducked in to answer it. It was a customer-service representative from Vodafone wanting to know if Ross was happy with their service.

THE GROVE HOSPITAL was a Gothic, red-brick edifice in a mishmash street of houses and offices behind Wellington Road in Maida Vale.

Oliver checked his mirror to make sure he wasn't being tailed, still aware he might be a target, then parked on a single yellow line just beyond the entrance. The Jeep's clock told him it was 6.10, twenty minutes before it was legal. Chancing it, he climbed out of the car, adjusted his tie, clipped his cellphone to his belt and locked the car. It was a warm evening, the cloying London air listless and muggy. Oliver wiped the perspiration from his face, walked up the steps to the panelled front door, turned the brass handle and pushed. It was locked. To the left there was a speakerphone with a surveillance camera lens visible above it; he pushed the button.

A crackly voice: 'Yes, who is it, please?'

'Dr Cabot—my secretary told you to expect me.'

The lock clicked. He pushed the door and entered a narrow, characterless hall, dominated by a high mahogany reception counter behind which was perched an elderly receptionist with prim hair.

The lighting was poor and the general ambiance stark, institutional: bare cream walls hung only with licences, certificates, First Aid procedures.

'Dr Cabot?' the woman said.

'Yes, I've come to see my patient, Mrs Faith Ransome.'

She handed him a visitor's log, asked him to sign in, then reached for her phone. 'Sheila, I have Dr Cabot in reception.'

Oliver scanned the log. The first visitor of the day had been Ross Ransome, in at 7.15, out at 7.35. Then further down he saw his name again. In at 12.32. Out at 1.05. He scrawled his own name, making it deliberately illegible and put down the time: 6.15pm. Then he glanced at a floor plan taped to the top of the counter.

The woman replaced the phone and said, 'Take the lift to the third floor, turn right when you come out, walk down the corridor, through the fire doors. Follow the signs to the nursing station.'

The lift was deep and wide enough for a stretcher, and painfully slow. Oliver stepped out into a windowless corridor and followed the directions. As he went through a fire door and approached the nursing station, a pretty ginger-haired nurse in a chequered blue uniform was talking to a serious-looking man in a white medic's coat, poring over a file. The nurse looked up at Oliver with the trace of a smile. On her lapel was a tag identifying her as Ward Sister Sheila Durrant.

'Good evening, I'm Dr Cabot,' he said.

The man put down the file. Giving Oliver a cursory glance, he left.

'Hello,' she said. 'We're a little confused. We have down on the forms that Mrs Ransome's GP is Dr Ritterman.'

'I believe Dr Ritterman has been the family doctor for some while, but Mrs Ransome recently registered with me.'

She held up a fax. 'Well, your secretary sent this through to us. It's just that we have instructions that no one other than the doctors and psychiatrists here—and, of course, her husband—is to see her.'

'You have a Mental Health Act section order?' Oliver asked. 'Can I have a look at it?'

She produced a file from under the desk and handed him a bunch of documents clipped together. Oliver read through them. Faith was being held for assessment under a Section 2 order for twenty-eight days. The applicant was Ross Ransome, as the nearest relative. The separate supporting forms were signed by Faith's mother, Dr Jules

Ritterman, as Faith's GP, and a psychiatrist, Dr DeWitt.

Patients had the right to ask for a review, he knew, which could either be reassessment by hospital managers or a Mental Health Act commission in a tribunal comprising a psychiatrist, a lay person and a chair. Oliver also knew that it was far harder to get such an order reversed than granted.

He glanced through the notes of the hospital's consultant psychiatrist. They confirmed symptoms of the advanced stages of Lendt's disease. Her current medication consisted of intravenous glucose solution, three milligrams of risperidone twice a day—a fairly heavy dosage—and two Moliou-Orelan N646329 Entexamin capsules, three times daily with food.

'How is she?'

'She's under our consultant psychiatrist Dr Freemantle. It would be helpful for you to talk to him, but he won't be here until nine tomorrow.'

'I really would like to see her.'

She glanced down and he could see the hesitation. 'Yes, well, I think you have every right to see her.' Then looking up at him again, she said, 'You seem familiar—your face. I'm trying to think where I recognise you from?'

'I've been in the news this week.'

'Ah—right. That's what—' The penny had dropped. 'Oh God. It was your brother?'

He nodded, with a lump in his throat.

'I'm sorry.'

Falteringly, Oliver said, 'Life has to go on.'

'I'll take you to her room.'

Oliver followed the nurse down a long corridor of closed doors, then right, along a further corridor, passing on their left, he noticed, a fire-escape external door. A male orderly wheeled a dinner trolley round the corner ahead of them, bringing out with him the smell of boiled fish and stewed cabbage.

'Here we are.'

Her name was printed on a card in the slot on the door. The nurse opened it and went in quietly in case Faith was asleep. When she could see she was awake she said, 'You have a visitor, Mrs Ransome.'

Faith was sitting up, propped on pillows, her food tray untouched on the swing table over the bed. She did not acknowledge the nurse, who walked across and checked the almost empty drip bag.

'I'll just replace this. You may be coming off it tomorrow. Dr Freemantle says your electrolytes are almost back to normal levels.'

In a slurred voice, Faith said, 'My husband changes it for me. He'll be here soon. He changes it.'

'Your husband?' Sister Durrant said, amused. 'I don't think that's your husband's job.'

'He changes it,' she said.

Oliver stared at her from the doorway, deeply perturbed. The room felt like a cell: stark white paint, the bed in the centre, making her look some kind of exhibit. But it wasn't the room that perturbed him, it was what Faith was saying.

She looked beautiful, even in the flimsy white hospital gown, her hair matted, and no make-up. He had to restrain himself from walking straight over to her, putting his arms around her and kissing her. Instead, from the doorway he said, 'Hello, Faith.'

There was no reaction.

Walking slowly over to the bed, he said, 'How are you feeling?'

It seemed to him there was just the faintest flicker of recognition.

'I'll pop back and change the drip bag, then I'll leave you,' Sister Durrant said, and went out, leaving the door ajar.

He waited, listening to her footsteps recede, before he spoke to Faith again. 'Do you recognise me, Faith?' Leaning close he could see that her pupils were dilated. From the medication she was on, this surprised him. 'It's Oliver.'

She spoke, suddenly, 'It's true what I said. Ross comes in and changes the drip bag. First the nurse changes it, then Ross changes it again. They don't believe me. They don't realise I can watch him sometimes from the ceiling.'

IN HIS HEAD Oliver carried a detailed summary of all the published material on Lendt's disease he had been able to find. Faith had returned from Thailand in late April. Today was 9 June. If she had contracted the disease out there, she should still be in the prolonged-nausea phase. She should not be in the psychotic state in which she appeared to be now. She should not have dilated pupils.

He strode over to the door, looked up and down the corridor, then dashed back to the bed, disconnected the drip line from Faith's wrist, put the tube to his mouth, and tested the solution tentatively with the tip of his tongue. It tasted innocuous enough. Then he gripped the tube in his lips, took a couple of hard sucks, swallowed and replaced the line.

Moments later the nurse came back into the room, carrying a fresh bag, which she exchanged for the almost spent one.

'Are you expecting Mr Ransome?' Oliver asked her.

'He said he would be here at about six o'clock.' She glanced at her watch. 'Twenty-five past.' Then, sensing something from his expression, she said, 'Shall I let you know when he arrives?'

'I'd be grateful.' Then he added, 'Tell me something—the drip, she's on a six-hour replenishment?'

'In the daytime. Dr Freemantle has it on twelve hours at night.'

Oliver thanked her. She left and closed the door.

It shimmered as she closed it. Oliver stared at it, puzzled. It was as if he could see every single atom in the door vibrating. And as he turned back to Faith, the door seemed to elongate and travel with him. The floor seemed to be swaying beneath him.

A voice that he wasn't immediately sure was his own said, 'What do you mean, Faith, that you watch Ross changing the drip bag?'

'He comes and he changes it. He thinks I don't notice.'

She seemed a long way away from him now, as if he were on the far side of the room. Something crawled down his back. It felt like a spider. As he reached behind him, he felt more creatures, down his chest, down his legs, down his neck. He took off his jacket, rolled up his shirtsleeves, but he could see nothing.

Now he recognised what was happening to him. Something in that drip was doing this to him. Ross was putting something in the solution he was substituting, but why? Was he trying to drive Faith mad? Was this his way of getting back at her?

The bastard was deliberately keeping her in a psychotic state—and doing it on a prolonged basis like this carried a severe risk of brain damage. Was this man crazy?

The most likely drug, he guessed, would be ketamine. It was frequently used for burns-trauma cases, and part of Ross Ransome's reputation was based on his work with burns cases. He would have easy access to the drug.

Ross Ransome, you are a sick man.

And where was he? Sister Durrant had been expecting him at six. He glanced at his watch: 7.17. Impossible. He'd arrived here before a quarter past six. No way could he have been here an hour, no—

The nurse had looked at her watch just before she had gone out. It had been 6.25. There was no way three-quarters of an hour had passed. He looked at the clock on Faith's bedside table: 7.18. Three quarters of an hour had gone from his mind.

'I don't want to be here,' Faith said.

Oliver looked down at her, and squeezed her hand. 'I don't want you to be here, believe me.'

The walls were glowing with an intensity of light. The drug was still working, and he knew the effects could go on returning for many hours after the initial effects had seemingly worn off.

He opened the door and hurried back to the nursing station. Sister Durrant was on the phone. Impatiently he waited at a polite distance until she had finished. Then he said, 'The drip bag you just removed from Mrs Ransome's room—where is it?'

She looked at him curiously. 'The drip bag?'

'Yes, the empty one. I need it.'

'I've thrown it into the incinerator chute. It'll be burnt by now.'

Thinking fast he said, 'Will you do me a favour? Will you take a blood sample from Mrs Ransome for me?'

'We have blood for our routine tests.'

'Could you please give me some? Just a small amount?'

'Yes, yes, of course.'

'Put the date and time on it, please. How do I get to the basement?'

'The lift—just press B.'

He was already on his way. He took the emergency stairs, running down into a long, poorly lit corridor. He took a step forward and nearly stumbled as the floor plunged away beneath him. *Just an illusion*, he told himself and took another step, then another, holding out his arms to stay upright.

He passed an open door to the laundry and ducked in. He saw several bins. One contained a stack of blue nursing tunics. He grabbed one, rolled it tightly and crammed it into his trouser pocket, then went back along the corridor to another door. It was marked DANGER, KEEP OUT. He opened it.

A blast of heat greeted him. A voice shouted, 'What you doing?'

He turned to see a bemused, grimy-looking man in blue overalls.

'I need something that was dropped down the chute in Park Ward.'

The man grinned. 'You got a problem with that one. You bring an asbestos suit with you?' He jerked a thumb at the metal casing of the thundering furnace. 'Because whatever you're looking for's going to be in there—and I'm afraid mine's at the cleaners.'

'LOOK, DETECTIVE SERGEANT, my wife is extremely ill in hospital. I was involved in an accident on my way there this afternoon.'

'Yes, you have already told me this,' Anson said.

Ross stood up and went over to the window of his flat. Five minutes' walk to the hospital. He looked at his watch: 7.30. The drip would have been changed an hour and a half ago. Faith might be returning to normal, although she had been on the ketamine for forty-eight hours. He was anxious to get to her. 'Could we continue tomorrow?'

'I'd prefer to wrap this up tonight, Mr Ransome. It won't take much longer.' The policeman's voice and demeanour were respectful, the courtesy of one professional to another. 'Were you aware that your wife was seeing Dr Oliver Cabot, the deceased's brother?'

Ross knew that he needed to be careful. Obstructing the police by lying was a serious offence, and he didn't want to say anything that might bounce back in his face. 'Yes, I was.'

'And how did you feel about that?'

'Are you married, Detective Sergeant?'

A slight frown. 'I am, yes.'

'Then perhaps you can understand how I felt. Our doctors are among the best-trained in the world and I want the best for my wife. I was furious when I discovered she was rejecting everything I had done for her and going to a charlatan.'

'How did you make your views known?'

'I told my wife.'

'Did you tell Dr Cabot?'

Thinking carefully, Ross said, 'I had no desire to get into a slanging match with the man.'

Anson smiled understandingly. 'Very restrained of you, sir. I'm not sure I would have had such self-control.'

Ross sensed that the two of them might just be on the same wavelength. 'Can I get you something?' he asked. 'I've got some Grolsch in the fridge.'

'Ah!' Anson looked at his watch. 'Well, I'm not supposed to drink on duty, but it's late and I'd like that very much, thank you.'

Ross fetched two lagers.

Swallowing a long draught of the beer appreciatively, Anson said, 'My father suffers from Parkinson's disease. A mate of his recommended an alternative doctor, who put him on some herbal diet. Didn't make a blind bit of difference. Cost my dad over two hundred quid by the time he'd bought all the stuff. Swallowed the first lot and threw up for twelve hours. Licensed con man, I'd say.'

Ross said, 'All these alternative medics are con men.'

Anson nodded in agreement.

Better, Ross thought. *This is much better.*

HE KEPT HIS HANDS jammed in his trouser pocket, trying to hide the bulge as he walked back past Sister Durrant at the nursing station. She was engaged in conversation and barely acknowledged him. She just pointed to an envelope on the counter and mouthed, 'Blood sample'.

He thanked her and pocketed it. Faith was asleep when he went into her room. He perched on the edge of the bed and watched her face. He looked at the fall of blonde tresses across her forehead, the beautiful pout as if she had fallen asleep waiting for a kiss. He would have loved to lean across and kiss her lips right now, while she slept. She looked so gentle and so beautiful. And so terribly vulnerable.

His thoughts were interrupted by the sound of the door opening, and he turned in alarm. It was sister Durrant. 'Dr Cabot,' she said. 'Mr Ransome has just arrived downstairs.'

Quickly, Oliver pulled the drip line out of her wrist and switched off the flow valve, then propped her upright.

She opened her eyes. 'Wh—what—wha?'

'We're out of here.'

He helped her into the nursing tunic he had brought up from the basement. Faith, in a state of confusion because of the build-up of ketamine, was of little help. He sat her on the edge of the bed, and rolled the bedclothes into the rough shape of a sleeping form. Then he grabbed her hand and half led her, half dragged her into the corridor. He stopped and looked in both directions, then took Faith to the fire-escape door, pushed it open and helped her through.

They were standing on a metal platform, with the fire escape descending below them into what looked like a loading area. Despite the hour it was still brilliant daylight, and he felt exposed. This was not smart. Helping a patient detained under a Mental Health Act order to escape from an institution could land him in serious trouble. But right now his only concern was to get Faith out of here before Ross arrived on this floor.

He led her down as fast as he could, and they finally made it to the bottom. Her coordination was so bad that walking was difficult. He was either going to have to carry her to the car or bring it round. Carrying her would draw attention; he would have to pass the front door of the hospital.

'Faith,' he said, 'I'm going to fetch my car. I want you to wait here. Don't move.'

He saw a gap between two large wheelie-bins. Not brilliant, but she'd be hidden. He pushed her in gently.

FAITH WRINKLED HER NOSE at the stench of garbage, staring along the grey slab sides of the bins that rose up either side of her. A fly buzzed in her face and she flapped it away. She was lucid again now. Lucid and scared. Scared of being in this horrible alley. Scared of what Ross would do to her and Oliver when he found out. He could come and get her. Take her away, lock her up, stop her from seeing Alec.

A sudden sweet smell: cigarette smoke. Footsteps. A dark shape crossed the gap in front of her. A security guard, hat under his arm, sneaking a quick cigarette break.

Go away. Please go away.

Her face felt hot. Oliver would be back at any moment. The walls of the bins were moving, coming in towards her. The sliver of daylight, which had been only a couple of feet away now seemed a hundred yards distant, and was getting smaller.

She pushed her way out with her hands, and suddenly she was free, standing in the loading bay. The security guard was walking away.

The roar of an engine. Big blue car, Jeep, familiar, halting.

Oliver! He was getting out.

The guard turned his head, stared at her, frowning. An elderly guy, he looked tired and hot. She realised afterwards that, in her nurse's uniform, she should have just raised a hand and waved, and he'd have waved back, thinking she was a staff member.

Instead she ran.

A shout behind her. 'Hey! Hey, you, hey, miss, lady!'

She fell into Oliver's arms, turned her head. The guard was breaking into a lumbering run.

Oliver flung her up onto the passenger seat and slammed the door. The guard was only yards away. The car lurched as Oliver climbed behind the wheel. He shut his door and with a squeal of tyres the Jeep lurched forward. She heard a loud shout, and saw the guard running alongside the car. Then suddenly he was gone.

OLIVER REACHED the end of the road and turned right, accelerating hard. No sign of the man in his mirrors. He went down the road for a quarter of a mile, then took a left down to Wellington Road, then turned right onto the busy thoroughfare.

He wondered if the guard had got his number. He wanted the shortest route to the motorway, deciding it would be safer to get out of town. Even if the guard hadn't got his number, he would raise the alarm. It wouldn't take long before Faith's absence was discovered.

'Faith, can you do up your seat belt?'

Looking bewildered, she groped above her shoulder for it. He leaned across with one arm, helped her pull it over and click it home.

Oliver followed the signs for the M40, and five minutes later was travelling at a steady fifty over the elevated section of the Westway.

Suddenly he felt as though he was outside his body. He could see the car in front, the road beyond it, but it was as if something else was driving and he was looking down, like a ghost, from above.

The drug again, he told himself. *I am here, I am driving, this is me, alive. I just have to keep calm, it will fade, just give it time.*

He thought for a while, then he reached forward and dialled his mobile phone. A sharp crackle, then he heard a male voice.

'Gerry?'

'Oliver! My friend, how are you? I was just thinking about you.'

Oliver began to feel better. Of all the people he had met in England, Gerry Hammersley was the one he had warmed to most. Gerry had come to see him six years back, after Oliver had been interviewed on a radio show about the treatment of acute anxiety through hypnosis. Gerry had been dumped by his fiancée and his self-esteem was then at an all-time low. Oliver had changed his life, Gerry told him.

'Gerry, your offer that I could use your place in the country if I ever needed some peace and quiet on my own—is it still open?'

'Of course. You can stay as long as you like. I'm not sure when I'll be down next, but it won't be this weekend.'

'I just need it for a day or two.'

'Fine. When do you want to go there?'

'Tonight, if that's possible.'

'Well, of course, yes. I'd have liked to have the cleaning lady air a bed for you but—'

'Not important.'

'There's bread in the freezer. Long-life milk. Wine in the cellar. Eat anything you can find. You remember where the key's kept?'

'Sure.'

'And the code for the alarm?'

'Uh-huh. Look, I need one other very big favour from you, Gerry.'

'What's that?'

'That you don't tell anyone where I am. Not a soul.'

'Absolutely. You've had the most appalling tragedy, and you must be sick of the media. My lips are sealed.'

As Oliver hung up, Faith said quietly, 'We have to collect Alec.'

'Alec?'

'Ross will use him against me if we don't.'

Incredulously Oliver said, 'You want to go to your house?'

'We have to.'

'Do you understand what's happened and what we're doing?'

'I—I think so.'

Oliver talked her through it, testing her to ensure that she was lucid enough to take it in. She seemed to be. But when he had finished, she was still adamant they had to collect Alec.

'Please, Oliver, I don't know what Ross is capable of any more. If something happened to Alec, I don't think I could ever—'

Oliver didn't like it but he understood. 'We'll get him,' he said. 'We'll go get him now.'

THE SECOND GROLSCH had been a mistake, Ross thought, as he rode up in the lift to the third floor of the Grove Hospital. Under its influence, Ross had let slip something to Detective Sergeant Anson about Faith and Dr Oliver Cabot. It was one of those off-the-cuff remarks that would have passed unnoticed if Anson had been a less observant man, but Ross could see that the policeman had registered it.

They had been talking about medicine men in primitive tribes, and how shaman healers whipped people into a frenzied trance state through the use of drums, and Ross had interjected that Dr Oliver Cabot probably achieved the same effect with his dick. He hadn't said enough to make it an outright accusation, but he had said more than enough for the inference to be clear.

Not smart.

He saw a ward sister standing at the nurses' station, strode up to her and read the badge on her lapel. Ward Sister Sheila Durrant.

'How's my wife?'

'Your wife has left, Mr Ransome.'

It took a moment to register. 'I—don't understand. Left what?'

'Here. She's gone. Disappeared.'

He backed away, fury erupting inside him. 'What?'

'Her doctor came to see her. Dr Cabot. They've both gone.'

'You're not serious?'

'I'm afraid I am.'

His fists balled at his side. 'How can she have left? This is a secure hospital for Chrissake—how? How? *How?*'

'No one knows.'

'She's sectioned—she can't bloody leave. Have the police been told?'

'Yes.'

'This creep Cabot, this charlatan, he's her lover. They're sleeping together. You let her lover come in and take her away!'

Ross turned in fury and walked away. He rode the lift to the ground floor, then walked out of the main door and slammed it behind him. Outside on the steps he reached for his mobile phone. He needed to speak to Caven. He had to stop him talking to the police.

Hugh Caven answered on the second ring. 'Yes, hello?'

'We—we didn't have a good meeting earlier. We need to talk. Meet me tonight, and I'll bring you the money I owe you.'

'Where are you?' Caven said.

'Grove Hospital—close to Wellington Road. Maida Vale.'

'There's a Hilton near you, opposite Lord's cricket ground. Do you know it?'

'I'll find it.'

'There's a coffee shop and a bar just off the lobby. I'll meet you there in half an hour, but don't keep me waiting, Mr Ransome.'

THE SAFETY CHAIN was on the front door. Rasputin was in a frenzy. In the porch of Little Scaynes Manor, Faith yelled over his barking, 'Mummy, open this door!'

'I'm phoning the police. It's for your own good!' her mother replied.

Faith turned wildly to Oliver, 'Your mobile—phone the number here, quickly! Phone it and block it so she can't call out!'

'Give me the number.'

She told him. Repeating it to himself, Oliver ran to the Jeep and dialled it.

'Let me in!' Faith shrieked. Through the bay window of Ross's study she could see her mother, picking up the phone. She was about to run across and pound on the window, when on the other side of the door she heard a little voice.

'Mummy! Mummy's home!'

'Alec! Darling! Undo the chain!'

The door opened and Rasputin leaped out, almost knocking her flat. Alec jumped up, hugging her.

Oliver went into the hallway behind her, mobile phone to his ear. Faith ran into Ross's study, grabbed the receiver out of her mother's hand, tearing out the wires.

'He's poisoning me!' she yelled at her mother. 'You stupid woman, my husband is poisoning me and you're letting him!'

'Faith, listen, Faith—listen to me, darling, you're—'

'You listen to me,' Oliver said. 'Mrs Phillips, I—'

'I know you, you were here earlier. Who are you? What are you doing with my daughter?'

'I'm your daughter's doctor.'

'My daughter is under Dr Ritterman.'

Oliver signalled to Faith with his eyes. 'Clothes,' he said to her.

As she made for the door, Oliver added, 'Tear every phone in the house out of its socket. Does she have a mobile?'

Faith shook her head.

'Two minutes and we're out of here.' He turned back to her mother. 'Mrs Phillips, please listen to me—'

'You listen to me,' she said. 'I had a phone call less than ten minutes ago from the Grove Hospital, telling me that my daughter was visited by a Dr Oliver Cabot—presumably you—earlier this evening and that she had vanished. They asked me to let them know if she turned up here, and that is exactly what I propose to do.'

'Don't you love Faith?' Oliver said.

'She's my daughter, Dr Cabot. I love her deeply.'

'Then help us. If you send her back to the Grove Hospital, her husband is going to kill her.'

'Oh, yes?' she said, sarcastically. 'And I suppose you're going to give her some miracle cure.'

'A cure,' Oliver said. 'Not a miracle, just a cure.'

There was an instant of hesitation in the woman's face. 'My daughter is under a Mental Health Act section order. If you are really her doctor, I expect you to act according to the law and return her to the hospital where she was being held.'

'Mr Ransome drugged Faith to get that order. I have the evidence.' Oliver pulled the envelope from Sister Durrant out of his pocket, ripped it open and held out the vial. 'Your daughter's blood is in there. When I take that to the Path Lab tomorrow it's going to show ketamine. Someone's going to have a problem explaining what that drug is doing in her system.'

'Whatever he may have done, he will have done it for the best of reasons. He's the most wonderful husband to her and I would trust him with my life. Do I make myself clear?'

'I'm taking Faith and she wants her son to come with us. I will take them wherever she wants to go, and if you truly love your daughter, you'll let her go and you won't inform anyone about this.'

'If you really are her doctor, I would suggest you leave Alec here and take her straight back. If you don't, I think you're going to find yourself in a great deal of trouble.'

'Mrs Phillips,' he said, trying one last time, 'please believe me, please trust me. Tell me what I have to do to convince you.'

Her arms folded, Faith's mother said, 'Ross has told me about you, Dr Cabot. You're a charlatan and you have some kind of hold over my daughter. I think you are a dangerous and evil man.'

'YOU'RE LATE, I was about to leave.' Hugh Caven said. 'I've been here forty minutes.' He was lounging on a sofa in a white T-shirt and jeans. His nose looked crimson and one of his eyes was half closed, with a dark blue ring round it. 'Did you bring your chequebook?'

Ross sat down heavily in an armchair opposite him, and pulled out his chequebook. A waiter came over. Ross ordered a glass of water then nodded at Caven. 'Can I get you—a drink?'

'No, thanks. But an apology might be appropriate.'

The waiter walked away. Ross was trying to think. He wanted to buy this man's silence. He also wanted to find Faith and Cabot.

'Listen, sorry. I was in a bad mood. We need to talk, you and I.'

'We *are* talking,' Caven said. 'We're talking for exactly ninety more seconds, then you're going to write me a cheque and I'm going home.'

'I think we understand each other. I think it would be better if you didn't mention to the police about working for me.'

Caven's demeanour changed. 'Is that what you brought me out here to talk about?'

Ross did not care for the man's expression. Alarm bells were clanging. 'I also need to talk to you because Cabot's taken my wife away and I need you to find her.'

'Dr Oliver Cabot has taken your wife? She's left you for him?'

Ross nodded, and opened his hands, helplessly.

'You don't know where they are?'

'No.' A waiter brought a glass and a bottle of mineral water and set them down on the table.

As the man walked away, Caven leaned forward, animatedly. 'In his car? Has he taken her in his car? In his Jeep Cherokee?'

'How the hell do I know?'

Caven sat back. 'I fitted a global positioning transponder to Dr Cabot's Jeep. It was one of the first things I did. I can plot his position on the computer in my office.'

Ross felt a boost of excitement. 'How accurate?'

'Call me in the morning and I'll look. If they've gone in Dr Cabot's Jeep, I can find them for you. For five thousand, I'll be able to tell you where the Jeep is, anywhere on this planet, to within fifty feet. Is that accurate enough for you?'

ten

Oliver drove in silence, one eye watching the mirrors for police.

Junction 15. Swindon. He turned off the M4, along the dual carriageway he knew well. He passed signs for Cricklade, then Cirencester, then Stroud, and turned off to head for the Cotswolds. He passed the Hare and Hounds pub, and slowed. Then to the left he saw the familiar sign, braked hard and turned left. A couple of miles along he turned right into a narrow lane barely wider than the car, which after half a mile dipped steeply downhill into a village of grey Cotswold stone houses.

It was easy to miss the entrance to the drive, and he kept his speed down as he left the village, going along the boundary of a walled estate. Then he saw the driveway ahead to his right. Breathing a low sigh of relief, he swung the Jeep in over the cattle grid.

Alec's voice startled him. 'Are we nearly there yet?'

'Just going up the track now. Couple of minutes.'

There was a shadowy cluster of farm buildings ahead. Oliver smelt a sharp tang of rotting straw and muck. He drove through another gate, and the track climbed for several hundred yards towards a copse of firs. Beyond them it levelled out, running over another cattle grid. The track continued upwards, more gently for a few hundred yards, the tyres rumbled over a third cattle grid and then they were mashing gravel. He brought the car to a halt.

Faith touched his arm lightly. 'Well driven,' she said.

Oliver smiled, stifling a yawn. He opened the door and climbed out, breathing in the sweet night air, the silence broken only by the distant bleating of sheep, the ticking of the hot engine, and the crunch of his feet on the fine white pebbles.

He unclipped Alec's belt, then helped the sleepy boy to the ground. Faith hugged Alec and looked around. 'It's so peaceful,' she said.

When Gerry Hammersley had bought the place twenty years back, it had been empty for over fifty years. A fire had razed the house to the ground shortly after the end of the Second World War, and the estate that had owned it hadn't considered it worth rebuilding. Gerry had converted the barn into a beautiful L-shaped house, the stable block into a garage, and he had put a swimming pool at the back.

Oliver hefted Faith's suitcase from the tailgate, retrieved the key from its usual hiding place beneath a flowerpot and unlocked the front door. Then he stepped inside, switched off the burglar alarm and turned on the hall lights.

'Wow!' Faith said, stepping into the tiled hall. 'It's beautiful.'

'It is,' he said. He had spent many peaceful weekends at Ampney Nairey Farm with Gerry, walking, mountain biking, playing tennis, lazing around the pool. If he had a favourite place in the whole world, this was it. You could spend a whole week at this house and not see another soul. Not even the postman disturbed the tranquillity, but by arrangement left the mail in a box at the village post office. And there was only this one track up to the place. Access across the fields at the back was only possible by tractor.

HUGH CAVEN'S SON Sean had taken to copying his dad. When his dad switched from Cornflakes to Shredded Wheat for breakfast, Sean switched too. His Dad had two pieces, and so did Sean. Then, as his Dad read the paper, Sean read his *Beano*, sipping his orange juice in the same grown-up way his dad sipped his, plastic mobile phone at his side on the table, just like his Dad's.

The private investigator liked to read the diary page. He told himself that it was purely a business thing: he needed to keep up to speed on the rich and famous because he never knew who might call on his services. But in truth he was fascinated. Which was why, every morning, the page of the *Daily Mail* he read first was Nigel Dempster's.

As he turned to it now, an item halfway down caught his eye:

I was much saddened to hear of the death, at 47, of my old friend, Lady Geraldine Reynes-Rayleigh yesterday at London's exclusive Harley-Devonshire Hospital. A spokesman at the hospital would only confirm that Geraldine had died following complications after rhinoplasty. The surgeon, society figure Ross Ransome, 42, was unavailable for comment.

There is no suggestion, of course, of any medical impropriety by Mr Ransome. But his long and glittering career as plastic surgeon to the stars has been a chequered one. Over the years, my enquiries show that as many as twelve other patients have died during or following surgery. In every case, the postmortem has established that Mr Ransome was not to blame. Nevertheless, it seems the quest for beauty has a high price.

In the kitchen the toaster popped. Sandy, in her dressing gown, called, 'Sean, hurry up, your egg is ready.'

Caven's mobile phone rang. He put down the paper, and lifted the phone to his ear. Across the table, Sean Caven brought his toy telephone to his ear and adopted a deeply serious expression.

'Good morning.' It was Ross Ransome.

'And what can I do for you?' Caven said.

'You said to call you in the morning for the compass coordinates.'

'I have them in my office, you'll have to hold for a minute.'

Caven went upstairs. They were written down on a jotter beside his computer. 'You still there, Mr Ransome?'

'Yes.'

'Fifty-one degrees, forty-eight minutes, fifty seconds, north, one degree, fifty-six minutes, fifty-one seconds west.'

'Where the hell is that?'

'Somewhere in Gloucestershire, in the vicinity of Cirencester.'

'Is that the closest you get it?'

'Like I told you, it'll be accurate to within fifty feet. You need to avail yourself of an Ordnance Survey map.'

'I thought I paid you last night to tell me where she is.'

'You did and I've just told you. Now I'm going to finish my breakfast with my son. Good morning, Mr Ransome.'

Hugh Caven hung up and went back downstairs. He picked up the *Daily Mail* again and continued to stare at the page throughout the rest of the meal, eyes flicking occasionally to Sean. In his wallet was a cheque from his client for £5,000 that he badly needed. Where was the borderline between decency and betrayal?

You're a killer, Ross Ransome. You killed Barry Gatt just as surely as you killed this Lady Reynes-Rayleigh and others before her. Don't ask me how I know, but I do.

AT SOME TIME around seven, Alec had found a television. Faith had been aware of him slipping out of bed, then she had heard distant shouts, laughter.

She slept on and when she woke again it was half past nine. She smelt bacon. Oliver was standing in the bedroom, in jeans, trainers and a pink polo shirt. He looked tired.

'Morning,' he said, and kissed her tenderly. 'Open the curtains?'

'Please.'

'It's a real English summer's day out there.' It was blustery outside with spots of rain on the glass. He turned towards her, and they held each other's eyes.

'Thank you,' she said, 'for all you did last night.'

He looked awkward. 'We got away with it.' He raised his arms apologetically. 'Had to borrow some of Gerry's clothes—just came down in the suit I was wearing and that was it.' He grinned. 'So, how are you feeling?'

'Rested,' she said. 'My brain feels clearer. We're fugitives, right?'

'You've broken a Mental Health Act order and I've helped you. It would not be too smart to get caught.'

'And what happens now?'

'Breakfast. I made Alec a fry-up. Hope that was OK.'

'I think I'd like a fry-up too.'

'Good.' He looked pleased. 'You need to eat.'

She sat up in the large, soft, sleigh bed, exposed wooden beams above her head. 'What happens after breakfast?'

'I have to go to London, see a lawyer friend. We need to move fast.' He dug a small vial out of his pocket and held it up to her. It contained what looked like blood and had a handwritten label on it. 'This is a blood sample the ward sister at the Grove Hospital took from you last night and dated. I'm hoping it's going to show that you were pumped full of ketamine, an anaesthetising drug.'

Alarmed, Faith said, 'Do you have to go? What happens if you get caught?'

'I have the blood sample—the proof. And I don't know where you are. So what are they going to do? Torture me?'

She smiled. 'And if you don't come back?'

'I'll be back. In a few hours. You just have to sit tight. Don't use the phone because that can be traced back. If I need to speak to you I'll call you. I'll ring twice, hang up, then call again. OK?'

She nodded, with deep reluctance.

'Good girl. Now, one egg or two?'

'Two, please.'

They were good eggs, cooked well, and after Oliver left she continued to sit in front of the warm blue Aga, at the refectory table, listening to the squawking voices of the Cartoon Network on Sky on the television in the next-door room. She felt scared. She was trembling.

Alec walked into the kitchen. 'Can we go home soon?' he asked.

She stared out of the window. The sky was darkening and a sudden volley of rain spattered against the pane, rattling like lead shot. She thought, with a shiver of both cold and fear, I don't know where home is any more.

MARGARET HAD LEFT a message on his voicemail, saying that the phones at home were out of order and she needed to speak to him urgently. *Bloody woman.* How was he supposed to speak to her? He had called his mother-in-law three times at Little Scaynes Manor; each time the phone rang four times and voicemail kicked in.

Ross hung up again and dropped the mobile phone back onto the passenger seat of the rented silver grey Vauxhall. It was eleven o'clock. He'd already spoken to Lucinda and cancelled his day's work. As for the clinic's problems, they could go to hell.

Rain was sheeting down and London's traffic was all snarled up. The traffic was always worst on Fridays, and Grosvenor Square was clogged up. He jabbed the horn in frustration.

Caven had told him to look up the coordinates himself on an Ordnance Survey map. Great. Five thousand pounds and he had to buy his own bloody map. He'd been to three places in London so far: two had nothing; one had Ordnance Survey maps for every square inch of England except the Cirencester area.

The traffic was inching forward. He finally reached the far side of the square, passed the American embassy, then turned left into South Audley Street, parked on a yellow line as close as he could to Purdey's, the gunsmith's, and ran into the shop.

In the dignified, handsome interior, the assistant recognised him immediately. 'Mr Ransome, what can I do for you?'

'I brought in one of my guns ages ago to have a scratch removed from the stock. I should have collected it in May.'

'I'll go and find it.'

Ross waited, drumming his fingers on the wooden counter.

'Here we are!' The assistant was taking Ross's twelve-bore out of its leather gun case. 'I'll show you what we've done, Mr Ransome. I think we've managed to polish it out pretty well.'

'Looks fine. I also need a box of cartridges. Number Six shot.'

Ross asked for the gun and bullets to be put in a bag, handed him a credit card and signed the slip.

The next shop he wanted was only a few doors away. Its window displays announced that it sold spying equipment, everything from night-vision goggles to briefcases with in-built recorders. He went in and asked if they sold global positioning systems.

They sold him a receiver, which looked much like a mobile phone, and an attachment into which the assistant inserted a CD of Ordnance Survey maps covering Gloucestershire and much of the rest of the west of England. The assistant helped him program in the two sets of coordinates Hugh Caven had given him this morning, and showed him how to get the computer to read them.

When he returned to his car, in addition to the GPS he had bought a pair of military specification Zeiss binoculars, and a slim pencil torch, which he had already clipped inside his breast pocket. There was a parking ticket taped to the windscreen. Ross tore it off, dropped it into the gutter, then climbed back into the car.

He removed the receiver and the computer from their bag and looked at the screen closely, adjusting the brightness. He saw a village named Lower Chedworth. Roughly a mile to the west of the village he saw a long track, finishing at a building marked Ampney Nairey Farm, at the epicentre of the coordinates.

He started the car and threaded his way towards Park Lane, the Cromwell Road and the M4. The hatred inside him was intensifying with every minute. He could see images in his mind of Faith and Dr Oliver Cabot naked in bed together as he stood over them in the bedroom with his shotgun in his hands.

A small flashing display on his new GPS told him that he was

116.075 miles from the target destination. As he approached the Hammersmith flyover, Ross saw a garage on his left and pulled onto the forecourt. He bought a five-litre petrol can from the shop and filled it. He also bought a cheap plastic lighter.

OLIVER KNEW that he needed a lab he could trust not to ruin or lose the blood sample, one with an established reputation for forensic work, whose evidence would stand up in court.

He left the Jeep tucked safely among a mass of cars in Swindon station car park, and caught a train that would get him into London shortly after eleven thirty. He would have just enough time to get to the lab then on to a meeting with his solicitor.

He sat alone in a first-class compartment and made a call on his mobile to the house, using the code he had agreed.

'It's me,' he said, when Faith answered. 'How are things?'

She sounded tense. 'OK. How soon will you be back?'

'I'm on my way to London. I have to use a lab that's accredited with the police and I've fixed a meeting with my lawyer, Julian—his firm are the top medical specialists in the country. I want to get this section order lifted on you today somehow. How's Alec?'

'He's sitting in front of the wide-screen television watching Sky and eating caramel-crunch ice cream I found in the freezer. That's about as good as it gets for a small boy on a wet Friday morning.'

Oliver laughed. 'And you? No relapses from the drug?'

'Some weird flashes, and occasionally the floor moves around. Nothing else.'

He was pleased how normal she sounded. 'Is there anything you need?'

'No,' she said. 'Just you. I love you, Oliver. I really love you so much.' She was breaking up, sobbing.

'I love you too. Everything's going to be all right, Faith. I promise.'

AT TEN PAST ONE, Oliver and Julian Blake-Whitney were seated in a cramped booth at the back of a packed wine bar just off Chancery Lane. The solicitor wore a grey chalkstripe suit, a Jermyn Street shirt, sombre silk tie, and half-moon glasses.

Oliver, in his polo shirt, felt underdressed.

'I'm sorry to hear about your brother,' Blake-Whitney said.

'Yup. Tough call.' Oliver swallowed. He found it hard when people spoke of Harvey's death.

The solicitor gave a sympathetic grimace. 'Anyhow, you're looking well, Oliver, you haven't changed a jot.' He summoned a waitress and got the ordering out of the way so Oliver could talk him through the events of the past few weeks, and in particular of last night. Their food arrived as he was finishing.

'OK,' Blake-Whitney said. 'It's good that you had the nurse sign the vial. You've had this blood sample analysed?'

Oliver shook his head. 'The lab won't be able to get a result until Monday afternoon at the earliest.'

The solicitor tore off a chunk of garlic bread then, munching hungrily, said, 'Well, as it's Friday afternoon, we're not going to get anything in motion until Monday at the earliest. Mrs Ransome will have to be examined in advance by at least one independent doctor and we're looking at two weeks after that if we go for a Mental Health Act commission.'

'There's nothing you can do faster?'

'Unfortunately it's a damned sight easier to get someone sectioned than to get it reversed. In the meantime, as your lawyer, I have to advise you to return Mrs Ransome to the Grove Hospital.'

'No way, Julian. I'd only return her to the hospital if you got an injunction preventing her husband coming within a mile of her. So now give me some advice as my friend.'

'You're sure no one knows where this lady is, other than this chum of yours who lent you the place?'

'Absolutely.'

'Then go back to Gloucestershire, make yourself scarce, give me a phone number and we'll talk on Monday.'

'THERE WAS A GREY CAR, Oliver. It came up the drive.'

Faith was stammering and he could hear the fear in her voice.

'What kind of a car?'

'A saloon—I'm not sure—a Vauxhall maybe.'

'How close did it come to the house?'

'I don't know—a few hundred yards, then it turned round. I saw it driving away.'

'How long ago?'

'About an hour.'

Concerned now, Oliver said, 'What car does Ross drive?'

'A blue Aston Martin.'

'So it wasn't Ross, right? Anyhow, Ross has no idea you're there.'

'Please come back quickly, Oliver, I'm really scared.'

'Are the doors and windows locked?'

'All of them.'

'Listen, Faith, don't worry. I'll be there as quickly as I can.'

IN HIS OFFICE overlooking the back garden of his home, Hugh Caven was staring at the rain on the paddling pool. He had just come off the phone after a traumatic conversation with Barry Gatt's widow.

The coroner was releasing Barry's body, and Steph had arranged the funeral for next Tuesday. He knew how hard up she was, and had persuaded her to allow him to pay for Barry's funeral, since Barry had died while in his employ.

His conscience was troubling him and it had been all day. Ross Ransome was a dangerous bastard. He was regretting having given him those compass coordinates. If Ransome was behind the killing of Cabot's brother and Barry Gatt, who was to say he wasn't intending to finish the job off?

Why the hell else would he want the coordinates?

Caven dialled New Scotland Yard and asked to be put through to the incident room for the Cabot and Gatt murders.

BITCH! Ross could see her clearly now, through the binoculars. He was lying, shielded by a clump of ferns, in a ditch close to the track, with a clear view of the house. A long green Barbour jacket, waterproof trousers, Wellington boots and a rain hat, which he'd bought in an outdoor shop in Cirencester an hour ago, were keeping out most of the weather, except for one persistent trickle of water down the back of his neck.

He thought back to the good times, those early years when they had been happy together. Before Dr Cabot had come on the scene.

Where are you, Dr Cabot? Is your car hidden away in the garage?

She was in what looked like a kitchen, wearing some kind of blue top, and her hair could have been tidier.

You look like a slut, today, Faith. Is that what Dr Oliver Cabot does to you? Makes you into a slut?

His mind went back twenty-eight years. To when he was a small boy. He remembered finding his mother lying on the bed in her small, grim flat, with her legs around her lover's waist.

A sharp clatter some way behind him startled him. The sound of wheels on a cattle grid, he realised, and now the sound of an engine. A vehicle travelling quickly.

He could see it now. A blue Jeep Cherokee, passing just yards from him, a tall man with grey curly hair driving.

Through the binoculars he watched the Jeep pull up outside the house. Faith, his beloved Faith, was there, opening the door to Dr Oliver Cabot, welcoming him back to their love nest.

You are going to be sorry, both of you.

He swung the binoculars. She was in that kitchen window again now. Dr Oliver Cabot was standing next to her. Faith was pointing in this direction, they were talking, discussing something.

For an instant he panicked that they could see him.

Impossible. The car was safely hidden away, parked in the thick of a copse, out of sight from every direction.

It was now ten to five. How long were they going to remain here? They had stayed last night, which meant they thought they were safe. He had a feeling they'd be here tonight as well.

If the weather held, it would be a dark night. The wind and the rain were a real bonus: they would mask any sounds he made.

'MUMMY, can I show you something? Please!' Alec stood at the bottom of the stairs, breathless with excitement. 'Can I? Can I?'

In the huge living room, Oliver was kneeling down, trying to light the wood-burning stove. Faith, relaxing on a sofa, was sipping a glass of Australian chardonnay that tasted like nectar.

It was the first alcohol she had drunk in almost a week, and the wine was going to her head. It was a good feeling. She felt safe now Oliver was back, and the room was filling with the crackling sounds and the cosy smell of burning kindling.

She smiled. 'What is it you want to show me, darling?'

'You have to come up and see it.'

Alec had been good all day, watching either Cartoon Network or the Trouble channel, and exploring the house.

'OK,' she said. 'Let's go—it had better be good!'

Standing up, she realised how tired she felt.

Alec scampered up the oak staircase and she followed him slowly, up to the galleried landing. The room Oliver had slept in was to the left, and the one she had shared with Alec was straight ahead. Alec ran down to the right and in through a door.

She followed him, and found herself in another bedroom, attractively decorated with antique pine furniture.

'Mummy's very tired, darling. What am I meant to be looking at?'

He ducked into a wardrobe and came out with a long pole with a hook on the end, then stared upwards. Faith followed his gaze and saw a loft door.

'Alec, I don't think this is a good—'

But he was already hooking the pole into the metal eye on the door. He gave a sharp tug and the hatch door lowered. A compacted metal ladder was attached to it. With another flick of the pole he had the ladder telescoping open to the floor. He began to climb up it.

'Alec, darling, I—'

He disappeared through the hatch. Never comfortable with heights, Faith gripped the ladder and climbed.

When she reached the top she stared round in amazement. It was a kid's paradise. A huge insulated loft with a wooden floor, a bed with a Batman cover, and toys bulging out of an open trunk. At the far end, side by side, were a huge electric train set and Scalextric track.

'The man said I could sleep up here tonight, Mummy. Can I?'

'Oliver said you could sleep up here?'

Alec nodded. 'Please can I?'

She went over to the bed and pulled back the counterpane. It was all made up and the sheets were bone dry. 'This isn't our house, I don't think we should use this bed.'

'The man said I could.' He went over to the Scalextric, pressed a switch, then picked up one of the controls and squeezed the button. With a sharp whir a sports car hurtled along the track and somersaulted off on a bend. 'Have a race with me.'

'Later. I'm going to get your supper now.'

Faith went downstairs into the living room. 'Alec's up in a loft that's full of toys,' she told Oliver. 'He said you'd told him he could sleep up there—did you?'

'If he wants to, sure. Gerry keeps the place for any kids who come down. He has a raft of nephews, nieces and godchildren who visit.'

She caught the look in his eye, and grinned. 'If he sleeps up there, we might get to spend a little time together?'

'Had crossed my mind.'

She put her arms around him, held him tightly, then stood on tiptoe and kissed the tip of his nose and his lips. 'I think that's a very good idea,' she murmured. 'Much the best idea you've had all day.'

THE LUMINOUS HANDS of his watch said ten to nine. There was light coming from three windows in the house: the kitchen window where he had seen the bitch looking out, a window beside the front door, and a Velux window up in the roof.

Ross raised his binoculars, training them on the house, lowering them. *Come on, you bitch, you have to come into the kitchen sometime, you need to feed your lover.*

At twenty past ten Faith came into the kitchen, and pressed her face up against the glass, staring out, looking worried. Then Dr Oliver Cabot came and stood behind her. Ross could see them, framed, as if he was watching them on television. Cabot slipped his arms around her waist and nuzzled her ear.

You're trying to ruin my life, Dr Oliver Cabot. You are screwing my wife and you are polluting her mind. You are killing her, you selfish bastard. Killing her with your charlatan mumbo jumbo.

Ross churned with anger. He lowered the binoculars. His chest was pounding and the whole night was a blur in his eyes as he marched back to the boot of the car, opened it, and with the light of his pencil torch, removed his shotgun from its carrying case, loaded it, and shovelled extra cartridges into each pocket. Then he took out the can of petrol and slammed the boot lid.

With the can in one hand and the gun in the other, he walked towards the house. After a few moments, the kitchen light went off. He walked at a steady pace, eyes fixed on the house.

He reached the cattle grid and stopped. Light spilled out onto the gravel ahead from the window by the front door. Too risky to walk on gravel, too much noise. Boots squelching on the boggy grass, he went round the side of the house to the back.

There was a light on in an upstairs room behind drawn curtains, and weaker light still showed through the Velux window in the roof. Keeping close to the house, he walked along, pausing to test a door, which was locked, then detoured around a massive rhododendron and approached a window. He shone the torch into it and saw a small study, with a desk, computer, photographs on the walls. The door was shut. This was good.

The wind was howling, tugging at his hat. The windows were all shut, but the panes were large. He set down the petrol can, held the gun by the barrel and waited. When the next gust struck, the wind howling even louder, he rammed the butt against the glass.

The crash sounded as loud to him as an entire greenhouse collapsing. He moved away from the window, pressed himself flat against the wall and waited, trying to hear voices, movement, anything above the wind and the roar of blood in his ears.

He didn't know how long he stood there. Five minutes, maybe ten. Still the same lights on, no sign that anyone had heard him.

He went back to the study window. There was a low sill, with a cloisonné vase which he moved to one side. He also tugged away a few jagged shards of glass and dropped them on the lawn. Then, holding the torch in his mouth, he climbed in quietly and reached out for his gun and the petrol. He laid them both on the carpeted floor and removed his Wellington boots.

He went to the door, lifted the latch, and peered out. He saw a long passageway and a closed door at the far end. No sign of anyone.

He carried the gun and the can into the passage, then closed the door behind him. In the silence as he walked he could hear the petrol sloshing about in the can. And there was another sound, right above him. A creaking sound. Steady, rhythmic.

He looked up, his mouth dry with hatred. Then he quickened his pace. Light spilled beneath the door at the end of the passageway. In his rough calculations of the geography of the place, he decided this must be the light from the entrance hall.

He was right. The door opened onto a wide hall, with a beamed ceiling, terracotta floor tiles, several fine Italian marble statues on plinths. A wooden staircase led up to the next floor.

Above him, he heard a moan as gentle as a summer breeze.

The creaking sound was louder now, and faster.

Then it stopped, abruptly. He looked up, confused. Suddenly he was eleven years old again. He was in the kitchen of a small flat; dirty plates were piled in the sink. He could hear his mother's voice, unmistakably her voice, crying out, 'Oh, yes, don't stop, oh, God, keep doing that!' In his right hand the young Ross held a heavy oil can with a round screw cap. It contained a gallon of petrol that he had siphoned from the tank of his father's Morris. In his pocket he had a box of matches. In his heart, hatred burned.

He climbed the stairs swiftly, stealthily, then stood at the top listening to his mother's voice coming through the door.

'Yes, oh, yes, do that!'

Ross unscrewed the cap on the can, and walked the length of the landing, pouring the petrol steadily out. Then he stood at the top of the stairs, listening to the screams of pleasure, and watched petrol flow down each of the wooden treads.

Scream, bitch. You'll be screaming differently in a minute.

'Oh, God, yes! Oh, yes, don't stop, oh, God, keep doing that!'

He opened the bedroom door, and let the last of the petrol gurgle out, watched it spread across the bare oak boards towards the bed. There was just a cosy glow in the room from one bedside lamp. In its light he could see two figures asleep. His bitch wife and Dr Oliver Cabot. Now, suddenly, they weren't asleep any more. He was back in his mother's bedroom, watching the white bony buttocks of a strange naked man pumping between her thighs. Saw her bare legs around his waist, her back arched, her hair scattered around the pillow, her cheeks red with exertion.

He let the can fall with a clank to the floor, and that was when Faith woke up and saw him.

'Oliver!'

The scream of terror was sweet music to his ears.

Dr Oliver Cabot was awake now, too, blinking in confusion. They were both sitting up in the bed, mouths open, holding the sheet up to their necks, trying to keep themselves covered.

He held the gun tightly, pointing it straight towards them.

'*Ross. No, Ross. No, please, Ross.*'

Ross smiled. For the first time in a very long time he felt calm. 'Get out of the bed, Faith, and put your clothes on.'

The charlatan smelt it first. Ross saw his eyes widen even more. Then the bitch smelt it.

'Oh, no, no, Ross, don't do this. Please, Ross, no.'

'I said, get out of bed and put your clothes on, slut.'

Without taking her eyes from his face, she slipped out, stooped, picked up her knickers, lost her balance trying to put them on and had to clutch a bedpost.

'Mr Ransome,' the charlatan said, 'don't harm your wife. I'm the guilty one. Let's talk about this.'

'Shut up,' Ross screamed, aiming the gun even more closely. 'One word and I shoot.' He turned back to Faith. 'Come on, hurry! You got them off fast enough.'

'Mr Ransome—' Oliver Cabot said.

Ross pulled the disposable lighter he had bought at the petrol station from his pocket and brandished it. 'I said shut up.'

Oliver stared at him in silence, eyes darting from him to Faith.

Faith had on her jeans and was pulling on her blue knitted top.

'Tie him up,' Ross said.

Trembling she said, 'How—how do you mean?'

Ross saw a dressing gown at the end of the bed. He reached forward, stripped the belt out of the loops and threw it at her. 'Around his wrist, then around one of those posts.'

Swinging the gun from Faith to Dr Oliver Cabot, Ross marched across the room to a wardrobe with sliding doors. He pulled one open and saw a rack of ties. He yanked a bunch down and flung them at her. 'Tie him with those.'

'Mr Ransome—Ross—' Oliver said.

Ross whipped the barrels of the gun into Oliver's jaw. 'I said silence!'

Faith tied Oliver, as Ross directed, an arm to each post and a leg to each post. Blood dribbled from Oliver's mouth. Faith looked at her husband. 'Please talk to me, Ross. This isn't any way forward for anyone—this is crazy.'

'Get out of the room, bitch.'

Faith looked at Oliver with desperation in her eyes, then back at Ross. 'I'm not leaving him, Ross.'

'Get outside.'

'No.'

Ross held up the lighter, his hand shaking. Faith looked at his face, at the gun, then at the lighter. There was a flicker of something in her eyes, and before he had any chance to work it out she launched herself at him, sinking her teeth into his hand.

With a howl of pain he released the lighter, which fell to the floor, and squeezed the gun's trigger. Nothing happened.

And he knew, in that split second, what the bitch had seen. He'd taken her shooting clays in the past, and she knew this gun. She'd seen that the safety catch was on.

Faith jabbed her thumb into his eye, and punched him with her free hand, then again. He staggered and went over backwards.

Pushing herself away from him, she grabbed the gun, and threw herself at the door. Out on the landing, she crashed against the banisters. Turned. Ross was lurching towards her. She lifted the barrels of the gun towards him, then realised. The petrol. Mustn't fire.

She hurled herself down the stairs, and ran over to the front door. *No!* Oliver had put on the safety chain.

Ross was halfway down the stairs now. She yanked at the chain, pressed the release button, grabbed the latch and the door opened.

His hand grabbed her by the throat, her legs were kicked away, and she fell face first onto the gravel. She heard the gun clatter down somewhere beside her, but before she could do anything, Ross was stumbling to his feet with the gun in his hands.

She stood, blocking the door. 'No, Ross, don't do this.'

He raised the barrels at her. 'Move out of the way.'

Suddenly, finding strength from deep inside her she said, furiously, 'Ross, you are bloody well going to listen to me.'

For an instant he looked startled by her sudden change of tone.

Softening her tone she said, 'Ross, if all these things you've ever said to me about how much you love me are true, then you've got to turn round and walk away from here. You have to let me go, so I can live whatever I have left of my life the way I want to. If you kill Oliver, Ross, you are killing me.'

Ross stared at Faith, then at the tiny red sight at the end of the barrels, then back at her. He saw her lying on her back with her ankles around the naked waist of Dr Oliver Cabot, heard her moans of pleasure . . . And then another sound. A wailing that was getting louder. A siren. He turned his head and over his shoulder saw a spangle of blue light shoot across the darkness.

'You called the police!' He hardened his grip on the gun.

'I didn't—for God's sake, how could I?'

He raised the barrels so the red sight was dead centre between her breasts. Then something hurled her sideways. The charlatan was coming out of the door, hurtling headlong at him.

Ross jabbed the safety catch, squeezed the trigger. The deafening boom of the gun sounded right in his ear as he crashed forward over Cabot's body.

The interior of the house erupted in flames. And searing heat singed his hair, sucked the air from his lungs.

Alec! Ross, our son is in there.'

Ross knew from Faith's voice she was telling the truth. Frantic, she ran towards the raging flames, and he stumbled after her, hauled her back, feeling the heat on his face. 'Where?'

'In the loft, you bloody fool.' She turned on him, raining punches on his face. 'Let me go! Let me go! My son, he's in there!'

Trying to hold her at bay, he said, 'How do you get to the loft?'

She tore free, ran again to the inferno in the doorway. Ross grabbed her and punched her in the face, knocking her out cold.

'You goddamn madman, your kid's in there.'

He turned. Dr Oliver Cabot was standing, dazed, blood pouring from his mouth and the top of his head where a swathe of his hair had gone as if he'd been scalped.

Ross pushed him away, ran to the right looking for a way in that was free of flames. The window he had broken. At the back.

He sprinted round the side of the house, calling frantically, 'Alec! Alec! Alec!' He climbed back in through the broken study window. No flames here yet. Then he crossed to the door he had shut earlier and opened it.

He'd operated in the past on burns victims who'd done exactly the same thing: they'd opened a door from a room with an open window, giving a fire the fuel it needed. Creating a tunnel of oxygen.

The solid wall of fire avalanched down the passageway towards him, sucked the air from Ross's lungs, and pulled him, screaming, right into the searing, blinding vortex of the flames.

Oliver, climbing up a drainpipe, heard an explosion of glass below him, and looked down. A man, alight from head to foot, was running in a crazed zigzag across the grass. *'Alec!'* the figure screeched.

Oliver looked away. He had to keep going up. *Alec, I'm coming, just hold on, I'm coming.*

Choking on the dense smoke rising all around him, he got one hand on the guttering, scrabbled for a foothold, found a tiny ledge, levered himself higher. Then somehow, he was up on the roof, climbing up the slippery tiles. At last he reached the Velux where the light was coming from, in the loft roof.

Through the glass he could see Alec standing by his bed in his pyjamas, flames licking up through the hatch. If he broke the glass, he risked a fireball. He ripped a tile from the roof and rapped on the window with it. Alec looked up.

Oliver pressed his face close to the glass and yelled, 'Alec! It's me, Oliver! Alec, you are going to have to be brave. Get a pillowslip, soak it in the washbasin, put it over your head, then reach down and pull that hatch shut.'

Alec shook his head, stammering with fear. 'No, no, no.'

'Alec, come close. Can you see me, Alec? Can you see who it is?'

The boy nodded.

Behind him, Oliver could see the flames starting to catch on the beams above the hatch entrance. 'OK, Alec, I want you to be calm, I want you to be calm. Look at my eyes, just keep watching my eyes, don't look at anything else, eyes, just my eyes.'

He was engaging him now. 'My eyes, just keep watching my eyes, just be calm, don't listen to anything but my voice, be calm, think about your eyes, just your eyes on my eyes, keep calm, keep your eyes on my eyes and do what I tell you. We're going to play a game. This is an important game. Keep your eyes on my eyes, keep your thoughts on my thoughts.' Staring at the boy, concentrating as hard as he could, Oliver continued for a full minute until he could see from the dilation of the boy's pupils that he was now under hypnosis.

'We are going to play fire-fighters, Alec. You are going to take a pillowslip, soak it in cold water, put it over your head, and go over to pull that hatch shut. Do that now, then come back.'

Alec did exactly as he had been told. He walked without fear towards the hatch, put the pillowslip over his head, ducked down, pulled up the ladder, and slammed the hatch door shut.

Oliver smashed the glass, grabbed the child, removed the pillowslip, scooped him into his arms and swung him up onto his back. He told Alec to hold on tight. He climbed down the roof. There was a ferocious crackle in the air and a smell of burning paint. All around him sparks and smouldering embers floated in the air. He inched his way down until his feet reached the guttering. Miraculously, the one part of the house that wasn't burning was directly beneath him.

A police car was parked just short of the cattle grid. He could see Faith slumped in the front passenger seat. No sign of Ross.

'Hey!' he yelled. 'Hey! Help! Help!'

Seconds later a beam was shining in his face. Then he saw two police officers below him. He yelled, 'There's a ladder—'

His voice was drowned in a massive roar, as if he was standing on an erupting volcano. The roof was moving. The house was collapsing. Both officers looked up in horror and stepped back. One cupped his hands and yelled, 'Jump!'

In sheer panic, Oliver lobbed Alec, like some giant rugby ball, straight at them, then leaped as far out into the darkness as he could.

*e*pilogue

Hugh Caven was restless. Among the envelopes in the morning post was one he didn't like the look of: a buff, letter-sized envelope with a police crest on the outside.

He didn't know what it contained, but there was a possibility it was to do with the bugging of Dr Oliver Cabot's flat.

He remembered back in June when he'd finally taken the plunge and phoned Detective Sergeant Anson, now promoted to Detective Inspector. It had seemed to him that the policeman was more interested in the fact that he had illegally entered Cabot's flat than in his information that Ross Ransome might be linked to the murders of Barry Gatt and Harvey Cabot. But Anson had taken down the compass coordinates and the address in Gloucestershire where Caven thought Ransome was going, and where he had warned Anson that there might be an ugly scene.

He took the post upstairs to his office, lit a cigarette and ripped open the envelope.

Notting Hill Police Station

5 September 1999
Dear Mr Caven,
Reference: 37 Ladbroke Avenue, London.

I am writing with respect to your activities in unlawfully entering the premises of Dr Oliver Cabot in June of this year, and in placing illegal surveillance devices in these premises.

Having given consideration to all the circumstances, I have decided to take no further action on this matter. However, I must warn you formally that any recurrence of offences of this nature will be viewed seriously, in light of your previous record.

Yours sincerely,
Detective Inspector D. G. Anson

NINE MONTHS LATER, Hugh Caven received a second letter from the same Senior Investigating Officer.

Notting Hill Police Station

8 June 2000
Dear Mr Caven,

I have the pleasant duty of informing you that a reward was offered in June of last year for information leading to the arrest and successful prosecution of the killer or killers of Professor Harvey Cabot. The award was sponsored by the late Professor Cabot's brother, Dr Oliver Cabot.

Our investigations have led us to conclude that the prime suspect, responsible also for the unlawful killing of Mr Barry Gatt, is now deceased. These same investigations, partly as a result of information supplied by yourself, have resulted in the issuing of a warrant for the arrest of Mr Ross Ransome, of Little Scaynes Manor, Little Scaynes, West Sussex, on a charge of conspiracy to murder.

As Mr Ransome's medical condition is such that it has as yet not been possible to serve any warrant, nor does it seem likely he will ever be in a fit state of health to attend trial, I am instructed by Dr Oliver Cabot to inform you that he would like to make you an *ex gratia* payment of £10,000 (ten thousand pounds sterling) as a token of his gratitude for your contribution.

If you are willing to accept this award, kindly contact the undersigned at your convenience.

Yours sincerely,
Detective Inspector D. G. Anson

THE CHEQUE ARRIVED ten days later. Hugh Caven paid it in at his bank. He allowed five days for the cheque to clear, then drew out the entire amount in cash.

Late that same night, he drove to the street where Barry Gatt's widow lived with her three small sons. He parked a distance away, so that he wouldn't be spotted if she looked out of a window. He was relieved to see that no lights were on in her little house.

He pushed the cash through the letterbox in a bag, then returned to his car. As he headed home, he kept the radio switched off, preferring to listen to the music playing inside his head. It was an old Bob Dylan song, and as he drove, singing the words with the window open and the air blasting his face, a weight lifted from his heart and began blowing in the wind.

IN THE SMALL ROOM in the burns unit of East Grinstead hospital, Faith glanced at the nurse, then back at the figure in the bed. Ross Ransome was a rare case, and the sheer strength of his will to live had amazed everyone. Few people survived sixty per cent burns. Yet two years on, Ross was still alive after suffering almost seventy per cent burns. He lay on his back and the only sound he made was a long, low moan.

Life-support had been switched off with Faith's consent as next-of-kin, three months after that June day when he had been transferred here, suffering second- and third-degree burns and severe damage to his internal airways and organs, in particular the kidneys and, by far the most serious, his brain. His vision had gone, but EEG tests showed that he still retained some hearing. The skin across almost all of his torso, arms, legs and head had fibrosed into scar tissue.

Ironically, instead of weakening and gradually slipping away, as the medics had expected, his pulse, month by month, got a little stronger. No one knew whether he was capable of feeling pain, but he was kept on a morphine drip.

Patches of his body were still covered in bandages. For the past two years he had undergone an endless series of grafts, as his former colleagues fought a constant battle against areas of his skin dying because of his damaged circulation.

Faith wasn't sure why she had come. The hospital said he had been calling her name as if he had something he urgently needed to say, but the thought of seeing him had scared her. He still wielded power over her, the power to come to her in her dreams and frighten her.

And she had seen the evidence that had been amassed against him on some of his patients, though it didn't appear likely he would ever be brought to trial. She slept badly most nights, lying in bed, thinking, unravelling those years of her marriage to him, looking for the signs and clues pointing to the monster she had failed to see. Oliver reminded her repeatedly of the words of the philosopher Sören Kierkegaard, that life can only be understood backwards but it must be lived forwards.

Standing as far away from Ross as the small room allowed, she watched him warily, glad of the company of the nurse, scared that somehow, even in this state, he could reach out and harm her.

One of the hardest things to bear had been Alec's persistent questions about his father, but they were becoming less frequent. She'd decided from the start to stick as close to the truth as she could. She told him his daddy had been badly injured and was in hospital a long way away, and did not want Alec to see him until he got better.

Oliver was good with him and Alec was clearly fond of him, but there were still times when she could see sadness on his face.

The words came out suddenly, sharp and clear. 'How's Alec?'

Faith wondered if she had imagined it, but she could see that the nurse had heard him too.

In a trembling voice, Faith said, 'He's fine.'

There was no response, just the ragged sounds of Ross's breathing.

She waited a full minute, maybe longer and then, she couldn't help it, tears welled in her eyes. 'He's just had his eighth birthday party,' she said. 'We had a bouncy castle, a conjuror and a barbecue.'

She glanced at the nurse, who encouraged her with a nod to continue. 'He scored thirty runs in cricket at school last week. He's going to be a good sportsman, just like his dad. He's shooting up now, too. He's going to be tall and strong, like you.'

She dug into her handbag, pulled out a handkerchief and wiped her eyes. 'And do you know what he said the other day? He told me he wants to be a doctor when he grows up. He said he's going to be a plastic surgeon, just like you. He wants to fix that bump on my nose—the one I got after you biffed me in the face to stop me running into the burning house to try to get him.'

Tears were flooding down her face. She turned away, racked with emotion, walked out of the door and quickly down the corridor.

THREE MONTHS LATER, on a fine autumnal morning, in the middle of breakfast, Faith received a phone call from the hospital, telling her that Ross had died during the night.

She thanked the duty houseman and hung up, unsure how she felt. Relief, certainly, but it was more complicated than that. Oliver would understand the jumble of emotions inside her; he seemed to understand so much about people, about life.

Heavy-hearted, she sat down at the kitchen table of the house Oliver had bought near Hampstead Heath, and watched Alec munching his cereal. Rasputin sat by his feet, ever hopeful that a stray cluster of granola might fall his way. He was usually lucky.

Both she and Ross had been living on borrowed time. In a way, all of them were, Alec, her mother and Oliver included. All of life was borrowed time, really.

It was two years and four months since her first diagnosis of Lendt's disease. The check-ups were down to every three months now. The last two had been clear. There were people who went into remission only to have the disease return and wipe them out, but two years was pretty much the outer limit. She had no way of telling whether the route she had chosen with Oliver Cabot was the right one to beat the disease, but every time she questioned it in her mind she remembered a conversation she'd had right at the start of her treatment from him.

'At this clinic we're not against science, Faith, anything but. Science is just a method of getting at the truth. But we also know that we're treating people, not cars. And we know from a number of well-run studies that if we make the mind feel good, with massage, good music, pure, natural foods and, of course, love, the body will have a much better chance of healing.'

'Is that what you want to do to me, Dr Cabot, cure me with love?' she had asked.

'Mummy, we're going to be late for school.'

Faith looked up and stared at her son through a mist of tears.

'Why are you crying?' he asked. 'Are you sad?'

She nodded. 'Mummy's sad this morning. She's very, very sad. But she's also happy.'

'You can't be happy and sad at the same time.'

'You can,' she said, dabbing her eyes with a napkin. 'It's a secret they don't teach you at school.'

She stood up. 'Come on, get your bag and your coat. You're right—you *are* going to be late.'

'What else don't they teach you at school, Mummy?'

She grabbed the keys off the hook on the dresser, got Alec's coat on him and his bag over his shoulder, then scooped her son out of the door.

In the car he repeated the question.

She didn't reply. The journey was too short and the answer was too long.

PETER JAMES

Peter James has been labelled 'the British Stephen King' in the press. Although the author has reservations about being pigeon-holed as a horror writer, he does share King's passionate interest in the occult and the supernatural, different aspects of which have have inspired his novels, including *Host*, *Alchemist* and *Prophecy*.

Recently, however, with his thrillers *Denial* and *Faith*, he has begun to move away from the paranormal. In *Faith*, for example, he explores the conflict between conventional and alternative medicine. About a year ago he was researching a book on alternative therapies when his mother became terminally ill with cancer. He encouraged her to try less conventional treatments as well as those prescribed by her consultant, and is convinced that they not only helped to prolong her life, but also improved its quality.

'I was surprised by the arrogance I came across in the medical profession. There are some very negative attitudes towards alternative medicine out there, and I've met a lot of Ross Ransomes,' he says, referring to the sinister doctor in *Faith*. 'Conventional medicine has improved our lives immeasurably over the past hundred years, 'particularly when it comes to things like infections or pain control. But it's also true that we have too much faith in it.'

As well as being fascinated by medicine and the paranormal, Peter James is also interested in science and technology. He is currently working on a new novel about genetic engineering. 'The potential for abuse is enormous in that field. In one sense, you can't progress without taking risks, but it's difficult to achieve a balance between risk-taking and the abuse of power.'

The author is also a successful feature film-maker and television and radio broadcaster who ran his own film company in Canada for a number of years, and in 1993 co-founded Pavilion Internet, one of the first internet companies in Britain. He now lives just outside Lewes on the South Downs with his partner Helen, her two teenage daughters and his Hungarian puli sheepdog called Bertie.

Eddie's Bastard

WILLIAM KOWALSKI

Old Thomas Mann always considered it would be a 'damn shame' if he was the last of the Manns, the end of a line of entrepreneurs, daredevils and wartime super-heroes. So when he finds a baby abandoned on his doorstep, with a note telling him the child is his grandson, his heart is filled with joy.

A new life. Another chance for the Manns to achieve the greatness they were destined for.

I arrived in this world the way most bastards do—by surprise. That's the only fact about myself that I knew at the beginning of my life. At the very beginning, of course, I knew nothing. Later, as I grew older and learned things, I began to make certain connections, and thus I discovered that among children I was unusual. Where others had a mother, I had none; father, same; birth certificate, none; name, unknown. And as soon as I was old enough to understand that babies didn't just appear from midair, I understood that my arrival was not just a mystery to myself. It was a strange occurrence to everyone who knew me.

Nobody seemed to know where I was born, or exactly when, or to whom. In the space for *mother* there is nothing but a blank. I know who my father is—or was, rather. He was Eddie Mann, Lieutenant, USAF (dec.). The 'dec.' stands for deceased.

In my imagination I see my mother, a pregnant young girl, panicked but with a strong conscience and some desire to see me succeed in life. She gives birth to me in secret somewhere. Then, after I'm born, she—a princess, a faerie queen, Amelia Earhart—deposits me on the back steps of the ancestral Mann home in Mannville, New York, where my father had been born and raised, as had his father, and his father before him. This is where my imagination is relieved of duty and the facts take over. This part of the story really happened.

It was August 3, 1970. My grandfather, the failed entrepreneur Thomas Mann, Jr. (no relation to the writer of the same name), who lived alone and abandoned in the farmhouse, found me there. Like some character in a Dickens novel, I'd been wrapped in a blanket and placed inside a picnic basket. Many years later I was to discover that Grandpa had saved the basket, a deed for which I've always been profoundly grateful. For years it was my greatest treasure. It was the one thing in the world I was sure my mother had touched.

It was just after dawn, and the day was Grandpa's birthday. Grandpa celebrated his birthday the way he celebrated every other day: he drank whiskey sitting alone at the ancient kitchen table. He drank whiskey in the morning, for his lunch, before dinner and after dinner. Sometimes he didn't bother to eat dinner at all. Eating sobered him up, and that was unpleasant; he preferred to be drunk. But today there was something unusual going on, something to break the monotony of his drunkenness. It was my crying. Grandpa heard it dimly, out of the corner of his ear, as it were. It sounded familiar. It was a noise he'd heard before, but couldn't quite place.

'Chickens,' he said to himself. I know he said this, because later he was to tell me the story over and over again. There were no chickens on our farm, hadn't been for years, but sometimes he forgot this. Grandpa, when drunk, remembered better days, when the farm was still operating, crops were still growing, ostriches had yet to wreak their havoc upon our future, and chickens roamed free. In Grandpa's inebriated mind chickens meant hope, and they had to be protected.

So he interrupted his drinking. He stepped out of the kitchen door to see if there were foxes in the chicken coop, which, though long deserted, still stood. Instead of foxes, however, he found me.

Years afterwards Grandpa told me he'd nearly stepped on me as he came out of the door. The sudden roar of a jet overhead caused him to stop his foot in midair as he looked up. It saved my life.

'Thank God for that jet,' Grandpa said, 'or I would have squashed you like the little bug you were.'

It was a military jet, an F-4 Phantom, the same kind of fighter jet my father, Eddie, flew in Vietnam. Grandpa recognised it as an F-4 from the photo Eddie had sent home several months earlier. In that photo my father is standing in front of his plane, a hotshot, a pilot *extraordinaire*. He was just twenty-one years old. He's bare-chested and muscular, teeth bared in a dazzling smile. The blueness of his eyes is noticeable even on black-and-white film.

There was no doubt in Grandpa's mind about whose son I was. I had the same eyes as my father, and Grandpa recognised them immediately. 'Mann eyes are always blue,' he said later as he was telling me the story of my arrival. 'And they're not the same blue as other families. Take the Simpsons up the hill. They've got eyes like muddy water. Blue but muddy. You can tell everything about a man by his eyes. As for those Simpsons—stay away from them. Folks with eyes like that have got plenty to hide.'

On that summer morning in 1970 Grandpa stopped and stared, completely astounded, at the spectacle of a baby in a basket on his doorstep. He looked around suspiciously. Nobody was in sight. The property, though not as large as it had been before the Fiasco of the Ostriches, was still large, and it would have been easy for anyone to hide behind one of the many trees and bushes scattered throughout the vast yard. But there was no one. Some poor young girl had left me there, Grandpa was thinking; doubtless she had her reasons.

Already his mind was working, turning over various possibilities. Eddie had had a lot of girlfriends; the girls of Mannville fell for him like dominoes. No one could blame them. My father was irresistibly handsome.

Grandpa focused back on me. Scotch-taped to my basket was a note. On one side it said in large printed letters: EDDIE'S BASTARD.

Well now, Grandpa thought, that's not a very nice way of putting it. On the other side, in meticulous Palmer script, the note read:

July 15, 1970
1 gallon milk
1/4 lb. cheese
1/2 doz. apples
1 loaf bread

It was a receipt from Gruber's Grocery. Grandpa could show the note to Harold and Emily Gruber and ask if they remembered who had bought these items on July 15. That way he could find out who had left me on the steps.

But he would do that later. At the moment my wailing filled him with paternal tenderness and anxiety. He picked up the basket, brought me inside, and set me on the kitchen table.

'Ah, Eddie,' he said, 'if only you'd lived long enough to see him.'

Then, Grandpa said, he began to cry, because my handsome and popular father had been shot down over the South China Sea months earlier, and no parachute had been sighted.

We sat crying together, Grandpa and I, the last remnants of the once great Mann family—I because I was hungry and Grandpa because he was sad. Then Grandpa dried his eyes, put me in the front seat of his Galaxie, and drove to the doctor's office in town.

The doctor's office was the first floor of the doctor's house, and Dr

Connor was Grandpa's best—in fact, his only—friend. Dr Connor looked up in surprise as Grandpa came marching through his front parlour with a screaming infant in a basket.

'Give 'im the once-over and see if he needs a tune-up,' said Grandpa, who was always a mechanic at heart. 'I aim to keep him.'

'Where in the hell—?' asked the doctor, interrupting his own question by peering into the basket at me.

'I don't know for sure,' said Grandpa. 'But he's a Mann. You can see that a mile off.'

'There's tests for that now, if you want me to run one,' said Dr Connor as he tickled the bottoms of my feet. My toes curled.

'I don't need any test to know my own flesh and blood,' said Grandpa. 'You just make sure everything's where it's supposed to be. I'll be right back. I got to go get some Formula One.'

'Formula,' Dr Connor said. 'Formula One is a racing car.'

'Right,' said Grandpa. 'Formula, then.' He was still drunk, but he was all business.

There had been no babies in the Mann home for over twenty years. There were tricks, secrets, inside information that one needed to know to raise a baby, and of the members of Grandpa's generation these secrets were known largely only by women.

Had Grandpa's wife still been around, no doubt she would have taken over the business of raising me. But she—my grandmother—was no longer present; she'd simply disappeared one day when my father, Eddie, was still little, just after the Fiasco of the Ostriches, and Grandpa had never heard from her again. He would have to do the best he could on his own.

Grandpa went to Gruber's and bought baby things, searching his memory for what else a growing boy might need besides formula: diapers, safety pins, bottles, talcum powder, a rattle, strained food, several beginning reader's books, and a .22-calibre rifle. He found himself growing more excited by the minute, leaping ahead in years to when I would be a young man.

'Havin' a baby, Tom?' asked Harold Gruber as he rang up my grandfather's purchases.

'Already had one,' said Grandpa. He suddenly changed his mind about showing Harold the receipt. He didn't want to know. And he didn't want people talking. 'Grandson, actually.'

'I didn't know Eddie had a baby,' said Harold.

'Neither did I,' said Grandpa, 'and I'll thank you to keep it under your hat until I get things all straightened out.'

Harold nodded and didn't say another word. Harold Gruber was a well-respected man; everyone trusted him. He heard all Mannville's gossip in his store, and he'd learned the value of keeping his mouth shut and his ears open. He was also one of the few Mannvillians—besides Dr Connor—who hadn't made fun of Grandpa after the Fiasco of the Ostriches in 1946. Because of this Grandpa knew he wouldn't go blabbing my sudden arrival all over town. People already talked about Grandpa enough: Crazy old hermit up there in that old house. Drinks all day, talks to himself.

Grandpa loaded his purchases into the Galaxie and went back to Dr Connor's office. The two men warmed some formula, put it in a bottle, and watched apprehensively to see if I would take it. I did.

'That settles it, I guess,' Grandpa said. 'He's a keeper.'

'I don't want to intrude on your personal affairs,' said Dr Connor, 'but how on earth do you expect to raise a baby on your own in that house? You can't even take care of yourself!'

'What else can I do with him?' Grandpa said. 'I can't give him to some agency. I couldn't sleep nights knowing there was a baby Mann out there somewhere. Besides, Connor, I don't mean to get corny, but he's the answer to my prayers.'

'You've been praying for a *baby*?'

'No, you dingleberry, I haven't been praying for a baby. But I've been thinking. We're all gone now—all of us Manns. I'm the last one. I always thought it would be a damn shame if I was the last of the Manns. Now I'm not the last one any more.'

'Is that so important?'

'I got stories to tell him,' said Grandpa. 'I'm sick of talking to myself in that house. He needs to know everything.'

'What are you going to name him?'

And Grandpa, as he told me later, answered immediately and without thinking, 'Connor, meet William Amos Mann the Fourth. But I'm going to call him Billy.'

'Hello there, Billy,' said Connor.

At this point, Grandpa told me, I spit up formula all over myself.

'Little fella can't even hold his liquor,' said Grandpa.

He had the doctor refresh him on the major points of baby raising while he cleaned me up. Then Grandpa put me in the Galaxie and drove us back out to the old farmhouse.

THE FARMHOUSE in which I was to be raised wasn't really a farmhouse. It was more of a wood-and-brick mansion. A curving driveway led up to it from the road, and the front porch boasted two immense pillars that flanked an oak door nearly eight feet high. The house was three storeys tall, not including the attic and basement. A huge, dilapidated, spooky place, it had been built in 1868 by my great-great-grandfather Willie Mann. Once, it had been filled with Manns, but now the house was empty except for Grandpa and me. Each floor was a wilderness of bedrooms, closets and parlours, some of which hadn't had a human occupant in fifty years.

I learned to walk in the kitchen. It was mostly bare except for a table and chairs, with a wood stove for heat, a single gas ring for cooking, and an icebox instead of a refrigerator. It's the first part of the house of which I have a clear memory.

I'm sprawled on my stomach, perhaps ten or eleven months old, and Grandpa is at the other end of the kitchen on his hands and knees. The floor is a gleaming expanse stretching away before me. I plant my hands on it and push myself up into a runner's crouch. Grandpa is shouting encouragement as though he's at a horse race and I'm the odds-on favourite. I work my way into a squat, and then, hanging on to a nearby chair for support, I'm standing. Grandpa erupts with joy. He picks me up and whirls me around. I remember the room spinning, and Grandpa's hat.

Grandpa always wore a battered tweed fedora set far back on his mostly bald head. His breath smelt of whiskey, and his eyes crinkled when he smiled. When I was old enough to walk unaided, he took me on tours of the house, from basement to attic, and told me stories about each room. He could recite the biography of every person who'd lived in the house from 1868 onwards.

The only room that really interested me, however, was my father's, the one room Grandpa kept dusted and scrubbed. The walls were lined with pictures of Eddie in his Boy Scout uniform, his football uniform, and his air force uniform. I spent several hours a week in there, looking at his pictures, hoping I would learn something of my father just by being there. All I gained was the overwhelming sense that he was not home. The room, for me, was empty.

I was free to wander through the house at will. The other bedrooms were thick with dust but still made up, as though the occupants of the house had got up *en masse* one day and walked away. The closets were full of moth-eaten clothing that hadn't been popular for decades. I became particularly attached to a polished walking stick that had belonged to my great-great-grandfather Willie, the builder of the house. His monogram was engraved on the gold handle: W.A.M. III—William Amos Mann III, founder of the town of Mannville, at one time the richest person in Erie County, and the man for whom I—William Amos Mann IV—had been unofficially christened by Grandpa. With—as he told me later—a drop of whiskey dabbed on my forehead.

In the evenings Grandpa sat in his rocking chair and I sat in his lap. There was always a large glass of whiskey within reach, and he breathed it on me as we read the paper together. These are the smells of my childhood: whiskey and newsprint. We started by looking at the photographs—in those days still of soldiers in the jungles of Vietnam—and Grandpa made me tell him a story about each one. I invented them as I went. They always had a common thread. They were always about my father.

Then we would plod our way through sentences from the Associated Press, I reading them out loud and Grandpa correcting me. By the time I was six, I could pronounce all the words in a three-paragraph article, though I understood few of them. I went around the house reading everything from detergent labels to instructions on how to dismantle the Galaxie. I was, Grandpa said, a prodigy. There were two rooms on the second floor devoted to Grandpa's books, and I began to plough through them, following Grandpa around from room to room, reading them in a sportscaster's voice. Grandpa would correct my pronunciation and define words for me. Despite his lack of education, there was nothing he didn't know, and he was determined that I should be even smarter and better read than he.

Our only visitor in those days was Dr Connor. He was a kind, soft-spoken man with large warm hands and white hair, and he arrived in a green Volkswagen every few weeks with his black bag full of medical instruments and lollipops. After he had examined me, he would give me a cherry lollipop, my favourite, and he and Grandpa would sit at the kitchen table with a bottle of whiskey between them. They would talk for hours, telling jokes and stories and sometimes arguing.

When they argued, their voices got louder and they banged the table with their fists. Sometimes, I knew, the subject of their arguments was me. Dr Connor kept trying to convince Grandpa of something, and Grandpa would sit with his arms folded, shaking his head while Dr Connor gesticulated and shouted and pleaded. I didn't know exactly what they were arguing about, so I listened from the living room with the hope of gleaning some clue.

'There's nothing they can teach him in school that I can't teach him at home,' said Grandpa. 'Just because of the ostriches, everyone thinks I'm an idiot.'

'You're not an idiot,' said Dr Connor. 'You're the most well-read man in the county. And Billy—he's incredible. I've never seen anything like it. But he needs to meet other children!'

'Time enough for that later,' said Grandpa. 'The world is full of people. He'll get his fill of them by and by.'

'Not if you keep him locked up like this,' said Dr Connor.

'He's not locked up,' said Grandpa. 'I'm not some lunatic like you read about in the paper.'

'That's what people are saying.'

'Let 'em! Let 'em say whatever they want. I don't care!'

'Tom,' said the doctor, 'how long are you going to sit and stew over something that happened almost thirty years ago? Why can't you forget it and get on with things?'

'Why can't *they*?' Grandpa countered. That, as far as I could tell, was the end of the argument for that day. I was always relieved when they stopped yelling.

Aside from Dr Connor and our occasional trips into town to buy necessities from Harold and Emily Gruber, we saw nothing of other people. Our nearest neighbours were half a mile away, at the top of the hill. They were the Simpsons of the muddy blue eyes, and Grandpa never spoke of them without bitterness, so I learned not to ask what they were like. When we went into town in the Galaxie, I was permitted to talk with the Grubers and nobody else. 'Walk tall,' Grandpa instructed me. 'Hold your head up and look straight in front of you. Remember you're a Mann, and we used to own this whole damn town and everything around it for a ten-mile radius.'

The Grubers were a kindly old couple who always fussed over me. Mrs Gruber smelt like perfume, and she used to pick me up and let me choose a piece of candy from the row of shining glass jars they kept. I thought she was an angel.

But Grandpa's warnings about not speaking to anyone were unnecessary, because nobody ever spoke to us. We passed people on the street who must have known who we were, but they ignored Grandpa and he ignored them. Sometimes grown-ups would sneak a smile at me. Later, when I got to recognise certain faces, I would smile back, but this was always surreptitious, and if Grandpa saw me do it, he would give my hand a quick tug.

So I spent my time wandering the house and grounds, which were reduced from their former size of 3,000 acres to one. That was big enough for me to be satisfied with. I climbed trees and built forts, talking to imaginary friends and conducting elaborate rituals to conjure up the spirit of my father.

As my seventh year came to a close, I took to wandering farther and farther from the farmhouse. I spent entire days walking in the remnants of the forests that had once spread over the countryside.

The trees existed now only in sparse patches of growth, cut down to make way for fields, which in turn gave way to suburban neighbourhoods. It was still possible, however, to walk from the farmhouse to the shore of Lake Erie, half a mile away, without leaving the cover of the trees, and I went to the lake frequently to play on the sand and to torture minnows. I also took to spying on the Simpsons.

The hill on which the Simpson house sat was surrounded by the original forest, and on one side the trees crept up the slope far enough to afford cover for my espionage missions. Concealed behind their trunks, I observed the goings-on of the Simpson family. I was deeply curious about them. Grandpa spoke of them with such contempt that I thought they must be fascinating. As far as I could tell, they didn't do very much. Their house was in far worse repair than ours, and the yard was strewn with the wreckage of old cars.

The Simpsons appeared to be a tribe of corpulent Neanderthals whose sole pursuit was to watch television. That is, they sat in the living room and stared at what looked to me like a blue flickering light. We didn't have a television, and I'd never seen one before, so the light was a mystery to me. There were several girls, most of them teenagers. The father had an impressive belly that extended far over his belt. The sight of him was terrifying. He had beady eyes, a walrus mustache, and a flabby white body. His daughters mirrored him in appearance with stunning genetic accuracy, except for one of them.

She was about my age. She had pigtails that bounced between her shoulder blades as she ran. She was the only Simpson who did run, simply because she wasn't fat like the rest of them. I watched her as she played around the yard. She had an imaginary life as vivid as mine, it seemed, for she spoke constantly to herself, as though she were surrounded by throngs of admirers. Sometimes she sang. There would on occasion come a loud male rumble from the house, and the girl would stop what she was doing and trudge back inside, her spirit suddenly gone. After that, there would sometimes be crying, not just from her but from the other girls too—a chorus of wails, sometimes hysterical. So I knew her father was mean. I vowed to rescue the little girl when I was big enough. She became the object of my fantasy. When I was bigger, I would lock her father in his room and she would run away with me and perhaps be my girlfriend.

I knew better than to reveal this plan to Grandpa. He would have been livid with rage had he known I was considering contact with the Simpsons. So I explained it all to my father, with whom I held regular conversations. He was fully in approval. My father always wore his uniform, and whenever we met he would remove one of his medals and pin it on my chest. 'I'm very proud of you, son,' he said. Sometimes we would take a ride in his F-4. I piloted it around the yard, up over the Simpson house, and far out above Lake Erie. I shot down enemy planes by the score and flew low over people's houses. My father thought I was a genius and said he would help me in my plans to liberate the Simpson girl. I was a chip off the old block, he said. He wished he'd had more men like me in Vietnam.

Grandpa sat in his rocking chair in the darkened living room and drank and whispered to himself. We were entirely alone now. Dr Connor didn't visit any more. The last time he'd come, there had been a tremendous argument, worse than any they'd ever had before, and Grandpa had thrown a whiskey bottle at him. Connor ducked just in time. The bottle exploded against the wall, and the shards of glass sat on the kitchen floor for days before I finally cleaned them up.

THERE'D BEEN A TIME, long before my arrival, when Grandpa wasn't yet a bitter and lonely recluse; when he wasn't a bottle-a-day drinker of whiskey; when he was, in fact, a charming young man, the apple of his mother's eye and Mannville's brightest star. This was before the Second World War.

In 1943, when Grandpa was nineteen, he joined the army and became a regular infantryman. He did this over the protests of his mother, Lily, who thought he ought to go to college instead. College, however, held no interest for Grandpa. He was more interested in the war. Mannville was full of soldiers and sailors strutting about in their fine new dress uniforms. In fact, it was becoming impossible to get noticed by girls unless one was in uniform, and getting noticed by girls was Grandpa's only real concern at the time. He burned to fight and to distinguish himself; perhaps, if he was lucky, he would get wounded just badly enough to develop an interesting limp, and he would be sent home to live out his days in glory like his grandfather Willie. Willie limped because there was a Confederate musket ball in his leg. Everyone, from the mayor on down, worshipped him.

Lily Mann despaired. The infantry, she believed, was below the station of the Manns, who were millionaires thrice over and whose landholdings were of legendary proportions. She thought Grandpa at least ought to have become a cavalryman; she hadn't yet grasped the concept of mechanised warfare. To ride, she pointed out, was much more dignified than walking.

Thomas junior dropped the subject. He knew better than to argue directly with his mother. She was the toughest person he'd ever met, man or woman.

Lily had been only sixteen when she married Thomas junior's father, Thomas senior. She was widowed a year later when her husband died attempting to prove that it was possible to drive an automobile across Lake Erie, when frozen, all the way to Long Point, Ontario, Canada, a distance of roughly twenty miles. Theoretically, this feat *is* possible, but Thomas senior picked the wrong night to do it. There was a raging snowstorm. Also, he was drunk. Also, the lake hadn't yet completely frozen over. But none of these factors seemed to deter him. We are daredevils, we Manns, every last one of us. The inebriated Thomas senior got in his Pierce-Arrow convertible, waved goodbye to a party of equally drunken friends onshore, and drove off gaily into the blizzard, never to be seen again.

Lily was pregnant with Thomas junior at the time. She absorbed the news of her husband's death with characteristic stoicism, and, as soon as her son was born, she single-handedly took control of the Mann estate with a firmness and sense of purpose her frivolous husband had never possessed.

Lily herself was born to a poor but fanatically respectable farming family in nearby Springville. She'd married Thomas senior not because he was rich but because he was irresistible. He had charm, wit and good looks; parties didn't pick up speed until he arrived, and after he left they began to wind down. Lily had married him for love, but she knew nevertheless that she was lucky to have married into such a fortune, and she was determined to keep her husband's farms and orchards and vineyards profitable.

Thomas senior's father, Willie, had retreated into his bedroom. He was old now, and he spent most of his time with his wounded leg propped up on a footstool, scribbling in his journal. Willie showed no interest in taking over operations again after his foolhardy son drove his Pierce-Arrow to the bottom of Lake Erie. Lily could, he said, run the whole show if she was so inclined.

Lily chose to take Willie at his word. She was barely eighteen years old, but her will was inexorable, and her business instincts were deadly accurate. Under her strong hand the Manns became wealthier than they'd been since Willie Mann made them rich after his return from the Civil War. By the time Lily was twenty, she was the reigning queen of Erie County, in social, economic and even political circles. Sheriffs and council members found it difficult to maintain their office if they didn't have Lily Mann on their side.

The US Army, however, had never heard of Lily Mann. After Thomas enlisted, against her wishes, he received orders to go to Buffalo. Eventually he would board a plane to San Francisco, and a transport to the Philippines, where he would do battle against the Japanese. At first Lily was outraged, but Thomas filled her head with as much anti-Japanese propaganda as he could make up and gradually her attitude shifted. Then she was not only in favour of his going to the Pacific but actually bragged about it to her friends at parties and Red Cross fund-raisers. 'My son is off to destroy the Yellow Menace,' she said proudly.

Thomas junior was the second Mann to travel to Buffalo to be inducted into the army. Eighty-two years earlier his grandfather William Amos Mann III had walked there barefoot to join the Union army and go down south to 'whup Rebs', as he put it. Thomas had known his grandfather well. Willie was a stooped old man with a tremendous white beard. He'd died only a few years earlier, at the remarkable age of ninety-five, still limping from the wound he'd received at the Battle of Antietam. Willie had finally finished writing his diary, and he gave it to Thomas a short time before his death, saying, 'Most of what I learned in my life, lad, I tried to write down, so's the next fella could maybe make some sense out of things. Bein' as your father's gone, you're the next fella. This is for you.'

Thomas had been only sixteen at the time. He put the diary in a safe place and promptly forgot about it. But when he was packing before going off to war, he suddenly remembered the diary and dug it out. It was a gift from one warrior to another, he thought grandiosely. He would take it with him. No doubt it contained stirring accounts of hand-to-hand combat that would give him courage to face the enemy.

On the train, Thomas reached into his duffel bag and took out the diary. It was bound in cracked leather. Inside, the paper was only slightly yellowed and still supple. The first entry, written in an unpractised hand, read:

May 21, 1866
My Naym is Willie Amos Mann I Learnt to Write from a Feller in the Army of the Union and I be Twenty One Yeres old the feller who learnt me to Write and Reed was a Scoolmaster. To-day tis hot and We half been Working at the Corn all day Hoing Wedes.

Thomas put the diary away. This was not glamorous war stories. This was boring farmer talk. Besides, the churning in his stomach made it hard for him to concentrate. Though he hadn't mentioned it to his mother, or to anyone else, he was desperately afraid. So he sat with his head against the window and his eyes shut until the train arrived in Buffalo, and he disembarked, along with several other men his age. A waiting sergeant lined them up and marched them off in single file to the induction centre. My grandfather walked into the open maw of the US Army, never to return in quite the same form.

THE REAL REASON Thomas junior had joined the army—as opposed to the other branches of the military—was not one of which he was proud. He'd never flown in his life and had no wish to do so, so anything to do with airplanes was out of the question. He'd grown up on Lake Erie and was familiar enough with water to know that drowning also terrified him; so the navy was out. And the marines were too crazy. He assumed that in the army he would spend his time on the ground, a medium with which he was familiar. As long as he had at least one foot on the earth at all times, he thought being shot at was something he could tolerate with a modicum of manliness.

However, after being inducted in Buffalo, Thomas was placed in a large cargo plane along with forty-nine of his fellow soldiers and flown to San Francisco. He spent his first flight vomiting behind a bulkhead. After basic training, which he handled well enough, he was placed on a troopship and sent to the Philippines. There was more vomiting. When he arrived in the Philippines, it appeared that there'd been a mistake; he hadn't been wanted there after all, but in the Marianas. He was placed in another cargo plane and flown there.

By this time Thomas realised he was in the hands of dangerous idiots. When he arrived in the Marianas, he reported for duty and was told that there'd been another mistake—he was supposed to be in the Philippines after all—and so he simply did an about-face on the runway and got back on the plane.

Not only was Thomas airborne once again, but he was flying over an ocean that afforded plenty of opportunities for drowning. When Thomas realised this, he resigned himself to death. He sat on his helmet, as he'd seen other soldiers do, to prevent any wayward shards of metal from doing damage to his nether parts in the event of an attack. Willie Mann's diary was wrapped in several layers of oilcloth and secured to his stomach by means of packing tape.

He was the only passenger on this flight. There was a pilot, a copilot, and a navigator with whom he chatted from time to time. The navigator was a twenty-three-year-old engineering student.

Incredibly, the first thing that happened was precisely what Thomas had been fearing: an attack by a Japanese fighter plane, the dreaded Zero. It came as a surprise to everyone. They were not in an area of heavy Japanese presence, and no trouble had been expected.

Thomas noticed first that the pilot was shouting loudly enough to be heard in the back of the plane. Then the plane reared upwards on its tail and began a creaking climb. Thomas was sent tumbling into the tail. The plane completed its climb and promptly dived almost straight down, so that Thomas was sent flying again. The navigator threw open a porthole and unstrapped a machine gun that was fixed there. As he pulled the trigger and swivelled his upper body, shell casings spewed from the breech of the gun and littered the floor.

When they levelled out, the copilot came into the cargo area. 'Put on your parachute!' he screamed. He helped Thomas struggle into the bulky backpack that contained his parachute.

'I've never used one of these before!' Thomas shouted.

'Hopefully, you won't have to,' yelled the copilot. 'But if we ditch, jump out that door'—the copilot pointed to the great sliding cargo door—'and pull this cord here.' He showed Thomas the rip cord and went back into the cockpit.

That was the last Thomas ever saw of him. There was a tremendous rattling, and several ragged holes appeared in one wall of the plane and then in the wall opposite as Japanese bullets passed through with the velocity of tiny meteorites. At the same moment, smoke began issuing from the cockpit. Thomas felt a sickening lurch as the plane headed downward.

The navigator fired one last burst from the machine gun and ran to the cargo door. Together he and Thomas managed to push it open.

'Wait here!' shouted the navigator. He ran into the cockpit and came out again immediately, his face the colour of milk.

'What about those guys?' my grandfather shouted.

'They're dead,' said the navigator.

Thomas turned and looked out of the cargo door, squinting against the fierce wind. Then he felt the navigator's hands on his back. Suddenly he was tumbling through open space. He felt frantically for the rip cord as he flipped over and over. Finally he found it. His parachute opened with a tremendous yank, and he stopped tumbling. He looked up at the underside of the canopy. The Pacific sun shone through the silk, lighting it up like a lampshade.

He looked down. He was, he guessed, about a mile above the sea. Not so very far off were a smattering of tiny islands. He tried to steer towards them but only succeeded in spilling air out of his parachute, making himself fall faster. 'I'm going to die,' he said.

Far below him he saw a minuscule splash as the cargo plane crashed into the sea. A sick feeling pervaded his body. Then he saw the navigator float past about a quarter of a mile away.

Thomas began to shout. 'Hey! *Hey!* Hey *you!'*

The navigator looked over. Ridiculously, he and Thomas waved at each other. Then the navigator realised Thomas's predicament and showed him, pantomiming furiously, how to control his fall. The ocean was growing closer, but so were the islands. Thomas hoped fervently that he would fall close enough to swim for it. He was a very good swimmer, perhaps because his fear of drowning was so keen. He began shedding as many articles of clothing as he could reach so they wouldn't drag him down once he was in the ocean.

He was only a thousand feet or so above the water now. The islands were still a good swim away, perhaps a mile. He could do it. He was sure of it. He looked at the navigator again. He'd drifted closer to Thomas.

When Thomas hit the water, he pulled himself up into a ball. His parachute was designed to come off quickly, and he shed it easily. He kicked his pants off, removed his shirt, and began to tread water.

Immediately he saw the navigator's chute. He'd landed closer to the islands than Thomas, but not by much; in fact, the islands now looked impossibly far away. It was going to be a hell of a swim. Thomas struck out for the navigator. He swam slowly, pacing himself, forcing his breath to come regularly.

It took him for ever to reach the navigator. When he got there, he found the man floating, his head protruding from the hole in the centre of the parachute, which billowed around him.

'Get me out of this damned thing,' said the navigator. He was crying like a child. 'I can barely move.'

'Right,' said Thomas. He began rolling up one side of the parachute until he reached the man's head. He slipped it over him and saw that the man was wearing a flotation jacket.

'They make us wear them,' said the navigator. 'Thank God. I'd share it with you, but I'd drown. I can't swim.'

'I'll be fine,' said Thomas. 'I'm a good swimmer. Let's unstrap you.'

The navigator struggled with the straps of his harness. After several minutes he was free. He was still crying, trying to stifle his sobs.

'Don't panic,' said Thomas. 'Hear me? Stop crying. If we panic, we're done for. We have to make it to those islands.'

'What's that on your stomach?' asked the navigator.

Thomas had forgotten about his grandfather's diary. He looked down. It was still there, safely secured around his middle.

'It's a book,' he said.

There was a moment of awkward silence.

'I should have joined the infantry and gone to Europe,' said the navigator. 'Instead I'm in the air force, and I'm sitting in the water, and we're going to be eaten by sharks.'

'No we're not,' said Thomas. 'Start swimming.'

'Yes we are,' said the navigator. 'I saw them when I was falling. Big ones. Back there.' He pointed over his shoulder.

A cold chill swept through Thomas. 'Are you serious?'

'Yes,' the navigator said simply. Then he glanced up. 'Look,' he said. 'There's another parachute.'

Thomas followed his gaze. There was indeed another parachute drifting gently above the islands.

'Oh my Lord,' said the navigator. 'It's the Jap. I must have got him. I shot his plane down!'

'Start swimming,' said Thomas. 'I'm going to go ahead of you. You'll be much slower than me, but you won't sink.'

'OK.' The navigator was smiling now. 'I shot down a Jap plane!'

'I'll see you over there,' said Thomas. He began swimming with strong, even strokes.

'I'm Phillip Neuberg from Kansas City,' the navigator called after him. 'If I don't make it, will you write to my family?'

Thomas didn't answer, but he made a mental note of it. He couldn't waste any more time talking. He just swam. He heard the navigator's splashes grow farther and farther behind him. He had been swimming for about fifteen minutes when the first shark hit.

The navigator let out a scream that pierced Thomas through to his soul. He forced himself to keep going; there was nothing he could do anyway. There came another scream, then another, and then the screaming abruptly stopped.

Thomas swam as he had never swum before. I'm going to make it; I will not by eaten by sharks, he repeated in his head. They won't come after me. They don't like me. They like Phillip Neuberg from Kansas City. I'm going to make it to the island, and I'm going to kill that damn Jap who shot us down, and I'm going to get rescued and go home to Mannville. Swim. Swim. Swim.

THOMAS WAS FLOPPED up on the beach by the surf like a sodden rag doll. He lay there for several minutes just breathing. Then he took stock of himself. He was nineteen years old and completely naked except for the diary strapped with packing tape to his stomach. He was half full of sea water, and he was lying on a beautiful white beach several thousand miles from Mannville. Somewhere on the island was a sword-wielding, idol-worshipping Japanese pilot. Thomas had no food and no gun. It might be that there was no fresh water on the island. It might be that there was nothing to eat either. It was two or three o'clock in the afternoon and the full brunt of the southern sun was blasting down on him like a thousand bonfires. The situation, to put it mildly, was grim.

Thomas crawled away from the surf into the line of bushes and trees. There he made a nest of leaves and went to sleep.

When he woke up, there was a small dark-skinned man standing above him. The sun was almost down, and the little man was silhouetted against the surf, which glowed a deep dark blue in the orange sunset. Thomas shot to his feet. He and the little man stood there looking at each other. Neither of them moved.

Technically, Thomas knew, he was supposed to kill any Japanese he met. That was what war was about. Failing that, he was to take them prisoner. But he didn't want to kill anybody, and he didn't know how to take someone prisoner. So they stood there looking at each other until the sun went down and blue faded to bruise-purple. A chill sea breeze began to blow across the island. Grandpa and the Japanese soldier began to shiver in unison.

Seeing this, realising Japs got cold too, Thomas decided to resign from the US Army. The war was over for him. He was exhausted and nauseated and hungry, and the only reason he'd wanted to go to the war was so girls would pay attention to him when he got back. At that moment it seemed like the stupidest reason in the world.

'We need a fire,' Thomas said. He pantomimed the rubbing together of two sticks.

The Japanese pilot nodded. 'That's a fine idea,' he said. 'It's getting a little cold.'

Thomas was flabbergasted. 'You're speaking English.'

'Do you speak Japanese?' enquired the pilot.

Thomas shook his head.

The pilot smiled. 'I didn't think so,' he said triumphantly. 'Therefore I'm speaking English.'

'Well, I'll be damned,' said Thomas.

'I am Enzo Fujimora,' said the pilot. 'Harvard class of '35.'

'Well, I'll be damned,' said Thomas again. 'A Jap Harvard man.'

'Exactly,' said Enzo Fujimora, and he bowed slightly from the waist. 'Shall we make a fire?'

Enzo Fujimora was thirty years old. He was a schoolteacher, the son of a well-to-do family in Nagasaki, and he had a wife and two children—a boy age three and another age seven. When the atomic bomb was dropped on his hometown two years later, all three of them would be wiped out in an instant.

It was three long weeks before Enzo Fujimora and my grandfather were discovered. In that time they became fast friends. They were both naturally amiable, and they shared a distaste for war. During their time together on that tiny Pacific island they told each other every detail of their lives, right up to the point where they had met in midair in their respective airplanes. Enzo had been separated from his squadron when he spotted the American cargo plane, and he had thought to cover himself in glory by shooting it down to avoid the disgrace of getting lost.

'It was a selfish action,' he told Thomas. 'I deeply apologise.' And he bowed again. Thomas, a fast learner, bowed back.

There was very little food on the island. Enzo had a pistol, and with it they managed to shoot two parrots. Other than those birds, which were musky in flavour and tough, the only things they had to eat were some sort of tiny fruit and a few herbs that grew near a freshwater spring.

Enzo recognised the herbs right away, and he taught Grandpa the Japanese names for the plants they found. In return, Grandpa read aloud to him from the diary of Willie Mann. They were both hearing it for the first time.

Far from being the monotonous account of farm life that Grandpa expected, it was fascinating. It got easier to read, too, as they progressed, for Willie had gradually mastered the mechanics of spelling and grammar. The slight Japanese pilot sat and listened, enthralled, for as long as Grandpa cared to read to him. When Thomas's voice grew tired, Enzo read it himself, silently.

One day an American fighter plane flew overhead, attracted by the smoke from the signal fire they kept burning day and night on the beach. The next morning a ship appeared on the horizon. Thomas and Enzo watched in apprehension as it approached. Enzo, they both knew, was about to become a prisoner of war, and my grandfather was probably going to return to active duty. Neither of them was thrilled with the prospect, but rescue by the Americans was better than the certain death that otherwise would have been their lot.

A flare went up from the ship as it anchored offshore. As a landing party made its way towards the island in a small skiff, Grandpa turned to Enzo impulsively. 'Here,' he said, handing him the diary. 'I want you to take this.'

Enzo looked at him in bewilderment. 'I cannot,' he said. 'This is the property of your ancestors.'

'You can give it back someday,' said Thomas. 'I don't want you to keep it for ever, but you seemed to get a lot more out of it than I did.'

He was thinking that Enzo would need something to keep his mind occupied while he was a prisoner. And the truth was that Thomas didn't want it. The diary contained many fascinating stories about his family, but it had also informed him of something he would rather not have known. In fact, he realised with a shudder, he was the only Mann to know the true story of his grandfather's Civil War experiences, the only Mann to know that Willie Mann was not a hero at all. That he had never been in battle. That it was not a Confederate musket ball that wounded him. That, in short, Willie did not deserve all the recognition and admiration that had been his all his adult life.

Enzo, however, was touched by the gift. To him the diary was a wonderful story that inspired him and made him think.

'I will return it if I live,' said Enzo. 'I swear it.'

'I believe you,' said Thomas.

The landing party made shore. Thomas, naked, saluted and reported Enzo, also naked, as his prisoner. Enzo was placed under guard and, once on board the ship, was locked in the brig.

'That was the last I ever saw of him,' said Grandpa to me some thirty-five years later. 'But he still has the diary. I made them let him keep it. And he's going to bring it back—I know he will. He was the most trustworthy fellow I ever knew.'

I first heard this story when I was about six years old. Grandpa used to talk me to sleep when I was little, his cracked bass voice lulling me. It was one of my favourite bedtime stories. I always felt the same thrill of security when he landed on the beach just ahead of the sharks that had consumed poor Phillip Neuberg of Kansas City.

WHEN GRANDPA RETURNED to Mannville at the end of the war, he was given an elaborate hero's welcome. His mother, Lily, had already spread the story of how he was shot down and survived on a desert island by his wits, omitting for the sake of Mann honour his friendship with Enzo Fujimora and embellishing other details here and there. When he disembarked from the train, there was a crowd of 400 people to welcome him. Several of them carried signs saying MANNVILLE SALUTES ITS HERO. It was December 1945. Thomas had finished out the war at a desk job, as he'd requested after his rescue, but nobody seemed to know that. He himself had no delusions about his role in the war. He'd only done what he had to do to survive, as had everyone else who'd made it home.

His mother, Thomas discovered, had aged a good deal more than the three chronological years he'd been gone; her hair was mostly grey, though she was just forty, and her heart was beginning to fail. She'd been waiting for Thomas to come home so that she could begin the gradual process of turning over the farm to him, her only son. That huge trust, combined with the awe with which he was treated in town, began to swell inside him until he walked with a strut and grew a fancy moustache. He never mentioned what he'd discovered about his grandfather in his diary, of course. There was no reason to upset his mother, and it had all happened so long ago that it didn't matter anyway. The diary was safe in Japan, where nobody in Mannville would find it.

Lily died of a heart attack in the spring of 1946. Thomas, married now to the lovely Ellen Hurley of Buffalo, was suddenly free to do whatever he wished with his money. He was not the type to waste it on useless luxuries. Instead he acted upon a plan that had been brewing in the back of his mind. Farming corn and vegetables had always seemed boring to him. He was therefore going to liquidate his assets, import ostriches from Australia, and begin an ostrich ranch. It couldn't fail, he told himself; he was just the sort of far-thinking man who could pull it off. He was a millionaire and a war hero, and nobody would dare contradict him. He'd eaten ostrich meat once while visiting Australia on leave and found it delicious. Mannvillians would soon follow his example, and then he would have an unshakable hold on the ostrich market. And he wouldn't do this on a small scale either. All his land would be converted to ostrich ranching.

Straight away Thomas imported 2,000 ostriches from Australia at phenomenal cost and hired seventy-five workmen to fence in the entire farm. Thomas and the rest of Mannville waited expectantly for the arrival of the birds. Two weeks went by, then a month, then three. Then came a telegram. Half of the ostriches had died aboard ship en route to America. Of those that survived the trip, another half died promptly after their arrival, victims of various New World diseases to which they had no immunity.

The rest of the ostriches milled about disconsolately in the huge area Thomas had ordered fenced. There they remained until they discovered the fences, which they promptly jumped over. Thomas had told the workmen of his plan, but none of them had ever seen an ostrich before, and they had no idea of the true size or strength of one. Most of the men had the vague impression that an ostrich was a very tall chicken. The fences were built accordingly, and the ostriches found them no serious obstacle to their freedom.

That was the end of that. After only three months Thomas found himself almost bankrupt and with not a single ostrich to show for it.

What was worse, however, was that his reputation among the people of Mannville had plummeted. People in town laughed in his face. Outraged farmers barraged him with phone calls—rampaging ostriches were ruining their corn crops, and they shot them on sight. The *Mannville Megaphone* carried weekly articles on the subject for the next year. Finally the whole affair came to be known as the Great Ostrich Fiasco of 1946. It is, I believe, still mentioned in history classes at Mannville High School as a colourful local legend.

Broke, depressed and suddenly friendless, Grandpa retired permanently to his farmhouse. My father, Eddie, was born in late 1947. Soon after, Ellen Hurley, whose name I know only from reading the wedding announcement on microfilm in the Mannville Public Library, returned alone and for ever to Buffalo, having discovered belatedly that her love had been for the Mann fortune and not for Thomas himself. My grandfather never mentioned her to me, and Eddie barely knew of her. All of Thomas's energy was focused on his son. It was through Eddie, Grandpa knew, that the Mann name could begin its long ascension from the muck into which he had plunged it.

Everything had to be sold to pay off his debts. The three main Mann farms were auctioned. The land was mostly purchased by developers. Within four years, by 1950, the 3,000 acres had been subdivided, built upon, and sold, and where once fields of wheat and corn had stretched across the landscape, there were driveways with shiny new cars parked in them and streets filled with children on bicycles. A new town existed, and all because of a lousy idea my grandfather had that never came to fruition.

My father entered kindergarten in 1952. His academic career from that moment on was brilliant. He could read phenomenally well at an early age, and skipped the first grade. In middle school he began playing football and baseball as well as working a part-time job at Gruber's Grocery. Eddie also learned to fight.

'Kids used to tease him on account of his old man was the laughing stock of the town,' Grandpa said. 'So they would say things to him, and he'd pound on 'em till they took it back. He was one of the strongest kids around, and after someone got a taste of him, they didn't come back for more. Then he started getting noticed on the field. By the time he was in high school, everybody forgot who he came from. He was just Ready Eddie. His name was in the paper every week. Girls used to call here all the time. God, he was something.'

He was more than something; he was a Mann. His natural tendency towards greatness could hardly be suppressed by a mere lack of money. If anything, it made him shine more.

'We don't have any money,' Grandpa would tell me. 'We don't have any friends. We just have this house, and you have me. And I have you. But we still have more than any other family in this town because we have Mann blood. And don't you forget it.'

'I won't,' I promised.

And I haven't, because it's my story too.

My father's old bedroom was on the first floor of the farmhouse. His was the only uninhabited room that was kept up—it was far cleaner than the kitchen, with its unwashed dishes, or the living room, littered with newspapers and sticky whiskey glasses. One wall of the bedroom was lined with shelves of golden trophies, thirty-eight in all, polished and arranged in order of height. Eddie competed in cross-country running, the breast stroke, shot put and football. He excelled at everything, but football was his love. He became the first-string quarterback for the Mannville Meteorites when he was only fifteen.

On another wall were photographs: Eddie in a boat holding a prize-winning walleye; Eddie wearing his football helmet and jersey; Eddie in his air force uniform, smiling brightly, an American flag stretched out gloriously behind him. Hey, son, he seemed to be saying to me, war is great, flying is great, America is great, everything is great. Isn't it fun to be a hero? Isn't it great to be a Mann?

I stared at this particular photograph for hours, wishing that I could jump into it. Grandpa allowed me into my father's room on the condition that I wouldn't mess anything up. Certain things on the desk had been left untouched since my father placed them there. As a result, the desk was thick with dust, a filthy oasis of sentimentality in a desert of spotlessness. The items themselves were nothing of note: a pen, some paper clips, a copy of *A Farewell to Arms*. Eddie had been a Hemingway fanatic, but it would be years before I picked up the book and read it for myself. For now it was enough to look at the dusty cover and know that the last person to touch it had been my dad, and that perhaps the only way for me to speak to him was to venerate these things as my grandfather did—to treat them as though they were some sort of radio transmitters permanently tuned in to the frequency of the afterlife.

My father had been a daredevil, Grandpa told me proudly. He was convinced at an early age that he could fly. Grandpa still had the collection of plaster casts to prove it. There were five of them—three legs and two arms. I inherited my father's madly suicidal tendencies, much to Grandpa's delight, although my courage—some might call it stupidity—took the form of high-speed stunts performed on the riding lawn mower, which interested me more than jumping off the carriage-house roof—my father's favourite routine. Grandpa had removed the blade from the mower to make it safe for me. It was a good thing he had. I was constantly practising such tricks as standing on the hood while steering backward, or attempting a headstand on the seat while steering with my bare toes. Grandpa roared his drunken approval. I fell off more often than I stayed on, and several times the mower rolled over an arm or a leg. Thanks to the foresight of Grandpa, I came through my childhood not only intact but entirely unafraid of anything the physical world had to offer.

Sometimes in the afternoons we played Munchkins. This was great fun because it was murderous and frightening, and I never knew exactly what was going to happen. But it went mostly like this:

Grandpa sat on the roof of the old doghouse, unoccupied now by any dog, with a glass of whiskey near by and his fedora pushed back on his head. I would stand next to him, and he'd put his hand on my shoulder. We would be absolutely silent. I was attuned, coiled, ready. Suddenly there would come a rustle from the bushes.

'There they are,' I whisper, pointing.

'Right!' Grandpa shouts. He begins pulling imaginary things out of the doghouse, handing them to me.

'Dynamite?' he says.

'Check.'

'Fuse?'

'Check.'

'Plunger?'

'Check.'

'OK,' he says. 'Go plant your charge.'

I would sneak off to whatever bush or tree or hedge the Munchkins were hiding in this time. The Munchkins were a band of ferocious creatures who'd lived in our yard since the beginning of the world. They were small, about my height, and they had long fangs and claws that could rip you in half. It was imperative that they be wiped out so the world would be safe for kids again. Blowing up Munchkins was my terrifying duty. I quickly planted my charge in the bush.

'How many are there?' Grandpa would shout from the doghouse.

'Eight hundred and eleven!'

'Holy cow! Report back to headquarters!'

I would race back to the doghouse.

'Ready on charge!'

'Right! Countdown!'

'*Ten nine eight seven six five four three two one!*'

'Kablammo!' shouted Grandpa, pressing down the plunger. The world would be shaken by a tremendous explosion. I'd be knocked off my feet, lie unconscious for a few moments, then return to where I'd set the charge to finish off any survivors or to take prisoners, depending on my mood towards them that day.

I loved to play the game over and over because it was a game Grandpa told me he'd played with my father, just the way he did with me—a man and a boy alone in the world, defying nature by pretending that what was real was not and what was not real was.

THE WINTER OF 1977 was a particularly bad one. Late that fall, before winter had even officially begun, there came a storm that encased everything in a solid inch of ice. Trees, shrubs, power lines, even the old farmhouse itself—everything was sealed in solid glass. The backyard became an acre of mirrors upon which I could slide with incredible velocity.

By propping open the kitchen door and running from the far wall of the kitchen, I could get up enough speed to launch myself onto the ice and skim gracefully on my belly almost a hundred feet across the yard. It was like flying. I flew again and again until I was exhausted. Finally I decided that I would make one last run and then find Grandpa so he could fix me some lunch.

I hadn't seen Grandpa all morning, but that was nothing unusual. Sometimes hours would pass without us encountering each other in the huge house. When one of us needed to see the other on some matter of importance, we rang the old iron dinner triangle that hung outside the kitchen door. After my last slide I'd ring for Grandpa, who would appear and say, 'Fried baloney all right?' It was what he always said. It was what we always ate, and it was always all right.

I never completed my last slide. Instead I ran smack into Grandpa, who was coming up the back stairs to ring the triangle himself. We collided just as I parted company with the last inch of runway. I heard the air go out of him in a soft, surprised '*Hooo!*' as my head drove into his abdomen. He was propelled backward, and we landed together, me on top of him. I heard a mighty crack somewhere deep inside his body, and he gave an anguished scream.

'My hip,' cried Grandpa. 'Get off me!'

'I'm sorry, I'm sorry, I'm sorry,' I said, crawling off Grandpa's poor broken body.

'Billy,' said Grandpa, 'stay calm.' His face was white, and he breathed in gasps. 'You have to call somebody for help.'

That was something I knew how to handle. I slithered my way over the slicked-up stairs into the kitchen. The phone was cold and black and very heavy. I held the receiver to my ear and listened. It was, of course, dead. So was every other phone in New York State. I slammed down the receiver and ran to the door.

'It doesn't work!' I screamed.

'OK, Billy,' said Grandpa, 'listen to me carefully. You'll have to take the Galaxie and get some help.'

'The Galaxie! No way! I don't know how!'

'Listen to me.' Grandpa's face was growing whiter as he spoke. 'I can't move. It's very cold out here, and I'm going into shock. Do you know what shock is? It's when you're hurt very badly and your body temperature drops. I could freeze to death, Billy,' he said. 'If I don't get some help soon, I could die.'

As soon as Grandpa said that, my fear was gone. Though I was only seven years old, I assumed the burden of Grandpa's life with the confidence of a man who'd lived my life span many times over. I ran back into the house, found some blankets, and arranged them on top of Grandpa. Not even he had thought of that.

'Good boy,' he said. He was in intense pain, breathing rapidly.

A flash of inspiration hit me. 'I'm taking the rider mower,' I said.

Even in agony Grandpa was impressed. 'Beautiful,' he whispered.

There was only one place I could go for help —the Simpson house. In ordinary circumstances I would rather have cut off my arm than appear at their front door. These, however, were not ordinary circumstances. Cautiously I piloted the mower down the frozen driveway. When I got to the junction of our dirt road with the county road, I peered hopefully to the east and west, looking for a car or a policeman or anything. There was not a living creature in sight.

The mower skidded only slightly on the road. It was far lighter than a car, so even when I did skid, there wasn't enough momentum to carry me into the ditch. The wheels spun maddeningly, however, and when I got to the base of the hill on top of which sat the Simpson house, they lost their grip entirely. I sat dejected. It would take me for ever to climb up the hill on foot. It was just too slippery. I could see the house far above me, glinting in the sunlight like a beacon of hope. I thought of Grandpa freezing to death in the yard. I almost began to cry. I wouldn't let it out, however. I must be brave, like my father, I thought. My father never cried. He would have flexed his bronzed arms, grinned his bewitching grin, spat contemptuously on the ground, and gone straight to it. I would have liked to go straight to it too, but I had no idea what it was I needed to do.

And then I hit upon the solution that would later be reported in the *Mannville Megaphone* as the heroic feat of the century, a stunning example of youthful ingenuity under duress. I turned the mower around and went up the hill backwards. I wish I could remember how I hit upon that idea. It was a true flash of genius, for with the mower reversed, the greater part of the weight was forward. This, combined with the fact that reverse is usually the strongest gear of any machine, allowed me to arrive at the top of the hill rear end first, having travelled exactly half a mile in about thirty minutes.

I manoeuvred the mower through the maze of junked cars in the front yard and stopped before the sagging porch of the ramshackle house. There, standing in the doorway, was the girl I had seen playing in the yard several times before. She stared at me in astonishment, her pigtails ratty and frizzed. I hopped off the mower and skated to the door in my boots.

'You better go get the man with the moustache,' I said. 'The mean one. My Grandpa fell down.'

She kept staring at me.

'I know who you are,' I said. 'You're the only pretty one in the whole family.'

Annie told me much later, when we were teenagers, 'I had no idea who you were, but I fell in love with you on the spot.'

'Annie!' came the voice—that deep, rumbling bass that always set the children crying. 'Who the hell is it?'

Annie didn't answer. Her eyes clouded over, and she stepped back from the door. In a moment I heard heavy footsteps, and the man with the moustache and large belly appeared.

'What the hell are you doing here on a day like this?' the man said. 'Who are you?'

'I'm Billy Mann,' I said. 'My Grandpa had an accident. He slipped on the ice, and he says his hip is broken.'

'Billy Mann,' he repeated. 'Oooh. Eddie's bastard.'

I wondered if he had read the note left by my mother. How else would he know my real name? He looked me up and down. Then he opened the door. 'Come on in,' he said gruffly.

I stepped inside. Every house has its own peculiar odour, but the smell here was almost overwhelming. It was composed of beer and stale cigarette smoke and old greasy cooking and just plain filth, and somewhere deep underneath it all was a layer of fear.

The man waddled into the living room and sat down on the couch. There were beer cans and paper plates and car parts strewn about the floor. On a coffee table sat a fascinating apparatus. It had knobs and dials and glass tubes in the back, and a microphone. Mr Simpson flicked a switch, and the tubes in the back of this thing began to glow.

I remained in the doorway next to Annie. I could feel her looking at me, but I hesitated to look back. I watched Mr Simpson instead. When the tubes were a bright orange, he picked up the microphone and, to my astonishment, began speaking into it.

He used a strange language, one I'd never heard before. But the words were made up of recognisable parts: he said 'niner' instead of nine and used numbers like 'ten-four'.

Annie took me by the hand suddenly. 'C'mere,' she whispered. 'I want to show you something.'

With another glance at Mr Simpson, who ignored us as he chattered into the microphone, we crept down a hallway to one of the back bedrooms. The door was open. A stronger smell issued from here. It was unfamiliar and very unpleasant.

'Look inside,' said Annie.

I did. There on the bed, under a sheet, was a man, or a half-man. He lay motionless because he had nothing to move. He had no arms or legs, and his head was perfectly still. I couldn't tell if his eyes were open or shut. If they were open, he was simply looking up at the ceiling. The sheet he was covered with was dirty and grey and showed signs of having been repeatedly soiled without being washed. Tubes ran into his body; they hung from several clear plastic bags.

'What is he?' I whispered to Annie.

'He's my brother. Don't worry. He can't hear us. He can't hear or see or talk or anything.'

'What happened to him?'

'He was in Vietnam, and he got blown up,' said Annie.

'Vietnam,' I breathed. 'My dad was in Vietnam.'

'Come on,' said Annie, taking me by the hand again.

We went back to the living room. The sight of the half-man had shaken me. If someone could have their arms and legs blown off and survive, how badly was my dad hurt for him to die? The image was horrifying. I was fighting the urge to cry again. Annie's hand in mine was soft and hot, and I squeezed it hard. She squeezed back.

Mr Simpson had finished speaking into the microphone. 'Idden 'at cute,' he sneered when he saw us. 'Annie got her a little boyfriend.'

Annie said nothing. I waited to see what would happen next.

'Ambulance is comin',' said Mr Simpson. 'But if you think I'm gonna take you back down the hill in my truck, you're outa yer mind. Too much ice.'

I hadn't expected him to do anything of the sort. I looked away, embarrassed. My gaze fell on another device, a large box with a glass screen in it.

My curiosity overcame my fear. 'What's that?' I asked.

Mr Simpson snorted, superior and supercilious. 'Ain't you never seen a TV before?'

'I've seen it plenty of times,' I said defensively. I almost gave away the fact that I'd been spying on him and his family.

'The damn women in this house have it on all day and all night,' said Mr Simpson. I wondered where these women were. As far as I could tell, the house was empty except for the three of us and the frightening creature in the back room. 'These damn women,' he went on. 'They don't do nothin' but sit around and watch TV. Annie too. She's gonna grow up just like her momma. Fat and useless and ugly.'

I felt Annie flinch next to me. 'No, she isn't,' I said before I knew the words were out of my mouth.

For a fat man Mr Simpson moved surprisingly fast. He was up off the couch and in front of me before I'd even noticed he'd moved, and one meaty hand was wrapped around my throat.

'You got a big mouth,' he said. 'Course, maybe you think 'cause you got all that money, you can say whatever you want. Well, lemme tell you somethin', you little bastard. You Manns ain't so great now that all those damn birds ran off on you, are you? You ain't got any more money anyway.'

I tried to swallow. My knees were trembling, and I knew that the tears were going to come no matter what I did to stop them.

Mr Simpson loosened his grip and went into the kitchen. I heard the refrigerator door open and the sound of a can of beer being opened. He came back out again, swilling from the can.

'You Manns think you're mighty fine,' he said. 'That old man down there always had his nose in the air. Too good to talk to us. His kid gets to be a pilot while mine has to join the infantry. Lemme tell you something, you little bastard. I was in the infantry in the big one, and there ain't nobody there but niggers and spicks and the white folks who ain't got the money to be pilots. My kid had to fight down on the ground while his kid got to fly around in a nice cosy airplane. If you were back there, I guess you saw my boy. He ain't much now, but at least he came home. *His* didn't make it. And that's what he gets for havin' his nose in the air.'

I couldn't even bring myself to say another word to Annie. I was out of the door and back on the mower before I knew my feet were moving. The motor started with a roar. I headed back down the hill, weeping furiously, going too fast. Before I was halfway down the hill, I lost control of it and went sliding into the ditch. I was thrown up onto the far bank, smacking my lip on the ice.

I left the mower in the ditch, crawled back on the road and scooted down the rest of the hill on my bottom. If I hadn't been so furious at Mr Simpson, I would have been delighted at the new game I'd discovered. But there was nothing in me but blind rage.

I skated on my boots once I reached the bottom of the hill, screaming and sobbing through the blood that trickled from my lip down my chin. The trip home was faster than the trip up had been. Long before I got to the farmhouse, I could see the flashing lights of the ambulance. When I finally arrived, I found the paramedics loading Grandpa into it on a stretcher. I tried to run, lost my balance and fell and hit my lip again, and that was how I got to ride in the back of the ambulance with Grandpa, because I needed to be stitched up.

I sat next to him and cried as he held my hand. I was too furious to explain any of it. It was all right, he said. He knew I was scared. He knew it was scary to be a kid when something went wrong. But it wasn't my fault. I mustn't worry, and I mustn't cry. I didn't have to tell him I wasn't crying because of my split lip. He knew I didn't cry over little things like that. I was a daredevil, and the son and grandson and great-grandson of daredevils. He understood that I was crying because today I had caught a glimpse of how the world could be sometimes, and because that sight is horrifying to children.

I hadn't intended to tell Grandpa about what I saw, but the words were flying out of me before I could stop them. Grandpa lay wincing in pain as I rattled on. He'd been doped up, but he was still conscious. The ambulance siren, much to my delight, was blaring.

'They have a man in their house with no arms or legs!' I told Grandpa. 'He was in Vietnam just like my father was! Do you think they knew each other?'

'Just because they were in the same war doesn't mean they knew each other,' said Grandpa.

'Yeah, but did they?' I sensed I was being put off.

'Did they what?'

'Know each other!'

'Billy, I'm tired,' said Grandpa. We sat in silence for a while.

'Yes,' he said finally. 'They did know each other. But not in Vietnam. They were friends here in Mannville when they were boys.'

'They played together?'

'Yeah.'

'What did they play?'

'I don't know. They ran around in the woods a lot.'

'Did you play Munchkins with them?'

A brief smile flickered across Grandpa's face. 'Yes, I did,' he said. 'The three of us played Munchkins together.'

'What's his name?'

Grandpa frowned. 'Why do you want to know his name?'

'Because! You never tell me anything, that's why.'

'Never tell you anything. Hah! Don't I tell you every story about this family I know?'

'I guess.'

'You guess. You know more about your own family than most kids do, my boy, so no complaints. Knowing the kind of people you come from is just as important as knowing yourself.'

I was confused. 'How do you know yourself? You can't meet yourself like how you meet someone else and get to be their friend.'

'No, you're right,' said Grandpa. 'It's not like that at all. You'll understand later, when you're big.'

'I'm pretty big now.'

'You're seven years old. That's not very big.'

'I'm going to be big enough someday to go back there and beat up that fat old man with the mustache!'

'What?' Grandpa was instantly alert. 'Why would you want to do that? Did he do something to you?'

I hadn't wanted to tell Grandpa about how mean Mr Simpson was. On the other hand, I couldn't keep Mr Simpson a secret from my grandpa. I couldn't keep *anything* a secret from him.

'He yelled at me,' I admitted.

Grandpa took my little hand in his big warm one. 'Did he?' he said, his voice soft. 'Did he yell at you?'

'Yeah.' I was feeling miserable again, but I was glad to be telling Grandpa about it. 'He was mad I was talking to Annie.'

'Who's Annie?'

'A little girl who lives there. She's my age. We're friends.'

'So there's another one,' Grandpa muttered. 'You say you're friends with this little girl?'

'Yeah.'

'And he was mad about it?'

'Yeah. And he was mad about the man in the back of the house with no arms and legs. And he was mad about my dad.'

Grandpa stiffened a moment and then relaxed. 'What did he say about your dad?' he asked, letting go of my hand.

'That he was lucky because he got to fly, and he didn't have to be in the intrafy—'

'Infantry,' Grandpa corrected me.

'And his nose was in the air, and Mr Simpson had to be down on the ground with the niggers in the war.'

'Don't say that word.'

'What does it mean?'

'It means black people, but it's not a nice word. Only white trash use that word.'

'What's white trash?'

'The Simpsons are white trash. Dirty and poor, but mostly dirty. There's plenty of poor people who aren't trashy at all, because they don't go around talking about other people who work harder than they do and calling them names. Mr Simpson is angry for a lot of reasons, Billy, but mostly because he never worked hard at anything in his life. He always expected everything to be given to him. A Mann never expects anything to be given to him. That's the difference between us and the Simpsons. That's what makes them white trash. It has nothing to do with money.'

'What's his name?' I changed the subject abruptly.

'Who?'

'The man with no arms and legs. You never told me.'

'His name is Frederic,' said Grandpa. 'We called him Freddy.'

'Did you like him?'

'Yes,' said Grandpa. 'He was a sweet boy, and he didn't take after his father at all. He was very polite. I used to take them on little trips and play with them, which that fat old drunk never did. Excuse me, Billy, I shouldn't talk like that about Simpson in front of you. But Simpson's real mean, and don't ever forget it.'

'He yells at Annie all the time.'

Grandpa eyed me suspiciously. 'How do you know that? Were you ever up there before today?'

'Yes.' I could feel my face getting red.

'Why?'

'I don't know,' I said. 'I get bored. There's nothing to do.'

Grandpa was silent.

'Are you mad at me?' I asked him.

'No,' he said. 'I'm mad at myself. Connor was right. You need to meet other kids. You have to start going to school.'

'School?' A sick feeling blossomed in the pit of my stomach. I'd spent my entire life doing exactly what I pleased. Grandpa read to me, and I read to him, and he taught me what I needed to know whenever the opportunity presented itself. If the Galaxie was in need of repair, we repaired it together and I learned how to work on cars. If the roof needed shingling, I learned how to shingle a roof. I thought I was learning plenty from Grandpa. I didn't see any reason to go to school. 'I don't want to go to school,' I said.

'We'll talk about it more later,' said Grandpa. 'Don't worry about it for now.'

'OK,' I said. But I worried.

The ambulance pulled into the driveway of the Mannville General Hospital. Mannville was really too small to warrant its own hospital, but my great-great-grandfather had built one anyway. It was an imposing four-storey red-brick structure. The back door of the ambulance swung open, and the attendants appeared.

They unloaded Grandpa's stretcher and wheeled it through the doors of the emergency room. I followed them. They stopped beside a woman in a suit.

'Get the boy stitched up. He's coming with me,' she said to the attendants.

'Yes, ma'am,' they said together.

'Mr Mann,' she said to Grandpa, 'I'm Elsa Wheeler from the county children's services office. I understand you're the sole guardian of this boy?'

'Yeah,' said Grandpa. 'Why?'

'We'll look after your grandson while you're recuperating.'

Grandpa had done a lot of talking in the ambulance, induced by the painkillers the paramedics had given him, and now he was fading out. His eyes fluttered like the papery wings of an insect.

'Take care of my boy,' he whispered.

Elsa Wheeler reached down and grabbed my hand. Her hand was thin and bony and cold. I struggled to pull free from her grasp, but she only held on tighter.

'Hold still,' she said sharply. 'I don't have time to go chasing you all over the place.'

'I don't want to go to school,' I said, because I was sure that was where she was taking me.

'You're not going to school today,' she said. 'You're going to stay with one of our foster families until your grandfather is better. But you're going to school soon.'

'The hell I am!'

Her hand flew loose from mine, swung around in a wide arc, and smacked me on the bottom. I was dumbfounded. It was the first time in my life I'd been struck by another human being.

'You just watch your filthy mouth, mister,' she hissed.

I knew I was going to cry now, and there was no helping it. My wails filled the emergency-room lobby. I saw Grandpa lift his head up briefly from the bed and search for me before he collapsed weakly against the pillow again.

Elsa Wheeler lost patience with me altogether. She dragged me by the arm into a large white room where a doctor was waiting.

'Now, then,' said the doctor. 'You're Billy Mann, and I've heard all about you. You're a very brave little boy.'

I stopped crying somewhat.

'Brave boys don't cry, do they?' said the doctor, and he stuck a needle in my lip and proceeded to sew it back together. He didn't do a very neat job. That's why I grew a beard as soon as I was able, to hide the jagged white line that ran from my lower lip to my chin. It was always a physical reminder of the worst day of my life, the day I was taken, if only temporarily, from my grandfather.

I AWOKE EARLY the next morning in a strange bed. The sun was not yet up, and the room was predawn grey. I couldn't see where I was. Then I noticed what had awakened me. A figure loomed over the bed. I caught a faint whiff of manure and milk and tobacco. Now, who did I know who smelled like that? Someone I knew. Oh yes. Now I remembered where I was. Relief flooded through me. I was at the Shumachers', and the Shumachers were nice.

Mr Shumacher was a large, beefy man, and as he clicked on the lamp next to my bed, I saw he was holding a copy of the *Mannville Megaphone*, the local paper. My eyes focused first on the headline. It read BLOOD OF WAR HERO RUNS IN SON'S VEINS.

I looked next at the picture under it. It was a picture of me.

'Look! You famous boy!' said Mr Shumacher. 'Mutti!' he shouted over his shoulder. 'We have a famous boy in our house.' He spoke with a heavy German accent. It sounded like he was saying 'Ve heff a famous poy.'

'Yah,' said a woman from the doorway. 'Famous Amos, we could call him.'

'We could if his name was Amos, like mine,' said the man.

I got up. 'Amos is my middle name,' I said.

'Yah, time to get up,' said Mrs Shumacher as if she hadn't heard me. She had an accent too, heavier than her husband's, and she wore an apron over her house dress.

Mr Shumacher led me to the bathroom and filled the tub. Mrs Shumacher began to scrub me down thoroughly while I stood in it. I'd never taken a bath standing up before, nor had I ever been bathed by a woman. Her hands were swift and sure, the hands of a practised mother. Mrs Shumacher seemed to have bathed a thousand children, and she was much better at it than Grandpa. She gave me a professional scrubbing all over, even digging into my ears with the washcloth, until my skin glowed pink and raw.

'There,' she said with evident satisfaction. 'Clean.'

Then she dressed me in strange new clothes that didn't quite fit, and I went downstairs with her to breakfast.

The Shumachers were a large and buoyant tribe of Pennsylvania Dutchmen, and they already had so many children one more could hardly be noticed. They'd been taking in children for over two decades, most of them victims of some tragedy or other, like me.

Besides the father and mother there were six Shumacher children, most of them teenagers. The Shumachers were loud and Teutonic and vibrantly healthy, and they greeted me with happy shouts as they came in from their early morning work about the farm and sat down to an unbelievably large breakfast. There were platters of bacon, sausage, fried potatoes, pancakes, bowls full of scrambled eggs, pitchers of ice-cold fresh milk and orange juice. Mr Shumacher drank two cups of steaming black coffee without flinching before he even began to eat. He set down his cup with a deeply satisfied, 'Ahhhh,' and wiped his impressive moustache with a napkin; here was a man who appreciated small pleasures in a big way. When he saw me looking at him, he poured a small amount of coffee into a mug, filled the mug the rest of the way with milk, and sprinkled in some sugar. He set this in front of me.

'Drink that, boy,' he said. 'It makes you strong like me.'

'It makes you fart like him too,' said one of the Shumacher boys, and the table instantly erupted with laughter, Mr Shumacher included. He picked up a sausage and pointed it like a gun at the boy. 'I've had enough of you,' he said, and this seemed to be the funniest thing the family had ever heard. They laughed until tears poured down their cheeks. Then Mrs Shumacher clapped her hands once, and the joking was put aside. Only an occasional giggle now interfered with the serious business of consumption.

I, however, didn't laugh. I sat in silence, overwhelmed by the attention and the sheer volume of food. Grandpa and I ate like birds compared to the Shumachers. Nor did I see what was so funny. In fact, I was beginning to feel lonely. The horror of the previous day was slowly revisiting me. I remembered Grandpa lying on the ground, old and soft and helpless on the hard ice that had nearly killed him. I remembered the half-man in the back of the Simpson house and the way Annie's eyes looked when her father yelled at her.

Then the eldest of the Shumacher children, also named Amos, who was in his early twenties, reached over and tickled me. I shrieked. More laughter. This time I joined in. After that everything was fine, and I ripped into breakfast as though I'd never eaten before.

That was how easy-going the Shumachers were. If they didn't know you, they tickled you, and then they knew you.

'You stay with us until your grandfatti gets better,' said Mrs Shumacher.

'Where is he?'

'In the hospital.'

'When is he getting out?'

'Soon,' said Mr Shumacher. 'Don't worry about him.'

'How do you know?'

'We know your grandfatti,' said Mrs Shumacher. 'He said you should stay with us while his hip gets better.'

'He did?'

'Yah.'

That was all I needed to be reassured.

DAYS ON THE SHUMACHER farm were predictable. Even though I was not expected to work—I was too young—I was awakened at the same time as the rest of the family, long before sunrise.

The Mr and Mrs called each other Fatti and Mutti—German for Dad and Mom—and insisted that I do the same. Each morning Mutti came into the room I shared with Jan and Hans, the eighteen-year-old twins, clapping her hands and shouting, 'Yah! This is a good time to get up!' So we got up. We formed a line outside the bathroom, the door of which remained open while we urinated in turn so that other members of the family could come in and out as needed. Life as a Shumacher included dealing on a regular basis with the facts of animal reproduction, and this translated into their daily affairs as a complete lack of modesty.

Then we went downstairs in our underwear to dress in front of the wood stove—the only source of heat in the large old house. Fatti generally appeared around this time, emerging from the subarctic wasteland that is upstate New York in winter, his eyes lighting up at seeing us out of bed. 'Yah!' he shouted. 'This is a good time to get up!' That, it seemed, was the Shumacher philosophy concerning mornings.

At mealtimes the family sat at the long kitchen table, with Mr Shumacher at one end and Mrs Shumacher at the other, the seven of us arranged in between according to age. Mrs Shumacher ran the kitchen with startling efficiency, and it never seemed to be dirty, even when production was in full swing. The food she created for each meal would have kept Grandpa and me in leftovers for a month.

I watched in awe as these giants consumed food as though they'd never been fed before. The Shumacher body, I was learning, was a mighty machine in need of constant refuelling. When I first saw on television those military jet planes that are able to refuel in midair, I thought immediately of the Shumachers. They would have benefited enormously from this method of eating while they worked, except that it would have deprived them of the opportunity to talk to each other, which they did unceasingly as they ate. Mealtimes were the high points of their day. They shouted, laughed, cried, belched, clacked, slurped, smacked and snorted. I'd never imagined there could be such a thing as a Shumacher.

THREE WEEKS PASSED, and Christmas drew near. I'd spoken several times with Grandpa on the telephone. His voice was strong and healthy now, and whenever I talked to him homesickness welled up in me. But I knew I'd be seeing him soon, because he was almost better, and we would live in the old farmhouse like we always had, and he would tell me stories. And after Christmas I was to go to school.

I was still opposed to the idea of schooling, but I had held several conversations on the subject with twelve-year-old Marky, the youngest of the Shumacher children, who told me that school was not at all bad if you kept your mouth shut and were polite to the teacher. So I was somewhat reassured about the whole business.

I went home on December 22. Mrs Wheeler came in a long red car to get me, and she sat at the kitchen table smoking thin brown cigarettes and sipping thick black Shumacher coffee. She smelled strongly of perfume and lotion; her foreign, citified odour had the effect of stupefying Fatti and of sending Mutti into a territorial cleaning frenzy at the kitchen sink.

'Are you packed?' Mrs Wheeler said to me.

'Yah, he's packed,' said Mutti, sniffling.

'Best to get it over with right away, then,' said Mrs Wheeler. 'They get attached quickly at this age.'

'Yah,' said Fatti.

'OK, then,' said Mrs Wheeler. 'Did you thank the Shumachers for taking such good care of you?'

'He doesn't have to thank us,' said Mutti.

'Thank you,' I said shyly.

'See what a good boy he is?' said Fatti proudly. 'He thanked us anyway.'

Fatti carried my suitcase out to the car and put it in the back seat. Mutti stayed in the house. Fatti put his hands in his pockets and then stuck one out to me. I took it, and we shook. Suddenly he picked me up by my armpits and crushed me against him.

'We love you, boy.' He said it simply, thickly (it sounded like 'Ve laff you, poy'). 'Remember everything you have seen here. Yah?'

'Yah,' I said. 'Can I come visit you after I go back with Grandpa?'

'Yah,' said Fatti. 'You come back soon. *Auf Wiedersehen.*'

'Auf Wiedersehen, Fatti.'

Fatti clamped me against his massive chest for a moment longer. Then he put me down and stepped backward a few paces from the car. The other Shumachers came out in the driveway; the boys shook my hand stiffly, unaccustomed to such formality. Mutti and the two girls, Elsa and Hildy, knelt down and drew me to them, crushing me against their pillowlike chests.

'Let's go,' said Mrs Wheeler gruffly.

I got in the car, and Fatti shut the door.

Mrs Wheeler started the car. We pulled out of the slush-filled driveway, and twenty minutes later we pulled into the driveway of my ancestral home. Grandpa was standing out in front of the house wearing only a thin sweater against the cold. He had lost a great deal of weight, and he looked much older. I got out of the car and walked slowly towards him.

He smiled shyly. 'Almost don't recognise me, do ya?' he said, and in truth I didn't, but his voice was still the same, and it all came over me in a surge of emotion. I ran and wrapped my arms round his waist.

'Oof,' he said. 'Careful. I'm still a little sore.'

'Sorry,' I said.

He put his hands on my head and looked at me. 'You've grown three feet, I think,' he said. 'Go get your suitcase.'

I ran back to the car and got my suitcase. Then Grandpa and I went into the house together. I heard Mrs Wheeler's car crunch out of the driveway. I hadn't said goodbye to her. Neither had Grandpa. She didn't exist any more. I was home again, amid the same familiar smells of living. I sat down at the kitchen table.

'Hungry?' Grandpa asked me.

'Yah.'

'Yah?'

'Yeah, I mean.'

'Whillikers,' said Grandpa as he stooped stiffly to retrieve the frying pan from a low cupboard. 'Can tell you been hanging around with a bunch of Krauts. Fried baloney all right?'

'Yeah,' I said. Fried baloney would always be all right, as long as Grandpa was the one who made it. We sat together at the kitchen table, and Grandpa watched me eat, and he asked me what I had been up to, and I began to tell him the whole story. I picked up speed and chattered away until the whole thing was told: the Shumachers, how much they ate, how big and loud they were. I went on and on until I arrived in the present, and the whole thing was history. It was just me and Grandpa again, sitting in the kitchen, and he ruffled my hair and made me another sandwich.

I returned from my sojourn with the Shumachers a changed boy. I'd ventured into the outside world and come back in one piece, proving to myself and to Grandpa that such a thing could be done successfully. I was learning that there were at least two kinds of people in the world: the Mr Simpson types and the Shumacher types, the bad and the good, the scary and the safe. And I learned also that even though the former could ruin things for you pretty quickly, they were made up for by the latter—by the kind, warm Shumachers. Perhaps I would like school after all. If Marky Shumacher liked it, then it couldn't be so bad. So I yielded to Grandpa's will and allowed myself to be enrolled in school.

Though I was only seven, I could read and write as well as any ten-year-old, and my mathematical abilities were decent. As a result, I was allowed to skip kindergarten, first grade, and the first half of what would have been my second-grade year and was put into Mrs Schmeider's second-grade class at Mannville Elementary, right where I would have been if I'd been in school all along.

I was late for my first day of school because the Galaxie wouldn't start. When I walked into the classroom, I was clutching a brown paper bag with a fried baloney sandwich and an apple in it, wearing a new pair of Zips sneakers. I hung up my jacket in my cubby and joined the class on the floor, trying to ignore the sea of curious faces staring at me. Fortunately, Mrs Schmeider was reading a story.

Although Grandpa read to me often, it was never children's material. I was spellbound by the bright pictures on the shining pages of the book the teacher held. And then I felt a cold little hand work its way into mine and squeeze it in welcome. I looked up. To my astonishment it was Annie—the little girl from up the hill.

To say that I was overjoyed to have found Annie again would be an understatement. For the first time in my life I had a friend. After that first day I bounced out of bed bright and early every morning, urging Grandpa to hurry up and make my lunch and asking was he sure the car was running today, because I didn't want to be late to school again.

'Of course it's running,' he barked one morning when he couldn't take it any more. 'It just didn't run that one day, because I was in the hospital for so long. A car needs constant attention, boy. Just like some people around here I could name.'

Meaning me, I suppose.

SECOND GRADE PASSED for Annie and me, and so did third and then fourth, and the years rocked along like the cars of a speeding train. None of my classmates seemed to mind that I was a Mann. The Fiasco of the Ostriches, it appeared, had been forgotten by everyone except Grandpa, and nobody made fun of me for it. And Annie's hand stayed in mine, or so it felt, right up to the year we turned thirteen, when I began to feel shy around her. But shyness notwithstanding, we were together, and before I knew it, we were in eighth grade.

Each morning Annie walked down the hill from her house and met me at the corner of Mann Road and the county road. Her father didn't know she and I were walking to school together. He hadn't spoken to me since the day Grandpa slipped on the ice, six years ago now. That was because I'd done my best to avoid his presence. He sat in front of the television all day, leaving the house just to buy beer, which he drank on the couch until he passed out. I knew this only from Annie, of course. I hadn't dared to set foot inside the Simpson house again. His belly, according to her, was growing ever larger, his skin turning the sallow shade of death. She shuddered when she spoke of him. I learned not to bring him up.

On the way to school Annie and I compared lunches, and if she didn't have enough, I would give her some of mine. Annie packed her own lunch every morning, but often there was little to put in it. Anything I had was hers, even my fried baloney sandwiches.

Annie asked me once if I didn't ever get tired of eating fried baloney sandwiches.

'No,' I said truthfully, although today, as a grown man, just the thought of eating one will make me nauseous.

'You do your homework?' I asked her.

'Yes!' Primly said, as though she was shocked I would have thought otherwise. Annie *always* did her homework. She did it in the public library or sometimes at my house. She couldn't do it at home, because she had no desk and she shared a room with three sisters.

Annie was a genius. She was teaching herself to speak French from language tapes she'd bought with money she saved from doing odd jobs for neighbours. She was, she said, going to become fluent in French and move to Montreal after high school. I had no doubt that, if that was what she wanted to do, then she was going to do it.

'Did you do yours?' she asked.

'I did some of the math,' I said. 'I already read this damn novel a couple of years ago, though.' I'd had to read *Lord of the Flies* for English class.

'Don't swear,' she said. 'It's mentally unhealthy. Someone with your vocabulary ought to be able to think of other ways to express himself.'

'Mentally unhealthy?'

'You need a sound mind in a sound body,' she said. 'So you can be strong enough to rescue me.'

I smiled at that. We were barely teenagers now, but she still remembered the plan to rescue her I had contrived when I was small. Many years later she would tell me that not only hadn't she forgotten it but she thought about it every night as she went to sleep. Sometimes, she said, it was the only thing that kept her going.

We were forced to meet in secret at the base of the hill, as we'd been doing almost every day since we were seven. The need for secrecy was something we never mentioned. We skirted around it. Whenever we said, 'Meet you later,' it meant 'See you at the bottom of the hill, safe from his eyes and close to the woods, so he can't get you and so we can hide if we need to.'

'So you can rescue me' was only half a joke. Annie was seriously in need of a rescue mission. The problem was, I was the only one who knew it, and I didn't know how to do it myself.

It was a three-mile walk to school. Grandpa offered repeatedly to take us in the Galaxie, but I shunned the idea. Mornings with Annie were a rosy, luxurious time, and I lengthened our walks as much as possible. I know now I was already completely in love with her. We'd stopped holding hands, and we never kissed, but I thought someday we might, and the anticipation hung over me. We brushed arms sometimes as we walked. Her skin was soft, her arms covered with a fine golden fuzz, barely visible unless the light struck them just right. They were lovely arms, although she often had to wear long-sleeved shirts to hide the bruises from where her father had grabbed her. Touching her sent a thrill through me so powerful I could scarcely breathe. Any boy who has ever been in love knows this feeling. It consumes you and pulls you along, leading you to your final goal. I myself had no idea what that final goal was, but I knew it was there, because I could feel it. I thought it probably was 'making out'.

Soon it would be time to make the move. There were some minor obstacles to overcome. Annie was four inches taller than I was, and I wasn't sure how I was going to circumvent that. I felt I ought to be able to sweep her into my arms and pull her to me so that her petite shoes were dangling just off the ground. First, however, I needed a magical growth spurt to bring me to the level of her lips.

'HOW OFTEN DO you see that Simpson girl?' Grandpa asked me one day as we sat at the kitchen table, he sipping a glass of whiskey.

'What do you mean?'

'Just what I said. How often do you see her?'

'Every day, I guess.'

'You ever kiss her?'

I blushed. 'Shut up,' I said.

'Did you or didn't you?'

'No! OK? No!'

'All right,' said Grandpa. He appeared relieved. 'That's all I wanted to know.'

'Why?'

'Never mind why. You'd just be better off not getting mixed up with those Simpsons.'

'There's nothing wrong with Annie,' I said.

'I'm not saying there's anything wrong with her. I'm just saying it would be better if you didn't get involved with her.'

'She's not like the rest of them.'

'No, you're right. She's beautiful. Smart too. Nobody would ever know she's related to that fat bastard up the hill. Oops. Forget I said that. Oughtn't to speak ill of folks,' he said.

'Everyone speaks ill of everyone, seems like.'

'Not everyone. White trash sit around saying things about people. Quality folks don't do that. Simpsons do.'

'Annie's a Simpson.'

'No she isn't,' said Grandpa. 'Being a Simpson is a state of mind.'

'Something has to happen to him.'

'I know it.'

'I've seen bruises all over her.'

Grandpa raised an eyebrow, not joking. 'All over?'

I blushed again. 'I mean on her arms and stuff.'

'Does he just hit her?'

'What do you mean? Of course he hits her.'

'But I mean is that all he does?'

'I . . . I don't know for sure. She doesn't say.'

'But you think he does more than that?'

I nodded.

'You should tell someone.'

'She told me not to. She said in a few years she'll be old enough to move out. She wants to move to Montreal. She's saving money, and she's teaching herself French.'

Grandpa had a faraway look in his eyes, and I could tell he was remembering something he didn't want to remember. 'Just remember what I'm telling you about the Simpsons. And don't ever get started on this stuff,' he said, pointing to his glass. 'Pure poison. It'll kill ya. You ever been drunk?'

'No.'

'Good.'

'I'd like to try it once, though.'

'What? Drinking?'

'Just getting drunk.'

'Why?'

I shrugged.

'It's ruined me, that's for sure.'

I said nothing. I didn't think he was ruined. I thought he was disappointed. No farm left, all the money gone, and not an ostrich to show for it. And me the only living descendant of the once great Mann clan—besides him, that is.

FALL ARRIVED, and then faded into winter. I had been skipped ahead to tenth grade, which meant that I would be in the senior high building while Annie was still in junior high. I wasn't looking forward to it. If anything, it was she who should have been ahead of me. Grandpa drank his way through his days. Time passed in Mannville.

During Christmas break of my fourteenth year I worked for Mr and Mrs Gruber, stocking shelves in their store and occasionally delivering groceries, and after vacation was over, they invited me to stay on as a regular employee. I showed up after school and worked for about four hours each evening.

I began to meet people now. I carried armloads of food to homes all over town, and by the time the old year had died and the new one was begun, I knew upward of fifty adults by name. Most were elderly, but they were all the more interesting to me because they *were* old, and it was exciting to talk to them. All of them had known my father, and they never failed to comment on how much I looked like him, acted like him, talked like him, and walked like him.

One day, as Annie and I were walking home after school, I said, 'Let's go on a date.'

She stopped in her tracks. 'Beg pardon?' she said.

'A date,' I said. 'A movie or something.' I was listening to myself in astonishment. Some new part of me was speaking, a smooth operator version of my old personality.

'You're a maniac,' Annie said. She began walking again.

'Just for fun,' I said, or the smooth operator said. 'What else is there to do around here?'

She smiled but said nothing.

'Life is short,' the smooth operator philosophised grandly. 'We might as well make the most of it. Besides, I've only been to one movie in my life.' It was true. Going to a movie was something Grandpa simply never thought of. I had money of my own now that I was working at Gruber's Grocery, and the smooth operator wanted to spend it lavishly. *Return of the Jedi* was playing at the Bijou, and I'd been dying to see it. 'Besides, you're the only girl in my life. You're the one for me, baby.' The smooth operator was speaking in a fake French accent now, deliberately bad. Annie shrieked with laughter and blushed. I continued. 'You are the one who makes the sun go up and down. You make the moon go round. You make the leaves grow and the white, white snow.'

Annie looked at me out of the corners of her eyes. 'Are you making that up?' she asked.

'We shall watch Luke Skywalker, the Jedi warrior, as he conquers the evil forces of the galaxy. And we shall eat popcorn.'

'Have we met?' Annie said.

''Ow do you do,' I said. 'I am Jacques le Snock.'

'You're crazy.'

'Not crazy. I am *French*, baby.'

'Oh my God.'

'Come on, Annie,' I said in my normal voice. 'It's no big deal. It's just a movie. Just come with me. Saturday night.'

Her face betrayed some emotion I'd never seen in her before. 'You had me with the white, white snow,' she said, and I knew by the sound of her voice that something had changed with us, and that I had caused it, and that it was good.

I walked whistling up Mann Road to the farmhouse. I could hear Grandpa murmuring to himself as I came in the kitchen door. He was sitting in the living room with a glass of whiskey.

Grandpa wasn't saying much these days. It seemed as if his drunkenness had reached the point where it never left him. Somewhere along the line he'd surrendered to it. I wasn't sure when this had happened. It was a gradual process, I guess. You never see these things when you're right on top of them, but when I compared the Grandpa I'd known as a little boy to the Grandpa of my early teenage years, I could see the difference right away. The old Grandpa sang, talked, laughed, bellowed challenges at the Munchkins. This Grandpa was a spectre who talked to himself instead of to me.

'I have a date,' I said. I liked to pretend that he and I were a normal family, who had conversations about things that mattered.

He looked at me with vacant eyes. 'Swell,' he said.

'Yuh. Movie. With Annie.'

He began to murmur again. He was telling himself stories.

'Quit it,' I said. 'Wait until I get my notebook.'

He fell silent.

'You hungry, Grandpa?'

I'd become the cook for both of us. I also cleaned the house, did the laundry and the dishes, and shovelled the snow from the driveway. Grandpa never asked me to do these things, but I knew that if I didn't, the whole place would fall apart.

'You hungry, Grandpa?' I repeated.

But he never answered.

I went into the kitchen and made two peanut butter sandwiches and two cups of hot chocolate. Then I went upstairs and got my notebook. I set one sandwich and one mug of chocolate next to Grandpa—though I knew he would never touch them—opened my notebook and waited. When he muttered loud enough for me to hear, I wrote down what he said. In this way I was learning the story of how Willie Mann found the money.

About once a week I gathered everything I had recorded from Grandpa and added things in the middle to make them fit. I was in the process of turning it into a story. When it was finished, I was going to send it off to a magazine and publish it. I wanted to be a writer when I grew up. This exercise with Grandpa was my first attempt at a short story. It seemed to be taking for ever, but in my own way I was enjoying it.

The week passed on without anything earth-shattering happening, and Saturday finally arrived. The movie began at seven fifteen. I began to get ready around three o'clock. First I took a shower. Then I brushed each tooth, back and front, and rinsed with mouthwash. I shaved, even though it was completely unnecessary, and then cauterised my raw face with aftershave, which brought tears to my eyes. Then, thoroughly sterilised and reeking of bay rum, I spent a further half-hour getting dressed. When I was ready, it was five o'clock. I still had two hours before I was supposed to meet Annie at the hill.

At 6.45 an idea occurred to me. I sneaked the keys to Grandpa's Galaxie from the hook on the kitchen wall, started it up and drove slowly to the base of the hill. Grandpa himself had been passed out all afternoon, and I knew he wouldn't notice that the car was gone even if he woke up. Driving was a brilliant idea; now I'd have a car in which I could make out with Annie should the opportunity arise.

She was waiting for me at the foot of a giant oak. The headlights of the Galaxie caught her like a rabbit, and for a moment she froze, confused. She'd been expecting me on foot.

I turned out the headlights and opened the door. 'Come on,' I called.

'Oh my God,' she said. I opened the passenger door for her, and she slid in next to me. 'Billy, this is *dangerous*.'

'Don't worry about it.'

'Do you know how to drive?'

'Of course. I've been driving since I was five.'

'Lawn mowers don't count, Billy. You have to be sixteen to drive a car! What if Madison sees you?'

Madison was Mannville's police officer. He usually spent his Saturday nights parked in the square, which was where the movie theatre was. But there was an easy way around that one.

'We'll park behind the bank,' I said. 'Then we can just walk across the square to the theatre. He'll never see us.'

Annie said nothing. I was crushed. Here I was, being gallant and manly and daring, and she thought I was just being stupid.

'Are you mad at me?' I asked her.

'It's not that,' she said. The tone of her voice had changed suddenly. It was flat and dead, as though another person were speaking. I knew instantly what that meant. Her father had been after her again. I stopped the engine and turned on the interior light. Then I took her chin in my hand and gently examined her face.

'No bruises,' I said. I brightened my voice to hide the sudden twist of apprehension in my bowels. 'You look all right.'

'Yeah,' she said. 'I look fine.'

She began to shake, just barely noticeably. I was still holding her chin. I thought now might be a good time to kiss her, but something told me not to; instead I put my arms round her and drew her to me tightly. Her arms remained at her sides.

'Hug me back,' I whispered in her ear.

'I don't know how,' she said.

'It's easy,' I said. 'You just pick up your—'

'Billy,' she said, 'I know how you feel about me.'

I pushed back from her. 'What do you mean?' I asked.

She smiled weakly, but there was no mirth in her eyes. 'You're the sweetest guy in the world, Billy,' she said. 'And I want to feel the same way about you. I really do. But I can't feel that way. In fact, I can't feel anything at all.'

'What are you talking about?' I said.

'Well,' she said, 'I want you to know something.'

'All right.'

She sighed. 'No. Wait. First let me tell you something else. I was really happy that you wanted to go on a date with me.'

'You were?'

'Yes, I was. You were perfect. The way you asked me. All silly and sweet. Just the way a nice boy should ask a girl on a date.'

'Well, good,' I said, thoroughly confused.

'But now I have to tell you the other thing. I'm not . . . I'm not a nice girl.'

'Well now, there you have something,' I said. 'You're not *always* nice. Sometimes you get kind of bossy.'

'I'm not joking around. I mean I'm not a nice girl like you meet at school. Or innocent.'

'You're not? I kind of thought you were.' I was still trying to tease her, but it was failing miserably, and I hadn't the slightest clue what she was talking about.

'Well, you were wrong,' she said. 'I'm not innocent.'

'What do you mean?'

'I mean,' she said carefully, 'that I'm not a virgin.'

I stared at her.

I'd always known what she was about to tell me, or at least I'd known it for long enough that it felt like always. But I didn't want to hear her say it. I was scared. Of her, a little bit. Of how she sounded so much older. 'You don't have to say anything,' I said.

'I have to,' she said. 'Please let me say it. If you really love me, Billy, and I know you do, you'll let me say it. I have to tell someone. And you can't tell anybody.'

'OK,' I said.

'Do you promise?'

When Annie told me the truth for the first time, there in Grandpa's old Galaxie, I looked her in the eye and flat-out lied to her. And this was my great lie: 'I promise,' I said, 'that I will never tell anybody.'

She turned her gaze to the windshield, looking out at the whiteness. 'The reason I'm not a virgin,' Annie said, 'is because of my dad. And that's why I'm not nice and innocent like the other girls at school. And you deserve someone like them. You're a sweet guy, Billy, and you're the best friend I have, but I'm not what you need. I'm a load of problems, and I'm going to be crazy when I get older. In fact, I'm probably crazy right now.'

'You're not crazy,' I said. It was all I could think of to say.

She looked at me again. 'My dad is raping me,' she said.

I must have flinched, looked away.

'You don't like to hear it, do you?'

I didn't answer.

'Well,' she said, 'then just imagine how it must feel to have it actually *happen*.' Her shaking was visible now.

'I can't,' I said. I was shaking now myself.

'No. You couldn't. Nobody can.'

Annie looked out at the quiet, frozen night. Grandpa was right; there was nothing Simpson-like about her, not a trace of the sloping brow or jutting jaw. Her nose was long and thin, her lips were filling out with the first flush of womanhood. Her hair fell down her back in a long braid, soft and clean and reddish brown. She was beautiful.

'You've always known, too,' she said.

'Yeah. Or I kind of knew.'

'I want to know what you think of me,' she said. 'Would you still ask me on a date now if I'd already told you?'

'Of course!'

She examined me closely. 'You're lying,' she said.

'Stop it,' I said. 'It's not a fair question. I always knew. You just told me that yourself. And you were right.'

'You didn't know. You guessed. That's not the same thing.'

'No. I always knew. I used to spy on you when I was little,' I said suddenly. 'I used to sneak up the hill and hide in the trees.'

'What on earth for?'

'Because I was in love with you,' I said. 'I've always been in love with you. You used to sing to yourself all the time.'

'You creep,' she said. 'You *spied* on me?'

'I was watching out for you. I used to hear him yelling. That was when I decided I was coming after you. I've always loved you, Annie,' I said again. 'I always will too. No matter what.'

'You were watching me? And you heard things?'

'Yes.'

'What kind of things?'

'Shouting,' I said. 'Crying.' I was shaking harder now, and I was afraid to look at her.

'Oh my, Billy,' said Annie. She reached over and took my hand.

I was ready to shriek, to start punching the roof. I began to choke on tears. I went on. 'I don't think you're crazy. Not in the slightest. You can get over this. I know you can. You're the only person in this town our age with any brains.'

'I will be crazy,' she said. She sat up demurely, looking suddenly like a little girl again, the way she had when I first met her. Had he been doing it to her even then? It was a chilling thought. How could something like this be allowed to continue? Why didn't someone kill him? Why didn't I?

'I will be crazy because I can't stand my life. As if this wasn't enough, I have to be a Simpson too? The poorest, dirtiest, stupidest family in town, the one that everyone makes fun of? And look at me with you! You're a Mann, for crying out loud. You're like super-people. Rich, smart, talented, popular, good-looking . . .'

'Come on,' I said. 'That's not us any more. You know that. My dad was the superhero, not me. Besides, Annie, look at yourself. You know you're the smartest kid in town.'

'Yeah? Then why did *you* get to skip a grade?' She was crying now too, tears for a life that had been disregarded, not by herself, but by others. It was the worst possible crime against her. Annie's life had been stolen, and she wanted it back. Her face was contorted in agony as she sobbed. 'Why is everything so easy for *you*? You never do any homework, and you still get all the grades.'

She was right. Things came easier to me, not because I was smarter, but because I was a Mann and she was a Simpson. No Simpson ever went to college. Plus, she was a girl. None of the other girls raised their hands nearly as much as Annie did, and even though teachers knew she was smart, they still acted surprised when she said something right.

I couldn't think of anything else to say, so we sat there in the car holding hands. Gradually her sobs quieted, and I put one arm around her shoulder and leaned over and rested my head against hers for a moment. Then I sat up again.

'I don't care if you're crazy or not. I love you,' I said. 'I mean it. I do. Do you still want to go to the movie?' What she had told me was almost too big to conceive. I could think only in little steps. Suddenly the next thing we did seemed very important, no matter what it was, and all I could think of to tell her was that I loved her.

She smiled, sniffling. 'I'm sorry,' she said. 'We've probably missed the beginning.'

'That's all right,' I said.

We parked behind the bank and walked across the square. Madison was where we thought he'd be. He greeted us by name, and we did likewise. Then we went into the theatre and watched the horrible truth of Luke Skywalker's parentage unfold. I'd known it was coming, but still couldn't quite bring myself to believe that Darth Vader was Luke's father. It seemed incredible, and yet somehow it made sense. When the movie ended, we walked out with the crowd, and I took her hand in mine. I wanted people to see us together. I was proud of her.

We drove out of town the back way to avoid Madison and went back to the base of the hill. I could tell she was thinking about what she would say when she got home. Her mind had already pushed the entire evening into the background.

'Good night,' she said. 'Thanks for the movie.' She got out. I watched her climb the hill, her long braid swinging like a pendulum in the headlights.

Then I went home. That was it. My first date was over.

Grandpa was still sitting where I had left him, lolling in his recliner, unconscious. I took the glass of whiskey from his side and dumped it in the sink. Annie had missed her childhood. How much of mine had I missed? I had no father, no mother, and my grandfather, though kind, was too drunk most of the time to take care of me. I sighed. I could have had it a lot worse, I thought. He could have taken me to an orphanage when I was a baby.

I scrubbed the whiskey glass and went upstairs to my bedroom. There I took out my notebook and scribbled away until midnight.

DR CONNOR and his wife lived on the first and second floors of a large Victorian mansion. Pasted to the front door was a small hand-lettered card that read PLEASE DO NOT RING DOORBELL. This meant you were just supposed to walk in. Underneath that it said, in smaller, less optimistic lettering, PAYMENT IS EXPECTED AT TIME OF SERVICE. That, as everyone knew, was just a formality. Dr Connor's patients were mostly those who didn't have insurance. As a result, payments were not only often not made at time of service but sometimes never made at all. That didn't bother Dr Connor. He was not in medicine for the money, he once told Grandpa. Any doctor who was could have done better becoming a stockbroker.

A bell tinkled behind me as I closed the door. There was a small waiting room that boasted a coffee table smothered in magazines, and a couple of easy chairs. Dr Connor himself was sitting in one of these chairs reading a fishing magazine. He peered at me over his glasses as I came in.

'Well, hello there, young William,' he said. 'Come for a checkup?'

'Sorta.'

'Um-hmm,' he said. He led me to his examination room, where he pointed to the paper-covered table. 'Have a seat,' he said.

'There's nothing really wrong with me,' I said.

'I know,' he said. 'I can tell just by looking at you. But it never hurts to check, as long as I've got you here.'

Dr Connor felt my throat and looked into my ears, eyes and nose with his light scope. He tapped my knee with his rubber hammer; obediently my leg swung out and back again.

'How old are you now?'

'Fourteen.'

'Yes,' said Connor. 'I knew that. I knew you before you were even born, practically.'

He sat down in a chair in the corner and indicated the other one. 'Hop down from there,' he said. 'Examination over. What is it you wanted to talk to me about?'

I looked around, not knowing how to begin. In fact, I'd forgotten exactly what it was I was going to say. In desperation I folded my hands in front of me and stared at them, hoping the answer would come. 'Grandpa's missed having you around,' I said. I don't know why I said that. I didn't even know if it was true, but it flashed into my head. 'He's sorry about everything.'

Dr Connor said nothing in response, but in the softening of his eyes I could see he had heard me.

'Something wrong?' he asked. His voice was kind, warm.

'Did you know my dad?'

It was still not what I had intended to say, but there it was. I'd meant to ask him about Annie.

Dr Connor took off his glasses and put them in the pocket of his white lab jacket. 'Yes,' he said. 'I knew him quite well.'

'What was he like?'

'He was a lot like you. About your height. No, shorter. Same eyes. Same personality, even. Intelligent, friendly, good-looking.'

'Am I good-looking?'

Dr Connor laughed. 'You really wouldn't know, would you?' he asked. 'You teenagers are all alike. So shy, so uncertain.'

'Was my dad shy?'

'Was he?' He cocked one eyebrow. 'Well . . . your dad was different from the rest of us, Billy. He had a kind of glow about him. He was always confident but never overbearing.'

'What do you mean?'

'He was never stuck-up. Didn't have a cocky attitude. He could have, you know. He was the most popular person in town, and he genuinely liked everyone. He was always going out of his way to do things for people. Helping little old ladies across the street. That sort of thing. Anyway, I never answered your question. Yes, Billy, you are good-looking, and you will be a handsome man, barring any unforeseen mutilation, of course. So be sure and always wear a seat belt.'

'What?'

'When you're driving,' he said sternly. He gave me a look then that told me that somehow he knew I'd driven Annie to the movie in the Galaxie. Had he seen us? Spooky, I thought. But I chose to pretend I didn't know what he was talking about.

'There's . . .'

'Hmmm?'

'Do you know who my mother is?' I asked Dr Connor abruptly.

He was silent.

'Because if you do,' I said, 'I have to know. I can't stand not knowing. Grandpa won't even hint if he knows or not. I'll never know my dad, but my mom is out there somewhere. I have to find her.'

'Why?'

'Why? Why do you think? She's my mother!'

'But what will you ask her when you see her?'

'I don't know.' I was exasperated. 'I just want to see her.' My voice was suddenly rising in volume. I could feel trails of wetness working their way down my cheeks. 'Tell me! Do you know?'

'No, Billy, I don't know who your mother is,' he said. 'If I did, I would tell you. I would tell you if I knew.'

'If you're lying—' I said, but I didn't finish the sentence. That was the boldest statement I had ever spoken to an adult in my life, and I was afraid he was going to be angry. But Dr Connor was not like most adults. He could see through me, right to who I was.

'Son,' he said, 'everything will resolve itself in the end. You have questions. You need to know things. That is what will give you purpose. Follow your nose. Someday you'll find out. Don't get disappointed when things aren't immediately available.'

We sat in silence while I wiped my nose and eyes.

'What are you going to do when you grow up?' he asked me. Coming from him, it didn't sound like the same mindless question adults always ask of children. He was actually curious.

'I'm going to be a writer,' I said.

'Ahhh,' he said. 'A writer.'

'Of short stories,' I went on. 'And maybe novels. I'm writing a short story now.' Not even Annie knew that about me.

A bell tinkled on the front door. Someone was waiting in the parlour. 'I would like to see it when you finish it,' said Dr Connor, getting up. 'Not to criticise it, just to read it . . . I know how hard it is to show these things to others, but I will always be interested.'

'There's one more thing,' I said.

'What is it?'

I took a deep breath. I wanted so much to tell him about Annie, to tell him everything she'd told me. That, I remembered, had been my original reason for coming to see him—not to talk about myself or my father or my mother. But there in the office the events in the Galaxie that night seemed unreal. I found myself unable to say it.

'Nothing,' I said. 'Never mind. Just— Thank you for talking to me. You're the only one I can say these things to. I appreciate it.'

Connor smiled, his wrinkled, kindly face creasing with pleasure. 'I've always felt like you were sort of a son to me, Billy,' he said. 'And I'll always talk with you about anything.'

If I'd been younger, I would have hugged him. Instead I shook his hand. He patted me on the shoulder and gripped my hand warmly, strongly, in his large fist. Then without warning he drew me to him and clasped me against his chest. After a brief moment he released me, and I went out of the examination room and down the hall and out through the front door.

4

Life was good. I walked whistling through the square, down Frederic Avenue, and up Mann Road, the same walk I had taken every day of my life since I'd started school. It was late spring, 1986, at about six o'clock. The air smelt of honeysuckle and swimming pools. A small boy rode by me on his bicycle, a beach towel safety-pinned around his neck like a cape. 'I'm Superman!' he shouted at me.

'I know how you feel,' I said.

The boy stared at me and then darted off down the street.

I had finally finished my very first short story. All I needed to do was type it out. I'd found an old Royal typewriter in the attic and fixed it up. When I got home, I opened a package of typing paper, set it next to me, opened my notebook to the beginning of my notes, and started typing:

WILLIE MANN AND THE RORY FORTUNE

Willie Mann was digging up his garden. It was early spring, and the weather in western New York State—along the southern shore of Lake Erie—was still cold and wet.

Willie grimaced in pain each time he forced the shovel into the ground. There was a Confederate musket ball buried in his thigh, which the surgeons on the battlefield at Antietam had been unable to remove. But Willie didn't pay any attention to the pain. He knew he was lucky to have kept his leg at all.

He was digging up a piece of land that his father had given him for when he got married. He was about to turn twenty-one, and although he had no immediate plans to find a wife, he knew it was wise to prepare for the day when he would have one. There were many rocks in the soil, which would have to be removed before planting could begin.

It was nearing noon, and Willie was hungry. He stabbed his shovel into the earth again and struck a rock. It was a big one. Sighing, he dug around it and dropped painfully to his knees. Then he began to scoop the loose soil out with his hands. Soon Willie forgot all about dinner. He focused his attention instead on the top of the ironbound chest he had just uncovered, which lay just a bare six inches under the ground. He reached down and touched it—the rusted iron almost gone, the wood eaten away by damp and decay. The thing looked *old*.

Far away, at the other end of the fields, his mother rang the iron dinner triangle, a shrill, nerve-jangling sound that usually sent him limping eagerly off to the house. This time, however, Willie ignored it. He picked up his shovel again and excavated the chest so that every inch of it lay exposed. It had large wrought-iron handles on either end, and a lock, all badly corroded. On the lock was still visible the letter *R*, moulded long ago by an English craftsman—if the legend was correct. Willie recognised the chest immediately. It gave him a tremendous shock.

He thought about the history of the chest and of how strange it was that he should be the one to find it. 'Well, well, well,' said Willie as he went to the pump and washed his hands. Then he went into the tiny house that he shared with his mother, father, grandfather, and two brothers.

The rest of the Manns, except for Daddo, Willie's grandfather, were already seated around the kitchen table. Daddo ate in the back bedroom, by order of Willie's father, because he had no teeth and made too much noise when he ate.

Willie hung up his jacket but did not sit down in his chair. 'Excuse me,' he said, and limped straight into the room where Daddo ate. He could feel four pairs of eyes burning at the back of his head. Something was going on, they knew, but they also knew better than to ask him what it was. Willie had been very quiet since his return from the fighting. He'd barely spoken at all, not even to tell them the story of how he was wounded. War did that to a man, counselled Father. Best let him work it out on his own, and he'll tell it when he's ready.

Willie sat down on the floor at Daddo's feet and tapped him on the knee so the old man would know he was there.

'Eh?' said the old man. 'Who would that be?'

'Me, Willie,' said Willie.

'Willie. What is it, then?'

Willie paused, unsure of how to begin. Daddo was very old, and Willie didn't want to excite him.

'You remember that story of the Rory treasure?' Willie said.

'Aye,' said Daddo. 'Why d'ye ask?'

'Tell it,' said Willie.

'What! Now?'

'Aye.'

Daddo had come from Ireland and, like many old folks from there, he was a wealth of ancient stories and legends. But the story of the Rory treasure was relatively new, having happened around the time of the War of Independence. Everyone for miles around knew the tale well, and all of them hoped that they would be the one to find the treasure, because it was rumoured to be a great one.

But few people Willie's age believed in the Rory treasure. This was why Willie wanted to hear the story again. He had to make sure of every detail.

Daddo pulled out his pipe and filled it. Willie lit it for him.

'There was once a Scottish clan by the name of Rory,' Daddo began. 'They were among the first to settle in the Colonies, brought here by the scent of money. They had a land grant from the governor of New Amsterdam, and half of their time and money went into farming there, with the benefit of free labour from Indian slaves. The other half of their money was invested in a different kind of slave. The Rorys owned a dozen or so ships, which loaded their hulls with stolen human beings, bought in African ports. The Rorys shipped these slaves across the ocean and unloaded them in the Colonies.

'This brought them huge profits until the Colonies went to war against England. Then the English tried to press the Rory ships into naval service against the rebellion. The Rorys themselves cared nothing for the rebels but, being Scots, their hatred of the English overcame even their love of easy profits. They scuttled all their ships so that the English couldn't get their filthy hands on them. The English king was so furious he sent a detachment of specially trained mercenaries—Hessians—to kill every Rory man, woman and child, seize all their goods, and turn them over to the Crown.'

Daddo paused to puff at his pipe. 'Among the Rorys that had come to the New World,' he continued, 'were two brothers. One of them was handsome and charming, named Malcolm. The other was as ugly as it is possible to be, and he was James. But they were the same in temperament, both being cruel, evil men. They hated each other deeply. However, they had no choice but to remain business partners, although they plotted against each other constantly.

'When word came that a squad of Hessians was after their heads, the brothers knew they had to be united against these soldiers. But neither of them cared for the safety of the other. They only cared for keeping the family fortune safe from the English. They took all their holdings to bankers to be turned into gold, and when this was done they had seven large chests filled with gold pieces. The brothers then set about the business of hiding the chests.

'They did none of the actual digging, of course. They had slaves do it for them, and when the hole was dug and the chest placed into it, they murdered the slaves and put their bodies on top of the chest, so that they could never tell where the gold was hidden. Six of the chests were hidden in this fashion. Finally there remained only one. Anyone could see what would happen next. Since the two brothers were the only ones who knew where the other six chests were buried, each hoped to murder the other and return after the war to dig them up.

'They put the seventh chest in a wagon and rode west until they were out of the territory of New Amsterdam and into what was then Penn's Woods. They wanted the last chest to be so well hidden that nobody would ever think where to look for it.

'What they hadn't counted on was their sister, Mary. Mary was a

Rory but, for all that, she had a good heart. She was half-witted, or at least everyone treated her as such, and she had never begged the difference. The brothers took Mary along when they buried the seventh chest.

'James and Mary rode in the wagon while Malcolm followed on horseback. They went on in this manner for several weeks, the brothers very much on their guard against robbers and each other. Finally it was agreed they had ridden far enough. This time, since there were no slaves with them, they had to dig the hole themselves. Early in the morning, with Mary still asleep, they dug deeper and deeper until the moment came at last.

'While Malcolm's back was turned, James took a shovel and struck his brother with the blade of it in the back of the neck. Malcolm never had a chance. His handsome head rolled off his shoulders and into the hole. Mary, waking suddenly, began to scream, but James ignored her. He threw his brother's corpse in after the head, dropped the chest of gold on top of it, and filled in the hole. When he had finished, he turned to Mary and was amazed to see her pointing a large pistol directly at him. "This is what you were to me, brother," she said, and she fired.

'To understand the bravery of such an act, you must remember that in those days pistols were matchlocks—big, slow and unreliable. They failed more often than they fired. But Mary had nerves of steel. The pistol fired, and her aim was true. The ball passed through her brother's heart, and he fell dead.

'Mary had known all along what the brothers were plotting, y'see. She wasn't half-witted; it was only to her advantage to pretend that she was so. Her plan was to avenge those whose lives had ended at the hands of her brothers and also to return someday for the gold. But she never returned. Soon after that the Hessians found her, cut off her head, and shipped it back to England for the King to gloat over. And that was the end of the Rory clan, as well as their fortune. The English found the first six chests of gold, but they never found the seventh, and from that day to this, men have sought it in vain.'

Daddo finished his story with a self-satisfied expression, saying, 'Now that the afternoon is wasted, ye may as well bring me a dram.'

Willie reached into his shirt and pulled out the lock from the chest. It was so rusty it had come off with only a few blows of the shovel. 'Feel that,' he said, handing it to his grandfather.

The old man squinted at it, turning it over and over in his hands. Then he traced the letter R that was worked into the face of the lock.

'Jaysus,' whispered the old man.

'Would you say that lock is about a hundred years old?' asked Willie. 'Would you say it came off the Rory treasure?'

The old man could not speak.

'You'll have as many drams as ye like, from now until the end of your days,' said Willie, struggling to his feet. 'Come on. I've somethin' to show everyone.'

That night, when Willie's entire family was drunk on whiskey, the neighbours began to stream in to see for themselves whether the story was true. Soon the kitchen was full of revellers. Willie looked at the open chest sitting on the table. His brother and father were guarding it fiercely, allowing no one close. Willie saw his brother snarl at a man who reached out to touch a piece of the money. The expression on his face was savage; not quite murderous, but close.

Nobody saw Willie limp out of the house and out across the field. He went to the hole he had dug earlier that day. There he lay down on his back, staring up at the clouded night sky. He found himself seeing into the future, and he wished, quite simply, that someone else had found the money. Nothing was going to be the same for the Manns from now on.

The End

'WILLIE MANN and the Rory Fortune' was my first short story. Writing it was the hardest thing I'd ever done. There was nobody to help me with it, nobody to talk to about it when I got stuck. In my more reflective moods I realised that I didn't even know why I was doing it.

I began work on that story the summer I turned fifteen, and I didn't finish it until just before my sixteenth birthday. Annie and I still walked to school every day that fall and spring, but we saw less of each other than we used to. I knew without asking that it was because of what had passed between us in the car that night.

She didn't look me in the eye any more, and she was quiet much of the time as we walked. Sometimes she didn't say anything at all. I decided she was embarrassed she'd told me.

'Have you told anyone?' she asked me once.

'No,' I said, because I hadn't, even though I was going to. Any day now. In fact, I didn't know why I hadn't yet. 'Of course not.'

'Good,' she whispered. Head down, feet shuffling through the dirt. She never used to walk like that. She was being beaten down. I was losing her. The time was coming for me to do something, but I still didn't know for sure if telling was the right thing. Maybe I had to do something myself. But what?

To my surprise I found myself dreading our morning walks to

school. Also, school itself had begun to seem so irrelevant that one day I decided simply to stop going. I made it in once or twice a week for roll call, and then I just went home. Amazingly, nobody seemed to mind. Certainly we never got any phone calls from the school about it, although that may have just been a period when I forgot to pay the phone bill. And Grandpa never noticed I was playing hooky; actually, I doubt he even knew I was home. He spent a good deal of his time in bed or passed out in the rocking chair.

Grandpa drank more now than I'd ever seen him drink before. Mr Gruber sold him the whiskey at a discount, a case at a time, and I brought it home. I guess if I'd known how alcohol, like a cat, will torture its victims mercilessly before dispatching them, I would have been alarmed at how much he was drinking. But I was a teenager, and teenagers rarely bother to look beyond the ends of their own noses. And it must be remembered that I grew up with Grandpa drinking. Constantly. I thought it was normal, so I didn't worry about it much. I thought instead about becoming a writer, and sometimes about Annie. That was about it.

Soon after I finished my story, I took it to Dr Connor. I needed the opinion of an adult. I wasn't sure if it was any good, and Connor was the only person I knew who'd been to college, so he was the logical choice. He read it in his consulting room while I toyed with the paper on his examination table. His eyes, when he finished, were glowing with excitement.

'Where did you learn to write like this?' he demanded.

'I taught myself,' I replied. 'Do you like it?'

'Like it? I love it! It's fantastic.'

I blushed. A warm feeling of success swelled up in my chest.

'What are you going to do with it?' Dr Connor said.

'Publish it, I guess.'

'Do you know how?'

'I'll just send it away to a magazine or something.' It had never occurred to me that I wouldn't become a published writer, even though it seemed like awfully hard work, and to turn out only a few pages in nine or ten months was not exactly the mark of greatness.

But Dr Connor dismissed these concerns with a wave of his large, hairy hand. It wasn't how much I wrote that mattered, he said, but how good it was. He promised to take me to the library and show me where to look up the addresses of publishers. It wasn't as simple as I made it sound, he said.

'You're coming along splendidly, my boy,' he said. 'Splendidly.'

I looked at him with gratitude, and I realised at that moment that I trusted Connor completely. It was then I knew I had to tell him about Annie.

'Doc,' I said, 'I have something to tell you.'

And I told.

IT WAS SEVERAL DAYS later that Annie appeared at the front door. I was in the kitchen when her shadow fell across the porch, and I caught it only out of the corner of my eye. She didn't knock or ring the bell. I went down the long hallway to the door. She stood turned to the side, so that I could see only her profile. That was how I knew she had something to hide again.

'Where have you been? You haven't been going to school,' she said, speaking away from me, out into the yard.

'Look at me,' I said.

'No.'

I stepped out onto the porch and gently turned her face towards me. Her left cheek was bruised black and green, swollen out of proportion to the rest of her face. Her eye was puffy and closed.

'What happened?' I said.

'I didn't go to school today either,' she said. 'And I have you to thank for it.'

'I'm taking you to the hospital. Right now.'

'No. You're not taking me anywhere. You broke your promise,' she said. 'You told.'

'Annie. Please understand. I had to.'

'I trusted you,' she said. She didn't say it vindictively. It was simply a statement of fact.

I felt my face begin to flush with rage—at her father but also at her. She was letting this happen. She was allowing it.

'How can you let him keep this up?' I asked her.

'It's nobody's business,' said Annie. 'OK? It's not yours or Connor's or the county's. It's mine.'

'It's not just yours. It's mine. It's everybody's.'

'I can't fight him, Billy,' she said. 'He's too strong. If I fight him, he hits me. So I let him drug me. That's how it happens.'

'What are you talking about?'

'When he does those things to my body,' she said. Annie was staring far beyond me, as if she were talking about someone else. 'I know he's going to do it to me. There's nothing I can do about it. So I let him drug me, and at least then I don't feel it. But after those people came, this is what he did to me. And he didn't drug me first, and I felt every bit of it.'

'I'm going to kill him,' I said.

'No you're not. Nobody is going to do anything.'

'If that's what you think, then you really must be nuts,' I said. I was in the grip of full-fledged anger now.

'I trusted you,' she said again. 'And you told. I'm never telling you anything again. Do you have any idea how it made me feel to have those people come to my house? To snoop around, interrogate us like we're some kind of criminals? Bank robbers or something?'

I knew then that Connor must have called the county, and the county had sent its people over. That must have been the only way Connor knew to go about it, and in most situations it would have been the right way. But not this one. I knew it couldn't happen for Annie the way it was supposed to happen. I'd always known I would have to take care of it myself. And I decided right then and there that I *would* take care of it myself, the way my father would have done it if it was him instead of me. This was a job for a superhero, a daredevil. This was a job for Billy Mann.

Annie stepped off the porch and headed back down the driveway.

'Annie,' I called.

She turned. 'Yes?' Her voice was vacant, void.

'I told because I love you,' I said. 'That's why.'

'That's nice,' she said. She turned again and headed up the road.

I felt, as she left, that Annie had not been there at all.

Well, I thought, if she wasn't going to save herself from her father, then I was. I was going on another mission to the Simpson house. An image of my own father smiled at me and slapped his hands together. He spat contemptuously on the ground and flexed his muscles. 'Let's get to it,' I said to him. 'We have a job to do.'

I SPENT TWO DAYS in preparation for my mission. During this time I stayed away from school and Annie stayed away from me, but I sent her telepathic messages: I'm coming, I would think, standing on my porch and staring up at her house. Don't give up.

I was ready on a Tuesday. I decided that I'd make my run early the next morning. If I didn't catch him on the first run, I would simply go back again and again until I got it right. But something told me morning was the right time. As I thought about it, I remembered that Annie was often subdued in the mornings.

I went to bed early that night, my gear laid out on a chair next to my bed: dark clothing, ski mask, sneakers, flashlight. My alarm went off at 4.00am. I sprang out of bed, dressed, and was moving up the road within fifteen minutes. When I hit the base of the hill, I entered the trees. This was why I'd brought the flashlight—to navigate among the large trunks and fallen branches. I calculated the time to be around 4.45. When I had finally cleared the trees and climbed the hill, it must have been nearly five. The sky was greying as false dawn approached. I was at the outer boundary of the Simpson yard . . . where I stopped and hit the ground like a man under machine-gun fire. I had caught a glimpse of orange on the porch. It was the glowing end of a cigarette butt. Annie didn't smoke, and her older sisters had all left home by this time. It had to be Simpson. I hardly dared breathe. I lay on my belly next to a large birch, certain he'd heard me.

But nothing happened. There was no shout, no approaching footsteps. I could make out the figure on the porch now as the eastern sky began to brighten. It was him, all right. I saw the orange cigarette butt arc towards me as Simpson flicked it away from him. It skittered to a halt several feet from my nose. I heard him grunt with exertion as he stood up and went into the house, the screen door on the porch closing quietly behind him.

This was the first time I'd seen Simpson since the day Grandpa broke his hip on the ice. He'd grown fatter, waddled more. The fact that he hadn't let the screen door slam gave me both fear and encouragement. Perhaps he was being sneaky, not wanting to wake his daughter up until it was too late for her to resist. My timing might possibly be dead-on.

I crawled on my belly towards the house. When it became apparent that he wasn't coming back onto the porch, I ran in a half crouch until I gained the front door. I waited there. I heard the thump of a glass being set down. He was close, in the kitchen perhaps. I edged the screen door open and slipped inside.

And I was back in the same living room where I had first met Annie, where she had held my hand for the first time. The house was filled with the same stench, but the living room was not quite as dirty as it had been eight years ago.

I moved across the living room to the back hallway, listening for the sound of Simpson. I went to the hallway first because I wanted to see if the half-man was still there.

I kept my hand over my nose as I approached his room; the smell was nearly intolerable. I opened the door. There he lay, staring up at the ceiling, the same as I remembered him, swaddled in filthy sheets.

I moved to the side of the bed and looked down. He was unshaved, longhaired, a perfectly blank expression on his face. The same tubes ran around him like so many plastic snakes, and the respirator hummed and hissed as it always had.

Frederic—that was his name, I remembered—just breathed away. In thinking back, I assume he must have had some sort of damage to the part of his brain that controlled his higher functions. He could blink, but that was about it. It might have been that his mind worked perfectly and he was merely paralysed, on top of being a quadruple amputee. I prefer to think that he was not capable of thinking at all. For to be trapped in that filthy bed, in that house, aware of everything that was going on around you and unable to do anything about it, would be a fate worse than the worst kind of hell I can think of.

Time to get out of here. I stole along the hallway again, then through the living room to the stairs. I stopped there and listened. There was an angry voice, muffled by walls. Then there was crying. My God, I thought, could it be happening right now? I sneaked up the stairs. The shouting seemed to be coming from a bedroom around the corner. I had just identified which door it was coming from, when it opened and Mr Simpson came out.

I drew back and froze. If he turned the corner to go down the stairs, he would see me. If he saw me, he would kill me. But he didn't turn the corner; he went into the bathroom, next to the door from which he'd come. I heard him turn on the faucet.

I peeked cautiously around the corner. The bedroom door was open, and the light was on. There was an item or two of clothing on the floor, and I could see the end of a bed. On it there was a small, slender foot. Annie's foot.

Without thinking, I crept into the bedroom. All instinct for caution had fled, and I was thrumming with adrenaline.

Annie lay on the bed in much the same attitude as her brother downstairs, staring vacantly at the ceiling, unblinking. She wore a nightdress, which was lifted halfway up her thighs. Was I too late? I wondered. Had he already done it?

'Annie,' I whispered. She didn't move.

'Annie!' Not a sound, not a glance. I reached down and touched her shoulder. She didn't flinch. I bent my ear over her mouth. Yes, she was breathing. There was a faint medicinal odour to her breath. He had drugged her. I was too late to stop that, but I wasn't too late to stop the rest of it.

Just then the sink stopped running. I opened the closet door and slid inside, pulling it closed just enough so that I could see through a tiny crack. Mr Simpson came back down the hall into the bedroom. I looked through the crack in the door.

Simpson was taking off his shirt. I was horrified by the sight of his flabby torso. And I learned something I hadn't known about Mr

Simpson—he had a long scar on his chest, extending the length of his sternum. It was the mark of heart surgery. Somewhere, sometime, some misguided surgeon had decided he would try to extend this miserable life by ten or twenty years.

I heard the unzipping of pants and the clink as the belt buckle hit the floor. I was afraid I was going to be sick. It was now or never, I said to myself. I didn't know what to do, but there was no way I could stay there in the closet and listen to this man rape his daughter. I wished for a gun or a knife or anything to kill him with. I was almost crying. This was too much. It was more than any fifteen-year-old boy could be expected to handle.

But I was not, I remembered, just any fifteen-year-old boy. I was a daredevil, and the son of a daredevil. The blood of heroes coursed through my veins. And what was more, I was a Mann.

I pushed open the closet door.

'GET OFF HER!' I screamed at the top of my lungs.

The effect upon Mr Simpson was immediate, and better than anything I could have hoped for. He was just about to get on top of Annie. He was naked and completely unprepared for the sight of a black-clad, ski-masked stranger emerging from his daughter's closet. A lifetime of hard drinking, heavy smoking and greasy food had already left its mark on his heart. He stood up rapidly, put one hand on his chest, and spun round to look at me.

'Waahhhh . . .' he said, and slowly, almost gracefully, he toppled over like a short, thick tree, hitting the floor with a thud.

I stood there for several long moments. Simpson, lying on the other side of the bed, was invisible to me.

I waited. His head did not reappear over the bed. He said nothing. Annie was still unconscious on the bed. Delicately I reached over and pulled her nightdress down, not looking at her as I did so. So far she didn't even know I'd been there, and it was beginning to look as if she never would.

I stepped around the end of the bed and looked down.

Simpson's pudgy hand was still pressed to his chest in a final, fruitless effort to encourage life to remain. I stood there for a long time, wanting to make sure, but not able to bring myself to touch him. After five minutes or so of stillness I was certain.

Mr Simpson was dead. I'd scared him to death.

I had very little time to waste on reflection.

I fled down the hallway, back down the stairs, into the living room, and out of the house. I ran down the hill, avoiding the road. It was more important than ever now that I not be seen.

Annie would wake up from her drugged stupor, see her father on the floor, and call the police. There was absolutely no reason for anyone to suspect that I'd had anything to do with it.

Back home, I hid my dark clothing in my closet even though there was no reason to hide anything. Nobody would be looking in my room for clues to Simpson's death.

It was now near 6.30am. From the direction of town I heard the whine of Mannville's ambulance. This meant that Annie had woken up and found him. What would she think? Would she be scared, or would she fall on her knees and thank God for delivering her?

It wasn't until late the next afternoon that I heard from Annie. Nobody had reported the death of Mr Simpson to me yet, and I was still playing dumb, but there were bags under my eyes. The suspense was already beginning to tell on me.

I went to work at Gruber's as usual. Mr Gruber was oblivious to any changes in me, as he was oblivious to everything that didn't involve football or his grocery. The Buffalo Bills had been victorious the night before, and that was foremost in his mind.

Heading home that afternoon, I saw Madison, Mannville's lonely police officer. He was sitting in his squad car, staring blankly down the street. A chill shot through me. I forced myself to wave at him.

'Hey, Billy.'

'Hey, Officer Madison.' He smiled at that; he was rarely called Officer. 'What's new?'

'Big news,' he said darkly. 'Jack Simpson's dead.'

'No!' It was the first time I had repeated the script I'd so carefully prepared. I hoped I wouldn't stumble over my lines. 'What happened?' Not too dramatic now, I cautioned myself.

'Well,' said Madison, 'they say it was a heart attack.'

'Wow,' I said. 'I can't believe it.'

'You're a friend of Annie Simpson, ain't you?'

'Yeah.'

'Seen her lately?'

'No,' I said. 'Not in a while.'

'How long?'

I thought hard and fast. 'Eight or ten days.'

'She didn't call you?'

'No. We never call each other,' I said. 'He wouldn't allow it.'

Madison nodded at that. There was no reason to ask who *he* was; Mr Simpson's temperament was well known.

'She called it in herself,' said Madison, 'but when we got there, she wasn't around.'

'That's kinda weird,' I said.

'And nobody's seen her. You sure you ain't seen her?'

'Yeah, I'm sure.'

'Reason I ask is, the circumstances under which he was found were mighty peculiar,' said Madison.

'What do you mean?'

'Well now, I can't reveal any details of the ongoing investigation,' he said pompously, 'but if you see the Simpson girl, tell her we need to talk to her.'

I was genuinely worried. 'I will,' I promised.

I walked on, my thoughts gathering momentum. I would have to start going to school again so that nothing would seem out of the ordinary. Sooner or later someone was going to notice I'd been skipping classes, and suddenly I didn't want anyone to notice me at all.

Annie would have realised immediately upon waking what had been going on when her father keeled over. She would know that he'd been caught by his heart in the act of raping her yet again. She would have had to look at him naked, lying on her bedroom floor. I wondered if she'd screamed. And where was she now?

'Annie,' I muttered, 'come out.'

We tried this sometimes, sending psychic messages to each other because we couldn't use the telephone. It had worked once, although it might have been coincidence. I'd called her name in my head several times, and a moment later she'd come walking up the driveway, claiming to have heard me.

It worked again, though not in quite the same way. In our mailbox I found a note containing only two words: '*My hero.*'

So she knew.

THE ENTIRE TOWN of Mannville searched for Annie for two weeks. Citizens formed rescue teams and combed through fields, woods and meadows looking for clues. Even though she was a Simpson, and the Simpsons were trash, she was one of our own. At least this is what people seemed to be saying to themselves. And we *knew*— that was the other thing they were saying, without saying it. We all knew what was going on in that house. There was an undercurrent of guilt running through our town, the feeling that all this could have been avoided if someone had had the guts to speak up. But guilt can be covered up by busy work, so everyone assuaged their conscience by walking through the woods and fields, wearing yellow vests that said VOLUNTEER on them, and calling Annie's name.

I participated in more of these searches than anybody else, but that was mostly for appearances' sake. I knew the whole business was a farce. Annie wasn't going to be found.

I was questioned once officially by Madison and perhaps two hundred times unofficially by everyone else. During these interviews I did my best to appear worried. But this was an act. I knew Annie was fine. I even thought I knew where she was, although I wasn't going to say anything to anyone. And I had no intention of showing the note she'd left me either.

There was a funeral for Mr Simpson, which was, to my surprise, very well attended. It seemed that everyone, not just Madison, found his death suspicious. Word had got out that he'd been found naked—and in his daughter's bedroom. These circumstances, combined with Annie's disappearance, made for the biggest gossip mine in Mannville since the Fiasco of the Ostriches, and nobody wanted to miss out on the closing ceremonies of Mr Simpson's scandalous life.

Grandpa and I went to the funeral in the old Galaxie. I'd roused him from his stupor enough to make him understand that Jack Simpson was dead. The news, amazingly, sobered him up.

'How'd you say he died?' he asked me slowly.

'Heart attack.'

'Huh.'

That was the longest conversation we'd had in years, or so it seemed.

Grandpa wore the same clothes to Jack Simpson's funeral that he'd worn to his mother's funeral when he was a young man, or so he claimed. Whiskey kept him thin, he said, by eating up his insides. But he drank no whiskey that morning. Completely sober for the first time in years, he stood stiffly at attention in the churchyard, ignoring the stares we received.

And boy, did people stare. They stared because Grandpa and I were never seen together in public. They were used to seeing me alone, of course, delivering groceries. But Grandpa had hardly left the house in five or six years. There were some older folks looking at him out of the corners of their eyes, with expressions that said 'He's still alive?' and I could tell they'd forgotten all about him.

'Why are you going?' I asked him as we were getting ready. 'I thought you hated him.'

'I don't *hate* anybody,' Grandpa explained. 'I just . . . Well, there's . . . there's an obligation.'

'What do you mean, an obligation?'

Instead of replying, Grandpa began muttering to himself. I knew better than to press him for details. I was just glad he was alive. I surprised him by throwing my arms around his brittle old frame and grabbing him tight. He stiffened, but after a moment he appeared to remember that I was his grandson, and he put his arm around my neck and clenched me to him.

There were, as it turned out, no Simpson family members at the funeral. Annie had disappeared, Frederic was simply Frederic, and Annie's mysterious sisters, whom I'd never even met, had stolen away over the years until it was just the three of them left: a ruined Annie, her demonic father and her vegetative brother.

Nothing exciting happened at the funeral, as folks seemed to have hoped—no sudden appearance of Annie, no thunderbolts from the sky. When it was over, we got back into the Galaxie, and as I was pulling out of the church parking lot, Grandpa said, 'Jack Simpson drank himself to death, didn't he?'

I shuddered. 'More or less,' I said.

'I'm headed the same way.'

I was startled to hear this. Grandpa rarely, if ever, indulged in reflections of this type. He knew he drank; I knew he drank. Everyone knew it, and that was the way it was. The end result of a life of hard drinking was well known. But this was the first time I'd ever heard him admit it.

'Yes, you are, I guess,' I said.

We drove in silence.

'How well did you know Jack Simpson?' I asked him after a while. 'I mean, were you and he ever friends?'

Grandpa snorted. 'No.'

'Then what was all that stuff about an obligation?'

Grandpa thought. 'We were never friends, but we knew each other,' he said finally. 'He was younger than me. Below me in school. Our boys grew up together. Eddie and Frederic. I told you that.'

'Yeah. I remember.'

'Freddy used to stay over at our place all the time—when things got rough. Simpson used to beat on him and the girls when he got drunk. Freddy came over whenever he felt like it. Didn't even need to knock. He knew he was always welcome. But he ran off and joined the army. Then he got hurt.'

'Do you know what happened to him?'

'Land mine. Or maybe a grenade. I don't remember which. Simpson was always mean,' said Grandpa, returning to the subject of his nemesis. 'He used to torture younger boys. He took to drinking early too.' There was a pause. 'Like me,' he added.

After another lengthy moment he said, 'You think it's too late for me to quit?'

'Do *I* think . . . No. Not yet. You could do it if you wanted to.'

'All right, then. When we get home, I want you to clean out the house. Top to bottom. Throw out every bottle you can find.'

'What?'

'I'm quitting,' he said. 'I'm going to check myself into the hospital for a while. When I come back, I don't want to find any temptations lying around. Will you do it for me?'

'I . . . You're serious?'

'Yes, I'm serious.' And to tell the truth, there was a determination in Grandpa's voice that I'd never heard before.

'Yeah. Yes, I'll do it. Of course I will.'

'Seeing Jack Simpson go to his reward without ever having made amends got me to thinking. I have some things to set right before I die. Drying out might kill me, but it would be better than living like I have been. And I owe you an apology.'

I was speechless. My eyes were growing wet.

'I've hardly been any kind of father to you at all,' said Grandpa, tears of regret welling up in his own eyes. 'I've been drunk for forty years. I saw the way folks were looking at me back there. Everyone thinks I'm a nut.'

'No they don't,' I said. 'They just think you're eccentric.'

Grandpa sighed. 'They're half right,' he said. 'But listen. I've wasted enough years sitting around feeling sorry for myself. It's time for that to stop. So clean out the house, boy. That's a polite order. I'd do it myself, but I don't think I'm strong enough. If I picked up a bottle, I wouldn't put it down.'

'All right,' I said, and with that simple acknowledgment the redemption of Thomas Mann, Jr., had its beginning.

He sat in his rocking chair for the rest of the day. I called the hospital and told them we would be coming in tomorrow.

'They're getting a room ready for you,' I said. 'You want me to start cleaning out the bottles now?'

'Don't leave me alone in here,' he said.

So I sat on the couch and watched him reach for where his glass would be about thirty times. After an hour he held up his hand.

'Look at this,' he said. It was shaking. 'I better have a drink.'

'No,' I said. 'You have to get over these shakes the hard way.'

We went to sleep early that night. I made sure his bedroom door was open, as well as mine, so I could hear him.

I was awakened sometime after midnight by shouting. Alarmed, I raced to his bedroom and flicked on the light. I found him sitting in his underwear in the corner, rubbing frantically at his arms.

'Grandpa!' I said. 'What are you doing?'

'Snakes!' he shouted. 'Get 'em off me!'

What was this? I wondered. 'There's no snakes in here, Grandpa,' I said.

But Grandpa continued to scream.

'There's no snakes in here,' I repeated. I was beginning to get scared. I sat down next to him and put one arm around his shoulders. My touch seemed to calm him; after a moment he relaxed.

'Oh, damned snakes,' he said. 'Oh, I'm seeing snakes.'

'I'm not afraid of snakes,' I said. I pulled him tight. 'Let them come on me. They won't bother you any more.'

Grandpa began muttering to himself. He rocked back and forth.

There was a phone in his room. I picked it up and dialled Dr Connor's number. He answered after the third ring.

'This is Billy Mann,' I said. 'Grandpa decided to go sober today, and now he's seeing snakes. Can you come over?'

'I'll be right there,' he said, and he hung up.

Several minutes later I heard Connor's Beetle pulling into the driveway. He came in the front door and headed directly up the stairs. He was in his pyjamas, and he was carrying his black bag.

'Howdy there, Tom. Haven't seen you in a while,' said Connor calmly. 'Billy says you laid off the hooch.'

'Oh Lord. Snakes,' said Grandpa. He was rubbing his hands over his eyes, as if trying to wake up.

'Here's a little something to help you sleep,' said Connor. He handed me a pill. I went into the bathroom and got a glass of water. When I came back into the room with it, Grandpa was in bed again, the covers pulled up to his chin.

'Here you go,' I said. Grandpa swallowed the pill with a sip of water and laid his head back down on the pillow.

'You'll sleep now,' said Connor.

'I'll sleep now,' Grandpa echoed, his voice already fading.

'It's the hospital tomorrow for you,' said Connor.

'We already called,' I said.

'Good. I can check in on you there, if you want.'

Grandpa nodded.

Connor motioned to me, and we headed out of the room. We were nearly through the door when I heard Grandpa's voice.

'Connor,' he said.

Connor turned. 'Yes, Tom?'

'That wasn't me that screamed at you that day,' Grandpa said. I knew he was talking about the fight they'd had when I was still small, before I'd gone to school. 'It was the booze.'

'I knew that all along, Tom,' said Connor.

'You're my best friend, Connor. I'm sorry.'

'I knew that too, you miserable old son of a bitch,' Connor said.

'All right,' said Grandpa. 'Just so you know.' And he fell asleep.

Connor shook my hand at the door and got into his Beetle. At another hour, perhaps, we would have talked, but it was late. I listened to him drive down the road, and then I went back to bed.

I may have slept for an hour or two. I was awakened by the sound of a timid knock at my door. When I opened it, Grandpa was standing there in his funeral suit, a small suitcase on the floor next to him. He refused to look me in the eye.

'Will you take me to the hospital now?' he asked.

I wanted to ask him how he felt, but something told me I should never mention the events of the previous night to him. Instead I dressed and drove him to Mannville General Hospital, where I waited while he checked himself in at the admissions desk. Then Grandpa and I shook hands formally.

'I'll come see you tomorrow,' I said.

'No visitors,' said the nurse.

'Can he call me?' asked Grandpa. He was looking jumpy.

'No phone calls tonight,' said the nurse.

'This is my grandfather,' I said. 'I'll call him when I feel like it.'

'Young man, we have rules here,' said the nurse. 'Particularly in *this* kind of situation.' She nodded at Grandpa.

'Forget about it,' said Grandpa. 'Call me tomorrow.'

'I will.'

'You'll be alone on your birthday.'

'That's all right,' I said. I would be turning sixteen soon. And he would be turning sixty-two. 'So will you.'

'I'm too old to give a shit about birthdays any more.'

'We don't allow profanity in this hospital,' said the nurse.

'I hope someday you can forgive me for all this,' said Grandpa.

'Knock it off,' I said.

'All right, then.'

We hugged.

I turned and walked out of the lobby to the parking lot. Then I turned around and went back into the lobby. As I'd hoped, Grandpa was gone, and the nurse was sitting alone at the desk.

'Yes?' she said.

'I wanted to tell you something.'

She looked at me expectantly, her eyebrows arched. I didn't like the way she'd spoken to Grandpa, so I said, 'My great-great-grandfather built this hospital. We used to own this whole town and everything around it for a ten-mile radius. So I'll thank you to remember that when you're talking to my grandfather.'

The nurse opened her mouth and then snapped it shut. I turned and walked out to the waiting Galaxie.

When I got home, I made a thorough search of the house and collected nearly seventy empty whiskey bottles and a few full ones. I took them out to the yard and threw them, one by one, into the old brick oven next to the carriage house. When I was finished, I built a bonfire of paper and wood on top of the shattered glass, soaked it with gasoline, and set the whole mess on fire. It burned for the rest of the day, black clouds of smoke roiling out into the Mannville sky. I sat in a lawn chair and contemplated the blaze and the snakes and the old farmhouse, and for the thousandth time in my life thought about what it was like to be part of the clan called Mann.

IN THE WEEKS that Grandpa was drying out in the hospital, I wrote fifteen stories. Solitude seemed to enhance my creativity. And I was waiting for news about my first story, 'Willie Mann and the Rory Fortune'. I'd sent it to a magazine that Dr Connor helped me pick out. When a month passed and I found a letter from the magazine in the mailbox, my heart leapt with joy. Inside was a form letter. 'Dear contributor,' it said. 'Thank you for your interest in our magazine, but . . .'

A rejection letter. It would not be my last, I knew.

Also, I bought a motorcycle. It was a 1977 Kawasaki KZ1000, an old cop bike I'd picked out of the newspaper one day. 'Needs work,' the ad had confided, but that was right up my alley. I'd inherited Grandpa's mechanical facility. I kept the bike in the garage. After I was done writing for the day, I went out to the garage and worked on it. Grandpa assisted me over the phone in our nightly conversations. The snakes, he said, had stopped crawling on him, and he'd actually made a friend at the hospital.

'Except for Connor, I haven't had a friend in decades,' he said. 'We watch the news together every night.'

'What's his name?'

'It's a she,' he said. 'Her name is Mildred.'

'You have a girlfriend?'

'I'm too old for that nonsense,' he scoffed. 'Boy, she's a smart one, though. You'd like her. What did you do on your birthday?'

'I forgot about it,' I said. My sixteenth birthday had come and gone without a nod of recognition from me. 'I think I just worked on my bike. I can't figure out how to straighten the handlebars.'

'I'll show you when I get back.'

'When are you coming home?'

'In ten days.'

'I cleaned out the house.'

'Good job. Thanks.'

'Don't mention it.'

What I meant, of course, was not 'Don't mention it'. What I meant was a million other things—such as 'What took you so long to do this? What would our lives be like if you'd quit sooner? What would they be like if you'd never started?' But I didn't know how to say any of those things to him, and I was still too young to understand the implications of the spiritual rebirth of my grandfather. I focused on small things. I just wanted him home with me so he could help straighten out the handlebars.

But I was able to straighten the handlebars by myself, and within a week the bike was running smoothly. My life was changed irrevocably and for ever. I soared along the back roads of Erie County, covering hundreds of miles, making up for all the places I'd never been. The taste for freedom began to expand in me like a slowly inflating balloon, and I knew the time for leaving Mannville would be coming soon. It was as inevitable as the approaching winter.

Grandpa came home from the hospital in early September. He'd put on weight, and his eyes were alert and clear. After cleansing the house of any traces of alcohol, I'd gone through it again with all the implements of purification: warm soapy water, bleach, oil soap, broom, mop, rags, lemon-scented furniture polish. It had taken me nearly two weeks to accomplish, but the house gleamed.

He stepped inside and inhaled. 'The old days are over,' Grandpa said. I knew he was talking about his drinking days. He put his hand on my shoulder. Tears came to his eyes. 'I have so much to tell you,' he said in a broken voice, 'that I don't know where to start.'

'There's plenty of time,' I said, embarrassed.

'Yeah,' he agreed. 'If drying out didn't kill me, nothing will.'

Grandpa was not alone; he'd brought Mildred with him. She was a tiny, pretty woman with sharp grey eyes and a birdy way of talking that belied her tremendous energy. She nodded in approval as she stepped inside our farmhouse for the first time. 'It's *clean*,' she said. 'And coming from me that's a compliment.'

'It's not always like this,' I said.

Mildred smiled. 'It will be from now on,' she said, and that was how I knew she'd come to stay.

Mildred had raised seven children over the course of thirty years, Grandpa told me later, and her husband had beaten her regularly all the way through it. She'd stayed first for the kids and later because she'd grown attached to drinking her way through her days, which was easier than leaving. I peered closely at her when I thought she wasn't looking. She didn't seem like the kind of woman who would drink at all, but alcohol doesn't choose its victims on the basis of appearance. I liked her immediately.

'Mildred's going to live with us,' Grandpa said to me late that evening. 'That is, if it's all right with you.'

'Are you guys getting married?'

Grandpa snorted. 'No,' he said. 'We know better than that.'

'You mean you're going to *shack up*?' I was only teasing him, but his face grew red, and he looked down at his hands.

'I didn't know you were so moral,' he mumbled.

'I was kidding,' I said. 'I think it's great. Really. I like her.'

'We're taking it slow,' he said.

I didn't understand what he meant by 'taking it slow' until I helped Mildred move her few possessions into a bedroom separate from Grandpa's. It was on the first floor, and it had last been occupied by one of Grandpa's ancient aunts. There would be no hanky-panky between Grandpa and Mildred, I gathered, at least not yet. They seemed to enjoy spending their evenings simply sitting together in the living room and reading aloud to each other, occasionally helping the other stifle the urge for a drink.

Mildred told me she was grateful that I hadn't objected to her moving in with us. 'Seven children I have,' she said to me, 'and not one of them has written or called in almost ten years. Not that I blame them. They hated their father, and I didn't lift a finger to change anything. I couldn't, you see. And my husband is dead now. So I would have been all alone in the world if I hadn't met your granddad.' Her explanation of her previous life went no further, but I understood. I knew something about cruel fathers.

Mildred gravitated naturally to the kitchen, which soon became a bustling enterprise that churned out cakes, cookies, roasts and stews on a grand scale. Grandpa and I both began to put on weight, and I gave silent thanks that I had eaten my last fried baloney sandwich. Grandpa spent most of his time in the garage, tinkering with machines and repairing everything he could get his hands on. Soon the house began to look as good on the outside as it did on the inside: shutters were painted; the yard was mowed. He also pruned the trees and ploughed up a garden.

'This is pretty near the spot where everything happened,' he told me one day, pointing to his little spaded-up patch of earth.

'What do you mean?'

'The treasure,' Grandpa said. 'This is where Willie found it.'

I stared at the spot, awe-struck. Somehow the notion that the events of 120 years ago had a physical location had never occurred to me. I was overwhelmed by the weight of our history.

'I want to read Willie's diary,' I said.

Grandpa sighed. 'Fujimora promised me he'd come back with it. He's not late yet either.'

Mildred came out on the back porch and rang the old iron dinner triangle. Grandpa and I looked at each other and grinned.

'It's nice to have a woman around again,' he said. 'Isn't it?'

'I wouldn't know,' I said. 'I've never lived in the same house with one before.'

'You'll like it,' said Grandpa. 'They make life worth living.'

We went into the house together for lunch.

6

Early in the fall of my junior year—it was a crisp Tuesday afternoon in mid-September—another strange wrinkle occurred in the fabric of my life. It announced itself as a letter in the mail.

Getting a letter in itself wasn't so unusual. I often received mail, mostly letters of regret from literary magazines. I was probably the only kid at Mannville High who raced home every day for news of whether or not he'd arrived in the literary world.

But this particular letter was unusual. It bore no return address, and it had a Canadian postmark. I was nonplussed.

Then I remembered. Annie.

I don't mean to imply that I suddenly remembered her. The fact was I hadn't forgotten her, not for an instant. How could I? Each morning I rode my motorcycle to school along the same route she and I had walked every weekday since we were small children. Without Annie I was alone. The boys of Mannville were generally suspicious of me, with my longish hair and my artistic pretensions, and the girls bored me with their endless nattering about who was going out with whom. Annie'd been the only person of my age in Mannville who understood me. Things had come full circle. My world was once again reduced to the farmhouse and to Grandpa. True, now there was Mildred and also my bike, but life in general seemed hollow without Annie to share it with.

Over three months had passed since the morning I murdered or did not murder her father. Nobody, including me, had seen or heard from her in all that time. It was as if she'd simply vanished. I knew very well that she *was* alive, but nobody else did, and though I felt vaguely guilty about leading everyone on, I knew it was better than telling them the truth. Nobody could know my suspicions about where Annie had gone. Her future sanity depended upon it.

All these thoughts flashed through my mind in less than a second as Grandpa handed this new letter to me. It was weighty and thick. I took it up to my room, opened it, and began reading:

Dear Billy,

I presume you got my two-word note on that awful morning, that you knew it was from me, and that you understood it. That's one thing about you I've always been able to count on—you understand everything about me, usually without having to be told, which is why it hurts me so much to tell you that I'm not sure I can ever see you again. And that too is something I hope you'll understand without me having to explain it, but I feel I owe you an explanation anyway.

I'm confused right now. At the same time, however, I feel free. That's a first for me, and I want it to make you happy for my sake. I'm in Montreal. All those years of studying French have paid off. I like it here. I think I'm going to stay for a long time.

I have so much to tell you. So I'll start where we left off, the last time we saw each other—or to be more exact, the last time you saw me.

I know you were in my house that morning. The drug my father used made me look unconscious, but I was still able to take in vague sensations. I remember seeing you bend over me to see whether or not I was dead. I could tell it was you even through the ski mask. I knew you were hiding in the closet, and I heard you jump out and scare him. I didn't want you to get in trouble, but all the same I had been hoping you would kill him, even though I'd told you I didn't want that, and you didn't disappoint me. Thank you, thank you, thank you. You really are my hero, Billy. You really did come to my rescue after all, just like you always said you would. And let your mind be at ease about the death of my father, because I know you must feel guilty. It was really his heart that killed him, not you. It was only a matter of time before it went out on him.

I'm not sure I'll ever be able to forgive myself for allowing those things to happen to me. I just didn't know what to do. There didn't seem to be anyone I could tell besides you. The shame I felt over what my father was doing to me was huge. I was afraid if I told someone, the whole thing would somehow backfire and be made to look like my fault. It's irrational, I know. But I've been doing some reading, and they say that kind of feeling is pretty common among people like me.

Despite the fact that you saved me from him, I'm not sure I can ever forgive you for having sneaked into my house and seen me at my most vulnerable. Does that make sense? I don't care that you saw me naked. That's not what I mean. It's hard for me to explain. You knew what was going on, because I told you, and I even felt shame over that.

There was a time when I thought you and I would grow up and get married. But what I told you that night in the car still goes. I don't think I can ever physically love a man, ever. The very idea of it repulses me. That's partly what I'm trying to tell you in this letter, to silence any doubts you might have about our future and make sure everything is clear. I love you deeply, truly, wonderfully, permanently, but we will never be lovers like you wanted to be that night. It's not because of a lack of feeling for you. It's not even that I don't find you desirable. Call it association. It's not you that disgusts me—it's me, my own body. I don't want anyone to touch it ever again. If you were to see me again—and that's a big if—I want to make absolutely sure you understand this.

I called the police only after I had managed to pack a bag and was sure I could get out of the house before they arrived. I would have just left him there to rot, but I had my brother to think of. It would have been weeks before anyone would have found out that I was gone and my father was dead, and Frederic would have starved to death. Poor Frederic. My father used to say he was the only one of us that was ever any good. I hope, wherever he is now, they're taking better care of him.

After I left the house, I disguised myself as best as I could and got on the main road and hitchhiked to Springville. I got a ticket to Montreal in the Springville bus station.

So here I am. I've been saving money for this move since I was little. I knew the day would come, and I dreamed of it every night. I didn't think it would come quite so soon, though. I was going to leave when I was eighteen. That way I knew there was no chance of me being brought back. If I had made it up here and he had found me and had me sent home, I would have killed myself.

I have a job and a tiny apartment. I work in a Middle Eastern restaurant, cleaning toilets in the mornings and serving food in the afternoons and evenings. I'm sure the owners know I'm here illegally and that I'm really too young to be working, but they don't seem too interested in who I am, and that is a valuable gift. Anonymity and secrecy are the things I value most right now. Please don't show this letter to anyone. I'm giving you my address, but don't write it down anywhere. Memorise it. You can write me if you want. I might even like you to come see me. But be warned that I am not the same person you knew in Mannville. I have no intention of being that person ever again. I will always have you in my heart, but things will be different with us from now on.

I always tried to be normal. I always wished I was a normal girl from a normal family. But the time for pretending is over now, isn't it?

> *Love,*
> *Annie*

IN OCTOBER I SAID to Grandpa, 'I think I'll take a trip up north.'

He raised his eyebrows. 'Really? Where did this idea come from?'

I shrugged, trying to conceal my unease. I didn't want Grandpa to know where I was going or why, but I had to tell him something, and it was useless to lie. 'I have my reasons,' I said.

'I'm sure you do,' Grandpa replied.

We were silent for a moment.

He looked at me carefully. 'Is it about that Simpson girl?'

'Not "that Simpson girl",' I said hotly. 'She has a name.'

Grandpa smacked his knee. 'Do you mean to say you've known where she's been all this time and you didn't tell anyone?'

'I couldn't,' I said. 'I promised her.'

'When? When did you promise her?'

Always, I thought. I promised her always, from the time I first knew what was going on in that house.

'Right before she left,' I said. It wasn't exactly true, but it was true enough. Some promises didn't need to be said out loud.

'Well, I'll be damned,' said Grandpa. 'You knew. All this time you knew!' He took off his fedora and scratched his head.

'Grandpa,' I said, 'think about it. If you were me, would you have ratted on her? After everything that happened up there?'

Grandpa knew that 'up there' meant up in the old white Simpson house on top of the hill. 'No,' he said, 'I wouldn't. But that's not the point. I thought she was gone for good.'

'Now wait a minute! That's not fair. Just because of her dad, you think she's a bad person. You told me yourself she wasn't like the rest of them. She's not! She's—'

'Calm down,' said Grandpa. 'I don't think she's a bad person.'

'Well then, why were you hoping she was gone for good?'

'I just don't want you to see her any more. Ever.'

'You can't stop me,' I said. My voice was low with rage. 'You have no right to do that. Not without telling me why.'

'I can't tell you why,' said Grandpa. 'I can't. It's not right for you to see her again. That's all. It's just not right.'

I was shaking so violently now that my vision began to blur. 'Not good enough,' I said. Then I turned and walked out of the house.

Grandpa came to the door. 'Hey!' he shouted after me. 'You get back here right now!'

'No!'

'Damn it!' Grandpa roared. 'Do as I tell you. Get back here.'

'You're not my father. I don't have to listen to you.'

'I raised you from a pup, boy. You mind me now!'

'You were drunk!' I shouted. 'You were drunk the whole time. I raised myself, and you know it.'

There was a stunned moment during which Grandpa and I stared into each other's eyes across the driveway. I'd always sworn I would never say that out loud. There'd always been something in me that wouldn't allow me to blame Grandpa for all his weaknesses. After all, he was my grandfather and my father and my mother all rolled into one. He was all I had in the world, my entire family. I can still feel the twinge of pain I felt then as I saw Grandpa's eyes go hollow. He turned away from the door as if he'd been shot in the gut, and then he went into the house.

There have been many nights since then when I wished I could go back and unsay that—long, lonely nights when I couldn't sleep in those dim, oddly reflective hours when we adults are haunted by the misdeeds we have done.

But there are other times when I think it had to be said. And you can't turn back the clock.

I turned my back on the farmhouse and began to jog. I headed down to the lake and threw rocks into the water for a while until I calmed down. The lake was good for that. Eventually I meandered back home.

When I came into the living room, Grandpa and Mildred were sitting in their rocking chairs. Mildred got up upon seeing me and went into the kitchen.

'Grandpa,' I said, getting right to the point, 'I have to go see her.'

'I know,' said Grandpa. He leaned back in his chair. 'Hell, don't I know it? Haven't I spent most of my life sitting here with a broken heart? If there was anywhere I could have gone to make it whole again, believe me, I would have.'

'If there's a reason you know of why I shouldn't go,' I said, 'I'd sure appreciate it if you'd tell me what it is.'

'Someday you'll know,' he said. 'Until then, forget about it. Live your life the way you need to live it. I can't stop you. I don't even want to stop you. You're a good boy. You'll be a better man than I ever was.'

I could say nothing to that, but I knew he was right. 'I'm sorry I said what I said,' I told him. 'I shouldn't have said it.'

'You had every right.' He was looking at the floor. 'I wasn't any kind of father to you. And now it's too late.'

'You did a good job,' I said. 'I'm gonna turn out all right.'

Grandpa got up from his chair and put his bony arms around me. I had to stoop nowadays to hug him. I had risen to the height of six feet, my long-sought-after goal.

That week I sent a letter to Annie telling her I wanted to come see her and asking if it was still all right. She replied, '*Yes. No. I don't know. You have my address. No promises. I have to warn you, I'm not the same person I was before. Come around Christmas if you want to. You might not want to.*'

Of course I want to, I thought. How could I not?

I BOUGHT A BUS TICKET to Montreal. I planned on going in mid-December, after school was out for the holidays.

The day of my departure Grandpa and Mildred drove me to the bus station. I carried a basket full of Mildred's cooking, a blank notebook, and a copy of Jack Simpson's obituary.

I shook hands with Grandpa—being older now, I had forbidden him to hug me in public—received a kiss on the cheek from

Mildred, and I was off. Ten hours later the bus pulled into the Montreal bus station.

Annie met me at the terminal. I barely recognised her. She'd cut her hair off. She hadn't just cut it—she'd shaved it. It had grown back some, but the sight of her skull under only a thin layer of hair was unnerving. I went to hug her, but she fended me off with one hand against my chest. 'First things first,' she said. 'Don't touch me.'

I stopped, my arms outstretched gracelessly in midair. 'All right,' I said. My arms fell to my sides. I looked aimlessly around the bus station. For the first time I was at a loss for words with Annie. 'Hi, Annie,' I said at last. 'Nice to see you, too.'

'I told you,' she said. 'I told you I wasn't the same as I was before.'

You were very right, I thought.

I picked up my bag and followed her out of the bus station. We walked for perhaps half a mile, she in front, silent and walking fast, I struggling to keep up behind her. It was unspeakably cold. Mannville got cold, but it was never anything like this.

'This cold hurts,' I said. 'I'm not wearing the right clothes.'

Annie said nothing.

'You could have told me how cold it was up here,' I said.

She turned and looked at me, a stony glint in her eye. 'Deal with it,' she said shortly.

We kept walking until we arrived at her place. My belly quivered with nervousness, and suddenly I wished that I hadn't come.

Annie lived in a first-floor apartment on Sherbrooke Street. Directly beneath her place was a Middle Eastern restaurant run by a couple of Palestinian women. Annie worked there twelve hours a day. Her apartment was a three-room affair, with a kitchen, bedroom, and small sitting area, and it was permeated with an odour of Middle Eastern spices that seemed to hover over everything.

I unpacked my picnic basket full of food. 'Grandpa has a girl-friend now,' I said. 'She loves to cook.'

'Does she love to cook or is it that she's supposed to cook?'

'What?'

'You know. Keep 'em in the kitchen? Barefoot and pregnant?'

'I don't know what your problem is,' I said, 'but I don't deserve this. You better get civil right now or I'm out of here.'

'Look,' Annie said. She ran a hand over her head. 'I don't know what you expected in coming up here, but—'

'Annie,' I said, thoroughly exasperated, 'do not assume for one second that I want anything from you. I told you already. I *missed* you. I wanted to see you, make sure you were all right, spend some time with you. Maybe I should go stay at a motel or something. In fact, you know what? I'm leaving.'

I picked up my bag and went towards the door.

'Wait,' she said. 'Please, Billy. Just hang on. Just—'

I stopped.

She sat down and put her face in her hands. I sat next to her. Automatically my arm went up around her shoulders.

She started like a colt. 'Please don't do that,' she said, but her voice was her old voice again—it was just a request, nothing more.

'I'm sorry. Habit.'

'*I'm* sorry,' she said.

'I'm on your side,' I said. 'I always have been.'

'I know,' she said. 'It's just—'

'I know what it is,' I said.

She was silent.

'Annie, you don't owe me anything, if that's what you're worried about,' I said. 'I didn't come up here to make you remember stuff you don't want to think about. I just wanted to make sure you were all right. I'm proud of you. I really am. Jealous. Do you know how much I'd love to have an apartment of my own?'

'You would?'

'Yes, I really would.'

'It gets really cold here,' she said. 'I mean, even worse than this. It's not as great as it looks.'

'Well, you know what I mean,' I said.

'Billy,' she said, 'I'm glad to see you. I really am.'

'Well, that's more like it,' I said. 'I'm glad to see you too.'

'Let's get out of here,' she said. 'We can go get a beer.'

'We can get beer?'

'You only have to be eighteen to drink here,' she said.

'We're not eighteen, though.'

'They never check,' she said. 'Just act natural.'

This struck me as a brilliant plan. We got dressed to go outside: jeans, flannel shirt, sweater, winter jacket, scarf, hat, gloves and two layers of socks. The sun was down, and when we emerged onto the street, the cold hit me like a fist in the stomach.

'Pull your scarf over your nose,' Annie instructed. 'Breathe through it. Don't breathe straight air. You'll freeze your lungs.'

The temperature had plummeted a further twenty degrees or so in the short time since my arrival. We walked rapidly to stay warm. Everyone else seemed to have the same idea. It was a Friday night, and the streets were filled with people.

We arrived at a small place with an unpronounceable name. Annie ordered a pitcher of beer. It was red and dark and glorious, and all the more delicious because it was my first beer in a bar.

'Be careful,' Annie warned me. 'This stuff is stronger than the beer at home.'

'Let me ask you something,' I said. 'Why did you cut off all your hair?'

She shrugged. 'Men,' she said simply. 'There's something about baldness that kind of makes you invisible. They don't look at you; they don't hassle you. I did it because I wanted to be invisible.'

'Did you really get hassled all that much?'

She looked at me in disgust, but it was no longer mixed with loathing. It was more pity for my ignorance. 'You will never understand in a million years,' she said.

'Understand what?'

'What it's like to be a woman.'

'Well,' I said, already a little drunk, 'that's because I'm a Mann.' I threw my head back and laughed uproariously.

'All right,' she said, and now she was actually smiling. 'I think we've had enough beer.'

We went home, wrapped ourselves in blankets, and sat on the couch talking. There were ten thousand things I wanted to tell her. It was impossible to get them all out, and I began to see that there was a segment of my life Annie had simply missed and would never understand, and that the same was true of me for her. But at least we were together again. We rubbed toes under the blankets. Words came more and more easily until we were talking freely and laughing. Annie began to seem more like Annie, and I realised I'd passed a sort of test, although exactly what it had consisted of escaped me. We fell asleep with our legs entangled, sleeping like children, and late in the night she awoke and led me to her bed and snuggled in next to me.

Once, three-quarters asleep, I thought I felt a hand stroking my hair and a voice whispering, 'You're still my hero, Billy Mann.'

But it was probably just a dream.

THE NEXT DAY, while Annie laboured in the kitchen of the Palestinians, I explored Montreal. The sheer magnificence of the city plunged me into a state of culture shock. Even the mailboxes, which were tall and thin and red, were fascinating. The influence of France seemed to be everywhere—in the architecture and the food and the language. I felt as though I'd got on the bus in Mannville and arrived in Europe.

It was an odd sensation, and I relished it thoroughly. I'd never been anywhere in my life. I realised with shame that I'd never even been to Buffalo, except to pass through it on the bus. The hunger to see more of the world was blooming in me like a ravenous flower, demanding to be fed. Compared with Montreal, Mannville seemed like a depressing backwater, its inhabitants a bunch of ignorant hicks. No great writers would ever come out of Mannville. I didn't want to go home.

I met Annie again at six that evening.

'Look at this,' I said, producing a magazine I'd bought at a bookstore. It looked to be a literary journal, but I couldn't be sure, because it was in French.

'*Le Journal des Lettres*,' she read out loud. 'It's local. They publish short stories.'

'How good are your translating abilities?'

'You mean from English to French? Why?'

'Do you think you could translate my story about Willie?'

Annie pursed her lips. 'Well, I suppose I could. I could do it literally, but it wouldn't be as good as it is now.'

'Don't sell yourself short,' I said. 'Will you try it?'

'Are you thinking of sending it to these guys?' She tapped the magazine with a finger.

'Well, I'm having no luck in America,' I said. 'Will you do it?'

'I'll try,' she said. 'But I can't promise you it'll be any good.'

'Trying is good enough,' I said. 'I have faith in you.'

She smiled at me shyly, her chin supported by one slender hand. I had a flash of how she was going to look when she was older. She'd be one of those women who attracts attention to herself without trying, the kind of woman who radiates a certain calm purpose in everything she does, and she would be beautiful besides.

'Nobody ever tells me that they have faith in me,' she said.

'You've been hanging around the wrong kind of people.'

'I was born to the wrong kind of people,' she said, and her face darkened for a moment. I recognised a storm approaching. We'd agreed that we were never, ever going to discuss her father again. She'd decided she would reserve that for the therapist she knew she would need someday. When we were together, it was my job to help her forget about it.

We spent the rest of that evening and the next several evenings in the same way: we walked, sometimes holding hands and sometimes not, and slowly I learned of all the little niches of Montreal that Annie had claimed as her own—bookstores, cafés, parks.

My last night we lay next to each other in bed, not speaking. In the last eleven days I'd crammed more sights and sounds into my poor provincial brain than it had ever known before, and now that I was going home, I felt a keen sense of loss.

The next morning Annie and I walked together to the bus station. 'Are you ever coming home?' I said.

'I am home,' she said. Her eyes were suddenly wide and glistening. 'I thought you understood that.'

'Force of habit,' I said, cursing myself for my careless words. 'I meant coming back to Mannville.'

'No. I'm not.' She stood with her arms folded in front of her thin chest, looking up at me both in defiance and in expectation.

'I think this is great, what you're doing,' I said, because I sensed she was waiting for me to say something. For her it was a question of survival, and I knew she would go on living alone in Montreal no matter what I said. And she would do it until she was ready to go on to the next thing. 'Really. I wish I was doing it too. I'm jealous.'

'Consider my life for a moment,' she said, smiling wanly. 'How could anyone be jealous of me?' But her smile contained a hint of relief, and I was glad I'd said it.

'I guess I just wish I had more time with you,' I said. I drew her to me and held her tightly for several moments.

She said into my ear, 'Thanks for coming.'

'It was my pleasure,' I said, releasing her.

'I was really nervous about it. It was like . . . my past meets my future, you know? I was afraid there would be a collision or something. But there wasn't. It worked out just fine.'

'I'm glad,' I said.

'I'm sorry I was so nasty when you first got here.'

'I understand,' I said. 'Don't forget to translate my story.'

'I won't,' she promised. 'Tell your grandfather I said hi.'

A garbled voice came on the loudspeaker and announced my bus: 'Toronto, Buffalo, Erie, Pittsburgh, and points south.'

'I'll write to you a lot,' I said.

'I'll write back.'

'I'll miss you.'

'I'll miss *you*.'

'Annie?'

'Yeah?'

Will you ever love me? Will you always hate men? Will we ever be together? Will you marry me? Isn't there something I can do to make things all right again?

'Bye,' I said. I couldn't say those things to her—not now, not ever.

We embraced again, and I got on the bus. I found an empty pair of seats and sat by the window. I amused Annie and distracted myself from my own despair by putting my lips to the glass and puffing out my cheeks, until we pulled out and headed, as the announcer had said, for points south.

BACK IN MANNVILLE I was met at the bus station by Grandpa and Mildred. Grandpa looked as if he had not slept in days.

'You leave for a while, and the whole damn world falls apart,' he said, his voice cracked with fatigue. 'I'm sorry to tell you this, Billy, but Connor's dead.'

I'd missed the phone call informing Grandpa of Connor's death. I'd also missed the wake, the funeral and the burial service, and now Connor was in the ground, and there was nothing I could do about it. We went straight to the churchyard from the bus station. We stood there, Grandpa and Mildred and I, before the freshly filled-in grave. The tombstone wouldn't be placed until the earth had settled.

'I had no way to get in touch with you,' Grandpa said apologetically. 'If I had, I might have just let you alone till you got back anyway. I didn't want to ruin your first trip outside of Mannville for a funeral. Connor wouldn't have wanted that either.'

'Annie doesn't have a phone,' I said, staring at the earth.

'I know this is sudden for you, boy,' said Grandpa.

Mildred remained respectfully silent. One thin, birdlike hand reached out to take mine, and she squeezed it for a long moment before she let it drop again.

'He never knew what hit him,' Grandpa went on. 'The docs at the hospital think it was a massive stroke. His wife found him in his examination room. He was sitting at his desk, writing.'

Writing. I squeezed my temples in my hands. 'How many people came to the funeral?' I asked.

'Whole damn town,' Grandpa said proudly. 'Even folks that owed him money.' He blew his nose.

'At least you made it up with him,' I said.

The sun was nearly down now, and the wind was cold and biting, though not nearly as cold as it had been in Montreal. I heard a clattering sound and realised it was Mildred's teeth knocking together. Then I heard another sound, a snuffling kind of sob, and I realised that Grandpa was crying.

'Yeah. And now let's get home,' said Grandpa. 'This weather is just plain obnoxious.'

7

Dr Connor had been writing to me when he died. Mrs Connor told me, in a note, that she took the letter from his cold hands, sealed it, and had it delivered to me the day after I returned from Montreal.

Dear Billy,

By the time you read this letter, I will be dead. I don't know when that will be, but it can't be too much longer now. I have seventy-two years under my belt, not so many by modern standards, but certainly more than enough by my own. Six months ago I suffered a mild stroke, which I told no one about because it didn't seem to harm me greatly. Last month I had another one. Then I knew it was only a matter of time. My father died in much the same way, having little strokes one after the other until a big one finally carried him off. I know that I will go the same way, and that it will be happening shortly. I am resigned to it. Curious, even. I've always regarded death as a great adventure. I have both a clinical interest and a spiritual curiosity in what lies on the other side of this life. But I have some items of business to attend to before I go, and writing this letter to you is one of them, because there are some things I need to tell you.

In the summer of 1970, very early in the morning, a pretty young woman whom I didn't recognise came to my office. I mention that I didn't recognise her, because that was unusual—strangers almost never come through this town, as you well know. This young woman was a complete stranger, however, and what was more, she was in the final stages of pregnancy. It was about five thirty in the morning. She pounded on the door for me to let her in and, when I did, told me that she was about to have a baby, and furthermore she intended to have it here, in my office. She'd been walking to the hospital but realised she wasn't going to make it. I offered to drive her, but she was vehement in her refusal. She was what you call a 'hippie'. She wore a fringed leather jacket and had long brown hair, and she was quite lovely. She told me that her name was Sky.

'Come now,' I said. 'Nobody names their child Sky. Surely you must have had another name at one point. What was it?'

It was with the greatest reluctance that she told me her real first name—Eliza—and she begged me to keep it a secret. On the subject of her family name she remained immovable.

I deduced that Eliza had another objection to going to the hospital. She knew that in the hospital she had much less chance of keeping her identity a secret. This was of the utmost importance to her. It didn't take me long to figure out what the story was. She was unmarried, the father of her baby was obviously not present, and therefore she wanted her pregnancy to be kept a secret— probably from her family, who no doubt would disapprove.

I rang upstairs and told my wife I would be needing her assistance. She and I prepared the birthing room, made Eliza comfortable, and settled down to the long business of waiting. I asked Eliza some questions on the pretext of needing a medical history. Thus I discovered that she was twenty-three, that this was her first pregnancy, and that she was not from New York State.

'And the father?' I asked. 'What do you know about him?'

'He's dead,' she told me, her eyes welling up with tears. 'He died in Vietnam.'

'I'm sorry,' I said. 'Do you have friends to help you once the child is born? Or family?'

She shook her head—unable to speak at the moment because a strong contraction had begun. She was brave and tough, and already I was developing a great respect for her. When the contraction was over, I asked her, 'Were you very close with him?'

She laid her head back on the pillow. 'He was beautiful,' she sighed. I sensed that she wasn't referring to his appearance, but to some quality he possessed. And I was right, for a moment later she went on, 'He was totally right on. Totally clear. He just zoomed in on you in an instant. No head games, no power trips.'

I translated this in my head. Her description, once I decoded it, sounded familiar. A few bells were starting to go off in my head. 'Was he from here?' I asked. 'From Mannville?'

But she couldn't answer; another contraction was gripping her.

Mrs Connor and I stayed with Eliza all that day, and she delivered the baby at around six o'clock that evening. It was a boy, nineteen inches, seven and a half pounds.

Eliza and her baby stayed for nearly six weeks—she had nowhere to go. Despite her reticence, she was very likable. We gave her one of the guest rooms upstairs. She begged us not to tell anyone of her existence, and my wife and I respected her wishes, though of course we were curious. We were also perplexed by the fact that she hadn't given the baby a name. When

we asked her about this, she said that it wasn't for her to decide
what the baby would be called. She would leave it up to those who
would know him better.

'There's something strange going on,' said Mrs Connor.

'I know,' I said. 'But it's none of our business. We promised we
would never ask for payment of any kind from girls like her.
That includes information, too. If she doesn't want to tell us, she
doesn't have to.'

'Well, I can still ask her,' said Mrs Connor.

It was then I did something I had never done to my wife before
and have never done since: I gave her an order. 'You are
absolutely forbidden to ask her anything at all,' I said.

My wife never quite forgave me for that. I wasn't just being difficult, however. I was reminding her of a promise we'd made. She
seemed to want to forget about that promise, and of course I
knew why. She was becoming attached to the baby and didn't
want him to go. Neither did I.

When Eliza was ready to leave, to my astonishment she produced a wallet full of cash, asking, 'How much do I owe you?'

At regular rates, including medical fees, groceries, and the
price of a room, her bill would have come to something like three
thousand dollars. I hadn't any intention of asking her for money,
of course. My wife was in agreement with me, but she wanted to
take things one step further. 'Tell her we'll forget about money if
she just tells us about herself,' she said.

'That's blackmail!' I protested.

'It's not blackmail,' retorted Mrs Connor. 'It's insurance. I
have a feeling this information will come in handy someday.'

'What are you talking about?' I asked her.

'It's just a feeling,' she repeated. And I'm sorry to say that I
contravened my wife's will and told Eliza she didn't have to give
us any money. Nor did I ask her any more questions. My wife
never forgave me for this either and, as it turned out, she was
right. This information would have come in handy later, simply
for the sake of satisfying the natural human urge to know something of one's origins.

The day Eliza left with her baby, Mrs Connor sat in the
kitchen and cried. I was moved to tears myself. We had grown
very attached to the young woman, despite her air of mystery, for
it was obvious that she was well bred, and we admired her grace
and strength. We'd also grown attached to the baby. Eliza's
departure was difficult for both of us.

Her last words to us were of thanks. 'You've helped bring a wonderful little man into the world,' she said. And she was gone.

As things would turn out, however, we had misunderstood her. What she was saying was not 'a wonderful little man'. She meant—and I'm sure you've deduced this by now, Billy—'a wonderful little Mann'. For this baby was you, William Amos Mann IV, and Eliza was your mother.

The very next day your grandfather came marching into my office with a baby in a picnic basket. I was hard-pressed to conceal my excitement, for I recognised the baby immediately as Eliza's. A few questions sufficed to prove to me that your grandfather knew nothing of the mother. It was obvious to him, however, that the father had been Eddie, his own son.

I said nothing to your grandfather about the fact that I already knew you, but I can never describe the joy that washed over me upon seeing you again and knowing that you were, after all, going to be part of my life. Your grandpa left you with me for a brief time to buy supplies, and as soon as he was gone I rang upstairs for my wife. She came down in a flash, and together we held you and cried tears of love and joy. There was no sign of Eliza, so we knew she'd abandoned you. It was one of the defining moments of my life. My wife and I have always loved you, and you'll never know how hard it's been not to show it more than we have. But we promised each other that we would never tell your grandfather— or you, until you were old enough—the real story of your birth.

You may be angry with me for not telling you the whole story sooner. Bit there were several mitigating factors that caused us to make our decision. First, Eliza had wanted her identity to be kept secret, and for all the anger we felt towards her for abandoning you, we had to admit we didn't know the whole story. There may have been a good reason for you not to know more about her. Therefore, since we weren't capable of making an informed decision, we decided on secrecy. I still feel we made the right decision.

Second, we didn't want to interfere in any way with the bond forming between you and your grandfather. We felt it was important for you to live your life with him and not be influenced by outside factors. Your grandfather was a very sad man, and to see him made happy again was deeply satisfying to both of us.

Perhaps these reasons seem silly to you, but consider finally the fact that I am a doctor, and ultimately I was bound by law not to reveal anything of Eliza's identity. That was the deciding factor. But I'm dead now and therefore no longer obligated to follow the laws dictated to me by the state.

You once asked me if I knew who your mother was. You will remember that I neither admitted nor denied knowledge. I did say I didn't know who she was, and that was the truth; I knew almost nothing about her. But I admit I am splitting hairs to assuage my conscience. I deliberately concealed from you the information I had concerning your mother, and that has, from time to time, caused me guilt. But I wanted to wait until you were ready before I gave out all the facts. You're ready now. Very soon, I feel, you will be leaving Mannville and setting out on the sort of quest that most young people undertake at one time or another—to find out who you are, what sort of material you're made of. In your case, the question of who you are is a literal one. To tell you earlier about your mother would have created problems of confusion and restlessness, and I didn't want to do that to you. You were always a happy child, despite the fact that you were raised in unusual circumstances. I didn't want that happiness to disappear.

One of the few facts I was able to establish about your mother was that she was from the Southwest. One could tell just by looking at her that she wasn't an easterner: Her skin had a tan glow to it, and her eyes—how do I say this?—were used to a bigger sky. She could see farther than most of us can. She mentioned in passing certain places she had been through: Santa Fe, Denver, Jackson Hole, Missoula—all out west. She was somewhat of a wanderer, I gathered. She was a captivating person, intelligent and quick-witted, and that made it all the more frustrating for my wife and me because she was the kind of person one would wish to know better no matter how well one knew her already.

I have no idea how she met your father. She would have been a year or two older than he, but there is nothing unusual in that. What struck me as really odd was the difference in their situations. Your father was the all-American type, clean-cut and proud to serve his country unquestioningly. That sort of person generally didn't associate with hippies. But it was easy to understand why any man would have been attracted to Eliza, and it isn't hard either to see how she would have been attracted to Eddie. I'm sorry it didn't work out for them to be together.

No doubt soon you will be ready to begin looking for her. If I were you, I would look out west, perhaps in the places she mentioned. Look for a tall woman, light brown hair, grey eyes, a Roman nose, a soft, husky voice. I'm sorry I can't tell you more.

And in closing I would like also to say that

The letter ended there. Connor had been writing at his desk when the final stroke came.

And I never got the chance to discuss the events of my birth with Mrs Connor. She was five years older than Dr Connor, and they'd been married for nearly fifty years, so it came as no surprise to anyone when she died peacefully in her sleep only a few days after Connor himself, in perfect health and with twenty years left in her if she'd wanted to live them. Apparently, however, she hadn't. She'd chosen instead to rejoin her husband.

'Who could blame her, poor dear?' said Mildred. 'Who would want to live alone after being happily married all that time?' And she put her birdy little hand on top of Grandpa's as they rocked side by side in their rocking chairs.

'Well, I missed this round,' Grandpa said.

'What do you mean?' I asked.

'This round of three. Death always comes in threes. Simpson, Connor, his wife. It's a fact.'

'That's ridiculous.'

'Of course it's ridiculous,' he said. 'But it always happens.'

'I've never heard of that,' I said.

'It's an old superstition, but it's true. Watch and see. The older you get, the more people you know start to kick off. And they go in threes. Anyway, what was in that letter?'

'News,' I said. It was then that I realised Connor had never told Grandpa any of what I now knew, so I let him read the letter. He read through it twice, right there in the living room. I expected perhaps that he would get angry or emotional or at least excited, but he only rubbed his forehead thoughtfully and said, 'I want you to finish high school first, before you go traipsing off.'

'What makes you think I'm going traipsing off?' I said, but before the words were out of my mouth, I knew he was right. I hadn't had time to think it through yet, but once I had, there would be only one possible course of action. I would have to go west and find my mother, and I wanted to get started immediately.

'That'll take for ever!' I protested.

'It will take exactly one and a half years,' he corrected me calmly. 'After that, you can do whatever you want. But if you leave now, you'll be screwed. You can't do anything without a diploma from high school. And you ought to plan on college too.'

'College, shmollege,' I said. 'I'm going to be a writer.'

'Writers go to college, too,' he told me. 'They even have special writers' colleges.'

'So what? That doesn't mean I have to go to one. It's experience that counts for writers, not some dumb piece of paper.'

'You don't have to go right away,' he said. 'See a little of the world first.'

'*You* never went to college,' I pointed out.

'That,' said Grandpa, 'is precisely the reason you ought to go.'

'This Eliza person,' I said. 'Does she sound familiar?'

'No,' said Grandpa. 'I can't figure out where Eddie would have met her. He didn't hang around with hippies.'

'But he might have if he'd met one,' I pointed out. 'And obviously he did meet at least one. He wouldn't have been the type to look down his nose at people just because they had long hair. Would he?'

'No,' Grandpa admitted. 'No, he wouldn't. What Connor wrote was true. Everybody connected with Eddie, and not just on the surface. It was a deep thing. He had a way of looking right into people.'

'Maybe she was the same way,' I said.

'It sounds like she was,' said Grandpa. I could see he was thinking, trying to remember back to the days when Eddie was home last. 'He would have to have met her while he was home on leave the last time,' he said. 'Which was for a month, in the autumn of '69.'

'Did he stick around Mannville his whole leave?'

'No. He went to Buffalo twice,' said Grandpa. 'To visit an air force buddy who was on leave at the same time. I'll try and remember his name. Maybe he would have met your—this Eliza person.' Neither of us could bring ourselves to refer to Eliza as my mother yet. The idea would take some getting used to.

'Yes,' I said. 'Try.'

There was something else nagging at me. She might have another family, one with legitimate children who would despise me for being illegitimate. 'It's me,' I could hear myself saying, 'Eddie's bastard—the one you didn't keep.' And then—what? Tears of welcome? Happiness? Remorse?

'This is not so simple,' I said. 'There's a good chance she won't want to see me again, isn't there?'

'Well, it's a big risk,' said Grandpa. 'You never know how these things are going to turn out.'

'Do you think she thinks about me?'

'I'm sure of it,' said Mildred.

It suddenly began to sink in that it was my mother we were talking about—my actual biological mother. Now she had a name and a face, and I had several details I could put together. Over the next few weeks these details became flesh and bones, until I had a real live mother in my head. I drew pictures of her based on Connor's description. Soon the walls of my room were papered with drawings of a young hippie woman with soft brown hair and a Roman nose. I was a terrible artist, but that didn't matter. What did matter was that I finally had a clue about where to begin looking.

I alternated between soaring to new heights of elation and grousing over my delay in leaving Mannville. I was ecstatic over Connor's revelation, furious at Grandpa. But by the time school began again in January, I was resigned to it, and gradually I realised—to my immense annoyance—that Grandpa was right again. I was at least comforted by the fact that my immediate future was laid out for me. Even if I had no idea where to begin looking for my mother, at least I had something to do when I graduated.

A few days later, up in the attic, Grandpa found a cigar box full of letters. He'd stuck it up there after the news came that my father was dead. My hopes surged when I saw it, but it contained only three letters of interest. They were written on thin blue military stationery and were dated September 1969, January 1970 and February 1970. During the interval between the first two, Eddie had come home and created me.

I took the letters to my room and read them. First I wanted to find names. Any name at all would be a possible lead. I was looking first of all for the name Eliza, but it didn't appear. Neither did Sky. It wasn't until the end of the last letter that I saw a name, and my heart leaped up into my throat and pounded there insistently.

> *You remember that guy Henry Hutchins I went to visit in Buffalo when I was home? Well, he got lucky. He got a million-dollar wound in the ass. A sniper snuck up close to the base and managed to nail three of our guys before we got him. Henry was one of them. He had just bent over to tie his shoe when the gook pulled the trigger. Bingo—he gets to go home for good.*

A clue. And Buffalo was only an hour or so away.

HENRY HUTCHINS'S HOME was one in a series of row houses in downtown Buffalo, all of them identical, separated by only a few feet of dingy cement driveway. I grew claustrophobic just looking at them. Henry Hutchins himself explained to me that the entire neighbourhood had been built by a tyre factory for the purpose of housing its workers; it rented the homes to them at exorbitant rates.

'My family worked for the tyre factory for three generations,' Henry told me. 'When I came home from the war, I bought the house. Who knows why? I always hated it. Come on in. You look just like your dad, you know. But I'm sure you hear that a lot.'

Hutchins was a small, balding man who spoke quietly but force-fully. He wore thick glasses, the lenses of which made his eyes look the size of half-dollars. We entered the house and came into a dark-ened living room. He indicated a couch to me and sat down opposite it. 'I presume you're not here just to reminisce,' he said, getting down to business. 'I don't mean to sound rude, but this is the first I've ever heard of you. I was kind of sceptical when I got your phone call. I never knew Eddie had a son. But I'm sure you are who you say you are. Which means you must have been born after he was killed.'

'That's right.'

'Which also means you never knew your father. I'm sorry.'

'It's OK,' I said. 'I mean, yeah, I guess I would have preferred to have him around, but I never knew him anyway, so it's not like I knew I was missing anything.'

'You're a tough kid.'

I smiled.

'Did Eddie get married?' Henry looked doubtful, pursing his lips. 'No, he didn't,' he answered himself. 'He never had time. Which means,' he said, a look of understanding coming over his features, 'that you're here to ask me some questions. Am I right?'

'Yeah,' I said. 'You should have been a detective.'

'That's what your father used to tell me,' said Hutchins. For the first time he smiled. 'Which proves you are who you say you are. Not that you'd have a reason to lie. If you don't mind my asking, who raised you?'

'My grandfather—Eddie's dad.'

'Ah,' said Hutchins. 'So what would you like to know?'

'I'm trying to find my mother,' I said.

Hutchins smiled again. 'An ancient story. Young man in search of his origins. Is she still alive? Do you know that for sure?'

'I don't know anything,' I admitted. 'I know her name, and I know what she looked like. That's it.'

'Tell me what it was.'

'Eliza,' I said. 'Or maybe Sky.'

Hutchins closed his eyes. 'Tall woman,' he said.

'Yes!'

'Strikingly beautiful. Long brown hair. A hippie.'

'You've met her.' A rush of elation surged through me.

'Yes,' said Hutchins. 'I met her once.'

'Only once?' I said.

'Don't be disappointed. It was a significant meeting.'

'When was it?'

'A party,' he said. 'When was that, now, let me think . . .'

'November 1969?' I suggested.

'That's right,' said Hutchins. 'We were home on leave.'

'And Eddie came up here to visit you.'

'Yes. We were out on the town, at a few bars. It was a weekend, I remember, a Saturday. Eddie and I were wearing our uniforms, and a few people shouted insults at us on the street. They were hippies. I don't know if you know this, but there were serious doubts in America about why we were in Vietnam in the first place. A lot of people had the idea that we were over there just butchering people left and right. Hippies in particular hated us. Anyway, we were walking down the sidewalk, kinda tipsy, and feeling too good to get into a fight. These hippies were shouting at us from the other side of the street. We went into this bar without paying any attention to them. No, wait—Eddie flashed them a peace sign. That made them even angrier, and they followed us in. There were four of them, three men and one woman.'

'What happened?'

'They called us baby-killers,' he said. 'Boy, was that a mistake. It was a blue-collar type of bar, and a lot of the patrons were veterans of Korea and the Second World War. Older men. They had an understanding of war that wasn't shared by these hippies. Most kids who had the leisure to grow their hair long and roam around the country came from families with money. They were able to afford college, and so they didn't get drafted, which caused a great deal of animosity among those who couldn't afford college. The war was not a moral issue for the working class back then. You got called; you went. You follow me?'

'I think so,' I said.

'So we're in this bar full of beefy ex-army and marine and navy guys, factory workers, and these hippies are hassling us, and suddenly they look around and think, Oh shit, what have we walked into? Everyone in there had gotten quiet. And then there was this sudden explosion of people towards the hippies.'

'You mean they rushed them?'

'Yeah. They were about to get their asses kicked.'

'Jeez.'

'Suddenly Eddie was in the middle of the whole thing. He was trying to protect them.'

'Protect the hippies?'

'Exactly,' said Hutchins. 'He didn't want to see them get beat up. It was really as simple as that.'

'Go on,' I said.

'Well, what happened next was the kind of thing you might see in a movie. Eddie actually gave a speech. He stood there in the middle of the hippies, waving his arms and talking.'

'What was he saying?'

'He was talking about peace,' said Hutchins softly. 'He didn't want any more fighting. He hated fighting. Odd, considering how many people he probably killed as a pilot. But he told everyone that he and I were home on leave for only a little while, and he told them how good it was to be home again, because America was a peaceful place and to him it meant safety. He said that even though war was a horrible thing, and maybe the peaceniks had a point, just for that night he wanted everyone to forget about it and be friends. He asked them to do that for our sake, so that when he and I shipped back in-country, we would have pleasant memories of home and not of more fighting. He was really eloquent when he got going.'

'So what happened?'

'Exactly what he wanted. He made them all shake hands.'

'You're kidding.'

'Hell no,' said Henry Hutchins. 'And then the hippies came and sat at the bar. The whole place was still quiet. Everyone was watching Eddie to see what to do next.'

'What did he do?'

'All he did was sit down. I think they were expecting something a little more dramatic. He ordered the hippies a round of beers, and we all moved to a table and sat around it.'

'And one of them was Eliza?'

'We didn't get to names right away,' he said. 'But there was only one woman with them. She was absolutely beautiful. I couldn't take my eyes off her. I never stood a chance with her, of course, not with Eddie in the same room. She was three or four inches taller than he was, but she was looking at him like he was a Greek god who'd just dropped by in his chariot for a quick drink. And Eddie kept looking at her, too. I think everyone knew right away there was something in the air between him and Sky. Some kind of chemistry.'

'So how long did you hang out with them?'

'We were in the bar for about an hour,' said Henry. 'Then we went with them to a party. Everyone there had long hair. They were drinking wine and sitting around playing all these musical instruments.'

'And Eliza came with you?'

'It was her party,' he said. 'It was her house. She didn't own it, but she lived there. But she didn't call herself Eliza. She was Sky. How did you find out her real name?'

I gave Henry a brief run-down of Dr Connor's letter.

'She went to Mannville to have you?' he asked, surprised.

'I guess. That's where I was born.'

'Why didn't she stay with your grandfather?'

'I don't know. She left me on the doorstep. With a note.'

'On the *doorstep*?' said Hutchins. 'That surprises me.'

'Why?'

'Because she seemed like a very responsible person,' he said.

'So you got to know her?'

'A bit,' said Henry. 'We actually ended up staying there all weekend. We were having too much fun to leave.'

'And is that when I was conceived?'

'Well, it must have been,' Hutchins admitted, 'because they spent most of their time in bed.' He blushed slightly. So did I.

'So what happened later? When you left, I mean. With Sky and my dad.'

'I don't remember too clearly, but I'm sure they exchanged addresses. They must have, for Sky to find out where your grandfather lived. Maybe they planned on getting together after the war. They sure would have been a beautiful couple.'

'What did they talk about? Did Eddie ever tell you?'

'No, and I didn't ask. But afterwards he was sort of glowing. I think he was very happy. Three days later we both shipped out again. And it was the next February that Eddie was shot down. I'm sorry. It must be hard for you to hear his death spoken of.'

'I'm used to it,' I said. 'I never knew him.'

'What a shame that is. He would have loved you, kid.'

'Anyway,' I said, 'you don't know where I might look for my mother?'

'I'm sorry, Billy,' he said. 'I never saw her again, and I don't think your dad did either. Maybe they wrote letters to each other. If they did, they should have been shipped home with his personal effects. Did your granddad get anything from the air force?'

'I don't know,' I said, feeling like an idiot. Why hadn't I thought to ask Grandpa that myself?

'Let me know how things turn out,' Henry said when I got up to leave. 'I've enjoyed talking to you, kid. You're a chip off the old block.'

'Thanks, Mr Hutchins,' I said. 'I'll let you know what happens.'

I walked out into the driveway and got into the Galaxie, which Grandpa had lent me. On the way home I mentally searched the entire farmhouse in Mannville for something, anything. I was missing a vital clue. I could feel its absence as though the gap itself was a palpable object, yet I didn't know what it was. But I was getting closer. I could feel that too.

We would never have known of Frederic Simpson's death if it hadn't been for Mildred's morbid habit of reading the obituaries each morning. She read them first thing, even before the headlines, and when she found a name she knew, she read the whole obituary out loud.

Someone had written a notice for Frederic, describing his service in Vietnam and mentioning that he was 'severely wounded', after which he was cared for by his 'loving father, whom he survived'. The notice made no mention of a sister named Annie. Most likely it was written by one of the nurses at the VA hospital where Frederic had been moved. Only a complete stranger could have made the mistake of calling Mr Simpson loving.

I felt as if a huge burden had been lifted from my chest. I breathed more easily knowing that poor Frederic was finally released from the prison of his body. It terrified me to think he might have had full use of his mental faculties all along. That morning I clipped the obituary out and mailed it to Annie in Montreal. My relief, I was sure, would pale in comparison to hers.

When Grandpa heard about Frederic, he knew his time was not far off, and he announced to me that he would be leaving soon. His liver had never recovered from four decades of hard drinking. It had been failing gradually for years, and according to the doctors at the hospital, it was about to go out on him completely.

'It could be another year yet,' he told me, 'so don't go around blubbering.'

'All right,' I said. I was trying to fight down the horrible feeling in my gut. It was the same feeling I'd had when Annie had disappeared, the same feeling I'd had as a boy when I thought about my lack of a father and mother. It was the feeling of being left behind.

'I do not wish to be hooked up to any machines,' said Grandpa. 'I feel very strongly about that. There's no reason for it except pure selfishness. Old people have a duty to get out of the way.'

It was strange to hear someone speak this way. Grandpa could, if he chose, prolong his life by many years, perhaps with a liver transplant. But the very idea made him snort in derision.

'Everybody ought to get one liver and that's it,' he said. 'Livers are like cars. If you can't take care of the first one, what makes people think they deserve another?'

'I don't know,' I said. I was searching desperately for some argument to counteract his, but he was right. It was time for him to die.

It was then spring of 1988. I was going to be graduating soon. Over a year had gone by since I'd visited Henry Hutchins in Buffalo. During that time I'd searched the farmhouse for anything the air force might have sent home after my father's death, and for other clues—anything.

I also wrote long, rambling letters to Annie. In retrospect I see them for what they were: a desperate bid to get her to change her mind, to love me the way I loved her. She answered them at first; then she only answered every other one; then she wrote rarely. Time passed as it always did. Then I heard nothing.

Forget about her, said an inner voice. It was a voice that had been speaking to me often lately. *Just let her alone.*

I knew the voice was right. I would never be able to forget about her, but maybe leaving her alone was the best thing. So I focused my energy anew on finding my mother.

Grandpa had told me nothing had been delivered to him, so there was no point in looking. There was nothing to be found. But now that I brought it up, he too wondered what had happened to Eddie's personal effects.

I knew the air force must have had a record of what he'd left behind, even if it was nothing important. I spent several months making phone calls to various government departments. Then I had to submit a request in writing, stating my reasons for wanting to know what Eddie's personal effects, if any, had been, and where they had been sent.

It took them nearly three months to respond, but finally, that spring, there came a letter. It was a photocopied list, typed in 1970 by a Sergeant Jackson. Apparently it had been Sergeant Jackson's job to catalogue the effects of dead men and mail them off to whatever address the deceased had put down for next of kin. The list contained mostly mundane items, but among them was the following entry: 'twenty-seven (27) letters, personal correspondence'.

'Did you write Eddie twenty-seven letters?' I asked Grandpa.

He frowned. 'I wrote him one a month.' Grandpa did some mental figuring. 'He was gone for eighteen months before he was killed. So I wrote him eighteen letters. If that many.'

'Who else would have written him letters?'

'I don't know, boy. Probably half the girls in Mannville.'

Of more concern than whom these letters were from, however, was where they'd been sent after Eddie's fighter jet disintegrated in a fiery cloud over the South China Sea. I was certain that was the next clue to the riddle of who my mother was. I imagined there must have been some kind of private agreement between Eddie and Eliza about what would happen if Eddie was killed. Henry Hutchins knew my father well, and if he thought they were in love, then they probably were.

But the address to which the letters and other items had been sent was not included. I seemed to have run into a brick wall. I fired off one last letter to the same department that had sent me the list of Eddie's personal effects, in the desperate hope that someone would read it and take pity on me.

Perhaps it would be months before I heard a reply; perhaps it would be never. I marked the date on a calendar. It was then Saturday morning, March 12.

'I DON'T KNOW how you could just give Willie Mann's diary away like that,' I fumed to Grandpa a few days later. 'I mean, did you think nobody else was ever going to be interested?'

'Think about it, kid,' said Grandpa. 'I was nineteen years old. Your father wasn't even born yet. I was an only child. I didn't think I was going to survive the war. You did things impulsively in those days because the moment was the only time that was. Plus, I didn't like what I read in it. I wanted to get rid of it.'

Grandpa had hinted before that there was something revealed in the diary that, at the time, he found too shameful to think about. He still refused to talk about it.

'You don't have an address for this Fujimora guy?'

'He was from Nagasaki,' said Grandpa. 'Nagasaki was nuked. Even if he'd given me an address, that house would just be a shadow on the street now.'

'How do you know he's still alive?'

'He's alive.'

'But what if he doesn't show up at all?' This was the big question, one that had been brewing in my mind for some time.

But Grandpa remained secure. 'He's coming,' he said. 'I can feel it. And it won't be long now.'

It wouldn't be long now, because, according to Grandpa, the next round of three had begun with the death of Frederic Simpson, and he was convinced he would go in this round. He was so sure of this that he asked for his grave to be dug now, while the earth was still thawing, so it could be drained periodically before he was put in it. He didn't mind the idea of being dead and cold, he said, but being dead, cold and wet was intolerable.

'Humour an old man,' he said, and so I called the cemetery, and the grave was dug.

I went out to see it without telling anyone. I had the crazy idea that I would get into the grave myself for a moment, just to see what it was like to be in there. But when I arrived, the grave looked so unpleasant I changed my mind about getting into it. Grandpa was right. The earth was soggy and cold and dank.

I decided to look around a bit, and that is how I found myself wandering among the dead, exploring a corner of the cemetery I'd never visited before. What I saw there took my breath away: dozens upon dozens of tombstones, perhaps one hundred of them, all bearing the name of Simpson. There were even more of them than there were Mann tombstones. Somehow it had never occurred to me that there might have been other Simpsons in other times.

I read with interest the names on the Simpson stones. There was, for instance, a Frederic Simpson who was born in 1848 and who died in 1864. The engraving on his stone depicted a pair of crossed rifles surrounded by a wreath, the sign of an infantryman. This Frederic had been a veteran of the Civil War, just like Willie Mann. I wondered if he'd known my great-great-grandfather.

Judging by the dates on the tombstones, there'd been many more Simpsons before the Civil War than after. Had they always been a bunch of fat drunks? I wondered. And what had happened to them?

Grandpa would know. I was sure of it. When I got home, he would have some questions to answer.

'SURE ARE A LOT of Simpsons up in that graveyard,' I said to Grandpa later that afternoon. 'There was even another Frederic.'

He was sitting in his rocking chair. In the old days he'd have had a glass of whiskey in his hand. Now he sipped herbal tea.

'Yeah,' said Grandpa. 'I kinda knew you'd find out sometime.'

'This other Frederic died in the Civil War?'

'Yes,' he said.

'Did he and Willie know each other?'

Grandpa put a hand over his eyes.

'Grandpa? Did they?'

He took his hand away. 'Yes, they did,' he said.

'How well? Were they friends?'

'Yes, they were friends. But they were more than that.'

'What do you mean?'

'They were cousins,' said Grandpa.

I sat in silence for perhaps a full minute, absorbing this. The connection this implied between Annie and myself was obvious, but my reeling mind chose not to look at it right away.

'Kid,' Grandpa said, 'there's a lot I haven't told you.'

'How could you not tell me that? Of all the things you had to leave out, how could you not tell me that?'

'How could I?' Grandpa said. 'How could I tell you the girl you were in love with was related to you by blood?'

'Did Annie know?' I asked.

'She might have,' Grandpa said, 'but I doubt it. Jack Simpson never told Freddy. He was as ashamed of it as I was.'

'That's why you didn't want me to go to Montreal to visit her,' I said. 'That's why you kept saying it wasn't right. Not because she's a Simpson. Because we're related.'

Grandpa sighed. 'Yeah,' he said.

'Lord,' I whispered. Simpson was family. *Family.* That meant I was related to Mr Simpson too. Nausea welled up briefly inside me. 'Did my father know about this?' I said.

Grandpa shook his head sadly. 'I never got the chance to tell him. I was gonna, when he was older. But he didn't get older.'

'So he and Frederic never knew they were related?'

'No.'

'You didn't mind that they played together when they were boys?'

'Hell no. In those days I thought there was a chance everything could be forgotten. I figured, let the boys grow up with each other, and that way, when they get to be men, once they found out the truth, they could just laugh it off.'

'But why keep it secret from me? Why? I'm the last Mann. I have to know everything. You told me that yourself.'

'I've never lied to you,' said Grandpa. 'But sometimes I leave things out. It's not because I thought you couldn't handle the truth. But there's some things that need to be pulled out of the world. If nobody knows something, then it isn't true any more. That's why there's things I haven't told you. To filter them out, like. Kind of clean things up. The only way to purge badness is to kill it. Or take it to the grave.'

He sighed. 'But I never figured on Annie entering the picture,' he continued. 'I felt god-awful bad for that girl, but I was relieved when she left town. I didn't know how much you cared about her. I should have seen it. I guess I just didn't want to. And now that you're asking, I can't lie to you,' he said. 'That was one thing I swore I'd never do. And I knew you'd find out someday, when the diary came back. But I figured by then I'd be dead and gone.'

'I understand,' I said. 'So where did all the feuding start?'

'It's a long story.'

'Grandpa,' I said, 'this is very very important to me. I need to know it. And you know I need to know it.' And, I did not add, time is running out. You're dying. Tell me now. Please.

To tell the truth, I'd never fully believed the diary was going to show up, and I was sure that if Grandpa didn't tell me himself, I would never know. And that was unthinkable.

'All right, boy,' he said. 'I'll tell you everything. OK?'

'OK,' I said, and Grandpa started talking.

'You know as much about Willie as everyone else in this town does,' he said, 'but you don't know as much about Willie as Willie himself would have wanted you to know. He would have wanted you to know the whole story. Willie understood how important it was to tell the truth. But he didn't go around town confessing to everyone about what he'd done during the war—not because he was ashamed of it, but because he was a hero, and Mannville needed a hero bad. Every town does. Look around you. We don't have much going for us. We have a grain mill, a bunch of farms, a few stores downtown. Willie built a hospital, a school, a library, all the stuff people needed to feel like they were important. Like living in Mannville wasn't a big waste of time. Willie wanted everyone to feel that way, and he knew that if people found out the truth about him, everyone would just want to curl up and die of embarrassment.

'But me—he wanted me to know the truth. He hadn't really been a war hero. That was just a story that got told around, kind of the same thing that happened to me when I came back from my war. Willie himself never made anything up. In fact, for years after he came home, he never said a word about the war to anyone. He clammed up tight, and that made everyone think he was just being modest. Next thing you know, he's a legend. Finding that money didn't help any, of course. Folks figured if he was lucky enough to find the Rory treasure, then he was probably also a war hero.

'Anyway. That wasn't the real Willie. The real Willie was a scrawny sixteen-year-old kid when he left home to join the army—underfed, wearing raggedy clothes, barefoot. In those days the Manns were so poor they couldn't afford shoes. In fact, one of the reasons he wanted to join up was so he could be sure of getting regular meals and having decent clothes. So Willie hears about the war, and heads off down the road to Buffalo, a good three-day walk. He had an old muzzle-loader his father gave him.

'On the way to Buffalo, Willie happened to meet up with his aunt and uncle, who were coming back from a revival meeting. If a famous preacher got within fifty miles, Willie's aunt was there, and more often than not she dragged her husband and son along with her. Her name was Elspeth Simpson. She was the hysterical type.

'So Willie stopped to talk with them. Young Frederic, their son, was with them. He was twelve that year. He and Willie were best friends, and they did everything together. It was no accident Willie had chosen to leave town while Frederic was away with his parents, because Willie knew Frederic would want to come along with him. As it turned out, that was exactly what Frederic tried to pull. But it was out of the question for him to go with Willie. Frederic was too young. Willie himself was just barely old enough, and he was afraid the army would turn him back.

'So he kept on his way, and his aunt and uncle and Frederic kept on theirs, and Willie camped the first night in a stand of trees along the road. He was lying awake, already homesick, hungry, tired, when all of a sudden he hears this voice calling his name. He listens, wondering who it is. And then it comes to him. It's Frederic. The little rat had sneaked off and set out to find his cousin, and as chance would have it, he found him. Willie tried to get Frederic to turn round and go home, but of course Frederic wouldn't do it.

'To make a long story short, Willie Mann and Frederic Simpson went to Buffalo and joined up. The army didn't want to take Frederic, but the boys lied and wheedled and whined, and finally Frederic was signed on as a drummer boy. They spent a month or so in camp, and then they marched down south.

'Now, on this march there was another soldier named Ferguson. Ferguson was a nasty son of a bitch, and the other soldiers didn't like him. He was drunk all the time, lazy, foul-smelling and a bully. They had chores to do every night when they made camp—one guy went for wood, another guy for water, and so on. Ferguson never wanted to go for wood when it was his turn, and if he was feeling particularly mean that day, he would make some other poor slob do it for him. It happened to Willie a few times. Ferguson was too big for Willie to fight, so he put up with it.

'That is, until one night when they were camped somewhere in southern Pennsylvania. It was Ferguson's turn to go for wood, and of course he decided he was going to get someone else to do it for him. Instead of Willie, though, he picked on Frederic. And to top it all off, Ferguson started smacking the boy around. Well, that was all Willie could take. He lit into Ferguson, and next thing you know, Ferguson is dead, and Willie gets taken off to jail—'

'Willie *killed* him?' I interrupted.

'Stabbed him to death with a big old hunting knife he carried. Said he didn't even remember doing it. The whole world just went red, and next thing he knew, he was in prison, with chains around his neck and his legs. Anyway,' continued Grandpa, 'Willie spent the rest of the war in a jail cell. With a schoolteacher. That was how he learned to read and write.'

'And what happened to Frederic?'

My grandfather's face grew dark. 'Frederic got killed.'

'In battle?'

'Yeah. Antietam. Willie didn't know that, of course. He didn't even know where Frederic was. In those days you rarely got notified of anything. Willie got out of prison on the very day the treaty was signed, and he spent a few months hunting for Frederic. Finally he found some fellows from his old regiment, and they told him Frederic was dead. So Willie headed home.

'Willie hadn't been home in four years. In all that time nobody back here had heard a word from either of the boys. So Willie's parents were overjoyed to see their son back safe and sound, if a mite silent. Of course, Willie didn't want to tell them where he'd really been, so he acted like he'd been through one battle too many and he didn't ever want to discuss it.'

'What about his leg?' I interrupted. 'His wounded leg?'

'Some farmer took a shot at him as Willie was stealing one of his chickens,' Grandpa said. 'Hit him in the thigh. That was the only time Willie ever came under fire in the whole war.

'When Willie got home, the first thing he did was limp on up to his aunt and uncle's place. Elspeth had been steadily losing her mind ever since Frederic ran off, and when she learned that he was dead, she lost it completely. She let loose with a curse on Willie and all the Manns—a real old-fashioned curse, calling down all kinds of horrendous things on Willie's head. He just stood by the gate and took it. When she was done, he went home. Soon after that, he found all that money. He tried to give some to Frederic's parents, but Elspeth wouldn't take it. She forbade any further contact between the Manns and the Simpsons, and she poisoned the minds of all her relations against us. Then the Simpsons started to die off. It was like her curse had backfired. They died of flu mostly. Measles too. Soon there were only a few left. And now they're all gone.'

Grandpa heaved a deep sigh of relief. 'I thought for a while that we were done for, too,' he said, 'but then you came along.' He grinned. 'Thank God for that.'

'Thanks for telling me the story,' I said.

'It's a hard story to tell,' said Grandpa, 'but I guess it doesn't seem that bad, now it's out. Willie never came out and told me this himself, you know. He put it all in the diary, and he gave me that, but I never got around to reading it until I was on that damn island. I never got the chance to talk to him about it. I wish—Well, never mind what I wish. You help me upstairs and put me in my bed now,' said Grandpa. 'All this talking has worn me out.'

TWO MORE MONTHS passed, and the end of the school year grew tantalisingly closer. With it would come my graduation and my liberation, and I would be free to search for my mother. But first I needed to know where to look, and I'd heard nothing further from the air force. I spent my days in a frenzy of restlessness.

I finally heard from Annie. She mailed me a package. Inside were several copies of a French magazine. The cover seemed familiar, and then it hit me—it was the Montreal magazine for which I'd asked Annie to translate my story. She wrote:

> *Dear Billy,*
>
> *I'm sorry I've been out of touch for so long. I don't think I need to explain. I never have, with you. You understand. Please keep trying to understand. Please never change that about you.*
>
> *I finally finished the translation, and guess what? They took it! They didn't offer any money, but they did send me ten free copies. I kept two and sent you the rest. This is sort of a triumph for both of us, I guess. Congratulations!*

So I was finally published—in a language I couldn't read. It was a triumph. A bittersweet one, but a triumph nonetheless.

And my suspicions about where I stood with Annie were confirmed. 'Please keep trying to understand,' she'd written. In our secret language that meant, 'Please keep leaving me alone. Someday maybe things will be different, but not right now.'

In the meantime, Grandpa grew yellower. His skin turned the shade of a maple leaf in autumn. His liver began to wind down, refusing to process the toxins that his body naturally produced. He'd made it do too much work for too long, he said, and now it was out of juice, or whatever it was that made it run. Grandpa's understanding of the human body was intimately linked with his automotive expertise. It was in these terms that he'd once explained to me the mechanics of sex, in the parlance of crankshafts and piston wells, oil and combustion, and he saw himself now as a machine that had been driven too long without the proper maintenance. His body was about to commit the human equivalent of throwing a rod, and there was nothing anyone could do about it.

Mildred showed little emotion at Grandpa's imminent passing. At least not in front of us. But walking by her room, I could sometimes hear her sobbing out her secret pain.

Soon he was unable to get out of bed. 'I feel like hell,' Grandpa confided when we were alone. It was the only time I heard him complain. 'I must look like hell too.'

'You don't look too bad,' I lied.

'Ha. I bet I look like I'm already dead.'

The truth is he was right. He looked more like a corpse than a living man. The feeling in my chest was worsening by the day.

'Listen, boy,' he said. 'Have you thought about what you're going to do after I'm gone?'

'You know what I'm going to do. I'm going to find my mother.'

'I mean in general. Like a career.'

'Writer.'

He sighed. 'I want you to go to college,' he said. 'This isn't the old days. Things are different now. A college degree is your only hope unless you want to be poor all your life. You're smart. Don't make the same mistakes I made.'

'I have some money saved up.'

'You'll get some from me, too,' he said, 'but that won't be enough. I took out a policy on myself right before I got sick. You'll get most of it.'

'What about Mildred?'

'I've talked it over with her. She doesn't need it like you will. She got some money from her husband, so she'll be all right.'

'But what is she going to do?'

'Retire,' said Grandpa. 'Take it easy. Move into that new home they built over in Forestville, where they wait on you hand and foot and you play checkers all day.'

'Will she like that?'

'Probably not,' said Grandpa. 'But she doesn't have any people.'

'What about her children?'

'You've heard her talk about them. They don't write; they don't call. She doesn't even know where they are.'

'Because of her husband, though. It's not her fault.'

'They blame her too—for putting up with him.'

'What about the house?'

'This house? It's yours, of course.'

'Mildred can stay here,' I said.

'Well, it's your place to do with as you see fit,' said Grandpa. He was trying to appear indifferent, but I could see tears welling up in his eyes. I pretended not to notice.

'She belongs here just as much as you or I,' I said.

'That's mighty nice of you, boy.'

'She's the closest thing to a mother I've ever had,' I said. Hardly were those words out of my mouth when their full import struck me. I put my face in my hands.

'Aw, shoot,' Grandpa said, and now it was his turn to pretend not to notice my tears. 'Sometimes I hate the way things turned out for you, boy. It wasn't fair, none of it. You got the raw end of the stick. Especially with me around.'

'Don't say that,' I said. 'You did fine.'

'I shoulda quit drinking years ago. When I got you. When I think of all the time I wasted—'

'Stop it,' I said. 'I don't blame you.'

'Anyway, boy, I'm glad you came along.' He closed his eyes.

I was suddenly alarmed. 'Hey,' I said.

'I'm not dead yet,' he said. 'I'm just taking a nap.'

I went downstairs to the kitchen and put the kettle on the stove for some coffee. Mildred appeared from the yard, where she'd been looking over her garden. She was short of breath, startled. Without a word she sat down opposite me at the kitchen table.

'What's the matter?' I asked.

'There's a man in the grotto,' she said.

'A what?' I sprang to my feet. The grotto was a small sunken area at the rear of the yard. It was a sort of tiny amphitheatre, no more than ten or twelve feet long, with a small bench in it facing a statue of the Virgin Mary. I ran to the kitchen window and peered outside. I could see a small form sitting hunched on the bench. It was a man, all right. He appeared to be deep in thought.

'A man in the grotto,' Mildred repeated, but I was already out of the door and running across the yard.

He was smaller than I'd imagined, somehow. In the stories

Grandpa had told me of him, he'd come to be larger than life, but now that he was here, he resumed his normal size. He couldn't have been more than five feet tall. I crossed the yard and stopped behind him. After a lifetime of preparing for this moment, I was tongue-tied and confused. I looked at the little man curiously from the back. He wore a dark overcoat with the collar turned up, and he was staring at the plaster Virgin with great curiosity. Suddenly he turned, alerted to my presence by my breathing.

'Ah,' he said, his Oriental eyes folded in pleasure, his face dissolving into a thousand wrinkles. 'And you are?'

'Billy,' I said.

He stood up from the bench and approached me slowly. Standing, he came only to the middle of my chest. He stopped at a respectful distance and bowed as far as his elderly spine would permit.

'Pleasure to meet you,' he said. 'Billy is short for William Amos Mann, I presume. Named after your great-great-grandfather.'

I bowed as low as I could in return. Instinctively I knew that a man of this age, who had come so far to fulfil an obligation, deserved my complete respect. When I straightened up, he was smiling even more broadly.

'For an American boy,' he said, 'you are very polite.'

'Thank you,' I said, at a loss for further words.

'Do you know who I am?' he enquired after a moment.

'Yes,' I said. 'Won't you come into the house?'

We walked slowly towards the house. He held my elbow with one hand. The yard was swimming before my eyes, and the chill of desperation in my chest was replaced by wild joy.

Enzo Fujimora had come to Mannville.

THE TRUTH WAS, as Enzo explained to me later, there was no great mystery to determining in advance the date of Grandpa's death. Long ago, when he and Grandpa were living on the Pacific island together, he had consulted a variety of signs to make his forecast. First, he read Grandpa's palm. The lifeline was long but intersected before its natural termination by misfortune or perhaps illness. Second, he asked Grandpa for the precise date and time of his birth and then correlated the information with his knowledge of Eastern astrology, which he had memorised. Finally, he improvised three coins of wood. Grandpa threw the coins, and then Enzo consulted the other vast work he had memorised—the ancient and mystical Chinese work called the *I Ching*. His pronouncement: Grandpa was probably going to die sometime between 1987 and 1990.

Of course, said Enzo, he said nothing of this to Grandpa at the time. It wasn't right for a man to know the date of his death.

But Enzo Fujimora's final means relied not on fortune-telling or wizardry, but on modern technology.

'I called the hospital in Mannville last month,' Enzo told me. 'After I introduced myself as a healer and told them I was hoping to encounter an old friend who I thought might already be sick, they gave me information concerning your grandfather. They were not supposed to do that, of course, but I convinced them.'

I brought Enzo into the house. Mildred was cowering in the kitchen, but when she saw him chatting familiarly with me and noticed how small he was, she relaxed. She too had heard the story of Grandpa's Pacific sojourn many a time, and when I introduced Enzo Fujimora himself, she was greatly impressed.

I took Enzo upstairs. I paused at the threshold of Grandpa's room and tapped lightly on the door. 'Grandpa,' I said, 'someone's here.'

Grandpa was too weak to raise himself up. He tried to see who was in the doorway behind me. 'Who?'

I led Enzo to the bed. He sat down next to Grandpa and put one tiny old hand on his. Grandpa's eyes grew wide, and the ghost of a smile wreathed his cracked lips. 'Enzo-san,' he said.

'Thomas-san,' said Enzo.

'You made it.'

'Yes.'

'I'm glad,' said Grandpa. 'You could have just mailed it.'

'I made a promise,' said Enzo. 'Besides, I've always wanted to see Mannville. The house, the garden and everything.'

'I'm dying, Enzo,' said Grandpa.

Enzo smiled. It was a smile of deep compassion. 'I know, Tom.'

The two old men stayed like that, one's hand on top of the other's. They said nothing further. They just rested.

I left them alone and went back downstairs to finish my coffee, which had grown cold. Mildred offered to heat it up for me.

'That's Enzo,' I said.

Mildred said nothing. She poured my coffee into a saucepan.

'I ought to buy a microwave,' I said. 'You can heat up coffee in one minute with one of those.' There were, in fact, a lot of things I wanted to buy. 'I want a television,' I said. 'And a VCR. And wouldn't you at least like a dishwasher? Don't you get tired of doing the dishes by hand?'

Mildred said nothing, her eyes filling with tears, and she looked away. Then I remembered I hadn't yet asked her to stay.

'You've earned a place here as much as I have,' I told her. 'You're the one who made Grandpa happy again. You have to stay. Please. Don't go to Forestville. Stay here.'

Mildred put her face in her apron. I sipped my coffee and pretended once again that I didn't notice. There had been a lot of crying lately, and I found it all very embarrassing.

'Thank you,' she said simply when her emotion subsided. We sat together sipping coffee and saying little else.

After half an hour had gone by, I went upstairs again. Enzo was seated in a chair by Grandpa's bedside.

'He was just in time,' said Grandpa with an effort.

I looked at Grandpa's eyes, his colour, listened to his breathing. His skin was growing translucent even as I watched him. He closed his eyes, and his breathing faded until it was nearly inaudible. It was then I noticed the book that lay on his chest, his free hand resting on it. It was an old book bound in plain leather.

Grandpa's eyes fluttered open once more. He grasped the book with both hands and pushed it up towards me with tremendous effort. I took it from him before he could falter. 'Read it,' he said after several tries. Then he closed his eyes for the last time.

Grandpa continued to breathe for three more hours. Enzo moved to one wall of the bedroom, out of the way, while I sat in his place and Mildred sat on the other side of the bed. We watched him until his breathing faded into nothingness. At the last moment Mildred and Enzo left the room and closed the door, and I was alone with my grandpa. I put his hand in mine and held it on the bed. At 3.43pm his breathing finally stopped, the tiny pulse in his hand disappeared, and his skin began to grow cold.

I got up and opened the window. A flock of birds, disturbed by the noise, flew silently from their roosts and fluttered skywards.

After a time I turned from the window and leaned against the sill. There was a mirror next to me on the wall and another one on the wall opposite; it was an arrangement Grandpa had insisted on, saying that this confluence of reflections would allow his soul a clear path to escape. I looked into the far one and saw myself stretching away into an endless corridor of windowsills, curving off to the right into infinity. I saw myself repeated endlessly out of sight, like the line of generations that had created me. It was like my own history. I could only see so far before it disappeared, before I lost the trail.

When I was sure that enough time had passed, I got two pillowcases from Grandpa's closet and placed them over the mirrors. Grandpa was on his way home.

We Manns bury our own in the old-fashioned way. According to Grandpa's stories, there was once a time when there was no such thing as a funeral home. People were waked in their own homes and then carried up to the church on the shoulders of their family.

Concessions to the times had to be made, of course. Grandpa was embalmed at the funeral home—you're not allowed to have unembalmed bodies just lying around the house any more—but then they brought him back and laid him out downstairs, right where he used to sit in his rocking chair.

No. Not Grandpa. Grandpa's *body*. I had to keep reminding myself of that.

So that was how it came to be that early the next afternoon Grandpa lay in his casket in the living room, his eyes covered with two heavy silver coins. The room had been cleared of furniture, and the walls were lined with rented folding chairs. Large brass candlesticks stood at either end of the coffin, each holding a white candle that in turn nourished a tiny yellow flame. Mildred had cleaned the old farmhouse, and every inch of it gleamed. I sat in one of the folding chairs staring dully out the window. I'd been up all night reading the diary, and my eyes burned with fatigue.

In death Grandpa achieved a state of relaxation that life had never granted him. The lines of tension around his eyes and forehead had melted. And there was something else, something odd about him that I couldn't put my finger on. Then it occurred to me: he was missing his fedora.

I asked the undertakers about it. They hadn't seen it, they claimed. I searched the house, but it was never discovered. Finally I gave up. It seemed that Grandpa had been allowed to take *something* with him, in defiance of the rules. I never saw the hat again.

Mannville being the small town it was, word of death—anyone's death—spread quickly. The news that Grandpa had departed, and that there would be an old-fashioned wake in the house, travelled across town within hours. To tell the truth, I was afraid nobody would come. Grandpa hadn't exactly gone out of his way to be friendly in the last forty years. Since he'd sobered up, he'd been re-establishing some old acquaintanceships, but you can't erase four decades of isolation in just a couple of years. So at first it was just Mildred, Enzo and me.

But around one o'clock the first tentative knock came at the door, and Emily and Harold Gruber entered. They came to me, and I shook their hands, and their condolences echoed fuzzily in the bright room. In addition to the absence of flowers, which Grandpa hated, he had insisted on open windows and natural light. 'I don't want a bunch of gloomy Gusses sitting around in the dark,' he'd said. 'Funerals are depressing enough already.'

An Irish wake means whiskey and food, and the old wooden table in the kitchen was laden with bottles, casserole dishes and silverware. Mildred flitted about with a bottle of Bushmill's and a tray of glasses. She wouldn't touch it herself, she promised me, but she saw no reason why her broken love affair with alcohol should ruin everyone else's good time. Mrs Gruber didn't drink either, but Harold cheerfully accepted a dram. Enzo joined him, wordlessly holding out his glass for Mildred to fill. Harold looked askance at Enzo for a moment; no doubt he was wondering what this tiny Japanese man was doing there. But the two of them, having the weight of years in common, soon fell into conversation.

'So this is Irish whiskey,' Enzo said. He sniffed at his glass, tasted it. His eyebrows shot up. 'My goodness,' he said. Then he threw back his head, tossed the contents of the glass down his throat, and smiled broadly. 'My goodness,' he said again.

'Say, Billy,' said Harold, 'how old are you now?'

I roused myself. 'Twenty-one,' I said.

'Well, I know damn well you're not twenty-one,' said Harold. 'Not that I care. Go and get yourself a glass and drink a toast to your grandfather with us men.'

'OK,' I said. I got a glass from the kitchen, and Enzo poured the whiskey for me himself.

I drank the whiskey down, all of it. 'My goodness,' I said.

'Exactly,' said Enzo.

The doorbell clanged again, and Mildred went to answer it. Several more people arrived. I poured myself another shot and offered the bottle to Enzo and Harold. Enzo declined, but Harold accepted a small one.

'Man,' I said to Harold, 'this makes you feel all right. No wonder Grandpa liked it so much.'

'Normally I never touch it,' said Harold, 'but at funerals . . . Well, you know. Funerals were made for drinking. Or drinking was made for funerals. One or the other.'

'Our condolences, Billy,' said a voice. I turned to see the Greenes. Mr and Mrs Greene were in their late sixties and wore twin crowns of silver hair. I delivered groceries to them once a week. They shook my hand and went to the catafalque and knelt in front of the coffin, where they crossed themselves.

I observed this with curiosity. I'd never prayed in my life, but it seemed as if this would be a good occasion to learn. When they were done, I crossed the room and knelt where they had been. If I was going to pray, I ought to do it now.

Dear God, I prayed. Here is the man who raised me from my infancy. He did the best he could, which I think was pretty good. I want his spirit to go free. That's why I covered up the mirrors. I want him to go on to whatever the next thing is, and I want him to tell every one of us Manns he sees over there, wherever he is, that I will be all right. I promise to tell all the old stories to my kids, when I have them. I promise to tell them about him too. So if you would pass that message on for me, please, God, I would be very grateful.

I wondered if I was supposed to wait for a response. After a moment, though, it appeared that none was forthcoming, so I crossed myself again and stood up.

The room had fallen silent, and everyone was watching me. When I turned around, they looked away. I heard sniffling. I could tell it was a poignant moment for them—the young orphan boy saying goodbye to his only known relative. At that moment I understood how I'd always been seen by the people of this town. I was never just Eddie's bastard to them. I was the kid who'd made it mostly on his own, and I could see they respected me for that.

Silence reigned for a time. It was my first wake, and I didn't know what to do next.

'He was a grand old man,' said Harold Gruber.

'I always did feel bad about them ostriches,' said Mr Greene.

'Hear! Hear!'

A toast was drunk by everyone, including me. It was my third. The doorbell rang again, and I went to get it myself. After ushering in Officer Madison and his wife, I hit upon the idea of propping open the front door with a chair. That way nobody would have to worry about answering the bell.

'Great idea, having a home wake,' said Madison. 'They used to do this all the time.'

'What customs do you have in Japan?' asked Mildred of Enzo.

'We cremate,' he said. 'Then we keep the ashes in a shrine. We worship our ancestors. We like to have them close by us.'

'How beautiful,' said Mrs Greene.

'Where exactly you from in Japan?' asked Mr Greene.

'I am from Nagasaki,' said Enzo.

There was another long and silent moment, during which I think everyone had the same image: a malevolent mushroom cloud glowing red and black in the Japanese sky.

'Friend of Tom Mann's, were you?' asked Harold finally.

'Oh yes,' said Enzo. 'We met during the war.'

'Is that right?' said Mr Greene. 'How'd that happen?'

'I shot down his plane,' Enzo explained.

Mr Greene began to choke on his whiskey.

'You were the fella that shot down Tom's plane?' said Harold, his eyes wide.

'Yes,' said Enzo. 'That was I.'

'It's all right,' I said hastily. 'This is the man Grandpa was marooned on that island with. They got to be good friends.'

'I apologised to him afterwards,' Enzo assured everyone. 'He understood. There was a war, after all. I had to do it.'

'Good American boys died on that plane!' said Mr Greene.

Enzo cleared his throat. 'My wife and children,' he said, 'were killed in Nagasaki by the atomic bomb.'

The silence that ensued now was aeons long. My face burned from whiskey and embarrassment.

'Well,' said Mr Greene finally, 'I am sorry about that.'

'It was a war,' said Enzo, 'and it was a long time ago. Things like that happen in wartime.'

'Did you fly one of them Zeros?' Harold asked.

This salvaged the situation. The three elderly men, their wartime animosities dusty from disuse, immediately embarked on a discussion of the Japanese Zero and the American P-40.

Then there were footsteps behind me, and I felt a hand on my shoulder. It was a familiar hand, large and heavy and hairy. For a moment I thought it was Dr Connor returned from the grave, but an odour assailed my nostrils, rising above the smell of whiskey and candles: manure. Manure and milk. And tobacco.

I stood and turned. It was Mr Shumacher. And behind him stood Mrs Shumacher and six Shumacher children, their round, pudgy faces emitting a mixture of excitement and sadness.

I couldn't speak. Mr Shumacher grabbed me by both shoulders and squeezed; he was hard-pressed for words. Mrs Shumacher came to his rescue by flying past him and taking me to her massive bosom. Neither appeared to have aged at all.

'It's good to see you, boy,' gasped Mrs Shumacher.

'Yah,' agreed Mr Shumacher. 'Good to see you.'

'Good to see you, Fatti, Mutti,' I said. Emotion was choking me, and speech was difficult.

Mr Shumacher was followed by Amos junior, Jan and Hans, Elsa, Hildy, and Marky, all of whom had turned into clones of their parents. They grabbed me to them as though I was a prodigal brother for whom they had grown tired of waiting.

The house was slowly filling now with people. I recognised all of them, some more than others, from my jaunts around town as an agent of Gruber's Grocery. The men pressed my hand, the women pecked me on the cheek, all of them muttering words of condolence under their breath. There were more people in the house than there had been at one time since I was born.

'You have begun reading the diary?' said a voice behind me that was both small and powerful. I turned to see Enzo. He seemed to have grown tinier in the company of so many burly Americans.

'Yes,' I said. 'I hope you slept all right last night. Was the bed OK?'

Enzo dismissed this question with a flick of his hand. I have survived far worse catastrophes than uncomfortable beds, it seemed to say. 'I wish to inform you of the arrival of the mail,' he said.

'What?'

'The mail. You have received letters.'

'Thanks,' I said. When he remained there staring at me, I said, 'I'll get them later.'

'You do not think it important?'

'Not now,' I said. 'Probably a few bills or something.'

'Perhaps you ought to make sure,' he said. His voice was barely audible yet impressed itself deeply on my mind. And suddenly his meaning became clear. I'd told him the story of my quest to discover who my mother was, right down to the detail of the air force having sent my father's personal effects to an address other than his home. And I'd said I was waiting to hear what that address might be. Enzo had seen the mailman arrive, and something had told him to go and check the mailbox himself and then to come and get me.

'I'll go check it right now,' I said.

Enzo smiled.

More cars pulled into the driveway as I walked out to the mailbox and opened it. The sounds of laughter were audible outside now, even where I was standing, holding an envelope in my hand. Laughter. At Grandpa's wake. He would be delighted.

Casually, feigning disinterest to myself, I opened the envelope and read the letter:

Dear Mr Mann,

Pursuant to your request of March 1988, enclosed please find the information for which you have been looking.

Good luck.

Following was a street address in Santa Fe, New Mexico.

It was once my mother's address. And it might still be.

There was a name above the address. A full name. Her name.

Occasionally our entire destiny hinges on something as insignificant as one thin piece of paper. It's at moments such as these that the machinations of fate are revealed to be as flimsy and pliable as a silk scarf. I could, I thought, throw the letter away, stay here in Mannville, and not know anything more than I already did. Grandpa had left me money. I could keep the house, get a job, get married, have more Manns.

But I knew that wasn't going to be the way it was. The future had always been blank to me, but it was not the obscurity of hopelessness; it was the darkness of what is unknown simply because it hasn't yet been explored. It was like looking down the corridor between the two mirrors in Grandpa's bedroom. I had to go into it; I had to explore. Otherwise I would never know what was around the bend, and I would live a miserable life.

I can always come back, I thought. There is no leaving so permanent that it cannot be undone by coming home again.

An image came to me then. It was the same image I'd had when I was seven years old, riding the lawn mower up the hill to the Simpson house to save Grandpa's life. It was an image of my father. He was tanned, as always, and shirtless, and grinning his bewitching grin. He flexed his arms, spat contemptuously on the ground, and slapped his palms together.

'Let's get to it,' he said. And he rubbed his hands in anticipation of the difficulty of the task ahead of us.

From where I was standing at the mailbox, I could just see Annie's house. For a moment I thought of going to her again. I had so much to tell her, and I wanted to let her know everything would be all right. But the same voice in my head spoke up again. Just let her be, it said. If you really love her, let her be.

I stuck the envelope in my shirt pocket and turned back towards the house.

My life has been made of stories, and just when it seems one is ending, a new one begins. The world itself is woven of stories, each of us—man and woman and child—threading our own brightly coloured tale into the bigger story that was already being told as we were born and that will continue to be woven by others long after our threads have run out. But I have no fear that the stories themselves will ever run out. Stories are what I was fed on as a baby, a young boy, a teenager. Grandpa was overjoyed that I'd come along, he said, because my arrival meant he'd finally have someone to talk to in the big old house, someone who would listen to his stories. And it meant also that he was not, as he'd feared, the last of the Manns, but that there would be more of us, and perhaps things would be different from now on.

I was alone now, the sole survivor of hundreds of years, but I knew that I wouldn't be the last of the Manns. More would come along. I would take them through the house as Grandpa had taken me, leading them through it by their tiny hands, room by room, telling them the stories of the Manns who'd once inhabited this place and were now long gone in body, but who lingered in spirit and would continue to do so for as long as their names were spoken aloud. I could see this happening already, sometime in the future. It was time to stop looking behind me and to turn my attention instead to what lay ahead.

And I knew that when I looked into their baby-blue eyes, I would feel about them the same way Grandpa had felt about me. I would feel pride, joy, completion. We are daredevils, superpeople, heroes, we Manns. Small-town heroes, but heroes nonetheless. And I would think to myself as I looked at them what Grandpa had thought when he looked at me for the first time: Perhaps our greatness has only just begun.

WILLIAM KOWALSKI

'Writing this book has changed my life in more ways than I can count,' says twenty-nine-year-old first-time novelist William Kowalski. Perhaps the most obvious change is that he has recently moved from Santa Fe, New Mexico, where he was a high school teacher, to Brooklyn, New York. 'I did that completely on a whim—all the writers I idolised as a boy have lived in New York for a while.' He has also been able to give up his teaching career to become a full-time writer. 'To my surprise, I found it wasn't entirely the blissful existence that it sounds. With my second novel, which I'm working on now, I had to teach myself to become a different kind of writer, a professional one. It was unnerving, at first, to realise that I was now expected to write all the time.'

Eddie's Bastard, in which the feelings of a young boy growing up in a small town in America are vividly described, seems as though it must, to some extent, be autobiographical. Kowalski, however, says this is not the case—his own childhood in Cleveland, Ohio was a very traditional one. Nevertheless, he does remember being impressed by stories about his ancestors when he was a child. 'My great-uncle served in World War II, was shot down over Yugoslavia and spirited to safety by partisans after hiding in a snowbank for three days. And my great-grandfather, who was from Poland, was kidnapped by Russians nearly a century ago to serve in the Tsar's honour-guard. To me these are stories of courage and great fortitude, and I intend to share them with my children some day as examples of what we, as a family, are capable of doing—or perhaps I should say putting up with.'

Many readers will wonder if *Eddie's Bastard*, which ends with Billy Mann setting off to find his mother, will have a sequel. The good news is that it will; *Somewhere South of Here* is due for publication in 2001.

ACKNOWLEDGMENTS AND PICTURE CREDITS: *The Visitor:* pages 6–8: Images Colour Library; Joseph Nettis/Courtesy of Stock, Boston, PNI; photomontage by John Calvert; page 147: Roth Child. *The Rescue:* pages 148–150: Digital Stock; Images Colour Library; photomontage by DW Design Partnership; page 269: Byron Holland. *Faith:* pages 270–2: photography by Piers North; page 417: Neil Phillips. *Eddie's Bastard:* pages 418–20: Kim McGillivray/Début Art; page 539: John Alexander.

DUSTJACKET CREDITS: Spine from top: Images Colour Library; Joseph Nettis/Courtesy of Stock, Boston, PNI: Digital Stock; Images Colour Library: Piers North: Kim McGillivray/Début Art. Back cover: (Child): Roth Child. (Sparks): Byron Holland. (James): Neil Phillips. (Kowalski): John Alexander.

Printed by Maury Imprimeur SA, Malesherbes, France
Bound by Reliures Brun SA, Malesherbes, France